THE CONVERSATION

THE CONVERSATION

Joshua Golding

A Novel

URIM FICTION

Jerusalem • New York

❧ To my wife, Ayala

The Conversation: A Novel
by Joshua Golding

Printed in Israel. First Edition.
ISBN-13: 978-965-524-066-5

*Book design by Ariel Walden,
based on a concept by the author.*

URIM FICTION / URIM PUBLICATIONS

Urim Publications,
P.O. Box 52287, Jerusalem 91521 Israel

Lambda Publishers Inc.
527 Empire Blvd., Brooklyn, New York 11225, U.S.A.
Tel: 718-972-5449   Fax: 718-972-6307   mh@ejudaica.com

www.UrimPublications.com

THE CONVERSATION

Freshman Year

9

Sophomore Year

137

Junior Year

309

Senior Year

427

ה

FRESHMAN YEAR

From: dgoldstein@cuniv.edu   Sent: 10/5/99 2:35 PM
To: rchgoldstein@rchgoldattorney.com
Subject: the usual

Hi Dad,

Things are going pretty well. How are you? What's going on with Mom? How is she? What did the doctor have to say? What's a good time to call?

You asked me to let you know what I'm taking. Bio with Lab, Calculus, World Literature, Music, Introduction to Philosophy. I think I'll have the most trouble with Bio and Calculus, but I'm really enjoying the philosophy course. Right now we're studying Plato's early dialogues. It's so different from anything I've ever studied before. Sometimes you have to read a sentence or paragraph over and over before it even begins to make sense. You really have to be patient with it. But it's really interesting and it makes you think.

I've made some friends in all of my classes, and one or two in the dorm.

I've been able to run five miles every day so far. I hope I can keep this up as the semester work heats up. Are you still doing tennis?

I'm planning a trip to DC with a friend during winter break. Do you think that'll be OK? It should be interesting. We'll visit the Capitol, the White House, the Smithsonian, etc.

I have a Bio exam tomorrow. Need to go study!

David

From: rchgoldstein@rchgoldattorney.com   Sent 10/5/99 6:10 PM
To: dgoldstein@cuniv.edu
Subject: Re: the usual

Glad you're excited about your courses. Have you given any thought to what your major is going to be?

Yes, I've been playing tennis pretty regularly. I've got a fantastic partner.

DC sounds like a great idea. Mom and I will give you some spending money. Where will you be staying in Washington?

I'm still in the office, and need to finish up so I can go down to the court. Mom will be OK, don't worry. Good luck on your Bio exam. Why don't you call tomorrow evening?

Dad

2
—

"Hey Simon! Come in, sit down. Thanks for visiting my humble dorm room."

"It's not bad, David. But next time you can come over to my apartment."

"I'd like that. At your age, you can really do college in style. Want a beer?"

"Sure, but watch it! I'm not much older than you, and I didn't make that much money working in theater. I bet your parents give you more money per week than I spend in a month . . . .which reminds me . . . how's your mother? Is she any better?"

"My Dad says Mom is OK."

"Good. That's a relief."

"I better call her soon."

"Yeah, you should. Want a smoke?"

"OK, just one. It's not good for my running."

"One cigarette won't kill you. Here, take one. So . . . what else is going on?"

"Uh . . . the usual. My father wants me to decide what to major in."

"Why don't you tell him? You already know the answer."

"Maybe I do. But what'll I do with a major in philosophy? Go to law school, I guess? That's what Dad wants me to do, but I'm really not sure I'm interested in law. I'm really not sure what I'll do . . . ."

"Forget *what I'll do*. Just do what you really enjoy most. You enjoy philosophy, so major in it! Look, the most important thing in life is to do what makes you happy."

"Yes, I know you think that. But what is happiness? That isn't so simple, is it?"

"It *is* simple. Or at least, it *should* be. This is one thing we disagree on. For you, happiness is a deep philosophical topic. For me, it doesn't take too much to figure this out: everyone knows what makes them happy when they feel it."

"So . . . you're saying happiness is whatever makes you feel good? Are you saying happiness is pleasure? Plato wouldn't agree with you."

"Too bad for Plato, I guess. Look, what's good is pleasure, happiness, enjoyment – call it what you want. Most people get pleasure from the same things – like sex, food. Of course, different people get a special pleasure from different things. Some people get pleasure from stamp collecting or cooking, some get pleasure from helping others or even going to church. I get pleasure from drama and the arts, you get pleasure from philosophy and running. Actually, I myself get some minimal pleasure from this philosophical discussion . . . though not as much as you do, I'm sure!"

"Very funny, Simon . . ."

"And speaking of pleasure . . . how's your girlfriend doing? What's her name again?"

"Helen. Helen Porter. She's fine."

"She's got it all, just what guys like you want. Real *shiksa* looks. Blonde, blue eyes . . . the works!"

"Yeah . . . well . . . thanks a lot . . . but that's *not* what it's about."

"Right, right, I know. She's really an intellectual disguised in a woman's body. And what attracts her to you is your philosophical mind, not your incredible, flaming red hair and your otherwise good looks. The fact that you could have made the track team if you really wanted to doesn't hurt either."

"Simon, that's one thing I like about you! You're honest, and you're blunt!"

"Speaking of being honest, have you told your parents about Helen?"

"Uh . . . no, not yet."

"Ah, well . . . the time will come for that. Anyway, sorry about the digression. Carry on with your inquisition, professor!"

"Seriously, Simon, do you think all that people care about in life is *pleasure*? What if I get pleasure from killing and raping? Does that make it *right*?"

"Hang on, David! Now you're talking about a case where what *one* person finds pleasurable, *most* people don't. The rapist happens to find something pleasant which is very painful for the victim and which most people do *not* like at all. So the overall happiness of society dictates that we catch this guy and stop him if we can. That's all we can do. Or we can try to reform him so that his desires are more consistent with what makes everyone else happy. Sometimes that works, and sometimes it doesn't."

"Simon, I don't deny that pleasure is a good thing. But I don't think that pleasure *is* the good."

"Then what, O philosopher, is the good?"

"I don't know."

"You don't? What does Plato say?"

"I don't know. We haven't gotten to that yet!"

"David! Isn't this a little ridiculous? If you don't *already* know what happiness is, do you think reading some ancient philosopher is going to give you the answer?"

"It's conceivable."

"Look. Isn't it obvious that we all want pleasure? Like I said, the basic pleasures are the same for most people. What's sometimes tricky is figuring out what gives you that *special* pleasure. It *is* simple if people weren't so screwed up, mostly by their upbringing, which usually stifles our personality, our individuality . . . ."

"What do you mean by that?"

"You know . . . your personality, your individuality – that's who you really are, what you really want to do. Society tells you: You can't do this and you can't do that, so you end up feeling guilty when you do what you really want to do. Like I've told you before, the arts were not encouraged in my family or school. Religion was not only encouraged, it was jammed down our throats as kids. Luckily, I've gotten beyond all that and I'm beginning to realize what I have a passion for, and that's what I'm going to focus on. You're focusing on philosophy, and I think it's great that philosophy gives you such pleasure. Happiness is simple enough if people are given a chance to want what they really want, and if they could only put guilt out of the picture. Really, David, I really don't get why you think this question is so complicated!"

"OK, I'll try to explain. What you're saying just doesn't click. First of all, you're right that *some* people are screwed up and their individuality is stifled by society. But some people are quite normal, yet they *still* have a tough time finding happiness in life. Why should that be, if you're right? People know what they find pleasurable – yes, *that's* simple. Like you said, food, sex, and things like that. But happiness? That's something else. And besides, did you ever experience something pleasurable, in fact, intensely pleasurable, that *didn't* make you happy at all, but actually made you rather unhappy?"

"Well . . . suppose I did. What's your point?"

"My point is: there's a *difference* between happiness and pleasure. What makes a person fulfilled – that's something much deeper than pleasure."

"Why? Why does there have to be something higher than pleasure? Isn't pleasure enough to make life worth living? Besides, you're confusing things by bringing up *fulfillment*. What's fulfillment?"

"I don't know. That's what I'm trying to figure out."

"Well, I'll tell you what I think it is. Fulfillment is the satisfaction of your deepest desires. When you get that, you get your deepest pleasure! So, in the end, the only thing we really want in life is *pleasure,* and the only thing we don't want is *pain*. That's why everybody's got their breaking point."

"What do you mean by that?"

"You know exactly what I mean. Some people can resist temptation more than others. But eventually, if the pleasure is strong enough, or if the pain is intense enough, everyone breaks down. Come on, admit that I'm right!"

"I'm not quite sure what to say. I still have to think about it."

"Don't think too hard . . . it might cause pain!"

"Painful as it is, I'll keep thinking . . . and thereby disprove your thesis!"

"Touché! Meanwhile, I'll have another cigarette. And I'll also take another beer, if you've got one . . . ."

3

"Hello? Dad? It's me."

"Oh, it's you . . . . Hi, Dave! How are you?"

"You sound surprised to hear me."

"No, not really. But I thought you would call tomorrow like we said. I was expecting a call from someone else just this moment."

"I see. So, anyway, is Mom there? I just wanted to say hello."

"Actually, she went to bed early. She was a little exhausted. But I'll tell her that you called. Is everything else OK?"

"Yeah, sure. Trying to study for the Bio exam."

"Get back to it, then. And good luck!"

"OK. Well . . . I'll call tomorrow night, I guess."

"Sounds good. Bye!"

4

"David, let's face it. Your pal Simon is an honest-to-God hedonist. It's grotesque."

"Don't be so tough on him, George. He's only saying what most people believe, not just now, but throughout history."

"I don't know about that. Sure, there have always been hedonistic societies, going back to the Romans and other ancient pagans. But recently, there's an obsession with the pursuit of indulgence. And I don't think people were so selfish and pleasure-seeking when my parents or grandparents were growing up. Don't get me wrong. I'm not saying I don't get pleasure from lots of things myself. I certainly do. But it's not the purpose of life."

"And what *is* the purpose of life?"

"I've told you before, my faith is in Christ. I think the purpose of life is to fulfill God's will and reach eternal life. True, God *wants* us to be happy on this earth, but not as an end in itself. You've studied the Bible, haven't you?"

"Very little. What about it?"

"Do you remember the beginning of Genesis? God tells Adam to 'be fruitful and multiply, fill the earth, *and conquer it.*' It's man's responsibility to fulfill this mission. And that entails working, eating, drinking, raising families, and so on. We have to live in the real world to fulfill God's will, and this means we have no choice but to enjoy the pleasures of this earth."

"So, you're saying it's OK to pursue happiness and pleasure, but only because God wants us to?"

"Exactly. God created us in such a way that we have certain natural drives and tendencies. But what makes it good to pursue those drives is not the fact that they give us pleasure. What makes it good is that God wishes us to fulfill them. And of course, there are some drives we have that God does *not* want us to fulfill. That's where the test of our faith comes: are we just pursuing pleasure for its own sake, or are we doing what's right just because of God? Consider sex, for example. I know this isn't a popular view around here these days, but I'll say it anyway. Sex outside of marriage is basically for the sake of pleasure alone. And therefore, it's wrong."

"Do you really believe that?"'

"Yes, I sure do."

"And do you . . . uh . . . practice what you preach?"

"I confess . . . it took a while for my fiancée and me to realize this, but it's really true. You've met Mary, haven't you?"

"Yeah, sure. How could I forget her? She's a knockout."

"Thanks. Anyway . . . uh . . . sorry, what I was saying?"

"You were saying that pleasure for the sake of pleasure is wrong, so sex outside of marriage is *wrong*."

"Right, exactly. Thanks, David. And sex within marriage is *right,* because it's for the purpose of procreation."

"But is that really so? That's the *only* time sex is OK? What about love? I mean, what if you're in love with someone – isn't sex OK then?"

"Hold on – what do you mean by *love*? If you're not married, you're not really committed to that person, so it's not love after all."

"So it follows you're *not* in love with Mary then, since you're not yet married. I find that hard to believe!"

"Well, uh . . . see . . . we *are* engaged, so we're almost there. But in the truest sense – no, we're not in love. Of course, I have feelings for her, and I am attracted to her and all that, but until you make that commitment, it's not true love. When a couple marries in the church, they commit themselves to a higher being – I mean, God. That's when it becomes true love. So, sex outside of marriage is basically an act of *lust,* not love."

"Hmm . . . I'm not so sure about that. But can I go back to something you said before? You said that the only thing that's right to do is to fulfill God's will. Now, let me ask you this: *why* should we fulfill God's will? You can't say 'because it's pleasant to do so' – can you?"

"Well . . . I do believe it *is* pleasant to fulfill God's will, if you truly appreciate it and if you have faith in Christ. Many people don't see it that way, because we're so stuck in our own desires for their own sake. But anyway, the pleasure of fulfilling God's will is a different kind of pleasure than the pleasure we get from anything else. It's . . . uh . . . a spiritual kind of pleasure. It's a kind of pleasure you have to work at cultivating. It doesn't come naturally. The body seeks physical pleasure, but the soul seeks something higher. Of course, someone like Simon won't admit there is this kind of pleasure because he won't admit that he has a soul, and he sure won't admit there's a God."

"He won't admit it because he doesn't think there's any good reason to believe in such things."

"No, I don't think so. Deep down he *knows* there's a God, but he won't admit it because he doesn't *want* to admit it."

"That's funny. Simon says something similar about everybody else – including you."

"Really? What's that?"

"Well, *you* say that deep down everyone believes in God, and refuses to admit it. And *Simon* says that, deep down, everybody just wants pleasure, and they refuse to admit it! See? It's just a little too easy to say that everybody agrees with you, but they just won't admit it! But I have another question. You were saying that it's pleasant, in a spiritual sense, to fulfill God's will."

"Yes."

"So, the reason we should fulfill God's will is . . . to obtain spiritual pleasure?"

"Uh . . . no, I can't say that. What makes it right to fulfill God's will is not pleasure, not even spiritual pleasure . . . ."

"So *why* should we fulfill God's will?"

"Just because . . . it's God's will."

"But George —"

"David, enough of this! You're driving me round and round in philosophical circles!"

5

October 13, 1999

Dear David,

I know this letter must seem old-fashioned to you. I still haven't gotten my email set up and we keep missing each other on the phone, so I just thought I'd write. Letter writing does have some advantages, you know. My experience is that people also tend to be more honest when they write than when they speak or even type. I'm not sure exactly why. I guess people tend to think a bit more before writing than they do before speaking (or even typing out those quick email messages)! Also, when you write an email, it's so easy to delete things and cut and paste, but when you write a letter it's harder to erase so everything comes out more natural. Even when you try to erase something, you can still tell something was changed.

I hope things are going well. This must be an exciting time for you – new ideas, new people. It reminds me of my college days. Some of the best in my life . . . enjoy it! That probably makes it sound like it's all down hill after college – which is, of course, not necessarily true. But your experiences and education in college will stay with you for the rest of your life. And so will some of the friends you make. After all, I met Dad in college!

I'm glad to hear you've developed an interest in philosophy – I wish I knew more about it. I never took philosophy and I probably should have. Are you learning profound things about the meaning of life? Clue me in if you are! Seriously, I'd like to learn more about it when you have the chance. In college I remember hearing about Plato's theory of the forms and the famous allegory of the cave, but I never quite understood what that was about. Have you studied that yet? If so, maybe you'll explain that to me some time?

David – it looks like I've got to go in for another procedure to remove something on my chest. Dad keeps ~~press~~ reassuring me not to be concerned. I can't say I'm not a little nervous about it. Lately also I've been feeling weak. I don't really know why. I'm actually in bed right now, writing this letter. I just wanted to tell you all this because I want you to know what's going on. And I confess I should have quit smoking a long time ago. I hope you're not taking up smoking (or drinking) which I know is a favorite pastime for college students! God knows I smoked up a storm in college. Don't make the same stupid mistakes I did!

Dad told me you're planning to go to Washington during winter break with a friend. Where will you plan to stay? Who's the "friend" you're going with? Anyway, I'm sure you'll have a good time. Washington's a great place to visit. If you have a chance, visit the Holocaust Museum. Last time Dad was in Washington for business, I got a chance to go myself while he was busy at one of his meetings. It's quite overwhelming, but really brings things home. I don't think I ever really understood the Holocaust that well until I went to the museum. In fact, It was at the Holocaust museum that I learned the tragic story of the Hungarian Jews. Did you know that for much of the war, the Hungarian community was relatively safe? It was only toward the end of the war, in the spring of 1944, when most of the Hungarian Jews were deported and sent to the gas chambers. Depressing stuff, of course. Why am I getting into all this? Anyway, I really recommend the Holocaust museum.

Speaking of home, when will we see you? I miss you more than you know. Now that both you and Jack are gone, the house seems so quiet these days. I put the TV or music on but it doesn't seem to fill the space. Dad always seems to be working extra long hours on some project or other. Or he's playing tennis, but that's good for him, I'm sure. I think of you a lot. Will you be coming home for at least part of winter break? You're welcome to bring your friend if you want to. Well, that's all for now. Keep me posted on any new developments in philosophy – and in your life as well!

Love,

Mom

6

"Ravi, this food is really interesting. It's different. But I like it!"

"I'm glad you like it. It's really quite simple cuisine."

"If you say so. It seems exotic to me. These cozy little Indian restaurants have a certain smell or scent about them. And there's that subtle music in the background. It's all so . . . enchanting."

"It's the oriental mystique. Or maybe the mystique of the unfamiliar."

"Maybe you're right. That's certainly part of the attraction for me."

"But to me, it's just good food . . . and it reminds me of my mother's cooking!"

"Great! So, at least you enjoy it. Actually, that reminds me . . . this is really the question I was curious to ask you about. I had a conversation with Simon about this, and with George. Are you familiar with the view called *hedonism*?"

"Ah! It's time for the philosophical discussion! I knew this was coming sooner or later. Yes, I think I know what hedonism is. But how would you define it?"

"Hedonism is the view that what's good is pleasure. Or that the purpose or goal of life is to pursue pleasure. Not necessarily physical pleasure, but any kind of pleasure. So – do you agree?"

"Well, I can tell you that one of the main teachings of the Buddha is that all suffering is rooted in that view."

"*What*? Suffering is rooted in the pursuit of pleasure? That sounds like a paradox, maybe even a self-contradiction."

"What's the difference between a paradox and a self-contradiction?"

"I learned this idea in my Intro to Philosophy class. A paradox is something that seems strange or absurd, but is actually true. A self-contradiction is something that isn't logical at all, and can't possibly be true. For example, it's a contradiction for something to be a square and a circle at the same time. That's just absurd, and no such thing can possibly exist."

"Well, I'm not sure I accept that. I think that there might be some things that aren't logical at all, but are still true.

"Really? That makes no sense to me."

"That's because you think reality must conform to logic. Anyway, what's an example of a paradox?

"I'll give you the example I got in my Intro class. It's a plain fact that *the more you learn, the more you realize how little you know*. Socrates illustrates this very well. His wisdom consists in realizing how *little* he knows. A fool thinks he knows a lot; a wise person knows how little he knows. Still, the more you know, the more you realize how little you know. That's not a logical absurdity. It's a paradox."

"I get it. Thanks. So, you're wondering about the idea that suffering is rooted in the pursuit of pleasure. Is that a paradox or a contradiction?"

"Exactly."

"Even if it's a contradiction, I think it could still be true. But let's not get sidetracked. I'll say it's just a paradox, since I think I can explain logically how the pursuit of pleasure is the root of suffering."

"Really? I'd like to hear that."

"It's simple. When you think about it, the source of all suffering is precisely that people *desire* things, especially pleasure, but they don't succeed in getting what they want. All suffering stems from the frustration or lack of fulfillment of desire. People *desire* to be free from pain, and they don't succeed very well in that either. In fact, as long as you are tied to desire, you can never be free. You might fulfill some desires here and there if you are lucky. But no matter how much or what you have, if you desire things, you always desire more. The Buddha taught there is no release from this bondage until you stop or cease desiring."

"*Cease desiring*? That's impossible! Maybe the Buddha could do that, but not most people."

"Look, on the one hand, the path to true freedom is not easy. Yet on the other hand, it is the easiest thing in the world, once you get started on the path. It is especially easy once you see it as a resolution to . . . your real question."

"My *real* question? Sorry — just what do you mean?"

"Your real question is: *what is the meaning or purpose of life*? In fact, this is the question that has been bothering you for some time. Am I right?"

"Yes. I guess that is right. You smoked me out, Ravi. I confess . . . sometimes I think there is no purpose — other than pleasure, of course. That's not so bad, except . . . somehow — I don't know . . . I'm kind of hoping there's more to life than that. Sometimes I even get a little depressed about it."

"Depressed? How long does that last?

"Oh, not too long. Usually a day or two, and then I'm back to normal. But then, in a few weeks or sometimes a month, it comes back."

"Well, in that case I congratulate you! It sounds to me like the kind of depression you have is actually a normal stage in spiritual maturity."

"Do you really think so?"

"Absolutely. Something's telling you that your ordinary life is . . . how I shall say . . . incomplete. But let's go back to the question: *What's the purpose of life?* If you come to view cessation of desire as the answer to this question, it becomes easier to follow this path. Of course, people are so bound by desire that they can't even comprehend this as a real possibility. It takes discipline, meditation, practice."

"I still don't see how it's possible, even with all the practice in the world."

"Ah, Mr. Philosopher! How do you know that cessation of desire is impossible? Aren't you just asserting your view without argument?"

"Well, what about you? Didn't you say you have desires? Didn't you say earlier that you enjoyed the food?"

"Ah! Now I see why you leapt from Indian food to a conversation about hedonism! You thought you could trap me in a contradiction! Seriously, there is a simple answer to resolve this contradiction. Actually, there are *two* simple answers to this . . . and then, there is also a deeper answer."

"You're thinking fast. What are the simple answers?"

"The first one is that I didn't say I *enjoyed* the food."

"I'm pretty sure you did."

"No. My exact words were, 'To me it's just good food, and it reminds me of my mother's cooking.' Then *you* said, 'So at least you enjoyed it.'"

"OK. Well, anyway, are you now telling me you *didn't* enjoy the food, even though it was *good*?"

"Hmm . . . well, let's suppose I *did* enjoy the food. Here's my next simple answer: *I admit that I am not a perfect Buddhist.* Indeed, I am bound by desire. The Buddha set forth a path of spiritual growth, you might say. Actually I don't really like the phrase 'spiritual growth,' but we can talk about that later. Now, some people are more attached to desire than others. The less you are attached, the better. Anyway, the hypothesis that *I* am attached to the desire for food certainly does not prove the Buddha wrong!"

"OK. If that's the simple answer, what's the deeper answer?"

"The deeper answer is that just because one *does* something doesn't mean one *desires* to do it. That's how something can be *good,* even though one does not *enjoy* it! Look, certain actions flow naturally, like breathing. A spiritual master does not breathe because he desires to breathe or enjoys breathing. *He just breathes.*"

"I still don't get it."

"Maybe it's impossible to explain it. You have to just experience it to know what I mean. David, have you ever done any meditation?"

"No. Why?"

"Maybe you should try it some time. For the Buddhist, that's what meditation is all about. First you become aware of the bodily and mental processes that are unconsciously going on all the time. Then you learn how to control or master those processes. With small steps, and with practice, you can reach a stage where you detach yourself from your desire to engage in those processes. Most of us don't even realize how attached we are to those processes. So, sure, a spiritual master *eats.* In fact, he acknowledges the food is *good.* But he is not *attached* to the object of his eating, that is, the food. Rather, *he just eats.* This is sometimes called the 'action of non-action' or *wu-wei* in Chinese."

"Sorry, Ravi. I've never practiced meditation, so I don't really know what you mean."

"Wait a second. Don't you run every day?"

"Yes, I do. Well, almost every day."

"Haven't you ever reached a state where you're not even thinking about what you're doing? You're just doing it, without thinking about the fact that you desire to do it?"

"Yeah, sort of. I enjoy running, and I want to run, so it's definitely something

I *desire*. But sometimes, when I've been running for a while, it just sort of seems to be happening, without my actually doing it."

"Ah! That's exactly what I'm talking about. That's the action of non-action. Colloquially, it's sometimes called 'being in the flow.' You are probably in a semi-meditative state when you run, at least some of the time. Now if you really learned to meditate more deeply, you could take that same process much further."

"I don't know. The idea of meditation has always sounded kind of intriguing. But I don't think I'm cut out for it. I tried it once in high school . . . and . . . I just found it kind of boring, to be honest."

"Perhaps you didn't have the right teacher."

"Maybe. But let me get something straight. You humbly admit that you are *not* a spiritual master."

"Of course. I am not."

"But this Buddhist path — is that something you aspire to?"

"I'm not saying I agree with *everything* the Buddha said or did. You know, I also have some Hinduism in my blood. Besides, there are many versions of Buddhism. But I do think there is a lot of truth in the way of non-attachment."

"Well, it sure explains why you always seem so relaxed, so composed."

"That's probably because I meditate. It *does* make a person more relaxed."

"You also have this uncanny knack of remembering exactly what a person said, and then quoting it word for word when the person misquotes himself later! And you know, you've already got a reputation in the dorm. They refer to you as 'the guru.' That's why people come to ask you for advice all the time."

"Really? I hadn't noticed."

"You're too humble. But let's get back to the point. There's something I still don't get. You seem to be saying that non-attachment is the goal of the spiritual path. Now, is this something that a person should desire or not?"

"You're trying to set me up to fall into a trap! If I say non-attachment is to be desired, I will have contradicted myself. If I say it is *not* to be desired, you will argue it is not worth seeking."

"You've got it, that's exactly where I was going! Well, what are you going to say?"

"I'm going to say that your argument begs the question."

"How's that?"

"I insist that non-attachment is *not* something to be desired, but that it is *still* worth seeking. And then we're back to square one. You will insist that if it is not an object of desire, I cannot pursue it. And I will deny that. By the way, that's what I meant before when I said that I don't like using the term *spiritual growth*. I think that's really a Christian or Western notion. That's the idea that the goal of life — salvation, bliss, heaven, whatever — is something to be *desired* and actively sought after. This is not really the Eastern or Buddhist way of looking at things."

"OK. Well, then, what *is* the Eastern way of looking at things?"

"The goal of life, if we can call it that, is *freedom* . . . freedom from desire, freedom from attachment. You don't reach this kind of freedom by actively striving for it. It's like the old joke about telling someone to forget thinking about a rhinoceros. The more you try to do it, the less you succeed! Rather, you reach this goal *negatively*, by ceasing to desire things. Very few people reach this condition perfectly. But it can be reached in stages . . . ."

7

From: dgoldstein@cuniv.edu   Sent: 10/20/99 10:46 PM
To : rchgoldstein@rchgoldattorney.com
Subject: Plato
Attachment: Plato's Theory of the Forms and the Good

Dad,

Mom had asked me to explain Plato's theory of the forms and the allegory of the cave. We just got through this in class and I had to write a 2–3 page explanation of the theory for my class. We also had to state what we find are the two most difficult or perplexing things about the theory. I just finished it so I pasted it into this email below. Can you print it out and give it to Mom?

Thanks.

David Goldstein

Introduction to Philosophy

Plato's Theory of the Forms, the Good, and the Allegory of the Cave

Plato used the character "Socrates" to express and explain his theory of the forms. He claimed that the world contains basically two sorts of things – namely, <u>forms</u> and <u>particulars</u>. Particulars are physical things that exist at a certain time and space. They are mortal – that is, they come into being and pass out of being, and they are merely possible beings (they could have not existed). Particulars include, for example, triangles, circles, trees, dogs, cats, planets, chairs, cars and so on. Any particular is imperfect first of all because it is subject to extinction, but also because it is limited. It is impossible to draw a particular triangle that is perfect, and even if one could, that triangle would have a specific dimension, color, and size, so it would not completely capture or express what it is to be a triangle. It is impossible to have a perfect dog, because it cannot be both cute and cuddly and also a watchdog at the same time. The same goes for all other particulars. Particulars are known through the senses or sense experience – that is, seeing, touching, hearing, etc. Plato claims the senses are imperfect sources of knowledge, for as we know, the senses often deceive us or mislead us. For example, we see something that looks like a circle and later it turns out to be an oval, and so on.

On the other hand, what Plato calls "forms" are the <u>essences</u> of things, such as triangularity, circularity, and so on. These are also called <u>universals</u>. We may not have a name for the essence of what it is to be a tree, or a dog, but still Plato claims that for any set of particulars that has a common nature, there must be a form. So we might use the terms tree-ness or dog-ness or cat-ness or chair-hood to talk about the form that makes these particulars be what they are. Even if no particular triangles existed, the essence of triangularity would still be a real essence that just happens not to be represented in the physical world. According to Plato, the forms are invisible, intangible, eternal, necessary (they <u>must</u> exist) and they are perfect. When we see a particular triangle, we are looking at something imperfect. But when we think of triangularity, we are thinking of perfect triangularity. The same goes for all the forms. According to Plato, we know about the forms not through the senses but through the intellect, or the rational part of the soul. We cannot see triangularity, but we can grasp it with the intellect. In Plato's view, the intellect when used properly never makes mistakes. When you think about circularity, there's no way you could be mistakenly thinking about ovalness!

Plato also believed in a very special form, called the form of the Good, or Goodness. He uses the theory of good to argue against hedonism (the view that the good is pleasure) and subjectivism (the view that what's good for one person or culture can be bad for some other person or culture). However, when the character Socrates is asked to explain the Good, he says he cannot because it is too difficult. Instead, he gives an allegory, which goes as follows.

Imagine a person inside a deep cave. He is seated in chains, facing the inner wall of the cave. Right behind him is a bonfire, the only source of warmth and light. Behind him, there is also a stage upon which puppets are passing. Because he is facing the inner wall, he sees the shadows of the puppets that are cast on the wall. He thinks the shadows are real. Now imagine that somehow, someone else gets inside the cave, unchains the person and gets him to turn around for the first time in his life. His first reaction is that he is blinded by the fire and can't see much else. But slowly he gets used to the light and starts seeing the puppets. Now he starts realizing that the things he had thought were real were only shadows of what he now thinks is real: puppets(!). Now imagine further that somehow he is pulled toward the opening of the cave. He is frightened, yet also fascinated by the fire. Somehow he gets around it without being burned or blinded. He is now partly dragged, partly coaxed up a dark and cold tunnel toward the opening. At this point he is frightened and wants to go back, still thinking he is deserting reality. But if he is courageous enough, he makes it to the outside. Again, he is blinded by light.

But slowly, he starts getting used to it and starts seeing things outside the cave. As he looks around, he realizes that the puppets weren't real either – they were only imitations of what is truly real. Finally, the last thing he will be able to look at is the most impressive thing – the sun itself.

Plato says a little bit about how to interpret the allegory. The things inside the cave stand for particulars, while the things outside the cave stand for the forms. The things inside are copies or imitations of the things outside. Furthermore, the sun stands for the form of the Good in two ways. This is where things get a little difficult to understand. Plato says that just as the sun makes the physical world visible, so too the Good makes the forms intelligible. Second, just as the sun makes the physical world grow and flourish, so too the Good makes the very being of the forms possible. The Good itself makes being possible, but it itself is beyond being. It's the standard by which the relative goodness of all other things or beings can be measured or judged. The more you partake of the good, the better you are (whatever that's supposed to mean). The goal of life, as Plato understands it, is to partake of the good as much as possible, particularly by focusing one's intellect on the forms, and especially the Good.

Plato proposes his theory of the good as an alternative to hedonism and relativism, but it has some problems. One problem I have with the theory is that even if there is a common nature for certain things, why should we assume that there is a form that exists that corresponds to that "nature"? Triangularity is a common essence possessed by all triangles, but does that mean that Triangularity is a thing that exists separately from all triangles? I don't think Plato has given a good argument for postulating the existence of the forms. Maybe triangularity is just an idea that exists in the minds of people who are looking at triangles. And the same goes for all other forms.

The second difficulty I have with the theory is that the Good remains very mysterious even after the allegory is given. Suppose we agree that there is a common nature for triangles and for dogs and chairs, and that there's a form for triangularity, dog-ness, etc. Still, why should we think that there is an ultimate form that makes all beings possible and intelligible? In conclusion, it might be nice if there were such a thing as the Good, but Plato's argument for its existence is not convincing.

$$\frac{8}{}$$

"David, this place is *really* nice. When did it open?"

"Just last week. I thought you'd like it, Helen."

"This espresso is perfect! And these chessboards on the tables . . . *so* nice. Thanks for bringing me here. You have *such* good taste."

"That's why I spend my time with *you*."

"Flattery will get you . . . nowhere."

"Sorry, Hel. I couldn't resist."

"So . . . anyway, I'm really excited about our trip to DC. Are you?"

"Of course."

"I've got it all planned out. There's an excellent Van Gogh exhibit at the Freer Gallery. My Dad is getting us tickets. And there's a show on Virginia Woolf's early manuscripts at the National. And there's the Mall, of course. Washington's got some of the most attractive architecture in the country, you know."

"It sounds like your favorite city. Is it?"

"My favorite? San Francisco, for sure. *Nothing* competes with that, at least not in the US. Have you been there?"

"No, actually I haven't."

"The hills, the bay . . . it's just gorgeous! I won't even try to describe it."

"Well . . . maybe our next trip?"

"I'd love it! Actually, I have an uncle in San Francisco. My mother's brother. He's really cool. He's an academic. He teaches at Berkeley. In fact, you remind me of him a little bit."

"Really? What field is he in?"

"Modern European fiction. I think he wrote a book on Trollope. He's also written some short stories and I think he's working on a novel right now."

"Fiction? Novels? Sorry, it doesn't sound like me at all!"

"Oh, *come on,* David! Anyway, I didn't mean his *field*. I meant *him*. He's even a runner like you. And besides, what's wrong with fiction?"

"I don't have anything against it."

"Yes, you do. You think it's inferior to philosophy. Actually, you think *any* activity is inferior to philosophy."

"Not exactly. You know . . . there's eating, running, and . . . a few other things."

"OK, let me put it differently. You think any *intellectual* activity is inferior to philosophy."

"Well, yes . . . I guess I do think that's true."

"And what do you have to say in your defense? I've heard some of this before, but I never quite get it. Remind me – why do you have this . . . rather snobbish view?"

"Hey, who's calling who a snob? Look, it's really quite simple. Basically, fiction is entertainment. Philosophy is the quest for ultimate truth. Now, which is more important? Obviously, the quest for truth! Of course, we all need entertainment. When I was little, I really enjoyed reading stories and even making up my own stories. Lots of kids do that. And I still enjoy a good novel every so often. One thing's for sure. It's a lot easier to read fiction than philosophy. Philosophy is something you have to work at to understand. But that's the cost of the quest for truth! The only fiction I read now is assigned stuff for classes. I haven't read a novel of my own free will in I don't know how long. As you know, I also enjoy going to the movies once in a while. Movies, theater, novels – it's all basically the same stuff. But like I said, philosophy is the quest for ultimate truth."

"The quest for ultimate *truth*? Tell me, how come there are so many different philosophies? How come philosophers keep changing their theories about what the truth is?"

"Good point, Hel. But this is the way my professor in Intro explained it to me. Sure, philosophers don't always succeed in getting at the truth, but at least they try to use *rational thinking* to get to the ultimate truth. And to some extent, philosophers *do* succeed. You've read Plato's *Apology,* haven't you?"

"Of course. What about it?"

"Socrates says the wisdom of the philosopher is that he recognizes *how little* we actually know. So he was closer to the truth than any one else at his time. Actually, I think Socrates knew or understood quite a lot, and he was being a little ironic when he claimed not to know anything. One thing he knew was how to ask some really tough questions. Sure, there are different theories about the truth. Philosophy changes and grows over time. Besides, I think there are *elements* of truth in the works of *all* the great philosophers, even though they may disagree. No one's got a perfect theory. But at least they're trying. In ancient times, philosophers had to struggle to break away from mythical thinking, the stuff found in religion, whether it's Homer and Aeschylus and all those other crazy poets. A novelist or short story writer is basically a modern mythmaker. The novelist is basically saying something like this: *I can't really describe the truth as it is. That's just too difficult or impossible to do. So instead I'll make up a story that's not true . . . but at least it's entertaining!*"

"David! You have a gross misconception about fiction! The best fiction is not simply stories that are 'not true.' The great works of fiction contain profound truths. The characters constructed by the great writers – Shakespeare, Henry James, George Eliot, Faulkner – they're *real* characters! Not literally, of course, but the things they do and the things that happen to them and the things they think about are just as real or true as you and me! What they do in the novel is an outgrowth of what they say and believe, or if it isn't, that's because the characters are flawed in some interesting and realistic way. And besides, you can't always present the truth by just describing it. In a novel, truths are presented or depicted the way people act and even by the way they speak. Even little things about the way characters express themselves can say a lot about what's going in their hearts and minds. Like for example, just the simple fact that a character in a novel speaks in a hesitating manner or pauses in between thoughts tells you something or hints at something that's going on in that person's mind."

"Very nice speech, Hel. But can I ask you a few questions?"

"Yes, Socrates. Or should I call you Sock, for short?"

"I'll ignore that. Look, you claimed that some works of fiction contain great truths. Now, tell me, what is the subject matter of these truths? Are they truths about mathematics or astronomy?"

"No, of course not."

"Are they truths about physics or chemistry? About the natural world?"

"No. Obviously, not. And you really *are* beginning to sound like Socrates."

"Thanks, you're beginning to sound like one of his typical interlocutors. Instead of attacking my argument, you're attacking me. But let's not lose track. You said that works of fiction contain 'profound truths.' But they are not truths about physics or chemistry or math or astronomy. Well, are they truths about history?"

"Sometimes historical truths, but that's not what fiction is really about. The great novels contain truths about relationships, about people, about love, about life . . . ."

"OK. So you're saying that these works of fiction, especially the characters in them, contain profound truths about human psychology?"

"Yes, that's mainly what it is."

"If that's so, why can't these great authors just drop the fictional characters and say what those 'truths' are directly? Why not just write an essay or book that describes these "truths" about human psychology and leave the fictive or false stuff out?"

"Well, for one thing, that wouldn't be as entertaining, and —"

"Ah! I knew it! *Entertainment!* So it turns out that the *only* reason for writing fiction is entertainment after all! And as far as I'm concerned, I find philosophy more entertaining anyway. Characters in novels don't really interest me."

"David! Will you *please* let me finish my sentence?"

"Sorry. Go ahead."

"I was going to say that a good author *can* find ways of revealing his own views about things. He or she might even place clues in his book about what his own views are. The author is in control of the sequence of events, the way things happen, what happens to the characters. And —"

"Ah! That's another thing I don't like about fiction. The author can pull the strings and make things happen exactly the way he wants to — that's not like real life at all."

"Excuse me — let me finish my point!"

"Sorry for interrupting. Go ahead."

"I was talking about how the author can find ways to reveal his or her own view. I was saying that sometimes there are little puzzles or things that don't make sense at first glance. And these can be clues to the author's own view about things. Sometimes you think you really know what's going on in a story or even a conversation. You think that certain things are important and certain things are not. Then it turns out later that something that was at first peripheral turns out to be really important. These are clues to what the author really thinks about life or about people. What the characters say — and sometimes, even what they *don't* say — can tell you things about what the author is trying to convey. And by the way, the same thing is true in movies. A good film maker will have a way of telling you what he thinks about things, and he doesn't necessarily have to *agree* with any of his characters. You know, that's why Alfred Hitchcock always appears in his own films."

"Why's that?"

"To remind the viewer that the film isn't just an entertaining story, but is also an expression of his own views about things. And to remind the viewer that the filmmaker is really there all along, even when you don't see him."

"Is that so? I always thought Hitchcock did that just for fun."

"No way! Everything Hitchcock did was very deliberate. I mean, it could be for fun, but there's also irony involved. Like, the irony of the fact that the director of the movie is in the movie. And besides, in a good novel or film, the characters are *inseparable* from the truths which the author is trying to depict. The 'truth' is not as simple to describe as you philosophers might wish. We talked about this just the other day in my Lit class. Sometimes, the 'truth' about human beings is multilayered or ambiguous. That's why if a novel is really good, people can come up with different interpretations of what's going on in the novel. And that's another thing that makes fiction so interesting."

"Well, I agree that truth is complex or multilayered. But you can also have multiple interpretations of a philosophical text as well. My point is, if a novelist has something in mind which he can't describe or explain directly, it's not clear that there's any 'truth' in his mind altogether. This is precisely Socrates's criticism of the poets in Plato's *Apology*. The poets come up with these brilliantly beautiful poems, but they can't *explain* what 'truths' are implicit in their poems. That makes you wonder whether there are any truths there at all! And that's not to say that the poems aren't beautiful or exciting or inspirational. But that's what I'm calling *entertainment*."

"How ironic it is that you keep mentioning Plato. Didn't Plato write dramatic dialogues?"

"Yes, but that was only true pretty much at the beginning of his literary career. He used the dialogue form to depict his teacher Socrates. And those dialogues are quite entertaining. But once Plato advanced in his own thinking, the dialogue form was just a vehicle to explain his own ideas. And that's why Aristotle and pretty much all later philosophers stopped using the dialogue form."

"I still disagree. I just don't think that *all* truth is explainable, if that's a word. I think the novelist or the poet is actually capturing a *higher* level of truth than the philosopher. Besides, I just thought of something else. How about if *I* ask *you* a few questions? I've studied a little philosophy as well, and in fact I've read a lot of the *Republic*. Remember that passage in the *Republic* where Socrates is asked to explain the Good?"

"Yes. What about it?"

"Doesn't Plato say the Good is the most important thing in the universe?"

"Yes."

"And doesn't Plato say that the Good is impossible to explain except by way of a metaphor, namely, that the Good is like the sun?"

"Yes, that's true . . . ."

"So? Doesn't that show that sometimes metaphor or allegory is *higher* than philosophy?"

"Hmm . . . no, actually that's not right. Socrates says he would *prefer* to explain the Good directly, but since he can't, he falls back on a metaphor. That proves my point. Metaphor is an *inferior* form of expressing the truth. Besides which, after giving the allegory, he then goes on to explain it in some detail. So it's really not clear that he's satisfied just with the allegory."

"But still, there is a level of truth or reality which goes beyond direct description."

"Wow, I'm surprised at what you're saying. Now you seem to be waxing mystical on me."

"Why? Not everything that is true can be described 'directly.' That doesn't make me a mystic."

"I agree. It's hard – perhaps even impossible – to describe all truth directly. But when we try to describe the indescribable, that's where we all get messed up and confused. Have you heard of the famous philosopher, Wittgenstein?"

"Of course. What about him?"

"You know what he said? Of that which cannot be spoken, *nothing* should be said."

"Well, then, I guess I'll just shut up and be quiet!"

"*Oops* . . . sorry, Helen. Really, I didn't mean to be rude. Did I say something wrong?"

"Forget it. Let's just finish our coffee and go."

9

"Well, David? Now that we're comfortable in my apartment . . . shall we try some of this stuff?"

"Yes, Simon. Let's do it."

"You know what I call it? The *good essence*. I can't remember where exactly I picked that phrase up. But I like it."

"Very nice. I like it too, Simon. Let it be called the good essence from now on!"

"Great. Here, smell this."

"Ah . . . that really smells good. The only thing is . . . this is not going to be good for my running."

"Not that again, David! Here . . . just take the lighter and try some!"

"Thanks. Hmm . . . . wow . . . that's some *good* essence!"

"Right! So good, I can't understand why it's illegal. It's a shame."

"Let's face it. It has different effects on different people. A lot of people can't really handle it too well. They overdo it."

"Maybe so. But what about liquor? How many people have trouble handling *that*? I think this is much safer than liquor. Would you rather drive drunk or stoned?"

"I agree with you on that one."

"Take another hit, then."

"Don't mind if I do . . . . Anyway, it's easy to see how a person might become dependent on it."

"Yeah, David. Like coffee . . . or running!"

"Hey, I'll admit that I'm addicted to running. But it's a lot healthier than smoking! Anyway, here you go . . . your turn."

"Thanks. Speaking of different effects, this stuff has different effects on different people. Some people become blithering idiots. Perhaps they shouldn't be smoking, but that's their business. Now, with you, for example, it has the effect of making you even more talkative than normal. You start asking more questions. You start lecturing a bit. It's really quite entertaining!"

"I'm glad you're amused. You're right. Smoking loosens me up. I get a little more creative. I see connections between things that I won't normally see. Somehow, certain things just start to click. Do you know what I'm talking about?"

"Of course. And it's another reason it shouldn't be illegal."

"But what about cocaine? Do you think that should be legal too?"

"Well, it's a big jump from this stuff to cocaine. But yeah. *All* drugs should be legalized."

"I'd be nervous about going along with that."

"Give me a break, David! People should have the right to do whatever they want to do in the privacy of their own home – or dorm room! – so long as they're not injuring anyone else. I agree that cocaine is potentially more dangerous than this stuff. But just because some people misuse or overuse a certain substance, that doesn't give the government the right to make it illegal. So long as *one* person can use that substance without causing any harm, why should the fact that others abuse it make it illegal for that one person?"

"You're a true libertarian."

"What's *that*?"

"You think that individual liberties should be as great as possible, even at the cost of social utility."

"Wow. Now you *really* sound like a professor!"

"Sorry. We've been doing some political philosophy in our Intro class lately. What I mean is, according to your way of thinking, even if twenty people are going to have their lives wrecked by cocaine, so long as *one* person can use cocaine as a recreational drug without causing trouble, it shouldn't be illegal."

"Yes, you've stated my position quite well. And I would add that if people choose freely to wreck their lives, that's their own business!"

"Well, you know, we don't live in a purely libertarian society. For example, we have to pay taxes that cover education, health care and things like that for other people. And we even pay to support things like scientific research, and, hey, what about support for the arts? I'm sure you won't oppose *that*! In effect, the government takes from the rich and gives to the poor. Individuals are forced to make certain sacrifices for the good of the whole. So, your privilege to smoke whatever you want can also be taken away if overall it is better for society not to have any smoking going on."

"I don't agree. It's one thing to make people pay for certain things like education and culture. It's another thing to make it illegal for them to use some substance because of someone else's problem handling that stuff. It's really not fair. In fact, for some people – like you – it's evidently quite an important tool in the creative process. Here . . . want some more?"

"Yeah, sure. Man, it's getting smoky in here."

"I thought you liked the smell."

"Yeah, the *smell,* not the smoke."

"Anyway, take George, for example. Perhaps he'd have a new perspective on things if he smoked."

"I'm sure he wouldn't do it. He's too strait-laced."

"Of course, he wouldn't. I'm just saying, it might be interesting to see how it affects his views."

"Maybe. He might just become more of the same. But you know, I'd really like to hear you talk to Ravi and George about some of these things we've discussed. You should hear what they have to say about hedonism, for example."

"Ah! The guru and the Christian! You've been interviewing them. What do they think?"

"I'm not quite sure I understand it, but Ravi thinks that you can just *stop desiring.* Actually, according to him that's *better* than desiring things."

"That sounds crazy to me. Why would you ever want to *stop* desiring things? You might as well commit suicide. What about George? What's his view?"

"Well, hey . . . something just clicked! I just had an incredible insight!"

"Oh? Tell me about it."

"I just realized how George's view is *similar* to Ravi's, yet also *different*! George thinks it's possible to do some things *not* in order to obtain pleasure. In that way he *agrees* with Ravi. But those are things that George thinks we do out of a desire to do God's will. And that's where he *differs* from Ravi!"

"*Profundis maximus*! Still, David, they *both* sound crazy to me! I don't see how a person can do *anything* unless it gives them *some pleasure* to fulfill that desire. George wouldn't be so religious unless he got some kind of pleasure out of it. Anyway, as I've told you before, I don't believe in God."

"Yes. I know. But can we discuss that a bit? Didn't you once tell me that your background was Orthodox Jewish?"

"Yes. But I've already told you: I think that belief in God is a myth. Don't you agree?"

"I don't know. I used to believe in God when I was little. For one thing, if God doesn't exist, then there's really no explanation for our existence."

"What do you mean, 'no explanation'? The world doesn't need an explanation. It just is."

"And there's no intelligent designer? No cosmic planner? No purpose?"

"No. I don't see any reason to believe that. In fact, there's a lot that indicates to me that there *isn't* any intelligent designer at all. Think about all the evil in the world, for example."

"True. But there is also a certain order and beauty inherent in the universe. Don't you agree?"

"No way. Order and beauty are in the eye of the beholder, as the old saying goes. We *impose* order on the world because we need it and want it. Look, for all the other species that never made it through the survival of the fittest, the world was definitely *not* an orderly and beautiful place!"

"So you're saying it's just an accident that we've survived?"

"Well . . . it's not a total accident. There's *some* kind of explanation for why we were the ones who survived, rather than other species. But, still, in the end, it has more to do with luck than planning!"

"Maybe . . . . Hey, let me have another smoke. Now what was I going to say? Oh, I remember! Why do you say we *impose* order on the world? Aren't there lots of orderly things in the world? Like – the sun rises, the sun sets. Or the law of gravity. Or any other fundamental law of physics. Nature has certain regular patterns. Order is something we *discover* in the world, something that is already there."

"I disagree. Look, what scientists believed years ago they don't believe today. People perceive a certain order in the world, and later they perceive a different order. It's subjective. And even more so for beauty. There's just no such thing as what is 'inherently beautiful.' Standards of beauty change over time."

"I'm not so sure that standards change completely. We talked a little bit about this in my music course. I think there are objective standards. Beauty always has something to do with harmony and unity."

"You've been reading too much Plato! And you need to learn more about modern art, music, and literature. Maybe you haven't gotten to the twentieth century in your music course! What counted as 'order and harmony' often gets thrown out the window."

"Hang on just a second. Actually, my music prof did talk about this a little bit. A lot of modern art is a conscious rebellion against traditional standards. New artists go out of their way to do things totally differently than everything that was done before. They purposefully try to break conventions. But that doesn't prove there isn't such a thing as order and harmony, or beauty, for that matter. It only shows that there *is* such a thing as order and harmony. For without that, there would be nothing to rebel *against*!"

"Hmmm, interesting argument . . . but I don't think that's right. Look, what

I'm saying is that there's no such thing as an objective standard of beauty. Sure, in any given society at any particular time, you'll have some generally accepted standards for what counts as beautiful. So there *is* always something for a new artist to rebel against, and those are the standards of beauty generally accepted in his society at that particular time."

"I see. Yeah, you could be right."

"Of course I'm right. And even if there are certain common standards that most people have had over the centuries for what counts as 'beautiful,' that still doesn't show that there is anything that is inherently beautiful, apart from how we perceive it."

"I guess so."

"So, if the world is not inherently beautiful, then there is no need to postulate an intelligent designer to explain the world. And anyway, like I said, there is a lot of evil and ugliness in the world too. How do you account for *that?*"

"Good question. I'm with you on that one. What did they tell you about that in Jewish school . . . what is it called again . . . *yeshiva*?"

"I only went to yeshiva till tenth grade, and then I dropped out. But anyway, the problem of evil had come up by then, and I assure you they didn't tell us anything intelligent. The only thing I ever got on that was that suffering is a punishment for our sins. God! That's ridiculous! I just don't see how that answers the question. Especially when most of the people suffering in this world seem to be the least sinful. Including innocent children, of course. That *really* doesn't make any sense."

"No, it doesn't. But maybe God isn't all-powerful. That's one idea I remember learning about in one of my bar mitzvah classes."

"David! I didn't know you had bar mitzvah classes. How nice!"

"Yep, I did. Anyway, I don't remember much about it, though. It wasn't very serious."

"Look. The idea that God is not omnipotent – that's *not* a mainstream Jewish view, as far as I know. And anyway, if God's not all-powerful, who needs him? Why bow and pray? Why plead with him to save us, if we don't think he can?"

"I see your point."

"Good. Anyway, the whole thing is ridiculous. We're better off just admitting that there isn't a God and moving on from there."

"Maybe you're right. I really don't know. Well, anyway, I guess your family must be rather upset with you for breaking away."

"Yep, they are. I don't see them too much any more. It's kind of like a divorce."

"Sorry to hear that."

"Don't feel sorry for me. It's really not so bad now. I've gotten used to the situation. It wasn't so easy when I was in high school. That's when I really began to think for myself, and when I started having problems with religion."

"Didn't you discuss things with your parents?"

"My parents? Hardly. Religion wasn't something you *discussed*. It was something you *did*, period."

"Wasn't there someone you could talk to? A rabbi or someone like that?"

"Not really. No one wanted to hear what I had to say. No one wanted to hear me *kvetch* about the problem of evil, or about any questions I had."

"*Kvetch*? What's that?"

"That's Yiddish for complain, nag, whine."

"I see. And what other questions did you have?"

"Well, lots of things. Like, if God is perfect, why does he need to create the world? And just think of all the stuff in the universe God supposedly created. There are thousands and thousands of species living just in the sea alone . . . what's the point of all that?"

"Hmmm . . . that's a good question."

"And the idea of the 'Chosen People.' Think of all the millions and millions of people that God supposedly created. All of these creatures are supposedly worthless, and the Jews alone are God's favorite. Really, I think it's all just an excuse to think you're superior to the rest of humanity. It's embarrassing. No wonder Jews were persecuted for so many centuries. If you claim to be superior to everyone else, what can you expect but that people will try to prove you wrong? And then, all the restrictions, like Shabbos and keeping kosher. What a pain! Do you know I didn't have a cheeseburger until I was seventeen?"

"Wait a second. I knew about not eating pork. But what's wrong with a cheeseburger?"

"You didn't know? Orthodox Jews don't mix dairy and meat."

"Oh, right . . . yes, I did know that, now that you remind me. And what did you say about Shabbos? You mean Shabbat, right? What's wrong with resting on Shabbat?"

"Well, it serves a function. Rest, recharging the batteries, and all that. But it can get quite dull and boring, especially in the summer when the days are long. You know, Orthodox Jews don't even use electricity on Shabbos. No television, no cars, no movies, no smoking, no nothing, except eating, sleeping, reading, and going to *shul*. It's really a hard day to get through."

"I can imagine. Hey, can you do exercise at least? Can you play sports or work out?"

"No, you really can't do that either. But then again, Orthodox Jews never do any exercise anyway. Basically, they're completely unathletic! The image of the traditional yeshiva student is that of a pale, gaunt kid poring over a book. Physical exercise – not to mention sex! – is supposed to be the very last thing on his mind."

"Hmm . . . that doesn't sound too healthy."

"No, it isn't. Here, have another smoke."

"Thanks. But Simon, still . . . there must be something about this tradition that has made people stick with it over the years."

"Yeah, sure. I just told you – the belief in your own superiority. Haven't you read Nietzsche in your philosophy class? I guess you haven't gotten there yet. Look, no matter how down and out you are, if you're God's chosen people – well, if you really believe that – you're special! No matter what they do to you – beat you, burn you, kill you – no one can take that belief in your own superiority from you – as long as you believe it, of course!"

"But Simon, look. If what you're saying is true, then eventually you'd think your belief in your superiority would unravel if you got persecuted enough."

"Of course it's crazy, and it's been unraveling for some time. But look, people will do anything to feel superior to others."

"Is that consistent with your hedonist perspective?"

"What do you mean?"

"Well, you remember, hedonism is the view that people do whatever they do only for the sake of pleasure, right? And according to you, Jews over the centuries were willing to make all sorts of sacrifices just because it gave them a feeling of superiority."

"Right. So?"

"So according to the hedonist, this feeling of superiority must be *so* pleasant that it outweighs all the sacrifices and suffering they had to undergo in order to stay faithful to Judaism."

"Yes . . . well, uh . . . that's exactly what I'm saying. Look, they don't do it consciously, you know. They don't sit there and say: 'Let's undergo all these strange and painful rituals just so we can feel superior.' Most of them really *believe* in the myth. But the real reason for why the myth has stuck for so long is because it makes them feel superior."

"Well, I don't know. I guess that could be right. I don't know if that makes sense."

"Whatever! The bottom line is: it's not for me, that's for sure. Look, religion is basically a crutch . . . ."

10

From: dgoldstein@cuniv.edu   Sent: 11/15/99 1:35 AM
To: hporter@cuniv.edu
Subject: Sorry!

Helen –

I know it's late and you probably won't read this till tomorrow morning. I just wanted to say I realize I was a bit obnoxious a couple of nights ago in the café. I got a little carried away in the heat of conversation. Please don't take it personally. We have different views about fiction and philosophy. So what? I still love you. Do you still love me?

From: hporter@cuniv.edu   Sent: 11/15/99 11:03 AM
To: dgoldstein@cuniv.edu
Subject: RE: Sorry!

I just read your message from last night. Love's got nothing to do with it. I don't mind a heated conversation, as you well know. Obviously you feel your opinion is superior – otherwise you wouldn't have it. Just try to be a little more thoughtful about how you express your own opinion.

From: dgoldstein@cuniv.edu   Sent: 11/15/99 11:04 AM
To: hporter@cuniv.edu
Subject: RE: Sorry!

So, are we still OK?

From: hporter@cuniv.edu   Sent: 11/15/99 11:34 AM
To: dgoldstein@cuniv.edu
Subject: RE: Sorry!

Is that an apology, or what?

From: dgoldstein@cuniv.edu   Sent: 11/15/99 11:35 AM
To: hporter@cuniv.edu
Subject: RE: Sorry!

Yes, I'm sorry I upset you.

From: hporter@cuniv.edu   Sent: 11/15/99 11:40 AM
To: dgoldstein@cuniv.edu
Subject: RE: Sorry!

OK, apology accepted. Do you want to meet in the library lounge tomorrow to study together for the next bio test?

From: dgoldstein@cuniv.edu   Sent: 11/15/99 11:41 AM
To: hporter@cuniv.edu
Subject: RE: Sorry

Great! See you there!

II

"Helen, I'm exhausted. I just don't think I can study any more."

"Come on, David. You just need a break, that's all. Take twenty minutes."

"I'm losing it, Helen . . .".

"Come on. You can do it! It's almost over. A couple more days and midterms will be over."

"You're very encouraging. I would have given up a long time ago without you."

"David, you know you can ace the Bio test tomorrow – if you really study hard tonight. After that, the Western Civ is a piece of cake."

"Yeah, really. If I don't die taking the Bio test."

"Look . . . let's talk about something else just for twenty minutes. Get your mind off the test. Think about something else . . . ."

"Like what?"

"Like, what interesting philosophical problems have you been wrestling with lately? Or are you too exhausted to talk even about *that*?"

"Let's see . . . philosophical issues . . . yes. Regarding the nature of human frailty – the fact that we are finite, limited creatures that need sleep . . . ."

"Cut it out! Come on!"

"The fact that we are doomed to fail, at least in certain respects. . . ."

"Very funny. We're not 'doomed' to anything. Will you be *serious* for a change?"

"OK, I'll be serious. You asked me what philosophical issues I am wrestling with lately. So, seriously, this is one of them. Do you think we are creatures of fate?"

"What's that supposed to mean? Sure, things happen to us that we don't want to happen. But basically, our life is in our own hands."

"Ah, so you believe in free will?"

"What do you mean, 'free will'? Do you mean, do people *choose* to live a certain way rather than another? Of course, I believe in that. Who doesn't?"

"Look, what about all this genetic stuff that we're doing in Biology? Your genetic make-up pretty much determines how you act."

"Well, it has an effect, of course. Your personality is shaped by genetics. But it doesn't completely determine your personality."

"OK. So in addition to your genetic makeup, your environment, your education, how your parents bring you up, the time and place you're born – doesn't all that pretty much determine who you are and what you're like?"

"No, I don't think so. You still have the ability to *choose* how to act."

"I'm not sure that's true. There's a dilemma here. Either your actions are determined by your genetic make-up plus the influences of your environment, or they are *not* determined by all that. Now, if they *are* determined by all that stuff, then you're not free to choose, right?"

"Right. That's obvious. You're not really free *if* your actions are determined by 'all that stuff.'"

"Fine. But now, suppose that your actions are *not* determined by your genetic makeup plus the environment. Suppose you have a case where a person chooses to act freely, as you would say. For example, take someone's choice to continue studying Bio after a break of twenty minutes. Now, here's the problem: what explains *why* the person chooses to continue studying rather than not?"

"What do you mean? What explains it is the fact that that's what the person *chose* to do! What's the problem with that?"

"The problem is, what explains why he chose to act one way *rather than another*? You can't say that something in his genes determined that he act that way. Right?"

"True."

"And you can't say that something in his environment explained his choice."

"Right. I guess not."

"So, what *explains* his action?"

"We're going around in circles! I told you, his own choice!"

"Yeah, but what explains his choice? *Why* did he choose to continue studying rather than to goof off the rest of the afternoon? Was it something in his mind? A motive? A desire, perhaps, to do well in school?"

"Yes, I guess so . . . ."

"Ah, so you're saying that something *does* determine his choice after all! I mean, a certain desire or motive in his head caused him to do what he did. And where did that desire come from? That wasn't something he chose to have, was it?"

"No, I didn't mean to say that. Wait, you're confusing me! Look, the desire to do well in school influenced him to act, but it was still his choice to act on that desire. He could have chosen to act on the desire to goof off."

"But now we're back to the same problem if you say that. What *explains* his choice to act on the one desire rather than the other?"

"Uh . . . nothing, I guess."

"So you're saying that in a case of free choice, *nothing* explains why the person acted the way he did."

"I guess not."

"So, he could have just as well decided to act on the desire to goof off as he did on the desire to do well in school. Then the act is really a random, inexplicable act. Sort of like an accident, right?"

"Yes, I guess so. That's how free choice works."

"If that's the case, why should we hold him responsible for his action at all?"

"Why not? It was a free action. He chose to do it."

"You can call it 'free' if you want, but according to what you just said, a free choice is a random accident. There's no reason that explains why he chose to study rather than goof off. In effect, he did not cause the action. It just happened, for no reason!"

"Hmm, that doesn't sound right. Look there must be something wrong with your argument. I'll have to think about it. Anyway, twenty minutes are up! Time to get back to Bio."

"All right, Ms. Taskmaster."

"Hey, watch it! Didn't I help divert you for a while?"

"Yes. I really appreciate it. I enjoy these conversations. And after all that, I feel myself *compelled* to get back to studying for Bio."

"I guess the desire to do well on the test won out over the desire to goof off."

"Actually, it was the desire to please my girlfriend that won out . . . ."

12

"David? Come in, come in. Have a seat. How are you?"

"Hello, Ravi. Sorry to barge in on you like this . . . ."

"No problem. You're always welcome. What's going on?"

"I was wondering . . . if you could give me some advice."

"Advice? From *me*?"

"Yes, O Wise, Holy and Ancient One!"

"Cut it out. Well, what's the problem?"

"This thing with Helen . . . ."

"Yes? What about it? Has something changed?"

"Not really. I'm just beginning to think maybe I should tell my parents already."

"So? What's the problem?

"I'm still not sure it's the right thing to do."

"Well, obviously something must have changed. Why do you want to tell them?"

"Just to be honest about it. You know, my parents are always asking, 'What's going on?' And it's on the tip of my tongue, but I can't bring myself to say it."

"But why force yourself to say anything until it comes naturally?"

"Well, I just feel it's dishonest to keep hiding this."

"So you want to be honest. How noble! But, you know, you're not *lying* if you just don't say anything about it. I'm sure your parents don't expect you to tell them everything that's going on in your life. They certainly don't tell you everything that's going in *their* life. And that's *not* lying."

"I guess so."

"Hmm . . . I see that you're confused and uncomfortable about the situation. Too bad you don't meditate. That might help, you know."

"Maybe you'll teach me how to meditate some time. But right now, I don't think meditation will help!"

"I don't know about that. Look, I really don't want to solve this problem for you. Listen, did you ever think about clarifying your own thoughts by keeping a journal? That helps a lot sometimes."

"I used to keep a journal when I was a kid. Then one day, I found myself sitting with a paper and a pencil, wanting to write something, but not being able to. It was a strange, uncomfortable experience. It's like . . . I felt I had something to say, but I had no idea what it was!"

"Hmmm . . . that's *very* interesting."

"But after that happened a few times, I stopped keeping a journal. To be honest, once I grew up, it struck me that keeping a diary is something for . . . uh . . . girls or kids to do."

"You must be joking! Are girls and kids the only introspective people? Anyone who takes himself seriously is bound to keep a journal – at least at some point in his adult life."

"I don't know. I guess I don't consider my own personal life all that interesting or worth writing about."

"Is your life interesting enough to *you*? If so, you should try journal writing. It might help. It's not something you have to write for publication! Journal writing is great. It helps clarify and solidify your thoughts. If you're honest with yourself, you begin to distinguish what you really believe and value most strongly from what you don't. You identify what things you feel certain of and what things are in doubt. You also begin to see connections between things that you've never noticed before. You'll be writing about something one day, and then you'll look back in your journal and find that you wrote about something similar yesterday, and you'll notice a surprising connection between the two passages. It's also a good idea to keep track of your dreams in your journal. You'd be surprised how just by writing them down, their meaning becomes clearer."

"More great advice for the long term, Ravi. Thanks a lot! But what should I do about the particular problem I have right *now*?"

"All right, all right. Let's go through this whole thing from the beginning. Explain to me: how in the first place do you know your parents would be so bothered if they knew about your relationship with Helen? Have you ever discussed this issue with them in general? What I mean is, putting Helen herself aside, have you ever actually discussed the issue with your parents about whether you should date or marry someone who is not Jewish?"

"Uh, no. Not as far as I can remember."

"So? Why are you so sure they will object?"

"I just know it. We never had to discuss it explicitly. Ever since I was a kid, it was just *assumed* that I would marry a Jewish girl. By the way, my cousin married a non-Jew. That was not pleasant, I can tell you that. My aunt was very upset."

"So it is established for sure that your parents would vigorously object."

"Yes, of course! I wouldn't be here asking your advice otherwise."

"Calm down. Tell me, *why* is it that they would object?"

"Ethnic ties, religion. That sort of thing."

"Hmm, that could be strong stuff. But what does that mean – 'ethnic ties, religion'? Is that two things, or one?"

"I'm not even sure."

"So you have some vague idea of why your parents would vigorously object, but you really don't understand why. By the way, have you discussed this with Simon? Isn't he Jewish?"

"Yes, I've talked with him. He thinks the whole thing is ridiculous. He's already told me I should tell my parents about Helen and be done with it."

"And why haven't you taken his advice?"

"Well, he's Jewish by birth, but he's a total atheist. He's utterly rebelled against his background."

"Ah! So, in effect, Simon's already made the very choice that you're having trouble with."

"I guess . . . yes, that's right. In fact, he's broken away from his parents completely. He refers to it as a 'divorce.'"

"Very interesting! And what about you? Are you an atheist too?"

"I don't know what I am. I'm not a total atheist, but I'm not a believer either. I don't know what I believe, really. I'm skeptical, but it's hard to rule out the possibility of God's existence, I think. And I really don't know much about Judaism."

"Hmm. Well, at some point you might want to have this kind of discussion with your parents."

"About atheism?"

"That's not what I meant, but that would be good too. I meant that you should have a discussion about having romantic relationships with non-Jewish women. Maybe your parents will surprise you and be more accepting than you realize. Who knows? But you can't do that right now without spilling the beans."

"Right."

"Well . . . let me ask you this, David. You say you're not an atheist, but what do *you* think of 'ethnic ties and religion'? Is that a good reason for not seeing or dating this person?"

"No, I don't really believe that. If I really love her, that shouldn't be a reason to give up the relationship. I mean, even if God exists, why should this be a problem? Don't you agree?"

"Let's focus on you, not me."

"But I'm asking for your opinion."

"I'm not going to make this decision for you. All I'm trying to do is help you sort out the confusion in your own mind. You just said, 'If I really love her, then this shouldn't be a reason to give up the relationship.' So, let me ask you this. Do you love Helen?"

"She's definitely under my skin."

"Is it lust? Or do you love her?"

"There's definitely some lust there, but it's not *just* lust. I really do enjoy her company. We have great conversations. We're planning a trip to DC together, and I've bought her a really nice pair of earrings, which I'm hoping to give her this week. And I get this . . . uh . . . certain twinge when I think of her when I'm not with her . . . ."

"Oh? What kind of twinge?"

"It's hard to describe."

"Behold the philosopher at a loss for words of explanation!"

"Sorry! I'm trying! At least I *admit* that I can't explain it."

"How noble! But can I ask you about this 'twinge'? I'm not sure I've ever had it myself. Is it painful or pleasant?"

"Both at the same time. It's a kind of pain at not being with her. Yet at the same time it's a good feeling because you know deep down that there's something out there that you really want . . . . I confess, I'm not explaining it very well. But I know that I *have* this feeling – it has a real physiological effect. It's sharp and gentle at the same time . . . ."

"This is getting more and more interesting indeed. It sounds to me like a kind of *yearning*. Well, is it love?"

"I don't know. I can't define love, so how can I really know if this is a case of love or not?"

"Look, Socrates! Are you ready to *commit* yourself to her? To get married tomorrow? To live with her for the rest of your life?"

"No, but –"

"So you might love her in some romantic sense, but you're not ready to commit yourself to her, to have a family with her."

"No way, not yet."

"So there is some sense of 'love' in which you do *not* love her."

"I guess so. But this reminds me of something I once said to George. You're just defining the word 'love' in such a way as to *include* a commitment. Is that fair?"

"Maybe, maybe not. OK, let's forget about the word 'love' for a moment. The point is, you're *not* ready to commit to her?"

"That's definitely true."

"Good. Now we're getting somewhere. We found something you know for certain, and we can build on that. Let me ask you this. Do you think there might come a point where you *would* decide to commit to her?"

"Yes, that could definitely happen."

"But how long do you think this indefinite relationship might go on?"

"I don't really know."

"Well, if it goes on for a really long time, obviously your parents will eventually find out."

"True."

"So, either you'll come to some point where you tell your parents, or you'll break up and perhaps they'll never know."

"Sounds true. So? Where does that leave us?"

"Let's go back to my first question. *Why* should you tell your parents? The only reason is because you want to be honest about things. But you're not dishonest as long as you don't lie. And besides, maybe you'll break up with her tomorrow or next week or next month."

"No, I don't think so, but I don't know."

"Well, what's the point of telling them now, anyway? If you break up, then what did you accomplish by telling them?"

"I accomplished being honest about what's going on in my life!"

"Look, I agree that you need to have a conversation about this issue with them at some point. Maybe they'll surprise you and say it's OK. But if they strongly object, then I doubt you'll convince them while you're in the midst of a relationship itself. The relationship itself is clouding your mind, and it will cloud theirs too."

"It's sure clouding *my* mind."

"The point is, why have this conversation with them *now,* when you're not even sure you are committed or will ever commit to her? Remind me – how long have you known Helen?"

"Since the beginning of the semester."

"That's not really a long time at all."

"True."

"Well, if you want my advice, here it is."

"I'm all ears."

"Obviously, you like her. So keep going out with her. Give it some more time. After two or three months, if you really think you might be committed to her, that may be the time to tell your parents. But right now, I don't see the point in telling them about her. And if you do break up with her, I suggest you talk to them about the whole idea of having romantic relationships with non-Jewish women. That way, you'll clear the air, and hopefully you won't have quite the same problem in the future. At least you'll find out where they stand. And don't forget what I said about the idea of keeping a journal."

13
—

"Helen, what do you think of all this snow?"

  "It's pretty, really pretty . . . like a clean sheet."

  "Hmm . . . great metaphor! And now, here's something for you . . . ."

"What's that you've got? A box? For *me*?"

"Go ahead, open it."

"Let's see what's in here . . . earrings! Nice! David, these are *really* stunning! Thanks *so* much!"

"I'm glad you like them. You know, Helen, I can't believe this is happening. Such a nice dinner . . . the wine . . . and now the quad . . . on this beautiful snowy night."

"Yes, I'm having a really nice time also. But David . . . I hope you don't mind, but . . . actually, there's something I need to tell you . . . ."

"Uh-oh. What is it?"

"It's nothing bad. Don't worry. I . . . uh . . . just want you to know that . . . um . . . if some kind of mistake happens and I get pregnant . . . ."

"Yes?"

"I just want you to know . . . that I'm not planning to go through with the pregnancy."

"Oh, I see. Well, I've got to admit . . . I hadn't really thought about that . . . ."

"I just wanted to clear that up. I hope you understand. I wasn't even going to bother bringing it up. But then I thought, since we're getting so close . . . well, maybe I should."

"Sure, no problem. I understand completely."

"Good. I'm glad we see eye to eye on this. So . . . let's just . . . continue the evening. David, this snow is all very nice, but I'm getting a little cold."

"Yes, it's cold just sitting here. Let's go for a walk around the quad."

"Yes. We'll make tracks in the snow."

"Hey, David, I have an idea. Let's write our names together in the snow!"

"What do you mean?"

"Just what I said! As we walk, let's print our names in the snow with our footsteps, in large letters, all across the quad!"

"That's sounds romantic. Let's do it!"

<u>14</u>

December 3, 1999

Well, here goes. Ravi's advice: write in a journal. This is such
a strange thing. Am I really writing to myself, or do I hope
subliminally that some day someone will read this? Part of me
dreads the idea that someone might find this and see what I'm
really thinking. But this is a good exercise. Can I be honest, even with
myself, even in the privacy of my own journal?

It sure is a good thing we can't read each others minds. How
embarrassing that would be. Every time I walk down the street
or ride the subway, what I sometimes think of other people! God
only knows what other people are thinking! I wonder if ninety-five
percent of the men are fantasizing about some woman who might
be sitting right across from them. Is there anyone out there with
really "pure" thoughts? If we could read each other's thoughts,
we definitely wouldn't (or couldn't) be individuals. Free will would
definitely go out the window. We'd be like bees, all acting in unison.
We'd be too embarrassed to have immoral thoughts.

I admit I can't get my mind off H. I'm practically obsessed with her.
God, that night was amazing! Writing our names in the snow, that
sure was romantic. Never thought this would happen to me, quite
like this. I admit, a lot of it is physical for sure. I've been thinking
about that a little more consciously lately. If she were a foot shorter,
would I be in love with her? What if she were six inches taller than
I am? What if she had red hair? She'd remind me too much of my
mom. If she were too thin or too heavy, if she were this or that, etc.,
would I be in love with her?

But anyhow, the fact is I'm obsessed with H. So what do I do about
it now? Tell Mom and Dad? I'm tired of not being honest, that's for
sure. If they don't like it, it's just too bad. Why am I so hesitant?

Ravi's advice: wait two or three months and see how it goes. His
reasoning: "You're not sure you love her since you're not committed
to her, so why upset them over something that's not sure?" But
now I feel that I <u>do</u> love her, even though I'm not committed. Am
I supposed to wait to ~~get married~~ be committed before I ever tell
my parents I think I'm in love? That's crazy! When will I ever know
that I'm in love for sure? And what is love, anyway? No one has ever

figured that out. Is there really a difference between love and lust? Maybe love is just socially-sanctioned lust.

Simon's right: People are motivated by pleasure, or the avoidance of pain. I don't see how humans can be "free" from these desires, like Ravi thinks. And what about Plato's idea of the good? It would be nice if it were true, but it doesn't really make sense. There is no such thing as an absolute good. Just go with what you really want, deep down.

Now, what's keeping me from being open about this with Mom and Dad (and it's really only Mom I'm worried about) is the _pain_ it might cause them. But why should it cause them pain? It's irrational. They're not religious at all. Why should it matter who I fall in love with? Obviously, it doesn't bother H that I'm Jewish. Why should it bother me that she isn't? I don't really believe in God. And even if I did, why should it matter whether she's Jewish? The whole thing is crazy. I need to be practical about this.

Here's a plan: We're going on this trip together to Washington and I'll be seeing her parents. Obviously, I'm pretty serious about her. So I don't need to wait two or three months. This trip will decide things. If I still ~~like~~ love her after I get back from the trip, that'll be it. I'll tell my parents once and for all.

This journal thing actually worked. Need to keep up with this.

15

From: dgoldstein@cuniv.edu   Sent: 12/15/99 10:32 AM
To: sschifter@cuniv.edu
Subject: Good essence?

Hey Simon,

Where are you? Tried your cell phone but no answer. Hopefully you're in the library working online. You know what? We're running out. Shouldn't I get some more?

From: sschifter@cuniv.edu   Sent: 12/15/99 11:05 AM
To: dgoldstein@cuniv.edu
Subject: RE: Good essence?

Yes, we need to get some. Will you take care of business or should I?

From: dgoldstein@cuniv.edu   Sent: 12/15/99 4:15 PM
To: sschifter@cuniv.edu
Subject: New request

It's my turn, isn't it? I'll do it, but by the way, I need a favor. Am going to DC with
Helen for winter break, as you know. They know I'm going to DC, but I don't want
to tell Mom about Helen quite yet. (Mom's condition, you know.) Do you mind if I
say I'm going with you and staying with one of your friends?

From: sschifter@cuniv.edu   Sent: 12/15/99 5:10 PM
To: dgoldstein@cuniv.edu
Subject: RE: New Request

I still think you're better off coming out of the closet. But if that's what you need to
do, you got it. No problem.

16

"Hi, Dad. It's me."

"Dave! How are you? What's going on?"

*"Nothing much. I just called home and there was no answer so I thought I'd try you at
work."*

*"No problem. Well, Mom should be home, but she's probably resting and turned off the
ringer. How did it all go? How were your finals?"*

"I think I did fine. How's Mom?"

"Mom? She's going in for the operation in January. Otherwise, she's great!"

"I see. . . ."

"So . . . you're off to DC soon, aren't you?"

"Yes, I am."

*"Well, before I forget to ask, Mom wanted to know, who are you going with? And, where
are you going to stay? Do you have all that worked out?"*

*"Oh, yeah sure. I'm going with . . . my friend Simon. He's got a friend who lives there,
so we're going to stay at his friend's house."*

*"Sounds great. But you know what Mom will say. 'Does Simon's friend have a name?
Does he have a phone number?'"*

"I'll get back to you on that. But look, I'll have the cell phone with me, so she can always reach me that way . . . ."

"Good point. That's fine, then. Well, have a great time. You did get the money I sent you, right?"

"Yes, thanks a lot!"

"Great. Bye!"

17

David and Helen sat close together in a small booth in the coffee shop at the National Art Gallery. A soft smile curved her lips. "This really has been a great trip. And I think my dad *really* likes you," she said.

"I'm glad. I like him too," David said, smiling back at her. "What about your mom?"

"Mom's harder to figure out. But I'm sure she likes you too . . . she just keeps her feelings to herself a little more. So . . . are you going to invite me over to your parents' during spring break?"

"Yes, I think that's a good idea."

"Great."

"Well," he said. "We still have a few hours before we leave for the plane. It's lucky we're traveling on Christmas Day. There really isn't a lot of traffic or crowds. What should we do next?"

Helen shifted in her chair, moving slightly away from David. She looked at her watch. For a brief moment she lost her usual poise. David noticed, and sensed the possibility of something strange about to happen.

"Listen, I . . . meant to tell you this before. . . ." Her voice trailed off.

"Yes? What is it?"

"I just need to see an old friend from high school. She's meeting me not too far away from here. The only thing is . . . she probably wants to catch up on . . . uh . . . personal stuff . . . you know what I mean?"

Now he got the picture. Helen wanted to be alone with her friend.

"Oh, yeah, sure. You go ahead. That's fine. No problem."

"Thanks for understanding, David. You're great! Well, what should we do, then? Meet at the airport?"

"Yeah, sure. At the gate?"

"Cool. I *knew* you'd understand. So, how will you kill a few hours in Washington?"

"Uh . . . I don't know. I'm sure I'll find something to do. Walk around, I guess. Maybe go for a run."

"Excellent!" she said, as she stood up and slipped on her jacket. She leaned over and kissed him. "See you at the airport! Bye!"

His eyes followed her as she disappeared from the coffee shop out the door and down the street. He sat for a while in the shop, sipping his coffee. He wasn't really interested in seeing another art gallery. But he needed to move. He paid the bill and left.

Outside, the sky was clear and the breeze was gentle. The sides of the buildings took the brunt of the afternoon sun. The glare was sharp and painful. He had his running gear in his backpack, but he wasn't in the mood to run.

He walked on aimlessly. Soon he found himself standing in front of the United States Holocaust Memorial Museum. Then he felt a tap on his shoulder.

"Hey, young man . . . ."

David turned around. A short, roundish-looking man stood before him. He seemed like a foreigner, yet not well-dressed enough to be a tourist. He was holding a cane in one hand and clutching an envelope in his other. David tried to be friendly.

"Yes? Can I help you?"

"No, no . . . you can't help me. *I* help *you*." The man spoke with an accent. He extended the envelope toward David.

"Here, take this. Ticket inside!"

"Oh . . . no, thanks. I don't need a ticket." David smiled.

"No, no, please take!" The fellow insisted. "Ticket to museum. Free."

"That's OK. I'm not going to the museum."

"Yes, take, take! I cannot use. I am late. I must go appointment. Very important to see museum. Hey, young man! You know how long line is? This special ticket — no line! You must use ticket *today*!"

The man held the envelope out to David.

"OK, OK." *I'll take it, just to get rid of the guy.* The moment David took the envelope, the man turned abruptly and left, scurrying away. David opened the envelope, not sure what he would find. But there indeed was the ticket, which read as follows:

UNITED STATES HOLOCAUST MEMORIAL MUSEUM
SPECIAL PASS
VALID ONLY ON: DECEMBER 25, 1999

David glanced down the street, but the man had already disappeared. *What a bizarre guy,* he thought. *Well, I do have a couple of hours to kill. Now that I have the ticket, I might as well use it.* And he went in.

18
—

January 6, 2000

Well, now I'm really in trouble. I'm really confused. I'll try to explain this to myself and see if I can work something out. Mom _was_ right. I thought I knew a lot about the Holocaust, but the Museum really brought things home. The pain, the suffering. And all so deliberate, so planned out. How could people do that to each other? A modern, so-called "civilized" state. And with all the technology. Unbelievable. And why such a phenomenal hatred for the Jews? I mean, even if they thought the Jews were bad, they couldn't have been bad enough to deserve all that!

And yet, of all the things I saw in the museum, the one image that keeps coming back to me is that picture of the Orthodox man with the beard and black coat, wearing his ~~religious stuff~~ prayer shawl and the little black boxes (what are they called?) calmly boarding the train to the death camp at Treblinka. The look of peace in his face. Really strange! This is what puzzles me more than anything else. What could motivate a person to act this way? How could a person remain devoutly religious – even to that horrible breaking point? Isn't it obvious that God – if he exists – has deserted the Jewish people? Or perhaps more obvious: that God doesn't exist at all?

What would Simon say? I can just hear him saying, "The guy was so secure in his belief that he had this special status – as a member of God's chosen people – and this feeling of superiority _outweighed_ the grief and pain he had to suffer in order to maintain this special status." Could that be right?

I guess the guy thought he was going straight to heaven, so as far as he's concerned, what's to be afraid of? Is that it? I don't know. And if that's the explanation, how could a person be so supremely confident about _that_? Besides, the guy wasn't exactly smiling either. He didn't look happy. He looked resigned, yet composed at the same time. Should I just say that the guy – and all the others like him – are just plain crazy? I really don't know.

On the topic of Helen. Well, what's the next step with that? The trip was great. Her family is nice. I must admit I'm a little sore at the way she buzzed off to see her friend at the last minute. Shouldn't hold it against her, though. Anyway, I feel like I still love her. It's hard to get through the day not thinking about her. But what am I going to do about the Jewish question? I know I can't live my life just for the sake of my parents' wishes. But if they (especially Mom) feel so strongly about it, I need to make sure how I feel about Judaism before I make the decision to detach myself from it.

So – how *do* I feel about Judaism? That's precisely the problem! I don't know. And why don't I know? Maybe because I don't really know enough about Judaism itself, I guess. (Socrates, again: In this respect I am wise: I realize that I don't have knowledge.) I know some Hebrew and a few things about some traditions, but very little else. Even George knows more about the Old Testament than I do. One thing is for sure: I need to know more before I can make a decision to detach myself from it.

There must be somebody I could talk to about Judaism, and get some answers. Simon knows so much, but he's so bitter about the whole thing, too. Maybe there's a rabbi on campus I could talk to?

Good idea: find a rabbi. Maybe I'll try the Campus Ministry.

19

"Hi there. Sorry but you look a little lost. Are you looking for someone? Can I help you?"

"Yes, maybe. I was just looking for a rabbi to talk to."

"Ah! Well, you found one! I'm Rabbi Abraham. Please, why don't you come into my office?"

"Oh, well . . . thanks."

"Come in, have a seat. Make yourself comfortable. So . . . what's your name?"

"David. David Goldstein."

"Great. Nice to meet you, David. I assume you're studying here at the college. Do you have a major?"

"I hope to major in philosophy."

"Wow, fantastic! Those are deep waters! I remember with great fondness my Intro to Philosophy course that I took many years back."

"I guess you're the Orthodox rabbi here."

"You're right. The black hat and the beard gave it away."

"Well, I . . . uh . . . I wondered if maybe I could ask you some questions about Judaism."

"Sure, go right ahead. But first, can you tell me a little bit about yourself? I gather you're Jewish, and you're interested in philosophy. What else can you tell me?"

"There's not much to tell. My family is not religious at all. But my parents identify themselves as Jewish. They've always been concerned that I be aware of Jewish things. And they're very big on supporting Israel. When I was younger, we always had a nice family dinner Friday night. As I got older, we stopped being so careful about that. For a while I went to Sunday school and I learned a little Hebrew. I even had a bar mitzvah, but it was more of a social event than anything else. I remember meeting all of my Dad's friends from his office. Anyway, I hope this doesn't offend you – but it seems I'm losing any conviction I ever had in God."

"First of all, I'm not offended. I've heard of such a thing before! In fact, I'm glad you've come to talk about this. But I wonder, why are you coming to me now? Something must have happened that led you to come talk to me. What was it?"

"Actually, you're right. One thing is, I have a friend who's from an Orthodox background, and he's told me a little bit about it and I've gotten kind of curious . . . ."

"That's nice. Maybe I know him?"

"I doubt it. He's no longer observant at all."

"Oh, too bad. But that's interesting. Although he's no longer observant, somehow he inspired your interest. Hashem works in strange ways."

"Sorry? What did you say? *Who* works in strange ways?"

"I said: Hashem works in strange ways. The Hebrew word *ha-shem* literally means 'the Name.' It's the customary Jewish way of referring to God."

"Oh, I see."

"Well, is there anything else going on that lead you to come look for a rabbi?"

"Yes, actually, there is. A few weeks ago, I was in the Holocaust Museum in Washington, DC. It was really an overwhelming experience, mostly for . . . uh . . . obvious reasons. But something strange happened. Of all the images I had in my mind, one kept coming back to me. It was a photograph of a traditional Orthodox Jew dressed in a prayer shawl and wearing – what are they called again – the little black boxes?"

"*Tefillin*. And the prayer shawl is called a *tallis*."

"Right. Anyway, evidently this man was in a group of people who were being forced to board a train for the death camp at Treblinka. And obviously, this man was quite religious. But I found this utterly horrifying and confusing. Why would a person cling to religion at that point? It made me think . . . what would I have done if I had been in his position? If I had been religious, I know I would have given it up."

"Don't be so sure. If you were in his position, you would have been a pious Orthodox Jew, and maybe, like him, you wouldn't have given it up!"

"No, no. I'm sure I would have given it up to save my neck if I could. And even if I couldn't save my neck, I still would have given it up out of anger and resentment. But there was something about the man in the picture. He didn't look like he was crazy or anything like that. He looked rather composed and serene."

"Hmm . . . I might be wrong, but it sounds like it might have been Hillel Zeitlin."

"Who's that?"

"Hillel Zeitlin. He was a very interesting person. He came from a secular background, but became very religious during the period leading up to the Holocaust. He wrote articles and books, even poetry. In fact, he's a personality you might be interested in learning more about. The story is that he was last seen alive on September 11, 1942. That was the eve of Rosh ha-Shannah – you know, the Jewish New Year. He was last seen wearing his *tallis* and *tefillin*, waiting on a platform just before he was deported to the death camps."

"Really . . . well, anyway, the whole thing was quite perplexing. So I thought I would come to you. I have a lot of questions to ask."

"That's great. But first, let me tell you what I think. The fact that you went to the museum and saw the photograph just at this time in your life was *not* an accident."

"Oh? What do you mean?"

"It's what we call *hashgacha pratis,* which means God's providence over the particular details of human life."

"You think so?"

"Definitely. And, what's more, something in you moved you to come here, in response to that photograph. Do you know what it was? I think it was your *yiddishe neshama,* your Jewish soul, your *pintele yid.*"

"*Pintele yid* ? What's that?"

"You said you know a little Hebrew, right? The *pintele yid* is the little point of the letter *yod.* The proper name of God begins with a *yod.* But the little point of the *yod* also stands for that spark of God in you, that little flame that can never be extinguished. That little flame, your Jewish *neshamah,* your soul, identified with the man in the photograph. The Jewish soul always seeks God, no matter how far it has strayed from its divine source."

"Well, Rabbi, that's an interesting theory. But right now I'm not even sure I have a soul at all."

"Oh? So you must have some other explanation for why you are sitting in this room, trying to find answers to your doubts about Judaism. What's your explanation?"

"You want an honest answer?"

"Of course."

"Guilt."

"What do you mean? Guilt about what?"

"I feel guilty that I am giving up, or about to give up, a family tradition which some of my ancestors died for."

"Ah, I see. So, you *are* contemplating giving up Judaism, *has ve-shalom.* You didn't say that before."

"Didn't I say that I'm losing any conviction I ever had? But what'd you say? Something about shalom?"

"I said *has ve-shalom,* which means 'Mercy and peace.' It's kind of like saying, *such a thing should never happen.* Anyway, earlier you said you were losing conviction, but just now you said you're concerned that you're about to give up the tradition. But what would that mean for you? Does it mean you won't support the State of Israel any longer?"

"No, I don't think it would affect my support for Israel at all."

"So, what does it mean, then?"

"I, uh . . . I guess it means I might fall in love with and marry a non-Jewish girl."

"I see. Well, yes, that would indeed be a serious break with tradition. For if you did that, you would end up not raising a Jewish family at all. There's no way you can transmit the Jewish tradition to the next generation if your children are not Jewish. So, you really *are* in a serious crisis. Let's see . . . you haven't already fallen for a non-Jewish girl, have you?"

"No, not at all. Not yet."

"OK, well, look. You're obviously sincere about searching for answers, but this is going to take some time. I'm willing to do the best I can to answer your questions. But let me ask you one favor. Please don't make any rash decisions during this process. This is not a one-shot conversation."

"I'm not sure I understand."

"David, let me try to say this as nicely as I can. I don't think you realize how much you have to learn about your own tradition. First of all, you didn't even know the most common Jewish way of referring to God is by the term Hashem. In other words, until you walked in this door, you didn't even know God's name!"

"True."

"And I presume, you barely know Hebrew. Right?"

"Very little."

"So, you've barely studied any Hebrew texts in the original language."

"That's true."

"Tell me, have you studied the Torah at all, even in translation? Have you studied the *Nevi'im* or the *Kesuvim*? That's the Prophets and the Holy Writings."

"You mean the Bible?"

"No, not the Bible. That's a Christian term. I mean the *Tanakh* – the Hebrew Scriptures."

"Well, parts of it, I guess. Not much."

"And you said you are interested in philosophy, right? That's the love of wisdom, right?"

"Yes."

"So, have you studied *Mishlei*? That's Proverbs. That's one of the books in the *Kesuvim* that discusses wisdom."

"No, I confess, I haven't."

"How about *Koheles* – that's Ecclesiastes. Have you ever studied that?"

"No, I've never read that one. Actually, I thought that was part of the New Testament."

"No, it's from the *Kesuvim*! It was written by Shlomo ha-Melech – that's King Solomon. See how little you know? Sorry, I don't mean to offend! And by the way, have you ever studied the Talmud?"

"The Talmud? I'm not even sure exactly what that is or when it was written."

"Ah! David! Do you see what I'm getting at? This is only the tip of the iceberg. Judaism is an extremely rich tradition. You've got so much to learn. My point is that this process of trying to see where you stand on Judaism is not something you can decide on overnight. As it says in the Talmud, you can't learn the whole Torah 'standing on one foot.'"

"That's a clever saying. And I see your point."

"The Talmud is filled with clever sayings, believe me! So . . . you agree that this process will take some time. Now, then, let's get some idea of your questions."

"I've got lots of them. I guess the main one is: does God exist? Or – why should I believe in God? Next, if God does exist, and he is perfect, why does he need to create the world? Next, what about the Holocaust? What about all the evil in the world? Doesn't that disprove God's existence? And even if there is a God, what about Judaism? Is Judaism true? I mean, even if I came to believe in God, why should I remain Jewish, other than to fulfill my parents' wishes? And what's the whole idea of the chosen people? Does that really make any sense? Why would God, if he exists, choose a special people? And what about other religions? Are Christians all wrong? What about Islam? What about eastern religions? By the way, I have a good friend who is Christian, and he seems OK to me. I have another friend who's seriously into his own version of something like Buddhism. He's probably the most spiritual person I know. So, are these other religions simply delusions? And also, even if God *does* exist, why would he care about what we do, as long as we are good human beings? Is God so petty as to care about things like whether I eat a cheeseburger? These are only some of my problems . . . ."

"Well, David, you certainly have a lot of questions! First of all, I have a number of good books to recommend on these subjects. But that shouldn't keep us from talking. May I first make one observation? Your questions are motivated by a desire to understand things rationally. You're a budding philosopher, and that's what philosophers try to do. Now, I think there *are* rational answers to your questions, but only up to a point. Ultimately, commitment to Judaism is a matter of *emunah*. David, do you know what *emunah* means?"

"No. What's that?"

"I guess they didn't teach you that in Sunday School. *Emunah* means faith. And the thing you have to understand is that faith is not completely rational. If you expect a completely rational solution to every question you have about Judaism

– then I think you will be disappointed. Reason can only take you so far. *Emunah* will carry you the rest of the way."

"Well, I guess I'll just have to see how far reason takes me. As for *emunah*, right now I simply don't have it."

"I'm not sure that's so true. Every Jew has *emunah*, built in to his soul. But there are degrees of *emunah*, and clearly, you have some *emunah* deep down. The highest kind of *emunah* is where you have faith *without any doubt*. Tell me, have you ever at any time in your life believed in God without any doubt?"

"Yes, I think so – when I was a child."

"Ah! Just as I thought. So in fact at one point in your life, you actually had real *emunah*. And when did your belief start to slip away? When you came to college?"

"No, around the time I went to high school. Then I started having doubts."

"We can talk about your doubts later. But first, tell me: why did you believe as a child?"

"Isn't it obvious? Because that's what my parents and teachers in Sunday School taught me."

"Just a second. Tell me something. Don't you think your parents and teachers are intelligent?"

"Of course, but I'm not sure they're right about everything. Besides, why do *they* believe in God? Only because they were taught so by *their* parents."

"Well, that's called tradition, or *Mesorah,* which means, that which is transmitted or passed down from generation to generation. The history of Judaism is the history of one generation devoutly transmitting the teaching of God – that is, the Torah – to the next generation. And this tradition goes back for centuries, all the way back to the revelation of God to the people of Israel at Mount Sinai."

"That all sounds very nice, but how do we know this tradition is right or true?"

"David, how do we know *any* tradition is true? How do we know that George Washington was the first President of the United States? How do we know that Julius Caesar was a powerful emperor? In general, our knowledge of history is based on tradition."

"But there's scientific, historical evidence that George Washington existed. The same thing isn't true about Moses. Besides, aren't there other religious 'traditions' just like Judaism that also claim to be true? Is Judaism any better?"

"I confess I'm not an expert on other religions, but I know enough to know that Judaism is unique in many ways."

"How so?"

"Judaism presents a unique story. It teaches that the entire nation of Israel experienced the revelation of God at Mount Sinai. This is a story that would have been very hard to fabricate. How could an entire nation be duped into believing this? And is there any other religion that even makes the same claim? Other religions, such as Christianity and Islam, make claims about *individuals* experiencing God or performing miracles in front of other *individuals*. These could have been easily fabricated or exaggerated accounts of unusual events that really have nothing to do with God. In fact, as I'm sure you know, both Christianity and Islam are based on the premise that God revealed himself to the people of Israel at Sinai. So, these other religions start by acknowledging the historical basis of Judaism. Then, they go on to claim that Judaism is no longer valid – in which case, the burden of proof is on *them* to show that God changed His mind! Seriously, can you imagine *that*? Can you imagine God changing His mind and giving up His beloved, chosen people, with whom He made an eternal covenant? The very idea is absurd!"

"Well, that may be true. But, Rabbi, I'm not so sure that, over a period of time, an entire nation couldn't be duped into believing that they had collectively experienced God."

"David, are you aware of how meticulously the Jews have preserved the text of the Torah over the last two thousand years?"

"Not really. I never gave it much thought."

"Well, that's precisely something to which you *should* be giving some more thought. Consider the fact – a fact with which no atheist can disagree – that the text of the Torah – the five books of Moses – is the very same text that was discussed and interpreted by the rabbis during the time of the Second Temple more than two thousand years ago. We know this because the rabbis refer to the text of the Torah countless times in the Talmud, which incorporates the teachings of the rabbis."

"I'm not familiar with the Talmud, so I'll take your word for it. But what's your point?"

"My point is this. If the text has been preserved for the *last* two thousand years without change, isn't it reasonable to assume that the same text had been preserved without change for the two thousand years before *that*?"

"I don't know. I'm not really sure. Perhaps once the story of the revelation was initially fabricated, after many years passed, it caught on so well that later generations came to believe in it."

"That's really impossible, or at least, highly improbable. Consider the character of the people involved. Let's go back to your parents. You've already said they're intelligent. How about their moral character? Are they good parents?"

"Sure . . . yeah."

"Are they kind? Compassionate?"

"Yes, sure."

"Are they truthful? Honest?"

"Uh, yeah . . . sure."

"Why are you hesitating? Are they truthful and honest?"

"Yes."

"And do they strike you as gullible or foolish?"

"No, not at all."

"Do they strike you as people who would deceive their children?"

"No, of course not."

"Well? Do you think your grandparents were different?"

"No, I don't."

"And your great-grandparents? Were they any different?"

"I guess not."

"You *guess* not? *Of course they were no different!* Consider also the content of the tradition. I mean, consider what the Torah itself says. It says *Be truthful and honest*. Now then, how could a document which teaches truthfulness and honesty be fabricated? How could a people or nation which upholds these values manage to fabricate the story of the revelation at Sinai? The very idea is nonsensical."

"I'm not sure. I think it's possible. Over time, even the wildest myths can become accepted as truth."

"Perhaps it's possible, but in this case, what does your gut reaction tell you? What does your *pintele yid* tell you? And, consider something else. Our tradition teaches that in the Torah, God makes many demands upon the Jewish people. In fact we are taught by the sages that God gave us six hundred and thirteen *mitzvos* – that means 'commandments.' Why in the world would a group of people fabricate *that*? If you're fabricating, wouldn't it make more sense to fabricate that God requires a much easier lifestyle? Why would one generation teach this tradition to their children unless they were *convinced* that it was accurate? And did you know, or did you ever realize, that the Torah is a system of law governing all aspects of life – social, familial, economic, military and so on – and that the Torah is the single, longest-living continuous legal tradition in the world?"

"Hmmm . . . are you really sure that's true?"

"Absolutely! Of course, there were plenty of other ancient legal systems – the Greeks, the Romans, the Babylonians, the Egyptians and so on all had legal systems. But where are they now? All gone!"

"That's interesting. I must confess . . . I never realized all this."

"So again, I ask you. Do you really think such a tradition could have been *fabricated*?"

"Well, I . . . uh . . . I really don't know, but I'm still not convinced that it's true either."

"David, I'm not surprised. Although you have *emunah* deep down, you've become accustomed to disbelief. Your doubt is *ingrained* in you. No matter what arguments I could give you to prove the truth of the Torah, if you sat around long enough you'd probably be able to come up with some theory about how the Torah could have been fabricated. I would disagree with it of course, but you'd have a theory. Look, let's shift our discussion a bit. Earlier you said you started doubting when you reached high school. Why? What made you start doubting?"

"Well, that has to do with the other questions I mentioned earlier. It was around the time that I started high school that I began to think for myself. I suppose the first thing that bothered me was when I finally realized the amount of evil and suffering that goes on in this world. If God really does exist, why does he allow bad things to happen? Like, the Holocaust, for example?"

"Well, first of all, I can tell you that a lot of things which seem evil turn out to be good in the end. In fact, I'll tell you that in my case, the reason why I *am* Orthodox has a lot to do with the Holocaust."

"Oh? How's that?"

"It's a long story. Maybe another time."

"Really, I'd like to hear it."

"OK, I'll tell you the story the same way my grandfather told it to me. Back in Germany, just as the Nazis were coming to power, my grandfather was not a particularly religious man. He was married, living with his family in a small town near Freiburg, not far from the Swiss border. He had some success as a businessman. The Nazis began to enact all sorts of anti-Jewish laws. So my grandfather made plans to leave with his family. But just then, the Nazis enacted a prohibition against the Jews from emigrating. My grandfather managed to get some false documentation papers for himself and wife, but he couldn't get false papers for his three children. But he still felt he had to leave. He drove to the German-Swiss border, with the intention of claiming that he was merely traveling to Switzerland for a brief vacation. At the border, the police stopped him and gave him trouble. The police called in a captain, and he too was skeptical of my grandfather's claim. But suddenly, the captain received an urgent phone call. He told my grandfather to wait in the car as he went into the back office. As I said, my grandfather was not a religious man, but as he waited he found himself praying silently. He kept repeating, silently, 'God of my fathers, save my family.' After a few moments, another officer came out and said that the captain had been ordered to close down the checkpoint and pursue some fugitives who had fled across the border somewhere in the area. The captain had no time to deal with my grandfather's case. But instead of sending him back, the officer suddenly and inexplicably waved him and his family through the checkpoint! The whole thing really made no sense. He should have sent them back. My grandfather and his family crossed the border into Switzerland, where they managed to survive the war. After the war, he came to the States, and though he himself did not become religious, he sent his kids to religious schools, and eventually they became Orthodox. One of those children was my father."

"Wow. That's quite a story."

"David, there were many stories like that coming out of the Holocaust. Of course, not everyone was so fortunate. All I'm trying to say is that for some people, the Holocaust turned them more toward religion than against it. Consider, for example, how even those Jews who are remote from observance – like yourself – find they have some tie with the Jewish people by having some connection, direct or indirect, with the experience of the Holocaust. You know, the Holocaust unified the Jewish people. It gave us a much stronger identity."

"Maybe so. But couldn't God have found a way of uniting the Jews *without* allowing the Holocaust? And, if there had to be a Holocaust, couldn't God have stopped the Holocaust after a thousand or even a hundred thousand Jews were killed – rather than *six million?*"

"David, let me ask you something. Have you read the portions of the Torah that describe the fate of the Jews in exile?"

"No, not recently."

"So you've read them some time ago. Do you remember those passages?"

"No, not really. Why?"

"Well, you should re-read them. In fact, like I said before, you should really start studying the Torah all over again."

"Perhaps I should."

"I'd be happy to help you do that. It's one thing to study the Torah as a child. It's another to study it as an adult. But anyway, the Torah describes in great detail how the Jews will abandon God and forsake the commandments. The consequence is that they will be exiled from their land and then suffer horribly at the hands of the non-Jews. The Torah says that God will hide his face from the Jews, and this is perhaps the worst punishment of all. My point is, all the suffering of the Jews has been foretold thousands of years ago. But eventually, God will bring them back to the land of Israel, and renew his relationship with the people of Israel. The same theme is repeated several times in the prophets."

"Now that you mention it, I vaguely remember those passages. So you're saying the Holocaust was punishment for disobedience?"

"I hesitate to say it, but that would appear to be true. After all, the European Jews were assimilating at a rapid pace, like never before. And you know, there's a theory that if the Jews had not attempted to assimilate, there never would have been a Holocaust at all."

"Why do you say that? Even when Jews kept to themselves, they were still persecuted. What about the Crusades and the Russian pogroms, and so on?"

"Yes, they were horribly persecuted by Christians over the centuries. But that was a different phenomenon from the Holocaust. It was a different kind of anti-Semitism. It was motivated mostly by religious zealotry and religious jealousy, if you will. But Hitler and the Nazis were up to something different. They believed, in their own sick, perverted way, that the Jews were poisoning their culture by intermingling with them. The whole idea of racial purity would never have been an issue if the Jews had kept to themselves. Deep down, of course, they were intensely jealous of the Jews, and they knew that the only way to 'prove' their own supremacy is to deny the supremacy of the Jewish people. That's the root of all anti-Semitism, by the way."

"What do you mean?"

"The non-Jews cannot stomach the fact that Israel is the chosen people and they need to disprove it by persecuting us and trying to eradicate our existence. But actually, every persecution is a backhanded admission that, in fact, we are the chosen people!"

"Rabbi, that's an interesting theory. But let's get back to the point. You were saying that the Holocaust was a punishment for assimilation."

"I can't say for sure, but it seems like a distinct possibility."

"But many of the Jews who suffered in the Holocaust were Orthodox!"

"Yes, but God holds the Jews responsible as a group. And besides, you should know that even among many Orthodox Jews in Europe there was a lot of denial about the anti-Semitism of the Europeans. In fact, Hillel Zeitlin – the person I mentioned earlier – prophesied years in advance that the Holocaust was coming and that the Jews should leave Europe if they could. Unfortunately, not enough Jews listened. It was a communal blunder."

"Then why did he stay?"

"He refused to leave his community behind."

"Well, anyway, it still doesn't seem fair. I mean, what about the children?"

"What about them? Children are here only because their parents bring them into this world. If the parents behave badly, the children suffer. It's not so much that the children are being punished, but that they suffer the consequences of the parents' behavior. That's the way God set up the world. Look, the same thing happened in the case of the Flood."

"The flood? What flood?"

"The story of the Flood in Genesis. Remember Noah? God destroyed almost the entire world because human beings were wicked. Of course, there, too, he commanded Noah to build the ark over a long period of time so that people would have a chance to do *teshuvah*, to repent. But in the end they didn't, and countless children perished in the Flood because of the sins of their parents."

"Well, even if all that's true, it still doesn't seem *right*. And anyway, there's so much other evil and suffering in this world, aside from the Holocaust. What about birth defects, disease, famine, and things like that?"

"Look, I'm not God. Neither are you. So why should we even expect to understand everything God does or allows to happen in this world?"

"If you say that, you're admitting you don't have an answer to the problem of why there is evil."

"It depends on what you mean by 'problem.' If you're asking why God allows evil things to happen, I *do* have an answer. It's part of God's plan and it's all for the good in the long run. If you're asking what *particular* good in the long run every evil serves – then I don't have an answer except to say that we can't expect to know every part of God's plan. Look, David . . . the problem of evil was not noticed by you for the first time. The problem of evil and why the righteous suffer is the main subject of the book of *Iyyov* – that's Job. Have you ever studied that book?"

"No, I haven't. I mean, I know the story that Job was a righteous man who suffered a lot. But that's about all I know."

"Well, again, you should really study the book some time. But basically, to make a long story short, I can tell you in simple terms what the answer is to the problem of evil as taught by the book of *Iyyov*."

"Oh? What is it?"

"It's basically what I just said. This is the teaching at the end of the book, when God appears to Iyyov: God is the absolute, eternal Creator of all things. Man cannot expect to understand God fully, and there are certain things he just has to accept as part of *emunah*. It says pretty much the same thing in *Pirkei Avos* – that's Ethics of the Fathers, which is part of the Mishna. You should really take a look at it. Anyway, it says there, '*Ein be-yadenu mi-shalvas reshaim, ve-af lo mi-yisuras ha-tzaddikim.*' That means: We don't know why the wicked prosper, nor even why the righteous suffer. But we accept it anyway because . . . God is God."

"Sorry, but I don't see that as an answer. If that's the answer, then belief in God's goodness is blind and irrational!"

"No, it's not blind and irrational, because belief in God has a basis in tradition, like we said earlier."

"Rabbi, the tradition teaches that God is all-good and all-powerful. Doesn't the existence of evil *show* that this belief is irrational, and that therefore the tradition must be mistaken?"

"No, because an all-powerful and all-good being might have reasons for allowing some evils that have a good purpose, but which we mortals simply cannot understand! Look, let me ask you something. You're claiming that the existence of evil shows that God doesn't exist. Don't you think Abraham, Isaac, Jacob *knew* about the existence of evil?"

"I . . . uh, I suppose so."

"What do you mean? Of course they *knew* about the existence of evil!"

"Yes. I'm sure you're right."

"And don't you think that Moshe, Dovid, and Shlomo – that's Moses, David and Solomon – knew about evil?"

"Yes, they must have."

"Don't you think all the *tanaaim* and *amoraim* – those are the rabbis from the talmudic period – don't you think they knew there was pain and suffering in the world?"

"Yes, you must be right."

"In fact, some of the most famous tanaaim were brutally tortured to death by the Romans. Have you heard of Rabbi Yishmael the High Priest? The Romans flayed the skin from his head with a metal comb. He died when they reached the part of his head where the *tefillin* are worn. Are you familiar with this story?"

"I am now."

"Have you heard of Rabbi Akiva? The Romans tortured him to death, too. But he died with the words of the *Shema* on his lips, affirming his faith till the very end. So, obviously, Rabbi Yishmael and Rabbi Akiva knew suffering! And what about the fellow you saw in the photograph in the Holocaust? Surely he knew pain and suffering most intimately."

"Yes, of course he must have."

"Well? If it's so clear that evil is logically incompatible with God's existence, why did these great people go on believing? Were they irrational? Were they less smart than you and me?"

"I . . . uh, I don't know what to say. Like I said, that puzzles me very much. Still, there's something here that still doesn't satisfy me."

"An interesting way to put things! Perhaps you mean, what I said doesn't satisfy you *emotionally*. But isn't what I said a *logical* response?"

"Rabbi, with all due respect, the fact that some smart people go on believing something is not proof that it's true or logical! And I just don't see what good purpose is served by so much evil that couldn't be achieved in some other way."

"But just because you can't see it doesn't mean it doesn't exist."

"Sure. I guess it's *possible*. . . ."

"Ah! Well, at least you now concede that the fact that there is evil does not conclusively *disprove* God's existence, which is what you said at first."

"Did I? Well, it's still a source of doubt. Let me put it this way. The burden of proof is on you – I mean, you as a *believer* – to show that God *does* exist. All those people you just mentioned – Abraham, Jacob, Moses, David, the ones that the Romans killed, the guy in the picture that I saw in the Holocaust Museum – they all *believed* in God. That's why they weren't bothered by the problem of evil. Now, if you could *prove* that God exists, then I would have to admit that all evils have some good purpose, which we cannot necessarily understand. But, so far, all you've offered as a proof for God's existence is the tradition of the revelation at Sinai. That's just not enough to convince me, because that could have been fabricated."

"*Oy* . . . what can I tell you? Like I said, your disbelief is *ingrained* in you. Even if I came up with a proof of God's existence, eventually you'd find a way to poke holes in it!"

"Rabbi, if you offered me a *good* proof, I wouldn't find holes in it."

"Look, let's set aside the problem of evil for a moment. What *else* makes you doubt your belief in God?"

"Well . . . to begin with, if God is perfect, he doesn't need anything, right?"

"True."

"If he doesn't need anything, why did he create the world?"

"I don't know if we can know the real answer to that question. How can we fathom God's reasons for creating the world? But I'll suggest something anyway. Look, Hashem is a God of *hesed,* or benevolence. In other words, God is inherently good. Since he's good, he wishes to share that goodness with a conscious creature, such as mankind. So, He can't share that goodness unless he creates the world!"

"Well, that only pushes the question back. *Why* does he need to share his goodness with others?"

"He doesn't *need* to. He *chooses* to do it out of his *hesed,* or goodness."

"OK, but why?"

"I just told you why!"

"I don't know – and even if that's true, it means that the whole world was created for man's sake alone. Can that be right?"

"I don't see the problem. And what else bothers you? What other questions do you have?"

"Well, this doesn't have so much to do with a belief in God, but with Judaism in particular. Like I said before, the whole idea of the chosen people is strange. If God exists, why would he choose a special people? That doesn't seem fair. And the whole idea of keeping separate from the non-Jews . . . it's not democratic, that's for sure. It promotes hostility and jealousy as well. Don't you agree?"

"I agree that it causes hostility and jealousy, but that's a secondary issue. The question is, *did* God choose a special people or not? If he did, then it's humanity's responsibility to treat Jews with respect, at least as much, if not more so, than they treat others with respect."

"But why *would* God choose a special people in the first place? That's the difficulty."

"Ah! Again, you're asking *why* God did something. You're looking for a rationale, and any rationale is going to be subject to criticism. Just keep that point in mind. I would suspect that if God chose Abraham, there must have been something special about his *neshamah* or his soul that made him worthy of being chosen. But if you read the Torah carefully, you will see no obvious rationale for why God chose Abraham. He just *did*. It was divine fiat."

"That's it? No reason at all?"

"One could argue that a reason emerges after the fact. When was the last time you studied Genesis in detail? Perhaps I should refresh your memory, then. Abraham turns out to be the only one who's really interested in worshipping God. Really, you should read the book of Genesis once again, if only to see that what I'm saying is correct. Actually, you have to read the book of *Shemos* – that's Exodus – as well."

"OK. I'll do that. But meanwhile, you can refresh my memory."

"In the beginning, God creates the world, and he creates man. Now, ultimately the purpose of creation is for everyone to serve God. Right away, Adam sins and gets kicked out of the Garden of Eden. Then, there are ten generations from Adam to Noah. By Noah's time, everyone is wicked except for Noah. So the whole world is destroyed except for Noah and his family. Then, after the Flood, there are ten generations to the time of Abram, or if you don't mind, I'll use the Hebrew, Avram. Again, the people are sinning left and right. They build the tower of Babel, worship idols, and so on. But evidently God saw something special in Avram. Avram had potential to really be a decent human being. So God makes Avram a promise. It amounts basically to this. "Walk in my way, follow my path, and I will make of you a great nation. I will make a covenant with you, that includes what will become the land of Israel – if only you commit yourself to a way of life that is just and compassionate, a life that is completely devoted to God." Avram agrees. Soon his name is changed to Avraham as a sign of this special covenant. Is this making sense so far?"

"Yes, I think so. Go on."

"So, Avraham is the first chosen one. He passes ten tests that show his total devotion to God. He's even willing to do something that doesn't make any sense at all – sacrifice his beloved son, Yitzhak, to God. But God makes it clear that although he appreciates Avraham's willingness to perform this action, it is not what he demands in general. Now, unfortunately, it turns out that not all of Avraham's descendants were fit to carry on this covenant. Esav and Ishmael are rejected. Only Isaac and Jacob are up to the task. Soon, Jacob gets a new name – Israel. All of his children are deemed fit for this special bond with God. That's why we're called Bnei Yisrael – Israelites, and not Abrahamites. Anyway, all the Israelites go down to Egypt and eventually become slaves. Of course, this is all part of God's plan. As a sign that he has chosen the people of Israel, God takes them out of Egypt with miracles and wonders.

"At Sinai, God reveals himself to the people and offers them another special choice. This time, it's not just about walking in God's way. It's about accepting God's law, the Torah. Essentially the choice is this: "Accept God's law, and God will show you special providence, from now until the end of time. Accept God's Law and you will be the *am segulah*, God's special, treasured nation." And, the people answered, "*Naaseh ve-nishma*," which means, "We will obey and we will listen." By the way, the sages of the Talmud derive from this that the Jews committed themselves to obey even *before* they heard what the Torah contains. Again, David, you see that faith precedes understanding. Ultimately, we're supposed to keep the Torah *lishmah*. Do you know what that means?

"No, I don't."

"*Lishmah* means for its own sake, for no other reason."

"I see."

"Anyhow, from that time on, God has a special relationship with the Jewish people. There are rights and privileges, but there are also responsibilities. Part of those responsibilities involves keeping a distinct identity. If someone wants to join up, and commit themselves to our way of life, that's fine. Judaism accepts converts if they're serious, but that's going to be pretty rare. Like I said before, there's something special, something elemental about the Jewish soul. There's a certain ethnic identity that Jews have – something that, as a general rule, non-Jews just can't identify with. Really, this goes beyond reason. It's why some people who are so removed from Jewish observance in many ways still find the idea of intermarriage deeply disturbing, even though they can't explain why. But anyway, what was I saying? Ah, yes. Jews are chosen to serve God, so God holds us to a higher standard of responsibility than the rest of the nations. We are, so to speak, God's children, and if we misbehave, we are punished more severely than if we were strangers. On the other hand, if we fulfill our responsibilities, we are richly rewarded, both here and in *olam ha-ba* — that means the next world."

"The next world? Is there really such a thing?"

"Of course. Absolutely! "

"I thought Judaism didn't believe in a next world."

"*Has ve-shalom!* That's dead wrong. The belief in the next world and the resurrection of the dead are central doctrines of our faith. It's clearly stated in the Talmud."

"Really . . . well, I must say that's hard to accept."

"Why is that? If God created *this* world, surely he can manage to create a *next* world. And if God created our bodies and our souls, surely he can manage to resurrect us after we die."

"I guess so. It all just seems too . . . uh . . . strange to me. Stranger than believing in God, even."

"There you go again. Don't you see? Your disbelief has nothing to do with whether it's rational or not. You just don't want to believe it because it's *strange*. I guarantee you that there are many truths in this world that are stranger than the idea of a life after this one!"

"Maybe so. But Rabbi . . . getting back to the question about chosenness – what you're saying basically is that only Avraham and his descendants—or rather, *some* of his descendants – were worthy of this relationship with God. But what about all the other millions of people in the world? Are their lives worthless?"

"No, of course not. Jews are special, but all human beings are created in the image of God. And, what's more important is that the nations are obligated to obey the seven Noahide commandments. Are you familiar with that concept?"

"No. I've never heard of it. What is it?"

"Perhaps I should have mentioned this before. According to Jewish tradition, there are seven basic commandments that are incumbent on all human beings. They are: do not worship idols, do not blaspheme God's name, do not murder, do not commit incest, do not steal, do not eat from the limb of a living animal, and establish courts of justice."

"I see. Very interesting. So there is a Torah for Jews and there's a Torah for non-Jews too."

"Yes, you could say that. This is where we get our concept of the righteous gentile. Any non-Jew who keeps the seven commandments out of a sense of obedience to God and the desire to worship him merits a place in the World to Come."

"Ah, so now you *are* saying that life is worthless without obedience or devotion to God."

"I know that's not very PC, but yes, ultimately it's true. I'm just telling you what traditional Judaism teaches without sugar-coating it. Look at it this way. If you *don't* worship God, you're essentially doing whatever you do for the sake of your own pleasure. And that, in the grand scheme of things, is worthless. That's the way animals act – for the sake of their own pleasure. So you're living the life of an animal if you do not serve God. That's what King Solomon says in *Koheles*. It's a famous passage, and in fact it's quoted in the daily prayers: The difference between a human and an animal isn't really that much. Life is basically *hevel* – that means 'worthless' – unless you have a relationship with God. In that case, life is very worthwhile indeed!"

"Rabbi . . . I can't accept that. Don't you think there are many non-religious people around who are decent human beings and who live worthwhile lives?"

"It may seem that way on the surface. But think about Germany just before World War II. Germany was considered the most cultivated society of the times, and look what happened. In just a few years, they descended to the depths of depravity and evil. And take a hard look at our own society today here in America. Secular people are nice and kind as long as it gives them pleasure to do so, and so long as it doesn't cause them any pain. But the minute people think they can get away with things, they will. The minute doing what's right entails some sacrifice – forget it! I'll give you an example just off the top of my head. People these days engage in premarital relations or even extramarital relations left and right. Isn't that so? They think it's all harmless fun and games. Or they think they're in love when really, all they're doing is satisfying their urges. It's really all about mutual self-indulgence. And what happens when the girl gets pregnant? Often, they get rid of the fetus without a second thought. Granted, having a child out of wedlock is very difficult. It's not easy going nine months of pregnancy, and then keeping the child or perhaps giving up the child for adoption. The only people who are willing to do what's right are real religious people, like Orthodox Jews or devout Christians, who are willing to do what's right even at great sacrifice."

"Rabbi, I think your example's a little unfair. I mean, the whole question of abortion is a moral dilemma. Some people don't think a fetus has any rights whatsoever."

"At least it should be a matter of concern! What I'm saying is that if you act for the sake of *pleasure,* you can easily end up twisting things around so that the pleasure of sex becomes more important than the conception of a human life! My point is that if you act for the sake of pleasure, sometimes your act will happen to be right and good. So, some non-religious people happen to be decent because they happen to find pleasure in good actions. But if they were to find pleasure in bad things, they'd do bad things just as quickly!"

"Well, I'm not sure about that. You're assuming that if there's no God, the only reason to behave one way or the other is for the sake of pleasure, and I'm not sure that's true. But let's go back to what we were talking about. I had asked: why did

God create all the non-Jews? Then you said that life is meaningless without God. So how does that answer my question about why God chose the Jews as special? That only makes the problem worse."

"No, you've got it all wrong. The Jews are supposed to be a 'light unto the nations,' as the prophet Isaiah says. And we've done that to a certain extent. The problem is that Jews have failed to some degree to perform their duty, and that messed things up. When we don't mess up, the nations of the world are faced with a choice. Those who choose rightly respect us and are inspired by us. In fact, they often seek to imitate us in one way or another. Those who choose wrongly persecute us and seek to destroy us. Unfortunately, Jewish history since the exile is largely a history of persecution. But eventually, we'll get it right, and then the whole world will be blessed through us. That's the covenant God made with Avraham."

"I guess what you're saying makes internal sense. But don't you think that there are non-Jews who are religious and spiritual people too? Let me ask you this. Does traditional Judaism grant any religious status to Jesus?"

"No, sorry. None at all."

"You mean, the Jewish prophets never predicted the coming of Jesus?"

"No. That's a totally non-Jewish interpretation of Jewish texts. From a Jewish perspective, it's nothing but a delusion."

"Hmm. Rabbi, isn't it arrogant to believe that the Jewish religion is true, and all other people on earth are suffering from delusions?"

"Well, not all other religions are *completely* false. They may be *partially* true and *partially* false. Like I said before, the Torah teaches that man is made in the image of God. So, deep down *all* human beings seek God, though they may not know it. There are some things many religions agree upon, such as that there is one God who created the world, and who demands our allegiance and obedience. Christianity and Islam agree on this, though I must tell you I have never quite figured out how Christians reconcile the oneness of God with the doctrine of the trinity and the incarnation. And that's a serious problem, because they may be violating the Noahide prohibition against worshipping multiple gods. But we don't need to go into that now. As for eastern religions, I confess I don't know very much about them. But the bottom line is, a religious Jew does not have to believe that all other religions are *completely* false. Rather, he is committed to believing that those teachings of other religions that *conflict with Judaism* are false."

"So an Orthodox Jew has to believe that other religious people are deluded about anything that differs from Jewish teaching?"

"Correct. What's so horrible about that?"

"Isn't it arrogant to believe that we have the truth and they don't?"

"David, people in any of these traditions believe that *they* have the truth, and the *other* guys don't! Look, either the founder of Christianity was God incarnate – or he wasn't. Either Mohammed was the greatest prophet to whom God spoke – or he wasn't. And so on. Someone's got to be wrong, and someone's got to be right!"

"Maybe the wisest thing to do is remain skeptical and not believe *any* religion. If you're going to be religious, which religion should you pick? There's no rational way to decide."

"Well, I think your own tradition is a good place to start. After all, it is *yours*."

"So what? Why does the fact that it's *my* tradition make it superior?"

"Well, between you and me, I *do* happen to believe it is superior, but right now I'm just saying that it makes sense for anyone to at least start with his own tradition before he abandons it in favor of something else. In a way, it's already evident that you are starting to take it seriously, perhaps for the first time in your life."

"But from a strictly rational point of view, why should I take my own tradition more seriously than any other?"

"First of all, there is no such thing as a 'strictly rational point of view.' And second, because your own tradition has molded and shaped your identity. It's your home, your family. Wouldn't it be ridiculous to ask, 'Why should I love my home and family just because they happen to be mine?'"

"Well, if there is something wrong or abusive about the family, people *should* break away."

"Of course. But just now you weren't claiming there is something wrong or abusive about Judaism. You were questioning why you should stick with Judaism versus any other tradition."

"OK then, here's another problem I have with the Jewish tradition. I find it hard to believe that God would really care about some of the things which Judaism teaches he does care about, such as, whether I eat pork or cheeseburgers, or whether I drive a car or watch TV on Saturday."

"Excuse me, but on what basis do you say this? How can you possibly know what the Almighty God, creator of the universe, might or might not care about?"

"I – I don't know. It just seems petty."

"Pettiness is in the eye of the beholder. In fact, it would be quite surprising if we could predict what God would or would not demand of his creatures. Look, children often find the commands of their parents incomprehensible and sometimes even cruel – such as when they're not allowed to have too much candy or have to have an injection at the doctor's office."

"That's true, but –"

"All the more so, a mere human cannot expect to know – apart from revelation – what God would command or forbid. You know, King Solomon was supposed to be the wisest man who ever lived. Yet our tradition says that he did *not* know the explanation of the commandment of the *parah adumah,* the red heifer."

"What's that? The red *what*?"

"The red heifer. A female cow. It's a little complicated. The bottom line is that in order to become ritually purified from contact with the dead, the Torah prescribes that we must slaughter a red cow and sprinkle a mixture of its ashes and water on the impure person. The person who sprinkles the water also becomes impure, and that doesn't seem to make sense."

"No, it sure doesn't!"

"Precisely. So not everything is rationally comprehensible to us. Like I said before, ultimately, we keep the commandments because God commanded them, not because we understand them. That's the idea of doing a commandment *lishmah*, just because God said so."

"Even – what did you call them – the Noahide commandments as well? At least some of those make sense, like not to murder or steal. Shouldn't we do *those* because we understand them?"

"No, not really. Those commandments seem to make sense to us, but then again, abortion might seem to make sense. So might euthanasia, pornography, homosexuality, and so on. Using reason alone, humans come up with different moral codes. That's why in the end, we need to rely on God's commandments to know what is right or wrong. You've studied philosophy. Don't you agree that there is no way that human reason can establish an absolute moral code?"

"I haven't studied ethics yet, but I do know that many different philosophers have tried, but yes . . . it is difficult to come up with an absolute moral code based on reason alone."

"Difficult? It's impossible! But getting back to the topic of reasons for the mitzvos, there *is* an explanation given for at least one of the examples you mentioned earlier."

"What's that?"

"The commandment to keep Shabbos. We are commanded to keep Shabbos partly because it reminds us of the creation. To violate Shabbos is in effect to *deny* that God created the world. So, it is understandable why God would care about the violation of the Sabbath. Now, there may be some reason for the prohibition against pork, but we just don't understand it. In either case, the bottom line is that we obey the mitzvos not because we understand them, but because God gave them!"

"Yes. Well, I guess it all boils down to the fact that I can't accept your earlier argument based on the tradition that God revealed himself at Sinai."

"What do you mean?"

"Well, *if* I were to accept the argument based on tradition, and *if* I believed in God and the divinity of the Torah, *then* none of these other problems – the problem of evil, the problem of how to reconcile Judaism with other religions, and the problem of why the Torah makes such strange demands – none of these problems would bother me. I would be able to dismiss those problems by saying that somehow God must have a reason for allowing evil, and that somehow all these other religions are just wrong or misguided . . . and that somehow God has reasons for commanding things that I don't understand. But the fact is that I don't accept the argument based on tradition, and I *don't* think I believe in God . . . so all these problems then become problems. Do you see?"

"Yes, I think so – but you have to remember what I said earlier about *emunah*. I agree that there is no air-tight rational proof of God's existence or for the truth of the Torah. You know, the Torah records how even the Israelites in the desert who experienced God speaking to them from the heavens and experienced countless miracles – many of them still doubted his existence and his word! Similarly, given *any* argument, a clever skeptic will always find some hole in it."

"Well, then, it looks like I'm just going to remain stuck where I am. You've essentially admitted that no argument will be convincing to me."

"You know, David . . . actually . . . there is a path – and really only one path – to be convinced of the truth of God's existence and the Torah."

"What's that?"

"It's a path that's very difficult in one way, but very easy in another way . . . and it's not an argument."

"What is it, then?"

"Like I said before, the Jewish soul knows deep down that God exists and that the Torah is true. But that knowledge is buried, so to speak, deep within the covering of the body. Now, if you were to study and observe the commandments and laws, the rituals and customs of the Torah, then that inner feeling would start to come to life. And then, if you worked on yourself really hard and developed your *middos* – that's your character traits – and if you refined yourself till your soul was very pure – then your *neshamah* would be like a flickering candle that is fanned to a burning flame. This is what's called the way of *mussar,* which basically means discipline. If you follow this path, you will feel in your heart of hearts that the Torah is true. Your *neshama,* your Jewish soul, would come to life and tell you that the Torah is right and valid, even though you couldn't necessarily prove it. That's what I call real *emunah,* real faith!"

"Hmm . . . so the only way to see that Judaism is true is to experiment with it?

"Yes – except that it's not a scientific experiment that you can do in a disinterested, impartial fashion. It's an experiment into which you must throw your entire self. After all, Judaism is essentially a way of life, not just a system of beliefs. The best way to judge the validity of a way of life is to *live it*. That includes learning and practicing it. Like anything else, *practice* is crucial."

"Hmm . . . I don't know . . .".

"*Nu?* What's holding you back?"

"Sorry? What did you say?"

"Excuse me. You're not familiar with the Yiddish word '*nu*'?"

"No. What's it mean?"

"It means, sort of like, *well?* But I didn't mean to be rude. I'm just asking, *nu,* what's holding you back from experimenting with the traditions of the Torah? I know you have doubts, but why should you let *doubt* hold you back? Maybe your doubt will dissipate if you make a commitment to keep Torah. And I'll tell you something else. If you start living a Jewish way of life, if you start fulfilling mitzvos,

I guarantee, *you will see effects in your life*. You'll start seeing God's providential hand at work in the most particular ways."

"What do you mean by that?"

"David, so much of what's important in our lives *seems* coincidental. You meet people, you see things, events happen that seem like accidents. But if you believe in God, you begin to see a pattern. Again, it's called *hashgacha pratis*. By the way, David, are you familiar with the codes discovered in the Torah?"

"The *codes*? No I don't think so. What's that?"

"I'll give you an article to read about that. Some people claim that current historical events are hinted at in the letters of the Torah. In other words, if you read the letters in certain sequences and combinations, you find references to events such as World War II, the death of JFK, and even the death of Prime Minister Rabin."

"What? That really sounds hard to believe! "

"It's really quite amazing. Some statisticians claim to find flaws in it, but I think it's pretty impressive. Anyway, it's something worth looking into. But that was really a digression. My main point was: if you let yourself believe in God, and you work at learning Torah and keeping mitzvos, you will begin to see God's hand in your life. Things will start clicking and falling into place, and eventually you will find your belief and your commitment becomes deeper and deeper. You will see what a great, tremendous thing it is to have a relationship with *Ha-kadosh Baruch Hu*, the Holy One, Blessed Be He."

"Maybe so. In a way . . . it would be nice to believe that what you're saying is true, but I'm still quite skeptical."

"Look, you're at a crucial stage in life. Either you make a serious effort to claim your Judaism now, or it may be lost to you forever. As Hillel said in the Talmud, 'If not now, when?'"

"Well, I'm certainly willing to study more about Judaism. But I'm not so sure I want to start taking on new commitments just yet."

"*New* commitments? Not really! You'd be returning to the commitments of your ancestors. *Ancestors?* What am I talking about! You'll be returning to the commitments of your great grandparents and probably your grandparents. Look, let me make a suggestion. I'll recommend some books for you to read. In fact, I'll lend you the books. And also, why don't you take upon yourself to fulfill just one or two mitzvos? By the way, you realize that there are negative and positive mitzvos, right?"

"What do you mean?"

"There are dos and don'ts, so to speak. The laws of kosher are basically don'ts, such as, don't eat pork, don't eat meat with milk, don't lie or make false promises, etc. Then there are do's – like, say the *Shema* every day, honor your parents, study Torah, be honest – those are positive commandments."

"I see."

"So what I was going to suggest was: how about taking on a commitment to do just one or two negative commandments and one or two positive commandments."

"Well, I guess there are a few of those that I already do. Like, honoring my parents and not making false promises or lying."

"Good. But do you think there might be any room for improvement in these areas?"

"Ah . . . well, I'm sure there's always room for improvement."

"Good. And what about some of the other commandments. For example, do you think you could try keeping kosher a little better? Pick one day out of the week when you strive to eat only kosher all day. Or pick one food that's not kosher and try to avoid it. By the way, did you know there's a kosher cafeteria on campus?"

"No, I didn't."

"You should try it. Anyway, how about just cutting out the cheeseburgers?"

"I . . . I guess that's not too hard. Can I combine your two recommendations and just not eat cheeseburgers one day a week?"

"Very funny! But seriously, David, even that's better than nothing. And look, are you familiar with the *Shema*? I mentioned it before. It involves the affirmation, "Hear, O Israel, the Lord our God, the Lord is one.""

"Yes, I'm familiar with it."

"Many people know that it's what religious Jews are supposed to say when they're about to die. But the recitation of the *Shema* is actually part of the daily service, or *tefillah*, of both the morning and evening. After one recites the first verse, there follows three passages from the Torah describing, the commandment to love God, the principle of reward and punishment for good and bad deeds, and the commandment to remember the exodus from Egypt. The reason that's so important is because that's when God chose us as his people. Anyway, I would suggest the mitzvah of reading out loud at least the first portion of the *Shema*, every day when you wake up, and every night before going to bed. Here, let me lend you this book. It's a *siddur*, a traditional prayer book. You can learn so much about Judaism by studying the *siddur*. And this is a recent translation with explanatory notes – it's really a fine edition. Another thing I was going to ask is: do you have a pair of *tefillin*?"

"No, I don't."

"I'd be happy to help you get a pair and show you how to put it on."

"Oh, no. I mean, no, thanks . . . . I really don't think so."

"All right. Well, in the meantime, why don't you look through the *siddur*? And, how about coming to services on campus this Shabbos? We have Friday night services and Shabbos morning services. In fact, speaking of Shabbos, I have another idea. When was the last time you really observed Shabbos? Why don't you join me and my family for dinner this coming Shabbos? There is no substitute for experiencing the sanctity of the Shabbos. I guarantee that if you start keeping

Shabbos the way you're really supposed to, you'll literally feel the special sanctity, the *kedusha,* of the day."

"Well . . . thanks, Rabbi, but . . . well . . . I'm going away this weekend."

"OK, no problem. Just remember, you have a standing invitation. Now, let me please suggest one more thing. In a few weeks, I'll be starting a class called Basic Concepts in Judaism. It's for beginners, so to speak. It will be every Wednesday at 7:00 PM. Do you think you'll be able to come?"

"Uh, sorry. I think I have an evening class on Wednesdays."

"Ah, too bad. Well, maybe we can study together on a regular basis. Look, you agreed to read Genesis and Exodus. But you have to read it with traditional commentary so that you get the genuine Jewish interpretation. Here, let me lend you this modern translation, also with commentary."

"Wow, thanks a lot, Rabbi Abraham. I'll definitely do some reading. I must confess – I'm a little overwhelmed. I'm not sure where it will all lead, but I really thank you for having this conversation with me. You've certainly given me a lot to think about."

"You're most welcome. I look forward to speaking with you again real soon. Oh, by the way, before you go, I wanted to ask, are you getting to hang out with any Jewish students here on campus? Are you familiar with the Hillel association?"

"I think I've heard of it. Is that the Jewish student group on campus?"

"Yes. You might be interested in some of their events. They have some interesting speakers from time to time. It's also a good way to meet other Jewish students. You know, Judaism is a social religion. It's not something you can do all by yourself. You should really stop by the Hillel sometime. And check out the kosher cafeteria. In fact, it's adjacent to the Hillel."

"OK. I'll look into it."

"Great! And remember – the invitation for Shabbos is always open."

20

January 12, 2000

Lots of thoughts about Rabbi Abraham. Both about him, and what he said. Seems like a nice man. Really knows a lot. Kind of anti-rational though. Got a little pushy toward the end. ~~Why did I lie to him about Helen?~~ But he got me thinking hard when he asked me about whether my parents are honest. I know that wasn't his intention, but it started me thinking. Are they really telling me the truth about things? And he sure understood Mom. There's some ethnic, elemental connection with the Jewish people, despite the fact

that there's virtually no observance of tradition any longer. Anyway,
I sure don't want to go to his house for Shabbat. Not ready for that.
But I must admit, I feel ~~guilty~~ self-conscious now every time I eat a
cheeseburger.

I started reading the Bible, or Torah, as Rabbi Abraham kept calling
it. I'm up to the birth of Joseph so far. Parts of the Bible are really
fascinating. Some are very odd, some are intriguing, hard to figure
out. I should really keep a section of my journal devoted to this
topic: Weird Things in the Bible. Anyhow, I never realized how much
was there. I always thought that the Bible was just like fairy tales for
kids. That's not true. It's all in there. Violence, lust, incest, duplicity,
love, hate. And the idea of faithfulness. Abraham sure is faithful. If I
had to entrust someone with something, no one would be better to
trust than Abraham.

I also looked through the siddur. I don't think I'd ever seen an
Orthodox prayer book before. It's amazing. All those blessings in
the morning, for everything — walking, breathing, seeing, getting
dressed, even going to the bathroom! The morning prayer is really
long, too. Longer than I would have thought. The part on sacrifices
and incense is bizarre, of course. (Got to ask Rabbi A. about that.)
Then, all those psalms, lots of Halleluyahs. I tried saying some of
these just for fun. Every time I say "Halleluyah" I feel like I'm an
old woman in a country church. But I guess this is where they
got it from! After psalms, more blessings, and then the Shema. I
like the part about thanking God for creation — the sun, the sky,
the heavenly bodies. That's kind of inspiring. (The part about the
angels is weird.) The Shema itself is pretty strong. "And you should
love your God with all your heart and all your soul and all your
might" — that's pretty heavy-duty stuff. And what does it really
mean, anyway? The commentary says "love" means keeping the
commandments, but I can't really believe that's all love amounts to.
(Relates to the question, what is love? Looking back, I see I wrote
about that earlier in my journal.) And then the second portion of
Shema: if you worship God, you'll be fine, but if you don't, you'll be
in deep trouble! That's tough to take. Then the Amidah or standing
prayer. Feet together, said in a quiet voice. And, it's long, asking
God for this and that and the other thing. The detail is unbelievable.
Do Christians or Muslims pray like this in such detail? Or is this
something only Jews do? I even threw in a prayer for Mom while
I was at it. Can't hurt, I guess. And finally the Alenu. The day
will come when everyone will worship the God of Israel. Wow. No

religious pluralism here! "And the day will come when God will be one and his name will be one." What in the world does that mean?

Getting back to Rabbi Abraham. One thing I meant to ask, but forgot: why should a person serve God, anyway? Is it about pleasure in the end? If not, what's the motivation?

I get the feeling that no matter what I ask, he's still going to say that in the end there are no convincing rational answers to my questions, and the only way to really get faith is just by learning and doing Judaism. Could that really be right? Reminds me of something Ravi once said about attaining enlightenment: it can be done, in steps, practice practice practice. I wonder. I'd call Rabbi A. an Anti-rationalist, but maybe I'm the one who's trying to be overly rational? But, that's why I'm trying Judaism, experimenting with it, at my own pace, of course. It's just kind of strange to be affirming things and doing things I really don't ~~yet~~ believe. Now I guess if it's all true, then it's fine to believe it. I mean, it would be nice if there's a God, if there is ~~"hashga prasi"~~ (find out what that term is again) divine providence. Like that story Rabbi A. told about his grandfather. And my ending up in the Holocaust Museum on my trip to Washington with H. And who knows what could be next? Maybe, if I keep more commandments, even more things will fall into place?

Still, after all this learning, I'm confused. Maybe even more confused than I was before. I feel like something in my <u>heart</u> wants to believe, but my <u>intellect</u> isn't letting me. It's sure comforting to believe that everything happens for a reason and that a just and compassionate God is looking over you at every turn. It's comforting to believe that life has meaning and purpose, which it really doesn't if there's no God. (Is that right? I'm still not even sure about that.) I guess it's also comforting to believe there's a solution to why there is evil, and that everything ends well in the end. But maybe that's where this belief in the next world comes in. Intellectually, I have trouble with that. Even if you could prove God's existence, that still wouldn't prove there's a next world. No, maybe that's not right. I guess <u>if</u> you could prove God's existence, and <u>if</u> you could prove that God has revealed that there is a next world, then it follows that there is a next world. But the bottom line is I still don't see proof for God's existence. Fascinating as the ~~Bible~~ Torah is, there's no proof of its truth.

Then again, maybe it all goes back to what Rabbi A. said: practice, and you'll become a believer. How seriously am I going to try this? And what I'm really wondering about is, how am I going to break *this to Helen? I was hoping the trip to Washington would settle the question one way or the other, and now I'm even more confused than I was before. I really don't know what to do!*

21

"So, David, what do you think of this place?"

"It's nice, Helen. It's . . . really nice."

"What about the food? Isn't it exquisite? What do think of these scallops?"

"They're . . . uh . . . quite good."

"*Good?* They're fantastic! And by the way, don't you recognize my earrings? You haven't said anything about them."

"Yes . . . the earrings I got for you. They look nice."

"David, you don't sound too enthused."

"I am. I *am* enthused . . . ."

"Come on, David. I'm not that thick! I can tell something's on your mind. What is it?"

"Nothing, really. I guess I'm just thinking about my mom."

"Uh-oh. I'm sorry to hear that. Is she worse?"

"I'm not sure. I'm getting mixed signals from home."

"You're not sure . . . but you're obviously worried."

"Yes. I guess it bothers me more than I thought it would."

"Why *shouldn't* it bother you? She *is* your mother. Speaking of Mom, what about spring break? Are you going home?"

"Yes, I am. But I . . . I don't think Mom would be up to company."

"Spring break is a little far away. Maybe she'll be better by then."

"I guess that's possible . . . ."

"David! *What* is going on? This isn't *just* about your mom, is it?"

"No, it isn't."

"Ah! So I was right! There *is* something else going on! Wait, don't tell me. I know what it is. You were upset about how I left you at that coffee shop in Washington. I could tell when I met you at the airport. Something was terribly wrong. I could see it in your face. And I can still see that same look now. You won't look at me directly. David, I'm really sorry about deserting you like that. But —"

"No, that's not it, Helen."

"No? Well, then, what is it?"

"Look, this is hard for me to say. But there's something we've never discussed. That is, the uh . . . the Jewish question."

"*What?* What Jewish question?"

"You know . . . the fact that I'm Jewish, and you're not."

"Oh . . . so *that's* it. You really had me worried there for a second. Well, what about it?"

"It's actually quite a serious thing. I've been thinking about it quite a lot lately."

"That's probably a good thing. You've got to deal with it sooner or later."

"*I've* got to? You mean *we've* got to."

"*We?* Look, for me it's a non-issue. I'm not religious at all, and that's that. But if it's an issue for you, then *you've* got to deal with it."

"I guess you're right. But what I'm saying is that I need some time to figure out what I think about Judaism."

"David, let me get this straight. Are you saying you need some time to figure out whether Judaism is more important to you than I am?"

"No. That's not how I'd like to put it."

"That's what it sounds like to me. I . . . I really don't know what to say. Here we are sitting in this restaurant having this elegant dinner. And now you're telling me that −"

"Helen, please calm down. I didn't want to talk about it tonight. I just wanted to enjoy the evening with you. But obviously you realized something's going on . . . ."

"Oh, my God. I really can't believe this. After all we've been through, you now need to sort out whether Judaism is more important to you than our relationship?"

"No, I told you. That's not it. I just need a little time to sort this Judaism thing out. I need to decide just how important Judaism is to me."

"And if it is important enough − that means our relationship is over?"

"I . . . I don't know what to say. It does create a problem. I mean . . . long term . . . . Don't you agree?"

"David, honestly, I'm a little shocked. It's not like you've talked a lot about your Judaism before, at least not with me. I didn't think it was all that important to you."

"Yeah. I'm to blame for that. I could talk about it if you want . . . ."

"Look, I told you, I'm not religious. I don't really get all that stuff about God and religion. It all seems like a crutch to me."

"Maybe you're right, but I'm not so sure. That's why I need time to sort it out."

"And just how long do you think it will take to sort it out? And what kind of relationship are we going to have while you go through this process? And how long is this going to last?"

"I don't know. I'm sorry, Helen. I just don't know."

"It sounds to me like you're saying you're not really in love with me."

"No, Helen, that's not true . . . ."

"Sorry, but I really don't think this is going to work. I'm not going to be placed on hold while you deal with your identity crisis. You know what? Maybe you should take your earrings back. Here. Let's just get the check, and go."

22

February 2, 2000

Dear David,

As you already know from talking on the phone with Dad, the operation went pretty well. It turned out to be a little more widespread than they had thought. But now the doctor thinks that not only is the cancer gone, but that the prognosis is good for remission. That was a close one, I guess. Someone upstairs must be watching over me.

It sounded to me like your trip to Washington was really a success. You really saw quite a lot, and I'm glad you managed to visit the Holocaust Museum. The only thing I regret is that because of your trip to DC, you didn't spend any time at home during the break. I missed you!

Someday you'll have to introduce me to your friend Simon. (That's the one you went to DC with. Right?) How's he doing? The way you described him, he sounds like a very interesting character. So does your friend Ravi, by the way. I'm glad you've made good friends so quickly.

Thank God, I'm feeling a little stronger each day. I'm no longer lying in bed half the time. Still, I don't see too much of Dad lately. He still seems to be working awfully long hours. Well, that's what he's got to do to be happy, I guess.

Write back and keep me posted on your philosophical studies!
Love,
Mom

23

"Hey, David. How are you?

"I'm OK, George. What's up with you?"

"Nothing much. Status quo. But I heard you broke up with Helen. Is that true?"

"Actually, I'm not sure what's going on with us."

"What happened?"

"Well, I . . . uh . . . it was starting to get serious, and I . . . got a little uncomfortable with the relationship. So I'm trying to figure out what I think about Judaism. I even had this long conversation with a rabbi. We had a really good discussion. I've started to read the Torah – you know, the Jewish part of the Bible – and I'm studying some of the traditional prayers. Anyway, I tried to explain to Helen that maybe we should cool things off while I try to figure things out. But she got really ticked."

"You can't blame her for that."

"I don't know. She could have had a little more patience with me. But it's really my fault for not bringing it up earlier."

"Well, I hope you can work things out. But on the other hand, I'm impressed."

"Impressed? About what?"

"Despite your feelings for Helen, you've realized there's . . . uh . . . a void that she can't fill. She's a great girl – but you've realized there's . . . uh . . . a bigger picture."

"I don't know. Maybe I'm acting more out of guilt than anything else."

"Guilt? Over what?"

"Guilt over what my parents would think about the relationship, guilt over a feeling that I'd be . . . oh, I don't know – deserting the Jewish people, or something like that. Simon thinks I'm crazy, you know."

"Of course he does. What did you expect? Don't pay attention to him. You know what? In my opinion, guilt's got a bad rap. People today don't really understand how important guilt is. If a person feels guilty, that's a sign something's wrong, something should change. People who don't feel guilty or who ignore their guilt feelings end up doing really disastrous things. Guilt serves a good purpose. In fact, I believe it's the main instrument God uses to prod us toward him."

"Really? If that's true, that's kind of depressing, isn't it?"

"Not if it leads you to God. Look, the real issue is, what is guilt? Basically, guilt is a recognition of one's limitations, flaws, failings. This is the first step toward spiritual growth. You can't grow if you don't recognize the human condition – if you don't recognize that you're imperfect. Once you recognize that, you realize that you need something or someone outside of you to bring you completion or perfection. And the more you realize how imperfect you are, the more you want completion! And you also realize you can't do it on your own. And you can't do it with the help of another human being. Because they're just as imperfect as you are, and two imperfections don't add up to something perfect. Don't you agree?"

"George, I think you're reading too much into my situation. I think I just feel guilty about what my parents would think, guilty about possibly deserting . . . uh . . . the tribe. You're making it sound much nobler than it really is."

"No, I don't think so. Your feeling of guilt is powerful and real. You can't deny that. But perhaps you've misidentified the true source of the guilt."

"What do you mean?"

"You seem to think the guilt has to do with going against your parents' wishes and deserting the tribe. But if that were all it was, then Simon would be right – it would all be superficial, and you should forget all about it. But I think that the guilt has a much deeper source, a spiritual source. All this time you've been involved with Helen, you – or a part of you – thought that this relationship would bring you some kind of completion, some kind of fulfillment. That's normal. It's what most people think when they first fall in love. I had this experience in high school, and my girlfriend and I went through it together. The point I'm trying to make is that right now, something inside of you is saying, 'No, this isn't what I'm after. There's something else I'm looking for.'"

"And you think that something else is God?"

"Well, basically, yes."

"It's funny, but you remind me of the rabbi I spoke with."

"That's not surprising. We probably have a lot in common. How do I remind you of him?"

"He thinks that my . . . uh . . . new-found interest in Judaism has to do with my 'Jewish soul.' I forget how he put it – some Yiddish phrase. Anyway, he thinks something inside of me is seeking God, and that's why I'm so bothered with this issue. But you're saying that the source of this quest is guilt."

"Interesting, very interesting. But hang on. What does he mean by your *Jewish* soul? Is that something different from the rest of your soul? Doesn't the rabbi think that everybody has a soul?"

"Yeah, I'm pretty sure he does, or at least, I think so. Yes, I remember what he said now. Everyone is made in the image of God, and so, deep down, everyone seeks a relationship with God."

"So, every human being has a soul. Not only Jews, right?"

"Uh . . . yes, I'm sure he'd agree with that."

"So why did he say it's your Jewish soul that's seeking God? Why not just say that it's your soul that's seeks God?"

"I'm not exactly sure. I guess he thinks there's something special about the Jewish soul."

"And do you believe that?"

"No, I don't."

"But you do think you have a soul, don't you?"

"I'm not sure what that means, so I can't really say."

"You do know that the Greek word for soul is *psyche*?"

"Yes. We learned that when we studied Plato."

"So, you *do* agree that you have a psyche, don't you? I mean, there's something in you that's conscious, that thinks, that makes decisions, has feelings . . . *that's* the psyche. Right?"

"Of course. But I'm not sure it's something that lives on after death, or is something that is non-physical."

"But the fact is, you do have a psyche."

"True."

"So why don't you admit that you *do* have a soul? Whether it lives after death or not is another question."

"I suppose so."

"But you also don't think your soul is particularly Jewish. Do you?"

"No, I don't think so."

"Well, that psyche or soul – *that's* the part of you that's seeking something higher. And the guilt is the recognition that you're failing in some way to do that. So I guess, except for the part about the peculiar 'Jewishness' of your soul, I do agree with the rabbi."

"Hmm. Well, assuming you're right that I am seeking God, how do *you* think I should go about this quest?"

"After recognizing your guilt, the first thing you've got to realize is that, like I said earlier, you can't do it on your own. You need help."

"What kind of help do I need?"

"You're not going to like my answer. Do you really want to know what I think?"

"Of course."

"You need Christ."

"Really? Why's that?"

"I told you. You can't do it yourself. You need help. Without Christ, you can't get to God. Without Christ, you'd be stuck with guilt forever. If it weren't guilt about this thing with Helen, it would be guilt about something else. This isn't just true of you. It's true of everyone. Human beings can't ever be perfect. Guilt is the normal human situation – until Christ came along, that is. Christ is the help we all need."

"And how's that supposed to work?"

"Very simple, in a way. You say the words, 'I believe in Christ, our Lord and Savior.' And then you let him into your heart. Most people around here make fun of the whole idea, but that's only because they're too arrogant to admit they need or want to be saved. If you just say those words, then, after a while, you'll feel a kind of inner peace, tranquility. It's almost as if the guilt just drains right out of you."

"Hmm . . . it all sounds very nice. But that wasn't exactly my question."

"What was your question, then?"

"I'm not asking what you do. I'm asking: *how* does it work? See what I'm getting at? How does believing in Christ take away one's guilt?"

"Oh, that's simple. God is all-powerful and all-merciful. So he has the power to wipe away sin, if he so chooses. God cleanses the soul by giving us the gift – the sacrifice – of Christ and the power to believe in him. All we have to do is accept that gift."

"OK, then let me ask you this. Why does God need to send Christ in order to cleanse us? I mean, why can't God just do the job himself?"

"Simple again. God sent Christ as a model for us all to follow in his actions and teachings, both during his life on this earth and at his crucifixion. Also, there has to be *something* we do to merit salvation. And that something is faith in Christ. That's why it says in the Bible, 'Let our faith be our salvation.'"

"That must be something from the New Testament. I was always taught that the Old Testament emphasizes deeds, not faith, while the New Testament stresses faith and not deeds."

"No, you're dead wrong. The verse I just quoted comes from the Old Testament. You know, faith isn't completely missing from the Old Testament either. For example, Genesis says something really important about Abraham's faith."

"What's that?"

"It says that when God promised him a child through Sarah, Abraham had faith in God, and God counted that as his 'righteousness.' The idea here is precisely that it's by faith that you merit salvation. I keep telling you – you should read the Bible. And just think, if you know so little about the Old Testament, you really will learn some amazing things if you study the New Testament! Anyway, getting back to your question about why God had to send Christ. Sure, God could have just waved a magic wand and we'd all be saved. But God wanted us to have something we could do to merit salvation. So he gave us the gift of Christ and the power to believe in him. Now all that's left for us to do is to accept Christ. When you accept Christ's suffering for us, you're acknowledging your guilt and you're gaining salvation – all in one step. And, actually, there's another reason God sent Christ."

"What's that?"

"To teach the world that we cannot achieve salvation just through our own deeds – not even by keeping the divine law or what the Jews call the Torah. God gave the Torah to the Israelites, but they couldn't manage to keep it. And that leads to another important point . . . which by the way is very relevant to your situation with Helen."

"Really? What's that?"

"David, don't you see? The whole idea of keeping separate from the nations . . . that made sense back then, but it no longer does, like the rest of the ritual law. Since Christ came to us, there's no need for the chosen people to remain separate from the nations."

"But still, even if what you say is true, why did God choose the Jewish people and give them the Torah if he was going to send Christ anyway?"

"That was all part of the divine plan to establish the need for Christ. History shows the Israelites couldn't keep the Law. That's quite obvious from the fact that the Israelites were exiled from their land. This shows that the divine experiment of the giving of the Law to the Israelites doesn't work – I mean, it was intentional, of course, all part of the plan to show that it can't work, and that salvation can't be achieved without divine grace. Do you follow?"

"George, this is all very interesting. But now you are admitting that I was right earlier when I said that the Old Testament emphasizes deeds, whereas the New Testament emphasizes faith."

"No, I'd put it differently. The Old Testament emphasizes keeping the Law, while the New Testament emphasizes faith. But deeds are very important for a

Christian. What you do displays your faith — or lack of it. The idea that you can be a good Christian just by merely believing something is not true. Belief isn't the same thing as faith. A person who has faith acts in a certain way, or at least aspires to do so."

"I see. Well, you've certainly given me a lot to think about. I guess I really do need to study the Bible more . . . ."

24

"David! Come in! It's good to see you again. How is everything?"

"Pretty good, Rabbi."

"Did you get some of the reading done?"

"Yes. I managed to get through half of the Torah, though not with all the commentary. Some of it seems so disjointed, it makes you wonder how one section is related to the next. And I noticed that sometimes there are little sections that are in poetry, and then it switches back to prose. Some of it really flows, and some of the stories are really interesting. I was just reading the story of Joseph again last night. That must be one of the most dramatic stories I've ever read. I mean, the dreams, the intrigues with his brothers and all that. Anyhow, I do have some new questions for you."

"Good, I'd like to hear them. Your observation about poetry versus prose is interesting. I confess I've never given that much thought. You're right, the Torah does sometimes shift into poetry — that's even more so the case in the *Neviim* — that's the prophets. But as far as the apparent disjointedness goes, that's a puzzle. It's meant to intrigue us. The sages and the commentaries are always wrestling with this issue — how does one section lead to another? You have to see it as a puzzle that we're supposed to learn something from. That's what we call *smichas ha-parshiyos,* or the juxtaposition of sections. By the way, did you read that article I suggested on the Torah codes?"

"Yeah, I did. I'm still suspicious of that whole thing, though. I think if you looked hard enough you could probably see similar patterns in other literary works."

"Well, it all seems pretty convincing to me. But I know that not everybody buys into it. And how about the *Shema*? Have you been saying it?"

"No, honestly, I haven't been saying it religiously. When I get up in the morning, I usually say it. At night I can't seem to bring myself to say it. I just don't have the conviction. I feel strange saying something I'm not sure I believe."

"OK, let's talk about that later. What about your questions?"

"Well, like I said, the Torah has some fascinating stories . . . but with all due respect, I'm not sure how any modern person could believe it."

"Why not?"

"I'm not even sure where to begin."

"Begin at the beginning."

"All right, I'll do that. First of all, the story of Genesis obviously conflicts with science. Genesis says that the entire world was created by God in six days, and that man was created on the sixth day. But science says that the universe is billions of years old, and that humans evolved from lower forms of life over a span of millions of years. How do you reconcile Genesis with science? The same thing is true of all the other miracles in the Bible – I mean the Torah. You know, like the splitting of the sea, manna falling from heaven, water coming from rocks, and all that. Modern science tells us these things just can't happen. Rabbi, do you really believe these things happened?"

"Yes, I do, absolutely."

"Every word? Literally?"

"Pretty much. First of all, the Torah comes directly from God – it is heresy for a Jew to say that even Moses himself made up or invented one word of the Torah. Now of course, here and there the Torah might use a metaphor or a symbolic phrase – like when it talks about God's hand or God's finger – but, basically, Orthodox Jews take the Torah at its word."

"Well, I guess that makes it very hard for a person to be Orthodox."

"Hold on. Your question based on science seems like a good one. But let's analyze it carefully. You really have two issues here – one is about the evolution of the universe and the human species, the other is about miracles. Now first, you should remember that the theory of evolution is just that: a theory, not a known fact. Scientists formulate theories on the basis of evidence, but their theories go beyond what the evidence dictates. That's why, for example, scientific theories change drastically as time goes on. What scientists believed three centuries ago is different from what they believed two centuries ago. What they will believe a century from now is very different from what they believe today."

"True."

"And that's because as new evidence is discovered, old theories are discarded. So it's quite possible, even likely, that the current scientific theory about the origin of the universe and the human race will eventually be discarded too."

"Yes. But today, right now, it is accepted scientific theory that the universe and mankind are a product of evolution. The fact that science used to be different or will be different does not change the fact that right now, it is unreasonable to doubt these theories."

"David, if all I had in my life were science, then I might agree with you. But the scientist considers only physical evidence such as the speed of light, distances between planets and stars, fossils, radioactive decay, and so on. As a Jew, I also consider the word of the Torah, which states that the world was created in six days and that man was created directly by God. Now, the Torah claims to be the revelation of the eternal God. On the other hand, science is an effort by human beings to know the truth, and, thus changes drastically. Which does it make more sense to believe? The eternal word of the eternal God, or, the ever-changing theories of mortal, fallible human beings?"

"Rabbi, if we *knew* the Torah was the word of God, then I guess I would have to agree that we should believe the story of Genesis rather than science. But the problem is that we don't know that the Torah is the word of God. So it seems we should believe in science and not the Torah."

"Quite the contrary! Look — last time I said that the way that we know the Torah is the word of God is first, through tradition, and second, through living a life of Torah we come to recognize its truth."

"I remember what you said, but I still have trouble accepting that, too."

"And my explanation for this is that you have not yet sufficiently cultivated a life of Torah. That's something we can still talk about and work on. But right now, you're trying to use a scientific theory to cast doubt on what Genesis tells us, right? You're claiming that the Torah is refuted by modern science, including the theory of evolution and the claim that miracles never happen."

"Yes, that's right."

"Well, to me what you're saying makes no sense at all. You will agree that the Torah purports or claims to be the eternal word of the Almighty God, the Creator and Sustainer of the universe. So it should not be surprising if what the Torah tells us about the origin of the world differs radically from what current science tells us. Again, science is basically man's effort to know the world in a manner that is unaided by divine revelation. If a scientist relies on revelation, he is no longer considered a scientist. But this does not mean that revelation is false! It just means that science, by its very nature, does not and cannot accept claims that are based on revelation!"

"I'm not sure I follow."

"I'll give you an analogy. Imagine a five-year-old trying to find an explanation for how a radio works. Suppose further that the child simply refused to listen to an adult's explanation of the radio. It would then be quite shocking if the child actually guessed how the radio actually works! To him, it might be very natural to suppose there is a little man in the radio, speaking through the speaker. He would have no conception of radio waves, transmitters, receivers, and so on. So, he would naturally think that, based on what he knows from his own experience, it is rational to assume that there is a little talking man inside the radio."

"OK. I'm with you so far."

"Good. So this is analogous to the case of the adult human in comparison with God. Science dismisses any attempt to rely on divine revelation. It is to be expected that a scientific theory about the origin of the universe and mankind would differ radically from what God might reveal to us about these matters."

"Hmm. OK, I guess I have to agree with that."

"By the same token, one's faith in God and the truth of the Torah should not be shaken even slightly by the theory of evolution."

"Why's that?"

"Because without revelation, one would naturally assume that the way things operate now is the way things have always operated in the past. And that leads naturally to the conclusion that the universe must have evolved over a long period of time to be the way it is. Basically, science doesn't *prove* that the Torah's account is wrong. It *presupposes* that the Torah's account is wrong."

"OK. I think I follow you."

"And as far as miracles go, science cannot and does not prove that miracles never occurred. Science only shows that as a general rule, nature operates according to certain rules – what scientists call 'laws of nature.' But science has no way of showing that exceptions to these laws *never* occur."

"Hmm . . . well . . . all this sounds very similar to the conclusion we reached last time when we talked about the problem of evil."

"How so?"

"We said that if a person already believes in God's existence, then the fact that there is evil and suffering in the universe does not create a logical problem, since an almighty God could have some possible reason for allowing evil – even if we have no clue as to what that reason might be. And, now we're saying that if a person already believes in the divine revelation of the Torah, modern science does not pose a problem, because it is bound to be the case that science differs from divine revelation."

"Yes. Actually, I think that's an excellent point."

"But rabbi, here's my difficulty. Don't you yourself believe in science? I mean, don't you believe that water is composed of hydrogen and oxygen? Don't you believe that oxygen is necessary for human life? Don't you believe that combustion of gasoline produces the energy that makes your car run? Don't you –"

"Oh, sure, I believe in science – up to a point! A lot of what science says does *not* conflict with the Torah, so there's no reason to deny that a lot of science is true. It's when science makes grand claims about the origin of the universe and the human race that I beg to differ – on the basis of the Torah. It's when science says that miracles *never* occur that I beg to differ."

"Hmm. Now I'm reminded of what you said last time about other religions. It's okay to accept what they say as long as they don't disagree with Judaism. That doesn't bother me so much because all religions make claims that other religions disagree with, and none of them can really be proven true. But science is based on experimental evidence – the kind of thing that any ordinary person can reproduce and observe in his or her laboratory anywhere, anytime. So it's arbitrary to accept some of what science says and not all of it."

"I disagree. I don't think it's arbitrary at all. As you just said, science is based on experimental evidence or observation. Now, observation always occurs at a given time and place. Scientists rely on observation of how the world appears at given times and places in order to formulate theories of what the world is like at all times and places. In fact, they go further and formulate theories about how the world came to exist. In doing so, scientists make an *assumption*. They *assume* that the way the world operates now is the same way the world always operated. They assume that the world will always operate that way in the future. Even more so, they *assume* that the way the world operates now is the same way the world operated when it came into existence! Now tell me, what justifies this assumption?"

"I guess it's always been that way, so why assume that the world was ever any different?"

"Wait a moment! This reminds me of Bertrand Russell's famous discussion of the problem of induction. Have you read that? The question was: is there any justification for the scientist's assumption that the way the world operates now is the same as the way the world always operated? If you claim that we should assume this is true 'because the world has always operated this way,' you would be assuming the very thing that you are supposed to be justifying!"

"Ah, I – I guess you're right. But still, what could possibly justify the assumption that the world has *not* always operated the way it does now?"

"You mean, what could possibly justify the assumption that the world was created by some being outside of the realm of normal scientific law – a being who has the power to suspend those laws whenever he wishes?"

"Yes."

"Well, that boils down to the question you asked last time: why should we believe that there is a God who created the world? And that brings up the more fundamental question – why should a person believe that the Torah is the word of God?"

"Right."

"Again, the answer to that is: first, tradition, and second, *emunah* or religious faith. Whether you accept this is another issue. The point I'm trying to establish is that science does not pose a real conflict for the religious believer. It poses a problem on the surface of things, but when you analyze the situation, you see that first, the religious believer anticipates the fact that what science teaches is not likely to be consistent with what God reveals, especially about creation, and second, the religious believer has no reason to doubt God's word because of science."

"You're saying that if someone truly believes that the Torah is the word of God, he will have no problem dismissing the scientific theory of evolution. Again, your argument seems to be going around in a circle. My problem is, I find it hard to believe that the Torah is divinely revealed."

"OK. But now you know that the source of your problem is not the fact that it conflicts with modern science."

"I – I'm not sure. To be honest, I'm a little confused. But let me ask you about something else. Something that really bothers me about the Torah is the way God punishes people. I mean, I can sort of accept the fact that there's punishment for sins. If people are really bad, they deserve punishment. But what about their children? For example, when God brings the Flood, what about all the innocent children that got killed in it? Or when God brings the plague against the first-born Egyptians, it implies that even the infants were killed. That doesn't seem fair."

"You're judging God based on assumptions that apply to humans. Maybe it doesn't seem fair to us. It would be wrong for a human being to punish children for the crimes of their parents. But who are we to question God's ways? God had infinite and infallible knowledge of what the generation of the flood would have done if they had grown up. He had the same knowledge of what the first-born of the Egyptians would do when they grew up. And I guess you could say the same about the Canaanites, whom the people of Israel were commanded to destroy. No one else could know this but God."

"Still, it seems really harsh to punish infants for something that they would do in the future."

"Well, to be honest, I don't know if that's the right explanation. Look, God's ways are not our ways. As it says in the Prophets, '*Lo mahshevosai mahshevoseichem*' – My thoughts are not your thoughts."

"By that reasoning, you could get around any potential problem or question that I might ever have about the Torah."

"What do you mean?"

"For any possible question that I might ask about why God does what he does, you can always say that we can't expect to understand God."

"Well, we can't. That's just the nature of God."

"Then your argument is circular."

"Hmmm. Well, you're right, in a sense. I *am* arguing in a circle. But, you see, we've come round to the same point where we ended last time. The bottom line is, there is no good rational argument *against* the belief in the divine revelation of the Torah. On the other hand, while in my opinion the argument from tradition is a good one, you do not find it convincing. And I don't think I'll ever be able to convince you that it's true by means of rational argument. Like I said, the only way you will find true *emunah* – faith in God and the Torah – is through living a Torah life. That's what I told you before. In order to do that you have to start 'keeping the Torah.' You know that it says in the Psalms – *ta'amu u-reu ki tov Hashem* – which means, 'Taste and you will see that Hashem is good.' If you don't try it, you will never develop a genuine belief in God."

"Even supposing you're right, I just don't have enough conviction to get motivated to keep the Torah."

"Sorry, but I really can't believe that. Again, here's my advice: start off simple. Make a commitment to keep some *mitzvah*. Say the *Shema* twice a day. You haven't really done that, have you? Or try keeping Shabbos. You still haven't taken me up on my invitation. Come to *shul* on Shabbos, and let me have you over for dinner. You'll experience the *kedushah,* the sanctity of Shabbos, and then you'll make a better judgment. I'm telling you, if you keep at it, I think you'll find after a while that your questions have answers. Or rather, that the questions simply don't bother you any more."

"Hmmm."

"I see you don't find what I'm saying too convincing. Listen, let me ask you this. Did you visit the Hillel at all?"

"No. I just haven't had the time . . . ."

"Well, I wanted to tell you, there's a guest speaker coming later in the semester. You might be interested in hearing him. Wait a second, let me give you a flyer. Ah, here it is! His name is Rabbi Low. I've heard of him, but I've never actually met him myself. He's originally from here – in fact he used to teach philosophy! Now he lives in Israel and heads a small *yeshiva* there. He might give you another angle on things. In any case, I'm sure you'd find it a stimulating event. Why don't you come?"

"Uh, OK. Sure. I'll try to make it."

25

March 5, 2000

Today, depressed. I'm feeling that sinking feeling. More than that: it's like a dull pain in between my shoulder blades. Almost literally, heartache. Is it because of my feelings for H? Did I act too quickly? Still can't get her off my mind. I called her yesterday and she really didn't want to talk. I called her later and she didn't return my call. But I'm not sure it's about her.

Depression. Or something like it. I don't know if it's clinical depression but it's definitely got physical symptoms. Mainly, lethargy. All I want to do is nothing. Smoke, sleep, lie in bed, or stare at the wall, waste myself away. Tried smoking and that only made it worse. Went for a run. It took my mind off things for a while. But now I'm back in the same place I started from.

Maybe Rabbi A. is right. Maybe life is meaningless without God. But I still don't think I believe in God, so that's too bad. I tried looking at Ecclesiastes. It seems pretty depressing. And also very confusing. God seems very distant in that book. Sometimes it seems the author isn't even sure there is a God at all. I gave up halfway through.

I wonder about that speaker Rabbi A. mentioned. A former philosopher who is now a rabbi. Could be interesting. I plan to go, but that's not for a few weeks.

Got to do something positive. Can't read. Don't have the energy or interest. What can I do? Write myself out of this mess? Is that really possible? Like Freud's "talking cure"? Maybe I should go talk to a shrink? No, I'm too embarrassed to admit I might have a problem. Anyway, I can't believe that talking or writing is the cure. But maybe it will get me focused. So here goes.

When do I really feel this pain most? Strangely, when I look out the window and see something like that beautiful sunset I'm seeing right now. Why should that be? Why would something beautiful intensify the pain? I don't get it. Maybe that beauty reminds me of H and I'm depressed over losing her? Is that why I'm depressed? Did I make a mistake with H? No, I don't think so. I didn't really love her. Did she love me? There was always a tension in the relationship. But so what? Tension is normal. It's a good thing, not a bad thing. Well, there are different kinds of tension. Still, if she loved me, wouldn't she have a little more patience with something that means so much to me? But on the other hand, can I blame her for her reaction? I can't deny that now I miss her. Well, maybe I did love her. I don't know. I'm confused.

Just forget her. Find another. But one can always theoretically find another. So what's true love, then?

Am I depressed about Mom? No, because she's so much better now. That operation was really lucky. It was strange how just a few days after I had the big blowup with Helen, Mom had the operation and came out fine. I also remember praying for her in the days leading up to the operation. Divine providence at work? Or just good luck? How can you really tell in the end? Of course I'm still a little worried about her, but I can distinguish the feeling of worry from this other, stranger, feeling. What is it?

Am I suffering from a bad case of what Simon calls "what's the pointism"? His approach: focus on pleasure. So what pleasures do I have? Right now I don't seem interested in pleasure at all. I can imagine what he'd say: "That's precisely the problem. You're thinking too hard again. You're trying to find some deep philosophical solution when really the answer is simple and right on the surface. Your depression is caused by a lack of interest in pleasure. Find another girlfriend. Throw yourself into work that you enjoy!" But is the lack of interest in pleasure really the source of my problem, or is it just a symptom of something else? Why am I in this sorry situation?

Got to start from somewhere. Positive points, think positive. Mom always used to say that, and I couldn't stand it sometimes, but actually, she's right. What's the point of being a pessimist?

I think I know at least this: Life is meaningful when you have something to strive for. So that's what I want: something to strive for. It doesn't have to be pleasure. Not that I have anything against pleasure. It could be, it might be pleasure, but it doesn't have to be pleasure. Maybe this depression stems from the fact that I have nothing I'm striving for. Well, I guess I am striving for something. I just don't know exactly what it is. Is it God, like Rabbi A. and George think? But intellectually, I don't really believe in God. So how do I fix this problem? Start praying? Start saying the Shema? I don't really think I can get myself to believe in all that stuff. I've been trying, but it just doesn't seem to be working. I have a hard time uttering things I don't really believe. Besides, how would keeping the Torah solve my depression? Should I even bother going to that lecture Rabbi A mentioned? I said I would go. I guess I should. I'm getting tired of lies. But anyway, that isn't for a few weeks.

Christianity. Can I even consider that as an option? Frightening. Should I start saying the little formula that George wants me to say? Could George be right after all? If it would upset my mom if I married a non-Jew, just imagine how bad it would be if I became a Christian! Unthinkable. But on the other hand, George makes some good points. Is what I'm feeling "guilt"? I sure feel inadequate. I feel a void. A pit. Emptiness. And if I were to become a Christian, I'd have no problem getting romantically involved with a non-Jew. That sure would make things easier. Maybe I could fix things up with Helen? No, this is all crazy.

Ravi's approach: "Your depression is natural. You're depressed because you're longing, yearning for something. Give up the longing and the depression will go away." But is it really possible to give up the longing? I still need to get him to explain this better. (But maybe it's something that can't be explained.) I sure admire him. He seems so calm, so well put together. (Does he ever think about girls? I wonder.) And if it weren't for him, I probably wouldn't even be writing these things down, trying to figure them out. You should meditate, he said, in order to reach the state of non-attachment. Maybe I should meditate? At least I don't have to affirm things I don't believe in when I meditate.

Conclusion: Ask Ravi to teach me how to meditate. I sure hope it helps. I don't know what else to do.

26
—

"David, are you ready?"

"I hope so, Ravi. I'm ready to try."

"Did you follow my instructions? Have you refrained from any intoxicants for the last three days?"

"Yes, just like you said."

"No alcoholic beverages?

"Not a drop."

"No smokes?"

"Well . . . just one, yesterday."

"What about coffee?"

"Nope. Not in the last three days. And it hasn't been easy."

"OK, let's get started. First, you need to find a relaxed position. Why don't you lie down on my futon? Now, if you'll wait a moment, I'll just put on a CD . . . a little *tambura* music to get us started. It's just a drone effect, to create a meditative mood. The music will taper off into silence later on, when we get into a deeper state of meditation."

"Great."

"Now, listen closely to my voice. I am your guide, and you have complete trust in me."

"Yes. Complete trust and total faith."

"No jokes, please. In fact, from this point onward, please do not speak, even if I ask you a question. Just mentally note your response. First, I'm going to give you some simple instructions. This meditation will have several stages, from lower to higher, from outer to inner. Each time I say, 'Listen closely to my voice,' that is a cue that we are going to a higher stage. Within each stage, there are also stages. At the beginning of each stage, I will tend to talk a bit more frequently. As the meditation progresses, I will talk less frequently, and there will be more and longer pauses of silence as I allow you time to meditate more deeply. In the final stage, I will talk very little at all, and toward the very end, I will be completely silent. My voice is a ladder. When you finish using the ladder, you will no longer need it.

"Throughout the process, avoid dwelling on any aimless thoughts or distractions that come to your mind. Since you are a novice, such thoughts and distractions are almost unavoidable. When they come, gently brush them aside. Apart from my voice, you may always come back to your breathing as a central focus. It is important to breathe calmly and rhythmically. Consider that your breathing is a process that goes on continuously, but that most of the time you are unaware of it. It is always there, but most of the time it is ignored. It is cloaked under the dress of everyday life, which is multiple and constantly changing. Also, in every day experience, the self seems divorced from that which is outside the self. The self thinks of itself as a *subject* that experiences the things outside itself as *objects*. But really, this duality is only an illusion. In truth, there is no subject and object. In truth, there are not *many* objects. In truth, reality is perfectly one. The purpose of this meditation is to move toward enlightenment, toward the realization that the self is ultimately at one with the single underlying reality, toward a place where subject and object are one. This is a place of total harmony and peace.

"Now, listen closely to my voice. Gently close your eyes. We will start with some simple breathing techniques. Breathe in through your nose, and allow your abdomen to expand. Hold the breath for a count of one . . . two . . . three. Good. Now breathe out: one . . . two . . . three. Good. Breathe in: one . . . two . . . three . . . breathe out: one . . . two . . . three . . . . Continue breathing at this same pace. Let the abdomen rise when you inhale, and deflate when you exhale. Do not allow your upper chest to rise. Breathe from the stomach. This is the proper way to breathe. When you breathe, consider that you draw in energy and life to sustain your entire being. When you exhale, expel any toxins within. Keep breathing in this fashion, and listen closely to my voice.

"I am going to instruct you to relax your body in stages. We shall start from the lowest part of the body, and move upward toward your head. When your body is completely and totally relaxed, you will experience your body as one unitary being, and not merely as a combination of different parts. Now, as you continue breathing rhythmically, say to yourself in your mind:

I am relaxing my toes...I am relaxing my toes...I am relaxing my toes....
I am relaxing my feet...I am relaxing my feet...I am relaxing my feet....
I am relaxing my legs...I am relaxing my legs...I am relaxing my legs....
I am relaxing my hips...I am relaxing my hips...I am relaxing my hips.

I am relaxing my fingers...I am relaxing my fingers...I am relaxing my fingers....
I am relaxing my hands...I am relaxing my hands...I am relaxing my hands....
I am relaxing my arms...I am relaxing my arms...I am relaxing my arms....
I am relaxing my shoulders...I am relaxing my shoulders...I am relaxing my shoulders.

I am relaxing my hips...I am relaxing my hips...I am relaxing my hips....
I am relaxing my back...I am relaxing my back...I am relaxing my back....
I am relaxing my stomach...I am relaxing my stomach...I am relaxing my stomach...
I am relaxing my chest...I am relaxing my chest...I am relaxing my chest.

I am relaxing my neck...I am relaxing my neck...I am relaxing my neck....
I am relaxing my throat...I am relaxing my throat...I am relaxing my throat....
I am relaxing my face...I am relaxing my face...I am relaxing my face....
I am relaxing my head...I am relaxing my head...I am relaxing my head.

"Now listen closely to my voice. Your body is now totally relaxed. But let us return to focus on your chest area. Consider that your chest area is the place of *animus* or spirit, the place where your emotions reside. Since you are calm and relaxed, as you are now, you breathe evenly and deeply. But if you were excited or angry, you would breathe quickly and sharply. Despite the fact that you are not excited or angry now, you still have the capacities for these emotions. And even though you are not actively experiencing these emotions right now, the fact is that you are experiencing residual effects of these emotions from past events, or even from future expectations. So . . . I am going to ask you to relax these capacities as well. This is in fact harder to do than to relax your body, so I will pause for a longer period of time after each emotion. And I will mention only a few typical emotions, but you will please relax all your emotional capacities. Now . . . say to yourself, in your mind:

> I am relaxing my capacity for anger . . .
> I am relaxing my capacity for anger . . .
> I am relaxing my capacity for anger.
>
> I am relaxing my capacity for joy . . .
> I am relaxing my capacity for joy . . .
> I am relaxing my capacity for joy.
>
> I am relaxing my capacity for hate . . .
> I am relaxing my capacity for hate . . .
> I am relaxing my capacity for hate.
>
> I am relaxing my capacity for love . . .
> I am relaxing my capacity for love . . .
> I am relaxing my capacity for love.

"Now . . . listen closely to my voice. Your emotions are now relaxed. Just as you have relaxed the body and the emotions, so now you must relax the mind. The bodily locus for your mind is your head. Of course, your mind must remain active enough to focus on my voice, and the complete relaxation of the mind will only be possible at the final stage of this meditation. But meanwhile you will relax the mind as much as possible. So say to yourself, in your mind:

> I am relaxing my power to hear . . .
> I am relaxing my power to hear . . .
> I am relaxing my power to hear.
>
> I am relaxing my power to smell . . .
> I am relaxing my power to smell . . .
> I am relaxing my power to smell.

I am relaxing my power to see . . .
I am relaxing my power to see . . .
I am relaxing my power to see.

I am relaxing my power to think . . .
I am relaxing my power to think . . .
I am relaxing my power to think.

"Now, listen closely to my voice. Your body, emotions, and mind are now relaxed. But there is still something left to relax, and that is your will, your ability or capacity to have any power at all . . . your power itself. There is no bodily locus for power, for it is spread throughout your entire being. It is through power that you move your body, that you have emotions, that you have sensation and thought. It is through power that you strive and seek. Once you have relaxed your will, you will find yourself on a precipice: on the precipice of merging with the One — the One that is beyond yourself, that envelopes yourself. I will now give you some final instructions. Then I will be quiet as you continue to meditate in silence. Say to yourself, in your mind:

I am relaxing my will
    I am relaxing all desire
        I am letting go of desire
            I desire nothing
                I am a leaf
                    floating on a pond
                        floating on calm water
                            The water is calmness and peace
                                The leaf is floating on calmness and peace
                                    My edges are moist
                                    My back is wet
                                        The leaf sinks gently into the water
                                        The leaf merges with the water
                                        I am the leaf
                                            I am floating on that water
                                                I am sinking gently into the water
                                                I have entered the water
                                                    I have become one with it

27

David came into the auditorium and was surprised to find the room quite full. The audience was boisterous and brimming with conversation. He had wanted a seat in the back, in case he needed to make an early escape. But almost every place seemed taken. He noticed an empty seat near the aisle close to the middle row, and he figured that was his best choice. He made a quick move for the space, and sat down.

Directly in front of him sat three female students. They all wore long, dark-colored skirts and long-sleeved blouses, and they all had dark hair. They were chatting away gaily, like sisters at dinner. When he leaned forward slightly, he could hear snatches of their conversation over the hubbub in the room. The one sitting to David's right spoke.

"So, *nu*, when is this going to start?"

"Are you in a rush or something? This is a rabbi's lecture. We're on Jewish time!" said the one on David's left.

"Give me a break. I have work to do. I can't sit here forever!"

"Stop complaining," said the one in the middle. "Look, this'll be really interesting. I've heard Rabbi Low speak before."

"Really? When?"

"In Israel, when I spent the year at Beit Bruria."

"Shh! Here he comes."

A tall, bearded man wearing a dark suit and a gray fedora hat strode quickly across the stage toward the podium. The audience quickly quieted down. The girls sitting in front of him briefly stood up, as did some others in the audience. David was a bit puzzled by this, until he realized this was a sign of respect. Before the man could start speaking, a student suddenly appeared on stage and politely signaled to the man to halt. The student stepped toward the microphone.

"Good evening! For those of you who don't know me, my name is Avi Green. Welcome to the monthly Hillel lecture! Tonight we are very happy to have Rabbi Dr. Yehudah Low with us. Rabbi Low is Rosh Yeshiva and Dean of Yeshivat Ahavat Torah in Jerusalem. Before that, he was a professor of Jewish thought and literature at Harbridge University. Before that, he was an instructor of philosophy at this great institution. Rabbi Low has lectured in Israel, Great Britain, South America and across the United States. He has written many articles both in Hebrew and English on many topics, from a Jewish perspective on the ethics of cloning to an essay on Messianism in contemporary Jewish Orthodoxy. His forthcoming book is entitled *How to Be a Thinking Religious Jew*. His lecture tonight is entitled 'Why I am a committed Jew.' After Rabbi Low's speech there will be a brief question-and-answer period. Let us all give a warm and gracious welcome to Rabbi Yehudah Low!"

The audience clapped politely. Before they could stop, Rabbi Low stepped to the podium and started to speak.

"Thank you very much and good evening to you all! It's a pleasure to be back here again. The college campus never ceases to be a place of intellectual growth and stimulation. I want to thank my wonderful hosts and especially the students for inviting me tonight. And thank you, Avi Green, for that very kind introduction.

"As Avi mentioned, my topic for this evening is 'Why I am a committed Jew.' Needless to say, some of the reasons for why I am a committed Jew have to do with my own background and upbringing. But I won't dwell on my autobiography. I don't think my personal history is all that interesting. Instead, I shall take a more universal approach. What I'll do is talk about why a person – any person – should be committed to a religious and monotheistic life, and in particular, why someone who is born as a member of the Jewish people should be committed to Judaism.

"I'll try to present my remarks in a so-called 'objective' manner. However, I am going to be arguing in favor of a certain view about how to live. Regarding such an issue, no one can be perfectly 'objective.' It may even sound as if I am trying to convince you to become religiously observant, or to be more of a committed Jew than perhaps you are right now. Let me make it clear that I firmly believe that sincerity and intellectual honesty are crucial to any kind of serious investigation, especially one about how to live. So I'm more concerned that you draw whatever conclusions you do from this lecture in a sincere and honest way than that you decide to become more religious after hearing this lecture. Another thing I want to say is that nothing in this lecture is particularly original. Most of what I have to say is based on ideas and arguments found in earlier philosophers. But I won't distract from my talk tonight with historical references and footnotes.

"Now, when we talk about 'rationales' for living a way of life, it's important to admit that we can know almost nothing, and perhaps entirely nothing, for certain. Some of you may be familiar with skeptical arguments such as the following. For all I know, it's quite possible that for the past forty years I've been lying somewhere in a dark room, with my brain hooked up to some virtual reality machine, controlled by a mad scientist or perhaps an alien, non-human creature. If so, all the images and sounds I'm experiencing right now are false! And if that's the case, none of you really exists, except as figments of my imagination. Alternatively, perhaps you are the one who's hooked up to the virtual reality machine, and everyone else in this room – including myself – is a figment of your imagination! At least since the time of Descartes, philosophers have puzzled over such skeptical arguments, and to be honest, there's really no way to refute them.

"These arguments and doubts may seem off the wall to you. Nevertheless, they show that the most basic beliefs we have about the world are ones which, somehow or other, we take for granted. Indeed, without taking certain beliefs for granted, we would never be able to make decisions about what to do. In other words, if we did not have to do anything, and all we did was sit around and think about what we should believe, then we might just as well be cautious and believe very little or nothing. But we are thrust into a world of action, a world in which we have to make choices. So we must decide what we are going to believe the world is like if we are going to make those choices and live. The result is the following key point: what we choose to believe about the world is based on what kind of life we decide we want to live.

"Now, let's explore some of the consequences of this key point. First of all, we want and need coherence in our lives. It would be impossible to act and function in a chaotic world. So we expect that our beliefs about the world should form a system that is coherent. This doesn't actually prove that the world functions coherently or consistently all the time. But a belief system that is incoherent is not pragmatically useful. So we expect our belief-system to be coherent, even though we can't be sure the world is coherent.

"Second, since we need and want to function in all sorts of different circumstances, we expect and hope that our belief system should encompass not just a portion of the world, but as much of the universe as possible – even those aspects of the universe that may be difficult or hard to figure out. Our belief system cannot remain noncommittal on profound questions such as: What is the nature of the universe? Is there a God? Is there life after death? Despite the fact that we may not be able to be certain about the answers to these questions, we need answers to them because we need to make choices about how to live, and we might make different choices depending on how we answer these profound questions.

"Third, and perhaps most important, we all want to live a meaningful life, or a life that's worth living. In fact, we want to live a life that's as much worth living as can be. So, one way of deciding whether to accept a given belief-system is to ask whether it serves as the basis for living the most meaningful life that we can possibly live. All other things being equal, a belief system that affords the greatest opportunity or possibility of living a most meaningful life is more preferable than a belief system which would, if true, make life less meaningful.

"It's mainly this last kind of consideration that I'll focus on here tonight, in order to address my topic, 'Why I am a committed Jew.' I'm sorry to disappoint you, but I'm not going to prove that God exists or that God gave the Torah to the Jewish people at Sinai. As some of you may know, medieval philosophy is replete with such attempted proofs. But the truth is that, for many of us today, these proofs just don't hold water. Instead, I will try to explain why a way of life that is based on monotheism, and in particular on Judaism, is eminently meaningful or worth living – indeed, about as meaningful as one can possibly imagine.

"But first, let's ask ourselves this question. What does it mean to live a meaningful life? It means to live a life that one has a strong motivation to live. The stronger the motivation you have for doing what you do, the more meaning there is to your life. That is why people who are fulfilled in their life usually *want* to live their life, while people who are depressed feel they have no motivation to keep on living. So a meaningful life is one that is filled with motivation.

"This leads to my next question. What sorts of motivations are there for doing things? I think there are basically two kinds of motivations for what we do. The first has to do with morality or ethics. Somehow or other, we believe we have certain duties or obligations, both to do certain things and to refrain from doing others. Obviously, people disagree over what is right or wrong to do in certain cases, and indeed, opinions on what is moral vary from society to society. Furthermore, there are vast philosophical controversies over what constitutes the basis of morality, and in fact many people are skeptical about whether any moral beliefs are really 'true' or 'valid.' I'll return to some of these points later. But the fact remains that moral beliefs or concerns motivate a large part of our behavior.

"The second source of motivation has to do with what brings us happiness or fulfillment or pleasure. By and large, we often do what we enjoy doing, or what we think will bring us happiness. Again, there are differences of opinion about what happiness is, and about what particular things will make one happy. There are also differences of opinion regarding the relationship between happiness, pleasure, and fulfillment. But the fact remains that people are motivated to do that which they enjoy doing or what brings them happiness.

"So we have established that there are two types of motivation: morality and happiness. Of course, many questions may be raised as to what is the relation between these two types of motivation. Are they wholly independent of one another? Is one reducible to the other? Sometimes they seem to conflict. Sometimes we feel that morality constrains our personal desires and interferes with the pursuit of joy or happiness. Yet it also seems that morality has a lot to do with happiness. It would seem strange if living a moral life had nothing to do with living a happy or joyous or pleasant life. But, the precise relation between morality and happiness is not our concern at present. Let's consider each of these sources of motivation separately, and see where they lead us in regard to the question, what way of life is most worth living?

"Let's consider morality first. Again, we think that a number of actions are morally binding upon us or morally forbidden. So we have 'moral motivations' to perform certain acts and avoid others. Now, notice that we rank certain actions as being more right or more wrong than others. For example, we think it's wrong to murder and wrong to step on someone's toe, but we think it's more wrong to murder than to step on someone's toe. We think it's right to repay debts and right to do someone a favor, but we think it's more of an obligation to repay debts than to do someone a favor. In other words, we feel that certain actions are more strongly binding or more strongly forbidden than others.

"So here's another key point: the more strongly morally binding we think a certain action to be, the stronger is our 'moral motivation' to perform that action. Thus, for example, given my beliefs about what is moral, I have a very strong moral motivation not to commit murder, and a less strong moral motivation not to step on someone's toe. In a similar way, different theories about the very basis of morality yield very different answers to the question of how strongly binding morality is upon us. Let me explain. In contemporary philosophy, one broadly accepted theory says that morality is a social institution that is a result of evolution: that in accordance with the Darwinian principles of the survival of the fittest and natural selection, only those societies with moral codes of one sort or another have managed to survive. Another popular theory says that over time, humans invented moral codes as a way of maximizing our collective preferences. Another theory says that morality springs from a sentiment of sympathy or empathy for our fellow human being. All of these theories of morality are 'non-theistic.' Such theories do not locate the basis of morality in a transcendent and divine source.

"Now, let's consider the degree of 'bindingness' that moral obligations have upon us according to such non-theistic theories. It turns out to be very weak. After all, what binds me to contribute to the survival of the society, or to maximize the collective preferences of society? Nothing, really. Perhaps it's true that, insofar as I am considered a 'member of a society' there are certain societal norms or rules which I 'ought' to follow. But what's the force or strength of the 'ought' here? Very little!

"Here's an analogy to make my point. Insofar as I choose to play the game of chess, I have to follow the rules of chess. But nothing requires me to play chess, and nothing except for physical force can stop me from moving pieces on the board in any way I please. Similarly, on any of the non-theistic theories just mentioned, there is nothing about me or about the universe that gives me an obligation to contribute to the survival of society or the maximization of collective preferences. It is only if my role as a member of society is assumed that I have any obligations at all according to such theories. But nothing binds me to assume this role.

"Alternatively, what if I don't happen to feel a sense of empathy or sympathy for my fellow human being? If so, according to the theory which finds the basis of morality in that sentiment of sympathy – I have no motivation to behave morally at all! So it turns out that the moral bindingness or 'moral motivation' involved in these non-theistic theories is very weak indeed.

"But consider instead a theory which says that the basis of morality is to be found in God – and let's define God as a single, transcendent, eternal, infinite, all-knowing being, upon which all things in existence depend — a being who has created and sustains the entire universe. In such a theory, morality consists of laws that are as strongly binding as one can possibly imagine. After all, if the moral laws stem from the creator of the universe, their basis lies at the very heart of things, so to speak. They are not controvertible or changeable or dependent on evolution or what people happen to prefer or feel. Rather, they have their source in an eternal and everlasting being. According to this theory, what binds a person to follow the moral law is the fact that the moral law is rooted in the eternal source of all being. So the 'moral bindingness' of a divinely-based moral law is as strong as can be. In other words, if you accept the view that morality is based in God, your motivation for behaving morally is as powerful as it can possibly be.

"Of course, this does not constitute a proof that God exists, nor a proof that morality really is based on God. But remember, I'm not trying to prove God's existence here. Rather, my argument so far is basically this: A lot of what we do is motivated by our moral beliefs. So the more strongly you think morality has a claim on you, the more strongly you are motivated to do a lot of what you do. And, since a theistic or God-based conception of morality involves the most strongly binding morality that is conceivable, the adoption of theism as a way of life gives you the strongest set of moral motivations that one can have.

"Let's turn now to the second source of motivation I had mentioned – namely, the happiness motivation. Obviously, all joy or happiness must come from somewhere. The joy or happiness a being may have depends on the kind of being it is, and also on the source of its joy or happiness. The greater the source of that joy or happiness, the greater the joy or happiness will be. So here's my next key point. For a finite or limited being, such as a human be-ing, the greatest conceivable joy or fulfillment would stem from an infinitely powerful but benevolent source – that is, God. In other words, an infinitely powerful and benevolent being could make you far more happy or fulfilled than anything else imaginable.

"Now, some of you might be wondering, what concrete sense does it make to say that one can find happiness, joy, or fulfillment by standing in some relation to an infinitely powerful and benevolent being? In other words, how might God make you happy, or rather, how could God make you more happy than anything else could? Perhaps the simplest way of looking at this is to think of happiness or joy as some sort of eternal state of bliss or pleasure in heaven. If there is a God – a being that is infinitely powerful and benevolent – then God would surely be capable of arranging things so that our soul lives on after death and that we enjoy eternal bliss in the afterlife. But there's another way to look at the matter. Let's consider the nature of joy more directly and see what conclusions we may reach regarding the question, how might some relationship with God make us incredibly happy or joyous?

"First we need to ask a more basic question. What, after all, is happiness or joy? In Hebrew, we call it *simha*. So, what is simha? First of all, joy or simha does not consist merely in the fulfillment of our desires, for it is notoriously the case that people who satisfy whatever passing desires they may have are not necessarily happy or fulfilled. Indeed, many such people are miserable, confused and not at peace with themselves. So if joy does not consist merely in the gratification of desire, in what does it consist?

"I propose that, first of all, genuine joy involves a kind of harmony or unity. A person is happy when he or she does not have inner conflict, and when he or she is in harmony with his or her environment. It follows that the ultimate or best kind of joy would involve, necessarily, the ultimate or deepest kind of unity or harmony. And that's exactly what the concept of God is all about. God is the being that unifies or harmonizes everything. All the great mystics of the world know that the ultimate or best kind of joy consists not necessarily in gaining heaven or eternal bliss, but rather in some kind of relationship with God Himself, the ultimate One that stands behind the diversity of the universe. According to Judaism, such a relationship with God can be attained not only in the next world, but in this world as well.

"But joy or fulfillment involves more than harmony or unity. I'm going to go out on a limb here because what I have to say next is a little vague, but I'm going to say that real joy or happiness also involves the experience and expression of the 'fullness of being.' Joy or fulfillment involves 'living life to the full' – that is, experiencing, behaving, and creating in the fullest possible way. For example, one may experience a certain level of joy by expressing one's powers in physical exercise. Did you ever notice how much fun little kids have just by running around? Of course, when you get older, running around in circles isn't so much fun any more! But what about sports? Some people just like running, even in a straight line! Or how about dancing? Dancing can be an incredibly joyous experience. Anyone who's been to a disco or, for that matter, a traditional Jewish wedding, knows this very well. Dancing is joyous because it is an expression of one's being. Another example is the exhilarating experience one might have in climbing a mountain and absorbing the magnificent vista upon reaching the top. In all of these cases, joy or fulfillment has to do with an active expression and experience of being, or life itself.

"Incidentally, this is one reason why people are not happy or fulfilled in life, if they are not in some way or another productive or creative. The human urge to create or to bring things into being stems from the very essence of our being. It's no accident that the paradigm act of physical creativity, that is, reproduction or what we call, not accidentally, procreation is an intensely pleasurable act – and if it is performed in the proper context, it can be an intensely joyous act as well. This also relates to the fact that people have an innate drive to be free, for true creativity requires the freedom of self-expression. You can't be happy unless you create, and you can't create unless you are free.

"I've been digressing a little bit, so let me get back to the main thread. I was saying that joy or happiness involves the experience and expression of the fullness of being or life. It follows that the deepest kind of joy or happiness would involve the experience and expression of the deepest or most profound being in a way that is in harmony or unison with all other powers in oneself and one's environment.

"Now, once again, the idea of God is that of a single, transcendent, infinite and powerful creator upon whom all things depend for their existence and order. So it follows that the greatest imaginable joy for a human being would consist in the active experience and expression of God Himself! For God is, by definition, the deepest and most profound being. God is that unity or oneness that underlies all things. So, here we reach another key point. A way of life which consists in the active experience and expression of God is a way of life that has the strongest 'joy motivation' that we can possibly imagine.

"Again, does any of this prove that God exists? Not at all. But what I'm saying is that a person who is committed to a theistic or God-centered framework has the greatest 'moral motivation' and the strongest 'joy motivation' for living his or her life. And so far, my argument leaves open the details about what God is like, and what the specific ways are in which God relates to the world and to people. It leaves open the details about what is moral, and about how one goes about finding joy in God. Indeed, in different cultures and at different times, the same basic set of motivations have given rise to vastly different ways of filling in these details about who God is, how God relates to the world, and how, in particular, people ought to live.

"So, you might ask, is this line of thought peculiar to Judaism? It would seem that the argument I've been giving may be used to justify any way of life that centers on a transcendent, eternal and infinite source upon which all things depend. In some ways, I agree with that point. But what I'd like to explain next is how Judaism uniquely fits the kind of argument I was just giving. And we'll also see how Judaism goes even further by adding another dimension to the same basic line of thought.

"I have argued that the most deeply binding kind of morality is grounded in a transcendent and eternal source, and that the greatest possibility for joy and fulfillment would consist in some kind of relationship with God – the unity and harmony behind all being. Now, Judaism takes these very ideas and pushes them to their utmost limits. Let me explain what I mean by talking about two fundamental aspects of the Jewish conception of God.

"The God of Judaism is conceived first and foremost as the single and only God. The oneness of God is perhaps the single most important tenet in Judaism. Furthermore, God is conceived as the Creator of the entire universe, who purposefully and freely brought everything into existence in an orderly arrangement and who continuously sustains everything in existence. The God of Judaism is the most supremely powerful being that can be conceived. God is infinite and eternal. The One, supremely powerful being is the single being which unifies all things into one single and harmonious universe. While several religions have borrowed or inherited this idea from Judaism, no religion stresses the unity and oneness of God more than Judaism does.

"A second aspect of Judaism has to do with its teaching about the relationship God has with the world and, in particular, with human beings. Although God is supremely powerful and infinite, God is intimately aware of and concerned with the most mundane affairs of human life. God does not remain aloof from the world and from people. Rather, God has a benevolent plan to bring about the ultimate perfection of the universe, that is, to bring about the expression of His own being and unity in the world itself, and most especially in mankind. Furthermore, God has designated the way through which this ultimate end may be achieved. These are first and foremost the laws of morality to which all mankind are subject.

"And finally, Judaism teaches that God has designated a crucial mission for the Jewish people: to play a special role in bringing about the revelation of God in the world, so that ultimately the day will come when all the people of the world will recognize that single and transcendent source from which the being of all things flows, and upon whose grace and power everything depends. That will be a day of moral enlightenment as well as one of great happiness and joy.

"Using fancy theological terms, we can say that according to Judaism, God is both 'transcendent' and 'immanent.' Indeed, this is the unique legacy that Judaism has given to the world. We can now tie this in with what we were saying earlier. Insofar as God is transcendent, God is the source of the most binding sort of moral motivation. On the other hand, since God is immanent, God is, so to speak, 'available' to us. Therefore, we can have an intimate relationship with God that is a source of infinite joy and happiness. In other words, the God of Judaism is precisely that kind of God which grounds the most powerful moral motivation and the most powerful joy motivation that the human mind can conceive!

"Finally, there's another dimension, another kind of motivation, that Judaism adds to this mix. We've talked at length about the moral motivation and the joy motivation. But Judaism also teaches that God *commands* us Jews to do certain things and not to do others. Let's think about that for a moment. Judaism teaches that God – the ultimate and supreme being, the infinite, transcendent and eternal creator of the world, the source and ground of morality, the source of supreme joy and happiness – God has not merely requested, or suggested, or even inspired us Jews to do certain things. Nor is it merely the case that God has a certain path or way that we can choose to follow, or not, and then take the consequences, whatever they may be. Rather, God has *commanded* us to do certain things and not do others. Not only that, but Judaism teaches that the purpose of our fulfilling these commandments is to play a pivotal role in bringing about the revelation of God in this world, and the perfection of all humankind. What an amazing thing! What could possibly be more motivating than the belief that what I am about to do now is fulfill a divine commandment in the sense which I have just described?

"To summarize this lecture, I am committed to Judaism because it gives me the strongest possible motivation for living my life. As a committed Jew, when I wake up every morning, I am going to serve the infinite and eternal creator of the universe. When I keep the Sabbath, I'm fulfilling the divine command of the infinite and eternal creator. When I help a friend in need, I am not only doing what is morally right, I am doing what God Almighty has commanded me to do. When I rejoice at a wedding or on a Jewish holiday, I am rejoicing, ultimately, in the underlying unity behind all being, God himself.

"Of course, a skeptic might say, 'But wait! You haven't proved that God exists! What if you're wrong? What if it's all a big mistake?' My first response would be, What if it's not a big mistake after all? Second, I would say to the skeptic: What other way of life do you propose that might make for a more meaningful life? All my life, I've been motivated to act in the most powerful way possible. My life will have been as meaningful as it could possibly be. What more could one ask from a way of life than that?

"Thank you all for your kind attention!"

As Rabbi Low finished, the audience applauded. David found himself applauding too. When the applause died down, Avi Green rose, took the microphone and spoke.

"Thank you, Rabbi Low, for that very interesting and engaging talk! I think we have time for a few questions." He turned to the audience. "Are there any questions?"

No hands went up immediately, but nobody moved from their seats. Many thoughts ran through his mind, but David could not formulate a question. Even if he did, he would have been too nervous to ask.

Rabbi Low smiled, and gently prodded the audience: "Well, how about a question or two? I'm sure I must have said something provocative."

Finally, a hand went up from the third row. Rabbi Low smiled and spoke.

"Yes, sir, what is your question? Please stand up and make sure we can all hear you."

A bright-looking, clean-shaven college student stood up and began to speak, but no one could hear him at first. The microphone was quickly passed to him and he started again. "Rabbi Low, I understand you're not trying to prove God's existence, and instead you're saying that being religious gives a person the strongest motivation for living one's life. But are you saying that Judaism is the best religion, the only religion, or just one way to be religious? Using your argument, couldn't you just as well justify being a Christian or a Muslim? These religions also teach that morality is based in God, and that true happiness is found only in God. So could you clarify your argument as to why Judaism is a superior choice over these other religions?"

The student passed the microphone back and sat down. *Good question,* David thought.

"Thank you," said Rabbi Low. "First of all, remember that my goal was to explain why I am committed to Judaism. This does not preclude someone else from giving some kind of explanation as to why he or she might be committed to some other religion. I did not claim that Judaism is a "superior choice" to other religions. I would be the last person to criticize any Christian or Muslim for being committed to their faith. But I do believe that Judaism uniquely fits the considerations I raised regarding what is the strongest motivation for living one's life. Now, as we all know, Christianity and Islam were outgrowths of Judaism. The notion of a single, transcendent God, that is both all powerful and all good, and that is available for us to have some kind of relationship with – that's a teaching which these other religions took from Judaism. So, as to why Judaism might be a 'superior choice' – my approach would be that since Judaism came first, the burden of proof is on Christianity and Islam to show why Jews should give up their Judaism in favor of some other religion. Also, I would add another point, particularly about Christianity. Remember: I concluded with the thought that the noblest motivation for human action would be to fulfill God's commandments. Well, Christianity essentially gives up on the idea that we can fulfill God's commandments. That is the whole rationale for rejecting the Torah and instituting what Christians call the 'New Covenant.' According to Christianity we are fundamentally sinful and can only achieve God's grace by accepting the deity's son as our savior. And that's without mentioning all the perplexing problems that the notion of a 'divine son' brings up. As for Islam, the situation is different, since Islam does teach the notion of a divine law or sharia, as it is called. In this way, interestingly, Islam has more in common with Judaism than Christianity does. But, as you know, Islam originated in the seventh century with Mohammed. Now I'm sure that for an Arab living at the time, Islam was a great breath of fresh spiritual air when compared to the animistic, pagan religions that were prevalent in the region. So I would not fault Arabs for becoming Muslim. But for the Jew . . . well, that's different! A Jew has to think about how Islamic teachings match up - or fail to match up - with the pre-existing Jewish tradition. The Koran would have it that after two thousand years of revealing himself to Jewish prophets, God suddenly chose to reveal himself to Mohammed and literally change the story he had been telling all along. For centuries, the Jewish prophets taught that Isaac was the chosen son of Abraham and that the people of Israel were his chosen people. Yet according to Islam, Mohammed suddenly taught that Ishmael was really the chosen one and that Israel had not really been chosen after all! Again, for someone who is not Jewish, or has no Jewish education and background, this may not be such a big problem. But for someone who is born Jewish – well, it seems to me that a Jew has every reason to remain committed to Judaism rather than to accept either Christianity or Islam, unless those traditions can overcome that burden of proof. I hope that this helps answer your question. Are there any others?"

Rabbi Low scanned the audience. Another hand went up in the middle of the audience. A short, stocky woman with dark hair and thick glasses stood up. Rabbi Low seemed to be familiar with her.

"Ah, Professor Maimon! Good to see you! Please pass her the microphone." The microphone was passed to her, and she began to speak.

"First of all, thanks very much for your speech. It was very engaging and, as you say, provocative. I have two questions. Your approach is to avoid trying to prove or rationally substantiate the claim that God exists or that the Torah is divinely revealed. Instead, you've argued that people, or, at least Jews, have a reason or motive to behave and live as religious Jews because that will give them the strongest motivation for living their lives. Is that correct?"

"Yes. That's exactly right."

"According to you, then, it really doesn't matter whether or not God exists or the Torah is divine. As long as people believe and act as if God exists and the Torah is divine, they will feel that their lives have meaning. But there are two problems here. One is what I would call a conceptual or philosophical problem, and the other is that Judaism itself seems to demand much more than your argument provides. Now, the conceptual or philosophical problem arises from the fact that surely there's a difference between believing that one's life has great meaning and actually having a life that has great meaning. To use a somewhat crude analogy, surely there's a difference between believing that I have a million dollars versus my actually having a million dollars. I'm sure if I believed I had a million dollars I'd feel wonderful, but that would be no where near as good as actually having a million dollars! Similarly, it might indeed make my life feel meaningful if I believed that God is the basis for everything I do in life. But it wouldn't actually make my life meaningful unless God actually is the basis for everything I do in life. Therefore, at best, your argument would only show that living as religiously observant Jews makes people feel as if their lives are more meaningful, and not that it is actually more meaningful. That's what I call the philosophical problem with your argument. I'll just continue with my second point and then you can respond to both if you wish.

"The second problem is that your position does not seem adequate to Judaism itself. Judaism teaches that we have an obligation – a mitzvah – to know God. This is, for example, the view of Moses Maimonides. In fact, some passages in the Torah indicate that the goal of keeping the Torah and mitzvot is just that: to know God. As it is written, for example, in Deuteronomy, '*Ve-*

yadata ha-yom, ve-hashevosa el levavecha ki Hashem hu ha-Elokim,' which means, 'You shall know today, and reflect upon it in your heart, that the Lord is God.' You yourself stated that what makes Judaism special is that it teaches that we can have a certain kind of relationship with God. I agree with you that this is one of Judaism's central teachings. But in that relationship, one is not only supposed to believe in God, but one is supposed to know God. What distinguishes believing in God from knowing God is precisely that a person who knows God has some kind of proof or evidence or justification for believing that God exists. So your pragmatic argument to the effect that the lives of Jews will be more meaningful if they believe in God will only hold up if the relationship with God is attainable. But it is attainable only if, at some point, knowledge of God is attainable. And that means that at some point, one must be able to provide some kind of rational proof or evidence or argument that there is a God! In sum, the pragmatic approach you've outlined is doomed to fail unless one is also prepared to give a more substantive justification for believing that there is a God. Excuse me. I've gone on more than I should have. Do you wish to comment?"

Professor Maimon passed the microphone back to Rabbi Low and sat down. The room was absolutely silent. *Wow,* thought David. *She just destroyed his whole lecture!*

"Well," said Rabbi Low. He cleared his throat and stroked his beard for a moment. Then he began to respond, slowly at first, then picking up speed. "As usual, your questions are penetrating. First, let me say that you're right. There is a difference between believing that your life has great meaning and actually living a life that has great meaning. For example, the terrorist who blows himself up on a bus filled with innocent passengers believes that his life has great meaning when he does that. But most of us believe he is radically mistaken. Nevertheless, from the point of view of human psychology, from the point of view of the motivation that a person has for doing what he does – you can't deny that a person who believes he is fulfilling the will of God Almighty has the strongest motivation for doing whatever it is he is doing. The problem with the terrorist is not that he believes in God, and not even that he believes God has a will and is interested in our devotion. Rather, the problem is that the terrorist believes God wants him to kill innocent people. Why or how the terrorist has come to believe this is a question for another time. But my point still stands that psychologically, people have the strongest motivation for living their lives if they're religious, God-oriented people rather than not. This leaves open the question of how one should be religious, or specifically what actions should one perform as a religious person. There's some debate about that, but I've already stated that for a Jew, the first and foremost choice should be to follow the path of the Torah rather than to go off in some other direction or concoct one's own ideas about how God wants to be served."

Rabbi Low paused a moment, then went on.

"As to your second question: well, I agree that knowledge of God is part of the goal of keeping the Torah. But first of all, I'm not sure I agree with your premise that a person who has knowledge of God is necessarily able to prove or even rationally substantiate the claim that God exists. Does knowing something require that one be able to prove or rationally substantiate it? For example, I know that my wife loves me, but is love a matter of proof or rational substantiation? I know that murder is immoral, but can I prove it? I don't think so. Similarly, knowledge of God is indeed part of the goal of Judaism, but that doesn't mean we'll ever be able to prove it. You know, the position of the Rambam – I mean Maimonides – is not the only option. For example, the Maharal and others speak of a certain kind of divine *sechel*, or intelligence, that is beyond the ordinary powers of natural reason or intelligence. Perhaps we can have knowledge of God even though we cannot prove God's existence.

"Secondly, even though knowledge of God is indeed part of the goal of Judaism, that doesn't mean that one already needs to have knowledge of God in order to keep the Torah, in order to be a religious Jew. One can pursue the relationship with God because one believes that to do so gives one's life infinite significance, even if one has doubts about God's existence. In fact, knowledge of God requires a very high level of spiritual attainment! Very few Jews really have knowledge of God these days. We have *emunah* – that is, belief or faith, but we don't have *daas* – that is, knowledge. As for the verse you quoted from *Devarim* regarding knowledge of God, I venture to say that knowledge of God is something that Judaism teaches will come only at the end of days, as the prophet Yeshayahu says, '*Ki mala ha-aretz deah es Hashem*' – that is, 'When the earth is filled with the knowledge of God.' At that time, when God's presence is revealed more fully, then we will come to know God. But until then, most of us can only have faith. Therefore, what I've argued here tonight is that Jews have good reason to have *emunah* because a Jew's life has infinitely greater significance if he or she is religious than if he or she is not."

Rabbi Low stopped, and looked at Avi Green, who came forward and stepped to the podium.

"I think we'll have to bring things to a close here. Please join me once again in thanking Rabbi Dr. Low for a very stimulating evening!"

The audience clapped again, this time with more fervor. When the applause died down, people began to leave. David was still sitting in his seat, trying to figure out whether Rabbi Low had really answered Professor Maimon's questions. The three young women in front of him stood up to go. The one in the middle turned around and bent down to grasp her jacket from her seat. David looked straight into her face, and for a moment their eyes met. *God, she's pretty*, he thought. He wanted to say something, to engage her in conversation, but he couldn't think of anything profound. Before he knew it, she and her friends were gone.

28

"Hello, Rabbi Abraham. May I come in?"

"Sure, of course. Glad to see you, David. Come, sit down. I noticed you at Rabbi Low's lecture the other night. Well, what did you think?"

"I thought it was very interesting. It made me think about a lot of things in a new way. I'm really glad I went."

"Great. So, what did you make of his . . . uh . . . pragmatic approach? I mean his idea that it makes sense to be a religious Jew because it adds meaning and purpose to your life?"

"I don't know. I'm still thinking about it. Like he said, even if it works, it still doesn't show that God exists and the Torah is really divine."

"Exactly. That's why I keep saying that you need to practice Judaism and study Torah in order to really develop that *emunah,* that belief that is within the Jewish soul."

"But another nice thing I liked was that he didn't insist that all other religions are wrong. He just explained why he felt Judaism was the best choice for *him.*"

"Ah, yes. His argument was rather tolerant in that way."

"The thing is, I wouldn't have minded asking some questions of my own. I was wondering if maybe you knew how to get in touch with him."

"It's too bad you didn't get a chance to meet him. I'm sure he would have loved to sit down and talk with you. But he's already gone back to Israel."

"Oh, well. Actually, I also thought that the woman who got up at the end – is she somebody you know? She really made quite an impression, don't you agree? Who was she?"

"That was Dr. Maimon. She's a professor of philosophy here at the university. I think her main focus is on philosophy of religion."

"Wow. Why didn't you tell me about her before? I'd really like to a take a course with her."

"I bet you'd learn a lot. Just remember though, she's a professor, a philosopher – not a religious guide."

"What are you trying to say?"

"I'm just saying that while she may be very bright, I would not recommend that you look to her for spiritual guidance. David, what you're looking for is something to satisfy your *neshama,* your soul. But her focus is very intellectual. It's all about the *sechel,* the intellect, as far as she's concerned. When you make that your focus, it's dangerous, because you try to rationalize everything. What can't be rationalized, you throw out. You end up making Judaism into something other than it truly is. In fact, I think that taking a course with her could easily undermine your *emunah* rather than strengthen it. The bottom line is: if you're looking for *information,* seek it from academics. But if you're looking for a relationship with *Ha-Kadosh Baruch Hu,* with *Hashem,* I suggest you stick with us rabbis!"

"I see what you're saying. I'll give it some more thought."

"Good. So, meanwhile, are you keeping up with what we spoke about last time?"

"You mean, the practices? Oh . . . it's going OK."

"Look, I'm not trying to pressure you. But what about *kashrus*? Are you eating kosher these days?"

"Uh, sort of."

"Have you tried the kosher cafeteria near the Hillel? The food is really not bad. It's also where all the Jewish students hang out."

"No, I haven't tried that yet. But that sounds like a good idea. I'll check it out."

29

"Excuse me — I can't seem to find an empty table where I can eat my lunch. Do you mind if I sit here?"

"No, of course not. Go ahead. I'm almost done."

"Thanks. Hey, haven't we met before?"

"Have we? I don't remember."

"I think I saw you at the Hillel lecture a couple of weeks ago. A rabbi from Israel came to speak about being a committed Jew. Don't you remember?"

"Oh, yes. You mean Rabbi Low. Yes, I was there. But I don't recall . . . ."

"That's OK. I'm David."

"Nice to meet you. I'm Esther."

"So, what did you think of it?"

"Sorry? What did I think of *what*?"

"The lecture."

"Oh! I liked it. But I really enjoy some of his other stuff better."

"His other stuff? What do you mean?"

"Most of the times I've heard him speak, he talks about some passage in the Torah, or he talks about something like Shabbat or the *hagim,* or he explains something peculiar in the *tefillah*. But this was different. It was more abstract."

"You mean his lecture was about being committed to Judaism overall as opposed to talking about some specific topic or text within Judaism?"

"Right, that's it. I guess I never really think about that issue too much."

"You don't?"

"No."

"You must be pretty confident about your commitment to Judaism."

"I guess so. That's the way I've been brought up, and that's just the way I am. Why? What about you? What's your background?"

"I'm Jewish. That's about it."

"Are you Conservative? Reform?"

"Not really. I'm not from a religious home. I had some Hebrew lessons, and I had a bar mitzvah, but it was really just a big party. I guess you could say that right now I consider myself . . . uh . . . a very interested agnostic."

"Well, in that case, what did *you* think of Rabbi Low's speech?"

"He's got an interesting approach. It's very pragmatic. I'm not sure I agree with it, though. I still have some questions I'd like to ask him."

"You should email him, then. He's approachable. I met him in Israel, and I even had lunch at his house on Shabbat a few times. Nice family, too. And he's very open to questions, that's for sure."

"Wow, that sounds great. How would I get his email address?"

"Go to his yeshiva's website. Do you have a piece of paper? Here, I'll write it down for you on my napkin."

"Thanks. I will email him. So . . . anyway . . . you're Orthodox, right?"

"Yep. FFB."

"FFB? What's that?"

"It stands for '*frum* from birth.' *Frum* is Yiddish for devout or Orthodox. So I'm FFB as distinguished from BT. You know what BT means?"

"No, I'm afraid not."

"BT stands for *ba'al teshuvah,* which means someone who's done *teshuvah* or returned to observe the ways of the Torah. Nowadays it's often used to refer to people who grew up in assimilated or non-religious homes, but who became religious on their own."

"So . . . if I were to become *frum,* I'd be a BT. Right?"

"Right! You've got it."

"It's my fine logic skills at work. Seriously, though . . . you've spent time in Israel, then?"

"Yes, sure. I was at Beit Bruria, a women's seminary. I spent last year there, after high school."

"A seminary? You mean you studied to become a rabbi?"

"No, of course not! Orthodox Jews don't have women rabbis!"

"Oh, yes. I knew that. But when you said 'seminary' I wasn't sure what you meant."

"It's an institution of advanced Jewish study for women. Some girls get a teaching degree. But most girls are there just to learn."

"I see. But that doesn't bother you?"

"What? What should bother me?"

"That women can't be rabbis."

"Ah! No, not all. Why would I want to be a rabbi? Sorry to be so blunt, but the whole idea of women rabbis is too strange for me to even take seriously."

"No problem. Well, do you want to go back?"

"To seminary?"

"No, to Israel."

"To visit? Sure."

"I mean, to live."

"Um . . . maybe. I don't know. It all depends. I mean, I'm *tziyoni,* but not that extreme."

"*Tziyoni*? What's that?"

"Zionist. I mean I'm Zionist, but not the kind that says everybody should move to Israel right away."

"I see. You mean, you support the State of Israel. My parents are Zionist, too."

"Well, I . . . um . . . I don't know your parents, but it's a little more than that. I'm not just 'in favor' of the State of Israel. A religious Zionist is someone who believes that the State of Israel has religious status."

"How so?"

"They believe that the State of Israel is the beginning of the *geulah,* or redemption, of the Jewish people. It's certainly *kibbutz galuyot,* which means, the return of the Jewish people to the land. This is a prelude to the days of *mashiah* – that's the messiah."

"I see. Well, maybe you can answer a question I have about the messiah?"

"I'll try."

"Orthodox Jews believe in a messiah, right? But what exactly does that mean? How do you tell who the messiah is?"

"Oh, that's easy. I learned about this last year in seminary. We went through Rambam's discussion of this in the *Mishneh Torah.*"

"Who's Rambam?"

"Moses Maimonides. Rambam is an acronym for Rabbi Moshe ben Maimon – Rabbi Moses the son of Maimon."

"OK, go on. What does he say about the messiah?"

"He says that the *mashiah* will be a great political leader of the Jewish people. The *mashiah* is not expected to do miracles or change the way nature works. And the *mashiah* is not a divine being. He is definitely human – an extraordinary leader, like Moshe or King David. He is supposed to be a descendant of David. Under his leadership, the Jews will re-establish themselves as a free people in the land of Israel and dedicate themselves to keeping the Torah. You can tell if someone is the *mashiah* if he successfully does all that."

"But hasn't that happened already? Haven't the Jews gone back to Israel?"

"Yes, but a few other things need to happen. Look at the Temple Mount, for example. There's a mosque on the exact site of the ruins of the *Beit ha-Mikdash,* the Temple. The *mashiah* will rebuild the Temple – that's one of his tasks. Besides, the State of Israel is basically a secular state, and most Israelis are secular. So, obviously the *mashiah* has not come. But the ingathering of the exiles looks like it's been going on for at least a century. Consider all the Jews who came to Israel from all parts of the world. So it does look like the beginning of the days of *mashiah*. But not all Orthodox Jews agree on this. Some are actually opposed to the State of Israel. They say that we should wait until *mashiah* arrives before taking charge of the land. They're also opposed to the idea of a secular Jewish state. For them, no state of Israel is better than a secular state. But these people are only a small minority within the Orthodox Jewish population."

"Wow. You seem to know quite a lot about this."

"No big deal. I've been brought up in this for years. Besides, I took a class on different religious approaches to Zionism last year at Beit Bruria. Hey, look . . . sorry, but it's getting late. I've got a class to go to. Besides, you'd better eat your lunch. You haven't eaten a single bite, and I'm sure it's getting cold!"

"Yes, well . . . it was really nice talking to you. I'd really like to continue our conversation. Could I . . . uh . . . maybe get your phone number?"

"Um . . . well . . . right now I'm kind of in transition, since I've just changed rooms on campus — so I don't really have a phone. Look, it was nice talking to you. Really, you should email Rabbi Low with your questions. Here's the website address. Take it."

"OK, thanks a lot. Nice talking to you, Esther."

"Gotta go. Bye!"

30

From: dgoldstein@cuniv.edu   Sent: 5/3/00 9:30 PM
To: rlow@ahavattorah.org.il
Subject: Question about Lecture

Dear Rabbi Low,

Please excuse my writing to you out of the blue. I was at the lecture you gave at the Hillel on my campus a few weeks ago. I especially liked your emphasis on being sincere and honest about what we can and can't prove. But I had a few questions. A friend of mine named Esther said that I should write to you. She said she had a few classes with you and also had some meals at your house in Israel. Do you remember her?

I'll start with this: At one point in your lecture, you said that all the great mystics say that the best kind of joy has to do with attaining some kind of experience of God himself. Since God is the ultimate harmony in the universe, anyone who attains this experience attains this harmony and joy. A friend of mine is into eastern religion. He says that the best state for a person to attain is "enlightenment" which means to merge or become one with the One, the ultimate reality. In order to do that, a person doesn't need to keep the Torah. So, using your own pragmatic approach, it seems that if we can attain enlightenment by becoming one with the ultimate reality without keeping the Torah, why should anyone bother keeping the Torah? Rather, we should all become eastern mystics.

Sincerely,

David Goldstein

From: rlow@ahavattorah.org.il   Sent: 5/4/00 4:23 AM
To: dgoldstein@cuniv.edu
Subject: RE: Question about Lecture

Dear Mr. Goldstein,

I'm glad you found the lecture interesting. As time allows, I will be glad to try to answer any questions that you have. It sounds like you met Esther Applefeld. Of course, I remember her very well. Please give her my regards. But I'm also curious to know more about you. What's your own background in terms of Judaism?

Your question is a good one. Ideally, I'd like to know a little more about which version of eastern religion your (other) friend is into. Not all eastern religions are the same. By the way, is your friend Jewish? I'm just wondering because, for the last thirty years or so, many young people who have been exploring eastern religions turn out to be Jews who are unfortunately unaware of the richness of their own tradition.

First, there's a very big difference between the Jewish conception of G-d and the eastern conception of ultimate reality. Judaism conceives of G-d as a Person – that is, as a "He." To say that G-d is a person doesn't mean G-d has a body, but rather that G-d has a will, and that he is rational. G-d makes choices, He plans, He creates, He communicates, He commands, and so on. And since G-d is a person, Judaism teaches that if we take the necessary steps we can have an **interpersonal** relationship with G-d that involves mutual love and respect. The necessary steps, according to Judaism, include following the way of G-d, following His commandments, respecting Him and loving Him – that is, keeping the Torah. On the other hand, generally speaking, for the eastern religions the ultimate reality is not understood as personal. Taoism is a case in point. The Tao is conceived as the ultimate structure or "way" in which the universe operates. The Tao is not a He but rather an "It." The "It" doesn't speak, doesn't communicate, it doesn't love us, and it certainly doesn't issue any commands. Most importantly, you can't have an **interpersonal** relationship with an It.

Some Eastern mystics teach that you can "merge" or "become one" with the ultimate reality. The idea that you can become one with the One is logically problematic. But let's suppose you *could* attain some kind of merging with the ultimate reality. Supposedly this is done partly through the process of meditation, but it also involves leading a very vigorous spiritual life. So I'm not sure it's any easier than keeping the Torah! But the more important point is that, according to Judaism, no saint, however great, can ever become **identical** with G-d. The best we can hope to do is attain a **relationship** with G-d in which we come close to the divine being, but not identical with Him. In my view, it is better to have an **interpersonal** relationship with a Personal G-d than to merge or become one with an Impersonal It. Therefore, to use your own terms, we should keep the Torah and not become eastern mystics.

Sincerely,

Rabbi Yehudah Low

From: dgoldstein@cuniv.edu   Sent: 5/8/00 10:29 PM
To: rlow@ahavattorah.org.il
Subject: RE: Question about Lecture

Dear Rabbi Low,

Thanks for your response. First of all, my friend – his name is Ravi – is not Jewish. In fact, his family is from India. He's someone I really respect and admire. I've learned a lot from him and he's helped me out a lot. He tells me that he believes in some kind of combination of Buddhist and Hindu teachings.

I get what you're saying about the difference between the impersonal conception of ultimate reality as taught by Eastern religion and the personal conception of God as taught by Judaism. Your explanation helped a lot. But I still don't understand why you think an interpersonal relationship with God is **better** than an impersonal merging with the One. I also don't get why you say it's absurd to think this merging is possible. Can you elaborate?

And by the way I notice you always write "G-d" with a dash. I've seen that somewhere before but what's the point of that?

David

From:rlow@ahavattorah.org.il   Received: 5/9/00 11:33 PM
To: dgoldstein@cuniv.edu
Subject: RE: Question about Lecture

Dear David,

I'm up early this morning and I just read your email which again I enjoyed very much. You sound like you're a philosophy student. Is that right?

I firmly believe that any interpersonal relationship with another person is far superior to an impersonal merging with the One. Basically, any person is superior to any non-person. A person is the most valuable entity we can think of. That's why we distinguish between persons and things. A person is a free, intelligent creature. I would go so far as to say that if Ultimate Reality is not a person, then, even a human being (a free, intelligent creature) is intrinsically more valuable than ultimate reality! Now, according to Judaism, G-d is not just a person, He is the best person of all, the Supreme Person. G-d is radically more free and more intelligent than anything else. I think that it's impossible to give a rational proof that it is better to be a person than a non-person. But let me ask you this. Given the choice, which would you rather be? A person? Or, a thing (a non-person)? Would you rather be a being that is capable of choice, capable of love and respect, capable of having interpersonal relationships with other persons? Or would you rather be a thing (non-person), that is, an entity that is not capable of choice, love, respect, interpersonal relationships? If your answer is that you would rather be a person than a non-person, this shows that, in practice, you agree that a person is better than a non-person!

Furthermore, it seems to me that the idea of merging with the One is a logical impossibility. If the One is really perfectly one, it is unchanging and non-composite (not made of parts). These are standard teachings about the One in classical Hinduism. In many ways this sounds exactly like what classic Jewish theologians like Maimonides would say about the essence of G-d. That is, He's perfectly one, unchanging, non-composite, etc. But whereas most Jewish theologians maintain a sharp distinction between G-d and everything else, many Hindu thinkers insist that somehow, *everything* is ultimately one. So, even the individual human self is the same as the One! (The theistic version of this strange view is *pantheism*: G-d is everything. There were some Christian thinkers and Jewish ones who advocated this, e.g., Meister Eckhart and at least in some places, Shneur Zalman of Liadi, the original Lubavitcher Rebbe. But this is uncharacteristic of most Jewish thinkers.) But if the One is unchanging and non-composite, nothing can "merge" or become one with it! For if something other than the one became one with the One, then the One would have changed, and it therefore wouldn't have been One after all. Another obvious problem is that if we are already one with the One, why would we need to bother engaging in a spiritual quest to merge with it? The whole thing doesn't make sense.

To answer your question about my spelling of the word G-d, actually that has a lot to do with our topic. For Jews, G-d is a holy being who is worthy of the utmost respect. Thus we do not "take G-d's name in vain" and we also do not erase even one of G-d's holy names, which of course are in Hebrew. There is a bit of a debate about whether the real English word for the divine reality may not be erased, or whether a text that uses G-d's name in English may be treated with disrespect. It has become standard for many Jews to use a dash instead of an "o" and then the name is erasable and any text which uses it may be discarded. By the way, if I am not mistaken there is no such prohibition in those eastern religions which regard the ultimate One as "impersonal." An impersonal being would not be subject to "disrespect" for it would not care about what humans do. Since we believe G-d is personal, respect for G-d matters a lot!

You've told me that you know Esther, and about your friend Ravi. Thanks! But I'm still curious about your own background. Can you tell me a little more about yourself?

All the best,

Rabbi Low

31

May 9, 2000

I'm writing in my journal under the influence of the good essence. Ideas are just popping and it's actually hard to write. All I really want to do is just think and talk. But no one's here to talk with, so I'll just talk to myself in my journal. I've been trying to meditate and it sometimes really feels like it's starting to work. Maybe my mind is playing tricks on me but the other night I really felt for a split second like I was going beyond into some other realm. Getting outside of myself somehow — it's really hard to explain but it's a little scary too. Ravi's right. Meditation is powerful stuff. Then again, sometimes I meditate, or at least try, and nothing happens. One time I think I just fell asleep. I guess if you practice, then it gets more consistent. Practice, practice, practice. So many things in life are all about "just doing it." Like what R. Abraham said about saying the Shema. But it's one thing to meditate, it's another to say a certain sentence over and over. I just can't get myself to keep repeating words I don't believe. Maybe the Shema is all true, but right now I don't believe it's true, so how can I just affirm, affirm, affirm? This really seems like an unhealthy way to go about acquiring a belief in God. HOLY SMOKES! Something really just clicked! It just dawned on me how Rabbi A's approach is exactly the same as George's approach. Rabbi A thinks you can't give convincing arguments for belief in God and the Chosen People and the Torah, and that in the end you just have to accept on faith. And George thinks you can't give convincing arguments as to why we need Christ for salvation, you just have to accept it on faith. The "arguments" work only up to a point — in the end you need to "just believe." It's *kind of like a doctor prescribing a pill. "Just say this formula and you'll see what an effect it has." So, according to both Rabbi A and George, it all boils down to a LEAP OF FAITH. My problem is that if it's all a leap of faith, why choose Judaism over Christianity? Low would argue that it's rational for a person to be religious since it adds to the meaning of life and gives you the strongest motivation for living. He also said that it's rational for a Jew to accept Judaism over Christianity, since the burden of proof is on the Christian to show that God changed his mind about having a special relationship with the chosen people. Of course Rabbi Abraham would agree that God didn't change his mind. But according to Abraham, belief in the Torah is all a matter of a leap, anyway. So, if that's the case, WHY LEAP ONE WAY RATHER THAN THE OTHER? For that matter, WHY LEAP AT ALL? But Low has an answer to this. He argues that being religious makes your life more meaningful. But then Low ought to have more to say about why <u>not</u> leap into Christianity. Maybe God (if he exists) had some reason to change his mind. It sure looks that way, given how successful Christianity is! Got to email R Low with that question. But why does Low keep nagging me about my background? Ugh! Need to stop and grab a smoke and a beer!*

32

"Well, here we are again, David. I got this stuff from downtown. I hope it's good."

"You always come through, Simon. I'm sure it's fine."

"Hey, will you chip in this time? I'm running out of cash."

"No problem. What you want? Look, here's a hundred bucks."

"Thanks. Well, are you going to light up?"

"Yes . . . . There. It's lit. Hmmm, not bad at all . . . ."

"Thanks. Well, what's been going on? I gotta tell you David, I'm getting a little worried about you."

"Why? About what?"

"First the breakup with Helen, then I catch you studying Torah, and lately you're eating all the time at the kosher cafeteria! You really seem to be really getting into Judaism. It's seems like nothing I've been telling you all along makes any difference!"

"Hang on, Simon. You've got to understand, it's different for me than it was for you. You were brought up in it, and you knew all about it. You made the choice to reject it and I respect your choice. But for me it's all kind of new and intriguing! Besides which, don't jump to any conclusions about what I believe. I only eat at the kosher place because it's an excuse to see Esther. In fact, at this point, I really can't even say that I believe in God. But let me ask you this. How come you're so certain that God *doesn't* exist?"

"Oh, come on. You know it's all a hoax, all a myth."

"No, Simon, I don't know that. Don't you see? You're just as certain that God *doesn't* exist as lots of religious people are certain that God *does* exist! Who's right? That's what I'm trying to figure out, at least for myself. I'll tell you this, though. One thing I've learned from Ravi —"

"Ravi? He's not Jewish! What's he got to do with this?"

"Just listen for a second. Have you ever noticed there's something deeply spiritual about him? He's got something very deep going on."

"Spiritual? *That* I can maybe accept — sort of. But that's different from being *religious*."

"Wait a second. You know what makes him so spiritual?"

"I wouldn't know."

"Look, have you ever meditated?"

"No, of course not. Jews don't meditate. They just mumble prayers. But what's your point?"

"Just hear me out! Ravi thinks there is an ultimate reality, a single, transcendent oneness that underlies all things. All the great religions of the world — or at least most of them — affirm this teaching. Now it's true that they all teach different paths toward the ultimate. Some religions are heavily into meditation. They also differ on what exactly the ultimate reality is. Obviously, Judaism has a different view on the ultimate from Hinduism or Buddhism. Instead of the impersonal One, Judaism says that God is the Supreme Person. So, in Judaism, you don't meditate on the Supreme Person, you pray to him. But still, there's something both traditions believe in common — the belief in an ultimate oneness of some sort. Are you following?"

"Give me the pipe, and maybe I'll follow you better. Thanks! Look, just because they have something in common doesn't prove that either of them is right!"

"True. Maybe all the great religions of the world are completely wrong and you're right, and there's no God or ultimate reality. And maybe all there is for us in this world is just to grab as much pleasure as we can before we die. That *is* your view, isn't it?"

"Yep. It is."

"Well, like I said, I respect your right to have your view. But I'm not yet convinced you're right. And, what if it turns out that they *are* right, and I end up living my entire life without realizing that there is an ultimate truth or a God?"

"What are you worrying about? Burning in hell?"

"No, I really don't think too much about death or what happens after death . . . . I really don't think there's a next world."

"I agree with you on that one. So, if there isn't a next world, what are you worried about, then? Just live life in the moment!"

"I'm not worried about the afterlife, but I *am* concerned about what kind of meaning my life has while I'm alive, in the here and now."

"David, I can sort of understand why a person might want to have some kind of spiritual life. It's not my cup of tea but I can sort of understand it. But even if there's no God or ultimate Oneness, it's no surprise that someone who spends time meditating is . . . um . . . bound to develop a certain kind of serenity . . . which I confess is certainly not something I have or even want. Still, I don't see how a person in today's day and age can even begin to believe in something like the Bible. What about all the stories? What about all those peculiar laws? Come on! It's all antiquated stuff!"

"I confess you've got a point there."

"And David, can I just ask you one thing?"

"Sure. What?"

"It seems like there was a sudden change in you. I mean, one minute you were about to tell your parents about Helen and break away from them once and for all. But I noticed when you came back from the trip to Washington, it was all over. What happened?"

"Well, actually, something *did* happen on the trip."

"I knew it! What was it? She must have ticked you off somehow. What did she do wrong?"

"Actually, it had nothing much to do with her at all. But there was something else. I didn't tell you about this, but I had a very odd experience. I ended up going to the Holocaust Museum. Not with Helen, I mean. She went off to see some old friend and I had nothing to do for a few hours."

"Ah! So it *did* have to do with her. She abandoned you, and it all went downhill from there!"

"No, no. Just hear me out. I'll tell you what happened. I was wandering around, and somehow I ended up in front of the Holocaust Museum. Then, all of a sudden, there was this strange guy offering me a free ticket. I had nothing to do, so I went in. Have you ever been there?"

"Yeah, sure. I went on a high-school trip. Anyway, what happened next?"

"Well, the museum had quite an effect on me."

"Uh-oh. There's a name for that. It's called 'Holocaust guilt.' OK, go on."

"Just listen. In the museum I saw this picture of an Orthodox Jewish guy, He looked like a rabbi, and he was being forced onto a train going to Treblinka. He was wearing his *tallis* and *tefillin*. But the look on his face . . . complete serenity. It made me wonder."

"Ah, now I get it! You think this whole thing was engineered by God to send you a message. *Dump the non-Jewish girl and return to your Jewish roots!* Is that what you think?"

"Of course I don't *know* that for sure. But Simon, the whole thing was eerie. I mean, I just went in to the museum by accident. And the guy who gave me the ticket, he was kind of strange, too. And it just happened that he was there, right at the moment that I happened to reach the museum, without my even intending to be there. And my mother had been telling me to go to the museum . . . ."

"Ah, so that's why you went! Look, I bet I could twist the whole experience around to mean something completely different. Let me see. When exactly did this whole thing happen? Over Christmas break, right?"

"Yeah. Actually, it was on December twenty-fifth, Christmas Day. I remember that because I was surprised that the museum was open."

"So! I've got it! We could just as easily say that this whole thing is not really about Judaism. It's really about *Christianity*!"

"*What*? Simon! What are you talking about?"

"Simple! You're trying to take this whole episode as a sign that God was sending you a message that you should return to Judaism. But a Christian could just as easily say that Christ pulled all the strings here. I can just imagine someone like George saying this: "David, don't you see what God was trying to tell you? You were involved with Helen for purely physical, sinful reasons. You were neglecting the religious dimension of life. So God brought you to your senses by guiding you to the Holocaust museum *on Christmas Day* in order to lead you to accept the true religion: Christianity!"

"No way! You're really stoned, man! I just don't buy that. It was just a coincidence that it happened on December twenty-fifth!"

"David! Don't you see how crazy the whole thing is? You can interpret any event like that any way you really want to."

"Well, I . . . uh . . . sorry, but I just don't really feel drawn toward Christianity at all. I just don't take it seriously."

"But why not? *Why* don't you take it just as seriously as Judaism?"

"I don't know . . . I guess because I'm not . . . never was Christian."

"Isn't that arbitrary?"

"Maybe so . . . but that's the way it is!"

"And the more important point is: don't you see how this attempt to see God's hand in your life is hopeless?"

"Well, I don't know. I can't prove that I'm right, but I'm not ready to agree with you either . . . ."

33

From: dgoldstein@cuniv.edu   Sent: 5/13/00 9:30 PM
To: rlow@ahavattorah.org.il
Subject: Question about Christianity

Dear Rabbi Low,

Hello again. Thanks for answering my question a few days ago on why you think
the conception of God as personal is better than the eastern conception of the
ultimate as impersonal. I'm still not sure persons are inherently better than non-
persons, but I do have to admit, I'm glad I'm a person, and not a thing!

If you wouldn't mind, I would like to ask a question on a different topic. You spoke
a little about this during the Q and A session after your lecture here. But I'm still
hazy on why you are so quick to dismiss Christianity. I get the point about how
Judaism came first and so the burden of proof is on the Christian to show that God
changed his mind and gave up on the Jews. I also understand your point that a Jew
should first have some solid reason to dismiss Judaism before he moves to adopt
another religion. But looking at it from an objective point of view, there seems to
be a lot of indications that God (if he exists) **did** change his mind and gave up on
the Jews. I have three arguments for this.

First, for thousands of years, the Jews have been scattered across the world,
oppressed and victimized by non-Jews in many countries, culminating, of course,
in the Holocaust. Doesn't this show that God has abandoned the Jews, or at least
that there is no special relationship between God and the Jews any longer?

Second, the success of Christianity seems to be an indication of its truth. Millions
and millions of people believe in Christianity all across the globe. The most
powerful country on earth, the US, has a substantial Christian majority and
some people even go so far as to claim that it's a Christian nation. Doesn't the
widespread success of Christianity count as a sign that Christianity is true? Besides,
given the success of Christianity, it seems unreasonable that the Jewish prophets
(if indeed they were genuine prophets) never even once predicted its rise. If they
could really see into the future, shouldn't they have foreseen how powerful it
would be?

Third, the Torah seems to contain so many laws and commandments that are
either hard or impossible to fulfill. There are so few practicing Orthodox Jews.
Many of the scriptural laws are not even practiced today at all, even by Orthodox
Jews. I've been reading through Leviticus, and there are a lot of examples there.
Like, for example, all the ritual laws of purity and impurity and all the laws
pertaining to the temple. Many of these laws are outdated (like animal sacrifices,
the one about eye for an eye and a tooth for a tooth, the law against interest or

usury, gruesome death penalties, etc.). The logical conclusion seems to be that God (if he exists) issued these laws only for a limited time to a premodern society. And that leads also to the conclusion that God decided to give the Torah only temporarily, and he knew ahead of time that he was going to change his mind, and abolish all the laws and commandments. And that's exactly what Christianity teaches. Basically, the Jews' failure to keep the law shows that humans are incapable of keeping God's law, and that the only way to have a relationship with God is by relating to God through some way other than the Torah.

Sorry this email has gotten so long. I'm really curious to know what you have to say. I hope you don't find any of this offensive. I'm just trying to ask honest questions.

Sincerely,

David Goldstein

From: rlow@ahavattorah.org.il   Sent: 5/14/00 6:23 AM
To: dgoldstein@cuniv.edu
Subject: RE: Question about Christianity

Dear David,

I gather from your email that you're Jewish and that someone's been talking to you about Christianity. Won't you please tell me a little more about yourself? Anyway, I'll try to answer your questions, which are so good that I don't think I can adequately answer them in one message. It's great that you're asking honest questions. Keep them coming. In this email, I'll address your first and second questions, which have to do with the length of the exile and the popularity of Christianity.

Your first question concerns the length of the exile. First, it is important to see things in historical perspective. You mentioned that the Jews have been oppressed for "thousands of years." The current exile began in 70 CE and therefore has lasted for somewhat less than two thousand years. But are two thousand years really such a long time in the grand scheme of things? Perhaps not. The Psalms (see Chapter 90) say that a thousand years is like a day from the divine, eternal perspective. Furthermore, according to Jewish tradition, the people of Israel received the Torah in the year 2448, counting from the time of Adam, which corresponds to 1312 BCE. This means that from the time of Adam, more than two thousand years passed before the people of Israel received the Torah. If G-d could wait two thousand years before giving the Torah to His people, perhaps it is not so strange that He might wait two thousand years before redeeming them. G-d's work takes time. Human beings needed time to grow and develop (just as children need time to mature) before the Torah could be revealed. Perhaps human beings need even more time to grow and develop before the final completion of G-d's plan – that is, the redemption of His people and the messianic era, which is supposed to be an era of peace and brotherhood for all humankind. Are we anywhere near that era? I hope so, but it's not surprising that it takes time – a lot of time.

Furthermore, consider the following. Many scholars date the exodus from Egypt at around 1280 BCE and the subsequent entry of the Israelites into the land of Israel under Joshua at around 1250 BCE. For the sake of argument, let's use these dates. From the time of Joshua till the time of King David, the Israelites were conquering the land. King Solomon built the First Temple in around 950 BCE. The Babylonians destroyed the Temple and exiled the Jews in 586 BCE. That means the Israelites were in the land for some 664 years, and within that time, Solomon's temple stood for some 364 years. After the Babylonian exile, the Jews came back and rebuilt the Temple in around 500 BCE. The Second Temple stood till around 70 CE, when the Romans destroyed it. So until the Roman exile, the people were in the land for the second time about 570 years. Thus, in total the Israelites were in their land for about 1200 years, and the two Temples stood for a combined total of almost one thousand years! Seen in this context, the current exile of less than two thousand years is long, but not absurdly long. Perhaps we are just about due for redemption! More on that point below.

About the suffering of the Jews, an important thing to remember is that the Hebrew prophets predicted the trials and tribulations of the Jews (including exile and oppression) well before the rise of Christianity. Those same prophets are equally filled with the promise of redemption, return to the land, and the oath of the everlasting covenant between G-d and the Jewish people. For a Jew, the exile is **not** a sign that G-d has permanently abandoned us. It is rather an already predicted sign that we are in a state of disfavor in G-d's eyes. And strangely enough it is also a sign that G-d cares about us. It may sound ironic, but you don't punish someone you don't care about. By the way, not to diminish the suffering of the Holocaust in any way, but a little perspective on that is also relevant. During the Holocaust, six million of our people died over the course of four years. But in Egypt, the Jews were enslaved for four generations, for some **two hundred years.** I don't mean to compare the suffering of slavery to the suffering in the Nazi death camps. Still, two hundred years is a pretty long time to be enslaved. Thousands, if not millions, must have also perished in the Egyptian persecution. This is not to minimize the suffering of the Holocaust, just to put it in historical perspective.

A final point on the length of the current exile. Many religious Jews such as myself believe that the time of the exile has finished or is coming to a close. As you know, in 1948 the Jews established the State of Israel. Although the Temple has not been rebuilt, Jews are now in control of their land for the first time in almost two thousand years. This is an amazing phenomenon. Many Jews see the state of Israel as the end of the exile, if not the beginning of the end. Not all Jews have this view about the religious significance of the modern State of Israel, but almost all religious Jews agree that one of the signs of the final redemption is the return of Jews to the land and its "bearing fruit" once again, which has clearly happened in a most remarkable – indeed, miraculous – fashion. Some of the passages in the prophets regarding the "blooming of the desert" have literally come true. Many Jews (and many Christians) see the State of Israel and the Six Day War as modern miracles. My point is that arguably, the exile is over or almost over. Granted, the Jews suffered horribly over the centuries, especially during the Holocaust. Granted, there is still a lot of anti-Jewish sentiment, particularly in the Arab world. But considering the number of Jews in the world, their economic, military, and pure brain power is quite remarkable. Consider, for example, how many Jews per capita have won the Nobel Prize. Or consider the per capita income of Jews worldwide. Or consider the number of Jews per capita who have advanced degrees. In many ways, Jews are more powerful and successful than they have been in the last two thousand years.

Furthermore, I don't think it's reasonable to argue that the widespread popularity of Christianity is a sign that G-d abandoned the Jews. Again, here is some historical perspective: Abraham was the original "iconoclast" – literally, a breaker of idols. The entire world was basically pagan, or polytheistic. The Jews, with their belief in monotheism, were a tiny minority. Moses in Egypt was a radical, going against the well-entrenched polytheism of the greatest civilization of the time, where Pharaoh himself was deified. You would not say that the widespread "success" or popularity of polytheism, paganism, etc. showed that it is valid or true. *It showed rather that there is something that the human being finds attractive about paganism*. Similarly, consider the fact that over two billion people (the population of Christians worldwide) on this earth believe, in one way or another, that *a Jewish man was the son of the divine being, a Jewish man died for the sins of humanity, and that a Jewish man is the vehicle of atonement for the entire world.* These are astonishing facts! Despite the overt paganistic nature of this claim, it is an indication that something about Judaism is probably true! And what's true is the fundamental teaching of monotheism, upon which both Judaism and Christianity and Islam agree. At the same time, the popularity of Christianity also shows how appealing paganism/idolatry is to the human being. People want to have their cake and eat it too. They want to have a transcendent, infinite, almighty G-d *who nevertheless assumes a finite physical form or image*. The deification of JC as the divine incarnation of G-d directly violates the Torah's prohibition against "*hagshamah*" – that is, depicting G-d in a physical form. (See Dueteronomy 4:16.) Basically, Christians want to have a relationship with the Creator, but at the same time *they don't want to commit themselves to monotheism in its pure form*. Now, as I indicated in my lecture, I do not begrudge the average Christian for being drawn toward such beliefs. But from the Jewish perspective, these yearnings are absurd and infantile. You should not be swayed or tempted by them.

Furthermore, your point about the widespread nature of Christianity is mitigated if you take Islam into account. It's interesting that Christianity had a tough time penetrating the Arab world, but Islam was immensely successful in the Arab world and also in the Far East. That should give you some pause regarding the "success" of Christianity. The thing that's really successful and impressive is the spread of *monotheism*. It is not an accident that Islam rejects the deification of Jesus and also insists on the notion of a divine law. From the Jewish point of view, Islam has other problems, but we don't need to get in to that right now.

As for your claim that the Jewish Scripture does not predict the rise of Christianity (or Islam), that is not universally accepted. A commentator from fifteenth-century Spain, Don Isaac Abarabanel, wrote a commentary on the Book of Daniel (Chapter 7) in which he reads certain passages as predicting the rise of Christianity and in particular the powerful domination of the Catholic Church. The great Jewish commentator, Ibn Ezra, and Maimonides in his *Epistle to Yemen* (something you should read), interpret some of the same passages as predicting the rise of Islam.

In sum, the success of Christianity and Islam does not show that G-d abandoned the Jews. It shows rather that a lot of people find the core idea of Judaism – monotheism – appealing. Well, that's all for now on your second question. Like I said, I'll write you something in a few days (*bli neder*) on your third question.

Sincerely,

Rabbi Low

From: dgoldstein@cuniv.edu   Sent: 5/15/00 9:30 PM
To: rlow@ahavattorah.org.il
Subject: Follow-up

Dear Rabbi Low,

Thanks for your message. I really appreciate your taking the time to write back in detail. I agree that the popularity of Christianity does not itself prove that Christianity is true. Nor does the length of the exile prove Judaism false. I'm now curious to see what you say about my third question, regarding the fact that so much of the Torah law seems outdated.

Based on what you said about the traditional Jewish date for the revelation at Sinai relative to the time of Adam, I've figured out that you must think Adam lived in the year 3760 BC which is 5760 years ago. Can you really believe that the first human lived such a relatively short time ago? And that also makes me wonder how you understand the whole creation story. Do you really believe the world was created in six days? This appears to be R. Abraham's view – he just dismisses the scientific theory of evolution as completely false. Is that also your view?

David

P.S. Sorry, but what does *bli neder* mean?

From: rlow@ahavattorah.org.il   Sent: 5/18/00 5:13 AM
To: dgoldstein@cuniv.edu
Subject: RE: Follow up

Dear David,

Good hearing from you. I still wish you would tell me a little more about yourself. Anyhow, your inquiry regarding creation and evolution and Jewish dating is a good one, but that's really another complicated topic. I'll have to postpone my answer on that to yet another email. I wanted first to respond to your third question, where you suggest that Torah law is obsolete.

First, you stated that the laws of ritual impurity and purity are no longer practiced today. But this is not entirely correct. One aspect of the law of purity (*taharah*) still practiced today is the immersion in the mikveh, or ritual bath, seven days after a woman has completed her menstrual period. It is forbidden (even) for a married couple to have relations from the time the menstrual period begins until after the immersion in the mikveh. This is very much a part of Orthodox Judaism to this very day. Another aspect of the laws of purity is that Kohanim (descendants of the priestly family of Aaron) avoid contact with dead bodies except in rare circumstances. In addition, almost all Orthodox Jews wash their hands ritually before eating bread, though this is mostly a rabbinic institution to remind us of the laws of purity and impurity. There is also a custom among many Orthodox men to immerse in a mikveh regularly. Some do so only before the festivals and High Holidays, others do it weekly before Shabbat and some do it every day. Finally, the laws of kosher food are based to a large extent on the scriptural teaching that certain animals are *tahor*, or pure, while others are *tameh,* or impure. You can see, then, that Jews practice certain aspects of the laws of purity to this very day.

Another mistake you make concerns the law of an "eye for an eye, a tooth for a tooth." Orthodox Judaism believes not only in the Written Torah (*Torah she-bichtav*) but also in the Oral Torah (*Torah she-be'al peh*). The Oral Torah is largely contained in the Talmud and in the writings of later generations of rabbis up through this very day. The Talmud teaches that the written law of an eye for an eye is not meant to be taken literally. It is meant to require just compensation for damages. So this law is still practiced today, when it is properly understood. A similar point may be of interest to you regarding the "gruesome" death penalties of Scripture. According to the Talmud, a person could be put to death by a court only if there were two witnesses who saw the act and who warned the person of the penalty just before he committed the act, and to whom the perpetrator replied, "Even so, I will still do it." The Talmud also states that a court that put to death one person in seventy years was a "murderous" court(!). This places those "gruesome" penalties in a different context indeed. Another relevant point concerns the law against usury. The Talmud provides for a way in which interest may be charged on a loan if it is done in a certain way and following certain regulations.

There is a deeper misunderstanding in your message, for you seem to assume that Orthodox Judaism involves following the written law almost literally, whenever possible. But this is a mistake. The Oral Tradition, the Talmud and rabbinic literature are the source of Jewish law, even more so than the written Law of Scripture. In fact, for an Orthodox Jew, the written Torah all by itself is a closed book. The Sadducees and, later, the Karaites were sects of Judaism that denied the Oral Law, but Orthodox Judaism regards these sects as heretical – that is, breaking radically with the tradition. Without the Oral Law, the text itself can be interpreted in any number of ways. (Even with the Oral Law, there is room for different interpretations as well, but the Oral Law provides a basic framework of interpretation.) This also goes a long way toward addressing your claim that the Torah is addressed to a premodern society. Maybe what you say would be true if all you had was the scriptural law. But Orthodox Jews understand that Scripture was given to be interpreted by the sages of each generation (as the text itself indicates in Deuteronomy 17). The Torah is more supple and pliable than you seem to think. Thus for example, although the written Torah provides for a man marrying more than one wife, that was banned – at least among European Jews – in the 900s. This ban occurred after the time of the Talmud. In short, the Law is adaptable to changing circumstances. But it takes careful study, erudition and piety to do this right.

With regard to the laws that pertain to the Temple, obviously, many of those are inapplicable today since the Temple has not yet been rebuilt. That doesn't make those laws obsolete. At present, they are on hold, so to speak. Even some of those very laws are still followed in one way or another. For example, the lighting of the Menorah in the temple is replaced (temporarily) by the lighting of the menorah on Hanukkah. The service and worship that took place in the Temple is replaced by the service and worship in the synagogue. The reverence for the Ark of the Covenant in the holy of holies is replaced by reverence for the ark containing the Torah scroll in the synagogue. Even the sacrifices and the burning of incense are replaced by the study of those laws and meditation on their inner meaning. Actually, speaking of sacrifices, I myself am not entirely sure that when the Temple is rebuilt, all the animal sacrifices will be reinstituted in precisely the same way (although this is what many Orthodox Jews believe). There is one Jewish tradition that says that no animal sacrifices will be reinstituted, and only the meal offering will be brought. (However, that seems to be a minority opinion.)

Also, you neglect to mention the obvious point that although many Torah laws are not practiced today, there are still many Torah laws that are. These include such basic ones as the commandments to love and respect G-d, to worship G-d, to study the Torah, to keep and observe the Sabbath and the festivals, the laws of kashruth, tefllin, tsitsis, laws of justice and ethics, the obligation of honesty, love thy neighbor as thyself, and giving charity, to name only a few. The list goes on and on. These laws are not arcane or obsolete.

You're right that keeping the Torah is, in some ways, a challenge. Perhaps it's with good reason that G-d didn't give the Torah to all humankind. It's not easy to be intimate with G-d, and G-d doesn't expect most humans to be able to reach this high level. But He does expect that His Chosen people can do this. Now if we assume that G-d is just and fair, would G-d command His chosen people to carry out a task which He knew ahead of time they could not fulfill, as the Christian suggests? This doesn't make sense. Sure, it's true that there have always been Jews who rebelled or assimilated. But throughout the ages, many Jews have loyally maintained their observance. When Jews were accepted into non-Jewish society, many were tempted to assimilate or convert. But this hardly shows that humans are *incapable* of living up to the demands of the Torah. It only shows that it's a *challenge*. But then again, anything really rewarding is bound to involve a challenge!

Sincerely,

Rabbi Low

PS. The phrase "*bli neder*" means "without making a vow." Jews try to avoid making a vow that they might not be able to keep, so as not to violate the commandment against making a false vow. We customarily use that phrase when making a statement of intention to indicate that we are not thereby making a vow. Sorry, but I've grown so accustomed to doing so that I did it without explanation.

34

May 20, 2000

Maybe it was the effect of that stuff I had with Simon, but last night I had a really strange dream. It took place in the Holocaust Museum. I was in the room which has the huge picture of all the shoes piled up from the victims of that town (I forget the name). I was just standing there, looking at the picture. But then I started to float slightly off the ground into the air, at first just a little, then higher and higher till I was floating at the top of the room. Then things started getting cloudy or smoky till I could no longer see anything below me. And I remember now a curious smell, kind of a sweet smell. This is strange because I once read that people don't usually have any sense of smell in dreams. Then I woke up.

I wonder what it all means. Maybe it doesn't mean anything. But I've still got to figure out what I think about Judaism. Maybe the cloud means I'm confused? (But then, what's that smell? Does this relate to the good essence? I wonder.) I should probably have taken a class with Rabbi A but I'm worried about getting brainwashed. I feel a little claustrophobic in his presence. Rabbi L seems so much better, but he also wants to know about my background. What difference does my background make? I want to make sure I'm making my own decisions and not what someone else guilts me into doing. But I have been taking some of Rabbi A's advice. I finally finished the first five books. Moses really gives it to the people at the end. Apparently God doesn't mess around. Also, I'm getting in to the siddur a little more lately. If I'm in the mood and I have time I read some of the prayers and just try to understand what they're saying. Sometimes I say Shema and sometimes I don't. I can't explain why all the time. (Do I really have a choice, anyway? I still wonder about free will.)

There really is so much detail in the siddur. It's amazing, but I've got so many questions. I should keep a list. In going through the morning prayers I discovered that the five "Halleluyah" chapters are actually the last five chapters of Psalms. Why are these five so special? And another thing I don't understand is the statement at the end of Alenu that one day, God will be one. That's a very strange thing. Isn't he one already?

I've been thinking about my courses for next year. One thing I'm going to take is a course in Moral Philosophy. I still haven't figured out what I think about hedonism. Even if there is such a thing as "THE GOOD" like Plato thinks, what's the motivation for pursuing it? Rabbi Low talked about two motivations for why we act, the moral motivation and the happiness/joy motivation. But how do these two relate? That's a tough question, and he never really got into that. Simon thinks the only motivation a person would ever have to act is for the sake of pleasure. I'm not sure I believe that. I think people sometimes act <u>not</u> just for the sake of pleasure. My ~~parents~~ mother seems like a good example of someone who doesn't act for the sake of pleasure. But what does she act for, then?

The problem is, I still don't understand why a person would act, if not for the sake of pleasure. If you believe that the purpose of life is to be morally good, the question is, why behave morally? Is it just for the pleasure you get from behaving morally? If the answer is yes, then, it's all about getting pleasure after all. And if the answer is no, then we come back to the question, why be moral? And even if you believe that the purpose of life is to have a relationship with God, the problem still remains, why pursue a relationship with God? Is it just for the pleasure derived from the relationship? If so, you're back to pleasure after all. I still don't see the answer. Except for maybe Ravi's approach, that you can transcend desire for pleasure in some kind of meditative state. It's hard to do but I think meditation is having an effect on me. There's something satisfying about meditation and it seems completely missing in Judaism. Do Jews ever meditate? Need to find out about that.

The other course I'm definitely going to take is philosophy of religion with Dr Maimon. It's obvious that Dr M is more intellectual than Rabbi A. Rabbi A admits that there is no convincing argument for belief in God, so you just have to make a leap of faith. It's only <u>after</u> you make the leap that you supposedly start feeling that God exists, you start seeing that things in your life fall into a pattern. I can see how that would be tempting to believe. (Like what happened with Mom: when I broke up with H, Mom got cured. But maybe it was just coincidence.) And I just ~~don't want~~ can't get myself to make that leap. But Dr. Maimon — she seems much more rationalistic. She said the whole point of Judaism is to <u>know</u> God, and in order to <u>know</u> God, you need to have a rational basis for your belief in God. So does she really think there is a rational basis for believing in God and the Torah? If so, I'd like to know what it is! That sounds even better than Low's pragmatic argument.

And the other thing I'd like to do next semester is hook up with Esther. Obviously she was trying to put me off with that story about being "in transition." She must have a cell phone, why didn't she want to give me her number? Maybe she runs or at least jogs? I hope she does. I can just see it now:

"Hey, Esther, how would you like to go jogging together?"

"Sure, David, I'd love to. "

"OK. Why don't we go for a five-mile run in the park?"

"Sounds great. I just need to change and I'll be right down . . . ."

OK, so I am fantasizing. Probably she doesn't want to have anything to do with me. Maybe she finds me a little threatening. But she seemed engaged in our conversation.

Conclusion: Try Esther again next semester. What do I have to lose? Now there's a good pragmatic argument. R. Low would be proud of me!

ו

SOPHOMORE YEAR

"Good afternoon, everyone. Welcome to Philosophy of Religion. For those of you who don't already know me, I'm Dr. Maimon. I'm pleased to meet all of you, and perhaps by the end of the semester I'll know all of your names. Today I just wanted to hand out the syllabus and describe briefly the topic and methods of this course. Here, will you please pass the syllabus around? Thanks. Since it's traditional to let you all out early on the first day of class, I'll do that, because I'm – well, very traditional! Does everyone have a syllabus? Good! So let's begin. Let me warn you that I have a tendency sometimes to talk too fast, so if there are any questions, please flag me down.

"Now, this is a course in philosophy of religion, so first let's talk generally about what is *philosophy* and what is *religion*. As I understand it, philosophy is the rational inquiry into the most fundamental truths. The philosopher attempts to ask the most basic, fundamental questions that can possibly be asked, and she attempts to answer those questions *with rational support*. Along the way, it is also the task of the philosopher to clarify basic or fundamental concepts – this is sometimes called *conceptual analysis*. Now, what counts as a fundamental concept or fundamental question is sometimes a matter of debate, but many would agree that this would include issues such as . . . well . . . let me write some of these on the board:

What is truth?
What is knowledge?
What is the nature of the mind and its relation to the body?
What is the meaning and purpose of human existence?
What is the best way to live? What is the best way to organize a society?
Is there any part of the human being that lives on after the body dies?

"And so on – you get the idea. Now, religion, at least for the purpose of this class, is a system of beliefs and practices that constitutes a way of life which centers on or around the belief in a deity or divine being of some sort. So, philosophy of religion is, firstly, the attempt to ask the most fundamental questions that can be asked *about religion, or about things having to do with religion*. But secondly, philosophy also attempts to *give answers to those questions with rational support*. Now, obviously, there are many religions and many different kinds of religion. In this course, we will focus on those beliefs that are held in common by the three major Western religions of the world: namely, Judaism, Christianity and Islam. So let us ask ourselves: what do these three religions have in common?

"Of course, the basic answer is *monotheism*. As I'm sure you know, monotheism is the belief in a single deity – commonly known as 'God.' Traditionally, God is conceived as all-knowing (that's *omniscient*) all powerful (that's *omnipotent*) and all good (that's *omnibenevolent*). God is also conceived as *revelatory* – that is, God reveals himself in some way and communicates with humans. God also *cares* about what we do, such as whether we act justly or unjustly, and whether we worship Him or not. This also means that God listens to human prayers, and under certain circumstances, God fulfills or answers those prayers. Finally, God performs miracles, at least under certain circumstances – though, as we shall find, it is not so easy to define precisely what a miracle is.

"Now, the conception of God as I have just described it is common to the three major monotheistic faiths. It is possible to conceive of God in other ways, and that is something we shall only briefly explore. I admit that I have little or no expertise in Eastern religions. So if you want to learn about Eastern philosophy of religion, you're in the wrong course. In any case, the three major Western religions differ over the *content* of what specifically God has communicated to humans, and over the content of specifically what miracles God has performed. These major religions also differ on what is the proper or best way to worship God. Thus, traditional Jews believe that the proper way to worship (at least for Jews) is by fulfilling the Torah. Christians believe that the proper way to worship God is through the teachings of what is known as the New Testament. Muslims believe that the Koran and the Sharia, or religious law, describe the true path. There are many other differences between the three religions, but we need not bother with them now. In any case, let's go back to our starting point: namely, *what is philosophy of religion?* For our purposes, philosophy of religion is the attempt to rationally scrutinize the major claims held in common by the three world religions. Thus we shall ask and explore answers to questions like – well, let me write some of these on the board:

Does God exist? How is God to be conceived?
Are there good reasons for believing in God?
Are there good reasons not to believe in God?
What is the nature of "faith"? What is the relation between
    "faith" and reason?
Does the existence of evil show or indicate that God does not
    exist? (The "problem of evil.")
Does God reveal himself and communicate with humans? In
    what way?
Are there good reasons for believing in revelation?
What are miracles? Are there good grounds for believing in
    miracles?

*Can there be different, multiple revelations that are all
    equally valid? (Does "religious pluralism" make sense?)*

"Well, there you have it. These are the major questions of this course, and, as
philosophers, we shall attempt to answer them *with rational support*. A philosopher
doesn't just give answers. A philosopher entertains discussion and rational debate
about possible answers. Now, in addition to the questions I just mentioned, there
are also secondary issues which will arise in the course of our discussion. I won't
write these on the board, but these include, for example, what is the relationship
between science and religion? Does science conflict with religion? What is the
relationship between ethics and religion? For example, does it make sense to
think that God is subject to ethical norms? Or does God somehow stand outside
of ethics? These are some of the questions we will be touching on in this class.
Any questions? No? Good!

"As to the method of this class, we'll be reading selections from classical,
medieval, and modern writers. For each class there will be a reading assignment,
on which I shall lecture, and then we'll discuss it. In each case what we're going
to try to do is understand a) what *view* the author is taking, and b) the author's
argument for that view. Now, how much of this class is discussion and how much
is lecture is going to depend on you folks. If you guys are quiet, I'll keep talking
. . . non-stop! Anyway, the other required work – I mean, papers and exams – are
described on the syllabus. As you can see, the papers count more toward the final
grade than do the exams. That's because I think writing is especially important.
When you write, or I should say, when you write *well,* you not only express your
ideas, you also sharpen those ideas through the process of writing. Writing brings
your thought to a deeper level of reflection. Speaking of the paper, I'd like each
of you to come speak with me in my office about a topic of your choice, to make
sure I approve your topic.

"Our first set of readings deals with some traditional, well known arguments for
God's existence. So your first reading for next time is from the medieval Christian
philosopher, St. Anselm, in which you will cover what is known as the Ontological
Argument for God's existence. Please read the first selection in the book, which is
a few pages from Anselm, and see what you make of it. I won't say anything about
it now. Just read it and be prepared to discuss it next time.

"Now, as you can see from the syllabus, I've got office hours and a phone number
on campus. In an emergency, you can get my home phone from the Philosophy
Department office. You can also email me if you have any questions or issues that
come up. Let's see – what else? Oh, yes – there's one day coming up in the fall
when I won't be able to be in class. That's October ninth. I'll have a video set up in
class for you that day. You'll be watching a film called *The Quarrel,* which bears on
some topics covered in this course, especially the problem of evil. I won't tell you
any more about the film right now. If for any reason you can't make it to class that

day, please watch the film on your own. You can rent it or find it in the library.

"Now . . . what else did I want to say? Oh, yes, one final thing. Ladies and gentlemen, I want to be very clear that the purpose of this class is *not* for me to tell you my philosophical views about religion, but rather for us to read and critically think about what some of the great philosophers have said about the issues. My aim is to get *you* to think as critically as you can about the claims and arguments in the texts that we'll read. Any questions? No? Well, I think that's enough for today. See you all next time!"

2
—

September 5, 2000

Dear Mom,

How are you? I'm doing pretty well. I thought I'd write you a letter for a change, just like you used to write me last semester. You're right. Writing is different from typing on the computer or speaking on the phone. Or even speaking in person, sometimes. There's something about the physical act of writing that makes you think longer before you say something. Writing by hand also makes you more likely to reveal something more personal. I don't think I told you this over the summer, but I started keeping a journal last year. (There's a revelation already!) And I can't imagine keeping a journal on the computer, though I guess there must be people who do that. Anyhow, it really is quite therapeutic. I was wondering, Mom, did you ever keep a journal?

I'm excited to be back here in school. It's great to see my friends, and how they've changed — or, actually, <u>not</u> changed from last year. In a way, they're just more of themselves, if you know what I mean. Ravi is still into his Buddhism/Hinduism thing. Simon is still into ~~the same stuff~~ theatre, and he's still sharp as ever. George (the really devout Christian guy) has still got the same girlfriend, except now they're beginning to talk about getting officially engaged. I've met some other nice people too, but so far no one else to write home about.

My courses look really interesting. I'm taking philosophy of religion, which is probably my favorite course. I've become kind of fascinated with the whole topic lately. The prof is a woman who I think is really brilliant. The course is about philosophy of religion in general, but sometimes she discusses particular aspects of Judaism, Christianity, or Islam. I've got to tell you, that trip to the Holocaust Museum last year (together with some other stuff) really got my interest in Jewish things going. Not so much the historical side of things, like how the Holocaust happened (which I am interested in too), but really the whole issue of Judaism itself. Like – is there a God? If God exists, why is there evil? Is divine revelation real? Is there something special about being Jewish? Why would someone be so committed to Judaism that they'd even be willing to give up their life for it? And other questions like that.

My other favorite class is Moral Philosophy, which is taught by a grad student who's really excellent. He's very different from all the other professors. He's quite comfortable with our calling him by his first name, Phil, and he has his office hours in a coffee shop just off campus. Sometimes he'll even treat students to lunch. Anyway, right now we're getting into some of the ancient Greek philosophers' views about virtue and wisdom. We're learning about the debate between moral subjectivists (the Sophists) and moral objectivists (Plato and Aristotle). The question is whether there is some kind of truth about what is moral, or whether morality is something that humans invent or make up as they go along. This is a question that interests me very much. We covered Plato last year in the Intro course, but this is the first time I'm learning Aristotle. I'm finding Aristotle harder to read than Plato. In fact, I have an appointment to talk with Phil about this tomorrow!

I'm really thinking seriously of majoring in philosophy. Like you said once, college is a great time to explore the really big questions, which is what philosophy is all about. Besides, I know Dad wants me to go to law school, and I've recently learned that philosophy is really a good major for that too, because it develops your "critical thinking" skills.

Meanwhile, how are you doing? I'm really glad you're feeling better and getting back to normal. Now that you've got your strength back, what are you up to?

Love,

David

<u>3</u>

"Hi, David. How are you?"

"I'm OK, Phil. How are you?"

"I'm fine. Have a seat. I'm ordering lunch. Want something to eat?"

"Sure, I'll have a cheeseburger. Thanks."

"So what's on your mind?"

"I wanted to talk about Aristotle's view on moral objectivism."

"Sure. What about it?"

"Phil . . . I'm sure you know there are a lot of people who say that if there's no God, then nothing is really good or bad. I mean, if there's no God, people just do whatever they feel like doing, and that's that."

"Yes, a lot of people say that. There's a famous line in one of Dostoevsky's novels that often gets quoted. It goes something like this: 'If God is dead, everything is permitted.' But it's no surprise that Dostoevsky was an Orthodox Christian. Actually, it's the kind of view I was brought up with myself."

"Oh? What kind of upbringing did you have?"

"Roman Catholic."

"Wow! Are you still practicing?"

"No. I haven't been for years."

"If you don't mind, I'd like to hear more about why . . . ."

"Some other time, perhaps. But truthfully, Aristotle and philosophy had a lot to do with my departure from religion. Aristotle doesn't believe in a personal God, and he doesn't believe that the soul lives after the body dies. According to him, there's no divine being looking over us to judge what we're doing. There's no hell or heaven, no divine reward or punishment. In fact, there's no divine providence over particular human individuals at all. What happens to us has little or nothing to do with how we behave. Scary thought, I suppose. But according to Aristotle, that's just the way the cookie crumbles!"

"And is that what you believe, too?"

"David, let's just try to get clear on what *Aristotle* believes. Despite the fact that he rejects all those beliefs, Aristotle does believe in moral *objectivism,* in the sense that there's an objective fact of the matter as to which character traits are good and which ones are bad. Just as it's objectively true that the earth is round and that two plus two equal four, it's also the case that, for example, courage is a virtue and cowardice is a vice."

"So he believes in moral objectivism *despite* the fact that he holds there's no such thing as God, and despite the fact that he rejects Plato's belief in the existence of the Form of the Good."

"Exactly! Really, the key to understanding Aristotle's position goes back to what we called in class Aristotle's doctrine of Teleology."

"Yes, I have that in my notes. But would you mind explaining that one more time?"

"No problem. That's why I'm here. Teleology is the view that all natural things have a certain *telos,* that is, a goal or purpose which is suited to their nature. Exactly what the *telos* of a thing is depends on its nature or its 'form.' For example, the nature of an acorn is to grow into an oak tree. The nature of an apple seed is to grow into an apple tree. If an apple seed doesn't grow into an apple tree, then, it hasn't reached its *telos.*"

"And where does a thing's *telos* come from?"

"It's there just because that's the way nature is. Nature is made up things that have forms or essences. Every natural thing just has a *telos*. Is there some problem with that?"

"No, I don't think so."

"Good. Well, now apply this doctrine of teleology to the human being. The human being is a part of the natural order. So, the human also must have a *telos,* an end suited to its nature or form. Now, the form or essence of a thing is that which sets it apart from other things, that which uniquely identifies some thing as a thing of a certain sort. For example, the essence of a square is that it has four sides. And, Aristotle thinks it's pretty obvious that what sets humans apart from other things is the fact that we are *rational animals*. Can you accept that?"

"I'm not sure. Dolphins and apes are pretty intelligent."

"But they have nowhere near the qualitative level of intelligence that humans have. They don't engage in abstract philosophical thought, for example."

"True."

"So it's established that the essence or form of the human being has to do with being a rational animal, where 'rational' is understood to mean, capable of abstract thought. And, it now follows that the *telos* or purpose of the human being has something to do with *living a rational life.*"

"OK. I get it so far."

"Good. Now, I need to remind you of something else we said in class, which is that Aristotle equates the human *telos* with human happiness. Of course, a lot of people think happiness consists in pleasure or wealth or honor or some emotional state of contentment, but Aristotle disagrees. Aristotle would admit that, for the most part, a rational life is a pleasant one, and that it brings about emotional contentment as an offshoot. But that's not what *makes* it a happy life. As Aristotle puts is, everyone agrees that happiness is our highest end, the thing we want most of all, and for the sake of which we do everything we do. In other words, happiness is our *telos,* the goal or purpose that is suited to our nature. Some modern Aristotelians like to call this 'human flourishing' or 'well-being.' Just as the apple seed reaches its state of 'apple happiness' when it becomes a beautiful, flourishing apple tree, so too the human being reaches 'human happiness' when he flourishes – that is, when he actualizes his potential for living a full human life.

Now an apple tree does not experience pleasure at all, but it *can* reach its *telos*! This illustrates the point that reaching a *telos* is entirely different from experiencing pleasure. Pleasure is a *sensation*; happiness is a *condition of one's being*."

"I think I follow what you're saying. But I'm not sure I agree. How can happiness be living a rational life? It sounds a little dry, doesn't it?"

"It's not dry at all, if you understand how broadly Aristotle understands what it means to live a rational life. It's quite a complex and rich thing and involves many components. We haven't gone into this in the class yet, but since you're interested, I can tell you a little bit more about what's coming."

"Yes, please do."

"OK. Basically, living a rational life involves developing certain character traits which allow a person to 'exercise reason' and to 'do it well,' as Aristotle says. Those character traits are the 'virtues' – the good character traits. The opposites of those good character traits are the bad ones, or the 'vices.' Now, the next obvious question is: what specific character traits are involved in living a rational life? Aristotle claims that there are basically two ways in which a human being can use reason. That's also the basis for his claim that there are two types of virtue, namely, *intellectual virtue* and *practical virtue*. Intellectual virtue involves using reason to pursue knowledge and understanding purely for its own sake. The main intellectual virtue is *wisdom*. A person is wise to the extent that he has developed his capacity for gaining knowledge and understanding of truth, just for its own sake. On the other hand, practical virtue involves using reason to guide one's actions and emotions. And that, in turn, involves following the doctrine of the golden mean, or the mean between extremes. So the practical virtues include things like *courage* (not too much fear, not too little fear), temperance (not too much pleasure, not too little pleasure) generosity (not giving away too much, not giving away too little), and so on. And, there's another important point to add – that a fully human life can only be lived in a certain kind of *polis,* or city. That's because, by nature, man is a social animal. So he can't fulfill his *telos* unless he participates in a social, communal life. The human has to develop those virtues or character traits which promote communal life, like the virtue of *justice*. Conversely, any behavior which is, so to speak 'anti-social,' is not consistent with the human *telos* and is therefore not virtuous but rather vicious, or 'bad.' Do you follow all this?"

"Yes, I think so."

"Great. Well, there you have it. According to Aristotle, you don't need God in order to believe in moral objectivism. You need teleology, but you don't need God. Now, you could dispute a lot of the details of his theory, but still accept his fundamental claim that teleology doesn't require God. As long as you hold that the human being has some natural end or *telos,* you can say that those character traits and actions which promote the *telos* are objectively noble, and praiseworthy, and those actions which fail to promote it are not noble, or praiseworthy."

"I think I understand it better now. So do you think the same applies when it comes to the search for meaning in life?"

"Sorry, I don't understand your question."

"As I said before, some people say that life is meaningless without God. So I'm asking: would Aristotle say that life is meaningful without God?"

"Oh! *Now* I understand your question! You've switched the terms from living a 'good life' to the more fashionable 'living a meaningful life.' That really doesn't change things. Aristotle would say that you don't need God to live a meaningful or purposeful life. Actually, your question reminds me of a conversation I once had in a bar."

"Can you tell me about it?"

"Sure. I was in college at the time, probably your age. I was having a drink with some friends when this guy sat down next to us. He was just a regular guy, you know. I think he worked in a magazine store somewhere. He seemed pretty bright, but he had never gone to college. Anyway, when he found out we were philosophy majors, he asked us to give an example of a philosophical question. So one of my friends said, 'Here's one that's really difficult. What's the meaning of life?' And without batting an eyelash the guy answered, 'That's easy. *The meaning of life is living.*' At the time we all just laughed and moved on to some other topic. But in effect, that's what Aristotle is saying, but with a certain twist. The meaning or purpose of human life is to fulfill one's human *telos,* to live fully as a human. Of course, according to Aristotle, the most important thing about a *human* life is that it's supposed to be a *rational* life. I don't know if the guy in the bar would have necessarily agreed with *that.* For Aristotle, just living like an animal would not be good at all! But living a rational life – that's an objectively good way to live, according to Aristotle. It's also the happiest kind of life as well. So, if you're looking for meaning, happiness, and the good life – whatever you want to call it – the best way to do that is to develop intellectual and practical virtue."

"OK, but let me ask you this. What exactly is the reason for being virtuous, or doing virtuous acts? I realize it's *not* about getting pleasure. But isn't Aristotle saying that the reason a person should be virtuous is because it makes him *happy*?"

"Well, yes, except that you got to remember that no matter what a person does, happiness is never guaranteed."

"Wait a second. Why not? I thought you said the human *telos* is living a rational life, and that's what Aristotle identifies as human happiness. So if you have virtue, you're living a rational life, and therefore it should follow that you're happy."

"No, that's incorrect. There's no guarantee that a virtuous person will *succeed* in living a fully human life. It's possible that you could have theoretical and practical virtue – you could be as virtuous as possible – but still not reach the state of human flourishing, due to factors beyond your own control."

"What do you mean? What factors?"

"It has to do with what Aristotle calls *external goods*. Let me explain. Let's go back to my example of the apple seed. The *telos* of the apple seed is to turn into an apple tree. But nothing guarantees that any particular apple seed will actualize its *telos*. A given apple seed could be doing everything right, but still certain external circumstances are required for it to become an apple tree. For example, it needs water and sunshine – these are factors beyond its control. Not to mention the fact that some little squirrel could come along and gobble up the seed, or the budding little apple tree plant, just as it's getting started."

"So your point is . . . ?"

"My point is that the very same thing applies to human beings. Remember, we said that the human being is a social animal. So you need friends, family and a certain amount of good luck or fortune to successfully reach the human *telos*. For example, suppose you are a virtuous person, but suddenly your family is destroyed by some natural disaster. If that happens, you're *not* flourishing and you're not happy."

"Well, that's a disappointing result, isn't it?"

"It's just realistic. David, if you look around the world, you see a lot of people who are virtuous or morally upright, but are not flourishing or doing very well."

"Yes, that's certainly true."

"Nevertheless, Aristotle would say that virtue is the most important component of a happy life."

"Why's that?"

"For several reasons. First of all, virtue is a condition of your soul or psyche. It's the most important thing about you, because it's your true self. And this is true despite the fact that according to Aristotle, the soul does not continue to exist after the body dies. Moreover, there's just no way to control external circumstances. All you can really focus on in life is developing yourself, that is, your intellectual and moral character. Besides which, Aristotle points out that a virtuous person will be able to handle adversity far better than a non-virtuous person will. A virtuous person is wise and balanced. He'll experience emotions of pain and anguish if he is struck by a tragedy, but he won't overreact, he'll bounce back. A person who lacks virtue or who identifies his happiness with something like pleasure or wealth or even something like peace of mind – such a person could be easily destroyed beyond repair if he experiences a tragedy. So, in the end, virtue is the most important component of a happy and fulfilled life. Well, what do you think? Does the view make sense?"

"Yes, it makes a lot of sense – assuming that you accept teleology."

"Precisely."

"But still, could I just go back to a question I asked earlier?"

"We're running out of time, but go ahead."

"We said earlier that according to Aristotle, the main reason a person should be virtuous is because it contributes to one's own happiness. Is that right?"

"Yes. Aristotle holds that whatever a person does, he or she does for the sake of personal happiness. No one is capable of acting out of anything other than self-interest. Of course, many people misidentify what their self-interest or happiness is. So they end up doing stupid, foolish, and even vicious actions under the false belief that those actions will bring them happiness. But someone who has a proper understanding of human happiness – in particular, the philosopher! – will always want to cultivate a virtuous character, because he knows that it leads to happiness in the long run, and he also understands that practical and theoretical virtue is the most important component of living a happy life."

"Are you suggesting that the philosopher is the one who is most likely to lead a virtuous and happy life?"

"Absolutely. The philosopher leads the best life altogether. Certainly, you can't have wisdom or theoretical virtue unless you are a philosopher. But this is getting way beyond what we've covered in class so far. And besides which, I think I need to cut this short, because there's another student sitting at the next table, and he's got an appointment with me ten minutes ago!"

"OK, sorry! I'll be on my way, then. Thanks a lot, Phil. I understand Aristotle a lot better now."

"No problem. Like I said, that's why I'm here."

4

September 15, 2000

It would be nice to think that there really is a God, but I'm still struggling with the question of whether it is rational to believe in God. In philosophy of religion we've started studying some of the classic arguments for God's existence. So far we've covered the argument by St. Anselm, known as the ontological argument. And soon we're going to start the famous "five ways" of St. Thomas Aquinas. Aquinas and Anselm were both serious Christians. I wonder if George really knows anything about them. They don't take the "faith only" approach, at least not when it comes to belief in God (but it's different when it comes to the belief in JC).

St. Anselm's ontological argument is amazingly simple. It's called "ontological" because it has something to do with the idea of being (ontos in Greek means being). Basically, the argument goes like this. I can think of a being that's perfect. By definition, that's the idea of God. Now I ask myself: does that perfect being exist? If I say no, that means I am now thinking of a perfect being as non-existent. And if so, I am contradicting myself, for I am now thinking of a perfect being that <u>lacks</u> something – namely, the property of existence! So if I am thinking of a perfect being, I <u>must</u> be thinking of a perfect being that exists!

What an amazing attempt to prove God's existence! Many later philosophers accept some form of this argument as well, including Descartes. Dr. Maimon won't say what she really thinks about this argument, but she presented a bunch of criticisms against it. It seems like the argument pulls a rabbit out of a hat. Just because you can think of a being does not imply that the being exists. Sure it's true that if you're thinking of a perfect being, you must be thinking of it <u>as existing</u>. But that quality of "existence" is still only attached to that idea in your mind. So it doesn't follow that such a being <u>actually</u> exists. The argument is ingenious, but it doesn't work.

I wonder if Thomas Aquinas's arguments are going to be any better. I am not optimistic. I think Rabbi Low, in his speech, mentioned that he doesn't think any of the medieval arguments work.

I'm beginning to see where Rabbi A was coming from. Basically, he said that if you study philosophy of religion, you'll find yourself becoming even more of a skeptic. But I still wonder what Dr M really thinks. She cancelled class for Oct. 9th, which is Yom Kippur. Why didn't she just say so when she made the announcement in the first place? I guess she didn't want to make a big deal out of canceling class on a Jewish holiday. Maybe she keeps the holidays just as an ethnic ritual? Or maybe she does believe in God. If she does, she must have her reasons. I wonder what they are.

<u>5</u>

"Esther? Hi!"

"Oh, hello. You're David, right?"

"That's me. How are you?"

"Good, thank God."

"Uh-oh . . . did some thing bad happen?"

"No, not at all! Sorry, I didn't mean to scare you. It's just a custom to say 'Thank God' for doing well."

"Ah, OK. So . . . I see you've got your books. Are you taking any interesting courses?"

"No, nothing really exciting. Just stuff for pre-med. Why? What are you taking?"

"Great stuff! Philosophy of religion, moral philosophy and comparative religion, and some other required things. By the way, I have regards for you."

"Really? From whom?"

"From Rabbi Low. I emailed him last semester after you gave me his email address. We had a long correspondence."

"Oh? About what?

"All about you, of course. Esther Applefeld, one of his star disciples!"

"*What?* You're joking, right?"

"Well, it wasn't *just* about you. But seriously, he *does* send you his regards, and he did say you were really outstanding."

"I told you he was nice! What else did he say?"

"Actually our correspondence was about lots of things."

"Like what?"

"Do you have time for a cup of coffee or something? I'd love to sit down and talk."

"Sorry, but I really need to get back to the dorm. Can't you just tell me briefly what you talked about?"

"You mean, standing on one foot?"

"Ah! I see you really have been studying! Seriously, what did you talk about with Rabbi Low?"

"Well, let's see. First we had a conversation about the difference between the Jewish and Eastern conceptions of God or the ultimate. We talked about whether God – the Ultimate, whatever you want to call it – is personal or impersonal. Then we talked about the length of the exile, the popularity of Christianity, and how that might be explained from a Jewish point of view, and . . . uh, let's see . . . some issues that arise concerning the Torah Law, its flexibility, things like that. We talked about the heresy of the Sadducees and the Karaites, and a few other things . . . ."

"Wow, that's a lot. I'm impressed."

"Thanks! I've got to say, Rabbi Low was really great answering my questions. Of course, I don't necessarily agree with everything he says. But he was very open to questions, which is great for me. Seriously, I owe you a lot for turning me on to him."

"No problem. If you write him again, send him my regards."

"I sure will. Actually, I've got some new questions to ask him, so I'll write soon. But – hey, are you sure you don't want to have a cup of coffee?"

"No, sorry, I can't. I really do have to get back to the dorm."

"OK, maybe some other time. You've sure got a lot of books. Do you need any help carrying them back to the dorm?"

"No, that's quite all right. I can manage."

"I'm sure you can manage, but why don't you let me help?"

"Well, if you really want to, thanks!"

6
—

From: dgoldstein@cuniv.edu   Sent: 10/4/00 9:30 PM
To: rlow@ahavattorah.org.il
Subject: Hello plus another question

Dear Rabbi Low,

Hello again. I've been meaning to write for some time. I was just looking over your email from last spring. I have some more questions for you. I still want to hear what you have to say about how to reconcile creation and evolution. But actually, that's not the thing I wanted to ask you right now.

Before I get to my questions, since you've asked me several times about my background, I'll tell you that my parents are Jewish, but not religious at all. When I was younger, I had some Hebrew classes, so I do know some Hebrew, but not as much as I'd like to. We had a big party for my bar mitzvah, but it was basically that – a party. The only thing I can say is that my parents were always big supporters of Israel, and that they drilled into my older brother and me that we were supposed to eventually marry Jewish girls. I always thought I was going to be a lawyer when I grew up. My dad is a lawyer. He works very hard and he's very successful at what he does. I think he wants me to work in his firm eventually. My mother studied psychology and got a master's degree. She never really had a career. I'm not sure how I got interested in philosophy, or as my Mom says, "the big questions." Last year, also for a combination of reasons, I got more interested in learning about Judaism. That's why I showed up at your lecture.

Now for the question. During your lecture you said that unless morality is based on God, there's really no solid reason to be moral unless a person happens to get pleasure from behaving morally or unless he doesn't want to get thrown in jail or punished in some other way. At the time, the idea kind of made sense to me. In one of my conversations with him, Rabbi Abraham used the very same argument: If God doesn't exist, morality is a man-made thing, and when you know you can get away with doing something that you want to do that may be wrong, why should you be moral? Rabbi Abraham also says that if we don't have a relationship with God, life is meaningless or worthless. He claims this is the teaching of the biblical book, Koheles. I tried to read this book myself and found it very puzzling. I gave up halfway through. The book sounds very profound when you start off, but then it gets pretty difficult (and, in some places, self-contradictory). But it does seem to say pretty much what Rabbi Abraham said: life without worship of God is meaningless.

Sometimes I tend to agree with that, and sometimes I don't. I'm really not sure what I think, but I do know that Aristotle didn't agree. In my Moral Philosophy class, we've been studying his idea of teleology. According to Aristotle, the human being has a goal, or telos. This goal is not based on God, but it's not man-made either. It's part of nature. Basically the telos is to flourish as a human being, which involves living a rational life. If you don't live a rational life, you're not living a fully human life. Aristotle also says that in order to live a rational life, you need to have virtue. He also says that a person who manages to live a rational life will basically be happy or fulfilled, assuming a certain amount of good fortune or luck. All this seems pretty reasonable. If Aristotle's right, you can have a moral and meaningful life even if God doesn't exist. I guess you must disagree with Aristotle. But why? Do you disagree with teleology? Is there something else I'm missing or what?

By the way, I have regards for you from Esther Applefeld. And since I've told you a little about myself, may I ask you a personal question too? I understand that you used to teach philosophy yourself. If you don't mind my asking, what happened? Why did you leave philosophy?

Sincerely,

David Goldstein

From: rlow@ahavattorah.org.il   Sent: 10/5/00 6:23 AM
To: dgoldstein@cuniv.edu
Subject: RE: Hello plus another question

Dear David,

I was very glad to read your email today. I was wondering how you've been. Thanks for filling me in on some of your background. I take it that your interest in Judaism is not only intellectual but spiritual as well. That's great.

Getting to your main question, let me clarify that in my lecture I did **not** assert that the only way there can be an objective morality is if G-d exists. I admit that life could have some kind of objective meaningfulness even if there were no G-d. If somehow tomorrow we discovered for sure that the G-d of Judaism were a hoax, I would **not** then say that objective morality goes down the drain and that life is meaningless (or that life is meaningful only from some arbitrary or subjective point of view). Rather, the claim in my lecture was that a person who believes that morality is rooted in G-d has a **stronger** motivation for behaving morally than a person who does not. Putting it in terms of meaningfulness, my claim is that the potential for meaning in life is **greater** if there is a G-d than if there isn't.

I did not explicitly address the Aristotelian approach to morality in my lecture. The main reason is that most people today who are not religious or theistic don't agree with Aristotle anyway. Most people who are not religious would say that morality is a human convention of some sort. In fact, many philosophers (some of them theists, some of them atheists) have argued that teleology is impossible unless there is at least some kind of G-d. Their argument is that if natural things indeed have a telos or goal, this implies there must be an intelligent designer of nature, i.e., something like G-d. The atheists conclude that since there's no G-d, there's no teleology. The theists conclude that since G-d exists, teleology is saved.

Personally I am not sure whether you can have teleology without G-d. For argument's sake, let's say you can. Still, we can conceive of two different types of teleology. One kind of teleology – let's call it Aristotelian or Naturalistic Teleology – says that nature itself has a certain structure, such that, all things including humans have a certain telos. The other kind of teleology – let's call it Theistic Teleology – would go further and claim that not only do natural things have a telos, but also that this teleology is rooted in the free choice of a supreme personal being, i.e., G-d, the eternal source and creator of nature. Now, I believe that both types of teleology would provide the basis for an objective morality. But I claim that Theistic Teleology provides for a stronger, deeper kind of morality. After all, which is superior or more fundamental? Nature? Or G-d, the eternal source of nature? Wouldn't you have far more reason to care about your telos if you knew it resulted from G-d Almighty, rather than just from Nature?

This leads to what I wanted to say about Koheles. Yes, it is a difficult work. I'll just say a little bit about how I understand it. Traditionally the author is regarded as King Solomon. Why didn't he use his real name? Why did he use a pseudonym? I believe he did this because he wanted to adopt a persona to write this book, as if to make clear that he was writing it from a perspective **other than his own,** in much the same way that a modern author might use characters in a book to express views that he may not fully agree with. In real life, the author of Koheles surely believed in prophecy, in the covenant between G-d and Israel, the Torah, life after death, the World to Come, etc. But the author adopted a persona because he wanted to write a book of human wisdom **without** relying on the prophetic tradition of Judaism. It is as if he was saying, "Here's what human wisdom comes to if you do not assume the traditional beliefs of Judaism, such as the covenant between G-d and the people of Israel, prophecy and the Torah." That's why there is no mention of these things in Koheles. And although G-d (*Elokim*) is mentioned in the book, the proper or personal name of Hashem is never mentioned (this is one of the few books in the Hebrew Scriptures where that is true). As far as the character "Koheles" is concerned, G-d is remote and hidden. From this perspective, there is no clear way of knowing whether the soul lives after death or whether there is a "next world." Sometimes it may seem that there is divine protection and providence, and sometimes it seems that there isn't. That's why the book is so pessimistic and that's why it also seems self-contradictory, because sometimes reason inclines one way and sometimes it inclines the other way.

Nevertheless, it's clear that even from this minimal perspective, Koheles believes there *is* a G-d (*Elokim*). In the end, the bottom line is that we should fear G-d, live an honest life, and be content with simple pleasures. Here's something important: *At no point does the author consider what life would be like without G-d's existence.* Such a hypothesis was unthinkable to Koheles. Hence it is mistaken to draw conclusions about what Koheles thinks the meaning of life would be if there were no G-d. What Koheles does say is that *even with* G-d's existence, human life is frustrating, empty, and exasperating – or, to use fashionable language, tragically tinged with "existential despair" (again that's on the assumption that there's no revelation, no Torah, no divine intervention in human affairs). But this doesn't mean that life would be meaningless or worthless! It means that life falls tragically short of fulfillment. The unstated implication is that life would be immeasurably more fulfilling if one could have a relationship with G-d. In real life, the author of *Koheles* knew that this was indeed possible through the observance of G-d's commandments.

Like I said, it is a difficult work. I hope this is clear.

Your last question was about why I "left philosophy." I always enjoyed philosophy and I still do. But after some years of teaching philosophy in an academic setting, I felt that I wanted to teach Torah in a yeshiva setting. For me, teaching Torah includes teaching philosophy, though in a broader sense. Basically, the modern academic setting shuns revelation and religious experience as a valid access to truth. The yeshiva setting allows and encourages access to a realm that goes beyond reason. Philosophy is a rational endeavor, and that's fine as far as it goes, but at a certain point one needs to move beyond reason. Human reason is a crucial tool in the quest for meaning, value, and purpose, but reason itself can recognize that it is not the only tool and it may not even be the primary one. For example, it may be rational to love someone because of that person's good qualities or traits. But reason itself realizes that love has a dimension that goes far beyond reason. This is a little paradoxical, but it's true.

Here's something else to consider. What are the two main texts of Judaism? The Tanakh (Hebrew Bible) and the Talmud. Neither is a philosophical work. Neither uses philosophical language to describe what Judaism is about. The Tanakh is a literary work, filled with narrative, poetry and, of course, law. The Talmud is similar, though with less poetry. Even those parts of Scripture with deal with philosophical issues such as the problem of evil (like the book of *Iyyov*) are not philosophical tracts but poetic works. The same is true for Scripture's wisdom literature, such as *Mishlei* and *Koheles*. Consider some of the features of poetic language. The music and sounds of the language are part of poetic expression, while in philosophy this is supposed to be irrelevant. Thus, for example, the fact that Scripture is in Hebrew, or *lashon ha-kodesh,* is crucial to its sanctity. But in philosophy, even in Jewish philosophy, the language is supposedly irrelevant. (Maimonides wrote mainly in Arabic, Hermann Cohen wrote in German, and so on.) This is because in philosophy, the "ideational" or propositional content is the most important thing. But in poetry, the mood and the emotion created by the words is crucial. Also, in poetry, the ambiguity of meanings and multiplicity of meanings is intentional, while in philosophy, this is (supposedly) to be avoided. A philosopher might say that this aim for precision is what makes philosophy superior to poetry and literature. But it could also be argued that poetic language is actually a richer and more genuine mode of expression than philosophical language.

Traditional, western philosophy suggests the notion of a kind of pristine rationality and objectivity. That is nothing more than a myth. We are all individuals who were born at a certain time and place (subjectivity is inescapable to a large degree). We are creatures of emotion as well as reason. What we rationally know or believe about the world is based largely on circumstantial factors such as when and where we happen to be born, whom we happen to meet, the schools that we attend and the books that we choose to read or study. I believe that genuine *emunah,* or faith, involves not a rejection of reason, but the acceptance of the limits of reason in the sense I just described.

Having said all that, I don't consider myself an anti-rationalist either. It's great that you're asking the big questions, and I admire your newfound interest in Judaism. As you continue to explore it, I guarantee you'll discover that it's a tremendously rich tradition. New doors will keep opening up for you, new levels, with layers upon layers. Keep asking the questions, keep up the learning. I believe that if you're persistent and honest with yourself, you'll find answers in Judaism that are intellectually, emotionally, and spiritually satisfying. That was my experience when I went through college (though I am from an Orthodox background). It sounds like you've got a lot more questions. Please keep them coming.

Sincerely,

Rabbi Low

PS. Even though I just admitted that there may be some kind of teleology even if G-d doesn't exist, a good question is whether you can really have free choice if there is no G-d. For the theist, nature is created freely by a supernatural being. It is G-d who gives human beings *behira hofshis* = free choice. Arguably, Aristotle's Naturalism does not allow for full free choice. Sure, Aristotle talks as if humans deliberate and make choices in some sense. But I'm not sure these choices are genuinely free if there's no G-d. If nature constitutes a purely rational system, then it's basically a determinate system. In fact, in any non-theistic view of the world, such as modern scientific naturalism (which drops teleology), it's not clear that genuine free choice is possible. If there's no free choice, a genuine moral life is impossible. So there's another reason for thinking that without G-d, morality – or at least, the best kind of morality – goes down the drain.

PPS. We still need to talk about creation and evolution. I will *bli neder* write you about that some other time.

7

October 7, 2000

I figured that one way to get a chance to speak to Esther again would be at services. So I went on Friday night, hoping to see her. I had forgotten they had separate seating. I tried glimpsing over the curtain but couldn't really see much. So I couldn't even tell if she was there. Meanwhile, the services weren't bad. Nice melodies. Everyone seemed pretty intense about "accepting the Sabbath," particularly when we reached the song "Lecha Dodi," which is actually a poem written by a sixteenth-century Kabbalist. (What is Kabbalah? Got to look into that.) The author of Lecha Dodi, Shlomo Halevi, managed to sign his name in the poem, by using one letter from his name as the first letter of every stanza. Interesting. And I couldn't help but notice how the Sabbath is compared to a queen. (If she's the queen, who's the king?) Anyway, soon after that, we said the evening Shema together. I can just see getting swept up into the whole thing and I'm nervous about that. Even if my heart is into it, I don't want to lose my head. When the services were over, I made a quick move for the door trying to find E. But of course Rabbi A noticed me and nailed me just as I was getting out. I had to be polite and I couldn't break away. He was so friendly I had no choice. He asked where I'd been, etc., etc. Then he invited me for dinner. I was really bummed that I didn't see E, but by that time I figured I had nothing to lose and maybe a nice dinner to gain. (Pragmatic argument again!) So I accepted. There were a few other guys who went over to his house for dinner and they seemed OK. They were all Orthodox, and all knew each other from before and were kind of in their own clique. But it turned out to be real nice. Rabbi A's wife was very quiet but she seemed very nice. His three little kids are angelic, and there's one on the way. The candles were still lit when we came in the house, and it reminded me of how Mom used to light candles when I was a little kid. We had Kiddush, which Rabbi A. explained is a verbal declaration that the day is "kadosh" or holy, together with drinking some wine, and the two loaves of bread, gefilte fish, soup, roast chicken, something else called kugel, and some other side dishes that I don't remember. The wine was traditional Jewish sweet wine,

and I couldn't drink that much of it. But in between the fish and
meat they had some vodka, and I sure liked that! Rabbi A didn't
seem to think twice about letting us have some. They sang some
nice Hebrew songs and then one of the guys said something about
the Torah portion of the week. I had to ask what the "portion of
the week" meant and the rabbi explained how, over the year, the
entire Torah is read aloud and so it is divided into portions for each
week or Sabbath. I asked some questions about keeping Shabbat,
and all the guys insisted that it rarely gets boring and they all
feel the day is kadosh, which means not just holy but separate or
special. They all claimed it was a great break from the work week.
As far as they're concerned, you literally <u>have</u> to relax on Shabbat
and not do any work, because it's not just an option like relaxing
on Sunday — it's a divine commandment! They also explained how
all the forbidden acts of work are based on 39 types of work that
were involved in constructing the Tabernacle in the desert. What's
forbidden is creative work, and creative work is defined by what's
involved in constructing the Tabernacle. Very interesting. I never
knew that. Practically speaking, I think the main problem I'd have
with keeping Shabbat is not writing or using the computer and also
not running, which is apparently not completely forbidden but just
one of those things the rabbis instituted as not in the spirit of the
day. Not smoking, too — that's considered a divine prohibition since
it involves burning. (At least you can drink!) I made up my mind
that I'd try to keep Shabbat for the rest of that night as best I could.
While all this conversation was going on, I was trying to figure out
how to ask in a nice way whether any of the guys or maybe Rabbi A
knew Esther. Finally as we were all leaving, Mrs. A said she planned
to be in ~~synago~~ shul tomorrow and that the Kiddush tomorrow was
being sponsored by a senior who got engaged to one of the girls he
had met at school here. (In addition to the Kiddush on Friday night,
there is also a Kiddush during the day of Shabbat. It's often held
in the shul after services and functions as a social get-together.)
I realized that Esther might be there tomorrow, so I decided to
go back to services the next morning, which I did. I got there a
little late but just in time to hear the Torah being read. Interesting
chant. The reader made a few mistakes which people corrected him
on. He didn't seem to get offended. I guess that's what's expected.
Also, they wanted to call me up to say the blessing over the Torah,
but I refused. I did agree to tie the Torah. That involved rolling it
together and tying it with a sash and placing the cover over it. Then
Rabbi A gave a more or less interesting speech about the portion

and he connected it to Yom Kippur which is coming up this week. During the latter part of the services, more singing. After it was over, I looked for Esther at the Kiddush, and there she was! She seemed pleasantly surprised to see me in shul, and we had a nice conversation. She really seemed more relaxed than before, and started to open up. We talked about classes, a few things about Judaism, some of her time in Israel. I even told her about Mom's condition. Unfortunately, it turns out Esther is not into running. But the good news is that when she had to leave, I asked her if I could see her again for lunch at the Kosher Café, and she said yes, and that I should email her. The next plan is to get her to go for a ~~jog~~ walk in the park. I was so high I figured I would try to keep Shabbat for the rest of the day. It wasn't as bad as I thought it would be. I read the portion of the week, did some other reading, and then did some meditating in the afternoon. While I was meditating, it dawned on me how keeping Shabbat is a perfect background setting for meditation! You've got not only one individual but an entire social group refraining from work, thereby getting into a relaxed, meditative mode. Got to talk to Ravi about this! Will email E on ~~Monday~~ Tuesday. (Don't want to seem too anxious.) So, as it turned out, my first Shabbos was a great success!

8
—

"Dad? Hi, it's me."

"Hi, David! How's it going?"

"Good. Hey, I didn't think you'd be home yet."

"Well, actually, I took some work home with me tonight."

"Oh, I see."

"So how are your classes?"

"Really good, Dad."

"Great. Did you speak to the pre-law advisor yet?"

"Sure I did."

"Excellent. And what else is going on? Did you make any new friends?"

"Yes. Actually, I—"

"Great! And how's the new dorm room?"

"It's good. Much nicer than last year. I was just saying that I've met —"

"Look, David, I'm really busy, but I know you're going to ask, so I gotta tell you, Mom's doing really well. She's out tonight, shopping or something . . . ."

"Wow! That sounds like a good sign."

"Yep, it sure is. Ever since she had that operation last January, she's been doing really well.

In fact, I think she's staying over in the city tonight with her friends."

"That's fantastic."

"You bet! Well, there's nothing else new here. Like I said, I'm busy with work as usual. Is there anything else you need from me?"

"Actually, there is, Dad."

"Oh, sure! I'll put a check in the mail tomorrow."

"Thanks, Dad! You're amazing!"

"What can I say? I know my own son! OK, David. Take care!"

"Bye, Dad. Thanks."

9

"So, David, do you have any of the good essence? In other words, where's your stash, man?"

"Simon, if you can answer this question, I'll tell you."

"Is this a riddle? What's the question?"

"Tell me, what stands behind the city of God?"

"Oh, man! This is not my field. I have no idea. I give up."

"Do you see that book on that shelf over there? That's the *City of God* by St. Augustine."

"Ah, I see it. It's a rather large tome. Well? What about it?"

"Take a look right behind it on the shelf. There you will find the answer to my question, *what stands behind the city of God?*"

"Ah, very funny! So that's where your stash is! Great! I'll take a look. Hey! This stuff looks – and smells – pretty good! Where did you get it?"

"Somewhere downtown."

"It must have cost you."

"No problem. Don't worry about it."

"Well, thanks. You can be the delivery boy from now on. I'm getting poorer. Meanwhile, you seem to be getting richer. Is this Dad's generosity at work?"

"Why don't you just light the pipe, please?"

"OK, I'll do that. But tell me: how is the old man? Still nagging you about going to law school?"

"Not so much any more. I told him I met with the pre-law advisor."

"Did you really do that?"

"No, but I guess I will sooner or later."

"David, you've outdone yourself! And how about your mother? How is she?"

"Pretty good. Last time I called, and spoke to my Dad, she was out . . . staying out with a friend overnight."

"A female friend, I hope?"

"Simon, *please*! Here, take another hit, why don't you?"

"Seriously, David, it's just a little strange. Finally, your mom gets well enough to go out, and it's *not* with her husband. Isn't that odd?"

"Dad stayed home. He had work to do."

"Since when does your Dad work at *home*? David . . . something's not making sense here."

"Look, why would he make up a story? Why would he lie?"

"Yeah, well, I can see this isn't going anywhere. Anyhow, speaking of women, who's that Orthodox girl I saw you walking with the other day?"

"How could you tell she's Orthodox?"

"David, don't be ridiculous! The long skirt gave it away. But she seems pretty nice looking. So? What's her name?"

"Esther. Esther Applefeld."

"How sweet! So, is this your replacement for What's-her-name, the *shikse*?"

"Yes, I hope so. We're supposed to go for a walk in the park next week. We'll see what happens."

"Oh, man! Are you in for a surprise!"

"Why's that?"

"Can I ask you a personal question?"

"I keep nothing hidden from you, Simon. What is it?"

"Have you kissed her yet?"

"No, not yet."

"Forget it! She's *shomeret negiah*. Do you know what that means?"

"Yeah, I think so. That means she won't have sex until she goes to the ritual bath. What's that called again? The *mikveh*?"

"No, sorry, that's not what it means! First of all, Orthodox girls – if they stick to the rules – they don't go the *mikveh* until they're married. So, they won't have sex until they're married!"

"Uh-oh. That *is* bad news."

"Worse than that. *Shomeret negiah* means they won't even *touch* a man until they're married to him!"

"What? Get out!"

"I'm serious."

"Not even a kiss?"

"Nothing. Nada. Zilch."

"But I don't get that. How can you know whether you want to marry someone until you see if you really like them?"

"Good point! I didn't discover who I was until I . . . uh . . . well, whatever . . . but that's another reason why I keep telling you . . . the whole thing is nuts."

"I'm not sure what to say. I'm a little stunned. Although some things are beginning to make more sense now."

"Well, you never know. Maybe there's a chink in her armor . . . some way to get through."

"What are you trying to say?"

"Look, she may be Orthodox, but you never know. Everyone has their breaking point."

"Simon! I'm *shocked* at what you're suggesting!"

"Oh, I'm sure you are. Well, what you gonna do?"

"We'll see. Meanwhile, pass me the pipe."

10
—

October 12, 2000

Dear Mom,

How are you? I'm doing well. I was glad to hear you're getting out and about. That's really great.

You asked me to keep you up to date about what's been going on in class, so I thought I'd write to you about this film I saw for my philosophy of religion course. My professor said she had to miss a class. It was actually Yom Kippur. Instead of having class that day, she had the class watch a film called "The Quarrel." I also missed the class, because I went to services part of the day at the synagogue on campus. So I watched the film on my own last night. I found it ~~very relevant to my situation~~ really interesting. It's different from so many other films I've seen. It really made me think about a lot of things. So I thought I'd tell you a little bit about it. I was thinking of writing a paper on the problem of evil, and that's exactly what the Quarrel is about.

The film takes place in Montreal, some time after World War II. It's mostly a dialogue between these two characters, Hersh and Chaim, who grew up together in Europe and survived the Holocaust, but ended up taking very different views about God and religion. It's interesting to see how two people can go through similar experiences and yet end up having a totally different reaction. The entire dialogue or "quarrel" takes place over the course of one day, the day of Rosh Hashanah. Both characters managed to escape death, but their wives and children were killed. Because they were separated for many years, each one thought the other was dead. At the beginning of the film, they meet by chance in a park in Montreal. They are shocked and relieved to find the other alive. They are saddened to learn about the deaths of the other's family. But once they get reacquainted, the rest of the film is basically their "quarrel" over what constitutes the right response to the Holocaust.

Chaim is an atheist because he's convinced that there's no way God could have allowed the terrible suffering of the Jews in the Holocaust. He's become a poet, a writer. He can't seem to remarry. I think because he can't forgive himself for not saving his wife. He left her behind when he escaped. Actually, even before the Holocaust, Chaim had turned away from the yeshiva and went off to the university to study literature, which became his great love. So I guess it wasn't really the Holocaust per se that made Chaim an atheist or a "rebel." It's just that he thinks the Holocaust proves he was right.

The other guy, Hersh, reacted to the Holocaust by becoming even more religious and devout. Although he lost his wife, he had managed to bring out some boys who had become his students. He's also become a rabbi of a yeshiva in Montreal. Hersh had always resented Chaim for turning away from Judaism, and he had basically shut down their friendship at that time. He'd refused to listen to any of Chaim's questions or problems with traditional Judaism. As the film goes on we find out that Hersh also resented the fact that his own father (the head of the yeshiva where they had both been studying) had favored the intellectually more brilliant Chaim to take his place as the head rabbi of the yeshiva. So there's a lot of bitter personal stuff that comes up in the film.

One thing I realized as I was watching the movie was how the personalities of the characters are so different, and that their personalities affect their views about God and about human beings. Still, what interested me most was their philosophical debate about the problem of evil. In the end they seem to come to some kind of deeper understanding and respect for the other guy's view. In the final scene they embrace, but they also walk away from each other. Who knows if they'll ever see each other again? I guess the message you're supposed to take away from the movie is that both views are valid. But that can't really be, can it? Someone's got to be right or wrong about whether there is a God! There is so much more to be said on both sides, and that's what I'd like to write my paper about.

Actually I have a test coming up in philosophy of religion, regarding proofs for God's existence. I better go study for that. I'll write again soon.

Love,
David

II
—

Philosophy of Religion

Midterm Exam

Dr. Maimon

October 18

Use the exam booklet to answer these questions: Summarize Aquinas's five arguments for God's existence. For at least two of the arguments, discuss "modern versions" of the arguments. Evaluate each of the five arguments. State whether you agree or disagree, and defend your position.

AQUINAS EXAM

David Goldstein

Aquinas's first argument is that the universe must have a "first cause." This argument is sometimes called the cosmological argument. Aquinas starts by saying that we live in a world where some things are caused by others. In other words, there are "causes" and "effects." A chain of causes and effects would be where one thing caused another and that second thing caused another thing. Aquinas then claims that there can't be an infinite chain or "regress" of causes and effects. An infinite regress is where Y is the cause of Z, and X is the cause of Y, and W is the cause of X, and so on and so on, without end. This may be symbolized as follows:

$$\infty \ldots W > X > Y > Z$$

Aquinas thinks that somewhere this chain has got to stop because otherwise there's nothing to support the whole chain. But the problem with this is why can't there be an infinite regress of causes and effects? If the chain is infinite, then there is no need for a "first" cause. Aquinas seems to be assuming what he was supposed to prove (otherwise known as "begging the question").

A modern version of this argument is that the best way to explain the existence of our cosmos is to postulate that it is the creation of an uncaused being. People who give this version of the argument admit that it's not a deductively valid proof, which means that they admit that it's possible that the premises of the argument could be true, even though the conclusion could be false. In other words, they admit that there is some chance that the cosmos could exist even if God doesn't. They claim that the best explanation for the existence of the cosmos is that there is an uncaused thing which caused the universe to exist.

An objection against this argument is that perhaps the cosmos doesn't really have an explanation, it's just a brute fact that it exists (a brute fact = something that's just true without any explanation). Could there be brute facts? I don't see why not, but there is something bothersome about the idea of a brute fact. Another objection is that if we say that God is the cause of the cosmos, another problem is: how can God be uncaused? God can't cause himself to exist, and he can't be caused by something outside himself. So is God's existence just a brute fact? If God's existence is a brute fact, we don't gain anything by postulating God's existence as the cause of the cosmos! Why not just admit in the first place that the existence of the cosmos is itself a brute fact?

Aquinas's second argument is that there has to be an "unmoved mover" – that is, something that itself does not move, but which causes other things to move. When we look around the world, we see that moving objects cause other objects to move, which then cause still other objects to move. Again, Aquinas argues that there can't be an infinite regress of moving objects that are moved by other objects that are moved by other objects and so on, going back infinitely. Hence, he claims there must be an unmoved mover – i.e., God. But aside from resting on outdated physics, this argument also relies on the idea that an infinite regress is impossible. But why should we assume that? Maybe there is an endless regress of movers and moved things.

The third argument starts with a definition of what's merely possible or contingent. The definition of a contingent being is one that might or might not have existed. Contingent beings are also dependent for their existence on something else. A being that is not contingent would be one that is necessary, meaning that it somehow must exist, something about its nature is such that it must be. This is not the same thing as saying that it is caused by itself, but rather that something about itself explains why it does not need an external cause. Now it seems that almost everything we're familiar with is contingent. For example, we can conceive of a world in which people, animals, plants and even planets and stars do not exist. But Aquinas argues there's got to be at least one being that's not contingent. His reason is that if every being is or was merely possible, there must have been some time in the past when no being existed at all. He seems to think that if a given situation is possible, then it must at some time or other be actual. His next step is to say that there could never have been a time when nothing existed, because then there would forever be nothing after that!

Again, Aquinas's argument is obviously flawed. Even if every being that ever existed was contingent, that does not imply that there must have been a time at which no being existed! The premise that "what is possible must at some point be actualized" is just false.

There is a modern version of this argument too. (Some people view this as a version of the first argument.) Samuel Clarke raised this argument. It is one of the better arguments for God's existence, in my opinion, but it still has problems. This argument starts by noting that for each contingent being that exists, the explanation for that being lies in some other being. Now, we can raise Clarke's question, which is: <u>Is there any explanation for why there are any contingent beings, rather than none at all</u>? Clarke says you cannot answer this question by saying that contingent beings are explained by <u>other</u> contingent beings, because then you're assuming the existence of the very things you're supposed to be explaining. So, if (and it's a big "if") there <u>is</u> an explanation for the existence of contingent beings, there has to be at least one thing that is <u>not</u> contingent — that is necessary, and that's God.

However, the skeptic could respond that maybe there is nothing in the universe that is necessary and there is just no good answer to the question, "Why are there any contingent beings at all?" Perhaps the existence of contingent things is just one big brute fact about the universe. Besides, the skeptic could also insist that the idea of a necessary being is itself absurd or contradictory. (I myself don't think it's absurd, but I do find it puzzling. What is it about a being that could possibly contain within itself the explanation for its own existence?) Finally, a skeptic could ask how a <u>necessary</u> being could explain the existence of <u>contingent</u> beings. If the existence of those beings somehow flows from the necessary being with necessity, it would seem that those beings would have to be necessary as well. On the other hand, if the existence of those beings does not flow from the necessary being with necessity, it is not clear how the existence of those beings is "explained" by the necessary being.

A problem with all three of these arguments (perhaps most famously pointed out by the great skeptic philosopher David Hume) is that even if there is a first cause or an unmoved mover or a necessary being, how do we know that there's only one such being? And how do we know it's an intelligent being? Even more, how do we know that this being is worthy of being worshipped? Maybe there is some kind of impersonal, eternal power and motion generator, kind of like an eastern conception of the Ultimate. And surely that's not the same thing as God. So even if these arguments work, they don't prove the existence of God. Some commentators suggest that Aquinas was well aware of this kind of objection, and it's partly because of these objections that Aquinas came up with the fourth and fifth arguments, which attempt to show that God is morally perfect and intelligent. But in my opinion these arguments aren't much better.

The fourth argument says that because we make distinctions between good and bad, there has to be some kind of <u>ultimate standard</u> by which we judge things to be good or bad. The ultimate standard is the good itself, that which is perfect. In other words, God himself. But this is really weak because the moral relativist can say that there is no ultimate standard. In other words, sure we make judgments about good and bad, <u>relative</u> to some standard in our society. But maybe there is no absolute standard of goodness. And even if you disagree with relativism and think there must be some ultimate standard by which you make all these judgments, all you really need is <u>the idea</u> of what is good or perfect, but it's not necessary to assume that a perfect being actually exists.

One modern version of this argument is sometimes called the Moral Argument for God's existence. It says that without God as a foundation, there could be no absolute moral standard for everyone to live by. Some people who give this argument claim that (somehow) we know that morality is absolute, so it follows that God must exist. This is a very popular argument among many religious people. Other philosophers who give this kind of argument make only a "hypothetical" claim, which is that <u>if</u> morality is absolute, <u>then</u> God must exist as a foundation. The argument is that if there is no God, absolute morality goes down the drain. But I'm not sure I agree with that claim. Some kind of Aristotelian view of morality could conceivably be true even if there were no God. I don't think objective morality requires God as a foundation. (Yet some people would argue that without God, there is no free choice, and without free choice, there can be no genuine moral life.)

The fifth argument is that the world has a certain order, so there must be some intelligent being who designed the world to be the way it is. This is also known as the "argument from design" or the teleological argument, from the Greek word telos, which means goal or purpose. This is also a popular argument among many religious people today. Like Aquinas says, an arrow doesn't fly right into a bull's eye without the direction of the archer. And if you look around the world it seems like many things work toward goals or purposes. Like, for example, the digestive system, or the way the human eye works. It seems like an amazingly complicated machine that was designed for a specific purpose, such as digestion or sight. But obviously, this argument is somewhat old-fashioned because it predates the theory of evolution, which shows how, over a period of long time, you can reach order from disorder. Originally, the universe may have been some kind of disorganized primal soup, and eventually over time things evolved in such a way that the more adaptable species survived and reproduced, until you have things like complicated organisms such as humans with brains. Given an eternity of time, perhaps a series of random events could eventually result in a stable, orderly universe. Besides, there seems to be a lot of disorder in the universe too, not to mention all the evil and suffering. How would Aquinas fit all that into his argument from design?

A modern version of this argument is to say that the best explanation for the apparent design in the universe is the intelligence and "agency" of a designer. Like the modern version of the cosmological argument, most people who give this argument admit it is not a deductively valid proof. Now it seems like the theory of evolution can be used against this argument too. But modern supporters of the argument from design say that the theory of evolution does not explain why there is any order in the universe rather than none at all. The theory of evolution explains why complicated organisms could have evolved from less complicated organisms, but it does so by relying on certain scientific laws or regularities such as the laws of physics, and chemistry. But why are those laws true? Is there any explanation? Again, this takes us back to the issue about brute facts. If there are brute facts, maybe this is just one of them. There is order in the world, and that's that. Why can't there be brute facts? And even if it were the case that postulating the existence of God explained something else (like why the world exists or why the world has order), you'd still be left with the problem of <u>what explains God</u>? It's like jumping from the frying pan into the fire. In order to try to explain something about the world, the theist postulates the existence of an omniscient, omnipotent, omnibenevolent non-physical entity. But then, the very thing you're postulating is even more bizarre than the thing you were supposedly trying to explain!

In summary, though it might be nice if there were a God, I have to say that in my opinion Aquinas's arguments don't work, even in their modern versions.

12

"Excuse me, Dr. Maimon. May I come in?"

"Yes? Who is it?"

"It's David Goldstein, from your philosophy of religion class. I came to talk with you about my paper."

"Ah, yes. Please come in."

"Thanks."

"Have a seat. So what are you planning to do your paper on?"

"I was thinking of doing my paper on whether it makes sense to believe in God given all the evil and suffering that exists in the world."

"Ah, the problem of evil. Very good. We haven't gotten to that yet in class, but evil is a good topic – pardon the pun! What texts do you plan to discuss?"

"Actually, I was wondering if I could write a paper on the film *The Quarrel*. Is that OK?"

"That's fine. In fact, there was a time when I would assign the class to do a paper on that film. My only comment would be that, somewhere in the paper, you must make reference to some philosophical texts on the issue."

"Sure, I could do that. What do you suggest? I guess I should have a look at the book of Job. Isn't that the classic work on the problem of evil?"

"I don't know about that. You can refer to the book of Job if you like, but it's not really very philosophical. It's more rhetoric and poetry than it is philosophy."

"In that case, what texts would you recommend?"

"First, why don't you tell me what you had in mind to do with the film?"

"OK. I'd like to write my paper in the form of a dialogue between the two main characters, Hersh and Chaim. Basically, Chaim thinks that the Holocaust disproves the existence of God, while Hersh thinks it still makes sense to go on believing even after the Holocaust. But I thought I could take their debate about the problem of evil a few steps deeper than what goes on in the film. A lot of the discussion in the film really has to do with their own personal stuff. The debate about evil could be deeper."

"Yes, you're right. It sounds like an interesting idea for a paper. In fact, there is a long history of great works in philosophy of religion that were written in dialogue form."

"Really? I didn't know that. Which ones?"

"I can think of several off the top of my head. First of all, the book of Job takes the form of a dialogue, but as I also said, in my view, Job doesn't count as philosophical. But Plato's *Euthyphro* can be considered a dialogue in philosophy of religion, since its main topic is piety. In the early Middle Ages, there's Boethius's *Consolation of Philosophy,* which I consider a very important work. That's also written in the form of a dialogue between Boethius himself and wisdom, personified as a woman. And there are many examples of dialogues in the medieval period, such as Judah Halevi's *Kuzari,* which involves a dialogue between the King of the Khazars, a Jew, a Christian, and a philosopher. There's also Peter Abelard's *Dialogue* between a Jew, a Christian, and a philosopher. Later on, David Hume, the great critic of religion, wrote his main work in philosophy of religion in the form of a dialogue."

"What about dialogues from modern times? Are there any?"

"Yes, in a manner of speaking. There's the *Nineteen Letters of Ben Uziel,* written by the German Modern Orthodox thinker, Samson Raphael Hirsch. It's a book of Jewish philosophy written in the form of a correspondence between a student and a rabbi. You might consider that an extended form of dialogue."

"Interesting. Why do you suppose there's so much in philosophy of religion that's written in dialogue form?"

"I'm not sure, but I'd speculate that since expressing controversial views about religion could often get a person into trouble, the dialogue form was used as a cloak or veil to protect the author from being accused of heretical views. The author of a dialogue can allow his characters to express views that he himself may or may not believe in, and he also cannot be blamed for the views of his characters."

"I see. So can I do it? Can I write my paper in dialogue form?"

"Like I said, the idea sounds nice, but quite frankly, I'd rather you *not* do a paper in the form of a dialogue."

"Oh, OK. No problem . . . but I thought you said that the dialogue form is very common in philosophy of religion."

"It's common, but of course, not all Jewish philosophy is written in dialogue form. In fact, most of it isn't. The greatest work in Jewish philosophy is Maimonides's *Guide to the Perplexed* – and that's not written in the form of a dialogue. And there's Bahya ibn Pakuda's *Hovot ha-Levavot,* or Duties of the Heart, which isn't in dialogue form either. Besides, writing in dialogue form is no longer in fashion in the academic world. So the assignment is to write a formal paper. I'm especially concerned that you take a very clear stance in the paper, especially at the end, as to what your own view is. It's just impossible to do that in a dialogue – and today, there's no need for you to cloak your personal opinion!"

"All right. Fair enough."

"But that doesn't mean you can't do your paper on the film."

"How would you suggest I do it, then?"

"Simple. Evidently, you think that each character – Hersh and Chaim – has a view about the problem of evil. That's really the main thing, philosophically speaking. For example, the fact that the whole film takes place on Rosh Hashanah – that's really irrelevant to the characters' views. Or the fact that most of the film takes place during a walk in the park – that's also irrelevant. After all, as philosophers, we're not really interested in the *personalities* of the characters as much as their *views*. Right?"

"Yes, I agree."

"And you think each character has an *argument* that he uses to support his view."

"Yes, that's true, too.

"And you also think that there's room for improvement in both cases. You said their conversation could be taken to 'a deeper level,' as you put it."

"Definitely."

"So this is my suggestion for your paper. Summarize the views and arguments on each side. Then compare the two positions and discuss their relative strengths and weaknesses. Briefly suggest in what direction each character would need to go in order to improve or develop their position. Then conclude the paper by giving your own view on the problem of evil. If you think there's a solution, state what it is. If not, then say why not. How does that sound?"

"That sounds great. That sounds exactly like what I want to do."

"Great. Now, as far as other things to read on the problem of evil, I could recommend a few things. I'll email you the references. And remember, I'm concerned that the paper be well organized. Make an outline of your paper before you do it. Section headings are also a good idea."

"OK, I'll make section headings."

"Good. And I'm sorry about not letting you do it in dialogue form. But this isn't a literature class, you know. It's a philosophy class. I want you to abstract from the characters and just focus solely on the views expressed, not on the personalities involved. So is that it, then?"

"Actually, there was one thing more I was curious to ask you."

"What's that?"

"Do you remember Dr. Low's lecture last semester?"

"Sure I do. Why? Were you there?"

"Yes. I was just wondering whether you thought his responses to you at the end were any good."

"Hmm, that's a while back, isn't it? Obviously, you must remember the exchange pretty well. Otherwise, you wouldn't be asking this question."

"I don't think I could restate your questions exactly. But I remember your saying there were two problems with his lecture – a conceptual problem and a problem that had to do with Jewish texts, I think."

"Ah, yes, that's right. It's coming back to me now. Actually, now that I think of it, he didn't respond to my questions very well at all."

"I had the feeling you'd say that. Can you explain?"

"I think so. On his pragmatic approach, he essentially admitted that all he really showed is that someone who is religious has a greater motivation to live her life, to do whatever she does. But that's like saying that it makes sense to be religious because if you're religious, you'll feel *as if* your life were more valuable, more joyous, more morally significant, or what have you. But he did not substantiate the claim that someone who is religious *actually has* a more valuable, more joyous, more meaningful life. You couldn't do that unless you showed or substantiated the claim that *there is a God* – which Low insisted could not be done. Second, when I pointed out that from the Jewish perspective it is a religious commandment to *know* God, he responded by interpreting the Torah to say that knowledge of God is something which will come only in the future. But this is just wrong and he knows better. Of course, the particular verse he quoted about the spreading of the knowledge of God throughout the world, among all peoples of the globe – *that* is indeed a reference to the future. But Scripture clearly states in Deuteronomy, "And you shall know *today,* and you shall consider it in your hearts, that the Lord is God in the heavens above and on the earth below; there is no other." Obviously, this passage is directed to the Jewish people, and it describes the obligation to know *today* that there is a God. His other response was that knowledge of something doesn't necessarily involve the ability to provide proof or rational substantiation. But that's absurd! If I claim to know something, I ought to be able to explain why I'm claiming that I know it! Otherwise I don't really know it, I just believe it. I think he used the example of knowing that his wife loves him. He said that he knows his wife loves him, but can't prove it. But surely he has good reasons for thinking his wife loves him! Surely she spends time with him, takes care of him while he's sick, nurtures him, raises his children, cooks his food, and so on. Anyway, my point is that since there's a commandment to know God, this requires that we have some kind of rational basis for our belief in God. And that's exactly what Maimonides would say. So, I don't think he responded very well to my questions. Why? What do you think?"

"Me? I . . . uh . . . I think you're right."

"Low's clever, and his argument has a certain seductive quality to it, but I think that in the end, the pragmatic approach fails. Anyhow, we'll be covering some of this material in our class later on in the semester, when we get to Pascal's Wager. Now, you'll have to excuse me. I've got to do some preparation for my next lecture."

"Oh! I'm sorry I took so much of your time."

"Not at all. See you in class."

13

"Esther . . . it's a beautiful day for a walk, isn't it?"

"Yes, it is."

"Do you walk a lot?"

"Sure, I like walking. Don't you?"

"I like running better. But I like walking too. It helps me think."

"You don't think when you run?"

"No. I'm totally focused on running when I run. That's what's so great about it. But I can think while I walk. I guess it takes less concentration to walk than to run."

"And what do you think about when you walk?"

"Oh . . . philosophy. God. Things like that."

"Hmm. Do you always think about such serious things?"

"Uh, yeah, sure. I'm always thinking about serious things. Unless I'm thinking about . . . ."

"What?"

"Never mind."

"What? What is it?"

"No, never mind."

"Come on. I won't hold it against you. I promise! What else do you think about?"

"OK. I'll be honest. Girls."

"I thought so! You guys are all the same."

"Tell me the truth. In the back of their minds, girls think a lot about guys. Isn't that true?"

"No, no way! At least, not in the same way that guys think about girls. When guys think about girls, it's usually about something physical. When girls think about guys, it's usually more serious, like about a relationship, or something like that."

"I don't know, Esther. But maybe you're right. Do you think girls take guys more seriously than the other way around?"

"Sure I do. In fact, I can prove it based on what you just said."

"Really? How?"

"David, don't you remember? You just said that when you walk, you think about serious things, like God and philosophy, unless you're thinking about girls. Therefore, girls are not a serious topic for you!"

"Ah, very clever! You're pretty sharp, Esther. But I think you broke your promise! You *are* holding what I said against me."

"Not at all! I'm just being honest . . . and David – d'you know what I like about you? You're honest. A lot of yeshiva guys think the same thing, but they'd never admit it!"

"Yeshiva guys? That means they're studying to be rabbis, right?"

"No, not necessarily. A lot of guys go to yeshiva just to study for a year or two, without becoming a rabbi. Studying in yeshiva is kind of like what I did, except that was a seminary for women, so they don't call it a yeshiva."

"I see. Hey, Esther, see that fork in the road? The one on the left looks like a nice, cozy path. Shall we . . . ?"

"No, thanks, David. Let's stick to the right side."

"OK, no problem. Hey, look . . . can I ask you something?"

"Go right ahead."

"You're *negiah,* right?"

"That's funny! You mean *shomeret negiah,* I think."

"Yes, that's what I meant. What's so amusing?"

"Nothing. It's just the way you put it. *Negiah* means touching. *Shomeret negiah* means a woman who keeps the practice of *not* touching a person of the opposite sex. Who taught you about that?"

"Not Rabbi Low, I can tell you that."

"Actually, I'm glad you mentioned it. I was trying to figure out a polite way to bring it up."

"Don't worry, I know what it means. No physical contact."

"Right. Not even an arm around the shoulder. Not even holding hands."

"Ah, I didn't know that part. It must be difficult to be – how did you say it?"

"*Shomeret negiah.* It's just part of what it is to be a religious Orthodox Jew. It's like not eating cheeseburgers. I don't miss them."

"Well, excuse me for saying so, but cheeseburgers taste very good."

"I bet they do. I wasn't saying they don't taste good."

"And besides, not eating cheeseburgers is one thing. Not having physical contact with the opposite sex until you're married – that's something else!"

"Well, they are not entirely the same, of course. But my point was – it's not hard to keep if you're brought up with it. Though I guess that once you break the rule, it might be hard to get back on track . . . . Anyway, it has advantages, you know. Like, for those of us who are *shomrei negiah,* when we get married, it'll be all the more . . . special."

"Maybe so. In the meantime, it sounds pretty tough."

"Only if you weren't brought up that way."

"But now, I have another question."

"Yes? What is it?"

"If . . . let's say . . . *I* were to kiss *you,* without *your* kissing *me,* would *that* be a problem?"

"Um, David, you *are* joking, right? Or maybe you still don't get it. Because that *would* be a problem. A big problem."

"Hey, Esther, I'm sorry. I was just asking a question. I didn't mean to upset you."

"David, if you want to be friends, that's fine. But you need to understand that friendship is all it's going to be. Nothing more."

"I do understand, Esther. I'm sorry."

"David, remember how I said before that I like how you're honest? Well, I appreciate the fact that you were honest about this, too, but now I'm a bit worried that I might have given you the wrong idea by coming on this walk with you. I'm starting to wonder if maybe it was a mistake, if I shouldn't have done it . . . ."

"Esther, please don't say that. We can still enjoy being together, can't we? I like you, and you like me. Isn't that true?"

"Yes. I do like you, David, but I don't think you understand how different we are."

"Maybe so — but why do we need to worry about that right now? Can't we just agree to be friends?"

"We can be friends, yes. But you've got to accept that it's not going to get physical."

"No problem, Esther. I accept that. No problem at all."

14

"So, David, you're interested in majoring in philosophy?"

"Yes, Phil. I am. And you can take credit for it. I really enjoy your class, and I'd like you to be my advisor."

"Really? What about Dr. Maimon?"

"I don't think so. She's not as approachable as you are."

"She's a little tough on the outside. But once you get to know her, she's really OK. I don't agree with her on practically anything, but that's another story. Anyhow, I'll be happy to be your advisor if that's what you want. But can you tell me why you want to major in philosophy?"

"I think you know why, Phil. I'm really fascinated by the whole idea of finding answers to the big questions. And that's what philosophy is all about."

"Ah! Just what I suspected. Very noble indeed."

"You sound a little sarcastic. How come? Isn't philosophy the love of wisdom, the passionate pursuit of fundamental truths?"

"Precisely! Philosophy is not wisdom itself. It's the *love* of wisdom. The philosopher *pursues* wisdom. He doesn't actually ever *possess* it. Philosophy is more about asking the questions than it is about answering them."

"Wait. I don't get it. What's the point of asking the questions if you can't find answers to them?"

"Why does there need to be a point beyond the activity itself? Actually, this question relates to my dissertation topic."

"Oh? What's your dissertation on?"

"It's called 'Writing and the Art of Philosophy.' It has to do with the purpose of philosophy, and specifically with whether genuine philosophy is done in writing, or rather, as I believe to be the case, in discussion or dialogue."

"Hmm. That sounds interesting."

"Thanks. You know, Socrates was really the greatest philosopher, the inventor of philosophy as we know it. And he didn't write a thing."

"Are you saying that he was a better philosopher than Plato or Aristotle?"

"No, that doesn't follow. I'm saying that philosophy in its highest, truest form, takes place in conversation and discussion rather than in the writing of tracts or works. Even Plato's dialogues – which of course count as written works – are artificial and secondary compared with the real activity of philosophy, which goes on in dialogue. It's one thing to actually have a dialogue, and it's another thing to write up a dialogue. My thesis does not exclude the possibility that when Plato and Aristotle truly philosophized – that is, when they held discussions and dialogues with their colleagues, perhaps then they were just as 'great' as Socrates was in his conversations with others."

"I see. But Phil, whether it's in dialogue or writing, I still don't see the point of asking questions if you can't find answers."

"Well, the way I look at it, philosophy is a form of thinking. In fact, it's the highest form of thinking, partly because of what you yourself said a few moments ago – philosophy deals with the big questions. But it's the activity of the thinking itself that makes philosophy so great. The philosopher engages in the highest form of thought because he contemplates the most universal or fundamental issues. And that involves seeking answers to the big questions – but not necessarily answering them! There's also something about the philosophical method that's important. The philosopher tries to think as rigorously and critically as possible about his subject matter. It's interesting that to this very day, logic is still considered a branch of philosophy. That's because no one is more interested in what counts as clear thinking than the philosopher. It was the philosophers who sharpened our tools of analysis to a very sophisticated degree. And only philosophers are willing to question any and all assumptions, unlike people in other disciplines who always have to make assumptions. It's the process of rigorous, critical thinking about fundamental questions that makes philosophy great, whether you find the answers or not!"

"Well, I admit that I enjoy the process of philosophy too."

"Good! I'm glad to hear you say that out loud."

"But are you saying that philosophers *never* find answers to the big questions?"

"Sometimes, philosophers come up with answers. But the answers are always temporary or partial, subject to revision. Of course, some so-called 'philosophers' have deceived themselves into thinking that they've reached the ultimate truth, the 'end' of philosophy. But look at the history of philosophy – it's always developing, always changing. Any proposed answer to a question has to be thought through and critically evaluated over and over again. As a philosopher, you never reach ultimate truth. If you did, philosophy would come to a halt. Sometimes the philosopher doesn't find answers, even temporary ones. Still, he's a philosopher as long as he's engaged in that fundamental inquiry.

"Some more great things about philosophy are its freedom and spontaneity, and the fact that it expresses freedom of thought. Socrates was the original freethinker. He had such an open mind about everything that it's no surprise he was put to death by the masses. Anyway, when you discuss things, you sometimes move from topic to topic. Something strikes you as important to say at that moment, so you say it, or you go off on a tangent, or whatever. But it doesn't make sense to write philosophy like that. When you write philosophy, you inevitably have to follow a structure or an outline. I think that's great too. It has a place. It can be developed into a highly sophisticated form, like Spinoza's *Ethics* or Kant's *Critique of Pure Reason,* both of which are highly structured works. But as I argue in my dissertation, once you write down your views in a tract or treatise, it becomes fixed and stale. And that's exactly what happened to Spinoza's and Kant's work. You can't set philosophy in stone like the Ten Commandments. If you set philosophy in stone, there's no chance for a second draft, and no revisions are possible. And then it's not philosophy anymore! That's why I say that genuine philosophy takes place in conversation. But I'm sorry, David – I've been lecturing you without letting you speak!"

"No problem, Phil. Look, I agree with you that philosophy's a great activity. The process of opening up everything to question without limit is so . . . um . . . liberating. And there's definitely something special about having a real live conversation as opposed to writing a book or reading one. But I'm still not sure I agree with your bottom line. If you can't find answers to the questions you're asking, why bother asking? Why bother having the conversation?"

"David, there's an unquestioned assumption implicit in what you're saying. Aren't you *assuming* that there is some point to answering the big questions?"

"Yes. I guess I am. But isn't that kind of obvious? There's got to be a point to answering the big questions."

"Tell me, David: what is the point of answering the big questions?"

"Well . . . uh . . . that's such a basic question. I – I don't know how to answer that . . . ."

"Let me help you out. Obviously, you attach some great value to *knowing* the most fundamental or important truths – assuming that we could ever have such knowledge. So the point of asking the big questions is to find out or know the most important truths. Is that right?"

"Yes, that's exactly what I wanted to say. Thanks."

"But then, consider this question: Why do you attach such great value to knowing the most fundamental truths, as opposed to attaching the same great value to contemplating or inquiring into what those truths are? If I could give an analogy, it may be a bit like playing a game. Do you have to win in order for the game to be worthwhile?"

"No, I guess not."

"So philosophy is like playing a game – a very serious game. But the activity of the game is worthwhile even if you don't win."

"But if you know ahead of time that you're not going to find the answers, that would be like playing a game without being able to win. And if you know or believe you can't win, it's not fun to play!"

"Not necessarily true, if you really love the game! Wouldn't you like to have a chance to race in the Olympics even if you knew you couldn't win?"

"I guess so. But in the back of my mind, I'd still be thinking . . . maybe I'll win!"

"Oh, come on. You're not being honest. A game can be exciting and fun, like playing chess against a grandmaster, even if you know you can't win. The same goes for philosophy, the passionate pursuit of wisdom. How shall I put this? Wisdom is like a woman you're pursuing whom you can never actually get."

"Now *that's* a very interesting thought. Actually, it kind of reminds me of my current situation."

"Is that so? Would you care to elaborate?"

"Well . . . I don't know if you really want to hear about this."

"Come on, tell me about it! You said you wanted me to be your *advisor*!"

"Very funny. Well, the bottom line is that I got sort of involved with this Orthodox Jewish girl. I'm pretty sure she likes me. But she won't even touch me or let me touch her."

"Very interesting indeed! Well, you must really like her, then. Right?"

"I find her very attractive."

"Is that it? Or do you really like her?"

"Actually, I'm not sure. I kind of do like her, but I think part of the attraction is her . . . unattainability."

"Ah! So that's how it reminds you of the pursuit of wisdom! Excellent parallel! But let me just tell you this. The main thing you should know is that the genuine philosopher isn't really interested in *women*. He's interested in *wisdom*. It's not an accident that many of the great philosophers remained single."

"Are you saying that a true philosopher remains celibate? Like a monk?"

"No, of course not. It's OK to have a girlfriend or an affair now and then. And it might even be OK to get married, under very unusual circumstances. But in most cases, having a serious long-term relationship – especially with a woman and especially having a family – that's a serious distraction from the philosophical life."

"Hmm. Do you really believe that?"

"Absolutely. But look, David, getting back to the other topic: if you're really looking for something that provides answers to the big questions, you know where you should go?"

"Where?"

"Not to philosophy."

"Where, then?"

"Where most people go. Religion."

"What? Do you really believe that?"

"David, didn't you ever hear the famous saying, "Philosophy consists in questions that are never answered. Religion consists in answers that are never questioned."

"Hang on, Phil. Now I'm really confused. Do you really think religion does provide answers in the end?"

"Sure, religion serves up answers. But they're not satisfactory to the philosopher – the real philosopher, that is! Of course, there've been so-called 'religious philosophers' throughout the ages, some of them very famous and also very clever. But insofar as they accept those 'answers,' they're not true philosophers in the proper sense. In fact, I think religion is inherently anti-philosophical."

"Why do you say that?"

"In my view, the genuine philosopher lives with the fact that there are no definitive answers to the ultimate questions."

"I see. So, you don't think we can have definitive answers to the ultimate questions."

"I'm afraid not."

"Wait a second, Phil. There's something I find puzzling. Do you remember the last conversation we had, about moral objectivism?"

"Sure. What about it?"

"Didn't you tell me that you believe that even if there's no God, certain things are objectively good because humans have a telos or end, which is to live a rational life? And it follows from this –"

"David, sorry to interrupt, but I did not say that I believe all those things. I was explaining Aristotle's view that you don't need to be a theist in order to believe in moral objectivism. But it doesn't follow that *I* believe in moral objectivism!"

"Oh, shoot! I thought I had you there for a minute."

"Nice try. One day, maybe you will. But look, I admit that most people can't accept the fact that there are no definitive answers. So they end up accepting certain answers on faith. This ties in to a point I make in my dissertation."

"What's that?"

"Tell me, David – in three of the world's major religions, Christianity, Islam, and Judaism, what is the single most important artifact?"

"That's pretty easy. In Christianity, it's the cross; in Judaism, it's the Jewish star or Magen David. Now, I'm not sure about Islam. Is it the stone at Mecca?"

"David, don't be absurd! The things you mentioned are relatively minor symbols! Think again. Quickly, name the one thing that if Christians didn't have it, there would be no such thing as Christianity?"

"Uh, I don't know. Christmas?"

"No, silly!"

"Sorry. What is it, then?"

"The New Testament!"

"Oh, right. Of course! That was so obvious I didn't think of it. For Jews it's the Torah, and for Muslims, it's the Quran. So how does this tie in with your thesis?"

"Don't you see? As I said before, genuine philosophy is never written down, and one reason is because there is no definitive philosophical statement of the truth. But religions have tracts or 'manuals' that purport to describe definitively what the truth is, what the answers to life's most important questions are. It's also no accident that in most religions, marriage is considered a good thing – you can, so to speak, have your cake and eat it too. Of course, the Catholics are peculiar on this matter. Anyhow, as far as the specific 'answers' that religion provides – well, that's where you get the variety of conflicting religions. That's not surprising, since religion abandons the use of reason in favor of faith. And notice how stifling religion can be, how it suppresses freedom of thought. In all of these three religions there's hardly any tolerance for free thinking. Some religious philosophers try to glorify this process by saying that religion goes beyond reason, but the truth is that religion falls beneath reason. The true philosopher is not willing to give up on reason. It's not easy to do, and most people just can't do it. That's why religion is infinitely more popular than philosophy. David, I'm telling you that the price of philosophy is living with doubt, and sometimes, perplexity."

"Well, right now I'd have to say I'm quite perplexed myself."

"So, do you still want to major in philosophy?"

"I – I think so."

"Then . . . you'd better learn to get used to perplexity."

15

November 1, 2000

Out of the good essence again. Just checked, and nothing stands behind the City of God. Need to get some more. Illegal, but so what? The risk of getting caught is ridiculously low, have to weigh that against how much I enjoy it. Think pragmatically! ~~Of course, it's not good for my running~~

Not getting anywhere with E. She really is committed. She's nice and attractive and knowledgeable and all that, but I don't know how long I can last without a real girlfriend. Maybe it just needs time, but how much more time can I give this? It's really getting bad. Last night I was drinking with Simon and some of his friends, and I met this girl L there, and the next thing I knew, we were in someone's apartment together and one thing led to another. E. had better not find out or it really will be over before it even got started.

Still reading the Scriptures, and now I'm reading Ethics of the Fathers, like R. Abraham said. Some of it seems so strange, but some of it seems so sharp, so true. (Examples on both sides. Need to make a list, some other time. Like my list of weird things in the Bible, so I can ask about them later.)

I'm still struggling to understand <u>why</u> a person should do what's good, or <u>why</u>, according to Judaism, a Jew should keep the Torah. In Ethics of the Fathers it says that a person should not worship God for the sake of a reward. One commentary I have says this means, a person should do what's right "just because it's right" (the Hebrew term for that is "lishmah") and not because of gain. Another commentary says it means that one should worship God out of love. But these commentaries only "push the question back," as Phil would say. Why should a person do what's right? Or why should a person love God?

Why should a person love anyone, for that matter? This is a problem I've been thinking about lately too, though it's surfaced only now, thanks to writing in this journal. If there is no gain in loving, why love? Is there such a thing as "true love" or "selfless love"? Maybe I should ask Dr. Maimon how she interprets that. Not the question about love, but the question about what it means to serve God, but not for a reward. She seems hard to approach, but I just have to take that plunge.

If I take a hard look at myself, and ask, why am I doing what I'm doing? When I'm brutally honest with myself I still have to admit that I do what I do because I enjoy it. If I didn't enjoy it then I wouldn't do it. Why did I have that fling with L last night? Why do I drink? Why do I smoke? Why do I hang out with Simon? Why do I run? Because I enjoy it. Why am I pursuing E? Because she's attractive. (Do I love her? Am I falling in love with her? What is love, anyway?) Still, why would I love her if I didn't gain something from it? And why do I spend all this time talking philosophy? Or even arguing about things like whether Judaism makes sense? Because I enjoy the intellectual stimulation of it all. That's why Phil engages in philosophy — because he enjoys it, too. Maybe it is "objectively good" to pursue philosophy because that is our true telos, but, even if so, the only reason to pursue your telos is because the intellectual stimulation gives you some kind of pleasure or joy in the end.

I guess I'm still a hedonist after all. Speaking of stimulation, need to find some more of the good essence. All I have are cigarettes and beer!

16

—

"Hello, Simon? It's David."

"Hey! What's up? Where are you?"

"Downtown. Where are you?"

"I'm in the library studying for my Psych test. What's happening? I thought you'd be back by now. Any luck?"

"Still looking. Didn't find anything in my usual spot. I've got to . . . uh . . . forage elsewhere."

"Well, keep looking. Listen — can you get some extra this time?"

"Maybe. What's up?"

"I got some friends who want some. We'll make it good for you."

"You got it, Simon."

"Thanks, man. You're great!"

"Right, I know it. Later!"

17

—

"Dr. Maimon? Excuse me, may I come in?"

"Mr. Goldstein? How are you? Are you all right? You look exhausted."

"I'm fine. I was . . . uh . . . just up late last night studying for a test."

"I see. Well, what can I do for you? Have a seat."

"Thank you. Dr. Maimon, there's something I wanted to ask you about. I hope you don't mind. It doesn't exactly pertain to our class . . . ."

"What is it?"

"I've been reading *Ethics of the Fathers*. And —"

"Are you studying it in a class?"

"No, I'm just reading it on my own."

"Good for you. Do you read Hebrew?"

"No, not really. A little, maybe. But I'm doing it in translation."

"I see. Have you ever seen Maimonides's *Eight Chapters*? It's his introduction to his commentary on *Pirkei Avot*. I think it's available in English. It's very worthwhile."

"No, I haven't seen that."

"You should look at it sometime. Anyway, what's your question?"

"Do you remember the passage that says a person shouldn't worship God for the sake of a reward, but rather *not* for the sake of a reward?"

"Of course. It's in Chapter One. Apparently, it means that one should worship God *lishmah* — that is, for its own sake."

"Yes, but I was wondering if you could possibly explain that. Does that mean worshipping God for no reason at all?"

"Of course not. That's absurd."

"Then what does it mean for a person to worship God 'for its own sake' and not because of a reward? It makes sense to me that someone would do something if it brings them happiness or pleasure. But what other motive could there be for doing something?"

"So you're asking about the nature of religious motivation – that is, why should a person behave religiously? You can ask the same question about ethics or morals, that is, *why* should a person behave morally or 'do the right thing,' aside from the obvious self-interested motivations such as wanting others to treat you in kind, not wanting to suffer social censure or go to jail, and so on."

"Yes. That's exactly what I'm trying to understand."

"Those are good questions. I think I may have an answer for you. But it's a rather long answer. In order to understand the true nature of moral motivation, one requires first an understanding of what is the true nature of the good, from an objective point of view. If you truly understand the nature of the good, you will recognize that certain beings are inherently better than others, and that certain actions are inherently better than others. And that in itself will make clear why it makes sense to do the right thing – not for the sake of some ulterior motive or reward, but just because it's right, that is, for its own sake."

"I think I understand what you're trying to say. But I'm not even sure I believe in this . . . um . . . objective good that you're talking about."

"I'm not surprised. Many philosophers, and indeed many ordinary people, reject the idea of an objective good. They think that the good is subjective, or relative. That one person's belief or one culture's belief about what is good is just as valid as any other person's or culture's. That what's good for one person may be bad for another, and so on. Actually, relativism is not a new view at all. It is actually quite ancient, as one can see from Plato's dialogues. And if you accept relativism, then perhaps there really is no adequate motivation for behaving morally, especially in those cases where doing so conflicts with self-interest. But, personally, I reject relativism. That's because I think there is a rational way of determining that certain things or beings are objectively better than others, and that certain actions are objectively better than other actions. Once you understand that certain actions are objectively better than others, you will understand why it makes sense to do good actions for their own sake."

"Wow. Well, I'd love to hear you explain your view."

"It might take a while. This is a very complex matter. But I suppose that if we don't get through it all today, we might just continue some other time."

"That's fine with me."

"All right. First, think about what it means to ask whether any given thing, call it x, is a good x. For example, if you're talking about a car, and you ask what it means for the car to be a good car, you probably have some idea in mind about what makes a car a good car."

"Yes. That sounds right."

"Or if you have in mind a tree, or a lampshade, or even a human being – in each case, if you ask what it means for something to be a good tree, or carrot or lampshade, you have in mind some set of characteristics that make for a good tree, a good lampshade, or a good human being."

"I follow so far."

"Now, the relativist claims that there is no objectively correct way of deciding which characteristics make for a good x of any kind. For example, one person might say that a good tree is one is that is tall and green, but another person might say that a good tree is short and has lemons. So it would be arbitrary to insist that we should judge the goodness or badness of a tree by whether it meets one set of criteria as opposed to another. And so, the relativist claims, there is no fact about the matter as to which set of characteristics is better for a tree to have. The same point applies to anything else, including humans. Hence, there is no objective standard by which we can judge whether a given human is a good human or not."

"Yes, that's the problem."

"Furthermore, the relativist insists there is no objectively correct set of criteria by which we can judge that a tree is better than a carrot or, for that matter, that a human is better than a lampshade . . . which, of course, can lead to some rather frightening consequences."

"Exactly, Dr. Maimon. You've stated the relativist position very well."

"Well, consider this. Instead of posing the question of whether some x is good insofar as it is an x, let us pose the question of whether a given x is good *insofar as it is a being*. Don't you agree that this is the most basic way one can possibly pose the question of whether something is good?"

"Sorry, I don't follow."

"Consider a lampshade, for example. The most basic way that you can speak about it is insofar as that thing is a *being* or *thing*. There's a difference between asking whether a lampshade is a good lampshade and asking whether it is a good thing or being. The latter is clearly more fundamental than the former. Isn't that right?"

"I guess so. But I still don't see where you're going with this."

"Be patient. So far, you've agreed that the most basic way in which you can ask about whether something is good is, insofar as it is a being."

"I'm not sure I even understand what that question is asking."

"Let's go back a step, then. The question on the table is whether there is some objective way of determining whether some things are better beings than others. Right? That means we have to be able to ask whether something is good not insofar as it is a certain kind of being, such as, a lampshade, a car, or a human, but rather insofar as it meets, or fails to meet, the criteria *for a better or worse being*."

"Ah! I think I understand the question now. But in what way might some being be better than another, just insofar as it is a being?"

"Very good. *Now* you're asking the right question: are there any criteria by which we can judge one being to be a better being than another? Well, suppose I could show you that certain features or properties would make one being a better being than another being, insofar as both things are beings."

"OK. Then what?"

"Then I'd go a long way toward refuting relativism. For, if it could be established that certain features or properties would make one being a better being than another being, *insofar as they are beings,* this would entail that in effect, it *is* an objective matter of fact that certain things are *better* than others, simply insofar as they are beings."

"Hmm. Maybe that's true. But, how can it be shown that certain things are inherently better than others insofar as they are beings?"

"Listen, and I'll show you. Consider the property of eternality, for example. Isn't it the case that a being that is eternal is less limited *in its being* than a being that isn't eternal?"

"I'm not sure. Why is that?"

"Simple. Something that is mortal is subject to death – in other words, the lack of being, or non-being! But something that's eternal is not subject to non-being in that way. Therefore, the being of an eternal being is in some sense superior to the being of something that is mortal."

"Yes, I suppose that's true."

"Well then! We've established something very crucial: it is an *objective matter of fact* – not a matter of mere taste or subjective opinion – that a being that is eternal is better *in its being* than a being that is mortal."

"Yes, that does seem right."

"And there are other properties like that. Do you recall the distinction we once made in class between necessary existence and contingent existence?"

"I think so. We learned about that when we did Aquinas's arguments for God's existence. A contingent being is one that might or might not have existed. A necessary being is one that, somehow, must exist."

"Exactly. Now, consider the property or quality of *necessity* or *necessary existence.* Clearly, a being that has *necessary existence* is superior *in its being* to a being that has merely *contingent* existence. It has, so to speak, a 'higher' kind of being."

"Yes. That seems true, too."

"Good. Now let's compare the notion of a finite or limited being with the notion of an infinite or unlimited being. Clearly, the being of an infinite or unlimited being would be better or superior to that of a finite or limited being."

"I'm not sure I even understand what it means for some being to be infinite in its being. But I guess an infinite being would be better in its being than a finite one. Dr. Maimon, this is beginning to sound a lot like God."

"No surprise! What else should you expect? Traditionally, God is conceived as *the best possible being,* which means that God should have all the properties that are good for a being to have, insofar as it is a being. But, let's be very careful here. I'm not saying that an eternal, necessary, infinite being actually exists. My point right now is only that conceptually speaking, and from an objective point of view, a being that has these qualities would be better in its being than a being that lacks these qualities. Do you follow?"

"Yes, I do."

"Now, let's consider a different property – namely, power. I propose that power – if understood correctly – is one of those properties that make a being better in its being than a being that lacks power."

"Hmm. That sounds like a scary thought. Somehow it doesn't sound very . . . um . . . Jewish."

"David, nothing I'm saying right now is based particularly in Judaism! What I'm saying right now is based on rational reflection. But since you brought it up, let me remind you that according to Judaism, the best being is God, who is traditionally conceived as supremely powerful. And besides, as you'll see in a moment, there's a distinction between power and brute force, which might be what you have in mind when you suggest that what I said doesn't sound 'Jewish.' But forget about Judaism for now, and just think very carefully about the nature of power. Don't you agree that power is a capacity or an ability that some thing or being has?"

"Yes."

"So, if a being has a certain power, that being must have the wherewithal, or causal resources, to do certain things. Let me give you an analogy just to establish this point. Think about the sun for a moment. The sun has the power to make the grass grow through the shining of its rays on the grass. But the sun has the power to do that only because it has a tremendous amount of energy, which it then radiates toward earth."

"True."

"In other words, the power that the sun has to make the grass grow seems to be an expression of something that lies within the sun itself. So, in other words, power is an expression of one's being. In other words, any power which a being has is a kind of potential energy that is stored in that very being itself. For if that potential were absent from the being, it would not have that power after all. Do you agree?"

"Yes, I think so."

"So it makes sense to think that if one being is more powerful than another, then, that first being is greater *in its being* than that other."

"I guess you're right, but I'm not sure."

"Let me give you another example. Suppose you have two beings: let's call them A and B. Now suppose that A can bring other beings into existence, but B cannot. It follows that A is greater in its being than B. That's because there must be something within A, but not within B, that gives A the wherewithal, the causal resources, to produce other beings, that is, to make other beings come to be. In other words, A is, so to speak, richer in its being than B."

"I guess that sounds right."

"So, having reached this stage, we can go back to the point about a finite versus an infinite being. You balked at this notion earlier, since you were puzzled as to what an infinite being would be like. Allow me to suggest that you think of an infinite being as one that is infinite in power, and a finite being as one that is limited in power. Again, I'm not asserting that such a thing exists. But conceptually, surely you can contrast these two notions in your mind?"

"Yes."

"Good. Now, once you've accepted the notion that a being that has power is better in its being than a being that lacks power, it clearly follows that a being that is unlimited or infinite in its power would be better in its being than one that is limited or finite in power."

"I guess so."

"I'll take that as agreement. Now, we're getting to a really important point. Suppose I could show that there are actually different kinds of powers, such that some powers are superior to others. It would follow that a being with the better kind of power would be superior in its being to a being with a lesser kind of power."

"I guess that follows from what we said before. But what do you mean? What kind of powers would be superior to others?"

"In particular, I'm thinking of intelligence. It's a special power for a number of reasons. First, a being that's intelligent can use its other powers with great effect. But a more important reason is that only a being that has intelligence can be an agent – that is, someone who understands, deliberates, and makes rational choices. A being that is unintelligent cannot be an agent, no matter how powerful it is. In other words, only a being that is intelligent has free choice, which is a very special kind of power. This is a kind of power that, I believe, human beings have."

"I see. So you believe in free choice?"

"Yes, I do. Basically, to have free choice is to be able to act rationally. A being that lacks intelligence doesn't choose to act. It just does whatever it's programmed to do either by biology or mechanics, like an elevator or a bumblebee. Animals have some degree of free choice, to the extent that they have intelligence. And since humans are by nature the most rational of all animals, we have the highest level of choice. Of course, the kind of free choice that we humans have is limited and highly conditional. It's not perfect freedom. That's because our power is limited, as well as our intelligence. A being that had unlimited intelligence – if such a being existed – would be the best possible being. But in any case, a being that has free choice is qualitatively more powerful than a being that lacks free choice. In fact, it could be argued that a being that lacks free choice doesn't have any genuine power at all! Alternatively, it could be argued that if a being lacks free choice, it may have 'power' in a certain sense, but it's not the kind of power that is an expression of one's being, and so, it is not the kind of power that is a mark of the greatness of one's being. That was the flaw, by the way, in my earlier example of the sun."

"I think I lost you somewhere in there. Can you run that by me again?"

"I'll try. Earlier, I mentioned the sun as an example of something that has great power. But obviously, the sun is not intelligent. So it doesn't have free choice. It does what it does due to circumstances beyond its control."

"True. So?"

"So, in a sense, the sun itself does not have any power at all. We should rather say that it has brute force. Alternatively, we could say that the sun has 'power,' but the kind of power that it has is not an expression of its own being. Any power that the sun exerts is really due to cosmic circumstances that far surpass the sun itself. The sun has energy, and radiates that energy outward, but only because of the laws of nature and other circumstances beyond the sun itself. Do you follow?"

"I think so."

"So compared to some being that has free choice, the sun is actually an inferior being. It also follows that, as a rule, human beings are superior in their being to anything else that lacks free choice. And —"

"Wait a minute, now. You're still going too fast for me. Can you restate why a being that has free choice is better in its being than one that lacks free choice?"

"I'll try this once again. A being that has free choice has the wherewithal, the causal resources, to make something happen that is truly a result of its own being. When you do something out of free choice, it is truly an expression of yourself. So a being that has free choice is truly powerful in a way that a being that lacks freedom is not. And therefore, based on the premise that we agreed on earlier — that power is an objectively good quality, it now follows that a being that has free choice is superior in its being to a being that lacks freedom."

"OK. I think I'm beginning to get it."

"Excellent. Then we've established a crucial point. Namely, it's an objective fact that human beings are superior, in their very being, to non-humans or at least to anything that lacks free choice. Another way of saying the same thing is to say that persons have a certain *inherent value* or *intrinsic worth* that non-persons lack. To say that a being has inherent value is to say that it has some feature in its being by virtue of which it is superior, in its being, to other beings that lack that very feature."

"So human beings have intrinsic worth . . . ."

"Exactly! And by the way, it also follows that if there is a being that has a higher kind of intelligence and freedom than humans do, that being would be superior, in its very being, to human beings."

"That would be God, I suppose."

"Precisely. Of course, let's be careful. Nothing I've said even remotely shows that God exists. But as you know, the traditional idea of God is the idea of an eternal, necessary, supremely free being. So based on what I have already said, it is an objective matter of fact — not simply an expression of taste or arbitrarily held opinion — that a being such as God would be supremely better than a being that is mortal, contingent, and not supremely free."

"Hmmm. Well, everything you've said seems to make sense, but I still don't know if I agree."

"I'm not surprised. Even if my argument were airtight and your intellect were totally persuaded, it would take some time for you to really start believing it. That's normal. Even after hearing a good argument, people don't change philosophical views overnight. We are not just intellectual creatures. We are physical creatures as well, and therefore creatures of habit. That's just the human condition! Anyway, let's go back to your original question."

"My original question?"

"Don't you remember? Your original question was: what does it mean for a person to worship God or do what's right just for its own sake."

"Oh, right! I got so absorbed in what you were saying, that I almost forgot about that. So how does all of this stuff about moral objectivism answer my question?"

"Well, we're almost there. As you said, *Pirkei Avot* teaches that we should serve God *lishmah,* for its own sake. Now, this teaching is based on the unstated premise that it is an *objective matter of fact* that God is the Supreme Being. The Talmud takes that for granted. So the teaching of *Pirkei Avot* is that one should worship God *not* for the sake of attaining some reward which God may or may not dole out. Rather, one should worship God just for its own sake, which is to say, purely out of the recognition of the fact that God is the Supreme Being. Do you follow?"

"Yes, I think so."

"And something similar goes for moral motivation in general."

"What do you mean?"

"We've established that it's an objective matter of fact that human beings have inherent worth: they are inherently superior to plants and animals. And that's true whether or not God exists. Because whether or not God exists, humans are rational creatures, and therefore, they have free choice, and they have inherent worth. Now, to act morally or ethically is to treat human beings with respect – that is, to acknowledge their worth. Human beings deserve respect because they have intrinsic worth as creatures with intelligence and free choice. And that's what morality is mostly all about: treating humans with respect."

"Wow. So you think objective morality doesn't depend on God's existence."

"That's correct. Like I said, whether or not God exists, humans have intrinsic worth, and they are worthy of respect. That is an objective fact even if God doesn't exist."

"Hmm. Do you think we can have free choice even if God does not exist?"

"Why not? Free choice depends on rationality or intelligence. We're rational, even if God doesn't exist. So we also have free choice, even if God doesn't exist. Do you see some difficulty with that?"

"I'm just trying to get clear on your view. Go on."

"Fine. So, getting back to morality, if you ask why a person should act morally, that's just like asking why we should treat people with respect. And the proper answer to that is: because human beings are worthy of respect – that is, because it's the right thing to do. In other words, one should do it for its own sake!"

"I think I see what you're saying. But can't I still ask why we should do that? Suppose I agree that humans have intrinsic worth and that they are inherently superior to plants and animals. Still, what's in it for me to treat people with respect?"

"Ah, but now you're asking what's in it for you, and that's obviously a question about self-interest. What do you have to gain by behaving morally? The answer to *that* question may very well be 'Nothing,' or it may be that behaving morally will benefit you somehow – but either way, it's beside the point. The real reason you should behave rightly is not for the sake of personal gain. It's rather because it's the right thing to do – or, to use the language of the *Pirkei Avot*, do it *lishmah!*"

"Hmm. I think I see what you're saying, but I don't know. Even if everything you say is correct, I'd still like to hear more about the what's-in-it-for-me question. Do you think there is a reward for behaving morally, or for keeping the Torah?"

"Ah! That's an entirely separate issue. And I'm sorry, but it really is time for me to go. I need to pick up my daughter at day care."

"Oh, sorry. I didn't even know you had a daughter!"

"How could you know? But I do have a daughter, and I do need to pick her up."

"OK, sure. Thanks, Dr. Maimon. Thanks so much for your time. That was really enlightening."

"No problem. I enjoyed talking with you. See you in class!"

18

November 15, 2000

Dear Mom,

I got your letter this morning. I'm glad to hear you're feeling so much better. Please write and tell me everything that's going on. Thanks to you, I've really gotten into writing. You were so right about letter writing, and also keeping a journal. It really helps to crystallize your thoughts and get out what's on your mind.

Things are sure busy here. School's hard, but I'm doing pretty well, working hard on my classes, and still reading and studying more about Judaism. Don't worry – I am staying out of "trouble." I am certainly not smoking or drinking. How could I do that and still be a runner? You really do worry about me too much, Mom.

I've gotten to know Phil a lot better. He's the grad student I wrote you about a while ago. We have great discussions about all sorts of things. What's so amusing about him is how he explains why the life of the philosopher is the best, yet he does it in such a cool and self-deprecating manner that it's hard not to like him. He's the most unsnobbiest snob I've ever met! According to him, the life of the mind, which is of course the philosopher's life, is the best and noblest form of human existence. Sometimes, I think I'm even beginning to agree with him! Speaking of writing, the funny thing is that Phil is writing his dissertation trying to support the claim that genuine philosophy only takes place in conversation and not in written works. I'm not sure I agree with that. Actually, now that I'm writing about it, I realize the irony of the dissertation is that since it is a written work, it has to fail in some way in order to establish its own conclusion that written philosophy is somehow not genuine. In other words, the dissertation has to fail in order to succeed! He also thinks philosophy is superior to religion, and I'm not sure I agree with that either. He sure makes a good case, though. It seems he can always win any argument I ever have with him.

Speaking of religion (or at least, philosophy of religion) I've been working on my paper on The Quarrel. Last time, you told me you were going to rent it. Did you watch it yet? I've also gotten to know Dr. Maimon a little better too. I had a really long conversation with her in her office in which she explained her view on moral objectivism. (This view is opposed to moral relativism.) It's hard to summarize her whole argument, but basically she thinks that it's an objective fact that some beings are inherently better beings than others. For example, an eternal being (if such a being exists is another question) is better in its being than a non-eternal being, and an intelligent and free being (i.e., a human) is better than a non-free or predetermined being (e.g., a plant). It follows from this that the better beings deserve "respect," and also that certain actions are objectively better than others since they promote the being or welfare of those inherently better beings. I think this is a kind of optimistic view because it says that being, or reality, is itself inherently good. It would be nice to think that we live in a world that is inherently good! Anyway, I'm guessing that Dr. Maimon believes in God (i.e., the ultimate being), but I can't even be sure of that. It seems to fit with her view. At some point I've got to just ask her about that. It's funny how in a certain way she is so much like Phil, yet obviously they're also very different.

I've gotten friendly with another sophomore, Esther Applefeld. Not a girlfriend technically, just a friend (so far). She really knows a *lot about Judaism and she's quite into it. She's taught me quite a lot already. I'm trying to teach her ~~a thing or two~~ a little about philosophy, but I don't know if I'll succeed.*

Please keep the letters coming.

Love,

David

19

"Dr. Maimon? It's me, David Goldstein. Sorry, I know I don't have an appointment . . . ."

"That's OK. Come in. What is it? Please, have a seat. Did you want to talk more about your paper? Or did you have another question about *Pirkei Avot*?"

"Well, no. It's something else."

"What is it?"

"Dr. Maimon, I think you know I'm enjoying your class very much. The thing is – every time you present the views of one philosopher, you do it so well that I think that philosopher must be right. But the next time in class, you point out all the flaws in their arguments. The same thing happens with the next philosopher and the next. So what I'm really curious about is, what do *you* think about the answers to the big questions?"

"I see. David, I think I'd better explain something. In this course, I aim just to present the material and let the students form their own opinions. At this level, it's not important for the students to know what *I* think. It's important for you to begin to figure out what *you* think. I don't want to be a guru. In my graduate courses and in my own writing, I'm not bashful at all about stating my own views. But that's not my role in this class."

"Sorry, but I'm not sure I understand. Last time we spoke, you gave me your own view about moral objectivism – which, by the way, I really enjoyed hearing. Why can't you tell me about your own views in philosophy of religion?"

"Ah, but that was different – your question was about moral philosophy, not philosophy of religion. I'm not your instructor for moral philosophy, so I feel a little more comfortable sharing my own views in that area."

"All right. Well . . . does that mean I have to wait till I finish the course before I get to hear your own views in philosophy of religion?"

"Either that, or you could read some of my articles."

"Are you sure? Is there anything I can do to change your mind? I like listening to you talk, and it gives me the chance to ask questions as well."

"David, I'd really rather wait until the end of the semester to have this kind of conversation with you. But since you're that anxious about it, I guess I can make an exception. All right, what do you want to quiz me about?"

"Thanks! OK, first of all, I noticed that you took off class for Yom Kippur."

"Yes, I did. What about it?"

"Is that because you're religiously observant?"

"Yes, I am."

"So, do you believe in God?"

"Yes, I do."

"And do you believe that the Torah is divinely revealed?"

"Yes, I do. However, exactly what that means is a complicated issue. David, I must say, you seem relieved."

"I guess I am. It's only because I respect your opinion so much!"

"That's exactly what I was afraid of. It's what I meant about not wanting to be a guru, or even a rabbi, for that matter! Well, anyway, I assume you have a follow-up question?"

"Oh, yes, lots of them."

"Fire away, then."

"Dr. Maimon, do you think your belief in God and the Torah are *rational* beliefs?"

"Of course. If I didn't think they were rational, I wouldn't have them."

"That's what I thought. So, am I correct in assuming that you think God's existence can be proven?"

"Ah, that's not a simple matter. Regarding certain aspects of God, such as God's reality, oneness, necessity, eternality – I think belief in God is eminently rational and, in fact, demonstrable – as long as you have the right understanding of God, which is a long story. In fact, I'd say that in a certain sense, I'm more convinced that God is real than I am convinced about anything else, including the belief that I am sitting here in my office! But regarding other aspects of God, such as divine freedom, providence, benevolence, justice – matters that concern God's involvement in human history, including the revelation of Torah – I think these beliefs are rationally defensible, but not rationally demonstrable."

"That sounds interesting, but I'm a little puzzled. Can something be rationally defensible but not rationally demonstrable?"

"Sure. A claim is rationally demonstrable if it can be conclusively proved. A claim is rationally defensible if I can describe good reasons for believing in it, and I can come up with reasonable responses to objections. However, those reasons and responses might not be convincing to everyone."

"How can that be? If you've got good reasons, everyone should find it convincing."

"Oh, no, not necessarily. David, perhaps you have an overly simplified view of rationality. There's a difference between what's rationally compelling and what's rationally defensible. There are many intelligent people out there who don't believe in God, and they're not all crazy! In fact, Judaism itself teaches that God is more evident to human beings at certain times in history than at others. For example, Judaism teaches that at Sinai, God revealed Himself directly to the Jewish people. If you had experienced Sinai in anything like the way it's described in the Scriptures, presumably you'd have to be irrational – or perhaps even sinful – not to believe in God's involvement in human history."

"Yes, I suppose that's true."

"According to the Talmud, something similar was true during the time of the first temple, at least in its heyday. God's involvement with human events was supposedly very evident. But the Talmud also teaches that, ever since the *galut* – the exile – God's reality is less obvious. And during some periods, such as during the Holocaust, God seems absent altogether. The Torah itself mentions the concept of *hester panim* – that God hides his face, so to speak. So I don't think anyone today can demonstrate there is a providential and benevolent God who gave Israel the Torah. But I still think it's rationally defensible to believe in God and the Torah."

"I'm still not sure I get it. Either something is provable or it isn't. How can there be a gray area between those extremes?"

"David, don't you find that rational people differ over controversial issues all the time? It's a sign of intellectual maturity to accept this fact. Only people who think like children believe that everything is either black or white. These are the same people who, at best, ignore any arguments against their beliefs – and, at worst, vilify their opposition as emissaries of the devil. Many beliefs we have today are genuinely controversial. Take, for example, the controversy over abortion. Consider the belief that abortion is morally permissible, especially in the early stages of pregnancy. That's a rationally defensible belief, even if it can't be proven. You can give reasons for it, you can argue for it, but you can't prove it. In fact, some philosophers would say that any moral or 'value belief' is going to be like this. Aesthetic judgments – judgments about art or taste – are also like this. For example, someone who really understands music could probably give a detailed argument about why Bach is better than Brahms. Still, that argument will persuade some people, but not everyone. Do you follow?"

"I think so."

"Well, the same thing holds in the case of religious beliefs. A belief in God is partly a 'value belief' – it carries with it a whole set of commitments about what is good and what is bad. So, how could you possibly expect anyone to prove conclusively that Judaism is true?"

"I never thought of it that way, but I guess you're right."

"Furthermore, you should recognize that the belief in God, or at least, the belief in the God of Judaism, is a belief in a world view – that is, a complicated, multilayered package of beliefs about lots of things. Judaism involves beliefs not only about God and the nature of mankind, but also some historical beliefs about the past, the present and the future. So it's impossible that there be one simple argument for it. Thus, while I might be able to give good reasons for belief in

God, I admit that I can't prove it in the way that I could prove for example, that sugar dissolves in water, or that the Pythagorean Theorem is true. You just can't expect that an entire world view can be argued for in that way."

"But then, how can you argue for a world view?"

"Good question! Perhaps the only way to argue for a world view is to articulate that world view in as clear and coherent a manner as possible. The articulation of a world view is an ongoing project, something that a multitude of scholars have to take on all together. It involves spelling out that world view in detail. The more completely and coherently the articulation, the more rationally defensible it is to believe and accept that world view. Furthermore, the point at which one person makes the judgment that a given world view is rationally defensible may be very different from the point at which another person makes that judgment. It's a judgment call that each intelligent person has to make for himself."

"I see. Dr. Maimon, what you're saying makes a lot of sense. Still, the bottom line is that you *do* think your belief in the God of Judaism is rationally defensible."

"Yes, that's correct."

"So you really *do* believe that's there's a super-power God, – a non-physical, non-spatial being who created the world and who watches over it, checking up on us to see how we're behaving?"

"David, it sounds like you're thinking of God as if he were the proverbial old man in the sky with a white beard. And that's pretty much the standard conception of God that you find among most religious people these days whether they are Jewish, Christian, or Muslim. But I must say, I personally don't think of God quite that way. In fact, I'm working on a book in which I describe my own conception of God . . . ."

"That sounds interesting. Can you tell me about your conception?"

"Oh, no. I'm afraid my theory is too complicated to describe in conversation. I think you'll just have to read my book when it comes out."

"Can't you just tell me a little bit about it?"

"I hesitate to do so. You might end up more confused than you started!"

"Please, Dr. Maimon, I'm really anxious to hear your views. I'll do anything you ask . . . and I promise not to get confused!"

"Very funny. Well, since you are so persistent, I'll try to explain my conception of God. There's no way we can finish in one day. But we can get started and I can finish some other time."

"That sounds great."

"All right, then. First, let's restate the popular or standard conception of God in a little more detail. Most religious people think of God as an *entity*, that is, a substance, or a being who interacts with the world. They think of that entity as having various attributes or traits. For example, God is conceived as perfect, one, infinite, necessary, intelligent, benevolent, just, and so on. The essence is the divine entity itself, and this essence causes certain actions. The so-called 'metaphysical attributes' apply to God's essence, while the 'attributes of action' describe the way or ways in which God's essence acts in the world. On this conception, God is a non-physical being who stands apart from the world and yet interacts with it. Does this sound to you like an accurate description of the standard conception of God?"

"Yes, I think so."

"Now, I admit that most religious people probably need to think of God as an entity. That's how I myself used to think of God. But it's got lots of problems. For one thing, if God is an entity, then it seems God is subject to the laws of logic. For example, God cannot create a square that is round, he cannot create a stone that is uncreated, and in general he cannot make some thing which has logically contradictory properties. And if so, God is subject to something outside of Himself – namely, the laws of logic. All this is a problem if one thinks of God as an entity. But that's not the way I think of God."

"So, how do you think of God?"

"There are two parts to my conception of God. First, I conceive of God's essence as *being itself*. And second, I conceive of God's character traits as consisting in certain principles which describe the way the universe operates, insofar as the universe is an expression of being itself."

"Hmm. The idea that God is being itself sounds interesting. But it doesn't sound like a Jewish view to me. It sounds more like an eastern conception of God."

"I thought you might say that. Indeed, on the surface, it seems that God is depicted in the Torah as a being. The popular conception of God takes the Torah literally on this. But not everything in the Torah needs to be understood literally. By the way, do you know the proper name of the deity in the Torah?"

"Yes. It's Hashem."

"No, not exactly. It's often referred to as Hashem, which means, simply, 'the name.' But the name itself is the one that's spelled *yod, heh, vav, heh*. It is sometimes known as the four-letter name, or the Tetragrammaton."

"Ah, right. Now I remember."

"And did you also know that the grammatical root of the *yod-heh-vav-heh* is the same as the word for 'being' in Hebrew?"

"No, I didn't know that."

"Indeed, all of the Hebrew words for being, such as *is, was,* and *will be,* are forms of the basic Hebrew root *heh-vav-heh*. So, arguably, the proper name of God in the Torah may be translated as *being itself*."

"Interesting. But, Dr. Maimon, if being is God, doesn't this amount to saying that God is everything? Isn't that pantheism?"

"No, that's incorrect. To say that God is being itself is not to affirm that God is everything."

"I don't get it. What does being itself mean, then?"

"Ah, well. What could be more difficult than explaining the very nature of being itself? I warned you this wouldn't be easy. But I'll try. David, have you studied Plato's theory of the forms?"

"Yes, we did that last year in my Intro course."

"Good. Do you remember that Plato distinguishes particulars from universals? For example, Plato would say that we can distinguish between particular red things and redness. Examples of red things are rose blossoms, drops of blood, and so on. These things exist at particular times and places. They come into being and they pass away. But redness is the property they all share. Redness itself isn't a particular red thing, redness is a universal. And redness does not mean 'all red things.' Redness is the property that all red things share. The same thing is true about triangles and triangularity. Triangles are particular things that take up space and time. But triangularity is not a triangle, nor does it refer to the collection of all triangles. Rather, triangularity is a universal. Are you following?"

"Yes."

"Good. So, in just the same way, we can distinguish between particular beings and the property of beingness – or, as I prefer to say, being itself. Examples of particular beings include you, me, and other creatures. Beingness, or being itself, is the property that they all have in common. In fact, some interpreters of Plato think that this is what Plato meant by the 'form of the Good.'

"I didn't know that. I don't think the professor mentioned that in my Intro course."

"That's because it's not a universally accepted interpretation. If that's what Plato meant, he certainly could have said so more explicitly. But whether or not this is an accurate interpretation of Plato's theory of the Good doesn't matter. The point is that we can make the distinction between particular *beings* and the universal *Being*. Do you agree?"

"Yes, I think so."

"Well, that's how I conceive of God's essence. God's essence is *Being itself,* or as I sometimes like to say, God's essence is *Being with a capital B.*"

"Very interesting. But, wait a minute. Are you saying that you agree with Plato's theory of the forms? Do you think that redness and triangularity are things that exist separately from red things and triangles?"

"No, I disagree with Plato on that point. I don't think that redness or triangularity exists. But I also don't think that triangularity or redness or Being are merely thoughts or concepts. I think that redness, triangularity, and all the forms are features of reality. Being is a feature of reality as well. In fact, it's the most basic feature of reality. In my view, Plato was mistaken if he thought that triangularity and redness exist as entities on their own. In fact, there are some scholars who think that in his later work, Plato rejected the belief in the separateness of the forms. Anyway, the important point is that the universe exhibits, or as Plato might say, 'exemplifies,' triangularity and redness. Similarly, the universe exhibits, or presents – or 'exemplifies' – being itself. In fact, any possible universe would exemplify being in one way or another. The same cannot be said for triangularity and redness. We can conceive of a world without any triangles or red things, but not without being!"

"But Dr. Maimon, if you say that God's essence is *being itself,* which is a universal, and you also hold that universals do not exist, then it follows that you can't say that God exists."

"Yes, that's correct."

"Sorry, Dr. Maimon, but now I'm really puzzled! Earlier you told me that you believe in God. Now you say that on your conception, you don't believe that God exists!"

"David, listen closely. What you take to be a criticism of my theory, I take to be an advantage! On my theory, it's just inaccurate to say that God *exists* – unless one is speaking loosely. In my view, God isn't *a* being! So God does not fall into the category of things that exist or do not exist. But just as redness and triangularity are real, in the sense that they are features of reality, so too, I would affirm that God is real."

"Ah, I think I get it. But wait – if God's essence is *being itself,* then, everyone should be a theist because it's obvious that there are beings, and that being is a feature of reality!"

"Right again! Do you realize that you've just stated a proof for the reality of God? That's why I said at the very outset that regarding certain aspects of God, demonstrable proof can be given. I think it's fair to call this a version of the ontological argument, which we discussed at the beginning of the semester. My claim is that if we think seriously about the very nature of Being itself, we realize the obvious fact that Being is real. This belief is more certain even than the belief that I am sitting here right now at my desk. As Descartes might say, perhaps I am dreaming right now and I am really lying in bed. But even if I am dreaming, and even if all of my life is a dream, there is no way I could be mistaken about the reality of Being itself!"

"All right. I guess it's true that everyone should accept the claim that Being is real in the sense that you have in mind. Still, that doesn't seem like much of a God. What about God's other properties?"

"Ah, *now* you're asking the right question. So let's think this through. Earlier, we said that on the traditional or popular conception, God is a being who is *ultimate, perfect, necessary, one, infinite, and transcendent* – meaning that God transcends time and space. We could also throw in the idea that God is radically *unique* – that is, radically unlike anything else. Now, it's very hard to prove that there exists *an entity* with all these properties. That's what Anselm apparently sought to prove in his version of the ontological argument. But on my conception of God, the metaphysical attributes are not properties of *a being,* but rather features of *being itself.* My argument here has its root not only in Anselm but in the pre-Socratic philosopher, Parmenides. It doesn't take too much effort to see that necessity, oneness, perfection, eternality – all the traditional metaphysical attributes – are features of Being."

"I'm not sure I get it. How so?"

"I'll try to explain. First of all, as I said before, anyone would have to agree that, in some sense, being is the most basic or fundamental aspect of reality. So everyone should agree that being itself is metaphysically *ultimate*. Being itself is also *perfect* – in the sense that it is complete, it cannot *be* any more than it already is, namely, being itself. Furthermore, it is a metaphysical truth that no one can deny that there are an infinite number of different possible ways in which Being could be exhibited or expressed. That is what it means to say that Being is *infinite*. At the same time, there are certain necessary constraints on what could be true in any possible universe. These are described in the laws of logic. In my view, that's what we mean when we say that Being – that is, God's essence – is *necessary*. And by the way, now you can see how my conception of God gets around a problem that plagues the standard conception. As I said earlier, if God were an entity, then God would be limited or bound by the rules of logic and necessity. But on my conception, when we talk about the essence of God, we are talking about Being itself. And necessity is a feature of being itself! There is no necessity *outside* of God. Rather, necessity is a feature of God, which is to say, it is a feature of reality."

"All right. I think I'm starting to get it."

"Furthermore, Being is unitary, or self-identical. Being is what it is, and it isn't not-being. Now, since it is identical with itself, then in some sense, it is one. That is what it means to say that, necessarily, Being is *one,* or *unitary*. Being is also *one* or *unitary,* in the sense that no matter how different you can imagine possible universes to be, they would all exhibit or exemplify Being itself. Even in our world, all things, no matter how different – rocks, water, fire, air, plants, animals, humans, planets, light waves – all these different things manifest or exhibit the very same *being itself*. In this way, Being is unlike anything else, and so we can say that Being is radically unique. We can also say that there is a clear and obvious sense in which Being is omnipresent. Wherever beings are, there you also find Being itself. Being is 'displayed' in any possible or actual being. And finally, being itself is not physical, it does not take up space, nor does it suffer change over time. Thus we can say that being itself – that is, God's essence – is transcendent. Oh, and by the way, based on all this, we can now say that it is objectively wrong to worship idols. For what that means in my interpretation is to treat anything other than Being itself as ultimate. But maybe we should leave my theory of idol worship for another time . . . ."

"Dr. Maimon, this all sounds very interesting. But I just thought of another question. You said something the very first day of class that stuck with me. In order to count as a theist, a person has to believe that God is *intelligent* and *free*."

"Yes, that's correct."

"So, how is *Being itself* intelligent and free? It seems to me that Being is impersonal."

"Excellent question, David. You're pushing me — I mean, my theory — in all the right places. In order to count as a theist, I *do* have to have some way of saying that Being is personal, that is, both intelligent and free. But first, let's take one step back and think about the popular conception of God as an entity. On the popular conception, God is conceived as intelligent, in the sense that he knows and understands all things, past, present, and future. Now, to my mind, this is one of the most difficult aspects of the popular conception. It boggles the human mind to fathom a being that can hold within it conscious knowledge of all facts – present, past, and future, all at the same time."

"Yes, I also find that difficult to grasp."

"Well, on *my* conception, we may understand all talk about the 'intelligence' of God or Being itself as a roundabout way of referring to the fact that *the universe has an order.* Not just *any* order, of course. The universe has a highly complex and pervasive order, one that runs through all things, past, present, and future. So, on my view, God is not an entity who *knows* all things in the way that a superhuman being might know all things. Rather, when we talk about 'God's mind' or 'God's intelligence,' that's really just a roundabout way of saying that the universe has an order. Do you follow?"

"Yes, I think so."

"Now, almost everyone agrees that the universe has an order. So, in my view, the statement 'God has intelligence' means something that is demonstrably true."

"I see. Well, I guess that sure makes things easier for your theory. But what about God's *freedom*? How are you going to say that Being is *free*? I can sort of understand what it means for *a being* to be free – it can choose to do certain things or not do them. But what could it possibly mean for *being itself* to be free?"

"Good question. But freedom may in fact be a little more complex than you think. So listen carefully to what I am about to say. Let's think hard about what God's freedom amounts to on the popular conception, which takes God as an entity. Basically, there are three elements involved in divine freedom. First, to say that God is free is to say that although God himself is a necessary being, at least some and possibly all of his actions are not necessary. In other words, they are contingent, which means that they could have been different from what they are. Second, it means that God is a being who has causal power, which means the power to produce or effect events for which he is solely responsible and that are not caused by anything outside of himself. Third, in claiming that God is free, the theist also affirms there is a reason why God chooses to do what he does, for otherwise those actions would not be freely chosen but rather arbitrary or capricious. In other words, even though God's actions are not necessary, there is still a *non-necessitating explanation* for why God caused those events. For example, traditionally, theists view God's creation of the world as a free action on God's part. This means that the existence of the world is *not* necessary. But it also means that God created the world for a reason. It wasn't merely arbitrary or capricious. Do you follow?"

"I don't know. I guess I'm not sure how can there be a 'non-necessitating explanation' for something."

"David, may I point out that your question here is just like your earlier question about how something can be rationally defensible, but not provable? Earlier, I pointed out that you were operating with an overly simplified view of what it means for a belief to be rational. Now you're operating with an overly simplified view of what it means to give an explanation!"

"Sorry, I really don't understand your point. What is a non-necessitating explanation?"

"I'll explain. A person, or even God, can have reasons for doing something even if he or she is not *logically compelled* to do that thing. For example, think of a creative artist, who expresses himself in his work. What the artist does is not logically necessary. If it were, we wouldn't call it creative. On the other hand, what the artist does must have some kind of rationale. It has to make sense in some way. Otherwise it would be merely random or arbitrary. In other words, once the artwork has been done, it has to make sense, even though, before it's done, it was not predictable. By the way, that's the secret to great art, and it's also the best answer to the age-old question of why God created the world."

"It is? How so?"

"Well, some theologians say that God had no reason whatsoever for creating the world. He did it out of pure will or something like that. But that makes for a capricious, absurd God. On the other hand, there is the emanationist theory that God necessarily created or gave rise to the universe, but that would imply that God is not truly free. I think that the only possible middle ground is to think of God's creation as a form of divine self-expression, in much the same way as an artist expresses himself in his work. To use the popular or vulgar way of talking, in which God is conceived as an entity, we would say that God didn't have to create the world. He wasn't logically compelled to do so. Still, there must be some kind of a rational explanation as to why God created the world. Otherwise, creation is arbitrary or absurd. And that's exactly what goes on in great art. You cannot predict what a great artist will do next. Otherwise, it would not be great art. Yet, once the artist does it, it somehow all makes sense that he did what he did! Indeed, if it doesn't make some kind of sense, it's not great art. It's just doing something new for the sake of doing something new, and that's not genuine creative art."

"Wow. That's a very interesting idea. I didn't think we'd end up talking about art, and I never thought about art quite that way."

"I'm glad you find it illuminating. But let's get back to God, and in particular let me explain now what it means for God to be free in my conception of God – where God is not conceived as an entity."

"OK, I'm listening."

"Now, just as there are three elements involved in what divine freedom means in the popular conception, there are three elements in my conception as well. In my conception, God is not an entity, so it's incorrect to think of God as having causal power. Being itself does not and cannot cause things to happen. Instead, in my view, to believe that God is free is to believe that, firstly, despite the fact that Being is necessary, nevertheless certain events happen which are themselves contingent. Again, almost everybody believes that there are some contingent events. Secondly, to say that God is 'free' is to say that there is an explanation for why contingent events happen, and that explanation has to do with certain features of *being itself.* That's something that I'll need to elaborate on later. Thirdly, to say that God is free is to say that the explanation for why contingent events happen is not a *necessitating* explanation, but rather a much looser, more relaxed kind of explanation. In other words, certain things that happen in our world *make sense* given the nature of being, but they are not *necessitated* by being itself. I caution you, this is one of the harder parts of my theory to grasp. But it'll make more sense after I go through the second part of my theory. So far we've been talking primarily about my theory of God's *essence.* We still need to talk about my conception of God's *acts* or *character traits.*"

"OK. But, Dr. Maimon, something puzzles me about what you've said so far. Can I ask one question before we go on? I was just thinking back to our conversation last time about objective morality."

"Yes. What about it?"

"I remember you said very clearly that your theory of moral objectivism does not depend on the assumption that God exists."

"True. I did say that."

"But didn't you also say that a being that is eternal, infinite, necessary, and free is inherently or objectively better than a being that is mortal, finite, and contingent?"

"Yes, I said that."

"And didn't you say that's what God is? I mean, didn't you say God is an eternal, necessary and infinite being?"

"No, actually I didn't. I was careful to say: that's how God is *traditionally* conceived."

"Oh, OK. But anyway, now you're saying that in your view, God is not a being."

"That's correct."

"So according to you, God is not the best possible being after all. Isn't that a strange thing for a theist to believe?"

"It sounds absurd only if you're fixated on thinking of God as a being or entity. In my view, God is not a being. In fact, God's better than that – God is being itself! Look, let me explain something. In our conversation last time, I was relying on the popular conception of God just for the purpose of discussion. My aim was to show you that there is a rational way to make distinctions about which beings are inherently better than other beings, or to defend the claim that certain beings are better than others *insofar as they are beings*."

"Yes, I remember that, and I really liked that part of your theory."

"Great. Well, now you should understand that nothing I said depended on the assumption that God is *a* being. If you thought so at the time, that was a mistake. Indeed, everything I said last time can be restated using the more sophisticated conception of God as being itself. Another way of putting the point is this. On the popular conception, God is the best being, because God has certain properties in virtue of which he is the best, insofar as he is *a being*. But in my conception, God *is* Being. So, it turns out that on my conception, God *is* the very standard by which one can judge the inherent worth or value of all beings!"

"OK, I think I get it. But I'm still puzzled. Is this really what it means to believe in God? What does this all have to do with things like divine revelation, the Bible, providence, and things like that? And why would anyone want to worship the kind of God you've described? Something seems to be missing here."

"David, I keep telling you there are two parts to my conception of God. We've only managed to get through the first part — namely, that God's essence is Being itself. The second part is how I understand God's attributes of action."

"OK, so how do you understand God's attributes of action?"

"The attributes of action have to do with the particular way or ways in which Being itself is made manifest or expressed in the world as we know it. Now — excuse me, but what time is it? Where is my watch? Oh, dear, it's three-thirty! I've got to leave immediately or I'll be late picking up my daughter from day care!"

"Dr. Maimon, I'm sorry I took up so much —"

"No, no, it's not your fault at all. We'll continue some other time."

"Yes, that would be great."

"Goodbye, then!"

"Goodbye. And thanks for the conversation!"

20

November 17, 2000

Dr. M is amazing. She's tough on the outside, but she softened up after a while. I'm actually starting to like her now. She mentioned her daughter again. Does she have a husband too? I wonder what he's like. But my head is still spinning. Can she be right? Does it really make sense to think of God as being itself? If it does, then I guess it's obvious that God ~~exists~~ *is real, at least in some sense. I still need to hear the rest of the theory. But now that I know she believes the Torah is divinely given, I want to ask her all sorts of questions* about Judaism, all the questions I was asking Rabbi A last year. She's obviously so different from Rabbi A or even Rabbi L.

I really liked the idea of God as creative artist. I was thinking that might explain the vastness of the universe — like, for example, the millions of stars and the millions of species on earth (even the ones that have died out) and the millions of species in the seas. If you say that the world was created just for man's sake, it hard to see why these millions are necessary. But if the universe is God's infinite self-expression, that's like saying that God creates the world "because he can." So the millions of stars and species are an expression of God, not necessarily for man's benefit alone. That makes more sense than saying that the entire universe was created just as a setting for the creation of man.

I was nervous at first but I'm glad I asked her about her own views. I'm not sure I follow everything she says, but she really seems to have thought it all through. Looking back in my journal I see that it was through writing that I came up with the idea of asking her about doing things for their own sake, and once I did that, it wasn't such a big deal asking her about God. I owe so much to Ravi. I haven't seen him in so long. I should really drop in. I miss his serenity. He's the one who suggested keeping the journal in the first place. He's also the one who advised me to stall on Helen until I figured out more or less what I'm doing with Judaism. Now I realize that's going to take much longer than I had thought. But still, he gave me good advice.

I need to get to work on my paper on The Quarrel. I finished reading Job (in English, of course). Very difficult and strange. I can't really follow a lot of it and it seems very repetitive. And I don't get the answer at the end, if it is an answer. Like Rabbi A said, the answer comes out at the end, when God says to Job basically this: "I'm God, you're not, so shut up and stop complaining!" It's not really an answer to the philosophical problem of how God can allow evil. It just begs the question about how can God allow suffering. Well, Dr. M warned me about it. It's not a philosophical work. Anyway I think I know what I'm going to say in my paper. I think the free will solution works up to a point but — oh, there goes the phone. Probably Dad. I'd better answer it. I'll come back to this later.

"Hello?"
"Hi, David. It's Esther."
"Esther, hi! What a nice surprise! What's going on? How are you?"
"Pretty good. What are you up to?"

"Oh, nothing much. Just working on my paper for . . . um . . . philosophy of religion."

"Really? What's it about?"

"The problem of evil."

"Deep stuff again! You don't stop, do you?"

"Actually, I've been talking a lot lately with my philosophy professor. We've gotten into some pretty intense conversations about God and things like that."

"You sure spend a lot of time with your professor. You must really like him."

"Him? No, it's Dr. Sofi Maimon! Don't you remember? She's the one who asked the questions at the end of Rabbi Low's lecture last spring."

"Oh, yes, I remember her. Well, that's great – but hey, look – are we on for coffee tomorrow or not?"

"Oh, sorry! I can't believe I forgot. I was supposed to call you . . . I'm really sorry . . . ."

"No problem, David. You've got more important things on your mind – just kidding! Seriously, are we still on for tomorrow?"

"Yes, definitely. See you at eleven o'clock?"

"Great. See you then!"

21

"Ah, it's the philosopher! Please come in. How are you, David?"

"Pretty good, Ravi. How have you been, O wise, holy and ancient one?"

"I'm fine. But I don't see too much of you any more. What's going on?"

"I've been busy with classes, and studying Judaism."

"Good for you. Have you been meditating?"

"Oh, off and on. I still have trouble getting into it. But actually, I wanted to thank you for a couple of things. First of all, you gave me the right advice about Helen. You know something? I'm not sure I was in love with her at all."

"Thanks for the compliment. But, as I recall, we never sorted out what love is, in the first place."

"Yes, that's true. But I still feel you gave me the right advice. And the other thing is – thanks for the idea about the journal. You were right. It's really been helpful."

"Indeed so. I found it to be helpful as well."

"You *found* it to be so? It sounds like you're talking about something in the past."

"It's definitely a help at a certain stage."

"Do you mean that you don't keep a journal anymore?"

"That's right. Sometimes I write a little poetry or maybe jot down an idea or two. But that's not really keeping a journal."

"Ravi, you're blowing my mind! I thought you said keeping a journal is always a necessary part of the spiritual journey."

"David, my friend! Once again you attribute words and thoughts to me that are not accurate. Do you remember that conversation in the Indian restaurant we had last year? The minute I said something positive about Buddhism, you assumed I was a Buddhist! Now, I never said keeping a journal is always a necessary part of the 'spiritual journey.' And I've already told you that I'm not comfortable using the phrase 'spiritual growth.' It makes it sound as if there is a certain goal in life that one is supposed to achieve or accomplish, when the truth is that enlightenment consists in ridding oneself of attachment to the objects of desire and in coming to realize that everything is truly one. I agree that for many people, journal writing is an important step in sorting out confusion, for finding the right path. But once you've found the path, the journal becomes irrelevant."

"Are you saying that once you've found the path, there's no room for change or growth?"

"Look, there's a time in one's life – usually around the late teens or early twenties – when a person struggles to determine what life is all about. At that time, a person is confused, so he needs to sort out what's true and what's false, what's important and what isn't. It's an incredibly exciting time, a time of turmoil. That's where change occurs. And that's where journal writing is crucial – to help sort out one's ideas. But once you find the path, the rest of life is just walking on that path. Of course, you *could* keep a journal all the way through, but it wouldn't serve the same purpose. It might even be a distraction and a source of self-absorption. At best, you might use it as a record of what's going on, rather than a means to achieving the goal."

"And what about meditation? You still meditate, don't you?"

"Yes, absolutely. I don't think I'll ever give up meditation."

"And how is that different from journal writing?"

"Oh, it's *very* different. Every time you meditate, you strip away the surface appearances and realize a unity with *that which truly is*. There's no getting around the need for meditation. But the purpose of keeping a journal is to sort out confusion. Once you're no longer confused, there's nothing more to sort out. Journal writing is like a ladder that's necessary for reaching a certain stage. Once you've reached that stage, you don't need the ladder any more. You just need to let the ladder fall away."

"Ravi, I think I follow you . . . but I don't think I agree. I think a person is bound to face challenges that confuse him and that he needs to sort out all through life, no matter how far advanced he is. Why would that ever stop?"

"Look. If a person reaches *enlightenment*, there just *is* no more confusion. At least, there's no more *existential* confusion. That's what enlightenment is all about! Of course, there may be challenges left in life, but those are only *technical* challenges, like, how to get food, how to get shelter, or even, things like how to make time for meditation, or how to help others reach enlightenment. And of course, a person who reaches enlightenment might conceivably write a book, such as a manual of instruction for others to follow. This is what many great spiritual people have done. But a truly enlightened person has no confusion about what the purpose of life is, or what is its meaning, or what is the nature of true happiness. So, at that point there is no need to keep a journal."

"It still sounds to me like you're saying that once a person reaches enlightenment, there's no more room for improvement. Can that be right?"

"David, the reason you find this puzzling is because you're still thinking of the spiritual life as a journey toward a goal, in which you achieve and accomplish things. And you're thinking about enlightenment as a state in which you achieve and accomplish even further things, maybe even, bigger and better things. But I believe this is a serious mistake. It is perhaps the crucial mistake of the West, which emphasizes *achievement, accomplishment, action*. Enlightenment is a state in which you realize that the apparent distinction between yourself and "reality" outside of you is false, and that there is a fundamental unity in all things. The way to reach enlightenment is precisely by *not*-doing, *not*-acting, *not*-accomplishing. And when you reach it – it's like descending into a calm, blissful pond. Once you realize this, there is nothing more to accomplish or achieve. In fact, all achieving or accomplishing is in some sense, a radical illusion. The truth is we are all part of a greater reality, which completely engulfs our individuality."

"OK, I think I follow. But now it sounds like you don't really believe in free will."

"Well, I certainly don't believe that humans are genuinely autonomous creatures, set over and against the rest of reality. Everything we do is merely an expression of *that which is* . . . that which is engulfs us and plays right through us. The false teaching of the West is the idea that we are all individual and autonomous free creatures, each with so called inalienable rights, each having intrinsic value. True enlightenment consists in being *aware* that there is no such thing as an autonomous self."

"Your view about humans fits very well with your view about ultimate reality."

"I should hope so. But what exactly do you mean?"

"Well, the western or Biblical perspective is that the ultimate reality is a 'person' in the sense of a free agent, a being who has the intelligence and freedom to choose what he does or does not do. That ultimate reality of course is God. But the eastern perspective is that the ultimate is *impersonal* – it's an *It*, not a *He*. So, it lacks freedom to choose."

"Yes, that's correct."

"And you were saying a moment ago that you don't think human beings are really persons either. I mean, they're not *persons* in the sense that they are not autonomous. Everything we do is really just an outflow of that which is beyond us."

"Right. Basically, personhood is an illusion."

"So, that's what I meant when I said, your view of the ultimate and your view of the human being go together. Both are really non-persons."

"Ah, now I see what you meant. Very true!"

"And all of this is related to why you think journal writing is only relevant at a certain stage."

"Well stated, David. You're a good student!"

"Thanks, Ravi. Well, anyway, maybe I'm stubborn, because I know free choice is a difficult concept. But I'm not sure I'm ready to give it up! And maybe that's why I'm having such a tough time with meditation."

"Maybe so. If you hold fast to your ego, meditation is very difficult indeed."

22

"David, how are you?"

"Good. What's new with you, George?"

"I'm doing great. How's your study of Judaism going? Are you still meeting with Rabbi . . . what's his name?"

"Rabbi Abraham? Uh . . . not too much lately. But I'm taking a course in philosophy of religion with Dr. Maimon. Have you heard of her? She's really brilliant. She presents things really well – all the arguments and positions on both sides. I've also been in contact with a guy named Rabbi Low – an Orthodox Rabbi in Israel. He's helped me a lot with some questions I've had."

"Oh? Like . . . what questions?"

"Basically, questions about the difference between Judaism and eastern conceptions of the ultimate, and actually about Christianity as well. In fact, I asked him some questions that have come up in our previous conversations. I asked him what he thought about the widespread success of Christianity, and the difficulty of keeping the Torah. I think he had some good responses. I can forward his emails to you on that subject if you'd like."

"Sure, please do. I'd be curious to see what he says. But I'm also curious . . . did he say anything about how Jews get atoned for their sins?"

"No . . . what do you mean?"

"How do Jews get atoned or cleansed for their sins, given that there is no longer a temple and no sacrifices, which the Old Testament says is necessary for atonement?"

"Hmmm . . . I don't know. To be honest, I haven't thought about that concept too much . . . it sounds kind of bizarre."

"Why? Atonement is an important concept, for Jews and Christians. Do you think people are morally and spiritually perfect?"

"No, of course not."

"Well, then they need atonement, somehow!"

"I guess so. I'll ask Rabbi Low about that too."

"Good. I'd also be curious to know what he thinks of Isaiah 53. That's where the prophecy occurs about the "suffering servant" who is going to come from the root of Israel. Have you read that passage?"

"Uh . . . no, I haven't."

"And there's also the passage about the new covenant. Are you familiar with that one?"

"No, I don't think so."

"I think it's in Jeremiah 31. God says that he will make a new covenant with Israel, and where he will 'write upon their hearts' the law. There are also similar passages in the book of Ezekiel. Do you know what I'm talking about?"

"Uh . . . sort of . . . you know . . . I'm still new at this."

"That's OK, no problem. I'm just suggesting these are things you should look into. Jeremiah 31 talks about God's purifying the people of Israel of their sins, turning hearts of stone into hearts of flesh, granting a 'new spirit' upon the people. What do you suppose all that means?"

"Uh . . . I don't know. Why? What do *you* think it means?"

"It's pretty clear what it means, if you just read the text and think about it in light of the gospels. Obviously, the new covenant is the New Testament. The word 'testament' is just another term for 'covenant.' It's a pact or agreement. And while the Old Testament represents God's pact with the Israelites, the new covenant is the pact made with all mankind through Christ. The writing 'upon the hearts of the law' is the internalization of the law within the soul, which occurs when a person accepts Christ. And through the sacrifice of Christ, and through our acceptance of that sacrifice – that's how atonement occurs. It's kind of like discarding the shell and being left with the kernel. Now I realize Jews don't accept all this. But I was just wondering, how do Jews think they get atonement these days, given that there are no sacrifices any longer?"

"I have no idea, George. I must admit, I'm not really up on all those passages you mentioned. I'll have to . . . uh . . . look into all these things . . .".

23

From: rlow@ahavattorah.org.il   **Sent:** 12/1/00 10:06 AM
To: dgoldstein@cuniv.edu
Subject: Creation, evolution, and the Torah

Dear David,

Sorry it's taken so long to get back to you. I hope you're well. Things have been somewhat hectic here in the yeshiva. A close friend of one of our students was killed in a suicide bombing attack a few days ago. The student was actually supposed to be on the bus with his friend when it happened, but his plans changed at the last second. As you might imagine, he has needed a lot of support. But things have calmed down a bit and I finally have a little time to write.

The question is: how can we reconcile the theory of evolution with the account of creation in the Torah? Actually, I think there are four separate but related issues where there seems to be conflict.

1. Modern cosmologists theorize that the universe or cosmos as we know it is billions of years old. But Scripture says that creation took six days, and Jewish tradition says the world is less than six thousand years old.

2. Modern science theorizes that the various species on earth evolved, while Scripture seems to depict each species as having been created separately.

3. Modern science says that there are fossils and extinct species that apparently lived millions or billions of years ago. How is this consistent with the claim that the world is less than six thousand years old?

4. The theory of evolution says that human beings evolved from apes, while Torah says that the original human being, Adam, was created singly and from "earth." (This may seem like it falls under the second issue, but I think it needs to be treated separately.)

The various approaches to these problems fall into three categories. The first approach holds strictly to a literal interpretation of the Torah and utterly rejects the theory of evolution. One can do so either by rejecting modern science altogether, by rejecting only the theory of evolution, or by trying to argue that evolution is not scientifically justified (this is sometimes called "creation science" or "intelligent design").

The second approach is to accept the entire theory of evolution as truth and to interpret the account of creation as a metaphor.

I will not say anything more about these first two approaches. It is the following third approach which I favor, which is to find some middle ground – that is, to accept the theory of evolution in part, but to reject other parts of it as not scientifically justified. In this approach, one interprets some passages of the Torah non-literally but holds fast to a literal interpretation of other passages. I will now address each of the four questions in detail, using this third approach.

The first question concerns the age of the universe. This is only a problem if you take the word *yom* in the creation story as a twenty-four-hour day. Although many traditional commentators and many contemporary Orthodox Jews do take it this way, there is no compelling reason to do so. The word *yom* can also mean a period of time, such as an eon, which is, of course, a very long time. (Elsewhere we find that the word *yamim*, the plural of *yom*, means "a year." See Leviticus 25:29, Numbers 9:22.) In fact, there is ample textual reason to think that in the creation story, the term *yom* does not mean a twenty-four hour period. The Torah indicates that the sun, moon and stars were created on the "fourth day." So obviously, the first three days were not normal days as we know them. Now, if the six days of creation are really six eons, and each eon was, let's say, a billion years, that would mean that there were six billion years **before** Adam, who was created at the end of the sixth eon. The traditional Jewish calendar that says we're now in the 5700s dates *from the birth of Adam,* not from the time of creation. This solves the first problem.

Let's move to the second and third issues. Actually, the Torah describes the creation of the species in a way which is consistent with the order as theorized by evolution. Namely, inanimate objects were created first, then simple life forms, then fish and birds, then animals, and finally human beings. Now it is true that the Torah seems to indicate that G-d created each species separately. But if each "day" is really an eon, or a billion years, then we can interpret the creation of the species as taking place at least partly through a process of evolution, yet guided by the divine hand. During this process, it is quite possible that the evolution followed the patterns of survival of the fittest, natural selection, random mutation, and other Darwinian mechanisms. Furthermore, it could very well be the case that during this process, some species, such as dinosaurs, passed out of existence, leaving fossils and other remnants behind. Why the Torah does not mention such things is a good question, but there is also a midrash (rabbinical teaching) that says that before G-d created this world, he created and destroyed many others. So this is a perfectly traditional idea. There is no reason to expect the Torah to mention every detail of the process of creation, and in fact that would be impossible. This answers the second and third questions.

The fourth question concerns the theory that human beings evolved from primates. I think there are two possible approaches here, and I'm not sure which is preferable. One approach is to extend the idea just described in the last paragraph. We could say that although the Torah says that G-d created humanity from the earth, what really happened is that first G-d created lower forms of life from the earth and that higher animals evolved from those lower forms until eventually human beings appeared. So it would still be true that G-d created human beings "from the earth," but it would also be true that there was a long chain of evolution that took place in between. But this is not a popular approach among contemporary Orthodox scholars. The idea that we actually evolved from primates seems ignoble. Another problem is that it seems from the text of the Torah that unlike the other species, the human being was created **individually.** The Torah indicates that one single human being was created from whom all other human beings descended. So it is strange to think of this one human being as evolving from an ape.

Here, then, is a second possible approach. We could admit that primates evolved from lower forms of life, and that proto-human or humanoid creatures evolved from primates. There are remnants of such creatures in various parts of the world, and scientists claim that these creatures lived much longer than six thousand years ago. That's not a problem because according the approach explained above, these humanoids could have been part of the fifth day (= eon) of creation. And even if such humanoids existed, it is still possible that G-d created a *human being* directly from the soil, and that this creature did not evolve at all from primates, and that all humans alive today are descended from this single ancestor and not from the other humanoids. This hypothesis is consistent with the fact that humans bear striking resemblances to primates. Yet this resemblance does not prove that we are descended from them. Indeed, scientists have not been able to prove demonstrably that humans are descended from primates. Rather, it is a theory based on the findings of humanoid fossils and on the hypothesis that the only way a human could have come into existence is by having evolved from them. Note that I am not rejecting the theory of evolution completely. I am just expressing skepticism about one of its claims: that humans evolved from primates.

You might ask: if everything I have said is accurate, why didn't the Torah say so? In other words, why doesn't the Torah describe the evolutionary development of the species more explicitly? Why doesn't the Torah mention, for example, that along the way, certain species died out? To this I answer that the Torah is not a scientific work. It would be absurd to expect the Torah to describe, for example, the composition of water and air, or the process of photosynthesis. G-d chose to describe creation in a way that is understandable to children and to earlier generations of people before the rise of modern science. The Torah is an expression of certain eternal truths, while science evolves and changes over time. The medieval scholar Moses Maimonides, who lived from 1135 to 1204, had to work to interpret Torah in light of the science of his day, which was Aristotelian physics. Similarly, we must interpret the Torah in light of current science, which includes the theory of evolution. But the Torah is not a scientific work. It is a manual of religious and moral instruction. We should not expect the Torah to provide a scientific account of the world. In fact, such a thing would be impossible, since science itself evolves over time.

Sincerely,

Rabbi Low

From: dgoldstein@cuniv.edu   Sent: 12/4/00 9:30 PM
To: rlow@ahavattorah.org.il
Subject: Atonement

Dear Rabbi Low,

I was very sorry to hear about the suicide bombing. Obviously, we know that these events are happening in Israel, but it's always different when you know someone who has a personal connection with them. It must be difficult living over there. I appreciate even more your taking the time to write.

What you said about creation and evolution was very interesting and I'll have to think about it. But I wanted to go back to a different topic, which is Christianity. I have a good friend who's a Christian, and in conversation with me he quotes a lot of passages from the Bible and gives me their Christian interpretation. I looked up some of the passages myself and I have no idea how to answer him. I was curious about how you deal with these passages. Basically there are three questions.

The first is, according to the Torah (Leviticus 16) the only way Jews can receive atonement for their sins is through the sacrifice of animals and the spilling of their blood on the altar in the Temple. Now, I'm not saying that I accept this idea. In fact, the whole ritual seems bizarre to me. But the Christian argument takes this text as given, and then goes on to make the following point. Since obviously there is no Temple today, there must be some other way of getting atonement, which is (supposedly) through the blood of Christ. Since Jews do not believe in Jesus, it follows there is no way for them to atone for their sins. That means the people of Israel remain in a state of sin. Again, I don't believe all this, but how do you respond to his argument based on the texts?

The second question is about Isaiah 53, which talks about the suffering servant. I looked it up and I have to say that as far as I can see, it fits very well with the Christian interpretation. What's your take on Isaiah 53?

The last question is about the idea of a "new covenant" which is mentioned in Jeremiah 31 and there's also something similar in Ezekiel 36. It seems like these passages foretell the teachings of the New Testament – i.e., that God will make a new covenant and "write the law upon our hearts" so that we don't need the external trappings of a legal system any more. This obviously makes the old law or covenant obsolete, and it seems to fit with the Christian idea that true spirituality doesn't require following the law of the Torah. How do Jews interpret these passages?

By the way, I've been working on a paper for Dr. Maimon's class on the problem of evil or suffering. I'd like to know your perspective on that problem sometime.

Yours truly,

David

From: rlow@ahavattorah.org.il   Sent: 12/5/00 8:27 PM
To: dgoldstein@cuniv.edu
Subject: RE: Atonement

Dear David,

Good to hear from you again. You mentioned you were doing a paper on the problem of evil. I would be interested in seeing what you come up with. Would you be willing to email me the paper when it's done? Then I could give you my perspective in response.

Before getting to your three questions on Christianity, I want to congratulate you on your persistence in looking up the passages. But I suspect you used an English translation – and one that doesn't have the traditional Jewish commentary. The Jewish commentators were very aware of Christian readings, and they offer alternative ones. Also, remember what I told you before – namely, that Judaism teaches there is an oral Torah as well as a written one, and that we cannot interpret the written Torah properly without the oral Torah. Your friend is trying to do exactly that.

Now to your questions. First, your friend is confusing the concepts of atonement (*kapparah*) with the concept of forgiveness from sin (*selihah, mehilah*). Let me explain. The passage in Leviticus says that in order to gain atonement for one's sins, the blood of the sacrificed animal must be sprinkled on the altar. In this context, atonement is related to a concept we call *taharah,* which translates as "ritual purity." In order to enter the grounds of the Temple, one had to be *tahor* – ritually pure. There is also the idea of purifying the Temple itself from the impurities that were generated by the people's sins. Throughout the Torah, the term *kapparah,* atonement, is almost always used in the context of cleansing from ritual impurity. So the Torah is saying that in order to be able to enter the Temple – that is, in order to be ritually pure, one must bring a certain kind of sacrifice. But this is only necessary if the Temple is standing. If there is no Temple, we don't need this kind of atonement. When the Temple is rebuilt, we will then reinstate some kind of atonement ritual. So it may very well be true that until the Temple is rebuilt and sacrifices are offered, there is something incomplete about our relationship with G-d.

However, atonement (= *kapparah*) is a different concept from that of forgiveness or pardon (= *mehilah* or *selihah*), especially for an intentional sin. Put simply, G-d forgives us for our intentional sins if and only if we do *teshuvah* (= return to G-d, repentance). We find numerous examples of this throughout the Torah. For example, when Moses prays for forgiveness after the sin of the golden calf, G-d says, *Salahti*, "I forgive." Later on, when Moses prays after the sin of the spies, G-d forgives the people. When David prays for forgiveness for his sin, G-d pardons him, but G-d punishes him too. Also, at the end of Devarim, the Torah speaks of the people returning to G-d and G-d returning to the people, and bringing them back to their land. Sacrifice is not mentioned here at all.

This shows that animal sacrifice is *not* necessary for forgiveness. Now it is true that on some occasions the Torah says that G-d forgives sins by virtue of our bringing a sacrifice. But this usually refers to atonement for *unwitting* or *unintentional* sins. I can't think of one example in the entire Hebrew Scriptures where someone sins *intentionally* and then gains forgiveness by offering a sacrifice. The Psalms

(*Tehillim*) teach this concept in several places. Take a look at Chapter 51, where the text clearly indicates that animal sacrifice is *not* required in order to achieve repentance. Yet at the end, this very same psalm indicates that the day will come when animal sacrifices are reinstituted. In general, the Torah indicates that animal sacrifice atones only for unwilling or unintentional sins, and not for intentional sins. This is totally opposed to the Christian idea that somehow a blood sacrifice is necessary for forgiveness for *intentional* sins. Not to mention that the radical Christian innovation is that the sacrifice is not that of an animal, but that of a human/demigod. That's the real shocking Christian claim which must always be kept at the forefront. This idea, which is totally un-Jewish, originates from pagan sources.

Now, to your second question. Isaiah 53 indeed refers to a "suffering servant," and it's not clear from the text who that might be. Over the centuries, there have been various Jewish interpretations of this passage: 1) The "suffering servant" is a metaphor for the people of Israel, who have suffered and continue to suffer at the hands of the nations. 2) The passage refers to the prophet Isaiah himself. 3) The passage refers to another individual such as Jeremiah, or some ancient Jewish king, such as Josiah or Yehoyachin, who also suffered at the hands of oppressors. 4) The passage refers to the Mashiach (messiah), understood as a human leader who has not yet arrived. (Although many Jews don't know it, this is one traditional Jewish interpretation of Isaiah 53 which of course the Christians took over. Remember, the concept of Mashiach is not a Christian innovation, so it's not surprising if it is hinted at in some Hebrew texts!) 5) The passage does not refer to a specific person, but is rather a metaphor for any righteous person, Jewish or non-Jewish, who suffers ill-treatment at the hands of the wicked.

Which interpretation is correct? Personally, I think that the first is the most reasonable. The suffering servant is the people of Israel. Of course, the passage speaks about a man rather than about a nation. But Isaiah often speaks of the people of Israel as "my servant" (see, for example, 41:8–9). We find this earlier in Exodus, where G-d refers to Israel as "my first-born son." If you start reading from Isaiah 52, it is obvious that in this context, G-d addresses the people of Israel collectively, using the singular "my servant." Note also that Isaiah 54 speaks of a childless woman who eventually gives birth, and shortly thereafter, Isaiah speaks of a "storm-tossed ship." It is eminently reasonable to understand these passages as referring, metaphorically, to the people of Israel.

Isaiah 53 seems unusual in that it seems to indicate that the suffering servant bears the sins of the wicked. But what does that really mean? The Christians say that it refers to some form of vicarious penance – that is, by suffering, the righteous person atones *for the sins of others*. But the plain meaning is simply that the "suffering servant" bears the sins of others in the sense that he is the target of their blows, just as any innocent person suffers at the hands of the wicked (as in interpretation 5 above). Nowhere in Isaiah 53 does it say that the wicked are somehow forgiven for their sins because of the suffering of the "servant"! Also, nowhere does it suggest that the suffering servant should be accepted or acknowledged as a savior! Most important, it never even comes close to equating the servant with G-d himself. These are the radical claims of Christianity that are not at all supported by this text, even if you go along with interpretation 4 that this passage refers to the Mashiach!

Finally, regarding the idea of a new covenant: it is true that Jeremiah 31 speaks of a new covenant. However, that does not mean that the content of the covenant is new. It certainly does not mean that the content of the earlier covenant has been abrogated or superseded. G-d does not abrogate past covenants when he makes new ones. This would make G-d a covenant-breaker! Rather, new covenants add to the old ones. G-d made a covenant with Noah and all of his descendants. Later on, he made a covenant with Israel. In fact, we find that G-d makes several covenants with the patriarchs, then with the people of Israel at Sinai, then in the desert, once more before they enter the holy land, and still later in the land itself, before the death of Joshua. We also find that after the first *luhot* (tablets of the covenant) were broken, God gave the Israelites the second set, which contained basically the same content as the first.

It is true that Jeremiah speaks of G-d's making a covenant that is unlike previous covenants. However, what is different about the new covenant is not the content. What is different is G-d's guarantee that it will not be broken by the Jewish people. That is what is meant by saying that G-d will write the Torah on our hearts. This is indeed similar to the passage in Ezekiel 36:26 which says that G-d will take away our heart of stone and replace it with a "new heart" and a "new spirit." Again, does that mean the content of the law will change? Not at all. In fact, the very next verse, 27, reads, "I will place my spirit in their midst, and I will make it so that *they walk in my statutes, and observe my laws, and fulfill them.*" This indicates that we will fulfill G-d's laws. It does not mean that we will somehow internalize them so that we don't have to actually obey them! Incidentally, this passage need not be interpreted as saying that G-d will take away our free will, but rather that ultimately G-d will arrange things in such a way that we will come to the point where we choose freely to keep the law because we really want to, and not merely to avoid punishment. That is what is meant by the "new spirit" that will be awakened in humankind.

In conclusion, some (liberal) Christians would not wish to see Jews convert. They believe that Jews may remain Jewish until some time in the future. With them, you really have no cause for argument. Even if they are right, we should remain religious Jews. But evidently your friend does not fall into this category. He sounds like a missionary who wants to change your mind. The missionary cites several passages in the Hebrew Scripture which seem to support Christian doctrines, such as the divine nature of the messiah, the breaking of the "old covenant," and so on. Now, we can argue over how those passages should be interpreted. Yet these same prophets say over and over that Israel is chosen, that Israel is G-d's special people, that they will return to the land, that the land will flourish with the people of Israel in it, that Jerusalem will be rebuilt, that happiness will spread throughout the land, that the people of Israel will fulfill G-d's laws, and G-d's name will be sanctified through the people of Israel. Thus, only four verses after Jeremiah speaks of a "new covenant," he states that the seed of Israel shall never cease to be a nation before Him. So on one side, you've got a few passages here and there that at best may be given a Christian interpretation, but can easily be given a Jewish interpretation. On the other side, you've got a huge number of texts proclaiming traditional Jewish doctrines, which the missionary writes off as metaphorical or ignores.

In short, the Christian missionary argument does not add up. There has to be some theological explanation for why we supposedly need to give up our Judaism and accept Christianity. The explanation is supposedly that w/out the acceptance of JC we are doomed, and that it is only through JC that we can achieve redemption. But then the crucial question is: what does JC offer that G-d himself does not offer? Why can't G-d himself forgive our sins and help us achieve our atonement? Why do we need JC's help? The answer can only be that JC is the embodiment or incarnation of G-d himself, and it is through JC's sacrifice that we win atonement. (Again, note that liberal Christians need not make this claim.) But if so, Christianity is a form of idolatry that any Jew should reject out of hand. Any attempt that Christians make to use the sources of Judaism as a basis for Christianity is belied by the fact that the main teaching of Christianity – the divinity of JC – contradicts the essential teaching of Judaism!

Sincerely,

R. Yehudah Low

24

December 12, 2000

Need to do work, but first I have to write down some things. R. Low answered my questions about Christianity pretty well. I really need to forward some of those emails to George.

Classes are just about over. We finally got to Pascal's Wager in Dr. Maimon's class. Very interesting. Obviously that's where Low got some of his ideas. The argument he gave during his lecture last year is like Pascal's, but not exactly the same. Basically, Pascal's Wager goes like this: Pascal rejects all the classic arguments for God's existence. So you can't tell whether or not God exists. But if you believe in God and he does exist, you gain eternal happiness, which is infinitely good. If God doesn't exist, the worst thing that could happen is that you will have lived a religious life in vain, and you would have lost out on some worldly pleasures. On the other hand, if you don't believe in God, you can't get the infinite good even if God does exist. So, you have everything to gain and nothing to lose by believing in God. Finally, once you've accepted this argument, if you find yourself having trouble believing, that's no problem. Just go to church (or shul? or the mosque?) and say the words "I believe" over and over, and eventually you will believe!

Dr. M pointed out several flaws in the argument: What if God rewards only non-believers? How do you know which version of God to believe in, or which religion to follow? Should it be Judaism? Christianity? Islam? Zoroastrianism? How do you know that the only way of gaining eternal bliss is if God exists? And does it make sense to believe in something for personal benefit? Is it morally acceptable to do this? Is it morally right to make yourself believe something that you don't have good evidence for? (But Pascal says you have no choice. Is that right?) This brings up the Ethics of Belief, which we're supposed to get into next time in class.

Meanwhile I'm almost finished with my paper on the Quarrel. It's the last serious thing I need to do before winter break. When I'm done, I'll email it to Rabbi L. Last night I watched the film again. I noticed a couple things I didn't catch before. One is that the film is based on a short story by the Yiddish writer Chaim Grade, "My Quarrel with Hersh Razeyner." I wonder if it was just an accident that he used his own name for one of the characters. Maybe I can find the short story some time. The other thing I noticed is that at the beginning of the film, before Chaim meets Hersh in the park, there's a snatch of conversation which he overhears from some Jews passing by. One of them says to the other: "And not too many people know this, but the very last commandment in the Torah is that every Jew is supposed to write a sefer (that means, a book)." And then his voice trails off. I wondered, could it really be true that every Jew has a mitzvah to write a book? After some digging I found out that actually the commandment is for every Jew to write a Sefer Torah, a scroll of the Torah. I asked Rabbi Abraham about this and he said nowadays it can be fulfilled by paying someone to write a Sefer Torah or by filling in the last few letters of the scroll or even just buying Hebrew books. But I wondered, what was the significance of this comment in the context of the film? I guess that since Chaim himself is a writer, the point is that in some way he has kept the tradition by being a writer, even though he's not Orthodox any more. Could that be? Can you in some way keep the tradition without really keeping it?

The significance of writing is so important in the Jewish tradition. That reminds me of the contrast with Ravi in that he no longer keeps a journal. Writing is an expression of one's self or will.

Idea! Once you come to enlightenment as Ravi understands it, you don't really believe in free will anymore, so you leave writing behind. But in Judaism, you don't give up the idea of free will, so you never leave writing behind!

Speaking of writing, I'd better get to work finishing the paper.

<u>25</u>

David Goldstein
Philosophy of Religion
December 13, 2000
Dr. Maimon

The Quarrel about God, Evil, and the Holocaust

I.   INTRODUCTION

A.   The Problem of Evil and the Problem of the Holocaust

For people who believe in God, and for people who are considering whether to believe in God, the "Problem of Evil" is one of the biggest stumbling blocks. Simply stated, the problem is this: If God is all powerful, and all good, why is there evil in the world? However, this is only a simple statement of a complex problem. There are different types of evil, and different versions of the problem.

There are two versions of the problem of evil: the *strong* version and the *moderate* version. The *strong* version uses

Do we really know that evil exists? What is "evil" if there is no God? the existence of evil to argue that God's existence[1] is *logically incompatible* with evil. This version argues that since <u>we know evil exists</u>, this conclusively *disproves* God's existence. This would imply that belief in God is *absurd.* On the other hand, the moderate version uses evil to argue that there is no good explanation we know of for why God would allow evil. This would imply that it is *probably* the case that God does not exist and that the belief in God is irrational, though not necessarily absurd.

While it may be relatively easy for the theist to escape the strong version of the argument, it is not so easy to escape the moderate version of the argument.

Hersh argues that evil can exist only if God exists. If successful this responds equally to the strong as well the weak version! (you get to this point later below.) Philosophers distinguish two types of evil: moral evil and natural evil. Moral evil is the result of human action, such as, murder, torture, rape, etc. Natural evil is any evil or suffering that is not the result of human actions, but is rather the result of natural causes, such as disease, earthquakes, tornadoes, etc.

The problem of evil also breaks down into (a) why would God allow *any* evil at all, and (b) why would God allow apparently huge or "massive" evils. For example, a small natural evil might be a child falling and scraping his knee, while a small *moral* evil might be a person hurting someone else's feelings. A massive natural evil would be a devastating earthquake that kills thousands of people, while a huge moral evil would be a person who blows up a stadium, killing thousands of people. This paper does not deal with natural evil at all. This paper deals only with a certain case of massive moral evil, probably one of the worst ever, namely, the Nazi Holocaust, in which six million Jews, among many others, were murdered. I shall refer to this as the Problem of the Holocaust.

While the Holocaust is a problem for anyone who wishes to believe in an all good and all-powerful God, it is especially a *provide the scriptural source of this idea* problem for traditional Judaism. That's because one of the main teachings of Judaism is that that the <u>Jews are God's chosen or beloved people</u>.

---

1   For the purpose of this paper God is conceived as an entity that either exists or does not exist. However, if God is conceived as Being itself then the problem would be restated as to whether there is a principle of supreme benevolence. *OK!*

So the problem arises: why would God abandon the Jews and allow them to suffer so horribly?

Just as there are two versions of the problem of evil, there are also two versions of the Problem of the Holocaust. The strong version tries to show that the God of traditional Judaism *definitely* does not exist. The moderate version tries to show that the God of traditional Judaism *probably* does not exist. Both versions of this argument will be discussed in this paper.

Good Intro. It's also worth noting that evil is nothing new. Suffering and evil didn't start with the Holocaust. Also, the suffering and evil perpetrated upon the Jews didn't start with the Holocaust. Surely, the Holocaust was unique in certain ways. But was it unique in any way that is relevant to the problem of evil?

B. Plan for the rest of this paper

The problem of evil has been addressed by many famous religious philosophers and atheistic philosophers as well. But the problem is also addressed in an entertaining way by the two main characters in the film, *The Quarrel*,[2] which depicts a discussion between two survivors of the Holocaust, named Chaim and Hersh. Both lost their wives and children in the Holocaust. Chaim is a secular Jew and a writer for a newspaper with an advice column. Hersh is an Ultra-Orthodox Rabbi who leads a Yeshiva in Montreal. Chaim takes the view that after the Holocaust, it is irrational to believe in the God of Judaism. Hersh takes the opposite view. In fact he claims the Holocaust only strengthened his belief in the God of Judaism. While there is a lot of emotional and personal content to the film, this paper focuses on the philosophical and theological views expressed by these characters about the problems of evil and the Holocaust.

The plan for the rest of this paper is as follows. Section II summarizes the views of Chaim and Hersh about the evil and *It's not* the Holocaust. ~~This is not a paper for a film class, so I will not~~ *necessary to* ~~get into the personal feud between the two characters~~. Section *say this!* III critically discusses their views. In particular, this section evaluates Hersh's responses to Chaim's claims and shows how his responses are flawed. Section IV describes what I think is a

---

2   *The Quarrel* (1992) starring Saul Rubinek and R.H. Thompson, directed by Eli Cohen.

better way for the Jewish theist to respond to the problems of
evil and the Holocaust. However, I will conclude by stating what
I think is a serious flaw or drawback in my own solution.

Plan for the paper is very clear! Good!

II. SUMMARY OF CHAIM'S AND HERSH'S VIEWS.

This section summarizes the parts of the dialogue between Chaim
and Hersh as it pertains to the Problems of Evil and the Holocaust.

Interestingly, it is Chaim who first brings up the idea that
some people say that the Holocaust was a result of man's free
will. However, Chaim quickly adds that if the Holocaust is a
result of man's free will, that does not get God off the hook since
God (if he exists) created humans with free will and can take it
away at any time. God is responsible for what humans do. In
other words, one can't respond adequately to the Problem of
the Holocaust by saying "God didn't do it, the Nazis did."

In response to this, Hersh says the Holocaust was a
punishment for the Jews' violation of the covenant with God.
Many Jews (such as Chaim himself) had abandoned Judaism
before the Holocaust started. Hersh says this punishment was
already predicted by the Scriptures thousands of years ago.
(Apparently Hersh has in mind Leviticus 26 and Deuteronomy
28.) The Jews were warned to keep the Torah and the covenant
with God, and they failed. So, bitter and horrible as it was, the
Jews deserved the punishment that they got.

In response to this, Chaim confronts Hersh with the following
question. If it's true that the Holocaust is a punishment, why did
religious Jews suffer just as much as non-religious Jews? Hersh
answers that the entire people of Israel is held responsible
for the actions of those Jews who strayed from the Torah. God
punishes the people as a whole, including the righteous, not just
the wrongdoers. He even blames himself for not being able to
convince Chaim not to abandon Judaism. Chaim quickly objects
that this cannot possibly explain the suffering of the Jewish
children in the Holocaust. How could they have been held
responsible for what adults did? They didn't do anything wrong
to deserve such suffering. Hersh responds that God's ways are
mysterious, and we can't expect to be able to explain everything
God does. Chaim does not respond to this.

He seems to dismiss it as not even worthy of a response!

Later, in the scene inside the shack during the rainstorm,
Hersh goes on the offensive and attacks atheism. He claims

Good!

that if there is no God, then, as Dostoevsky said, "Everything is permitted," that is, nothing is really right or wrong. In other words, if there is no God, and as Protagoras said, "Man is the measure of all things," it's inevitable that men will differ on what they think is right or wrong. So, if there is no God, what the Nazis did was not inherently wrong after all. In other words, if you want to claim that what the Nazis did was really wrong, you have to believe in God. He further argues that a world without God is a world in which people are vain, selfish and amoral. All those who abandon God end up serving themselves, their selfish needs, and/or end up like Nazis. It seems that according to Hersh, the Holocaust and things like it are the natural outcome of loss of belief in God. The point of this argument is that even if it's difficult to believe in God because of the problem of evil, it's still a better view than atheism.

In response to this, Chaim says that instead of faith in God, he has faith in *man.* Of course, man is fallible. But he claims that faith in man is more rational than faith in God. God by definition is perfect, so if he exists, we should expect the world to be free from evils such as the Holocaust. Sure, man is fallible and does horrible things, but that's no surprise – he is mortal and fallible. Further, Chaim argues that you don't need to be religious to have a high standard of morality. As witness of this, he says he personally knew of an atheist who helped Jews during the Holocaust at great risk to her own life. In other words, Chaim claims that life is worthwhile, meaningful, and moral, even if God does not exist. *Good summary of the dialogue as it relates to the paper topic.*

III. CRITIQUE OF HERSH'S RESPONSES TO CHAIM'S CHALLENGES

These texts may have been written by biblical writers living after the destruction of the first temple and the Babylonian exile.

Hersh's main response to the problem of the Holocaust is his claim that the Holocaust is a punishment for the Jewish people's disobedience. The Biblical texts say that the Jews will be scattered to foreign lands and will suffer horribly at the hands of the non-Jews if they "break the covenant." Hersh's claim is that mass assimilation by Jews in the modern period constitutes a form of "breaking the covenant." Could this be a reason for the Holocaust? A critical question is whether the punishment fits the crime. As Chaim says, what possible crime could warrant such horrible punishments? The idea of collective punishment seems questionable, especially when it comes to the suffering of innocent

Can you say why it is questionable?

children. Hersh responds that God's ways are beyond us. This is
what we might call the "Job" response. The book of Job teaches
the answer to the problem of evil is that God is beyond us, and we
simply cannot expect to understand him. In the book, this seems
to satisfy Job, but it is not necessarily a philosophically satisfac- *I agree!*
tory response to the problem of why the innocent suffer. It also
seems that Hersh should have said this in the first place, without
Very good points! bothering to claim that the Holocaust was a punishment at all.

Earlier, I stated that there are two ways the problem of the
Holocaust can be raised: the strong way, and the moderate
way. One can use the Holocaust to argue that the belief in the
Jewish God is logically *absurd,* or to argue that this belief is
irrational. It seems to me that to escape the *strong* version of
the problem, Hersh's Job-style response actually works. So long
as there is some possible reason why God might allow such evil
(even if we have no idea what that is) the strong version of the
problem of evil is defeated. Given the concept of God as infinite
and humans as finite, we have to admit that it's possible there's
some explanation for even such gross evil, even if we have no
idea what it is. We might not like it emotionally, but we have
Interesting point; I'm to admit that perhaps there's some possible reason we don't
not sure I agree. know which might explain why the children had to suffer.

However, in my opinion, Hersh's response is not sufficient
to escape the *moderate* version of the problem. That problem
is not solved by saying, "it's all a mystery" or "God's ways are
beyond us." For that is in effect to admit that the belief in God,
while perhaps not absurd, is nevertheless irrational. Until we
have some reasonable explanation for why the Jewish God
would allow the Holocaust, and especially the suffering of
innocent children, it is unreasonable to believe in the God of
Excellent point! Judaism.

Another problem with Hersh's view is that if you say the
Holocaust was a divine punishment, you have to say that the
Nazis did God's work, and that seems odd, to say the least. It
seems that if God wanted to punish the Jews, he didn't have to
make anyone do such terrible things. Given the Jewish idea of
God as omnipotent, He could have punished the Jews by diseases
or locusts or some natural penalty. How can God make people
wicked in order to administer a punishment? This doesn't make
sense. Still, the main problem is that the punishment is out of
proportion to the crime.

Next let's consider Hersh's claim that if there is no God, we cannot say that what the Nazis did was objectively wrong: all we can say is that we don't like it. This is the claim often made by theists that if God does not exist, morality is subjective or relative. Chaim's response to this is not very convincing. He claims that instead of faith in God he has "faith in man," but that doesn't really answer the question.

He cites a case of a woman who was an atheist and who did "good things," but still if Hersh is right, her "good deeds" are merely her doing what she happens to like doing (saving people) while the Nazis did what they liked doing (killing people). This does not directly answer Hersh's claim that without God, morality is subjective. *good point*

However, there are better responses Chaim could have given to this claim. First of all, Chaim could have admitted that atheism results in subjective morality, but that still doesn't ~~get God out~~ *solve* of the problem of evil. Chaim's argument is that *if* God exists, *then* there are certain things which if they exist are objectively very evil *and* which an omnipotent God should not allow to take place. Second, Chaim could have challenged Hersh to explain why he thinks God is necessary for objective morality.

Perhaps Hersh would have said that only a being such as God is intrinsically worthy of our obedience. But if so, the atheist could insist that an objective morality does *not* require the existence of God.[3] For example, he could say that even if there's no God, certain beings (such as humans) are inherently good beings, and deserve a certain degree of respect. If so, it is wrong to wantonly murder humans, even if there's no God. This is just as rational as the idea that only God (if He exists) is intrinsically worthy of our obedience.

At the very least, Hersh needs to defend his view much more than he does so in the film!

In summary of this section, Hersh may have a good answer to the *strong* version of the problem of evil, but he does not have a sufficient answer to the *moderate* version of the problem. He does not adequately respond to Chaim's challenge that the belief in the Jewish God is *unreasonable* given the Holocaust.

Good critique of Hersh's views.

---

3   This idea is based on conversation with Dr. Sofi Maimon. *OK!*

IV. MY OWN VIEWS

Run on sentence

Although I think Hersh does not answer the challenge, I think there's a better solution, though it's also got one major flaw which I'll get to at the end of this paper. For the purpose of this section, it's important to restate the fact that there are really two separate problems, which are not very well separated in the discussion in the film.

A. How could (any) God allow such an evil as the Holocaust?
B. If the Jewish people are God's beloved or chosen people, how could God allow this to happen to them?

These are two separate problems and so I shall discuss them separately.

A. How could God allow any evil such as the Holocaust?

It's interesting that it's Chaim who raises the idea of free will, if only to knock it down. Hersh does not develop this idea further, but I ~~feel~~ *think* the "Free Will Solution" to the problem of evil is worthy of further discussion. *In a philosophy paper, you don't feel; you think*

It is hard to define free will, but basically it is the power to choose between good and bad, without being predetermined to do so one way or the other, even by God, or any power outside one's own will. Some people don't even believe in free will, but many theists do, and we shall assume that the idea makes sense for the purpose of this paper.

We can understand why God would want to create man with free will, because otherwise man is just a robot or puppet doing whatever God makes him do. Without free will we cannot be moral creatures, we cannot deserve or merit anything. Without free will, there could be such a thing as pain and pleasure, but there really would be nothing we could do that is morally good or morally bad, and nothing we would get would be morally deserved. Some philosophers have gone so far as to say that free will is our best, most divine-like trait. Furthermore, if free will is a good thing, it also follows that the more free will we have, the better we are. (Up to a point, of course. And we can't have perfect free will. Only God has that.)

integrate this parenthesis into the paragraph; it's an important point!

Now let's assume that God makes the decision to give people free will. Once he does that, he cannot always control what people do. Some people will do good, some will do evil. If God were to intervene every time a person or group of persons was about to do evil, man would no longer have free will. Therefore, free will requires that man be free to do evil as well as good. Of course God might intervene on some occasions. But the more he intervenes, the less man has free will. So, God will have to allow for some moral evil. How much evil is too much? This is a tough question. The only thing we can say for sure is that it would be "too much" evil if humans completely destroyed one another, or committed such horrible acts that the world was beyond repair. However, terrible as the Holocaust was, the world did not become so depraved that it was beyond repair. Perhaps God made the decision at the beginning of creation to allow as much freedom as possible without allowing the world to become so depraved that it would be beyond repair. This could be viewed as a morally justifiable decision, given the great value of free will. Hence, the theist can say that the price we pay for maximum free will is, unfortunately, such heinous or massive evils as the Holocaust. This is what Hersh should have said, but he didn't. *Interesting suggestion.*

As much as I like this solution, there is still a problem with it, which I'll get to in the conclusion of this paper.

Your reader wonders: Why do you save this for the conclusion rather than discuss it here?

B. If the Jewish people are God's beloved or chosen people, how could God allow the Holocaust to happen to them?

Even if the above solution works to explain why God allows such evils as the Holocaust, someone like Chaim could still argue that since God chose the Jewish people as special, He should have protected them. According to the Scriptures, God promised the people of Israel special protection or providence. How is it then that God could allow His people to suffer on such a massive scale?

To this I think Hersh can rightfully respond that the promise of protection is conditional upon the collective obedience of the Jewish people to the covenant. If the Jews break the covenant, they are no longer under God's special protection. God was under no obligation to provide the people special protection, so when he removed that protection, they revert to the normal situation of mankind. They are then subject to the free will actions of human beings in the world, just like all other human

beings are. This interpretation is supported by a passage in
Deuteronomy 31:17:

Nice quote for your And I will be angry with [the people] on that day and I will
purposes (but see my point abandon them, and I will hide my face from them, and they
just below) will be consumed, and many evils and afflictions will befall
them, and [the people] will say, "Surely it is because God is
not in my midst that these evils have befallen me."

The idea here is that the punishment for the breaking of
the covenant is that God will "abandon" the Jewish people to
whatever fate they suffer without that special protection. This
solution is different from what Hersh says: In Hersh's view,
the Holocaust is a *punishment* for the sins of the Jews. In this
view, the punishment is the *abandonment* of the Jews, who now
revert to the situation of not being protected. At that point, the
suffering caused by the Nazis is due to the free will choice of the
Look again at the Nazis, which is explained or justified by the free will solution
Scriptural passages you already described above.
cited and see whether Another advantage of this solution over Hersh's is the
you think Hersh's view following. In Hersh's view, it turns out that the Nazis carried out
or your view is more God's work, which seems absurd. But in the present view, the
consistent with those Nazis did not do "God's work." What God did was to "abandon"
texts! (based on those the Jews by removing their special protection. What the Nazis
texts it sometimes looks did was to exercise their own free will in a negative way. So
like the punishment is the present solution avoids an absurdity which is present in
the suffering, not just Hersh's view.
the abandonment itself)

C.   A Problem with this solution

Although I have defended the free will solution to the problem of
evil and the Holocaust, there is one major problem that I wish to
point out. The main idea of this solution is that free will is such a
We'll have to discuss this valuable thing that God is justified in giving free will to man, even
at some point. If God at the cost of allowing such horrible suffering as the Holocaust.
exists, surely He could The problem is that only some people enjoy the benefit of
manage to arrange some having free will, while other people end up suffering horribly.
kind of "afterlife." The This is especially true of the children, which is one of Chaim's
deeper question is, what major points. A million Jewish children were killed in the
does it really mean to Holocaust, many of them horribly. Surely they were innocent.
believe in an afterlife. The free will solution says that these children suffered so that
Hersh could have easily people could have free will. Is that fair? Is that just? I don't see
appealed to it. It's a bit how that could be. These children did not have the benefit of
surprising that he does
not.

developing their free will at all. It seems they are being used as tools for others' moral and spiritual growth. How could God allow the children to suffer in order to give others the benefit of having free will? An analogy would be a parent who allows one child to harm another without intervening in order to allow the first child maximum freedom. Everyone would agree that this is wrong. It seems to me that the only way to escape this problem is to say that there is a next world or life after death or some other way in which the souls of the innocent children can have another chance at developing their free will and becoming moral individuals. If the children have another chance, theoretically that would solve the problem that they are not being used as pawns for the moral development of others. The analogy with the parent would break down because the parent does not have the ability to grant life after death. God, however, has the ability to do that if he grants life after death.

However, the obvious problem is that the whole idea of an afterlife or next world or something like reincarnation is very questionable. It's one thing to believe in God, and quite another to believe in an afterlife. It may not be an absurd belief, but it seems highly improbable that there really is an afterlife.

So, the overall conclusion of my paper is the following. If (and it's a big "if") there is an afterlife or reincarnation, then there is a solution to the problem of evil and the problem of the Holocaust. But if there isn't, there is no good answer to the problem. Since I am skeptical of the afterlife, I must conclude that I remain skeptical that the Problems of Evil and the Holocaust can be solved.

Good question, but I disagree with your answer below.

I disagree with this. See below at the end of your paper.

But we don't think it wrong to let an older child take care of a younger child, whilst knowing full well that abuse is a real possibility.

...lief in the afterlife is ...a tenet of traditional Judaism

I disagree; the analogy breaks down because only God is in a position to grant free choice even when he knows that free choice will result in evil.

I don't think an afterlife helps to handle the problem you've raised. If I use someone as a tool for an end, it doesn't make it any better if later on I give them something good. (I could apologize to them, but that's another matter.)

In my view, the suffering of the children is not inherently evil. (Pain is not the same thing as evil.) Surely, the act of intentionally causing senseless suffering is evil; and the act of allowing suffering without a moral justification is evil. If God has a moral justification for allowing the evil (e.g., it's the only way God can give humans free will) then it's unfortunate the children suffered, but that is not an evil act! What is evil is the Nazis' intentional causing of that suffering. As to why God allows that suffering – that is explained by the free will defense as you yourself suggest.

Overall comments: The paper is well organized and in general well argued. I disagree with your final conclusion, but that in itself does not constitute a flaw. The assertion at the end that an afterlife is improbable is the weakest claim in the paper; it is asserted without argument. Good use of sources, though more footnoting to those sources would be helpful.

A−

26

"Dr. Maimon? Hi. It's me, David. May I come in?"

"David, nice to see you! But I'm surprised you're still here. Sure, come in. Aren't your finals over?"

"Yes. I've got to catch a plane later. But I thought maybe I could see you one more time this semester. I was hoping I could hear some of the rest of your theory of God before the break."

"Well, it just so happens my afternoon is free. Sit down."

"Don't you have to pick up your daughter at 3:30?"

"Nope. Her father's getting her today."

"I see. So can we talk more about your conception of God?"

"Yes, I suppose now is as good a time as any. I need to fill you in on my conception of God's attributes of action."

"Great. But before we get into that, there was something else I wanted to ask you."

"What's that?"

"Dr. Maimon, I know you're very busy, but next semester I really wanted to take a course with you on Jewish philosophy."

"Sorry, I'm not offering it next semester. But the year after next I will be doing a course on classic works in Jewish philosophy."

"I know about that, and I'd like to take that too, but that's going to be my senior year, and it seems so far off. I was wondering if we could do an independent study course together."

"Hmmm. What did you have in mind as a course of study?"

"There's a whole bunch of topics in Judaism that I'd just love to hear your views about, like the issue of the chosenness of the Jewish people, and the question of what attitude does Judaism take toward other religions, what is the rationale for the commandments, especially things like the dietary laws, animal sacrifices, ritual purity and impurity, and lots of other things. . . ."

"That sounds more like a course in Jewish theology than Jewish philosophy. But I confess I have no shortage of things to say about those matters."

"So? Will you do it?"

"David, you should really first get a grounding in the classics."

"Dr. Maimon, I can't tell you how much this would mean to me. Isn't there some way we could work this out?"

"Well, since you're so insistent, I guess we could do it."

"Great! Thanks so much, Dr. Maimon!"

"We'll figure out the details early next semester. Right now, we'd better talk about God's attributes of action."

"Yes, let's get into that."

"First, let's talk about how the attributes of action are understood in the popular conception of God. Let me emphasize that I am *not* going to try to show that such a being exists. Indeed, I think it is very difficult to do so. I am just going to describe the concept of God as traditionally conceived. For, only then can you really appreciate the advantages of my . . . uh . . . non-standard conception of the divine attributes of action."

"OK. I'm listening."

"Recall that in the popular conception, God is conceived as an entity – that is, a being who is necessary, perfect, and all-powerful. God is one, but God is also infinite. These are what I called the metaphysical attributes of God. Now, the attributes of action are basically the ways in which the divine entity acts. In particular, the divine entity is conceived as creative and *providential*. The idea is that the entity, God, supposedly creates or causes the world, and also directs and guides the orderly processes of nature. For the theist, the ultimate explanation for why the world exists and why it has an order lies in the creative and providential properties of God. Of course, the question may be asked: why did God create the world, and why did God design it in the way that he did? There are different possible answers to this question, and, as I said last time, the one I favor involves the idea that God is engaged in a process of *self-expression*."

"Yes, I remember all that."

"Good. So let's talk a little more about the concept of self-expression. Recall my analogy between God and the creative artist. The artist doesn't create because he's forced to create, nor does he create for the sake of benefiting or pleasing others – though that might happen incidentally. Rather, God creates in order to express himself. As I mentioned last time, a genuine artwork is a true expression of the artist."

"Right. I really liked that idea."

"Now, when an artist truly expresses himself in an artwork, it doesn't mean that he reproduces himself in the artwork. For example, when Rembrandt paints a great self-portrait, the portrait is not a reproduction of Rembrandt himself."

"Obviously not."

"Yet at the same time, in a great work of art, the artist successfully expresses himself, as a whole, not just in part. The self-portrait is in some sense an expression of Rembrandt – that is, the whole person, and not just part of Rembrandt. Anything short of full self-expression is not a genuine expression of the self. Do you follow?"

"I'm not sure. Maybe even the best portrait can only partially represent the artist."

"Perhaps you're right in some sense. But, ideally, the best form of self expression would be an expression of the entire self. Can you accept that at least provisionally?"

"OK. I'll agree with that for now."

"Thanks. Now, let's turn to God. In the standard or popular conception of God, the idea is that the entity, God, expresses himself by creating the world. Since God is perfect, it stands to reason that the expression should also be perfect, though of course not in the same sense that God himself is perfect. Despite the fact that it is an expression of God, the world is not a reproduction of God's perfect being. Do you follow?"

"Yes, but there seems to be a problem. Either the world is perfect, in which case it is exactly like God, or it is not perfect, in which case it doesn't completely express God."

"Hold on, and I'll try to explain a way out of that conundrum. We said once before that there's a special connection between being and power. God expresses his infinite power by creating an incredibly diverse and complex world. In doing so, God expresses His infinite being. Of course, the universe itself is in some sense finite. But still, in some way, this incredibly complex world is an expression of the infinite power of God. And, in particular, God expresses himself by creating the human being, who is made "in the image of God." To say that the human is created in the image of God is to say that the human being has intelligence and free will. So, despite the fact that the human being is finite and limited, the human being is, in some sense, the paramount expression of God."

"OK. I think that makes sense."

"Furthermore, God expresses his oneness and necessity by having providence over the world. Can you see how that might work?"

"No, I don't."

"Let me explain. The traditional idea is that God's providence over the world – in Hebrew, the term is *hashgaha* – is exhibited in the fact that the world has order and design. Furthermore, the orderliness of the world exhibits the fact that there is one God who controls the entire cosmos. That's why I say that it is through his providence over the world that God expresses his unity or oneness."

"OK, I see."

"Furthermore, the orderliness of the universe also exhibits necessity in the following way: Given the orderly structure of the world, certain things must happen in a certain way. For example, if I throw a ball up in the air, it must come down. Now, the "must" here is not a matter of *logical* necessity. For, we can logically conceive of the possibility that the ball would go up and never come down. Rather, the ball "must" come down, given the law of gravity. So, we might call this *natural regularity* or *natural necessity* rather than logical necessity. The point is that natural regularities or so called "laws of nature" are an "expression" of God's necessary nature, even though the laws themselves are *not* logically necessary. Thus, on the standard conception, God expresses his necessary nature through his providence, that is, through his ensuring that the world has an order or structure."

"OK. I think I follow."

"Good. Now, I said before that since God is perfect, it stands to reason that the expression of God in the world would also be perfect. And you asked how it could be that the world, which is in some sense not perfect, could be an expression of God's perfect being. So here's at least part of the answer. As I said, God's providence is an expression of his unity and necessity. But God is not provident in some kind of half-baked or incomplete way. Rather, God is supremely provident. In other words, the unity and necessity of God are not expressed in some kind of partial ordering of nature. Rather, the order and design of nature are pervasive and universal. In this way, even though the universe is not identical with God, the universe still is a complete or full expression of God."

"Hmm. Very interesting."

"Now, still working with the popular conception of God, another thing we need to add is that God's self-expression is a process that takes place over time. God's initial creation of the world and mankind was only the first step in God's self expression. As time goes on, God expresses Himself further and further in the cosmos. Using traditional Jewish terminology, we may say that God's self expression takes place through the two secondary divine attributes, namely, benevolence and justice. In Hebrew these are the *middot* or divine attributes of *hesed,* which means benevolence, and *din,* which means justice. The way I look at it, benevolence stems from God's creative capacity, which in turn stems from God's power and infinite being. On the other hand, justice stems from God's providential capacity, which in turn stems from God's necessity and oneness. Get it?"

"Sorry, Dr Maimon. I definitely did not follow that last part."

"Here – this might make things easier to follow. Let me draw a little diagram on this piece of paper."

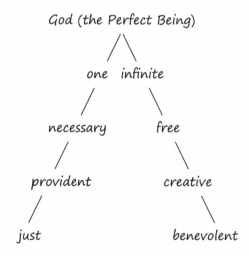

"Look at the diagram and I'll summarize what I've said so far. Again, I am speaking now about the standard conception that takes God to be an entity or a being. Starting from the top, God is conceived as the perfect being. The rest of the diagram shows some of the attributes of God, starting with metaphysical attributes and moving down to the attributes of action. This list is not exhaustive, there are other attributes as well. But the diagram shows how certain attributes are dependent on other attributes. Speaking metaphorically, we may say that the lower attributes flow from the higher attributes. Starting from the top, there are at least two primary facts about God's essence – the first is that God is one, the second is that God is infinite – and I'm not going to try to say which one is more important. Now, because God is an infinite being, he has infinite power or freedom to create. As I've said before, power is an expression of being. And, because God is one, and only one, there are certain ways in which God is restricted by his own nature. For example, God cannot duplicate himself. God cannot split himself in two, and so forth. Thus, there is a connection between God's oneness and his fixed nature, that is, his necessity. Are you following so far?"

"It's a little hard, but I think so."

"Good. So much for God's metaphysical attributes. Moving down the diagram, the remaining attributes or properties flow from the metaphysical attributes of God. In virtue of God's power, God freely creates a universe – something that was decidedly not necessary. Thus, God's creativity flows from his power. On the other hand, in virtue of God's necessity – the fact that God must be a certain way – God is provident: that is, he designed the universe with a certain order which it must follow. Thus, God's providence flows from his necessity. Does that make sense to you?

"Yes, I think so."

"Great. Now, I still need to explain how benevolence flows from God's creativity, while God's justice stems from God's necessity. To say that God is benevolent means first of all that God causes undeserved good things to happen in the world. As you know from our previous conversations, I understand goodness as having to do with being. In fact, you could say that the very existence of contingent beings is itself an example of benevolence at work. But here I am using the term benevolence to designate a certain way in which God manages the world once it has been created, and in particular, how God relates to human beings. In any case, benevolence is an expression of God's being and power.

"I see."

"Furthermore, God is conceived not merely as benevolent, but as supremely benevolent. It's not enough to say that undeserved good things happen. Rather, the idea of divine benevolence is that ultimately, God will bring it about that some supremely good outcome will be reached in the realm of created being. Obviously, we haven't gotten there yet. As I said a moment ago, there's a cosmic process going on that takes place over time. We have not reached the end of the process. Now, while benevolence involves the causing of undeserved goodness, justice involves the causing of deserved or merited goodness. So, to say that God is just is to say, at least in part, that God causes a situation to exist whereby creatures – that is, people – can merit or deserve that which is good. The way God does this is first by creating human beings who have free will, and second, by providing responsibilities and duties for them to fulfill. This is the creation of the realm of objective morality or ethics, so to speak. And third –"

"But Dr. Maimon, I thought that your view is that ethics does not depend on God."

"Ah, let me clarify. I hold that even if there were no God, there could still be objective ethics. But since I do believe in God and that everything is in some sense dependent on God, it follows that, like everything else, objective ethics depends on God."

"Oh, I see – sort of. Well, anyway, go on."

"Next, to say that God is just is not merely to say that God created the conditions for ethical behavior. It's also to say that God is engaged with the world in such a way as to bring it about that people behave more and more ethically – though this is a tricky matter, since God does not want to tamper with human free will. God cannot always intervene when someone is about to do evil, for that would destroy free choice. By the way, I could see from your paper on the problem of evil that you appreciate this point quite well."

"Oh, thanks!"

"And the point I wanted to explain next is that God's justice is an expression of God's necessity."

"How is that?"

"Well, since humans have free choice, they can do things by which they earn or merit what is good. When a person behaves ethically, he or she does what he ought to do. It's not logical necessity, of course, nor is it natural necessity either. We may call it moral necessity, which mimics logical necessity. People are not logically bound to fulfill their duties, nor are they bound by the laws of physics to do so. But once God sets up a situation in which people can freely choose to fulfill their duties, they are morally obligated to do so. That's a kind of necessity. And so that's why I say that God's justice is an expression of his necessity."

"OK, I think I get that."

"And once again, we need to add that not only is God just, rather, God is supremely just or perfectly just. Over the course of time, the most just outcome possible is achieved in creation. The idea is that God is providentially guiding and occasionally intervening in the world, in just such a way as to bring it about that there will come a day when human beings attain the best good that they could possibly deserve or merit. Are you with me?"

"Yes, I am."

"Finally, to complete the popular conception of God, there is at least one very important divine attribute that needs to be added, which is not on the diagram. Since God is supremely providential, benevolent, and just, it is also the case that, supposedly, God is communicative. This involves two things: first, that God listens to what people say – in other words, that God responds to prayer – and second, that on some occasions, God speaks to certain people – meaning that

God engages in revelation. Does all this sound like an accurate description of the popular conception of God?"

"Yes. I think you've described it very well."

"Fine. Now, there are several things that bother me about the popular conception. The main one is that I have problems with the idea of a non-physical entity that causes things to happen in the physical world. Also, it's extremely difficult to rationally support the belief that there is such a being or entity as the one I have just described at some length. How do we know that there is a supreme eternal being who is supremely benevolent and just? It's notoriously difficult to prove or even rationally support that belief!"

"I agree."

"So then let's move to my non-standard conception of God. On my conception, there is no divine entity, and so there are no acts of the divine entity either. As I already told you, I conceive of God's essence as Being itself. Again, Being itself is not a being. So, instead of talking about God's acts, or ways of acting, my theory is that the world has a certain structure or pattern. More specifically, there are certain metaphysical or divine principles in accord with which the universe operates. Instead of saying that the entity, God, expresses himself through his actions, I wish to say that the divine principles describe the various ways in which Being itself is expressed in the world."

"I think I follow, but I'm not sure. It sounds more complicated than the popular conception."

"It may sound that way at first, but conceptually speaking, my theory is actually simpler than the popular conception. Let me reiterate some of the things we've already discussed last time. Almost everyone, even the atheist, agrees that the universe has a certain structure or pattern. Everyone believes that there are certain laws in accord with which the world operates. Firstly, there are logical and mathematical rules (like 2 plus 3 equal 5) that govern the way things are structured or organized. These principles are *necessary*, since they could not possibly be other than they are. They describe the ways in which any possible universe would have to be. So the logical and mathematical principles are, so to speak, rooted in the very nature of being itself. Are you with me so far?"

"Yes. I remember this from last time."

"Good. Now, in addition to the logical and mathematical laws, there are also natural regularities or "scientific" laws – like the law of gravity and the other laws of physics that are discoverable through the scientific method. These laws are merely contingent, since it is logically possible that they could have been otherwise than they are. And these laws govern the way things behave in our world. Actually, this way of speaking is somewhat metaphorical. Scientific laws don't really govern anything. It's more accurate to say that all things are structured in accord with certain principles or that all things operate in accord with laws. You could also say that some or even all of these laws aren't really laws but rather general regularities, and it won't affect my argument. The point is that almost everyone would agree that the universe has not only a logical and mathematical order, but also a contingent order or structure, which is partly described, to the best of our current knowledge, by science. Are you with me so far?"

"Yes, I follow. "

"So, in my conception, to believe in God is in part to believe all the things I just said. That is: there is a structure or pattern to the universe. To which you might say, 'Big deal! Everyone believes all that.' In fact, that's what you said last time we spoke."

"Yes, and that's exactly what I was thinking right now."

"Well, here's where the theist sticks his – or her – neck out. The theist believes that, in addition to the scientific laws, there are certain underlying principles that are even more fundamental or ultimate, and not just the principles of logic or math. These underlying principles are themselves not scientific laws. Rather, they are what I call divine principles. The theist believes that it is by virtue of these principles that the scientific laws are the way they are. Differently stated, we can use the divine principles to explain why the scientific laws are the way they are."

"Sorry, I don't get it. Science explains the world. But you're saying that science itself needs to be 'explained.' Why's that? Doesn't science itself explain the world?"

"No, not completely. Science does a good job of explaining certain things in terms of other things. But there's a lot that science does not explain at all. For example, science explains why the earth goes around the sun in terms of the law of gravity. But it doesn't explain the fundamental laws, such as the law of gravity itself. And let's suppose that one day science could explain the law of gravity. It would have to do so by explaining it in terms of some other more general law of physics. And if so, science wouldn't be able to explain why that law is true. What's more, there are certain fundamental things that science can't explain, such as why there are any contingent beings rather than none at all, or why the universe has any order rather than none at all. Science also does not explain why the laws of nature are such that they are hospitable to human life. Theoretically, there are an infinite number of logically possible worlds – I mean, an infinite number of possible ways the world could have been. Some possible worlds are orderly. Yet even very few of those orderly worlds are hospitable to human life."

"Wait a second. What's so special about human life?"

"David! Surely you jest!"

"No. I really mean it. Any possible world would have something in it. Why is the fact that there's human life such a big deal, something that needs an explanation?"

"Don't you remember what we said some time ago about the intrinsic value of humans? I've already explained to you that, in my view, because we have free choice, it follows that humans have a certain kind of worth insofar as they are beings. What's special about humans is the fact that we are intelligent and that we are moral agents. That makes us quite special indeed, and that's an objective fact!"

"Oh, yes, I remember all that. So let's suppose I agree that humans are special. Still, why do you say that science cannot explain the existence of human life? What about the theory of evolution?"

"Look. The best that science can do is to try to explain how human life evolved, given certain laws of nature. But science does not and cannot explain why the basic laws of nature are what they are. In fact, it's not clear that science has a good explanation for the origin of life from inanimate life. And let's suppose that one day science could do even that. The bottom line is that, first, science cannot explain why there is any contingent order in the universe, second, it cannot explain why the natural laws are the way they are, and third, it cannot explain why the natural laws happen to be just those that are hospitable to human life."

"OK. I think I follow what you're saying."

"Then let's get back to my conception of God. In my view, to be a theist is to believe that there is an ultimate explanation for those things which science itself cannot explain. The explanation lies in what I've been calling the divine principles, which describe the ways in which being itself – that's the essence of God – is expressed or made manifest. Now, I caution you that while I hold that it is rationally defensible to believe in the divine principles, I concede there is no demonstrable proof that these principles are true. I do claim that these principles have implications and so they can be confirmed, but they cannot be confirmed in the same quantitative and repeatable fashion that scientific theories can be confirmed. After all, they are not scientific laws. They are divine or 'meta-scientific' principles – they take us beyond science."

"OK. So, what are these divine principles?"

"The divine principles are parallel to the divine attributes on the popular conception. Instead of saying that there is a non-physical being who has the properties creative, providential, benevolent and just, I would say that there are certain principles which are true, and which describe how Being is expressed. Here, let me draw a new diagram for you, which will illustrate my view."

"If you recall our discussion last time, I've already explained to you that unity, infinity, necessity and freedom are features of being itself."

"Yes, I remember that."

"So, now I need to explain the four principles on the bottom of the diagram. By the way, there may be other principles as well, but these are the main ones. They describe how the universe is structured in just such a way as to express the features of Being itself. What I call the principle of divine creation states as follows: *Being itself is continually expressed or made ever more manifest*. In other words, there is a process going on in the universe, such that Being is continually expressed. In my view, that's what it means to believe in creation."

"Dr. Maimon, you keep using that phrase, 'being itself is expressed.' I think I get that, but I'm not sure. What does that mean?"

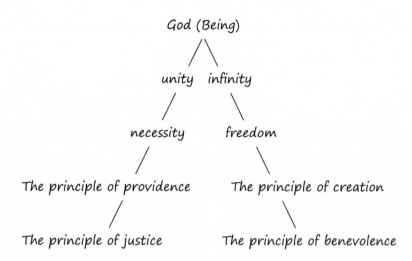

"I'll try to explain. Any contingent being is, in a limited sense, a representation of being itself. By the way, are you familiar with the Hebrew poem 'Yigdal'? It's printed at the beginning of the traditional prayer book, and it's actually a poetic codification of Maimonides's thirteen principles."

"Yes, I remember seeing that in the *siddur*."

"Well, in some versions, one verse runs as follows: '*Kol notzar yoreh gedulato u-malchuto.*' It means, 'Every creature indicates his greatness and his kingship.' At first glance, this is puzzling. One might ask: is it really the case that every creature, even a pebble or a gnat, indicates God's greatness? But the answer is that indeed every being, no matter how small or insignificant, is a being of some sort, and so it indicates or points to Being itself in all its myriad possible manifestations."

"I guess that's true. It's an interesting idea."

"But surely, not every creature fully expresses Being itself. There is so much about Being that the gnat or the pebble does not fully express!"

"Yes, that's also true."

"So the principle of divine creation says not only that Being is represented, but also that there is a certain process going on in the universe, such that all the features of being are expressed or made ever more manifest in the contingent world. The world we live in is incredibly complex and diverse, from the galaxies to the planets to the myriad creatures of the sea to the blades of grass to the grains of sand on the beaches."

"Dr. Maimon, that was very poetic!"

"Thanks. I'll take that as a compliment. Anyhow, my claim is that to believe in 'creation' is to believe that our world is an expression of the infinite and perfect nature of being. More accurately stated, to believe in creation is to believe that the cosmos is heading toward a fuller and fuller expression of Being, until that expression is, in some sense, as complete as can be. This goes back to the point I made earlier – namely, that a true self-expression is a complete one."

"Wow! I think I'm beginning to understand what you're saying. But it sounds like a pretty strong claim to say that the universe is headed toward some kind of completion or perfection. How can you possibly back up that claim?"

"I've already admitted that there is no way to prove it demonstrably. But I do think it is rationally defensible to believe that the cosmos is heading toward fuller and fuller expression of Being. For one thing, not only do contingent beings exist – they are constantly developing, evolving, unfolding. This is particularly true in the case of human beings, who, in a way, express Being most of all."

"Why is that?"

"Once again, humans are intelligent, so they can think about the idea of being, infinity, necessity, and so forth. Second, humans have the ability to recognize and respect beings insofar as they are greater or lesser beings. In other words, humans have moral awareness. Finally, humans have free choice, and so they are moral agents. This mimics the expression of Being itself in contingent being. Now, as the world grows and gets more complicated, and as the history of human existence unfolds, the expression of Being itself is continually unfolding. It is not an accident that humans have flourished and, to use the Biblical phrase, 'conquered the world.' Of course, we haven't quite succeeded yet, but we're getting there. This is all part of the metaphysical process which the theist claims is at work in the universe, namely, the expression of Being itself."

"I'm not sure I agree, but this is all very interesting."

"Glad you think so. Now, so far I've discussed the principle of divine creation. I still need to discuss the other divine principles. What I call the principle of divine providence says that there is a process going on, such that the *necessity and oneness of being is continually expressed or made ever more manifest in the contingent world.* Think back to what we said before. The world is an incredibly diverse place. Yet despite its diversity, the world is also an orderly place. It obeys not only the rules of logic and mathematics, but also it has a contingent universal order as described by science, though science itself cannot explain why there is such an order. The contingent orderliness of the world is an expression of unity and necessity. And the order is pervasive and universal. In other words, divine providence is not half-baked. It is supreme."

"OK, I think I follow."

"Good. Then the next thing for me to do is to explain the principles of divine benevolence and divine justice. These principles describe more particular ways in which being is expressed or made manifest. But they follow plausibly from the principles I've already mentioned – namely, creation and providence."

"How so?"

"The principle of divine benevolence says simply that *the universe is ordered in such a way that it is headed for the best end.* Part of what this means is that the universe is ordered in such a way as to promote the physical, moral, and spiritual development of humankind. Thus, for example, rain falls, crops grow, the world flourishes, humans grow and multiply and become ever more developed, and so on. At a deeper level, perhaps, we may say that the solar system is constructed in just such a way that human flourishing is possible. Again, science does not really have an explanation for this. In my view, if there is an explanation for it, it is the principle of divine benevolence. In some sense, it's obvious that, from a human point of view, undeserved good things happen. But what I mean when I assert this as a principle is that the explanation for why certain things happen in the world is rooted in the very nature of being. Of course, an atheist will admit that undeserved good things happen at least partly because of the scientific laws of nature, which are orderly. But the atheist has no explanation for why the laws of nature are the way they are. In fact, he has no explanation for why there is any contingent order at all. Do you follow?"

"You're saying quite a lot. But I think I follow."

"Good. Next is the principle of divine justice, which follows from the principle of divine providence. It goes like this: *the universe is ordered in such a way that the most just end possible is reached.* What this amounts to is that human beings are given free choice or responsibility to do good or evil, and they are held accountable for their actions. In this way, people can deserve or merit some good. Again, this is one way in which necessity is expressed in the contingent world. Furthermore, the universe is structured in just such a way that the most just end possible is reached. An example of divine justice is the fact that, over the long run, human history evolved from primitive, pre-moral status to greater and greater cultural and moral refinement. We can see that as we head into the twenty-first century – that universal justice and universal human rights are becoming more of a real possibility than ever before. In my view, this historical development is not an accident, nor is it merely a result of blind evolutionary principles. It is rather a manifestation or expression of something that is rooted in being itself – namely, the oneness and necessity of being."

"This is all very interesting, and I think I follow most of what you're saying. But I have an objection. Suppose I agree that it's rationally defensible to believe in some principle of benevolence – in order to explain the things you mentioned, such as the fact that the laws of nature are hospitable to human life. And let's say I agree that it's also rationally defensible to believe in some principle of justice – in order to explain the moral development of mankind. But why should we believe that God's benevolence or justice is supreme or perfect?"

"Well, look here. If God is Being itself, and if there is a process going on such that there is an expression of Being, then it stands to reason – although it is not logically necessary – that this expression should be as complete and perfect as can be. This is just normal explanatory procedure. The same thing holds in science. When you postulate a theory to explain some phenomena, you postulate a general rule or universal statement. To explain why the apple falls from the tree, you postulate that the force of gravity operates pervasively in nature. Similarly, it does not make sense to postulate a half-baked divine self-expression. Therefore, it does not make sense to postulate a half-baked divine providence, benevolence, or justice."

"Hmm. I'm not so sure I follow you there. But let me see if I'm clear on the overall difference between your theory and the popular conception. On the popular conception, there's a divine entity, who creates and manages the world, does good actions, and ultimately gives people what they deserve. God is a being that stands outside of time and space, yet intervenes whenever he wishes. But, on your view, there isn't a super-being or super entity out there at all. Rather, to believe in God is to believe certain things about the world – such as, that the world has an order and it is headed for the best and most just end."

"That's correct. But you need to add that on my view there is an explanation for why these principles are true, and the explanation lies in the nature of being itself – which is to say, God's essence."

"It sounds like you're saying that the universe has a grand scheme or design, even though there isn't really a designer."

"Yes, that's an excellent way to describe it. I am saying that the world exhibits signs of design and order, which cannot be explained by scientific principles alone. Yet we need not postulate a *designer* to explain the design. Rather, the world can be explained in terms of certain features of Being."

"But does that make sense? Can you have design without a designer?"

"I don't see why not. Postulating a designer to explain the design or structure in the world is both unnecessary and unhelpful, and raises more problems than it solves. Now, then – there is still one more principle we need to discuss, and that is the principle of divine communication."

"OK. What's that?"

"Let's go back for a moment to the popular conception of God. In the popular conception, God has freely chosen to create a world in which he acts differently, depending on what people freely choose to do – including whether they pray or not. Thus, God is a being who listens to our prayers and then makes some kind of calculated decision about whether to grant them or not. Sometimes he does and sometimes he doesn't. Of course, we can't always fathom why God grants some prayers and not others. But even if God doesn't grant a prayer, he still listens and takes it into consideration in governing the world."

"OK. So, what does 'God listens' mean in your view?"

"In my view, there is no entity out there who listens and then reacts to our prayers in some way. Rather, as I see it, it's part and parcel of the very structure of our world that prayer is efficacious. In other words, the world is structured in such a way that when people pray, it has a real effect on what's going to happen or not happen in the future. This is not because there's a logically necessary connection between the prayer and its effect. Nor is there a scientific connection between prayer and its effects, as if one could correlate the two by engaging in a scientific study. It's rather that the universe has a certain structure, such that, under certain circumstances, when certain prayers are said, the result is that those prayers are 'answered' – that is, fulfilled, either fully or partially. Of course, there are also circumstances under which prayers are not fulfilled. Whether and how prayers get fulfilled depends on how those prayers play into the ultimate goal – that is, the cosmic plan – which, as I said, is the fuller and fuller expression of Being itself. By the way, this would be the explanation for why it is so hard to predict when a prayer will be fully answered. In any case, the universe is ordered in such a way that sincere prayers always have at least some effect on the direction that reality takes."

"Hmm. Well, it's certainly an interesting way to look at prayer. In your view, a person doesn't really pray *to a being*. Rather, he prays that certain things might or might not happen."

"Yes. To put it a little more precisely, one prays that Being itself will express itself in a certain way rather than another."

"But why would you need to pray for that? In your view, shouldn't Being automatically express itself in whatever way is best or fullest without our prayers?"

"You're forgetting what we said about freedom. The structure of the universe is such that being manifests itself more fully if and when humans engage in free actions that help bring about that manifestation. And, the manner in which Being expresses itself depends on how people freely act. Prayer is no different on that score than any other free action. Do you follow?"

"I'm not sure. But let me ask you this. What's the rationale for believing that prayers are answered at all?"

"It follows from the principle of divine benevolence, for which I argued earlier. It's rationally defensible to believe that the universe is headed toward its best end, that is, the fullest possible expression of Being. So, it's rational to believe that in those cases where the fulfillment of a prayer will promote or tend toward this end, such a prayer will be fulfilled."

"Hmm. I guess I need to think about it."

"No doubt you do. This is complex material. Anyway, finally, let's talk about what it means to say that God speaks. On the popular conception, there's a being out there, God, who occasionally speaks to his followers or prophets. When he decides to do this, he causes his followers or prophets to become inspired and hear his message. But in my conception, to say that God speaks is to say that on some occasions, certain people are inspired to have unusually perceptive insights regarding important truths – truths about the being itself, truths about the divine principles, truths about the details of the divine plan, and perhaps other truths as well. Of course, it is all part of the divine plan itself that these moments of inspiration should occur. At a low level, this is called 'divine inspiration' or *ruah ha-kodesh* – that's the holy spirit. At a higher level, *nevuah* – prophecy – occurs.

In a prophetic experience, a person hears a voice or sees an image – sometimes in a dream, sometimes possibly in a conscious state – that teaches the person about some important truth, usually something that is crucial to the divine plan itself. Through this experience, a person or group of people might learn something they would never have known using ordinary means of reason and perception."

"OK. I think I get the idea."

"And, according to Judaism, the main claim based on prophecy is the claim that God revealed himself to the people of Israel and gave us the Torah."

"So, you do believe that the Torah is divinely given?"

"Of course. I already told you that once before. Second to the belief in God, the most important tenet of Judaism is *Torah min ha-shamayim* – that is, the Torah was given from Heaven, or divinely revealed."

"And how do we know –"

"Excuse me, David, but do you realize it's now 5:15? Didn't you say you had a plane to catch?"

"What?! God, it's late! I totally lost track of time! Sorry, but I really got to get going!"

"No problem, David. You have a good break."

"See you next semester!"

"I'll look forward to it. Take care."

27

"Hi, Esther. How are you?"

"Good, thank God. How was winter break?"

"Fine, but I'm glad to be back. I missed you!"

"Well, I missed you too. How is your mom?"

"Pretty good so far. It really seems they caught it in time."

"*Baruch Hashem!*"

"Say again?"

"*Baruch Hashem*. It means: blessed be the name of God – or, more conversationally, 'Thank God!' You say it when you hear good news. Sometimes I say it without even thinking. So – what classes are you taking?"

"I'm taking Political Science, Art History, Modern Philosophy, Math, and an independent study in Jewish thought with Dr. Maimon."

"Oh, Dr. Maimon again? You must really like her."

"Yes, I think she's brilliant. Hey, you're not getting jealous, are you?"

"Of course not, David!"

"Just kidding."

"Seriously, though, what I'm thinking about is . . . isn't she Conservative?"

"I'm not sure what she is. Why?"

"You should be careful about what she tells you. I'm not an expert on Conservative Judaism, but they don't believe in *Torah min ha-shamayim*. That means —"

"It means the Torah comes directly from God and it's not invented by man. But Dr. Maimon says she does believe in it."

"Well, Conservative Jews believe that part of the Torah is divine, but not the whole thing. That's why they think they can change things so easily."

"Is that so? Like what?"

"Like, for example, they say you can drive on Shabbat in order to get to shul, which is a radical change."

"OK, and what else?"

"They think that men and women have interchangeable roles. They even have women rabbis."

"Goodness gracious! What *will* they think of next!"

"David, you're not taking me seriously."

"Look, Esther, if you want to be serious about it, actually this is something I wanted to ask you about. I was reading over some of the prayers from the Orthodox *siddur* I have. There are a lot of blessings. The detail is amazing. But I noticed there's a blessing that men say praising God for 'not making me a woman.' Doesn't it bother you that women have a secondary status in Orthodox Judaism?"

"I don't consider the role of women secondary. It's just that men and women have different roles. David, let me explain something to you. Tell me — what do you think is the most important concept in Judaism?"

"That's easy. It's the idea of monotheism, the belief in one supreme God."

"No, I don't think so. Lots of people believe in one God."

"OK, so what is the most important idea in Judaism?"

"It's the concept of a *mitzvah,* a divine commandment. It's the belief that God has commanded us to do certain things. According to Judaism, the most important thing a person can do is fulfill a *mitzvah.*"

"OK, suppose I agree with that. So?"

"Are you familiar with the concept of positive and negative commandments?"

"Yes, I am."

"And did you know that both women and men are equally obligated in all the negative commandments?"

"No, I didn't know that."

"And that means that women have the same responsibilities as men do, as far as the negative commandments go."

"Interesting. And what about the positive commandments?"

"OK, first I need to explain something. The positive commandments can be divided into those that have a specific time when they must be performed and those that don't. For example, the positive commandment to love God does not have a specific time frame. It's always applicable. The same goes for the obligation to fear God and to have faith in God. These commandments are applicable at all times. Now, women are obligated in all those *mitzvot* too. The obligation to love God, to fear God, to believe in God – these are all equally important for women just as for men."

"OK. That's an interesting point."

"Now, some positive *mitzvot* are only done at certain times. There's a name for these commandments. They're called *mitzvot aseh she-hazman geraman*. For example, putting on *tefillin*. This is done only during the day, as I'm sure you know."

"No. I didn't know that."

"Sorry. Well – by the way, do you have a pair of *tefillin*?"

"No, but I know what you're talking about. I've seen them. And I've even put them on a few times."

"I see. Well . . . anyway . . . I was saying that some commandments are done only during certain times. Another example is the commandment to eat in a *sukkah* on the festival of Sukkot."

"That's the festival of booths or huts, right?"

"Exactly. There's a commandment to eat something on the first night of Sukkot in a *sukkah*. Like *tefillin,* this *mitzvah* can be performed only at a certain time."

"OK, I get it so far."

"Now, in general, women are exempt from positive commandments that are time-bound. There are some exceptions. For example, women are obligated to eat matzah on the first night of Pesach and to hear the Megillah on Purim. Are you familiar with these things?"

"I know about eating matzah on Pesach, but what's the other one you mentioned?"

"The Megillah – that's the biblical Book of Esther. It's read every year on Purim. Have you ever gone to a Megillah reading?"

"No."

"Ah, well – maybe you will sometime. It's coming up in the spring. Like I said, women are obligated in some of these positive time-bound commandments, but the general rule is that women are exempt from them."

"I see."

"And so, this is one explanation for why men say the blessing 'who has not made me a woman.' It's not because women are inferior or have a secondary role. It's because only men are obligated to perform the positive commandments that are time-bound, and that's something to be thankful for."

"That's all very interesting, Esther. But why are women exempt from those commandments?"

"Well, historically, women were responsible for bearing children and taking care of the home. So it's unreasonable to expect them to fulfill *mitzvot* that have to be performed at a specific time. Of course, in our day and age, with modern technology and with birth control where people can choose to have only two or three kids, this may seem strange. But historically, women often would have ten or twelve children, and being a homemaker in the old days was literally a non-stop occupation. Men had much more time on their hands. At least, their time was much more flexible. You couldn't reasonably expect a married woman to show up at morning, afternoon, and evening services! Just the nursing and feeding schedule would make it impossible to be punctual. Even now, that would be a crazy expectation. After all, women are still the ones who give birth and nurse the children. Basically, women have a more intimate relationship with their children than fathers do. I'm not saying fathers don't love their children, but their love is more about sustaining the family financially, providing for their education, and things like that. A mother's love is more intimately involved with the child's emotional and character development."

"Do you really buy all that? Haven't things changed?"

"I realize that not everybody today agrees with the idea of different roles for men and women. I'm just trying to explain that according to Judaism, the roles of men and women are different, but equally important."

"But if what you say is true that the most important thing in Judaism is to perform *mitzvot,* is it fair that there are quite a few *mitzvot* that only men perform?"

"Fair? You might as well ask the same question about the non-Jews. There's a blessing which the Jew makes, thanking God for not making me a non-Jew."

"Right. I noticed that one too."

"And the reason we make the blessing is not because we're superior, but rather because God gave us the Torah and the opportunity to do *mitzvot.* So you might as well ask: is it fair that God gave the Torah to the Jews, and not to everyone else?"

"Exactly! That is another problem that still bothers me. What's the explanation for God's choosing a special nation?"

"David, don't you see? Not everyone can be chosen. That's just the way it is. Not everyone can play the leading role. Not everyone can be the President. But that doesn't mean the President is inherently superior to or more important than anybody else."

"I don't know. Somehow that doesn't sound very convincing."

"I'm sorry, but I've explained it as best as I can."

"It's OK. Look, I still like you anyway!"

"I'm glad. And I still like you too, David."

28

"How are you, Dr. Maimon?"

"Fine, David. Have a seat. Let's see, what are we supposed to talk about?"

"The concept of *Torah min ha-shamayim.*"

"Right. A very central concept in Judaism."

"So you believe it's all directly from God? Every word? Every letter?"

"Just a second. Let's get clear on something. The Torah is the record of the revelation which takes place between God and Israel. But remember also that the term 'Torah' includes both a written and an oral part. These are called *Torah she-bichtav* and *Torah she-be'al peh*."

"Yes, I'm familiar with that."

"So, the script or text of the Torah which we have in our possession is only the *written* record of that revelation. The Talmud and the rabbinic tradition passed down and developed throughout the generations is the embodiment of the *oral* Torah. Like a living tree, the oral Torah is an evolving, changing organism. And therefore, our understanding of Torah – even of the written Torah – may change or evolve. The oral Torah includes how to interpret and re-interpret the written Torah. So, the doctrine of *Torah min ha-shamayim* applies not just to the written but also to the oral Torah."

"That's all very interesting. But getting back to the written Torah itself, the text of the Torah as we know it today – do you believe that it's all directly from God?"

"Sorry, but we still need to make another clarification before I can answer your question. The phrase *Torah she-bichtav* or 'the written Torah' has different uses or applications. In a general sense, the 'written Torah' refers to the Tanakh – that's all of the Hebrew Scriptures. These are traditionally divided into three parts: the Torah in the narrow sense or the first five books of Moses otherwise known as the Pentateuch; the Nevi'im, or writings of the Prophets, who followed after Moses; and the Ketuvim, or 'Writings,' which are believed to be divinely inspired or written with *ruah ha-kodesh* – the holy spirit. The latter group includes things like Psalms, Proverbs, the Scroll of Esther, Job, and so on. Now, no one – not even the most Orthodox Jew – believes that the latter two parts come directly from God word for word. The Nevi'im and Ketuvim were written by human beings, though – among other things – they include records of divine revelations. So when you ask whether the text of the Torah was divinely given directly from God, I presume you're asking about the first five books, or the Pentateuch."

"Yes. That's what I meant."

"Well, first of all – in my view – it's pretty obvious that Moshe did not receive the entire text of the Pentateuch as we have it directly from God. The text itself indicates that Moshe wrote the text, or at least most of it. But the content is divine. That's what's crucial."

"You're saying the text says Moshe wrote down most of it? So you don't think that every word of our text was divinely dictated to Moshe?"

"No, I can't believe that. First of all, it's obvious there have been some interpolations, additions, and corruptions of the text. Many Orthodox Jews try to deny this but there's really no way around it if you look at the text with an open mind. For example, there are references to personalities who existed after Moshe passed away, such as the kings of Edom mentioned in Genesis 36. Of course, Orthodox scholars try to find some way around such passages, such as saying that Moshe foresaw with prophecy what will happen after his death. Alternatively, they try to say that all of these kings came and went before Moshe's demise. But there's more. The book of Kings describes an episode in which King Josiah found an ancient text, or part of the text, of the Torah. This supports the thesis that well before the canonization of the Hebrew Scriptures, different texts were in use, and at some point an attempt was made to achieve uniformity. Later, in the rabbinic period, differences cropped up between different manuscripts of the Torah. For in the Talmud and other early rabbinic literature there are occasionally citations of certain passages from the Hebrew Scriptures that are quoted in a slightly different way from what we have in our texts today. If you're really curious, I can give you the references some other time. And to this very day, we also have some different traditions about the spelling of certain words, within the Pentateuch. Different Torah scrolls in different communities contain some differences – albeit minor ones – in the spellings of words."

"But wait a second. Someone once told me that according to the Talmud, anyone who says that even one letter of the Torah was not divine but was invented – even by Moshe himself – is considered a heretic. So by that standard, you're either a heretic, or you disagree with the Talmud."

"Hang on, David. You're referring to a passage toward the end of Tractate *Sanhedrin*. I agree that my position is not the conventional one you'd find among most Orthodox rabbis, but I don't think it's fair to call it heretical from a Talmudic standpoint. Sure, the Talmud makes that statement, but one needs to understand it properly. Did you know there is also a view stated elsewhere in the Talmud that not Moshe, but Yehoshua – that's Joshua – wrote the last eight verses of the Torah?"

"No, I didn't know that. But that would seem to make sense, since if I remember correctly, it describes Moshe's death."

"Right. Well, if Joshua wrote the last eight verses, how would that fit with the other statement that every single verse of the Pentateuch was transmitted from God to Moshe?"

"Hmm. I guess whoever said that meant that nearly all of it was from God to Moshe. One could say that God told Joshua exactly what to write. The point is that every word comes directly from God."

"But if so, it still remains the case that not all of our Torah text was given to Moshe."

"True."

"Well, then – here's one possible interpretation of the doctrine of the divine revelation of the Torah: There occurred a series of revelations in which God revealed the Torah – to Moshe. The Talmud in Tractate Sanhedrin is saying that Moshe did not interject or manufacture any part of that revelation. In other words, the Torah in its entirety was divinely ordained. None of it was man-made. Furthermore, when Moshe wrote down the original revelation, he did not interject a single letter of his own invention. Now, this does not exclude the possibility that Joshua may have written the concluding eight verses of the Pentateuch. Furthermore, in subsequent generations, the text may have undergone – indeed I believe it did undergo – many revisions and transcriptions, as the centuries wore on. During this period, other things may have been added as well, such as the names of the Kings of Edom. And finally, over the course of time, a plurality of texts may have evolved with slight variations. But none of this changes the claim that *there was an original revelation to Moshe, which was completely and wholly divine in origin.* To deny *that* is to be a 'heretic.' Perhaps that's what the Talmud is saying. Do you follow?"

"I think I get what you're saying. But on that view, the text as we have it is *not* completely written by God. Doesn't that cause some serious problems for being a committed Jew? I mean, why should we pay such serious attention to the text if it is not an accurate record of what God said or did? If things crept in to the text in later years, maybe some of the dos and don'ts in the Torah as we know it are just plain mistaken!"

"Not at all. As I've already explained, I believe in divine providence as well. So, the text as we have it today, which is substantially the same text we've had for two thousand years, it is that text – warts and all – which divine providence has given to the Jewish people. And that's what I believe it means to say that the text of the Torah is divinely given."

"Sorry, I'm not sure I understand."

"I'll explain it another way. Suppose – just suppose for the sake of discussion – that there really was no such historical person as Moshe. I'll go further – suppose it was proven by some kind of irrefutable archeological evidence that, as a historical person, Moshe never existed."

"But then the whole thing would be a fraud!"

"No, that doesn't follow. In fact, as far as I'm concerned, it wouldn't change matters all that much."

"Sorry. I don't get that at all!"

"Look, the main principle at issue here is *Torah min ha-shamayim* – the Torah is divinely revealed. But what does that *mean*? In my view, it means that God's providence has directed that the written and oral Torah as we have it – and as we develop it – is the essential teaching or law which God has given as a way of life for the people of Israel. Hence, it is immaterial whether Moshe the person actually lived! So, even if one *knew for a fact* that Moshe never lived as a historical figure, one could still believe in Torah from heaven in the sense I have just described. For, it's entirely possible that God could communicate or transmit a way of life to the people of Israel through the device of myth."

"What do you mean by that? When I think of myth I think of the gods and heroes of the ancient Greeks . . . phony stuff like that."

"Ah, no, David! Myths aren't phony stuff at all. Mythology is a very complex process whereby people invent or imagine profound tales about their past that have implications for their present. You should not underestimate the significance of myth, or fiction in general. Despite the fact that tales are *invented,* they may contain values and principles by which people should live. There is a sense in which some myths may be 'truer' than others. Indeed, some myths may be deeply perverse or false. Judaism teaches that God is more closely involved in the formation of some myths than others. Or as I would prefer to say, perhaps some myths are a more true expression of Being itself than others. But, whether you think of God as *a* being, or as Being itself, there is no reason why the divine plan couldn't be worked out through the process of mythmaking."

"Hmm. This is very interesting. But I'm not sure I follow."

"Look. Let's assume – let's speak as if – God is a being who wishes that a certain people should follow a certain way of life. Surely, God could easily bring it about that the people construct a myth about themselves involving the figure 'Moshe,' and containing precisely whatever guidelines or directives God wished to give them. And it could very well be an important part of this myth that the figure, Moshe, does not fabricate or invent any content of the divine message. This is the teaching of the Talmud that you mentioned earlier. What it really means, properly understood, is that the Torah is the divinely ordained path for the Jewish people. It is not a man-made invention or construction. Now, of course, this process of mythmaking would take some time. Myths aren't created overnight. Like any good myth, it would be based on actual historical personalities and events. It wouldn't be totally fantastical. But the bottom line is that, in theory, God could have ordained the Torah as a way of life upon the people of Israel *even if much of the story line of the Torah is itself historically false.* Isn't that a coherent possibility, David?"

"I guess so. Somehow it seems to me that if there is a God, and if he really wanted to give the Torah to the Jewish people, he would have taken a more direct approach – pretty much like the approach actually described in the text."

"On the contrary, David! I think there are good reasons for why God might choose to express himself in this mythical way. But look, I'm not insisting that all the stories or even some of them are literally false. All I'm trying to say right now is that one need not believe that the stories of the Pentateuch are literally true in order to believe in *Torah min ha-shamayim.* Actually, what I'm saying is just an extension of the idea that God communicates to prophets through the imagery of dreams and visions – an idea which is found throughout the scriptures and is very well accepted by traditional Jewish writers. Maimonides explains that the dreams and visions themselves are not literally speaking 'true,' but they convey information to the prophet which is true – profoundly true, for that matter. Something similar takes place in the formation of myth. A myth itself isn't historically true. To use the same example again, perhaps there really was no such person as Moshe who went to the top of Mount Sinai for forty days and forty nights, and so on. Despite this, the bottom line is that God communicated to the people of Israel that we ought to live in a certain way, that is, that we ought to follow the Torah."

"I guess that's possible. But there still seems to be some questions. Like, what would be the point of forty days and forty nights, then? I mean, if Moshe didn't actually stay on Mt. Sinai for forty days and forty nights, why does the text say that? Just because it sounds poetic?"

"First of all, don't underestimate the value of poetry. Second, I'm not sure what the forty days and nights signify, but whatever that significance is, does it really *depend* on the literal truth of the story? Suppose for a moment that Moshe *was* a real person and he did actually go up for forty days and forty nights. Don't you still have the same question, anyway? Namely, why did he go up for exactly forty days and forty nights? Or rather, why did the Torah record this fact?"

"Well, I would assume there must be some deep truth or lesson to be learned from the fact that he was up there for forty days and nights."

"Precisely! But if that's so, why couldn't the same significant message be implied by the text even if the story was a myth produced under divine guidance, and in fact Moshe never did go up for that length of time?"

"I'm not sure what to say, but somehow what you say doesn't strike me as right."

"David, let me put it this way. What I'm suggesting is that the Torah has an *exterior* meaning and an *inner* meaning. The exterior meaning could actually be historically false or inaccurate. But the inner meaning could still be profoundly true and valid. This is true of many great works of literature. Suppose, for example, that Hamlet never existed as a real person. Does that mean Shakespeare's *Hamlet* contains no profound truths? Of course not! Whenever Shakespeare introduces some small detail about what Hamlet said or did, or even some minor gesture that Hamlet made, there might be some profound meaning underlying that detail. The fact that Hamlet never lived would be irrelevant to the profundity of that detail. Either it would be profound or not, but that wouldn't depend on its historical or literal truth. Don't you agree?"

"Dr. Maimon, this is weird, but I'm getting a feeling of déjà vu. Somehow, I think I've heard this argument before, but I can't remember where. Anyhow, right now I must admit I can't think of anything wrong with what you're saying."

"It's simple enough. A fictional work can contain profound truths, illustrated through the lives and speeches of its characters, even if none of those characters are historically real. And even the details may carry some great significance, even if the story never occurred in actual historical time."

"I guess. I need to think about it."

"Fine. While you're thinking, I'm sure you can realize the advantage this approach has over the more conventional Orthodox view."

"What's that?"

"To put it bluntly, it's much easier to believe in *Torah min ha-shamayim* in this view rather than in the more traditional view. In the conventional Orthodox view, you have to believe that Moshe was a real person, and that all the events and personalities described in the Scriptures are historically true. You have to believe that God's voice issued from the heavens and was heard by the people, telling them to do certain things and avoid other things. And it follows that in order to know that God revealed the Torah, you need to have good reason to believe that a specific, real-time, historical event actually occurred some three thousand years ago."

"I think I get your point."

"Generalizing the same point, if one insists, as a matter of Jewish doctrine, that the stories of the Scriptures be taken as literally accurate, we then face the problem that Judaism is subject to criticism that stems from the sciences of cosmology, biology, history, archeology, anthropology, philology, and so on. But if you take the approach I'm suggesting, none of these things constitutes an obstacle to Jewish belief in the divine origin of the Torah."

"I think I follow, but can you explain that a little more? If you don't take it literally, how do you interpret the creation story, for example?"

"Actually, I don't have a detailed interpretation of the creation story that I am fully satisfied with. But I certainly don't take the six days of creation as an historical or scientific account. All the attempts to try to reconcile the details of the creation story with modern science have failed. But that doesn't bother me in the least, because I don't take the stories literally. And I don't take the Garden of Eden story literally either. Do you really think that a snake spoke to Eve and Adam? Do you really think that the snake used to walk around, and then got its legs chopped off? That's ridiculous – if it is taken literally. Rather, I take the whole story as a metaphor for the human condition. Maybe it tells us something about how humans are subject to temptation, and how God needs to suppress the urges of human beings so that they won't sin as much as they would otherwise. I don't really know, and to be quite frank, it's not something I really spend much time worrying about. It's all very interesting to speculate what the story really means, but I don't have a definitive view about it – other than the fact that it's not to be taken literally!"

"I see."

"And the same thing goes for the flood story. Look, do you really think there was an ark that could have held all the existing species of the time? That's very hard to believe! My interpretation is very simple. The flood story is a metaphor for the teaching that if humanity sins or becomes corrupt, our lives are worthless because we are not fulfilling the purpose for which we were created – that is, to express divinity. But if we are righteous, all of creation is thereby blessed and worthwhile. That's the inner meaning of the story of the flood. So, whether Noah actually got all the species into the ark is irrelevant to this teaching."

"Well, I see how your view certainly makes it a lot easier to believe in the divine origin of Torah. But you still need to explain your reasons for believing that the Torah is divinely given. Maybe the whole Torah was cooked up through pure fantasy, sort of like a bad novel as opposed to a good one. If the Torah is a myth, why should we believe in it any more than in mythical stories of the ancient Greeks, or Grimm's fairy tales?"

"Good question, David. All I've done so far is describe my understanding of what it means to believe in *Torah min ha-shamayim*. But I haven't given an argument for why I think it is rationally defensible to believe that the doctrine is true."

"Well, I'd love to hear it."

"OK, here goes. It's really very straightforward, because it follows from things we've previously discussed. I've already argued that it is rationally defensible to believe in God and to believe in the divine principles of creation, providence, benevolence, and justice. It's rationally defensible to believe that the world is structured in such a way that there is a continual expression of God or Being itself. And remember that the principle of providence says that the necessity and oneness of being is continually expressed or made ever more manifest in the contingent world. In addition, the principle of benevolence says that the cosmos is headed toward the best end, and the principle of divine justice says that the world is structured in just such a way that the most just end possible will be reached. Do you remember all this?"

"Yes, pretty much."

"Now, obviously the Torah exists as a phenomenon. I mean, the people of Israel *have* the Torah. No one can deny that. And the Torah purports to be the expression of God's directives to the people of Israel. In fact, the Torah is the only putative document that purports to be the expression of God's will in a written document. The only possible competitors are the teachings of Christianity and Islam, since these religions make claims about what is God's will for all humankind, including the Jewish people. But even these two religions presuppose a pre-existing tradition in which God communicated the Torah to Israel. So let's put Christianity and Islam on the back burner for a moment. Are you OK with that?

"No problem."

"Good. Now, as far as I'm concerned, it doesn't matter whether the Torah is mythical in the sense that the characters and stories described in the Torah are not literally true. It doesn't matter whether the characters and stories were invented or imagined by people over some long period of time. The only crucial question is *whether or not the Torah represents God's communication to Israel regarding what we must do to advance God's will*. And remember that in my conception, to say that *God speaks* is to say that on some occasions, certain people are inspired to have unusually perceptive insights regarding important truths – truths about Being itself, about the divine principles, about the details of the divine plan, and most significantly, teachings about what we must do or not do in order to advance the expression of Being itself in the world. Are you with me?"

"Yes, I am."

"Great. Well, given that it's rationally defensible to believe in divine providence, benevolence and justice, I claim further that it's also rationally defensible to believe that the Torah really does represent the expression of God's will for Israel. The revelation of the Torah is precisely what we would expect to happen if it hadn't happened already. In fact, it would be strange if divine providence had allowed the Torah to occur unless it is indeed a genuine expression of God's will for Israel. Do you follow?"

"Sorry, but I'm really not sure I do."

"Hmm. Well, I really hate to do this, but the only way I can think of to explain it any better is by giving you an analogy in the form of a story."

"Yes, please do. After all, I'm trying to get used to the idea that stories might contain profound truths."

"Touché! But listen here. Suppose I had rationally persuaded you to believe that there was a very wise, powerful, benevolent, and just king who lived somewhere across the sea. Suppose I also persuaded you that he was responsible for your existence and everything you have, and that all the good things in your life really came from him, and that he was guiding all the events in your life toward some good end. Got it so far?"

"Yes. It sounds kind of like God."

"Of course – that's the idea! Now, assuming I've convinced you of all this, you'd still be entitled to wonder why the king hadn't contacted you personally in some way, and why he hadn't told you about himself more directly. You'd be entitled to expect that someday he would do just that. Indeed, the fact that he has not contacted you in any direct way might cause some lingering doubt in your mind as to whether he really exists. If he hasn't contacted you directly, that would seem to be something of a flaw in his providence? Right?"

"OK, that sounds right."

"Now let's suppose that one day someone showed up with a document that purported to be a letter from the king. It described and confirmed some of the facts about the king which I had already persuaded you about, but it also contained instructions about what you must do in order to advance the king's plan for you. Suppose it was the only document of its kind. What would be your reaction?"

"Well, I'd look it at pretty closely and try to see what it contained and whether it made any sense . . .".

"Good, good. Is that it?"

"I don't know. The document might be a fake, I suppose."

"How likely could that be, given what I've already told you about this king? Remember, I've already persuaded you that the king is responsible for your existence and for everything you have, that all good things in your life come from him, that he has a plan for you, and that he is guiding your life toward some great end. So I ask again, what would be your reaction to the document?"

"I don't know . . . I'm not really sure."

"May I remind you of what we said just a minute ago? Namely, that on the assumption that such a king existed, you would have expected that at some point he would contact you. And now, the only plausible candidate for that commu-nication from the king has apparently arrived! We've also assumed that the king has control over everything that happens in your life. So a fake would have to be sent by the king himself, or at least allowed by the king himself. Given that the king is provident and just, that would be extremely unlikely. Hence it is rational to assume that this is indeed the communication sent to you by the king himself. And – oh dear. It's coming up on three-thirty again!"

"That's OK, Dr. Maimon. You'd better go pick up your daughter."

"All right. Anyway, I think you can work out for yourself what the analogy is supposed to prove."

"Yes, I think I can."

29

"Hey, David. How are you? Are you still smoking?"

"Sure, Simon. It does wonders for my running."

"Right. Well, here you go. Try this."

"Thanks! Hey – this is pretty good!"

"Don't you remember? It's the stuff you yourself got downtown."

"Oh, right. I almost forgot!"

"So, any progress with Esther?"

"Yes, definitely. She's almost there."

"What does that mean?"

"I think she's in love with me, despite our differences."

"But it's all platonic."

"So far. But that'll change."

"Sure, sure. How long has it been since you met her? You know what's changing? *You* are!"

"Am I? Maybe you're right."

"You're going to end up more like her than she will end up like you. Look, why don't you find some other nice Jewish girl? Why'd you have to pick Esther?"

"I don't know. It was just my luck I happened to meet her. But there's just something about her. I don't know what it is."

"Man! I'm really getting worried about you. You're getting completely shnookered."

"*What*? What's that mean?"

"Shnookered. That's like 'snookered' except it means to become a shnook, which is Yiddish for a fool or a dope."

"I see. That's pretty strong language, Simon."

"Sorry, David. Really, I'm just concerned about you. And I don't understand you. Look, what about Christianity? Remember our conversation about that? How did you rule that out?"

"Oh, I'm completely beyond that, Simon."

"Really? Why?"

"Have I told you about my conversations with Rabbi Low? He's the guy in Israel I was telling you about. He explained very well why it doesn't make sense for a Jew to adopt Christianity. Do you want me to forward his emails to you or print them out? If you'll read what he says, I'd love to discuss it with you."

"That's OK. Don't bother. I'm sure he's very good at disproving Christianity. But can he show that Judaism is any better? Can he prove there's a God?"

"Simon, I've got to tell you, my belief in God is really getting more solid. A lot of it has to do with Dr. Maimon."

"Ah, yes – your other Jewish girlfriend!"

"Seriously, Simon. She's given me a better way of understanding God, and she has a very interesting take on why it's rational to believe in God. Instead of understanding God as an entity, she understands God as a principle or structure of the way things are. Her idea –"

"Sounds very nice but spare me the details. As someone once said, *I'm completely beyond all that.* Besides, let's say you do believe in God – what about the idea of the chosen people? Why would God – assuming he exists – choose a special people?"

"Uh, I'm still working on that one."

"Right. Well, when you come up with a good solution for that, there will still be some other problems left over. Look, you can believe what you want. All I can say is, I hope you don't change too much more. I like you the way you are. If you become more and more religious, sooner or later you won't want to hang out with me."

"Simon, whatever happens with me, let's just promise we'll still be friends, the way we've always been."

"Yeah, sure. I promise. Look, will you still smoke with me, even after you become Orthodox?"

"Man, you really are stoned! Who says I'm becoming Orthodox? And of course I'll still smoke with you, no matter what!"

30

"Dr. Maimon, I'm really anxious to hear what you have to say about the idea that the Jews are God's chosen people."

"OK, let's talk about it. Evidently, you think there's a problem with chosenness. Why don't you state the problem in your own words?"

"It's simple. Basically, if God is not just God of the Jews, but the God of all mankind, and if God is fair and just, why would God choose a special people? If the Torah is such a valuable and precious thing, why didn't God give the Torah to all humans? If, as you yourself have said, the Torah represents the expression of God's will – if it describes the path or way in which we can advance the manifestation of Being itself in the world – why wasn't it given to humanity as a whole?"

"Good statement of the problem, David. Well? Can you think of any possible answers?"

"Not any good ones. I know that some Jews believe that Jews are inherently special, and that the rest of humanity is so inferior that they are unable to keep the Torah. But isn't that incredibly arrogant? And if it's true that Jews are somehow better than others, why would God create humans in such an unfair way? Anyway, I'm confident you have an answer. How does your alternative conception of God take care of this problem?"

"David, I'm sorry to hear you have such faith in me! But seriously, I think the question of chosenness can be handled just as easily whether in my conception of God or on the standard conception. A lot of it has to do with a proper understanding of the Noahide Law. Are you familiar with that concept?"

"A little. How does that solve the problem of chosenness?"

"I'll explain. First, tell me: what do you think is the most important or fundamental teaching of Judaism?"

"I'm not sure, but I think it's the idea of *Torah min ha-shamayim,* the belief that the Torah is from heaven."

"No, that's not correct. Without God, you could not have *Torah min ha-shamayim.* Obviously, belief in God is prior to belief in *Torah min ha-shamayim.* Rather, the fundamental teaching of Judaism is *ethical monotheism.* This is basically belief in God, and belief that God is the supreme moral agent, who requires ethical behavior of all humans. This is basically the teaching of the Noahide Law, which applies to all human beings, not just Jews. In my view, the Noahide Law is co-extensive with what humans can rationally know about God and about morality without revelation. In other words, the Noahide Laws are exactly what humans, using their rational capacities, can know about right and wrong in terms of action and belief. As I've explained to you before, I hold that, using reason alone, people can know that God is real, and that there are certain basic things that are right or wrong to do. Everyone can know that idol worship, blasphemy, murder, incest, theft, and cruelty to animals are wrong. Everyone can know that it is objectively right to have a just society. That's exactly what the Noahide Laws are all about."

"That's all very interesting. But someone once told me that God gave the Noahide Laws precisely because humans could not figure out what's moral or immoral on their own."

"I don't know who told you that. But I'm suggesting quite the opposite."

"Yes, I see. But if humans could figure it out on their own, why did God have to give the Noahide Laws to human beings at all?"

"Because not everyone knows in fact what they might know in principle. Not everyone uses reason to full capacity, either out of neglect or out of willful disregard. So God helped humans out, so to speak, by revealing the Noahide Laws. Even if God had not revealed them, we could have, and eventually would have, figured them out using our rational capacities."

"Still, if what you say is correct, what is the point of God's giving the Torah to the Jews? It seems like the Noahide laws should have been enough."

"I'm coming to that. Although the Noahide Laws are binding on all humankind, human beings have free choice to observe or fail to observe these commandments. Now, I believe that, as a matter of contingent historical fact, humans failed to keep the Noahide Laws. This brought about the need for the giving of the Torah to the Jewish people. As you know, Judaism believes in divine providence. The history and fate of humanity are directed toward a goal – namely, the continual unfolding or expression of God, whether you think of God as a Supreme Being or as Being itself. This unfolding or divine expression takes place through the divine attributes, or, as I prefer to say, through the divine principles of benevolence and justice. So despite the fact that we have free choice, humans are not left completely to their own devices, so to speak. In fact, this is the main message of the story of Noah and the Ark. If people were left to their own devices, then, through their poor use of free choice, the entire world could theoretically reach such a low level of depravity that it would need to be utterly destroyed in order for the divine plan to be carried out – that is, in order for God to be fully expressed or actualized. However, God has promised never to let that happen. This means that despite our free choice, things are rigged in such a way that the divine plan will come to fruition. Are you with me so far?"

"Yes."

"Now, let's stay with the story of Noah for another minute. In my view, it doesn't matter whether Noah was a real person or not, or whether the flood actually took place. Noah stands for someone who was committed to God and to an ethical way of life, but who was not interested in teaching that message to others or in changing the world around him. Many commentators have noted that there's no account of his trying to convince others to change their ways. That's the big difference between Noah and Abraham. Abraham called on people to come 'under the wings of the divine presence,' as the Talmud says. Among the descendants of Abraham, some of them followed in his way and some did not. The ones who followed in Abraham's way became the early Israelites. Divine providence protected, guided, and also goaded the early Israelites along the proper way in their dedication to the divine plan. Then, something crucial happened at the time of the exodus from Egypt: the divine ordination or selection of the people of Israel as a nation to carry out a certain mission. After the exodus, another crucial moment was the revelation of the Torah at Sinai. As you know, I don't think we need to take the story literally. But the bottom line is that God made a covenant with the Jewish people, *as a people,* to be a light unto the nations, that is, to *carry out the mission of spreading ethical monotheism throughout the world.* Of course, this does not mean we're supposed to go out and force the non-Jews to be ethical monotheists. Rather, by living an exemplary moral life and by recognizing God, we are supposed to inspire humankind to do the same. Do you follow?"

"Yes, I think so."

"Well, that's the rationale for chosenness. And it's important to understand that God didn't choose a group of individuals, like a society or a club. Rather, God chose a *people*. There are lots of good reasons for this. The main one is that a people can accomplish much more than what a society or a club can accomplish. A people can follow a way of life that is sustained for many generations. A people is bound together by a common history, heritage and destiny in a way that is impossible for a group or a collection of individuals. So, that's the explanation for why so many laws in the Torah have to do with reinforcing Jewish peoplehood. For example, this explains the prohibition against marrying outside of the fold – unless, of course, the non-Jewish partner converts and becomes a Jew – that is, a member of the Jewish people. It's all about preserving the integrity of the people. And the same thing is true for many other rituals, such as the dietary restrictions or laws of *kashrut*. It's all about keeping the people together. After all, there's nothing more ethnically defining than cuisine!"

"I suppose that's true. But there's still another question. Why did God choose the Jews, specifically? Why not some other nation?"

"Again, the answer goes back to free choice. The Torah makes clear that the Jewish people were chosen mainly because Abraham 'walked in God's way,' as did the other patriarchs and matriarchs. The ordination of the Jewish people was a divine response to humanity's quest for God. It just so happened that Abraham was the first one to freely choose to play a role in the fulfillment of the divine plan."

"So, in your view, there's nothing inherently superior about Jews which led God to choose them."

"Absolutely not! I reject the view that there's anything inherently superior in Jewish blood or in the Jewish soul. That's racism. And the proof that there's nothing special about Jewish blood or the Jewish soul is that Judaism accepts converts. Anyone from any ethnic or racial background who's willing to take on the mission with which Jews are charged can become Jewish. That conclusively proves that the selection of the Jewish people is not about race or genes. It's about commitment. It's about choosing to follow a certain way of life. Abraham was the first to make a total commitment to God. That was a result of his choice, not his genes."

"Then let me ask you this. If the Jews are supposed to teach ethical monotheism to the world, then, I guess according to you it's a good thing that Christianity and Islam evolved. Is that right?"

"Yes, that's true to a large degree. Maimonides wrote that if the Jews had completely fulfilled their mission at an earlier time, those religions might not have evolved. Thus, divine providence had to find other ways of spreading ethical monotheism across the world. He refers to these religions as a 'divine ruse' to spread monotheism across the globe."

"Do you agree with Maimonides on that?"

"I myself take an even more positive view of these other religions. I believe that these religions might very well have evolved even if Jews *had* done exactly what they were supposed to do. While from a Jewish perspective these religions are somewhat flawed, nevertheless, they both teach ethical monotheism. In Christianity and Islam, Abraham is considered a spiritual hero. Because of these religions, there is no corner of the globe that is unfamiliar with the name of Abraham. That could be considered a fulfillment of the divine promise in Genesis that the name of Abraham would be 'made great' among the nations. In fact, we can even interpret the scriptural passages which say that Abraham's descendants would be 'exceedingly numerous' as referring to these 'spiritual descendants' as well."

"But you just said these religions are flawed."

"They are flawed *for Jews*, but as far as the non-Jews go, the flaws do not really matter as long as they don't lead to the desecration of Judaism or the persecution of Jews."

"I don't understand. If they're flawed, they're flawed! How can you have it both ways?"

"I'll try to explain. Let's focus on Christianity first. From a Jewish point of view, there are two main flaws in Christianity. The first is the deification of Jesus — that is, the belief that he is somehow the embodiment of God. There is a certain pagan element at the heart of Christianity. In fact, I believe that's one reason why it caught on so well in the ancient world. Nevertheless, today most Christians are really monotheists — or, at worst, they are, in a manner of speaking, confused monotheists. They view Jesus as somehow a partner with the one God. Or they say that God is really one, with two or maybe even three aspects. But in the end, they really believe in one God. Of course, Jews cannot accept that God has a partner. But it's not a problem for non-Jews to believe God has a partner. Judaism does not mandate that the nations have to believe everything that we must believe about God. So it's not a flaw for them if *they* believe it."

"OK. And what's the second flaw in Christianity?"

"The second flaw is the traditional Christian belief, which not all Christians share, that keeping the Torah is a bad thing for Jews to do, or even the belief that it would be better for Jews to adopt Christianity than to keep the Torah. Again, this becomes a real problem only if Christians impose that view on us. The Torah was not given to them anyway, so if they don't believe they need to keep it, that's fine as far as we're concerned. In fact, today many Christians believe that the Jews *should* keep the Torah. The problem begins when they start claiming that Jews must accept Jesus in order to be saved or in order to have the right relationship with God. But in fact, many Christians today no longer believe this either."

"What about Islam? What's flawed there? Is it their claim that Mohammed was a prophet?"

"No, not at all. The Scripture and Talmud are very clear that in principle the idea of a non-Jewish prophet is a real possibility. For example, Balaam was a non-Jewish prophet. Of course, he was evil, but the idea of a non-Jewish prophet who is good is entirely conceivable. For all I know, maybe Mohammed was a prophet in some sense. To the extent that Muslims believe that *they* need to follow Mohammed's teaching, that is not a flaw. The main flaw from a Jewish perspective is insofar as they believe that Jews must accept Mohammed's prophecy and reject the earlier tradition of Moshe. Jews believe that the prophecy of Moshe regarding the Torah was in some sense final, and that no prophet will supersede Moshe. Muslims disagree. They regard Mohammed as the 'seal of the prophets' – that is, the last and greatest of them. But the fact that *they* believe that they must follow Mohammed's directives is not a problem from our point of view. Islam only becomes a problem if they insist that we must follow them. Some Muslims go that far, but others do not."

"All right. I think I get what you're saying. Still, the bottom line is that in some sense, from a Jewish perspective, these religions are flawed. Yet you're trying to provide a rationale for why God would have allowed these religions to flourish."

"Correct. Speaking colloquially, we can say that God realized that the only way to get the message of ethical monotheism across the globe without wiping away free will was to . . . bend the truth, so to speak. As you already know, I believe this is the case within Judaism. God uses myth to convey deep truths. So why shouldn't that be true of other religions as well?"

"I see. Well, do you think eventually the Christians and Muslims will realize their . . . um . . . flaws?"

"Like I said, many of them already have tailored or modified their views to accommodate Judaism. As long as they don't impose their views upon us, there really is nothing flawed about them."

"So you don't think that eventually everyone in the world will be Jewish?"

"No, certainly not. That's preposterous! But I do think that in the end, everyone will recognize and respect the role that the Jewish people has played in the divine plan. And in the end, everyone will recognize God, acknowledge the truth of the divine principles, and build a world of peace and harmony. This is beginning to happen already. Obviously, we still have a long way to go. It may take another five hundred or perhaps a thousand years. But when it happens, it seems to me that the differences between the different religions will recede further and further into the background. Finally, the Jewish people will have no longer any reason to remain distinct from the rest of humanity. Their mission will be accomplished."

"Wait – so now you're saying everyone *will* become Jewish, then."

"Not at all. I can't say for sure, but it seems to me that Jews will no longer need to remain separate from the rest of the world. If ethical monotheism should spread universally across the globe, it seems to me that there will be no need to maintain the differences between the religions."

"So Jews have a special role to play now, but when that role is fulfilled, the rationale for chosenness will evaporate."

"I really can't say for sure. But that's a fair statement of my view."

"Dr. Maimon, your mentioning the idea of special roles reminds me of something else I wanted to ask you about."

"What's that?"

"The idea of the roles of men and women in Judaism. Do you have anything to say about that?"

"Ah, that's opening up a completely different can of worms. I think we've done enough for one day. We'd better talk about that some other time. Will that be all right?"

"Sure. Thank you, Dr. Maimon."

31

From: dgoldstein@cuniv.edu   Sent: 2/14/ 01 9:30 PM
To: rlow@ahavattorah.org.il
Subject: Chosen people?

Dear Rabbi Low,

How are you? I haven't heard from you in a while. I know you're very busy. But I'd really like to hear what you have to say about the issue of chosenness. What's the rationale for God's choosing a special people? I'm taking an independent study with Dr. Maimon on Jewish thought and she's given me her approach to this issue. She says that the Jews were chosen to live an exemplary moral life and to show by example to the world how they ought to live. I'd like to hear what you think.

Could you also answer a question I have about the Noahide Laws? Rabbi Abraham once told me that the Noahide Laws were given because humans cannot know what is right or wrong without God's revelation. On the other hand, Dr. Maimon says that in her view, humans could in principle know what is right or wrong without God's prophecy, and that God just made it easier for humans by revealing the Noahide Laws. In fact, she thinks that the Noahide Laws are "co-extensive," as she puts it, with what humans could know about what is moral or immoral, just using our rational capacities. Who do you think is right?

By the way, did you get a chance to look at my paper on the problem of evil?

David

From: rlow@ahavattorah.org.il **Sent:** 2 /16/01 6:23 AM
To: dgoldstein@cuniv.edu
Subject: RE: Chosen people?

Dear David,

Sorry I haven't gotten back to you sooner. I've been terribly busy.

The independent study you're taking with Dr. Maimon must be fascinating. You must be learning a tremendous amount from her. The question about chosenness is a tough one and there are many different legitimate approaches. Some might say there's no reason for it except divine fiat. But I do think there is a rationale for why God chose a special people. The best way I can explain my view is with an analogy.

Imagine a powerful king of a vast empire. Imagine that in addition to being powerful, he is noble, benevolent, just, and compassionate. Naturally, he expects the citizens to act justly and properly, for the citizens have an innate sense of justice. In addition, the king makes certain rules that all the citizens must follow. The people understand some of these rules, but do not understand others. The king rewards those who follow these rules and punishes those who wantonly break them. Now, imagine also that the King is unmarried. His relationship with his citizens is noble and grand, but somewhat impersonal. Hence the king seeks to have an intimate relationship with someone. He wishes to marry a woman and have her rule with him as queen. Of course, the king cannot have an intimate relationship with every woman in his kingdom. For this reason, he must choose one woman to be his wife and queen.

Naturally, the queen will occupy a very special place in the empire. She will have great privileges, but great responsibility as well. She will live in the royal palace, sit at the king's table and be intimate with him, and she will be able to ask him for things that no one else can ask for. At the same time, certain things will be expected of her that are expected of no one else. She will have to dress according to her station, she will have to wait on the king, and so on. Also, she will be judged according to a higher standard. What would count as vulgar behavior on her part is far different than for an ordinary citizen. If the queen were to be unfaithful, the consequences for her would be far more devastating than for an ordinary citizen. On the other hand, if she is faithful, the rewards of intimacy with the king are far richer than those that await even the most devoted ordinary citizen. While the queen may assist the king in carrying out his plans for the kingdom and provide an example for the citizens by living an especially exemplary life, that is not the main reason for why the king has chosen her as his beloved. Rather, he has chosen her out of the desire to have an intimate and personal relationship.

You can probably guess where this is going. The king stands for G-d, the empire is the world, the citizens are human beings, and the queen is the Jewish people. Like the citizens of the empire in my analogy, all human beings have an innate sense of justice. They instinctively know certain basic things about right and wrong, even without being told. Finally, the rules which the king legislates to the citizens are like the Noahide commandments, while the rules that the queen must follow are the 613 commandments of the Torah.

Of course, the analogy is not exact. First of all, G-d is not a human being, so he does not have the needs and requirements of a mortal. G-d does not need a queen in the same sense that a king of flesh and blood does. Second, the Jewish nation is not an individual person – it is a people. But certain points in the analogy are valid. Since G-d is the Supreme Being, he is interested in the welfare of all human beings and ultimately he is also the judge of all humankind. We must also remember that G-d is in some sense a person. Even if G-d does not have deficiencies, he does have plans, intentions, and preferences. I would even say G-d has desires, as long as we understand that G-d's desires originate in G-d himself (he is not subject to desires that stem from anything outside himself). And, since G-d is a person, he has the desire for an intimate personal relationship with a beloved.

Now, G-d cannot have this intimate relationship with all human beings. For one thing, intimacy requires uniqueness, or chosenness. Like the King in my analogy, G-d would be intimate with no one if he were intimate with everyone. Furthermore, the Torah teaches that G-d created humankind with the plan that human beings should spread across the earth and flourish. All human beings have certain basic responsibilities: to acknowledge G-d at some basic level and to live a moral life. But humankind also has the mission to "be fruitful and multiply" – i.e., to develop and grow in the arts, technology, science, culture. Can you imagine how limited the world would be if everyone had to be Jewish and keep the Torah? If everyone were Jewish, we wouldn't have Plato or Aristotle, Copernicus or Galileo, Isaac Newton or Louis Pasteur. For that matter, we wouldn't have Bach, Beethoven, or Mozart. Of course, there have been great Jewish scientists (Einstein) and philosophers (Maimonides, Spinoza) as well, but they have all piggy-backed on the work of non-Jews. And the most famous scientists and philosophers who happened to be Jewish, such as Spinoza, Freud, Marx and Einstein, have almost all been non-observant Jews. (Maimonides is an exception.) Why is that? It's because the essence of the Jewish people is to serve G-d in an intimate way. That's a full-time occupation that doesn't allow for too much else. The greatest Jews have been prophets, Torah scholars, and devout individuals. As I see it, G-d does not want everyone to be Jewish and keep the Torah. That would frustrate the overall plan of creation. The proof of this is that we do not have a mitzvah even to attempt to convert non-Jews to Judaism. Of course, any individual non-Jew who wants to join the Jewish people in order to have that intimate relationship with G-d through keeping the Torah is welcome. But mass conversion of the non-Jews is not part of the divine plan.

It's hard to say what will happen in the "end of days," but I if I had to guess, I'd say the distinction between Jews and non-Jews will remain. Those who wished to pursue the intimate relationship with G-d would convert, and those who did not wish to take it on would remain non-Jews, but pious or "righteous gentiles." Jews do not have an explicit mitzvah to persuade non-Jews to keep the Noahide commandments, but it is certainly a praiseworthy thing to do. Perhaps it can be seen as an offshoot of the commandment Jews have to love G-d. For, if you love someone, you try to help advance his plans, and it is part of G-d's plan that non-Jews keep the Noahide commandments. But there are many ways in which one can express one's love for G-d, such as learning Torah, working on one's own spirituality, etc. Therefore it is not an obligation per se to spread the word about the Noahide commandments.

Regarding the Noahide commandments, I respectfully disagree both with Rabbi Abraham and with Dr. Maimon. I disagree with Rabbi A in that I think that humans can know without any special divine revelation that certain actions, such as murder and theft, are wrong. I tend to believe we know this innately, without any argument or rationalization. But perhaps there is some argument by which we can know that some actions are right or wrong. On the other hand, I disagree with Dr. Maimon in that I do not think that all the Noahide commandments are co-extensive with what human reason judges to be morally right or wrong. I don't think, for example, that the prohibition of eating a limb from a living animal (which is one of the Noahide commandments) is rationally knowable. This should not be confused with the prohibition against cruelty to animals (tsa'ar baalei hayyim). Using reason alone, you might think that you could anesthetize an animal and then eat a limb without being cruel to the animal at all. Also, in his Code of Jewish Law, Maimonides says (Hilchot Melachim or Laws of Kings 8:11) that a gentile is considered righteous only if he keeps the Noahide commandments out of a sense of obligation to G-d and not merely if he keeps it out of purely rational considerations. This does not fit with Dr. Maimon's view that the Noahide commandments are co-extensive with rational moral principles. If she is right, then keeping these commandments out of reason should also make a person righteous.

In my view, the Noahide commandments and the Noahide covenant constitute an intermediate stage between rational morality on the one hand and the Torah given to Israel on the other. At first, God expects people to behave morally on their own, without any revelation. Then, G-d gave the Noahide commandments to elevate humans a step higher than common sense or rational morality (if there is such a thing). Through the Noahide commandments, man is able to have an interpersonal and covenantal relationship with G-d. The Noahide commandments are also a backdrop and preparation for the revelation of the Torah and the 613 commandments, which allows for an even more intimate relationship with G-d. For the reasons I explained above, the Torah of the 613 is not feasible for all mankind. G-d's plan is fulfilled when the nations of the world keep the Noahide commandments and the people of Israel keep the Torah. The king wants both the queen, and the citizens, to fulfill their distinctive but complementary missions.

Keep the questions coming. I haven't had a chance to read your paper on the problem of evil. I hope to get to it soon, *bli neder*.

Rabbi Low

32

"So, David, did you enjoy the Megillah reading?"

"Yes, Esther. It was fun. I never imagined a synagogue service could be so rowdy. Thanks for inviting me to go with you. Sorry we couldn't sit together, though!"

"If we had sat together, maybe your focus would have been elsewhere!"

"Wherever did you get that idea?"

"Anyway, how d'you like the pizza here?"

"It's pretty good, actually."

"You sound surprised. Why? Why should kosher pizza be any different from non-kosher pizza?"

"I don't know. Is pizza Jewish food?"

"No, but so what? Jews can make anything! There are lots or kosher restaurants downtown – Italian, French, Chinese, whatever. There are even kosher sushi bars."

"Great. Let's try them all. But, you know, I'm still wondering . . . ."

"About what?"

"Oh, never mind. Let's just have a nice time."

"Come on, what is it?"

"I was just going to say, I remember your point about not eating cheeseburgers. If you're used to it, then it's not so bad. I think I could get used to not eating cheeseburgers myself. It's really not a big deal. But I'd still like to know more about the *why* of kosher . . .".

"Simple. The reason we keep kosher is because God said so!"

"But surely God didn't just say so for no reason. Do you think God commands things arbitrarily?"

"Maybe it's for a reason, but not for a reason we can fully understand. But if you're looking for reasons, there are a few good reasons I know of. Food's important, you know. We eat all the time. So, the laws of *kashrut* give us a discipline, a structure for eating. In this way, eating becomes a holy act."

"Right. I've heard this theory before. It makes sense up to a point."

"Also, it's a way of separating us from the non-Jews. It's not like we can't interact at all with non-Jews, or even be friendly with them to a certain extent. But the dietary laws provide a barrier. So in that way, it makes us holy, too."

"Yes, I've heard that theory too. But if that's the only reason, eating kosher doesn't make you holy, it just keeps you separate. You'd still have to maintain your holiness because of something *else* you're doing."

"I guess that's true."

"Well, there's got to be more to eating kosher than just keeping us separate. It's also got be more than just giving us some discipline in our eating habits. Because if that were the whole story, then God could have just as well commanded us to eat *only* pork and shellfish instead of cattle and chicken. Or he could have commanded us to eat rarer things rather than things that are so common. It seems like God did it the other way around."

"Hmm. That's a good point, David. I don't have an answer for you there."

"Besides, the Torah says that God commanded Jews not to eat certain things because those things are *tameh* – ritually impure. Rabbi Low pointed this out to me in one of his emails. I looked up the passages and I found something else also. The Torah says pretty explicitly that certain creatures are disgusting. Remind me . . . what's the word the Torah uses for that?"

"*Sheketz.*"

"Yes, that's it. Anyway the idea seems to be that certain creatures are disgusting, and that's why they're forbidden. So the real question is, what is the whole concept of *tahor* and *tameh* about?"

"Yes . . . . Well, have you asked Rabbi Low about that?"

"No, but I guess I should. Obviously, it doesn't have to do just with food or animals, because the category of *tahor* and *tameh* comes up in other things as well – like, for example – uh . . . sorry to bring this up . . . but a woman who menstruates is also ritually impure . . . how do you say it? *T'meah?*"

"Right again! Very good! But maybe *tameh* or *t'meah* simply means 'forbidden.' Like I said before, the reason certain foods are forbidden is because God wants to give us a discipline, to be holy. For the same reason, God wants marital relations to be restricted in some way, to give a husband and wife a certain kind of discipline."

"But if that's what it's all about, what is the ritual of purification for? Why does she have to go to the *mikveh*? Why not prohibit relations just for a certain length of time, since that would accomplish the same purpose? Obviously, the Torah claims that there is something inherently unfit in having relations with a woman who is ritually impure, just as there is something inherently unfit in pork or shellfish."

"Maybe so. But look – isn't it possible that we'll never know or understand the reasons for these things, and that God commands us to do things which we simply take on faith and are right to do? Did you ever hear about the idea of a *hok*? There are some things that God commands that we just don't understand."

"Yes. I've heard that idea. You mean, like the red heifer."

"Exactly. I'm impressed, David. But look. God is the creator of everything. So doesn't it make sense to think that there are certain things only God knows are best for us to do or not do? Why is that such a difficult concept for you?"

"If God doesn't make sense to me, I have trouble accepting him."

"How can you expect God to make sense to you if he's really God?"

"Esther, let's — maybe we can talk about something else? Hey, let's talk about Purim."

"OK, no problem, David. That reminds me: are you coming to the Purim party tomorrow afternoon?"

"Yeah, sure. I told you I was coming."

"It might get a little wild."

"Great! I've been to a few of those. But what do you mean by wild?"

"I think Purim is the only time in the Jewish calendar when there's a *mitzvah de-rabbanan* to become . . . um . . . intoxicated."

"Intoxicated? Wow! I'm up for that. But what did you say? What kind of *mitzvah*?"

"A *mitzvah de-rabbanan* — that's a rabbinical commandment, you know, as opposed to a *mitzvah de-oraita,* a divine commandment — one that's directly from God."

"Oh, yes. I'm familiar with that concept. Either way, it sounds great. Is there any specific kind of intoxication that's prescribed?"

"Wine or some alcoholic beverage. Why? What else is there?"

"Oh, I don't know."

"Anyway, this does create a problem with the issue of the legal drinking age."

"Yes, I bet it does. And just how intoxicated does one need to get in order to fulfill this obligation?"

"You're supposed to be so intoxicated that you don't know the difference between 'blessed be Mordecai' and 'cursed be Haman.'

"That's *very* interesting."

"Actually, some authorities say that you really should get drunk, while others say that all you need to do is drink enough to make you fall asleep. Once you're asleep, you don't know the difference between the two, so that way, you fulfill the *mitzvah*!"

"I think I prefer the first interpretation!"

"I'm sure you do."

"But wait — aren't you also supposed to drink four cups of wine on the first night of Passover?"

"Good question! But the point on Pesach is not to get intoxicated. The wine on Passover is celebratory, a sign of freedom. It's not necessarily meant to be intoxicating. In fact, some people use grape juice on Passover, which is not intoxicating at all."

"I see. So Purim is very unusual. Why is it such a celebration?"

"Didn't you read the Megillah? It's quite a story, don't you think?"

"Yes, the Jews of the Persian Empire at the time were saved, and they had a party."

"Is that all you could see in the Megillah? Look, first of all, at that time all the Jews lived in the Persian empire, that means all the Jews were saved . . . and thereby, all future generations of Jews were saved from annihilation as well, including us."

"Fine. So what's the difference between Pesach and Purim?"

"On Pesach we were redeemed from slavery, but on Purim we were saved from actual physical destruction. Therefore, the celebration of Purim is in a way more important than the celebration of Passover!"

"You know . . . you talk about these things as if all these events actually happened, in just the way they are described in the Bible."

"Of course! That's what it means to be Jewish – to believe in these things."

"And you also talk about these events as if we were there."

"Well, we were, actually. If the Jews of that time hadn't been saved, we wouldn't be here having this conversation! But you know, there's another thing special about Purim. The sages discuss the fact that unlike the exodus from Egypt, during the time of Purim there was no obvious miracle – that's called a *nes nigleh* – through which God saved the Jews. All of the events of the Megillah could be interpreted as coincidences or normal events. Even God's name – even the name *Elokim* – is not mentioned once in the story of Esther."

"I guess that *is* odd."

"Of course it is. There's only one other book in the Tanakh like that – *Shir ha-Shirim,* or the Song of Songs. But the point is that God worked a hidden miracle – that's a *nes nistar* – through which the Jews were saved. In fact, Esther's name is a hint to this. Esther – is related to the word *hester,* or hiddenness."

"Very interesting. And obviously you have some special affinity for Esther, since you're her namesake!"

"Actually, I'll tell you something else. Tonight is my birthday! It's actually my secular and Hebrew birthday at the same time. The dates coincide every nineteen years."

"Esther, I can't believe it! Why didn't you tell me before? I would have gotten you something. No wonder you seem so alive tonight. You're . . . like . . . glowing."

"I'm glowing because you're making me blush!"

"And your name is Esther! What a coincidence!"

"It's not a coincidence at all, David. My parents named me Esther because I was born on Purim!"

"Ah, of course. How stupid of me! Still, you do have an affinity for your namesake. After all, she *was* very beautiful."

"Oh, please . . . you're really too much!"

"Anyway, I've got to get you a birthday present. I've got just the thing for you. How would you like a pair of earrings?"

"Oh, please, *please* don't do that. I couldn't accept that from you."

"Why not?"

"I just can't. It's not done."

"Is this another rabbinic restriction?"

"Well . . . sort of. If an unmarried girl accepts a gift from a guy, it might be misinterpreted as a marriage gift. That's how a marriage takes place. The guy gives something of value to the girl, which puts the betrothal into effect."

"OK, I won't give any gifts just yet, then. But . . . I have a question – just a theoretical question, of course. I'm just asking out of curiosity. Can an unmarried man accept a gift from a woman? In other words, would you be allowed to give me a gift?"

"It would be unusual, but actually, I could. Why? When's your birthday?"

"In a couple of months. May 28. I'll be turning nineteen also."

"So I guess I'm older than you by a few months!"

"That's OK. I like older women."

"I know you do. But seriously . . . what's your Hebrew birthday? I mean, what's the Jewish date of your birthday? You probably have no clue."

"I have no idea."

"I can figure it out. You were born in 1982, just like me. Like I said, this year, your Jewish and secular birthdays must fall on the same date. I have a pocket calendar right here in my bag. Let me look. May 28 . . . hey, that's Shavuot! David, you were born on Shavuot. Did you know that?"

"No, I didn't. What's that?"

"Shavuot celebrates the day the Torah was given to the Jewish people. It's a major festival! "

"Ah! So we were both born on Jewish holidays! Amazing! So, anyway, are you going to give me a present?"

"Actually, I think I know just the right thing, but I'm not sure."

"Great! What is it? Now I'm intrigued. Are you going to give me something I really want?"

"It's not what you think."

"Come on! You've got to tell me!"

"Never mind. If I can get them, it'll be a surprise."

"*Them?*"

"Yes, *them.*"

"Hmm . . . you've really piqued my interest. Not earrings, I hope?"

"David! Of course not! Anyway – what were we saying before we got side-tracked?"

"Let's see. You were saying, that the fact that there was a hidden miracle makes Purim even more special than Passover. But shouldn't it be the other way around? I mean . . . can you explain that a little more? It would seem more likely that an open miracle would be more impressive than a hidden one."

"But that's precisely the point. One might think the fact that there was no obvi-ous miracle places Purim on a lower level than festivals such as Pesach. However, actually this places Purim on a higher level precisely because the miracle took place within the ordinary, natural scheme of events. The idea that God can contradict nature is actually less powerful than the idea that God works through nature."

"Really? That sounds like a paradox. Can you elaborate?"

"I'll try. By definition, a contradiction of nature can only take place rarely. Otherwise, nature wouldn't be what it is. Now, God works through nature all the time. But since it happens all the time, we don't always notice it. So, in a sense, a hidden miracle is more elevated than an obvious one. If God could only perform obvious miracles, that might lead us to think that God is not the source of all nature, but rather that God is a force who competes with nature. It is precisely the hidden miracles which indicate that God works within the natural world. Does that make sense?"

"Wow, this is deep stuff. You didn't make this up yourself, did you? Where'd you learn all this?"

"In seminary, of course. Probably from Rabbi Low, actually. I remember his giving a class on the significance of Purim."

"I knew it! It sounds very much like him. He really is quite an interesting guy."

"Yes, he is. Are you still in touch with him?"

"Of course. I just recently had a correspondence with him about the Noahide laws."

"Great. You know, David, I must say – I'm really impressed with your learning and how you've delved into Judaism. I was just wondering . . . you never talk much about your parents. How are your parents taking your interest in Judaism?"

"Well, my mom's been very supportive. My father . . . I don't think he really knows or cares about it that much."

"They sound very different from one another."

"You're right. I guess I'm much closer to my mom than my dad. My dad . . . I guess I just don't know what's with him, exactly."

"Do you speak to him often?"

"Sure. We talk on the phone all the time. But Mom and I . . . you know, it's a little old-fashioned, but actually, we write each other letters."

"Letters? That's wonderful! I love writing letters. But nobody does it any more."

"It was her idea. Last year, when she was ill, she found it uncomfortable to speak on the phone. And she never uses the computer, so she doesn't do email. So she started writing me letters. So I wrote back. Actually, she's the one who encouraged me to study philosophy and also Judaism. Meanwhile my Dad's major concern seems to be whether I can get into a top law school."

"She really *does* sound very different from your dad."

"Yeah, they are different, but somehow they get along. I don't know, really. Now that I think of it, they really don't spend too much time together. I think the cancer really didn't help the relationship."

"Sorry to hear that. By the way . . . how is your mother, health-wise? Is she OK?"

"It seems she's almost out of the woods. She's supposed to go in for another checkup pretty soon. We'll see what the doctor says."

"Let's hope for the best. David, I'm sorry if I got you upset. I didn't mean to pry . . . ."

"Never mind. It's quite all right. Hey, how about some more of that great kosher pizza?"

33

"Dr. Maimon, you said something a few days ago that I wanted to go back to."

"What was it?"

"Something to the effect that God might have reasons for revealing his will through the device of myth."

"Yes. What about it?"

"Well, honestly, I'm a bit puzzled. For centuries, Jews did believe in the literal truth of the stories in the Torah. And lots of Orthodox Jews continue to believe the stories to this very day. But in your view, they're all mistaken."

"David, let me clarify what I said. I didn't claim that the stories aren't literally true. I said that the belief that the Torah is divine and that it represents God's way for the Jewish people is *compatible* with the belief that the stories described in the Torah are not literally true. Now, even if the stories are not literally true, that doesn't mean they are silly or a waste of time. On the contrary. The stories contain profound truths about God, human nature, and how God relates to the world."

"Still, you are saying that one can believe that the stories are false and still believe in the divinity of the Torah. But it seems odd for God to operate in the way you describe. Isn't God kind of sneaky, if your theory is correct?"

"Not at all. You've got to take into account the way that humans have evolved over time. Primitive humans were kind of like children. Their way of looking at the world and interpreting it was bound to be childlike. Children can't sharply separate truth from fantasy. Their critical abilities are not yet formed. It's not their fault, of course. It takes time for children to grow up. And it takes time for human society to mature or develop. So it shouldn't surprise us if God had to interact with primitive humans in a primitive manner. It seems plausible to me that, under divine guidance, the early Israelites constructed myths about their past that contain profound truths. Of course, at that early stage, the Israelites didn't even make the distinction between mythical and non-mythical forms of thinking. So they just took their tradition to be 'true' without even raising the question of whether it was literally true or mythically true. Do you follow?"

"I still think that if God really wanted to, he could've found a way to communicate his message without using myth."

"And I think you're underestimating the primitive nature of mankind. You're also underestimating the significance of myth, and the role that imagination and even fantasy play in human existence. By the way, this has a lot to do with the question of *ta'amei ha-mitzvot,* or the rationale for the commandments."

"I'm glad you brought that up. I wanted to talk about that, too. I'm sure you believe that there are reasons for all the commandments."

"Of course. God wouldn't command them if they weren't rational. And if they are rational, they have to make sense to us. I don't buy the idea that some things might be rational to God but not rational to us. But here's the point I wanted to make regarding the reasons for at least some of the commandments. Do you know what Maimonides said about all the ritual sacrifices mentioned in the Torah? Basically, Maimonides thinks that God would have preferred not to bother with ritual sacrifice at all. He goes on to suggest that the early Israelites were so steeped in idol worship that they needed some elaborate form of ritual in order to make the transition from idolatry to worship of God. In fact, Maimonides interprets much of the ritual law in this way. And I already mentioned some time ago that you can interpret the prohibition against eating certain foods as a way of compelling the people of Israel to remain separate from the other peoples. There's nothing inherently magical about kosher food. But maybe people need to believe that there is, in order to follow this commandment."

"I don't know, Dr. Maimon. I don't really find that too convincing an explanation."

"You're entitled to your opinion. Like Maimonides, I hold that the early Israelites were – no surprise – a primitive people, and they needed all sorts of crutches, if you will, in order to reach the right path – that is, the Torah, the way of God. The theory that the early Israelites operated under mythical forms of thought is just an extension of Maimonides's approach. By the way, I don't know whether he personally would have accepted this theory, but that's a historical question about how to interpret Maimonides."

"Well, let me ask you this. Why would God create humans in such a way that they were so primitive that they needed to believe all sorts of false stories in order to reach the truth?"

"Again – I keep saying this – the stories aren't false. They are only false *when they are taken literally.* They are metaphorically or symbolically true. That's the beauty of Torah – it can be read at different levels. But when you ask, 'Why couldn't God have created people differently?' – that's raising a completely separate question. You might as well ask why God created a world that needs time in order to be brought to completion or perfection. That's a traditional theological conundrum – to which, by the way, I think there's a good answer. Namely, once God chooses to create a world, it has to be temporal, or subject to time. So it is inevitable that the world will need to develop in order to reach completion. We talked about this last semester in class. Even an omnipotent God can't do the impossible. Finite creatures, such as human beings, need time to develop and grow and reach perfection. This is especially so if you believe, as I do, that it is part of our task to perfect ourselves.

If we were born complete or perfect, there would be no work for us to do. The transition from primitive, mythological modes of thought to intellectual maturity is just part of that process."

"Well, if that's the case, Orthodox Jews who continue to believe in the literal truth of the stories of the Torah are still primitive or childlike . . . ."

"In a certain sense, that's true."

"But it's precisely those people who seem to be the most devoted to keeping the observances and the laws."

"When it comes to the ritual aspects of law, you're probably right. I won't deny that. They also remain the most rigid and unchanging in their interpretation of those observances, too. Look, maybe some people *need* to believe in the literal truth of the stories. I don't really have anything against that if that's what they believe. Where I have trouble is when people insist that if you don't believe the stories literally, that implies that you've rejected *Torah min ha-shamayim*."

"But if your theory is correct, why do some Jews insist on literal interpretation as the only correct way?"

"You'd really have to ask them. But I can speculate a little bit. First of all, you're absolutely right that for many centuries Jews traditionally believed in the literal truth of the Scriptures. So Orthodox Jews today also assume that they need to believe it as a matter of dogma. Anything that's been believed for centuries becomes a matter of dogma! This is completely wrong, in my opinion. Taken to its extreme, this results in the idea that the sages in the Talmud must have known everything about the entire universe, including modern science and medicine. Secondly, Orthodox Jews use the slippery-slope argument. They worry that if you admit that one story isn't literally true, then maybe later on you'll admit that all of it isn't literally true, and the next thing you know, you'll just say the whole thing isn't even mythically true. Finally, there's a sort of reactionary movement in the Orthodox world against anything that is believed by people on the 'outside.' Since many people who believe the stories aren't literally true are not observant Jews, it is felt that it is just too risky to promote that idea within the Orthodox community. But you know, I think there's something else going on too."

"What's that?"

"A lot of people just want to believe in the literal truth of the stories of the Scriptures because they want to believe in the kind of God that they depict. People want to believe in the kind of God that literally turns water into blood, splits the sea, and so on. This is a kind of God that actually comes down on Mt. Sinai with thunder and lightning. This is a Super-God, an interventionist, a God who tinkers with nature at will. If one suggests that the stories are only metaphorically or symbolically true, then it undercuts this picture of God."

"It sure does."

"But in my opinion, I think that this is really an immature way of thinking about God. It's one that we're supposed to have gotten away from. In fact, that's what I think is the true, inner lesson of Megillat Esther and the story of Purim."

"Really? What's that got to do with it?"

"David, are you familiar with the story of Esther?"

"Yes, I am."

"Did you know that the Book of Esther is one of the only two books in the entire Hebrew Scriptures that make no explicit mention of the name of God in any form?"

"Yes. The other one is Song of Songs."

"Ah, I'm impressed! How did you know that, David?"

"Well, I – um . . . have a friend who gave me a whole explanation about that."

"How does the explanation go? I'd like to hear it."

"OK, I'll try to summarize it. The story of Purim is unique in that no obvious miracle occurs. The Jews are redeemed by a hidden miracle, or what appears to be a series of coincidences. A skeptic could claim that all the events of the story happened without God's intervention. This is very different from the kind of miracle that occurred during Passover. In that case, God performed obvious miracles, like the splitting of the sea and the smiting of the first-born Egyptians. But that's why the name of God is missing from the scroll of Esther – to emphasize that God's hand in the story is hidden. The name Esther also hints at this, since it means 'hidden.' That's pretty much a summary of the explanation my friend told me."

"Excellent! Your friend is quite knowledgeable. But did he also tell you about the *midrash* which contrasts the acceptance of the Torah at Sinai with the re-acceptance of the Torah during the time of Purim?"

"Uh, no, she didn't."

"Oh, excuse me. Sorry about that. Your friend is a woman?"

"Yes. She's a student here. In fact, her name is Esther!"

"Ah, what a coincidence! Now, what was I saying? Oh, yes – do you know what a *midrash* is?"

"A *midrash* is a story, isn't it?"

"Not exactly. A *midrash* is an interpretation. Actually, the word has several uses. Basically, a *midrash aggadah* is a rabbinic interpretation that involves a story of some sort, usually reading between the lines of the Scripture to make a point. There is also *midrash halacha* – that is, rabbinic interpretation of the halachic or legal portions of Scripture. *Midrashim* are found in the Talmud, but are compiled also in several collections that were put together after the Talmud was composed. Anyway, the particular *midrash* I have I mind goes something like this: The Book of Exodus states that when the Israelites came to Sinai to receive the Torah, 'They encamped under the mountain.' Usually the word 'under' is taken to mean at the foot of the mountain. But Rabbi Yitzhak, one of the sages of the Talmud, says something quite shocking about it. He says, 'This teaches that God lifted the mountain over the people and turned it over like a dome, saying, "If you accept the Torah, fine; but if not, let your grave be right here!"'"

"Hmm. That *is* rather extreme."

"Indeed. What's so shocking about this is that while this *midrash* seems to indicate that essentially God forced the people of Israel to accept the Torah, the plain meaning of the Scriptural text would seem to indicate that the acceptance of the Torah was voluntary. In fact, in other places in the Talmud, the Jews are praised for having accepted the Torah freely. Anyway, the Talmud continues by asking the following question. If Rabbi Yitzhak's view is correct, and the Jews were essentially forced to accept the Torah, how can they be held responsible? How can they subsequently be punished for failing to keep the Torah throughout the generations?"

"That's a good question."

"The Talmud's answer is even more bizarre. The answer is that the Jews accepted the Torah anew during the time of Mordechai and Esther."

"What? That sounds very weird. I don't remember seeing that in the Scroll of Esther."

"Well, you see, again this is a rabbinic interpretation, a *midrash* – reading between the lines, so to speak. The idea is based on a verse in the Megillah which says '*kiyyemu ve-kiblu,*' which literally means, 'they established and they accepted.' In context, this phrase means that the Jews of the time 'established and accepted' the festival of Purim. But the Talmud interprets this to mean 'they established *what they had already* accepted.' In other words, at the time of Mordecai and Esther the Jews *reaffirmed* their original acceptance of the Torah at Mount Sinai. And this time, they did it freely and not under duress."

"That's interesting. The Talmud sounds like quite a book. I didn't know the rabbis could take such liberties with the original meaning of the text!"

"They do it all the time. But there's something bigger going on here, I think. As I said earlier, there's a certain immature conception of God which, in my view, we are supposed to evolve away from. This is the conception of God as an entity, and, if I may say so, a *masculine* entity who pulls the strings of the world from on high like a puppeteer. This is tied together with a certain immature notion of what is involved in our acceptance of Torah. The immature conception is that of God as an *interventionist,* a deity who breaks the laws of nature at will – this is the older, more mythological conception of God that the Israelites had before the time of Esther. This kind of God comes down with fire and brimstone from the heavens, essentially compelling the people to accept the Torah. In my opinion, this is the real, inner meaning of the *midrash* which says that God 'turned the mountain over them' and basically made them accept the Torah. I don't think Rabbi Yitzhak meant this literally. What he meant is that, for the early Israelites, God was conceived in such a way that they had no choice about whether to accept the Torah. In effect, the early Israelites did not accept the Torah voluntarily because they were under the sway of their own immature preoccupations and notions of what God is supposed to be – the old man with the white beard in the sky, so to speak. But with the story of Esther, a new conception is forged. Esther represents a critical development in the Jewish theo-historical consciousness – the *naturalization* of divine providence. In the story of Esther, God works through natural means to bring about redemption. No longer do we need to experience a radical break in nature in order to believe that there is a divine, miraculous process at work. And that is why the re-acceptance of the Torah during the time of Mordecai and Esther was genuinely free. It is free because it is not done under duress – the duress of a primitive conception of God!"

"Well, I must admit that's a very interesting interpretation, Dr. Maimon."

"Thanks. And, by the way, I don't think it's accidental that while the main hero of the exodus is a man – I mean Moshe, of course – the main heroine of the story of Esther is a woman."

"Oh? What do you think is so important about that?"

"It represents a major shift. We're familiar with some heroines before her, in the Bible and after, but Esther is a first. She essentially saves the entire Jewish people from death. So in a way she's kind of like Moshe, who saves the Israelites from slavery in Egypt and from death in the desert – several times, in fact. But of course, Moses performs miracles right and left, throughout the desert, using his staff. Clearly, the staff is a male symbol. Of course, Esther has no staff, and she performs no obvious miracles. In fact, do you remember the part in the story where Esther reaches out and touches the King's scepter? It's almost like she's disarming him, neutralizing his power. That symbolism is very important."

"I see. Well, speaking of Esther and women, do we have time to talk about the issue of women just a little bit?"

"Ah, yes, we're supposed to talk about that today as well. We've got some time left. What's your question about women?"

"In a nutshell, it's about the role of women in traditional Judaism. My friend says that despite what it looks like, traditional Judaism treats men and women as different but equal. Do you agree?"

"Your friend is Orthodox, right?"

"Yes."

"Sorry, David, but I don't think there's any way around this one. In Orthodox Judaism, women are separate and *unequal*. Both in the Scripture and in the Talmud it's pretty clear that women have a secondary status in terms of rights, responsibilities, and privileges. I'll just give you a few examples. According to Scripture, a man may marry more than one woman, but a woman may not marry more than one man. According to the Talmud, a woman cannot function as a witness in certain legal cases because they do not have the ability to testify. Often, they are viewed as having the intelligence and capabilities of a minor. Even the great Moses Maimonides, quoting from the Talmud, writes that women are less intelligent than men as a whole. Of course, this was a common belief in most cultures throughout history. Another example is that a man can divorce a woman at will, but a woman cannot divorce a man at will. During the rabbinic period, certain protections for women were built into the system. Still, women are second class in many ways."

"I see. How do you deal with this problem?"

"Well, I admit that the Torah and the Talmud were affected by the prejudices of the age. After all, you find rules about slavery in the Torah as well. What should we say about that? Apparently, the Torah condones slavery. You don't go along with that, do you?"

"No, of course not. So how do you square that with your belief that the Torah is divine?"

"I've already told you: the belief that the Torah is divine does not imply that everything in the Torah is literally true or correct. It just means that the text as we have it and the oral tradition as we have it comprise the teaching that divine providence gave us as a basis for leading our lives. And I emphasize the word *basis*. I believe that just as we can come up with novel interpretations of the stories in the text, so too we can modify and change things in Torah law in accordance with the principles of justice and equity that the Torah itself teaches."

"Wait a second. Doesn't that amount to saying that the Torah is flawed?"

"Look. God created humans – and they're flawed too, aren't they? Similarly, the Torah is an evolving tradition. Although the Torah is *min ha-shamyim* – that is, from heaven or divine, the Torah is given to humans. Once the Torah is given, it is not in heaven any longer. As it says in the Torah itself, '*Lo ba-shamayim hi*,' which means: 'It is not in heaven' any longer. I'm willing to say that at the time the Torah was given, all the laws that were in place were suited to the people of that age. Do you remember Maimonides's view on the rationale for animal sacrifices in the Torah? They are essentially a concession to the primitive tendencies of the ancient Israelites. According to that view, there was every reason to think that the time will come when ritual sacrifices would be abandoned altogether. Similarly, the ancient Israelites had primitive ideas about the capabilities of women. Maybe there are deep anthropological reasons for that, but it doesn't really matter. The Torah was given at a certain time to a certain people at a certain level of development. But times change, people change, and a living legal system has to make room for change as well. It is up to scholars and jurists to develop the Torah in a way that they see fit."

"But if you can change it, then anything goes. The Torah can be made to say whatever we want it to say."

"No, that doesn't follow. Legal scholars can't just change things at whim. They have to use principles based on the Torah itself, and they have to use reason and common sense as well. This is true of any legal system. There are mechanisms for change within the system. As long as the mechanisms are used, it is still the same system even if some things are changed."

"I guess that's true."

"Besides which, the process already started during the time of the Talmud.

The rabbis found ways of toning down the harsh punishments of the Bible, and they found ways of giving women greater rights in marriage. For example, the marriage contract is a rabbinic institution that is designed to protect the rights of the woman. It doesn't go as far as equalizing the relationship, but it's a start. At a somewhat later period, a rabbi known as Rabbenu Gershom, who was the rabbinic leader of the time, issued an edict banning polygamy. His ban was widely accepted, at least among European Jews. In our time, we need to carry this process a few steps further. For example, in traditional circles it's still very hard for a woman to get a divorce without her husband's consent. This could be fixed by having the marriage contract amended so that the husband commits himself ahead of time to grant his wife a divorce should certain circumstances arise. While some Modern Orthodox rabbis advocate such a change, in general, the Orthodox establishment is quite rigid about this point. I know some Orthodox rabbis who admit deep down that certain things could and should be changed, but they are afraid of being run out of their pulpits if they make their views known. I wish they were more courageous and spoke out more."

"What kinds of changes do you believe in?"

"Well, I'm not a rabbi or a Torah scholar. I'm a philosopher. But I would advocate an equalization of men and women in all aspects of family, marital, and communal life. I believe that women should have the option of leading prayer services and becoming rabbis, teachers, public leaders, and so on. Or if they wish to play a role that is more confined to the home, that's fine too. There are other areas in Jewish law and practice where I believe change is appropriate too."

"Such as?"

"The prayers. Classically, Jews pray a lot for themselves. You told me once that you've read the Orthodox *siddur,* or prayer book. Did you ever notice that Orthodox Jews never pray for the betterment of humanity at large? They pray for their own welfare, but never for the welfare of others. Perhaps it's a carry-over from ancient times, when the Jews suffered terribly at the hands of the nations. So maybe it made sense at that time that you wouldn't want to pray for the non-Jews. But now things are different, of course. I feel that we should be praying for the welfare of humanity. Yet the Orthodox establishment is so rigid that they can't contemplate introducing any changes or modifications. This is really a shame. Even in the late medieval period, changes and insertions were made all the time, such as introducing new poetry for special occasions such as holidays, fast days, and so on. In our day, we ought to be modifying things even more. We ought to be praying for the peace of the world. And that's just one example."

"Why do you think the Orthodox establishment is so rigid and resistant to change?"

"Fear of change, perhaps? Really, I can't explain it any more. You'll have to ask one of them."

34

From: rlow@ahavattorah.org.il   Sent: 4/15/01 10:52 AM
To: dgoldstein@cuniv.edu
Subject: book of Job

Dear David,

I finally got around to reading your paper on the problem of evil. I enjoyed it and I think I agree with it. I agree that without the hypothesis of an afterlife, it is difficult to explain the suffering of the righteous. And as Dr. Maimon pointed out, belief in an afterlife is part of traditional Judaism. Whether it is a rational belief or a belief based totally on faith is another issue.

The only criticism I have of your paper concerns what you say about the book of *Iyyov.*

I think this very difficult book is commonly misunderstood. In my opinion, the book is really not about the problem of *"tzaddik ve-ra lo"* – i.e., why the righteous suffer. In fact, the book is about a related but different problem. I'll try to explain.

Many people believe that the book is about why the righteous suffer, and that the "answer" at the end is that G-d is absolute and it is not our place to question him. In other words, we must accept that he allows the righteous to suffer for reasons that we do not understand. Now, there are several factors that count against this interpretation, and I'll mention only one. If the book is really about why the righteous suffer, then, given the stage setting at the beginning of the book, we should have expected a different answer from the one that is provided at the end. Let me explain. The reason for Iyyov's suffering given at the beginning of the book seems quite obviously this: to test Iyyov and see if indeed he is really righteous. So at the end of the book, it should have been the case that G-d says to Iyyov, the reason why you suffered is because it was a test to determine how righteous you are. But nothing like that appears at the end when the supposed "answer" is given to the problem of why the righteous suffer!

We need to think more deeply about Iyyov. Here's something very telling: The beginning of the book says that his sons and daughters had parties every day, and that Iyyov sacrificed animals to appease G-d, "just in case one of his children might have perchance cursed G-d's name." In the Tanakh, and indeed in rabbinic Judaism, cursing G-d's name is one of the worst things a person can do. Yet Iyyov was worried that his wealthy and apparently happy children might be tempted to curse G-d. That's very bizarre! How did he bring his children up? What kind of relationship did he encourage his children to have with G-d? Evidently, not a very deep one. In fact, a little reflection shows that Iyyov himself had no personal relationship with G-d whatsoever.

This may come as a shock, but I don't think Iyyov was really such a *tzaddik* (righteous person) in the sense used by the Talmud when it talks about the problem of why righteous people suffer. In the book, Iyyov is a not referred to as a *tzaddik,* but rather as *tam ve-yashar, yare Elokim,* and *sar me-ra.* That means he was "whole, straight, G-d-fearing, and one who avoided evil." He never did anything wrong, but then again he didn't go out of his way to do anything right. He certainly was not a *hassid.* He did not serve Hashem out of love. Even his *yirah,* or fear of G-d, was deficient. The sole reason for why he behaved well is that **he expected G-d to reward him with material blessing and protection.** In other words, Iyyov was just, but he was so only for selfish reasons. He had no concept of doing the right thing for the right reason, or for its own sake. While he is referred to as a servant of G-d, I would say he was a servant *'al menas lekabel pras'* that is, on condition of receiving a material reward. The implication is that if he could have secured material prosperity without being just and whole, perhaps he would have done so. He had no concept of worshipping G-d for its own sake. He did not go out of his way to improve the world, as did Abraham for example. He did not serve G-d out of love.

Given this, Satan's complaint about Iyyov was valid. The complaint is that Iyyov served G-d only because he gained material reward by doing so. Take away the material reward, the Satan tells G-d, and he will become your worst enemy. In fact, he will curse you. So G-d permits Iyyov to be tested, allowing his material rewards to be withdrawn and his physical suffering to begin. After bearing his grief in silence at first, Iyyov curses the day he was born and now claims that his whole life has been worthless. He does not curse G-d, and for this he is given credit. Yet a truly righteous person would have said: Life was and still is special. I had my children for some time, and as long as I'm alive, I can still do good deeds. I had a relationship with my family and G-d, and so on. But here's the key point: Iyyov seems to have no concept that doing good deeds might be valuable for its own sake. His whole life was worthwhile, and all his "good deeds" were worth doing, but only on condition that those good deeds brought about prosperity! What Iyyov can't seem to understand throughout much of the book is why it would make sense to worship G-d for any reason other than material gain.

The "friends" who visit Iyyov were right when they pointed out that if Iyyov were to reflect, he might reach the conclusion that he could have improved. But they also claimed, wrongly, that G-d must have some reason for punishing Iyyov and that Iyyov should beg G-d's forgiveness for having done something wrong. Iyyov steadfastly denies any wrongdoing, and as the discussion goes on he gravitates toward a deeper and deeper desire and willingness to encounter G-d personally, something that he had never pursued in his life. Again, the friends (in my reading) discourage this. They think it would be fatal to Iyyov because they think he has done evil and will be destroyed if he encounters G-d before repenting. The friends were wrong though, because (even in my view) Iyyov had not in fact done any evil. They, too, operate mostly under the assumption that the only reason to worship G-d is to win material gain. The friends were too coarse to realize Iyyov's true failing, which had to do with his mind-set rather than anything that he had actually done. Iyyov's problem was that he did not appreciate the value of doing good for its own sake. But he's in good company. A lot of people feel the same way. Perhaps you yourself have thought of this problem: Why should I serve G-d or be righteous if not for the sake of my own welfare, whether that means material prosperity or even spiritual bliss in the next world? *That* is the problem raised by Iyyov. The problem of why the righteous suffer is a different problem altogether.

The answer at the end of the book is that finally Iyyov understands that we are supposed to do the right thing *lishmah,* out of respect for G-d, because G-d is supreme. G-d is worthy of worship and obedience not because he has the power to reward us materially or even spiritually, but because he is the Supreme Being and therefore he is intrinsically worthy of awe and worship. You're supposed to be willing to do what's right even at the cost of self-interest. I agree that this is not such an easy thing to grasp. In Iyyov's case, he didn't really get it until G-d himself appeared to him in a revelation.

For whatever it's worth, that's my interpretation of Iyyov. Like I said, despite the criticism, I enjoyed and agreed with most of your paper.

Sincerely,

Rabbi Low

From: dgoldstein@cuniv.edu   Sent: 4/23/01 9:30 PM
To: rlow@ahavattorah.org.il
Subject: some views of Dr Maimon

Dear Rabbi Low,

Thanks very much for your interpretation of *Iyyov.* Yes, I have thought about the problem of why it makes sense to serve God or be righteous for its own sake. And I see your point that it's a different problem from the suffering of the righteous. It's amazing how a person can read through an entire book and not realize that the main topic of the book is different than what he thought!

I have some other questions. As I told you, I'm doing an independent study with Dr. Maimon. She's expressed some interesting ideas, some of which I tend to agree with. But I was wondering what you had to say about the following five issues:

1. Dr. M suggests that instead of thinking of God as an entity or a being, we may conceive of God's essence as being itself, and we may conceive of God's attributes as the principles or ultimate rules that govern the way the universe operates.

She claims this is not a heretical conception of God, and that all the traditional attributes of God, such as intelligence, power, benevolence, justice, etc., can be thought of as fundamental aspects of the way Being itself is expressed in the universe. I'm not even sure I understand it completely, but I tend to like this conception. One advantage is that if I think of God this way, I am absolutely positively certain that Being is real, and so I am absolutely positively certain that there is a God! What do you think of this conception of God?

2. Regarding the text of the Torah, especially the Pentateuch, Dr. M thinks that the text that we have cannot be the very same one that was given by God to Moses (if there ever was such a text at all). There are interpolations, emendations, and other signs that the text was changed long after Moshe's death. There are different texts in existence to this day, and not all of them can be right. How do you respond to this?

3. This concerns whether the Torah needs to be interpreted literally. I understand that even the most Orthodox agree that some passages need to be interpreted metaphorically or allegorically. For example, where the text says that God has a "mighty hand" and an "outstretched arm," it doesn't mean that literally. But what about the stories and even the personalities in the Torah? For example, Dr. M thinks you don't even need to take the stories of Moses and Pharaoh literally. In fact, she thinks you don't even need to believe that there really was a person such as Moses. Moses could be a mythological figure who is meant to stand for some truth or teaching. (I'm sure Rabbi Abraham would find this view totally unacceptable. That's why I haven't even bothered asking him his opinion.) But Dr. M claims this view is not heretical, and that as long as you believe that the Torah is divine in origin, it doesn't really matter whether you take the stories literally. According to her, to say that the "Torah is divine" means that the Torah represents how God wants the Jewish people to live. She believes that it is through divine providence that the people of Israel developed a myth about their history which resulted in their "receiving the Torah" – i.e., getting a code of law or way of life through which they could fulfill God's purpose. In this theory, it seems much easier for a modern person to be a religious Jew since you don't need to believe in the literal truth of the stories any more (which modern Biblical scholarship has shed some serious skepticism on). I'm sure I'm not describing the theory very well, but it seems like a reasonable approach for a modern person to take toward the Torah if he's going to be religious. Do you agree?

4. About the role of women in Judaism and also the question of whether the Torah law can change over time. Thanks to Esther Applefeld, I am familiar with the idea that women are obligated in all mitzvot except for positive time-bound mitzvot. There is some rationale for that, but I still don't think that answers the question. It seems to me that women are treated unfairly in Orthodox Judaism. This seems like something that should be changed and could be changed, just like other things.

Why are the Orthodox so rigid about this? Do they believe the Torah as it is given is unchangeable? Surely that can't be true. There are things in the Torah that don't seem right, like slavery, polygamy, and so on. Also, Dr. M pointed out that the traditional Jewish prayers never ask for the welfare of the world at large. Isn't that something also that should be changed? And if it can't be changed, doesn't that show something is wrong with Orthodox Judaism?

5. Finally, on the issue of keeping kosher. Dr. M says that the reason for the dietary laws has to do with separating from the non-Jews and getting away from certain pagan practices. This is one area where I find that what she says does not make sense. I don't buy the idea that these laws are just meant to keep us separate from the non-Jews, though they certainly have that effect. As you once pointed out in a previous email, the Torah says that we should eat only animals that are tahor and not animals that are tameh. This implies that there is something intrinsic about the animal that is either good or bad in some way. But the only thing I can really think of is that the ancient Israelites had some superstitious, pre-scientific "reasons" for thinking that certain animals or creatures are somehow "inferior" to others. So, what do you think is the true explanation of tumah and taharah?

Sorry this has gone on so long. Any responses will be appreciated!

David

From: rlow@ahavattorah.org.il   Sent: 4/25/01 6:23 AM
To: dgoldstein@cuniv.edu
Subject: RE: some views of Dr. Maimon

Dear David,

As usual, your questions are interesting and important. I don't know if there is only one single correct way to answer them from an Orthodox point of view. I'll do my best to give my approach. I don't have the time to answer all your questions at once. I'll aim here to tackle the first three, and I'll write you later about the other two.

1. I am familiar with Dr. Maimon's concept of G-d from conversations I used to have with her when she was first working out these ideas. Everyone, including Dr. M, agrees that Judaism conceives of G-d as a supreme person who has free choice and intelligence, who issues commands, who is capable of judging us, and who is capable of entering into a relationship of mutual love with his creations. But regarding whether one may think of the Supreme Person as an entity or as Being itself, you may be surprised to hear that I think it really doesn't matter as long as one keeps the Halacha. Judaism doesn't dictate a single answer to all philosophical and metaphysical questions. For a pragmatist like myself, as long as a person keeps the commandments, what difference does it make whether he thinks of G-d as *a*

being or as *Being itself*? Perhaps the only practical difference is that if you agree with Dr. Maimon's approach, then, when you use the word Being to refer to G-d, you will have to write it as "Be-ing." (Just joking!) Seriously, I myself have difficulty seeing how you can enter into a personal relationship of mutual love with a non-entity. The idea of having a relationship with Being itself leaves me cold. When I daven (pray), I cannot help but think of G-d as *a* being. But if her way of thinking about G-d makes sense to you, I don't see why you can't think of G-d that way and still count yourself as a traditional Jew — as long as you are committed to keeping the mitzvot. When we get to heaven, we will hopefully find out whether G-d is an entity or not! (And maybe not even then!)

2. Though many of my Orthodox colleagues seem to have difficulty doing so, I myself am quite ready to admit that the text of the Torah as we have it now might not be *exactly* the same as the text that Moses had or that Ezra had or that even Rabbi Judah had during the rabbinic period. In fact, some of the proposed cases of "interpolations" (such as the Kings of Edom) are actually pretty debatable, but in principle I could admit that there were some minor interpolations from later times. But there's no question that over time there were some variations in texts. The Talmud itself teaches this. Are you familiar with the *Sifri*? This is a collection of rabbinic literature which is a running commentary on Deuteronomy. Commenting on *Deuteronomy* 33:2, the *Sifri* records without embarrassment an episode in which, during the Second Temple period, the sages found three Torah scrolls with slight variations of three different passages in the Pentateuch. In each case, the sages established what the correct text should be based on the majority of texts. Basically, the doctrine is that every verse in the Torah as we know it came directly from God to Moses. The existence of a few interpolations and letter variations here and there doesn't substantially affect this doctrine. As a practical matter, we follow and accept the version of the Torah that the sages in our generation declare to be the most exact text. Orthodox Jews should not be embarrassed to admit this.

3. You're absolutely right that not every passage and phrase in the Torah should be taken literally. (I'll pass over the controversial issue of what exactly it means to take something "literally." This issue is not as simple as it seems.) However, from an Orthodox point of view, the question is: what are the limits of non-literal interpretation of the Torah? This is a very difficult question to answer, and I don't think there is a simple rule or criterion that can easily be formulated to describe the exact limits of non-literal interpretation of the Torah. But it seems to me that Dr. M pushes things too far. It's one thing to suggest the account of the six days of creation, or even the account of the Flood, need not be taken literally. But it's quite another to suggest that the accounts of the lives of the patriarchs and the account of the life of Moshe need not be taken literally. Let me explain why.

First, there is a general principle regarding communication that seems applicable here. Normally, you take a person at his word unless you have some good reason not to. Hence, we should take the Torah at its word unless we have good reason not to. This is not religious dogma, but a principle of communication. So in general, we should take the Torah at its word unless we have good reason not to. (Saadia Gaon says this in his classic work, *Emunot ve-Deot*.)

Related to this is the following point. If the Torah need not be taken literally, why does it provide numerous details of names, places, and dates? All of this information would seem superfluous if it were not a record of history. This point is made in the Talmud in connection with the book of Iyyov. When one authority suggests that the book of Iyyov is a *mashal,* or metaphor, an objection is raised, that if it is, what is the need for mentioning Iyyov's lineage, place of residence and so on? As you may know, Maimonides took the book of Iyyov as a metaphor anyway. In fact, it is possible to understand the names of Iyyov's lineage and his birthplace to be hinting at certain conceptual themes. One can even construe the Talmud's "objection" as hinting at this very point. But still, can this apply to the rest of the Torah? For example, the Torah recounts ten lineal descendants from Adam to Noah and ten more from Noah to Abraham. The Torah states how long each person lived and provides the names of his eldest children. Surely these are not allegorical names! What would the point of all this be if the Torah were meant to be taken metaphorically?

Second, the idea that you can take the Torah non-literally at will is problematic in that it opens the door to interpreting it however one likes in order to conform to any random theory that one may have. Given any theory I might have about G-d or the world, I can always say that the Torah points to my theory when taken non-literally. This is what the Christians have done. For example, they interpret references to the eternality of Israel as metaphorical references to the Catholic Church. If I were clever enough, maybe I could find a non-literal interpretation of the Torah that would point to atheism or the latest theory in physics, or perhaps the latest episode in American politics. Where does this stop?

Third – and this is a more important point – one of the main teachings of Judaism is that Hashem is involved in the everyday life of every Jew and, indeed, every human being. This is the concept of *hashgaha pratis,* or divine providence, over particulars. Perhaps you have heard this term before. In layman's terms, this is the idea that G-d is watching over each and every one of us at each and every second. He knows where you're going and what you're doing and he knows what's going on in your mind and heart at all times. Now, a person might reasonably ask, how do we know this is true? This is a critical question that raises many issues, not all of which can be discussed here. But, for a religious Jew, at least part of the answer to this question is that *this is the way Hashem is depicted in the Torah.* For example, Hashem is depicted as intimately aware of and involved in not only the lives of the patriarchs and Moshe, but even of the lives of wicked people, such as the Egyptian Pharaoh (who wanted to take Sarah from Avraham and add her to his harem, as we read in *Bereishis* 12). The Torah recounts that G-d brought a plague upon the household of Avimelech, who tried to do the same. Now, if we do not take the Torah literally when it talks about these people and events, this undermines the idea of *hashgaha pratis,* the idea that G-d is involved in the most minute details of human affairs. I suppose in theory it's possible for someone to believe in *hashgaha pratis* and still believe that the Torah is largely an allegorical document. But that doesn't make much sense to me. Basically, too much allegorical interpretation of the Torah undermines the basis of our belief in *hashgaha pratis.* In fact, you might ask Dr. Maimon to tell you her view on *hashgaha pratis*. I could never quite figure out what her view is on this. If she abandons this idea, then she is abandoning a central teaching of traditional Judaism. Also, if she allows too much allegorization of the Torah, that leads to an abandonment of *hashgaha pratis*.

Even more important, too much allegorization of the Torah undermines another teaching of traditional Judaism: namely, the doctrine that G-d commanded the people of Israel to abide by the Torah. We don't believe just that the Torah is merely a good way of life, or a way of life that is in some sense "divinely inspired," or even just a way of life that in some sense allows us to walk in G-d's path. We believe that the Torah is a divinely ordained law that G-d commanded the people of Israel to follow, starting with the first words of the Ten Commandments and through the rest of the Torah, through Moshe. (By the way, this is one of the things that makes Judaism uniquely different from other religions, with the possible exception of Islam. Other religions teach that a certain way of life is divine in some sense, but not quite in this way.) To my mind, this doctrine requires that we believe there was a specific time and a specific place when G-d actually commanded us to follow the Torah. Now, if we say that Moshe never lived, *has ve-shalom*, then *when and where did G-d give us the Torah?* On the other hand, if we say that the sentence "G-d commanded Israel to follow the Torah" is not literally true, or at least not true in the plain meaning of this sentence, what then does it mean? I can't think of any non-literal interpretation of this sentence that would not weaken it. In sum, while here and there it is permissible to take the Torah non-literally, too much non-literal interpretation undermines and dilutes the major teachings of traditional Judaism.

Again, *bli neder*, I will write later on the remaining issues.

Sincerely,

Rabbi Low

35

May 1, 2001

Dear David,

I am so happy to write this letter. As you know by now from talking with Dad, the cancer is completely gone and I have a clean bill of health. It really shows the power of prayer and having a positive attitude, which I've learned to cultivate finally.

So many things have turned around in my life. Not only have I quit smoking, but I don't even crave cigarettes any more. I haven't taken a single drink in weeks, except for maybe a glass of wine or two at dinner. Now that this cancer thing is over I'm hoping to spend more time with Dad. I'm trying to get him to go on a cruise in the Caribbean. I was also hoping we could visit Jack in Florida for at least a weekend. I know Dad is reluctant to leave his work, but maybe we can convince him anyway. Am I too optimistic? I hope not.

Anyway, I'm also going to sign up for some courses at the university next fall. I don't know if I'm quite ready for philosophy but I was thinking of taking something in literature. What do you think of your mom going back to school at this age? Any advice?

Well, enough about me. How about you? What's going on in your life? How's your running going? And how's your friend Esther doing? You said you were going to try to teach her some philosophy. Did you succeed? What about your inquiries into Judaism? Where is this taking you? I'm really interested to hear about your spiritual quest. Write back with more details.

I almost forgot to tell you that I rented The Quarrel and watched it. I found it very interesting. I really liked the way the film developed the views of the two main characters. And the nice thing is how they were able to come to see each other's point of view and part friends at the end. I'd really like to see your paper on the film. Can you send it to me? Just email it to Dad and he can print it out for me.

By the way, I was thinking of coming to visit you toward the end of the semester. Maybe I'll drive in and spend a few days in the city and then drive back home with you. What do you think?

Love,

Mom

36

"Dr. Maimon, I'm really anxious to ask you something about your view on divine providence."

"Yes, David. What about it?"

"I know you don't believe that there's a being, God, who watches over the world from somewhere beyond it. You think that there's a structure to the universe and that, in accordance with that structure, certain things happen and certain things don't happen, which are ultimately heading toward a better end. So that means you still believe in divine providence. Is that correct?"

"Yes, that's correct."

"But to what extent do you think divine providence covers us? I mean, on a daily basis, how involved is God in our lives as individuals? Traditionally, Jews mostly believe that God sees us all the time and watches everything we do, and everything that happens to us is part of a divine plan. Do you believe in that kind of divine providence?"

"In other words, do I believe in what's sometimes called *hashgaha pratit,* or particular providence?"

"Yes, that's exactly my question."

"Yes, I do believe in *hashgaha pratit* – in the following sense: The universe has a structure, and everything operates in accordance with the divine principles that underlie the universe. These principles apply everywhere and without exception. So even the minutest details of every day life are governed by these principles. Look, the same is true in the scientific realm. Whatever the laws of nature are – take the law of gravity, for example – these laws govern the tiniest trivial events, such as an insect falling from a leaf. The same is true of the divine principles, such as the principles of benevolence and justice. Everything in the universe, even the smallest details, is governed by these principles."

"Your view on this issue sounds pretty traditional after all."

"Well, I can tell you where my view does differ from the view commonly held by many religious people – not just Orthodox Jews, but also many Christians and Muslims. There's a certain kind of pietistic religious view that I reject."

"Oh? What's that?"

"Let me describe two features of the pietist view. First, this view says that since God's providence is total, that means everything that happens is part of the divine plan. There are no accidents or coincidences, so to speak. According to this theory, the fact that I sneeze now rather than two seconds later is part of the divine plan. Or if you bump into someone in the subway or stub your toe, or if a book you're holding falls on the floor and opens to a certain page, there is a divine reason why it happened precisely as it did."

"And you disagree with that?"

"Yes, I do. I believe that there are some genuinely accidental truths and some genuinely random events that have no religious, spiritual or ethical significance whatsoever. However, it may be difficult to tell precisely what are the accidental truths or random events —"

"Dr. Maimon, I'm sorry to interrupt. But if, as you said before, the divine principles govern everything, even the most minute details of the universe, then how can there be any genuine accidents?"

"Remember, David: my view is that the world is governed in accordance with certain divine principles, such as benevolence and justice. Those divine principles constitute the divine plan. But there could very well be many events that are immaterial to the divine plan. Similarly, there could be some truths which, despite the principles of benevolence and justice, are immaterial to the divine plan. Take, for example, the exact number of hairs on your head. I strongly believe that the specific number of hairs on your head is not relevant to the divine plan. The same goes for the precise number of birds on the planet or stars in the sky. Now, the fact that there are stars, or that there are birds, might very well be relevant to the divine plan. But the precise number might not make a difference to the divine plan. So the precise number is a matter of chance. Using more ordinary religious language, we might say, 'God doesn't care about the precise number of hairs on David's head.' Do you follow?"

"I think so."

"The same point may be made regarding coincidences – that is, pairs of events that happen to occur at the same time, or coincide. There are literally billions of pairs of events that occur at the same time. But just because two events happen at the same time does not necessarily mean they are significantly related. For example, if I were to sneeze at the very same moment that an apple falls from a tree some twenty miles away, that would be a coincidence, having no divine significance whatsoever. In fact, the Torah itself warns against seeing too much in coincidences. There's actually a name for it – superstition! For example, the so-called 'Bible Codes' – have you heard of them?"

"Yes, I have looked into it a little."

"In my view, that's superstitious as well. Now, the second feature of the pietist view has more to do with knowing or figuring out what God's plan is. Many pious people have a tendency to think that God's plan is transparent. I'll give you an example I read about some time ago. There was a fire in an Orthodox Jewish family's home, and unfortunately, four of their six children were killed. It was reported in the Jewish news that after the tragedy, a rabbi asked whether the mezuzah scroll on the outside door was still intact. He said that if it was, it should be checked to see whether it had been written properly. It turned out that the scroll was intact, but when it was checked, four letters were found to be missing. The implication was that because those four letters were missing, four children were killed. Isn't that absurd?"

"Yes, I think so."

"The point is that we don't have a handle on God's will in such a precise way. Don't mistake my position, though. If there is a fire in a Jewish house and someone gets hurt – I think that this event is not random, and that its occurrence must fit in to the divine plan somehow, though I don't know exactly how. It may simply be that the parents didn't take proper precautions for fire safety, and the deaths were a result of poor parenting! Anyway, I think it is arrogant to say that we can know precisely why God allowed such an event to happen – that is, precisely how it fits into the divine plan. To use old-fashioned terminology, in the case of the fire I just described, I'd say that God knew about the fire and that in effect, God allowed it to occur. But I don't think we can always pinpoint why God let it happen. All we know is that when human beings behave well, and when Jews follow God's way, things go well for us overall. Furthermore, this is true on a collective basis, not on an individual basis. That means there are times when good people suffer and bad people prosper. But over time, over the course of history, that is generally not true."

"So are you saying it's impossible for an individual to see God's hand in his life?"

"The only way you can do that with any reliability is by focusing on your inner life – that is, the life of the mind, rather than your outer life. I believe that if you are a moral person and if you follow the Torah, you will see the effects on your own mind and your personality. You will become more and more solid and secure in your knowledge of God, and your life will become richer in meaning. The effects of divine worship on one's inner life are almost always immediate and clear. But as far as what happens to you in your life – I mean, events transpiring outside of you, I don't think there is any way of telling why God does what he does, to use the vulgar mode of speaking. It's our job to pursue God regardless of what he throws in front of us. Consider the ten trials that Abraham had to pass. Are you familiar with that concept?"

"Yes, I read about it in *Pirkei Avot*."

"Ah, very good. So, on each one of those ten occasions Abraham didn't wonder, 'Why is God doing this to me?' He didn't try to figure out what he had done or not done to bring about each challenge. This very important lesson is taught at the beginning of Abraham's career. God tells him to go to Canaan, and almost as soon as he gets there, there's a famine and he has to leave. But he doesn't complain or try to figure out why this is happening. He recognizes that he has to leave temporarily and come back later. Abraham always rose to the occasion and did what needed to be done – meaning that he served God without trying to figure out why what was happening was happening. I don't think we can or should expect to do any better than Abraham. The bottom line is that we don't have a handle on the precise details of how divine providence works . . . ."

37

"Hello, Phil. How are you?"

"Good, David. Long time no see. What's going on?"

"Well, there were two things I needed to ask you about."

"Fine. But I'm ordering something for lunch first. I'm getting a cheeseburger. Do you want one?"

"No, I'll just have coffee."

"What? Why not? Have you gone veggie?"

"No – actually, I'm trying to keep kosher these days."

"Ah! I should have known."

"Actually, that's one of the things I wanted to talk to you about."

"OK. I'll do my best."

"But first, Phil, let's get the other thing out of the way."

"What's that?"

"I have to register for next year, and I need to figure out which two philosophy courses to take."

"Am I still your advisor? I thought you switched to Dr. Maimon."

"No, you're still my advisor."

"Oh, OK. Well, for one thing, you need to take Epistemology. You probably covered some of that already in your Intro course."

"Yes, I think I did."

"Well, let's give you a little test. Quick, tell me – what's epistemology?"

"It comes from the Greek word *episteme*, which means knowledge. Epistemology is the philosophical investigation of knowledge. It deals with questions such as: what can we know for certain, what is the role of sensation versus reason, are there innate ideas that are prior to sensation, and stuff like that."

"Excellent! You pass, and you don't have to take the course!"

"Very funny, Phil. And I still need to choose another course. What should I take?"

"How about *Philosophy of Mind*? Do you know what that's about?"

"Let me guess. The mind?"

"Very sharp! Yes, it's about the nature of the mind or the soul, and its relation to the body. You will get into questions like whether the mind is a bodily thing or some mental substance; does its existence depend on the body; what is the nature of personal identity. It's the ideal course for someone who's trying to figure out who, or what, he is."

"How appropriate. I guess I'll take the course, then."

"Good. So, that settles your first problem. Now, shall we talk about your other problem? What was it? Something about keeping kosher?"

"Well, it's related to that. Like I said, I'm trying to keep kosher now. Or at least, I'm experimenting."

"It must be a difficult experiment."

"They say you get used to it after a while."

"A person can get used to almost anything. Anyway, you must really be getting into Judaism."

"You could say that. But that's what I wanted to ask you about. Phil, you know I really respect your opinion about things. So I'm wondering whether I could ask you to lay your cards on the table."

"What do you mean by that?"

"I mean – what do you really think about religion? We had this conversation a while ago, and as far as I get it, you think that if we are philosophical and rely on reason alone, there is no way to answer all the ultimate questions. Yet that's exactly what religion tries to do – it tries to give definitive answers to all the ultimate questions. So religion is inherently anti-philosophical. This is related to the fact that in many world religions, a written text or 'scripture' is so important because it symbolizes the fact that religion tries to give a fixed or concrete statement of ultimate truth."

"I'm impressed. You remember my position very well."

"You also said that the common man is not satisfied living in a world of doubt, so he feels the need to go beyond reason and accept certain things on faith, which in your mind is really to fall beneath reason. You're also skeptical about any particular claim to revelation, partly because there are conflicting religious traditions about what God has supposedly revealed."

"Very good. Well? Isn't that enough? What do you say to all of that?"

"Well, first of all, if you think of God as Being itself, then –"

"Ah! I see you've been schooled by Dr. Maimon! I know her whole shpiel on that. Sure, you can use the word 'God' to refer to Being itself if you want, and then you can consider yourself as someone who 'knows' that God is real. That's basically what Spinoza did. But suppose I grant you all that. I'll even grant you that in some sense, Being is benevolent. Still, what does Being itself have to do with keeping kosher or any of the other non-rational commandments? The only way you can make that link is if you also believe in revelation, which Spinoza essentially rejected. That's where Maimon's argument gets problematic. I know she makes some attempt to argue that revelation is an expression of Being itself. But there's a serious problem with that."

"What's the problem?"

"Hang on a second – here comes my cheeseburger . . . . What I was about to say was: aside from the problem of how you tell whether any given revelation is authentic, you're faced with the following dilemma. Consider some purported revelation. Now, either the content of what God reveals is rational, or it is not rational. Right?"

"Yes."

"Now, if it isn't rational, then there is no reason to follow it. In fact, there's no reason to think that Being itself would express itself in any way that is not rational. If it does, we should just take that as a sign that Being itself has an imperfect way of expressing itself, and in that case, we should ignore the 'revelation' as a freak of nature – or should I say, a freak of Being. Do you follow?

"Yes, I think so."

"I assume you reject this horn of the dilemma. That is, you don't think that God or Being or whatever you want to call it would reveal irrational laws."

"Right. I don't think so."

"Now, on the other hand, if the content of the revelation is rational, then the problem is that we shouldn't have needed revelation to tell us about it. We should have been able to figure it out on our own."

"Why's that? Maybe there are certain things that are rational, but which we could never figure out on our own, and for which we need God's revelation to make known to us."

"Sorry – that doesn't make any sense. Even Dr. Maimon disagrees with that notion. If something is rational, it's got to be comprehensible to us in principle. It might be complicated and difficult, but sooner or later, we should be able to figure it out on our own.

"You're right. I'm not sure I agree, but that is her view. All the commandments are rational in principle."

"So, then, if they are rational, what do we need revelation for? Anything that is rational could have been known without revelation. Anything that is not rational is not worth obeying. That means that revelation is useless either way!"

"I'm not sure what to say. I'll have to think about it."

38
―

From: rlow@ahavattorah.org.il   Sent: 5/1/01 6:23 AM
To: dgoldstein@cuniv.edu
Subject: Women, halacha, change

Dear David,

Getting back to you on the remaining issues from your last email. First, on the issue of keeping kosher. Remember that first and foremost we keep the commandments out of love and devotion to G-d. Whether we understand them or not is secondary. But still I agree with Maimonides that G-d doesn't command things arbitrarily, and it behooves us to think about and even speculate what the reasons might be for the commandments.

Regarding mixing meat and milk, I think Maimonides was probably right that the prohibition against this had to do with getting away from some pagan ritual. But regarding the kosher vs. non-kosher animals, you're absolutely right that there appears to be some quality in the animal that makes it either *tahor* or *tameh.* And indeed the *concept* of *tumah* and *taharah* has much broader application than just to animals. I think this whole area is the most mysterious part of Torah law. Even the translation "pure" and "impure" is not accurate, in my opinion. This is evidenced by the fact that the word *tumah* is not simply the negation of the word *tahor.* I think a better translation would be "complete" versus "defective." In my view, the best available explanation is that the *tahor* animals are complete specimens of a certain type, whether they are land, water, or air, while all of the *tameh* creatures are defective specimens or "in-betweeners," so to speak. (See the book by Leon Kass entitled *The Hungry Soul* for an exposition of this theory that cites the work of anthropologist Mary Douglas.) For example, the sea creatures that have legs and walk out of the ocean and the river creatures that crawl are neither purely sea creatures nor purely land animals, so they are regarded as "in-betweeners." Similarly, reptiles slither and don't really walk, so they are not full fledged land animals. Rodents are also "in-betweeners" because they don't walk properly but only scurry along. Only the animals that chew their cud and have split hooves (basically, the ruminants) are considered full-fledged land animals, whereas those that do not chew cud or have split hooves are not. This is really only the start of a theory and it has some holes, but the overall thesis seems plausible to me. G-d created a universe of creatures, both complete and defective. The defective ones, or "in-betweeners," are *tameh* and the whole or complete ones are *tahor.* As you know, Judaism teaches the sanctification of the physical realm through the observance and performance of *mitzvos.* I'd speculate that since the Jewish people are supposed to live an especially devout form of spiritual life, they are commanded only to eat from the *tahor,* or complete, animals. However the connection between the complete animals and the spiritual life still needs to be developed. That's the best I can do on *kashrut.* I realize it's only a start.

Regarding your question of why don't we pray for the welfare of non-Jews – this premise is not entirely correct. First of all, Tehillim (Psalms) is replete with prayers for the welfare of all those who live a just life. This includes both Jews and non-Jews. As you may know, many devout Orthodox Jews recite Tehillim on a daily basis. This means that many Orthodox Jews pray daily for the welfare of the non-Jews. Furthermore, three times every weekday in the Amidah prayer, we ask G-d to have compassion on all those who are *tzaddikim* (righteous). I believe this refers to righteous non-Jews as well as Jews. On Shabbos in many synagogues there is a prayer for the welfare of the government. This comes from an ancient source (*Pirkei Avot* 3:2). In the second paragraph of the *Alenu* prayer, recited three times daily every day of the year, we pray that one day the world will be "fixed" through the universal kingdom of G-d over all humankind. This is the concept of "tikkun olam," or repairing the world. Finally, the liturgy of the High Holidays includes a prayer that one day *all* the righteous and pious people of the world will exult and rejoice in the kingdom of G-d and form *agudah ahat,* one unified group, to do G-d's will with a full heart. This is clearly referring to all humankind, not just the Jewish people.

Now, it is true that most of these prayers are for the "righteous" of the world, not for just anyone. I think the explanation for this has to do with something profound about the nature of prayer itself. The whole idea of prayer itself is in a way problematic. If G-d is the king of the universe, and G-d decides, let's say, to cause a hurricane or cause someone to get sick, then G-d must have a divine reason for letting that happen. Why should we mortals think that we can pray to G-d to "change his mind" and cause the hurricane to be diverted or the sickness to be healed? In effect, if G-d answers a prayer and changes the natural course of events, then that's an intervention in nature – in other words, a miracle. The only reason that Jews are in a position to pray at all is by virtue of the special relationship we have with G-d through keeping the Torah. Righteous non-Jews are also in a position to pray. That's very clear from many passages in the Prophets (for example, see 1 Kings 8). But if the purpose of humankind is to be righteous and serve G-d, it is not proper to pray for the welfare of those who are wicked and idolatrous. Prayer on behalf of the non-Jews doesn't make sense unless they are committed at least to keeping the Noahide commandments. If they do not, then *"olam ke-minhago noheg"* – the world operates in accord with its natural way, and they are subject to the course of nature. It is only the Jewish people and committed Noahides who have a special relationship with G-d, and by virtue of that special relationship, miracles (i.e., changes in nature) are feasible. That's why we pray primarily only for the Jewish people and for the righteous of the world.

On the role of women and change in halacha: these are both very complex issues, and there is some controversy even within Orthodox circles about these matters. I will just give you my own perspective about it. The Torah teaches that man and woman were created as one, so basically man and woman share the same fundamental nature. Women are not inferior to men. But the Torah also teaches that woman was created as an *ezer ke-negdo* that is, as a "helpmate" (literally, a "help in opposition to man," which is a very interesting locution indeed). Men and women are different not only in terms of anatomy. They are also psychologically and spiritually different. That's not in line with certain modern sensibilities, but that's what the Torah says. Men and women have different roles that are in some sense equal, in some sense not. I think it's a pointless issue to debate who has it better or worse. In some sense, men have it better, in some sense, women have it better. Some have argued that women do not have all the same duties as men not because they are inferior to men, but because they are naturally more in tune with G-d already. For example, it is said that women do not need to wear a kippah since by nature they are more humble than men. They do not need to work as hard as men do, so to speak, in order to reach the same level of connection with G-d. Still, there's no denying that in some respects, women play a secondary or facilitating role. The woman's role is primarily in the home, while the man's is more public. I do believe that there's some room for change in this area in our time, but not as much as some Jewish feminists would like. More on change below.

Regarding slavery, I know this may sound like a shocking question, but just think about it for a minute: what exactly is immoral about slavery? True, it's an "unfair" situation, but so is the fact that some people are wealthy while others are poor. Which is better – having a job as a laborer that pays barely minimum wage, or having a master who is responsible for providing for all one's needs? I believe that in our time, slavery is no longer acceptable, but in other times and places, slavery was not inherently immoral as long as certain guidelines were followed. (It's like polygamy in this regard. Polygamy is not inherently immoral, but since it often works out that way in practice, it was banned.) When you think of slavery, you probably think of an inherently abusive situation, but that's not necessarily the case. The Torah provides specific rules for the humane treatment of slaves. Under certain circumstances, if a non-Jewish slave was abused, he would go free. (There were two kinds of slaves, Jewish and non-Jewish, and the laws concerning them are somewhat different – see Exodus 21.) A Jew could become a slave by selling himself voluntarily, or the courts could sell him involuntarily if he was in debt and could not pay. This would only be a temporary situation. A non-Jew could become a slave by being bought from another non-Jew or by having been taken captive in war. But here's something amazing: A non-Jewish slave would become partly Jewish in that he would be obligated in all commandments in which women are obligated. This is an astonishing thing when you think about it. Also, see Maimonides, *Code of Law*, Hilchot Avadim 9:8, where he talks about proper and compassionate care specifically for non-Jewish slaves.

Now on the issue of change. Although divine commandments themselves can't be changed, the rabbis still have the power to ban certain things and to institute other things. So, for example, they could ban polygamy when they saw that it was causing problems, and they could institute the marriage contract to protect the rights of women. Furthermore, at least according to Maimonides, it is theoretically possible that rabbinic *interpretations* of the written Torah can change over time (see his *Code of Law*, Hilchot Mamrim 2:1). He writes that the Sanhedrin – the Jewish high court – of one generation may reject an interpretation of the Torah that was made by a previous Sanhedrin. Now, I believe that it is an *interpretation* of the Torah that women are excluded from being witnesses. Like all other ancient peoples, the Jews had certain prejudices about women – for example that they were less intelligent and more childlike than men. (Yet, interestingly, a passage in the Talmud states that women have an extra dose of *binah* – intuitive understanding – see BT *Niddah* 45a.) I think that possibly, this prejudice against the intelligence of women influenced and colored their interpretation of the Torah. In a future generation, this interpretation could theoretically be changed. However, until the Sanhedrin is reinstituted, which is presumably the time of the Messiah, such an interpretation cannot officially be changed. (You should also know that there are technical ways around the exclusion of women from serving as witnesses. For example, a judge can listen to a woman and take into account what she says in rendering his decision.)

Regarding customs and generally accepted practices, there is much more room for change and evolution within halacha. I believe that women can and should be studying Torah, and though I believe services need to be separate, I think women can and should have their own prayer groups if they want them. However, some rabbis hold that since men have an obligation to pray, it is actually better for a woman who wants to pray to attend services where she can hear and participate but not lead the services. Also, since men have an obligation to study Torah for its own sake, resources for establishing places of study will be given to men first rather than women.

There is another reason why change is difficult in Orthodox Judaism. Since the advent of Reform Judaism and also because of large-scale assimilation in the modern period, there is a greater desire to show resistance to change. Many Orthodox rabbis are nervous about any kind of change at all because, as they believe, who knows what will happen next? In theory, this view is too rigid for me, but there is a practical problem in that we can't all go off instituting whatever changes we want without compromising Jewish unity. From my point of view, this is what is most seriously wrong with Conservative Judaism. Even if I could be convinced halachically that mixed seating is really permissible or that women could function as rabbis even though they are not obligated in all the same mitzvot as men, I myself would not go off and establish mixed seating services until a majority of Orthodox scholars and rabbis signed off on it (which is not likely to happen anytime soon). A group of Jews has no business going off on their own and changing Jewish practice. Doing so divides the Jewish people. In fact, I believe that if it weren't for Conservative Judaism, the Orthodox establishment would be much more willing to accept change than it is today. This is not an excuse, but a fact.

Getting back to the issue of the role of women, the bottom line is to remember that the Torah is given to the Jewish people as a whole – men, women, and children. Do you know about the three classes of Jews? There are Kohanim (priests), Levites, and Israelites. This was especially important during the time of the Temple. The Kohanim play the central role in the Temple, the Levites play a facilitating role, and the remaining Israelites play only a lesser role. There are different roles for different people. For example, it is also a tradition that a legitimate Jewish king must come only from the tribe of Yehudah and be neither a Kohen nor a Levite. So there is no way that a Levi or Kohen could be a king (so the Messiah cannot be a Kohen or Levi). My point is that there are different roles for different groups. It's the *people* of Israel as a whole that must follow the Torah. I don't gloat over the fact that I am a man and have responsibilities that my wife does not have. I am awed and humbled by the fact that I have these responsibilities, and I try to do my best to fulfill them. Similarly, my wife doesn't burn with envy over the fact that she doesn't have my responsibilities. She knows that she has enough to handle as a Jewish woman. Together, we try to serve G-d with a full heart, and we believe that if we do what we're supposed to do, we will both end up together in the same place – the right relationship with each other and with Hashem.

Sincerely,

Rabbi Low

39

"So how do you like it here?"

"It's nice, really nice, Esther."

"And the food?"

"It's fantastic!"

"I told you, David! There *is* good kosher food!"

"You're right."

"So, do you still wonder about keeping kosher? Does it still bother you?"

"Actually, I took your advice and asked Rabbi Low."

"What did he have to say?"

"He shared with me a very interesting theory about kosher animals. The basic idea is that the kosher animals are perfect specimens of their type, whether land, air or sea creatures, and the non-kosher animals are what he called 'in-betweeners.' The idea is that *tumah* and *taharah* have something to do with completeness and incompleteness. The creatures that are complete, or perfect, are *tahor* and therefore kosher, while the 'in-betweeners' are incomplete and therefore *tameh*. Have you ever heard this theory?"

"Now that you mention it, it sounds familiar. Yes, I remember that Rabbi Low once gave a talk about that idea when I was in Israel."

"Esther, I can't believe it! Why didn't you say anything about it before? Really, it's the most reasonable theory I've heard so far."

"Sorry – I guess it just slipped my mind. I told you before – as far as I'm concerned, the real reason for keeping kosher is because God said so. But it's an interesting theory. So – do you think it works?"

"Maybe it does. One problem I have is that even if it's true that the non-kosher animals are somehow incomplete, what's so terrible about eating them? But the basic idea that *tumah* has to do with incompleteness of some sort makes a lot of sense to me. For example – and I don't mean to be morbid – this idea fits very well with the fact that in the Torah, there's a strong connection between *tumah* and death."

"What do you mean? I know that a dead body is considered the most serious case of *tumah*. But what does that have to do with Rabbi Low's theory about non-kosher animals?"

"Simple. His idea is that the impure animals are ones that are somehow incomplete. But death is also a form of incompleteness. A dead body is seriously incomplete, since it has lost its life. That's why it's *tameh*!"

"Ah, I see. Good thought!"

"Also . . . I hate to bring this up, but a menstruating woman who has just lost one of her ova is considered *t'meah*. This also fits with the theme of death and incompleteness."

"Right. That fits, too."

"The same goes for some of the diseases mentioned in the Torah that make a person *tameh*. A disease is a form of imperfection."

"Yes, David. I recall a *midrash* which says something just like that. Leprosy is a kind of death."

"Perfect! That's more confirmation of the theory. The basic idea is that *tumah* is a form of incomplete being, or something like that. The rest of the theory would be to explain how the kosher animals are complete while the non-kosher animals are incomplete. Hey – another idea just hit me."

"What's that?"

"It follows from what we were saying that there's some connection between eating and – um, no offense intended – sexual relations."

"Uh, OK. Why's that?"

"It's forbidden to eat an animal that is *tameh,* and it's also forbidden to have relations with a woman who is *t'meah*. You have to eat kosher food, and you can only have relations with . . . um . . . a kosher partner . . . ."

"Ah, yes. I see. I can't believe I'm having this conversation! You know, David, I've got to tell you . . . I just wanted to say . . . I really admire how you're really delving into the study of Torah. You're obviously learning, you're studying and reading, you're making so many connections. It's great!"

"Thanks, Esther."

"And I've got to admit . . . when I first met you, I didn't think things would head this way. I'm really impressed with your commitment to learning."

"Thanks again. And now that you've flattered me, can I flatter you? I just wanted to tell you how important you've been in my spiritual quest."

"Me? I haven't done anything at all."

"Sure you have. And also, I want to tell you how stunning you look tonight."

"Come on, David – that's really too much. You've got to stop."

"Why? Can't I compliment you? You know what's so strange? From the moment

I saw you, it was so obvious how attractive you are. Yet there's some taboo about my saying what is obviously true. Isn't that strange?"

"David, there are good reasons for these things."

"I'll tell you something else. The last time I was in a fancy restaurant with a girl, it was when I broke up with my non-Jewish girlfriend."

"Oh? You've never told me about that. That probably wasn't easy to do."

"It wasn't easy at the time, but I'm glad I did it. The strange thing was, the day after that happened, I got a letter from my mom, saying her operation was successful."

"Wow! That's really *hashgaha pratit* – God's direct hand. By the way, how is your mom doing these days?"

"She's great. In fact, her doctors said that she's completely cured."

"*Baruch Hashem*!"

"I agree. In fact, the last time she wrote, she really sounded good. She even said she'd like to drive down here and visit when the semester's over."

"Wow, that's nice!"

"She also asked about you in her last letter."

"About *me*? You're not kidding, are you?"

"No, I'm not."

"So – you've actually told her about me?"

"Yes, a little bit. No gory details, but a little bit."

"David, I really think that maybe when she comes, I'd like to meet her."

"Sure. No problem."

40

"*Hello?*"

"*David? It's Dad . . . .*"

"*Dad? Hi! How are you? What's going on?*"

"*David . . .*".

"*Yes?*"

"*David, I . . . .*"

"*Yes? What is it? You don't sound too good. Are you OK?*"

"*David, I'm sorry . . . but what are you doing right now? Can you sit down?*"

"*Sure, but why? Dad, you sound very strange. Are you at work?*"

"*No, I'm at home.*"

"*What is it? Is something wrong?*"

"*David, you've got to come home as soon as you can.*"

"*Why? What's happened?*"

"*Just come home as soon as you can, and then we'll talk.*"

"*Dad, what is it? What's going on? Come on, Dad. Tell me what this is about! Is it*

Mom? What's going on? Is she depressed again?"

"No, David. I'm afraid it's much worse than that."

"What is it? Did the cancer come back?"

"No, David, it's worse . . . much worse . . . ."

"Dad, just tell me! What happened? Is she all right?"

"David, I'm sorry . . . I didn't want to tell you this way . . . but Mom passed away last night . . . ."

"What? I don't think I heard you right. What did you say?"

"I'm sorry David . . . . Mom passed away last night."

"Dad, no . . . I can't believe it . . . ."

"I'm sorry . . . I guess it was an accident . . . ."

"An accident? What do you mean? Why? What did she do?"

"Took too many pills . . . drank too much . . . at the same time. It's a bad mix . . . . I'm sorry, David. Just please come home."

41

The grave was covered with a large canopy. David, his father, Richard, and his brother, Jack, stood close to each other. The rabbi spoke softly and soothingly, but David barely heard a word he said. When the rabbi stopped speaking, the casket was lowered slowly into the grave. Soon, all those assembled were asked to place some earth on the casket.

When the burial was completed, the rabbi spoke again. "The family members may now recite the burial *Kaddish*. Please follow along with me on page 28."

Richard and Jack remained silent as the rabbi intoned the *Kaddish*. David was somewhat familiar with the prayer, having heard it recited by mourners in the synagogue, but he felt unable to speak. Out of the corner of his eye, David sensed that someone was moving toward him. A young, bearded man, dressed in the traditional black garb of an Orthodox Jew, approached David and stood on his right. He held a prayer book open and showed David the place on the page.

"My name is Chaim," he whispered. "I'm a relative from your mother's side. If you'd like to say the *Kaddish*, I'll help you."

David took the book from Chaim's hands and slowly started to read the words.

The Burial Kaddish

Magnified and sanctified may His great name be	יִתְגַּדַּל וְיִתְקַדַּשׁ שְׁמֵהּ רַבָּא
in the world which He will renew,	בְּעָלְמָא דְהוּא עָתִיד לְאִתְחַדָּתָא
when He revives the dead,	וּלְאַחֲיָאָה מֵתַיָּא
raises them up to eternal life,	וּלְאַסָּקָא יָתְהוֹן לְחַיֵּי עָלְמָא
rebuilds the city of Jerusalem,	וּלְמִבְנֵא קַרְתָּא דִירוּשְׁלֵם
perfects His Temple within it,	וּלְשַׁכְלָלָא הֵיכְלֵהּ בְּגַוַּהּ

uproots idol worship from the earth, וּלְמֶעֱקַר פֻּלְחָנָא נָכְרָאָה מֵאַרְעָא

and returns the worship of Heaven to its place. וּלְאַתָבָא פֻּלְחָנָא דִשְׁמַיָּא לְאַתְרֵהּ.

Then the Holy One, Blessed be He, will reign וְיַמְלִיךְ קֻדְשָׁא בְּרִיךְ הוּא

in His sovereignty and glory – may this happen בְּמַלְכוּתֵהּ וִיקָרֵהּ

during your lives and in your days, בְּחַיֵּיכוֹן וּבְיוֹמֵיכוֹן

and during the lives of the whole house of Israel, וּבְחַיֵּי דְכָל בֵּית יִשְׂרָאֵל

swiftly and soon, and now respond: בַּעֲגָלָא וּבִזְמַן קָרִיב. וְאִמְרוּ

Amen. May His great name be blessed אָמֵן. יְהֵא שְׁמֵהּ רַבָּא מְבָרַךְ

forever and ever. לְעָלַם וּלְעָלְמֵי עָלְמַיָּא.

Blessed, praised, glorified, exalted יִתְבָּרַךְ וְיִשְׁתַּבַּח וְיִתְפָּאַר וְיִתְרוֹמַם

uplifted, glorified, elevated, and praised וְיִתְנַשֵּׂא וְיִתְהַדָּר וְיִתְעַלֶּה וְיִתְהַלָּל

be the name of the Holy One, Blessed is He שְׁמֵהּ דְּקֻדְשָׁא בְּרִיךְ הוּא

beyond all blessing, and song, לְעֵלָּא מִן כָּל בִּרְכָתָא וְשִׁירָתָא

praise and consolation that is said in the world, תֻּשְׁבְּחָתָא וְנֶחֱמָתָא דַּאֲמִירָן בְּעָלְמָא

and now respond: Amen. וְאִמְרוּ אָמֵן.

May there be abundant peace from heaven יְהֵא שְׁלָמָה רַבָּא מִן שְׁמַיָּא

and life upon us and upon all Israel: וְחַיִּים עָלֵינוּ וְעַל כָּל יִשְׂרָאֵל

now respond: Amen. וְאִמְרוּ אָמֵן

May He who makes peace in His heights עוֹשֶׂה שָׁלוֹם בִּמְרוֹמָיו

make peace upon us and upon all Israel: הוּא יַעֲשֶׂה שָׁלוֹם עָלֵינוּ וְעַל כָּל יִשְׂרָאֵל

now respond: Amen. וְאִמְרוּ אָמֵן

As the last words of the *Kaddish* faded, David began to weep.

42

May 27, 2001

Mom is dead.

I write this sentence and stare at it on the page.

Mom is dead.

Sometimes this single thought just fills my mind, for an hour at a time. It's hard to think of anything else or anyone else at all.

MOM IS DEAD.

I still don't understand it. The coroner ruled it accidental suicide. But was it really an accident? Why was she drinking and taking pills like that? Why was she depressed? It doesn't make any sense. Why won't Dad talk about it? And where was he? Not just that night, but all the other nights?

Dealing with death. Never thought I'd write about death in my journal. Not like this. Why does God – if he exists – let things like this happen? Couldn't he have stopped her before she took that final pill, that last drink, the one that was too much?

But this is once again the question of human suffering. Is Mom's death the first tragedy to ever happen? Of course not. And what about the Holocaust? Didn't I already say that it wasn't the first major tragedy either, even if it was unique in certain ways? Yet when it happens to <u>you</u>, then, suddenly things are different. It's so much easier to try to explain someone else's suffering. But when it's your own suffering, suddenly it's not so easy.

The rational answer: the free will defense. (It seems like a selfish thought now, but it just hit me: I wonder if she ever read my paper on evil? I'll never know.) I know what I would say if I were trying to explain this to a friend. "God gives us choice, God gives us responsibility. The conditions for living a virtuous and spiritual life require that we be free, that we have the opportunity to bring about joy, but also that we be able to cause suffering. Having choice enables us not only to ruin our lives, but the lives of others around us." Blah blah blah. Does this really make sense? I still disagree with Maimon. If there's no life after death, it doesn't make sense in the end. The price, the suffering of the innocent, is too high to pay. And then the question is: Can there be life after death? I want to believe it, but does it make sense? Is this just wishful thinking? I don't know.

Crying, finally, at the funeral. That was a relief. Never liked crying, but sometimes, you've got to. It helped. And I don't think I would have cried if I hadn't said the Kaddish. Got to look into the Kaddish. What's all that stuff about praising the "great name"? And for all that stuff about the great name, it doesn't use the Tetragrammaton even once. Theoretically, I'm supposed to say Kaddish every day for almost a year. No way that's going to happen. Well, maybe I'll try to do it once a week.

Chaim. Who is he? Never knew I had relatives quite like that. I'm not even sure how we're related. Need to find out about that. If not for him, I wouldn't have even said the Kaddish. Nice of him to show up at the funeral, and then once again at the house, to "console the mourner." He didn't speak much, but when he left he gave me a piece of paper with his telephone and address and told me to visit any time. He reminded me of the man in the photo I saw last year in the Holocaust Museum. Not that he looked exactly like him, but there was something about his look. The man in the photo was old, Chaim is young. Yet there was a resemblance. Well, all those guys kind of look the same. Also, being in a cemetery is kind of like boarding a train to Treblinka. Death was all around us. I couldn't help but make that association.

Speaking of the Holocaust, I had the same dream again last night. (Maybe triggered by this connection of Chaim with the Holocaust? Didn't think of that till now.) But this time, slightly different. Started as usual in the museum. I'm in the room with the shoes. Suddenly, I'm floating off the ground, into the air, over the museum, into the sky. There's the smoke and that odd, sweet smell. But this time, as I'm floating above, I hear something too. A rushing sound, like the wind, together with another sort of high pitched sound, almost like a voice. (Is it the voice of a Holocaust victim? I don't know.) As I'm floating, I look down. I can see through the smoke the rough outlines of the museum building below me. Very strange. Is there a meaning to this dream? Or is my mind just spinning out some fantasy?

Mom's death has had a paradoxical effect. I feel so much older now. Death really ages a person. Actually, tomorrow is my birthday, and I almost forgot about it completely. That means it's Shavuos tomorrow, and I completely forgot about that too. On the one hand, her death makes me question God's existence, and even more, to ask why, why, why. Especially since things seemed to be going so well. When I broke up with H, Mom got better almost overnight. Now that I was on the verge of introducing her to E, she dies. Where's the providence?

What would Dr M say? I guess she would say there is no problem at all. You can't expect things to go the way you want them just because you act right. That's the immature way of thinking about God. Actually, at the funeral itself I felt oddly religious, spiritual. All my doubts about God and all those issues about whether the Torah needs to be taken literally or not, all those arguments for God's existence and counterarguments, suddenly seemed irrelevant. As the casket was lowered, I thought of Mom's letters. They all compressed together in my mind, as if she had written me one long letter during the whole time in college. I almost felt I could sense Mom's soul.

But now those feelings are over, and the rational, critical mind has taken over again. Maybe all that stuff was just wishful thinking.

Maybe there is no hashgaha pratis, and Mom just died because she died, period. Maybe I wasn't sensing her soul. I was just remembering Mom as she was in the past. Or maybe it really was her soul? I don't know.

God, if you exist, help me.

ה

JUNIOR YEAR

August 29, 2001   BS''D

Dear David,

I really hope you're doing all right. There isn't much I can say except that
I know it must still be really difficult for you. I haven't called because
to be honest I don't really know if you're interested in hearing from me
now. I called you a few times over the summer and you seemed really not
in the mood to talk. Of course I understand that. But now the new term
has started so I just thought I would write and tell you that whenever
you're ready to get together, talk about things, or just be together, call me
up. I am there for you when you ~~want me~~ need to talk.

Sincerely,

Esther

September 5, 2001

Trying to throw myself into my classes, which are pretty interesting,
if I can keep my mind focused. But it's hard not to think about
Mom.

I had this idea of trying to write in my journal about things I'm
learning in class. Maybe it will help me focus better. (Therapeutic
writing.)

For my epistemology class I need to write a short paper on the
differences between "rationalism" and "empiricism" as we've covered
them so far in the class. So here goes.

Rationalism: this is the view that reason or the intellect is the
most important thing about the human. Reason is very powerful,
and can discover the most important truths. What we can't
understand thru reason, we have no knowledge of. Rationalists

tend to believe that reason is infallible if used properly. Plato and Descartes are classic examples of rationalists. They also believe in innatism (innate=inborn). That's the idea that the mind has within it certain ideas and knowledge that it must discover by a process of introspection. This kind of knowledge is certain (infallible) and eternal.

Empiricism: whatever we know, we know through sense experience or sensation. The Greek word <u>emperia</u> means trial or testing out. We have no idea ahead of time what the world is like until we find out through <u>experience</u> (same root, <u>per</u>). The mind is a blank slate (<u>tabula rasa</u>) at birth, there are no innate ideas. According to the empiricist, reason is just a tool that helps organize, combine, or break down ideas that are taken in through the senses. Reason itself doesn't come up with knowledge. To some extent, Aristotle is considered an empiricist, especially when compared with Plato. Aristotle said the mind can form no idea on its own without some sensory experience. John Locke and David Hume are considered empiricists. The empiricists tend to be fallibilists — we could be mistaken about almost any belief we have because sensation is liable to error.

This ties in with what I'm doing in philosophy of mind. The questions are: What is the self? What is the mind? Rationalists tend to identify the essence of the self with the intellect, the "thing that thinks," as Descartes says. Many empiricists identify the self with the thing that experiences, the thing that has sensations and feelings.

Am I basically a thinking thing, as the rationalists say? Or am I an experiencing, feeling thing, as the empiricists say? Or is there some other alternative?

Many rationalists believe that the self — that is, the intellect or the rational part — can exist independently of the body. Descartes argues that the soul can live on after the body dies. His argument: there is a conceptual distinction between thought and extension or body. The definition of a thinking thing is that it thinks. The definition of an extended thing is that it takes up space. The two ideas, thought and extension, are totally separable in the mind, just like the idea of 'green' and the idea of a 'triangle' are separable. So, he argues, it is logically possible that a thing that thinks should not have a body. This shows that logically, it is possible for my mind to exist without my body. If my body and my mind happen to go out of existence at the same time, that would just be a coincidence. Interesting. I don't find the argument convincing, but I can't exactly say why!

On the other hand, empiricists see the self, the consciousness, as an experiencer or feeler, and they tend to see the self or mind as tied more closely to the body for its existence. Some modern empiricists go so far as to identify the mind with the brain, or mental processes with physical processes. The mind or self is a bodily thing. In which case, when the body dies, the self goes down as well. This seems to be Hobbes's view.

I tried to escape it but I came back to death. I guess it's unavoidable!

Really, I should call Esther. She's trying to be helpful. What a nice note she wrote. Why do I keep putting this off? What's going on with me? That reminds me: what does BS''D mean? She wrote that on the top of her letter. Find out.

Don't want to admit I need consolation. It's a weakness. That's it. That's the explanation.

Ridiculous! Got to call her. She's been real kind and patient with me. Also, got to speak to Low again. I wonder what's his take on the afterlife? And of course, what is Dr. M's view? I have no classes this semester with Dr. M and I miss her. Got to go see her soon.

Beginning to feel better. I guess the therapy worked.

<u>3</u>

From: dgoldstein@cuniv.edu   Sent: 9/6/01 9:30 PM
To: rlow@ahavattorah.org.il
Subject: not good news

Dear Rabbi Low,

I haven't written in a while, it's because I've been distracted with the death of my mother. She passed away a few months ago, at the end of last semester. She was ill for some time. I won't go into the details. I'd like to think of myself as strong and able to get over this but it's been difficult for me. I thought I'd finally write just to let you know I'm still here and I'd like to get back to our conversations. I guess this is the first email I've written you that doesn't ask you a question! Which makes me think – what a pest I've been all this time, without realizing it.

Sincerely,

David Goldstein

From: rlow@ahavattorah.org.il   Sent: 9/6/01 9:52 PM
To: dgoldstein@cuniv.edu
Subject: words of consolation

Dear David,

I am truly sorry to hear of the passing of your mother. My sincere condolences to you and your family on this loss.

You mustn't be ashamed of your grief at all. It is important to go through the grieving process and it will take time. Perhaps you know that, in Judaism, the most intense form of mourning is during the week after the burial. Thereafter, a less intense form takes place during the ensuing thirty days, but in some fashion mourning continues for almost an entire year. And even then, the anniversary of the death, or yahrzeit, is always important. Please don't be so hard on yourself.

Regarding our conversations, I assure you there's nothing to apologize for. I have enjoyed all of our conversations. Please feel free to ask me anything at all, whenever you're ready to do so.

May the soul of your mother find eternal peace with G-d.

Sincerely,

Rabbi Yehudah Low

From: dgoldstein@cuniv.edu   Sent: 9/7/01 11:22 AM
To: rlow@ahavattorah.org.il
Subject: RE: words of consolation

Dear Rabbi Low,

Thanks very much for your note. I confess I do have a question, which your last email actually helped me put into words. I can't deny the fact that reading or hearing somebody say something like, "May the soul of your mother find peace with G-d" is strange to me. I'm not trying to be skeptical, but I really wonder about the idea of the soul and things like life after death. I guess if I really believed in all that, I wouldn't really grieve in the same way, would I? Anyway I don't know much about this part of Judaism. Someone once told me that these beliefs are not even original Jewish teachings, and that somehow they crept into Judaism from non-Jewish sources. I see references to the next world and the resurrection of the dead in the prayer book, but I can't find the idea of the next world clearly stated in the Hebrew Scriptures. If it's part of Judaism, why isn't it in the Scriptures? When did it become part of Judaism to believe this? And anyway, is it rational to believe in life after death? How can such a thing be proved? Is this one of those things that we just take "on faith"?

David

From: rlow@ahavattorah.org.il   Sent: 9/7/01 9:30 PM
To: dgoldstein@cuniv.edu
Subject: life after death

Dear David,

First let me say that grief for a loved one is always normal and appropriate, even for those of us who believe very deeply in the afterlife and the world to come or *olam ha-ba*. There is no denying the fact that your loved one is departed – i.e., no longer present among us, and that is very difficult and painful. But you're also right in thinking that there is some comfort in this belief as well. It does mitigate our grief to think that the soul of our beloved still lives on in some other form, and that there is a way to be reunited at some future point.

As to your questions about the afterlife, I'll try to be succinct. Remember, traditional Judaism is not defined only by what's in the Scriptures, it includes the oral tradition as well. According to the Talmud (*Sanhedrin,* Chapter 11) one who denies the revival of the dead or the next world loses their portion in the next world. This indicates that at the very least, one is not permitted to deny these doctrines overtly. My interpretation of this is that the Talmud accepts that a person could have some doubt regarding these matters. That's not ideal, but as long as one doesn't overtly *deny* them, one is not considered a *kofer*, or heretic. Many of the medieval Jewish philosophers considered these beliefs as required dogma. In his commentary on the Mishnah, Maimonides suggests that *any doubt at all* about this or any other doctrine constitutes heresy. Although I disagree with that rather harsh view, it is certainly the case that belief in this doctrine is part and parcel of traditional Judaism.

You wrote that the doctrine is not found in the Scriptures, but that's not entirely true. See, for example, Isaiah 26:19 and Daniel 12: 2–3 which state pretty clearly that the dead will be resurrected and that the righteous will live forever. Also, take a look at the episode described in I Samuel 28, where you'll find a very peculiar and interesting story of communication with the dead. There are also numerous hints to the afterlife elsewhere in the Scriptures, especially in *Tehillim* (Psalms). Take a close look at Psalm 30 (which is recited daily in the morning prayer). See especially the last verse: "Lord, my G-d, I will praise you *forever*." This implies life after death. See also Psalm 37, which says, "The righteous shall inherit the earth and live on it forever." The commentaries take this as a reference to the next world. Also consider the verse *"G-d watches over the bones of the righteous, not one of them has been broken."* (34:21) Or consider this one in 37: "*I never saw a righteous man abandoned or his children begging for bread."* It's very hard to take these verses literally. Rather, they refer allegorically to life in the next world. Several other psalms hint strongly at a next world for the righteous, and a loss of eternal life for the wicked. See, for example, Psalms 42, 55, 73 and 112.

Having said all this, still it is quite remarkable that such a profound doctrine is not found more clearly and unambiguously stated in the Tanakh. In my opinion, the Tanakh only hints at the next world, precisely because G-d wants us to fulfill the commandments not for the sake of a reward in the next world, but rather for the sake of our relationship with Him. G-d wants us to focus on this world, not on the next world. By the way, the situation is very different for Christianity and Islam, whose sacred texts talk very explicitly about the next world. Evidently, there is a strong human desire, or need, to believe that physical death is not really the end. The truth is that for many people, it's hard to live a moral and religiously devout life without a belief in the next world. Judaism affirms that there is a next world, but also that worship of G-d is proper and right even in the face of doubt about whether there is a next world.

As for any details about what the afterworld is like or what the nature of this revival of the dead will be like, we don't have much to go on. The Talmud does not give details about the afterlife, except to say that the righteous are rewarded and the wicked are punished. As the Talmud says regarding *olam ha-ba*, based on a verse in Yeshayahu, "*Ayin lo raatah Elokim, zulatecha*" – "The eye has not seen it, except for G-d." In other words, we don't know what the next world will be like, and it's a futile effort to speculate about such matters. As I'm sure you know, Plato and later many other philosophers tried to prove the immortality of the soul, but I don't think these proofs work. I think if we could prove the immortality of the soul and the next world, that would seriously damage our free will because then everyone would automatically do what's right in order to make it to the next world.

The bottom line is that our belief in the next world is based on the fact that the Oral Torah teaches these things and therefore we accept them. (The passages from Daniel and Isaiah and many of the other passages mentioned above could be read metaphorically, perhaps.) If you then ask why we accept these teachings, you're back at the question of why we accept the Torah in the first place. As you already know, I advocate a "pragmatic" rationale. We can neither prove nor disprove the truth of the Torah, but pragmatically, the potential for living the most meaningful and valuable life is through the Torah. Since the doctrines of the revival of the dead and the next world are part of the Torah, we should therefore accept them as part of the package of Torah.

One could also directly examine whether it is rational to believe in a next world from a pragmatic point of view. Does belief in a next world make life potentially more meaningful or not? The American pragmatist William James argued that it does, or it least it can, and I agree (see James's famous essay, "The Will to Believe"). If I assume that my soul has the chance of living eternally with G-d after I die physically, then I will live a certain kind of life – that is, a much more meaningful and happy life – than I would if I assumed that my life ended with my body's death. On the other hand, if I assume there is a next world and it turns out that there isn't, what have I lost? Nothing much, really. If James is right, we have a pragmatic rationale for belief in the next world.

That's my view, for whatever it's worth.

Sincerely,

Rabbi Low

$$4$$

"Dr. Maimon? Hi . . . may I come in?"

"Certainly, David. Please come in. Sit down. I heard from the dean about your mother's passing. My deepest sympathies."

"Thanks, Dr. Maimon."

"Are you doing OK?"

"Yes. I'm doing OK, really . . . not too bad."

"Good. So . . . how are your courses going?"

"Pretty good. I'm enjoying Philosophy of Knowledge and Philosophy of Mind."

"Excellent. What can I do for you?"

"Dr. Maimon, there are a couple of traditional Jewish doctrines we didn't get a chance to talk about during our independent study. And I was curious as to what you thought about them."

"Oh? What doctrines do you have in mind?"

"The belief in the resurrection of the dead and the next world."

"Ah, indeed! We did not get a chance to discuss those doctrines."

"Also, in your comments on my paper on evil, you said you thought the problem of evil had an answer even if there is no afterlife."

"Yes, that's correct."

"That made we wonder – do you reject the belief in an afterlife?"

"No, not at all! I do believe in a resurrection and a world to come. As to what all that really means – that's another story. Why? What's your view? I remember that you expressed some skepticism about those doctrines in your paper on the problem of evil."

"I don't know. I want to believe in these things. You know, over the past couple of years I've definitely gotten much closer to believing in God. But resurrection and the afterlife . . . these ideas seem so foreign to me."

"Well, it certainly is an interesting fact that there is no explicit and unequivocal mention of the world to come in the Scriptures. But these doctrines are taught in the Talmud. Anyone who rejects them is considered a *kofer*, or heretic. So, regardless of the historical question of whether the idea crept into Judaism from outside or not, the afterlife is definitely part of Torah."

"Wait! Are you saying that even if it crept in to Judaism at some time after the revelation at Sinai, it could still be part of the Torah?"

"Don't you remember my theory from last semester? The historical question of what God actually said to Moses at Sinai is irrelevant to what constitutes the religious doctrines of the Torah. What's relevant is what the Torah – both written and oral – says and teaches. So even if, historically speaking, the doctrine of the afterlife crept into Judaism, it was still part of the divine plan that it happen just that way."

"Ah, yes, I remember now. But anyway, you're saying that you do believe in an afterlife."

"Yes – although not in the same sense that most ordinary religious people do."

"That's what I suspected."

"You know me too well."

"So, in what sense do you believe it? Can you elaborate?"

"Well, I'll try. But first I need to explain my conception of the soul, which, like my conception of God, differs substantially from the standard conception of the soul held by most religious people. Actually, I'd better first describe the standard view of the soul within traditional Judaism. You've studied Descartes, right?"

"Yes. Why?"

"Descartes's view of the soul and its relation with the body captures very closely the conventional religious view about the nature of the soul. According to this view, the soul is conceived as a *substance* or a *thing* – of course, a very special thing. In particular, it is a non-physical or 'metaphysical' entity that pre-exists the body. At some point, God pairs up a given soul with a certain body. Two things are crucial about the soul. The first is that it is conscious. The other is that is has power, the ability to act, especially on the body. The body is essentially a lifeless hulk of matter that is enlivened by the soul residing within it. Of course, the soul doesn't literally reside physically *within* the body. Yet somehow, this non-physical soul *interacts* with the body. When the body dies, the soul departs and goes on living, or at least it can, if God wishes that it do so. God can then do all sorts of the things to the soul after the body dies. He can punish it, reward it, or just put it in a metaphysical holding cell. Many believe that at some future time, God will return at least some souls to their bodies – that's 'resurrection.' Some go so far as to say that the actual bones of specific dead people will be reunited to form the resurrected persons. This is sometimes given as the reason for burying people intact. But this is really strange. What about people who've been blown to bits? Can they never be resurrected? And there are even some who believe that souls can go through many bodily lives before resurrection happens. This is the Kabbalistic idea of reincarnation or transmigration of souls or *gilgul neshamot,* which in my opinion is definitely a concept of non-Jewish origin altogether. You won't find *that* in the Talmud! Anyway, some people believe that at some future stage after the resurrection, the souls will depart from their bodies once again to live forever in the realm of *olam ha-ba* – the world to come. Alternatively, some say that the resurrected bodies themselves will live forever. Either way, this is the standard or conventional view. Needless to say, it has difficulties."

"Yes, I agree. For one thing, it's impossible to prove."

"Right, but there are other problems as well. As I've already told you once before, I have difficulty with the very notion of a *non-physical entity*. I'm not saying it's logically absurd, but I just think it's problematic. How does the non-physical entity interact with the physical entity? This is a classic objection raised against Descartes. On top of that, the standard view conceives of this non-physical entity, the soul, as that part of the human being that thinks and feels. Now, to me, the part of us that thinks and feels is intimately wrapped up with the body. I mean, my consciousness as Sofi Maimon – my memories, my experiences, my beliefs, my sensations – all that stuff is intimately connected with my physicality, my brain processes. I'm not a biologist, but I believe that the power that surges through a person's body is a certain form of electricity or energy that runs through the nervous system. And that power is *not* something immaterial or non-physical! Of course, I *don't* think a purely mechanistic, deterministic account of the self can be given. But still, I don't see how postulating a non-physical 'soul' adds any explanatory power to one's theory of the self. Do you follow?"

"Sort of. I'm not sure what you mean when you say that a 'mechanistic' account of the self cannot be given. Doesn't that mean that in the end you agree that there is such a thing as a non-physical soul?"

"No, that doesn't follow. In fact, I think we can give a different account of the soul which is conceptually clearer, more economical, and theologically just as meaningful and powerful as the standard conception, *without* the view that the soul is an entity."

"Hmm – I'm not sure I followed you there. Can you explain?"

"I will try, but first I need to talk more about the idea of the *psyche*."

"That means *soul* in Greek, right?"

"Right. But as you will see, what I call the psyche is *not* the same thing as the soul. Now, consider this. Any given human being has a body – that is, the physical stuff they are made of. But there's also something else important about a human being, and that's the fact that they are rational, free agents who have thoughts and feelings. In other words, they have a psyche, a consciousness. Of course, some would say that the psyche is merely a function of the body, or that it is wholly explicable in terms of bodily processes. I'm not sure that makes sense, but let's leave that question aside. Anyway, my point is that everyone agrees that everyone has a psyche. Also, there are certain features of the psyche that all humans generally share, and there are certain features of individual psyches that seem unique or idiosyncratic. For example, on the one hand, all humans are rational; we have beliefs and desires. We make choices, and so on. In this way, we're all alike. On the other hand, each individual human being has his own particular set of beliefs and desires, his own particular way of behaving and acting. In other words, each particular human has a unique character. In this way, we're all different. Are you with me so far?"

"Yes, I think so."

"Now, the standard religious view asserts that the soul *is* the psyche, and then it adds – absurdly – that the psyche – i.e., the soul – is a non-physical entity! It seems abundantly clear to me that the psyche of a person *dies* or *ceases to exist* when the body dies. So if I were to say that the soul just *is* the psyche, then I would *not* say that the soul lives on after the body dies. Do you follow?"

"Yes – but then, what *is* the soul, according to you?"

"In my view, when we talk about the soul of a person, we are *not* talking about the psyche itself, but about the *structure* of that person's psyche."

"Ah. That's kind of like what you said about your conception of God."

"Exactly! My conception of the human soul is analogous to my conception of God. Again, most religious people think of God as an *entity*, a *being* who stands outside the world and sustains it. God is usually conceived as the powerhouse of energy that runs the entire universe. But in my view, all talk about God's attributes is really talk about the *structure* of the universe. Now, the *structure* of the universe is *not* identical to the universe. On the other hand, the structure is not an entity that exists apart from the universe. In fact, one might say, the theist believes the universe is 'permeated' by structure. You remember all this, don't you?"

"Yes, of course."

"Then you also remember our discussion of the fact that for anything that exists – let's say a circle, a painting, a tree or what have you – there is the physical stuff of which the thing is made, and also its structure or 'form' – the way in which the material is put together, and the characteristic set of ways in which that thing acts or behaves."

"Right. I remember that too."

"So, similarly, the *structure* of a person's psyche is *the way or set of ways in which the psyche acts.* That structure is *not* identical with the psyche itself, nor is it a thing or entity that exists. Again, in my view, the soul is *not* an entity that 'powerhouses' the body or the psyche. Rather, the psyche operates in a certain way, *in accord with a certain structure.* It is that structure that I call the soul. Do you follow?"

"I'm not sure. According to what you're saying, everybody – even atheists – should believe in the soul, because obviously every person's psyche has some kind of structure."

"Exactly! Indeed, I take that to be a strength of my view rather than a weakness. In other words, in my theory, the reality of the soul is pretty much self-evident."

"But in your theory, the soul isn't something that exists. It's just a structure."

"*Just* a structure? Why do you say that? As if 'structures' were not important! Look, without structure, nothing would be what it is! If your psyche didn't have a structure, you wouldn't be a person. You'd be a blithering idiot, a mass of chaos! It's of the utmost significance that we live in a universe that has a certain structure.

So you'd have to clarify why you think it's a *problem* for my theory if I say that the soul is the structure of the psyche."

"Hmm. Well, I'm . . . uh . . . still not sure what to say. Your theory sounds interesting, but what does it have to do with the idea of a next world or afterlife?"

"I will explain. In my theory, to say that the soul 'lives on after death' is just to say that the structure of the psyche is in some sense *independent* of the psyche, and of course of the body as well."

"I'm sorry, but I don't understand how that could be. How can the structure of the psyche be independent of the psyche itself?"

"I'll explain. Let me make an analogy with numbers, though the analogy will not be perfect. Suppose you have two marbles in a bag. So the marbles are structured, if you will, in accord with the number two or two-ness, so to speak. Now, when you destroy the marbles, you *don't* destroy two-ness. Plato made this point. Right?"

"Right."

"The same thing goes for their roundness. If you destroy the marbles, you don't destroy the form or structure of roundness. Now, the number two is *not* an entity that exists, nor is roundness an entity either. Two-ness is independent from the marbles, even though it is not an entity. That's where it appears Plato made a mistake, when he postulated the existence of two-ness or roundness as entities. Rather, two-ness is a structure – that is, a way in which the world of objects may present itself. But the point is that even if you destroy the two marbles, you don't destroy two-ness."

"All right. I think I get it."

"Well, then, the same thing is true in the case of the soul. *The structure of the psyche is independent of the psyche itself.* Of course, there are some limitations to the analogy with numbers. One difference is that two-ness is a structure that is represented by *many* sets of marbles (and other things) *in exactly the same way*. On the other hand, for each and every human being, the psyche, and therefore the soul, is different. But the point is that the structure of each and every psyche does not cease to exist when the psyche dies with the body. In fact, it can hardly cease to exist, because it's not an entity!"

"But if what you're saying is right, then *everybody* ought to agree that souls, in your sense of the term, live on after death."

"That's correct! In my view, belief in the soul and its independence from the body is not a matter of revelation. It's a belief that is rationally grounded independently of revelation. Of course, this was the view of many medieval Jewish philosophers. It also fits with the fact that the Talmud does *not* mention the belief in the independence of the soul from the body as a religious doctrine. Rather, it mentions *resurrection* and the *next world*, which are something else, beyond the mere belief that the soul is independent from the body."

"Ah, OK. So in your view of the soul, what then is resurrection? I don't see how a 'structure' could be resurrected."

"Yes, you're absolutely right: a structure can't be resurrected. Only a *person* can be resurrected. But, as you just said, the real question is: *what does resurrection mean*? Here we're getting into deeper waters. Now, in the conventional or standard religious view, resurrection means that the soul or psyche of someone who dies comes back to 'inhabit' another body at some later time. For example, if at one time a certain person – let's call him Jacob – lived and died, then, for him to be resurrected would mean that Jacob's soul comes back to inhabit another body – let's call him Jacob #2. Some go so far as to say that Jacob #2 would have not only the same traits and qualities that the first Jacob had, but also the same memories, experiences, and beliefs that Jacob had when he died. Of course, you could always say that the memories might be buried so deep that he can't recall them. But if so, in what sense does he really have the memories? Anyhow, I reject this outmoded conception of the soul, and along with it, I reject this understanding of resurrection. Instead, I have a different interpretation of resurrection."

"And that is?"

"Instead of saying that the souls of the dead actually come back to life, I would say that the doctrine of resurrection comes to this: *the lives that people have lived in the past play a significant role in determining the character of the lives that are brought into being in the future.*"

"Say again? What do you mean by that?"

"Let's take a step back for a second. Remember that in my view, God is the ultimate structure of the universe, and it is in accord with this structure that all events are to be explained. So the fact that certain people are born at certain times with certain psyches and certain souls – that is, structures – that's all part of the divine plan. Now, the nature of those souls at birth – by that I mean their innate qualities or characteristics – are determined by God's plan. Also, the kinds of events that happen in peoples' lives – those are also determined by God's plan. Do you follow?"

"Yes. I'm with you so far."

"OK. Listen carefully, then. In my view, the doctrine of resurrection teaches that the universe is structured in just such a way *that the souls of those who have died in the past play a significant role in determining the character of the souls that come to life later on.* In other words, it is part of the divine plan that the ways in which people live their life in one generation have an effect on the people who are born in subsequent generations. To put it somewhat colloquially – speaking of God as if he were *a* being – I would say that God ensures that those who have lived in the past have not lived in vain, because their projects will be continued by people who live in the future. Do you follow?"

"I think so, but if *that's* what resurrection means, isn't that a misuse of the word 'resurrection'?"

"No, I don't think so. I'll give you an example of a similar use of the word 'resurrection.' Imagine a play that was performed a long time ago. Many years

later, a director decides to unearth the script and perform the play again. It would
not be inappropriate to say that the play has been 'resurrected.' That would be a
perfectly good use of that term. Don't you agree?"

"I guess so."

"The same applies in the case of souls. To believe in the resurrection of souls
is to believe that the structure of the universe is such that the lives of those who
have lived and died in the past are 'resurrected' in the sense I've described. And if
you look at the history of the world, you see that this is in fact true. For example,
even the mere fact that you're named David shows that the lives of our ancestors
has had a profound impact on the lives of people living today."

"Yes, but even an atheist would agree with *that*. Of course people alive today
are influenced by people who lived in the past. That's just the way history works!"

"David, I don't think you're getting what I'm saying. I'm saying that it is part
of the divine design that the way people have lived their life in the past plays a
role in determining the qualities and characteristics of people who are born in the
future. For example, there is something about your very psyche which is the way
it is precisely because of something that had to do with the structure of someone
who lived in the past. This is much more than what atheists generally believe!"

"Hmm. It's an interesting idea. But do you really think it's what the rabbis of
the Talmud had in mind when they thought of resurrection?"

"Look, they weren't philosophers, and they didn't articulate any theory with
conceptual rigor. So it's hard to tell what they had in mind. And anyway, it really
doesn't matter. As a religious Jew, I accept the central teachings of Judaism. But
that doesn't mean I need to understand the *meaning* of those teachings in the same
way that the ancient rabbis, or even the medieval Jewish philosophers, did."

"OK. Well, let's see – so far, you've explained your concept of resurrection.
What about the doctrine of the next world?"

"I'll explain. Most religious Jews think of *olam ha-ba* as a future state where the
entity, the soul, will reside – basking in the glow of God's being. In other words,
the soul will go from this world, or *olam ha-zeh*, into the world to come, or *olam
ha-ba*. So, *olam ha-ba* is something that is *yet to be*. But I don't think of it that way
at all. Instead, I regard *olam ha-zeh,* or this world, as a way of talking about *the
universe as we ordinarily perceive it and see it*. And I regard *olam ha-ba*, or the next
world, as a way of talking about *the universe as we understand it intellectually, from the
point of view of divinity and eternity*."

"Sounds interesting. Can you explain that a little more?"

"Let me put it this way. Forgive me if what I'm going to say sounds somewhat
moralistic. Just imagine for a moment that I'm a rabbi giving a sermon, let's say on
Rosh ha-Shannah. So here goes: A person who believes only in *olam ha-zeh* believes
only what his senses tell him. He is a slave to the moment, to his immediate passions
and desires. He fails to see his life in the context of the whole universe. He lives
just for himself, or perhaps for some passing cause. His life is shallow because he

doesn't reckon his life in terms of eternal values and ideals, that is, in terms of God, eternal truth, divine revelation. Such a person may have a great deal of superficial pleasure in life, but no real joy or inward happiness.

"On the other hand, a person who believes in *olam ha-ba* approaches the world from a divine, eternal perspective. Such a person appreciates what is truly good and has a kind of inward joy or happiness, no matter what happens in *olam ha-zeh*. In fact, sometimes the sages refer to *olam ha-zeh* as *olam ha-sheker*, a world of falsehood, and *olam ha-ba* as *olam ha-emet*, the world of truth. It's a realm in which no falsehood and deceit exist, where truth is evident and clear. All who make it into *olam ha-ba* have an unveiled knowledge of God. Or at least, they do not have the veil that they had in *olam ha-zeh*. In light of this knowledge, any person who makes it to *olam ha-ba* truly understands the significance of all their good actions – even the small ones– and they also understand the significance of their bad actions – again, even the small ones. That in itself is their true punishment or reward. It's not easy to make it into *olam ha-ba*. It requires hard work, devotion, keeping the commandments, being a good person, and above all intellectual study, including philosophical understanding of the fundamentals of Judaism. This is where I agree with Maimonides. If you don't make it to the *intellectual understanding* of what *olam ha-ba* really is, you can't get into *olam ha-ba* at all! Of course, there are levels in *olam ha-ba*. Some people are 'higher' than others, so to speak. But the righteous and thoughtful ones of the earth – both Jew and non-Jew – definitely make it to *olam ha-ba*. The wicked and the unphilosophical never make it. They condemn themselves to be excluded by their own actions and lack of thought.

"OK, the sermon is over. Did you follow?"

"Yes, I think so. Good sermon! But seriously, I think what you're saying is that *olam ha-ba* is not a place or time in the future. It's rather a realm you can go to *now*."

"Perhaps it's more a state of mind than a realm that you can go to. When you get into that state of mind, you sense the ultimate significance of things, at least at some level. Do you know what I'm talking about?"

"I think so. I've had that experience myself. It's that experience you have when suddenly things click into place."

"Kind of like that, but even higher. It's hard to explain, but you know how most of the time you're kind of focused on what's in front of you and what's immediately around you . . . like how, right now, we're sitting here, focusing on this discussion. Of course, this is a very deep discussion, not chit-chat or small talk. But still, our focus is very intently on right here and right now, so to speak. But sometimes you can sort of pull yourself out of yourself and get a more universal perspective. It's an incredibly liberating, uplifting experience. I can't really explain it much better, I'm afraid."

"I think I understand what you're saying."

"Good. Well, then, can you also see how a belief in resurrection and *olam ha-ba* follows naturally from a belief in God – as least as far as I understand these concepts?"

"Uh, no. How's that?"

"Remember my theory of God? To believe in God is partly to believe that the universe is structured in accord with the principles of divine providence, benevolence, and justice."

"Yes, of course."

"So, if it's reasonable to believe in God, it is reasonable to think that the righteous are rewarded and the wicked are punished. It is also reasonable to believe that God does not allow the righteous to live their lives in vain."

"That should follow."

"Well, if all this is correct, something like 'resurrection' and *olam ha-ba* must be true – at least in the sense that I understand them. So if it is rationally defensible to believe in God, it follows that it is rationally defensible to believe in these doctrines. Also, as I mentioned earlier, the doctrines of resurrection and *olam ha-ba* are to some degree confirmed by experience. That is, we know from experience that the lives of people who lived in the past indeed have a tremendous impact on the lives of people living in the future, and it is possible to grasp the universal perspective, that God's-eye point of view which is, in my theory, what it means to be in *olam ha-ba*. Do you follow?"

"I think so. Still, there's something a little disappointing about the theory. If what you're saying is correct, then, when you die, you don't really go to *olam ha-ba*. It's basically over. I mean, when you're dead, you're dead."

"Yes and no. Indeed, the particular person who dies is *dead*. That's why we grieve for the dead. But we just have to accept that. No miracle could make the *very same person* come to be at some later date. On the other hand, don't forget the other part of my theory. Again, the soul or structure of the psyche is independent from the body and the psyche. So your soul doesn't die when your body dies. Furthermore, your soul may be resurrected, so that someone else continues where you left off, so to speak. A new person will come into being whose psyche has the same structure as yours. Your life will not have been lived in vain. Finally, if you did lead a righteous life on this earth, then you've already made it to *olam ha-ba* while you were on this earth. And that means your life as it was lived had eternal significance. Now, why should all that be disappointing? What more could a person reasonably ask for?"

"I don't know, but thanks, Dr. Maimon. You've really given me a lot to think about."

5

September 17, 2001

I'm in shock.

Did it all really happen? Almost a week has passed since 9/11 and I still can't believe it. I don't want to believe it. But it happened.

Like a bad dream, like a nightmare. Am I asleep? Can I pinch myself, wake myself up? This didn't really happen, did it?

In my dreams, all I can see over and over again is the image of the planes going into the towers. First one, then another. And the people, jumping from windows, the flames coming out of buildings, the smoke, the dust, the people running scared on the streets, screaming.

And the worst at the end, when the towers collapsed, first one, then the other.

God? Are you there? What is going on?

Tomorrow is Rosh Hashanah. I was planning to go to Rabbi A's shul but now I'm not sure. I think of all the people who couldn't make it. Reminds me of Hillel Zeitlin. He couldn't make it to shul either that year.

What should I do? I don't know.

6

"Good Yom tov, everyone!

"My dear friends, in a few moments we will listen to the blowing of the Shofar. The shofar reminds us that Rosh ha-Shannah, the first day of the New Year, is a time for renewal, but also a time for introspection and reflection. It is a time when Hashem looks down and judges us — as we say in our prayers, *hinei yom ha-din* — 'Behold the day of judgment!' It is also a joyous time, when the people of Israel proudly blow the *shofar* and crown Hashem not only as King of the Jewish people but also as King of the universe and of all humanity.

"Yet for many of us, it is hard not to think about the horrible tragedy we experienced just a few days ago. In fact I will tell you that yesterday afternoon, a young man I know called me on the phone and said, 'Rabbi Abraham, I don't think I can sit through all the services on Rosh ha-Shannah. I'm just too upset over what happened on September 11, and I won't be able to focus on the prayers.'

"At first, I didn't know what to say. Indeed, we've been through a lot over the last few weeks: pain, grief, shock, fear, tears, much anger, and many questions, such as: what is the meaning of this terrible event? Why did it happen? How could it have happened? What kind of human beings could have perpetrated such a horror? What could we have done to prevent this? And let's be honest: for some of us, a tragedy such as this is a test of our faith. How can God allow such events to happen? Why didn't God intervene and foil the terrorists' horrible plan? Questions such as these are swirling in our minds as we come together on Rosh ha-Shannah. Perhaps we are still so close to this tragedy, we are still in a period of grief and mourning, we cannot yet think clearly about what happened — we are still in a state of shock.

"But to return to the phone call. After thinking for a few moments, I told this young man on the phone: one thing I do know: *the proper way to react to this horrible event is not to withdraw into ourselves, not to hide from God on Rosh ha-Shannah.* Surely, it is not accidental that this terrible event happened so close to the New Year. Tragic though it was, it was also an event of epic proportions, a watershed event in history. And coming so soon before the *Yamim Noraim,* the Days of Awe — the main question that we need to ask ourselves is: *what is the meaning and significance of this event, especially from the vantage point of Rosh ha-Shannah?* This is the crucial question that we need to ask.

"My friends, from the vantage point of Rosh ha-Shannah, we must remind ourselves of one of the central teachings of our Jewish faith: *this earthly existence is only a gateway to the next world.* When we pray today that God judge us as righteous and inscribe us in the *sefer ha-hayyim,* the Book of Life, what does that mean? Does it mean that God should grant us another year of earthly existence? No, it does not! For if that were the case, it would imply that anyone who passes away this coming year would have been judged as wicked, and surely that is not so! Many people who will unfortunately pass away this coming year are righteous. So it must be the case that the life that we are speaking about when we ask to be inscribed in the Book of Life is the true life - *closeness to God both on this earth and even more so in the hereafter.* As it says in the Talmud, 'The wicked, even during their lifetime, are called dead, and the righteous, even when they are dead, are called living.' For God himself is the *makor hayyim,* the Source of life. And that is why, when we speak of the righteous, we do not say that they died but rather that they passed away.

"Now, for many of us it's hard to grasp the idea of *olam ha-ba,* the next world. For we only see the immediate physical world that is directly in front of us. How then can we try to understand some inkling of the next world?

"Let me tell you the story of a *yeshiva bochur*, a young student, who lived some years ago in Europe, who wanted to know what life would be like in *olam ha-ba*. So he went to the famous Reb Zusha of Hanipoli because it was said that Reb Zusha visited *olam ha-ba* in his dreams. The disciple made the long journey and arrived late at night. He found Reb Zusha studying the holy book, the *Zohar*. Gently he interrupted the Rebbe and asked him, 'What is life like in the next world?'

"Reb Zusha said, 'It's difficult to explain. If you work very hard and become a righteous, pious Jew, you will understand something of what it's like in the next world.' But the student pressed on, insisting that the Rebbe say something further, something more tangible. Finally, the Rebbe said, 'Let me explain it this way.' He picked up the holy book he had been studying and said, 'Do you see this *sefer*, this book? This book is a made up of paper and ink. But do you recognize the difference between the book itself and the *ta'am* – that is, the *meaning* – of a book? The book itself you can destroy or burn. One day, this book will fall apart. But the *ta'am*, its meaning, is something you cannot destroy. Do you understand now?'

"The student nodded. 'Well, then,' said Reb Zusha, 'life in this world – our earthly existence – is just like a book. Our flesh and blood are like the letters and pages of the book. Just as the book will eventually disintegrate, the body, too, will die one day. But life in the next world – that is the true *ta'am*, the true meaning of our earthly existence.'

"The young student was satisfied with Reb Zusha's answer.

"My friends, events such as those of September eleventh remind us that the measure and value of a person's life is not how long he lived or how much wealth he acquired or the pleasure he obtained. The measure and value of a person's life consists in whether he lived in a holy and Godly manner! Of course, only God himself can be the true judge of whether, and to what extent, a person lived righteously, and this is the purpose of Rosh ha-Shannah.

"But there is more. From the vantage point of Rosh ha-Shannah, the tragedy of September eleventh reminds us of something else we already knew. Of course, the way it all happened was new and shocking, the manner of the attack was diabolical, the magnitude of the attack was unique. Never before have so few attackers caused so many deaths. Never before have we seen human beings – if we can call them human beings – willfully flying hijacked planes, packed with civilians, into buildings. But the thing that we already knew, and of which this event once again reminds us, is that in the end, the world is divided into two groups of people: the *tzaddikim* – those who do good – and the *reshaim* – those who do evil.

"September eleventh calls out to us: There are evildoers in this world! There is a real, stark choice between good and evil! No one can possibly justify what these vile terrorists did. It is not evil for the sake of greed, which we could surely understand. It is not evil for the sake of pleasure or indulgence, which we could also understand. No! This is evil *for the sake of evil itself* . . . a mad, enraged craving to attack what is good just because it is good. What is the source of this craving? Jealousy, perhaps? Yes, I believe so. It is the kind of jealousy that says something like this: 'You are prosperous, wealthy, secure and at peace. You are spiritually rich. I am impoverished and torn apart. I am spiritually destitute. Therefore, I will tear you down. I will destroy you, even at the cost of my own life, so that neither of us will be able to live in peace!'

"Indeed, many people are asking: why do so many Muslims hate the United Sates so much? One reason is because the United States stands for democracy and tolerance, which the terrorists abhor. But that's not it alone. There's another reason that some people are too timid to admit: the Muslims are angry with the United States for its support for Israel. And the truth is, indeed, the United States is today the greatest ally that Israel has ever had. Why? Let me let you in on a little secret. Despite all the talk about separation of religion and state, the United States is the greatest – yet at the same time most tolerant – religious country on earth. Despite all the academics and skeptics, despite all the liberals and atheists, it's a documented fact that the citizens of the United Sates are among the most religious in the developed countries – but they are also the most tolerant and respectful. And so, the people of the United States know deep down that God exists, that Israel is the chosen nation, and that the land of Israel belongs to the Jews! And now, after September 11, the fate of Israel and the fate of the United States are bound together more closely than ever.

"Indeed it is true that the hatred of the US is based on a hatred of Jews. Again, some people wonder: why do the Muslims resent the Jews so much? Why can they not accept that the Jews are entitled to their own tiny country amidst a sea of Muslims? I will tell you why: Because they know that if they acknowledge the legitimacy of Israel, they thereby acknowledge that Islam is in fact *not* the true universal religion! And if they acknowledge that Jerusalem belongs to Israel, then it does *not* belong to the Muslims. This they cannot accept!

"Still, let the children of Israel take heart! The war between good and evil has a long history. What we are witnessing today is only the drawing of a new battle-line in an age-old conflict. Israel's ancient enemy was Esav and, later, Laban, who sought to destroy our father Jacob. Still later, it was the idolatrous Egyptians who enslaved the Israelites, and then the people of Amalek, who attacked Israel without provocation. In much later years, during medieval times, it was the Christians who falsely accused us, of all things, of deicide! But the idolatrous Egyptians disappeared from the face of the earth. The Christians eventually did *teshuvah* – they repented their deeds and recognized the Jewish people as worthy of respect. In the twentieth century, our main enemies were the racist Nazis. They, too, were destroyed, with America's help. Still more recently, we faced the Soviet scourge – the atheist Communist regime, whose rotten and false ideology crumbled under its own weight. And now we are facing what I believe is our final enemy: the fundamentalist Muslim. But all of our enemies have come and gone, and, as it says in Tehillim, "*Va-anahnu kamnu va-nisodud*" – we, the Jewish people, have survived and reconstituted our community. Some of our enemies were destroyed, while others have chosen to make peace with us. This will happen to the Muslims as well. So let us take heart!

"My friends, the world is facing a battle between good and evil. Now, more than ever, those who are on the side of good must step forward and actively choose good. The righteous non-Jews must stand up and say: We are with the forces of good. And we, the Jewish people, must accept and reaffirm our destiny as the chosen people. I am happy to say that I see the young man who called me on the phone sitting here today in shul! *Yasher koach* to you for coming, young man, and *yasher koach* to you all for being here! Let us use Rosh ha-Shannah together as God intended: to reaffirm our commitment to Hashem, to crown Hashem as King of the world, and to accept our role as the chosen people. With these thoughts in mind, we turn now to the blowing of the *shofar*. May God bless us and inscribe all Israel in the Book of Life!"

7

"Dr. Maimon? Hello. I wanted to talk with you about . . . about what happened on nine-eleven."

"Oh, dear . . . if we must. Come. Come in and sit down."

"Dr. Maimon, are you feeling all right?"

"I've got to admit – I am feeling somewhat depressed. Lots of my colleagues are, too. I have to confess: I'm finding it difficult to do any work."

"Well, that's only normal. I mean, it really was quite horrible."

"It's more than that."

"What do you mean?"

"Look, I'm not just depressed about the human tragedy. I feel disoriented. It seems like the world I thought I lived in is not the real world after all. I'm experiencing difficulty connecting my present self with the self that I used to be not so long ago. But maybe the world hasn't really changed. Maybe I was just mistaken about what I thought the world was, and now I'm realizing what the world truly is. Do you understand?"

"I'm not sure. Do you mean you didn't think people were capable of doing such a horrible thing?"

"No, that's not exactly it. Look, there have been greater tragedies, worse acts of violence. One thinks of the Holocaust, of course, but this is very different. First, this is a global campaign of terrorism. Second, these people are also suicidal. As fanatical as the Nazis were, they didn't believe in martyrdom. And there's something else. This is motivated by religious beliefs. The Nazis weren't religious. You could assume that they were interested in their own material well being, and you could fight them on that basis. But that doesn't work with these people. And it's not just a few people, either. Evidently there are thousands of people out there, across the world, who are only a few steps away from being willing to do what these people did. So, catching one or two people or even a few leaders is really not going to make much difference."

"I guess not."

"And no matter what we do, there's a limit to how secure we can be. How much does it take for someone to plant a huge bomb in a shopping center or train station somewhere? The Nazis wanted to defeat the US in war. But these terrorists aren't even trying to do that. They're just interested in creating as much terror and horror as possible – which makes them harder to fight than the Nazis. And there's something else, too. In a way, it is the most bothersome and depressing thing of all."

"What's that?"

"Well, a lot of us – a lot of my colleagues – thought we were making progress. We thought people out there were changing . . . ."

"People *out there*? Who do you mean?"

"Well, I mean everybody – but in particular, the Muslims. Of course, the people who perpetrated the horror of nine-eleven are hard core extremists, and we've got to be careful not to confuse Islam with this extremist, radical version of Islam. Actually, that's something else I'm really worried about – the potential for an irrational, violent backlash against Muslims – but that's not something I'm *depressed* about. What I'm depressed about is the apparent popularity of the terrorists in the Arab world. If you read the paper, you'll find there seems to be a lot of sympathy for the extremists in the Muslim world. And the sad thing is that just a few years ago, we thought we were getting somewhere, closer to peace. It's similar to what's happened with the Palestinian-Israeli conflict."

"What do you mean?"

"Many of us thought we were heading in a direction of compromise. It was not too long ago that peace seemed to be breaking out all over. But it turns out that – while the Israelis themselves are by no means perfect – the other side has some radically extreme, hard-core terror elements that are really quite popular throughout the Palestinian population and the Arab world. And now we've got these new extremists to deal with as well. It's all so profoundly disappointing . . . ."

8
—

"So, Phil, are you also depressed like everyone else?"

"I don't know if I'd go that far. But sure, it's a real bummer!"

"Well, what's behind it all? What's your take on all this?"

"Simple. This is just one of those periodic moments in history when religion raises its ugly head. This is what I've been telling you all along. Religion is essentially a non-rational phenomenon. So you never know where it's going to lead or what it's going to cause. Sure, it's depressing, but it's not surprising. I'm sure you, as a Jew, know plenty about the atrocities committed in the name of religion."

"Yes, I do."

"Well, those atrocities and persecutions have always been driven by deeply irrational beliefs and ideas. And the same thing is happening here. The Muslim extremists and fundamentalists have a completely warped sense of reality. They believe that by doing these things they'll go straight to heaven. What's even crazier, maybe, is that they believe that by doing these things they'll get their way in the Middle East. All this is just going to come back on their own heads. But that's just my political prediction. My point is that religion is inherently irrational, and you never know what it's going to produce."

"So you think religion is to blame for this?"

"Yes, David. I do."

"But lots of atrocities were perpetrated by non-religious people. The Holocaust was perpetrated by the Nazis, who were definitely not religious."

"First of all, I didn't say all irrational people are religious or that religion is the only form of irrationality that might lead to devastation. But surely, the roots of the Nazi ideology lay in religious superstitions. A lot of historians argue that the ground for the Nazi destruction of the Jews was laid by centuries of virulent hatred for Jews that stemmed from a certain nasty version of Christianity. Without the Christian-based demonization of the Jew, the Holocaust probably couldn't have happened. So, in fact, religious beliefs did play a role in enabling the Holocaust to happen."

"Maybe you're right about that. But still, don't you make a distinction between good religion and bad religion?"

"Look, I told you once before that basically, I believe that some form of religion is necessary for most people. I haven't changed my view on that. And in some sense you're right – there's good religion and bad religion. Good religion is peaceful and tolerant. Bad religion is the opposite. The problem is that there's no telling when a 'good religion' will turn sour. And besides, there's a limit to how friendly any religion can be to philosophy, since religion, as I've told you before, is inherently anti-philosophical. Now, the main world religions often take the form of 'good religion.' Most Muslims are peaceful and not interested in perpetrating attacks like these. During the early Middle Ages, the Muslims were the most philosophically and scientifically advanced peoples in the world. But they never got out of the Middle Ages. They never experienced the Enlightenment. The Christians were actually much worse in the Middle Ages, quite horrible for many centuries, but finally they were tamed and rationalized – by philosophy, I might add! We're still waiting for this to happen to Islam. But this is my main point: once you leave reason behind, who knows where the craziness will lead?"

"Has Judaism ever led to this kind of craziness?"

"David, haven't you read the Bible? There was a time in ancient history when the people of Israel were quite violent. The conquest of the land of Canaan was bloody, wasn't it? And even today, sometimes you see Jewish militants who sound almost like their Hamas counterparts. Don't you agree?"

"I guess so. But that's really a minority of Jews who talk like that. It doesn't seem to be quite on the same scale as what we've seen from other religions."

"I grant that over the centuries, Judaism has been better in this regard than other religions. By nature, Judaism is tolerant of other religions since it does not preach universal conversion to Judaism. But as we both know, both Christianity and Islam are daughter religions of Judaism."

"True. So?"

"So even though Judaism itself may be relatively tolerant of peoples and religions other than itself, it nevertheless gave rise to Christianity and Islam – which in turn gives rise to things like the craziness and bloodshed of nine-eleven . . . ."

9
─

From: dgoldstein@cuniv.edu   Sent: 9/30/01 1:10 PM
To: rlow@ahavttorah.org.il
Subject: Doubts and related matters

Dear Rabbi Low,

I must confess I'm having a difficult time lately. I'm turning to you because I just don't know who else to talk to. Everyone around here seems to be depressed or otherwise preoccupied with themselves. I'm feeling listless and de-energized.

I must say I'm really having trouble saying the words of the prayers. I just don't feel that I believe them enough to say them. I know what Rabbi Abraham would say. He'd tell me to say the prayers anyway even if I don't believe them. This is sort of like Pascal's recommendation at the end of the Wager argument: "Say the prayers often enough, and eventually you'll come to believe them." And I guess you'd accept this. But I can't.

I also feel very constricted by the do's and especially the don'ts of Judaism. Lately I have trouble keeping Shabbat. Yom Kippur was really tough. The system seems so tight and restrictive. Isn't there some room, ever, for breaking out of the system and just doing, spontaneously, what feels right? If I don't feel like praying one day, am I still supposed to force myself to pray? Why is it so important to talk to God (assuming that He exists) especially if I don't feel up to it?

David

From: rlow@ahavattorah.org   Sent: 9/30/01 2:22 PM
To: dgoldstein@cuniv.edu
Subject: Re: Doubts and related matters

Dear David,

We're all going through a hard time right now and I urge you to be patient. In your latest message, several threads are getting tangled together, and it's worthwhile trying to separate them. You were in the midst of recovering from a personal tragedy when you were suddenly thrust into the midst of an awful national tragedy as well. Please be patient and give yourself time to think clearly.

To answer your questions, first of all, it's important to "talk to G-d," as you put it, because, according to Judaism, G-d is in some sense a person, and Judaism is all about the Jewish people's cultivating an interpersonal relationship with Him. The primary way we relate to other people is through speech. If you were married, could you imagine getting up one morning and not saying "Good morning" or "I love you" to your wife because you weren't in the mood? You might be tempted to, but hopefully you'd overcome your mood and say it anyway. Or, at least, you should. It's always appropriate for the Jewish people to speak to G-d or to cry to G-d, and maybe even to argue with G-d.

However, while it's one thing to be in a lousy mood, it's another thing to be in a situation of real doubt. I mean that if you don't love a certain person, or you're really not sure you love her, or if you're not even sure that person exists, then maybe you shouldn't say "I love you" until you really mean it. Liberally paraphrasing a verse in Song of Songs (2:7), one should not incite or force a feeling of love that is not really there. One should wait until it takes hold naturally. So, if you personally feel you can't say the words of the davening or the Shema, then perhaps you shouldn't force yourself to do so.

In fact, while I advocate a pragmatic argument for religious commitment, as you know, I do not agree with Pascal's recommendation at the end of the Wager. The fact that you're thinking and working on the whole issue of whether you should daven or not is part of your spiritual process. I once knew a Jewish woman who felt so much doubt she couldn't even go into a shul. Yet she would come and stand outside the door just looking in and wondering what it must be like to really be a believer and feel that one had a relationship with G-d. That woman was probably on a higher level and closer to G-d than many of the people who actually were in shul and who were going through the motions of prayer out of habit. I advised her to keep visiting the shul and to pray only when she felt ready to do so.

However, by the same token, you should not do anything that counters the spiritual process either. For example, I would encourage you to keep Shabbat at the highest level you can. After all, if you keep Shabbat, you are not verbally affirming something that you don't yet believe. You may be keeping Shabbat in the hope that the day really is special, or in the hope that by keeping it, you will discover its sanctity. You wrote me once that you felt that keeping Shabbat made the day special. But if you violate Shabbat, that feeling may begin to crumble. I suspect that if you maintain your observance and keep learning and studying and thinking, you will find yourself naturally wanting to daven sooner or later. Going back to the analogy above, if you're in doubt about whether you love a certain person, maybe you shouldn't force yourself to say "I love you." But it would not be right to go off and have an affair with someone else just because you're in doubt, because that in itself could ruin the relationship.

Finally, I can't deny that some of the do's and don'ts may at times feel "constricting." Otherwise keeping the Torah would not be a sacrifice – and it is supposed to be like that in some sense. You mention feeling listless and de-energized. But your dissatisfaction with this only indicates to me that something in you, like in everyone else, craves a way of life that is rich and full. Judaism teaches that you can't get that richness or fullness without do's and don'ts. Trust me: on the spiritual journey, the old slogan "No pain, no gain" is always true. You also made a critical remark about the systematic nature of Judaism. Actually, there is a tension which I think you are going through that is really very profound. On one hand, humans crave system and structure. We want a recipe or step-by-step process for living a good life or doing the right thing. We also want to understand and articulate the reasons for why we do what we do and how it all fits in to the plan. Yet at the same time, we want freedom and spontaneity. We want to be able to do what we feel like doing at a given moment. From this perspective, reasons become secondary. I think that Judaism provides a balance between these two extremes. There is a lot of structure and system, a lot of do's and don'ts in Judaism. But there is still room for personal expression and spontaneity **within** that system. Finding the right mix is part of the spiritual struggle that we all go through as religious Jews.

I hope this helps. Keep in touch. And, if I may say so, try to enjoy Sukkot, which I'm sure you know starts tomorrow night!

Sincerely,

Rabbi Low

10
—

"Hey, Esther . . . it's me, David."

"David! How are you?"

"Uh . . . so-so. What are you doing now? Are you busy? I really could use some company."

"David, I'm sorry, but I'm studying, or at least I'm trying to. I've got a test tomorrow."

"How long will it take you to study?"

"I don't know, exactly. There's a lot of stuff to go over."

"OK, so what about tonight? Can we meet after you study? I could just come over to your apartment. Esther? Are you there?"

"Yes, I'm here. What did you say?"

"How about I come over later to your apartment?"

"No, I don't think so. That won't work."

"Come on, Esther. I just want to see you, to talk to you."

"Yes. I'd like to see you, too, but not here. That's not a good idea. Besides, I need to study."

"So when can I see you, then?"

"Let's see. I'm going away right after the test to my uncle's house for Sukkot. But I'll be back the week after next. How about then?"

"A week?"

"Yes, I'll be away all week. David, hang in there. I'm sure you'll be OK. Look, I've got to go."

11
—

October 4, 2001

A student committed suicide last night. He jumped out of his dorm window. They found his body near the trash bin below. It's really bad. Dr. M is right — everything has changed since 9/11. I feel changed, too. Can't pray. I just feel like I'm mouthing the words, and no one is listening.

I just smoked some stuff, and that was really stupid. It just made things worse. Emptiness. Very intense emptiness.

I tried reading Descartes. But I can't get into it. It all sounds very sensible and reasonable. But there seems to be something missing, something that I found in Plato's dialogues. Is it the personality of Socrates? He was such a rich character. There's something impersonal about Descartes's philosophy. What does he say about the "I"? Who is the self? The self is the "thinking thing" which comes pre-packaged with innate ideas, including the idea of God. Very nice. But how is my self any different from any other self? Essentially, my self is exactly the same as any other. But is this Descartes's fault? Is he more impersonal than the other rationalists or the empiricists? I don't know.

I can barely talk to Dad, of course. What is going on with him? I still have lots of questions about Mom's death. I can't even write them down in this journal. (I hope no one ever reads this.) Nothing will ever be the same between me and him.

Esther. Cold of her to brush me off like she did. But she's just being consistent, I guess. She must have been afraid that I'd try something on her. That's ridiculous, of course. But can I blame her for thinking that? Anyway, she's gone for Sukkot, and she won't be back for another week. So what should I do meanwhile?

Mom. I feel like writing ~~you~~ her a letter. Who knows? Maybe her soul is out there somehow, just like some people think. I wish it were true. But I ~~can't~~ refuse to operate on wishful thinking. If I had to accept anybody's view about the "next world" and the "afterlife", it would have to be Dr. M's. That makes the most sense to me. The soul doesn't <u>really</u> exist after death. Why don't I just accept that? People live on in the values and truths that they've lived by. That's why people write books — to leave something of themselves behind. That reminds me of the Book of Life that Rabbi A talked about on Rosh ha-Shannah.

So how does the Book of Life relate to the Torah? It can't be the same thing. Or can it?

I haven't said Kaddish in a while. It had so much meaning when I first said it, but lately I have trouble. It's one thing to say it once at the funeral, and another thing to say it every day.

God! I keep going through these phases, up and down. Into it for some time, then out of it again. I was reading my journal from last year when I kept Shabbat for the first time. I was so into it and now the fire seems gone. What's wrong with me? Why can't I be consistent?

This is no good, sinking deeper and deeper. Guess I'll have a few beers. Another smoke, go for a walk somewhere, go downtown.

But if I do that, God knows where I'll end up. No, I won't go there.

Maybe I'll go bother Ravi. But what help can he give me now?

I just re-read Low's last email. "Enjoy Sukkot." God! How am I supposed to do that? Maybe I should go visit my relative, Chaim. He invited me to come see him some time. I think I still have his address somewhere. Why didn't I think of that before?

12

David arrived at Chaim's house in the late afternoon. He rang the bell and knocked several times, but there was no answer. He was just about to give up when he heard a voice calling from somewhere outside.

"Be right there!"

In a moment, Chaim appeared in the driveway. He was wearing almost exactly the same garb he had worn the day he had visited David's house: dark suit pants, dark suit jacket, white shirt, black dress shoes. Yet this time he wasn't wearing a tie, and instead of the black hat, he was wearing a large black velvet *yarmulke*. When he saw David, his eyes lit up and his face broke into a smile.

"Dovid! Please come in! Just come right around to the backyard. I was about to have a little snack in the *sukkah*. Come, please join me."

"Thanks. I hope I'm not imposing," David said.

"No problem! You came at a perfect time. I have to go off to the yeshiva in a little while. But the kids are still in school and my wife is still out. So come in, come in."

In a few moments they were sitting together in the *sukkah* in the back yard. The walls were made out of green canvas, and the roof was made from bamboo poles covered with greenery. Chaim insisted that David have a cup of hot tea and some of his wife's honey cake. David sat down while Chaim poured the tea from a large hot urn that was hooked up inside the *sukkah*.

"Here's the cake. It's really, really good, I promise. Wait a second. I just need to say some *brachos* . . . you know, blessings."

"Yes, I know. Go ahead."

Chaim held a piece of cake in his hand, and recited intently:

"*Baruch atah adonai elohenu melech ha-olam boreh minei mezonos.*"

"*Baruch atah adonai elohenu melech ha-olam asher kideshanu bemitzvosav vetzivanu leshev ba-sukkah.*"

Chaim took a quick bite from the cake. Then he continued:

"*Baruch atah adonai elohenu melech ha-olam she-hakol nehyah bi-devaro.*"

Chaim took a gulp of tea. David found himself answering *amen* at the end of each blessing.

"I'm really glad you came," said Chaim. "So, Dovid — you don't mind if I call you by your Hebrew name, do you? *Nu*, Dovid, how are you getting along?"

"Well, first I wanted to say — it was really nice of you to come to the funeral and to visit after my Mom passed way. You could have hardly known my mother, right?"

"Actually, I never met your mother at all. My grandfather asked me to go."

"Your grandfather? How old is he?"

"He's 68. He knew your mother's father, and in fact he met your mother when she was a kid. He would have gone himself, but he's been ill. He wanted someone from the family to go, and my own father was busy with work. So I offered to go."

"Well, thanks. Chaim, you seem to know more about the family than I do. Can you explain exactly how we're related? And I'm curious — how is it that your side of the family became Orthodox, while my mother's side did not?"

"You mean: the question is, how is it that my father's side remained Orthodox, while your mother's side did not?"

"Yes. I guess that's what I mean."

"Well, I can certainly tell you what I know about the family. My great-great grandfather was your mother's grandfather. He was known as Reb Dovid Alter, and he was a rosh yeshiva in Hungary. That must be the person you're named after, I suspect. Anyway, Reb Dovid Alter had seven children. Two of them were Chaim and Shlomo. Chaim was my great-grandfather and Shlomo was your grandfather.

"Now Chaim was the eldest in the family and Shlomo was the youngest. In fact, Chaim got married and had children before the war. One of his children was Reuven, and that's my grandfather. In 1938, Shlomo was only eighteen and still unmarried. Reb Dovid could see what was happening in Europe, and he wanted the whole family to leave. But it wasn't so easy to move. But he thought maybe at least Shlomo should leave before starting a family. He agonized over this because he really didn't want Shlomo to be separated from the family. Also, he worried about the influence of America — the *treifa medina* — that's the unholy country — on Shlomo. Unfortunately, that's exactly what happened, but I'll get to that in a minute. In the end, Shlomo did go to America, while the rest of the family stayed behind. In 1944, the Nazis deported many Hungarian Jews including Reb Dovid, his wife and daughters, and also Chaim. None of them survived except for my grandfather, Reuven, who was only twelve at the time."

"Wow. How did he survive?"

"He was in the countryside visiting friends when the Nazis came to his father's town. Then he was hidden by some righteous gentiles. It's really a miracle. Anyway, after the war, he came to America, with the help of his uncle Shlomo — your grandfather — as his sponsor. Now, by that time, Shlomo was no longer *frum* at all. He didn't even go by Shlomo any more. He went by Solomon or Solly. My grandfather Reuven was still a teenager and he went to stay with Shlomo. While Shlomo had become *ois-frum*, Reuven had become even more committed to *yiddishkeit* even though he had lost almost his entire family in the Holocaust. I'm sure Reuven was shocked to find that his uncle was not *frum*. I'm sure they must have had some long discussions!

"But Shlomo was very good to my grandfather. He helped him until he could stand on his own feet. As the years went by they grew farther apart, but they always stayed in touch. Like I said, my grandfather met your mother when she was a little girl. And when Shlomo died in 1995, my grandfather made sure there was a kosher burial and someone to say *Kaddish*. Then, when he heard that your mother had passed away – well, like I said, he couldn't go himself, but he wanted one of us to go to make sure that someone said *Kaddish* the right way."

"I see. Well, that's all very interesting. I didn't know any of this. And it's amazing how you know all these things so well. The truth is that I was a little shocked to find out that I have relatives like you."

"What can I say? Death brings people together. Speaking of relatives – tell me, how is your father?"

"He's OK, I guess."

"And you? How are you getting along? You didn't really answer my question earlier."

"Well, it's really hard to focus on things . . . especially after nine-eleven."

"*Ach!* Dovid, don't let that pull you down! You know what I think? Everyone's walking around so depressed about nine eleven. I think we're making a big mistake!"

"Why? What do you mean?"

"Look. Sure, we need to mourn for the dead, and we need to act, do what we can to defend ourselves, go after the bad guys and all that. But let's not be depressed about it. That's the worst thing!"

"Sorry, but how can you *not* be depressed? Don't you think nine-eleven changed the world? Don't you think it's a watershed event, like everyone keeps saying?"

"A water – *what*? Sorry, I don't know what that means."

"It means an event that changes the course of history."

"Oh! Well . . . no, I don't think it's that important. Look, evil isn't new. Death isn't new. You know what? It's just another challenge that we have to get over. You mentioned something about losing your focus. You know what the most important thing is? *Ivdu es Hashem be-simcha!* You know what that means? *Serve Hashem in joy*. That's what we needed to focus on before nine-eleven, and that's what we still need to focus on now. Maybe people who didn't realize this needed to be shaken up. But as far as I'm concerned, nothing's really changed. We just have to say *baruch dayan emes* and move on."

"What's that? We have to say *what*?"

"It's the blessing you say on bad news. It means, "Blessed is *Hashem*, the true judge." If you remember, you said this blessing at the funeral of your mother, may she rest in peace."

"I did? Sorry, I don't remember that part."

"That's OK. Look, the point is, just as we say *baruch Hashem* when we hear good news, we also say *baruch Hashem* when we hear bad news."

"Really? I've heard of the phrase *baruch Hashem*, but I thought it meant 'Thank God.' I didn't know you were supposed to say it on bad news too!"

"It doesn't mean 'Thank God.' It means 'Blessed be *Hashem*.' And we say it even on bad news because even bad news is ultimately from *Hashem*, and in the end it's all for the best."

"Very interesting. That reminds me of something else I was wondering about. Have you ever seen someone write the letters BSD at the top of a letter?"

"Yeah, sure. That stands for *be-siyata de-shamaya*, which means with the help of heaven. Some people write it at the top of any text they're writing, like maybe a letter, or especially if they're writing something that has to do with Torah."

"I see. Actually, I'm noticing it right now on some of your sukkah decorations."

"Right. By the way, d'you like the sukkah?"

"It's very nice. Who did the art work?"

"The kids, of course. They really got into it this year."

"How many kids do you have?"

"Three. Moishe is seven, Rivky is five, and – what's his name – Yankel is . . . let me see . . . almost three."

"Wow. That must be a handful for your wife."

"My wife? I don't know about that. She works full-time and the kids are in school or preschool almost the entire day. Usually I pick them up at five o'clock down near the yeshiva where I learn. We also have a cleaning lady and mother's helper. The only housework my wife does is cooking. And she's a good cook, let me tell you. You'll have to come over some time – maybe for a Shabbos? Anyway, usually I'm home through dinnertime and then I go back to the yeshiva when the kids go to bed."

"I see. What kind of work does your wife do?"

"Something with computers. She's really very sharp, she's sharper than I am. But don't ask me to explain what she does. It keeps us going so I can learn full-time!"

"So . . . you don't work?"

"Work? Why should I? I'm studying in yeshiva full time. I'll probably get *smicha* – become a rabbi within a year or so. Actually, I do a little work. I play the keyboard at *simhas* . . . you know, weddings, sometimes a bar mitzvah, that kind of thing. It pays OK, but there's no way we could live off that!"

"So your wife supports the family."

"I'm very fortunate, *baruch Hashem*."

"And you're into music, also."

"Yeah, sure. It's an important part of my *ruchnius* . . . that means my spiritual life, as you might call it. Life without music would be like life without a sense of humor. It wouldn't be worth living!"

"That's an interesting thought."

"And what about you, Dovid? Do you play an instrument?"

"Nope, never did."

"What do you for recreation?

"Well, for one thing, I run."

"You run? Where to?"

"Nowhere. I just run. You know, jogging."

"Ah, I see. Do you find that fun? Do you really enjoy it?"

"I don't know if I'd call it *fun*. It's invigorating, it's a challenge. It's really important for my health and psychological well-being. You don't do any sports yourself, do you?"

"Nah, not really."

"That's something I don't get. How can you guys not do any exercise?"

"*You guys*? You mean us *frum* Jews?"

"Yeah, sorry. That's what I meant."

"That's OK! Well, lately more and more of 'the guys' are getting into exercise. Lots of the younger guys at the yeshiva play basketball on a regular basis. But you know, there's also *simha* dancing, if you consider that exercise. I'm always into that when I have the chance."

"What? What kind of dancing?"

"*Simha* means joy or celebration. Like at a wedding or on holidays. Like I said, I go to a lot of weddings, and there's always dancing. I get into that, if I'm not playing the keyboard. Come to think of it, it's the ideal Jewish exercise."

"Why's that?"

"Look, I can't imagine my *rosh yeshiva* – that's the head of my yeshiva – playing basketball or jogging, but I can imagine him – in fact, I've *seen* him – dance up a storm at a Jewish wedding. When you dance at a Jewish wedding or at *Simhas Torah*, you're dancing for the joy of a mitzvah, or the joy of worshipping *Hashem*, for the joy of a *choson* and *kalah*. When a really pious, holy Jew exercises, what do you think he's going to do? Throw a ball through a hoop over and over again? Run nowhere five miles until he's exhausted? No way! He's going to move every limb in spiritual ecstasy before God."

"Chaim, my recollection of Jewish dancing from the few pictures I've seen is a lot of Jewish men going around in a slow circle."

"You haven't been to a traditional Jewish wedding, have you?

"No, I haven't."

"Look, there are different kinds of Jewish dancing . . . slow, medium, fast, with others, and individual as well. It's just like music. Maybe some time you'll come to a wedding with me and you'll see for yourself . . . ?"

"Maybe . . . . thanks."

"Of course, we'd have to wait till your period of mourning is over. Now, meanwhile, would you like another cup of tea?"

"Yeah, sure. It's getting a little chilly in here. It *is* a nice *sukkah*, but it must get cool in here at night. You don't sleep in here, do you?"

"Nope. These days, the custom is that married men don't usually sleep in the *sukkah*. The main thing is to eat in the *sukkah*, not to sleep in it. But when I was younger, I did sleep in the *sukkah*. Actually, Moishe's sleeping in the *sukkah* for the first time this year. It's a good experience. You should try it while you're still single!"

"Maybe I will sometime. But why don't married men sleep in the *sukkah*?"

"Um . . . well . . . never mind."

"No, please tell me. What's the reason?"

"OK. One reason is that a married man really should sleep in the *sukkah* with his wife. It's just that it's . . . bound to be immodest."

"Immodest? Why? What do you mean?"

"Look, it's really a complicated story if you look into all the halachic sources, but basically, a married man is supposed to sleep with his wife. And unless you have a really private sukkah, it's immodest to have relations in the *sukkah*. It's too exposed."

"But wait a second. How long is Sukkot? Only a week, right? So, why can't you skip the marital relations for a week? That should be easy enough, especially for a pious Jew!"

"Good question. But listen: in general, it's a *mitzvah* to have relations with one's wife. That *mitzvah* is so important that, together with the principle of modesty, it outweighs the *mitzvah* to sleep in the *sukkah*."

"Interesting. I knew there was a *mitzvah* to be fruitful and multiply. I didn't know there's a *mitzvah* to have sex at least once a week!"

"Excuse me, Dovid! I didn't say there was a *mitzvah* to have sex! I said 'a mitzvah to have relations with one's wife.'"

"Of course. That's what I meant."

"Actually," Chaim continued, "there is a whole discussion in the Gemara about how often a man should have relations with his wife. It depends on his profession. For a Torah scholar, once a week is the minimum. Usually, Friday night is considered the most appropriate time for this. Of course, we're assuming that his wife is at a time in her cycle when she is permitted to him. You know about that, don't you? Anyhow, that's one explanation for why married men don't sleep in the *sukkah*."

David sipped his tea and took a bite of honey cake. David watched as Chaim's gaze drifted away and up toward the thatched roof of the *sukkah*. He seemed absorbed in thought. Slowly he brought his gaze down toward David. He narrowed his eyes and frowned slightly as if he were struggling with some mental puzzle.

"What's on your mind?" David asked.

"I never quite thought of it before, but there's an interesting irony about the fact that one doesn't have marital relations in the *sukkah*. In a way, it's really too bad."

"What? Why do you say that?"

"Well, I'm not sure you're ready for this."

"What do you mean by that?"

"I'll tell you what I'm thinking, but only if you promise you'll take it seriously. It may seem frivolous to you but I assure you it's not."

"Of course I promise to take it seriously. What is it?"

"Did you ever learn about the *gematria* of the word *sukkah*?"

"The *what*?"

"*Gematria*. You know what that is?"

"No. What's that?"

"*Gematria* has to do with computing the values of letters and words. Each letter in the Hebrew Aleph-Beis has a numerical value. The letter *aleph* is one, the letter *beis* is two, and so on up through *yod* which is ten. The next letter *kaf* stands for twenty, *lamed* is thirty, up through *kuf*, which is a hundred. The letters *resh, shin,* and *tav* are two hundred, three hundred, and four hundred respectively."

"Right. Now that you explain it . . . . I think I did learn about that once. But what does that have to do with married men not sleeping in the *sukkah*?"

"Wait a minute. Be patient! Do you know how to spell the Hebrew word *sukkah*?"

Chaim took a pen from his jacket pocket and grabbed a napkin from the table. He wrote the following and showed it to David:

סוכה

"Look," Chaim continued. "Here's the word *sukkah*. And now below it I will write the numerical value or *gematria* of each letter:

5 = ה   20 = כ   6 = ו   60 = ס

"So, all together, the word *sukkah* adds up to ninety-one."

"Right. So?"

"Now, in the Torah the *shem ha-meforash*, the proper name of God is . . . what? Do you know?"

"The Tetragrammaton. That's the four-letter name, *Yeho* —"

"Dovid! Please! Don't pronounce it!"

"Sorry. It's holy. I forgot."

"Next time, say *Havayah*. That's how we say it. Or you can call it the "*shem ha-meforash*" which means the explicit name, or the name that requires explanation. I won't write it on the napkin. You know how it's spelled? First a *yod,* then a *heh,* then a *vav,* then another *heh* at the end. So, that equals how much in *gematria*? Ten, plus five, plus six, plus five. That's how much?"

"Twenty-six."

"Good! They really are teaching you something at college after all! Now, do you know what the *mekubbalim* say about that name?"

"The *who*? What did you call them?"

"*Mekubbalim*, from the word *Kabbalah* or reception, receiving. Those who've received the secret tradition regarding the *sod*, the inner meaning of the Torah. They are sometimes known by the outside world as Kabbalists."

"Oh, yes, I've heard of them. That's the Jewish mystics. My Jewish professor spoke about them briefly in my philosophy of religion course."

"Really? What did your professor say about Kabbalah?"

"First of all, the professor is a *she*, not a *he*."

"Ah! A woman professor. Great! So, what do you know about Kabbalah?"

"I don't know much about it. We didn't spend too much time on it at all."

"I see. Well, Dovid, how much do you know about *Yiddishkeit*?"

"You mean Judaism?"

"No, I mean *Yiddishkeit*. It's not the same thing. Judaism is a subject you study at college. *Yiddishkeit* is a religion, a way of life. You don't study it, you *learn* it."

"Ah . . . well . . . I guess I've been doing both."

"Good answer, Dovid! And how long have you been learning? Is this a recent interest?"

"Well, yes – actually in the last couple of years I've kind of rediscovered it."

"Oh? That's great! Fantastic! What, may I ask, got you interested?"

"It's a long story. As you know, I wasn't raised with a religious background. But a couple of years ago, I got interested in philosophy and starting asking questions like what's the purpose of life, and stuff like that. Then, I visited the Holocaust museum, and something inside me just clicked. I decided, at first, just to learn more about Judaism, and as I did, it started growing, though I'm not sure where it's all headed. I have to admit that I go through some pretty strong phases of doubt and belief."

"And what phase are you in right now?

"More doubt than belief."

"I see. Well, are you at least keeping some of the *mitzvos*?

"Yes, some of them."

"Good! Do you *daven*? Do you pray? Do you say *Kaddish* for your mother?"

"I try, at least once or twice a week."

"Do you put on tefillin?"

"Sometimes."

"Do you keep Shabbos?"

"Uh, sort of."

"OK, well, that's good. And who are you learning with?"

"There's the professor I just mentioned, Dr. Maimon. She's taught me quite a lot. And there's Rabbi Abraham, the Hillel rabbi at school. I've gone to a few of his classes. And then there's this other guy, Rabbi Low, who's in Israel, but I don't really learn with him. We just converse a lot through email."

"That's all very nice! But it sounds like you don't have a *chevrusa*."

"What's that?"

"A learning partner. That's what you really need. You know what it says in the

Talmud? "*O chevrusa o mitusa,*" which basically means, "Either you have a *chevrusa* or you have death."

"That's a pretty strong statement. Anyway, I don't know anything about Kabbalah. I don't remember Rabbi Abraham mentioning it at all, in fact."

"What can you expect? He's a typical Ashkenazi!"

"A typical what?"

"Ashkenazim are Jews of Central European descent. Most of them really don't understand or appreciate Kabbalah. The only thing they think it's important to learn is Talmud and *halacha* and maybe a little *mussar*. You've learned something about *mussar*, maybe?"

"Yes, I learned a little bit about that from Rabbi Abraham. *Mussar* means discipline, working on yourself, developing and refining your character – that sort of thing."

"That's right. Sorry, I really shouldn't be so hard on them. Actually I'm an Ashkenazi myself."

"What? Now I'm really confused!"

"Look, not all Ashkenazi Jews ignore Kabbalah, but it's a stereotype that happens to be generally true. The Hasidim and the Sefardim have a different approach."

"Sorry, I didn't follow all that. Hasidim and who else? I don't know much about these different groups."

"Never mind that for now, we're getting off the track. Look, I wanted to tell you what the Kabbalah says about the name of *Hashem*. In fact, some say that all of Kabbalah is one long commentary on the divine name!"

"Wow. That's interesting."

"The thing I wanted to say right now is that the name *Havaya* signifies the masculine aspect of *Hashem*. In this aspect, God is sometimes referred to as *Hakadosh barch hu*, or in Aramaic, *Kudshah brich hu*, which means 'the Holy One, Blessed be He.'"

"So God has a masculine aspect? I've never heard that before. Does God have a feminine aspect too?"

"Of course. Don't you remember what the Torah says? "God created Adam in his own image . . . male and female he created them." In other words, God is in some way represented in the human being, both male and female. The feminine aspect is basically what the *mekubbalim* call the *Shechinah*, the divine presence that is most accessible to us."

"Very interesting. OK, continue."

"Now, I'm sure you know that when you see the *shem ha-meforash* in the Torah or in the prayers we usually pronounce it like this: *Ah*, then *do*, then *nai*, which is spelled, *aleph, dalet, nun, yod*. The *mekubbalim* say that the feminine aspect of *Hashem*, or the *Shechinah*, is signified by this name. And the *gematria* of this name is as follows:

$$10 = \prime \quad 50 = \int \quad 4 = ? \quad 1 = k$$

"And that equals what, David?"

"Sixty five."

"So, the masculine name is twenty six and the feminine name is sixty five. So the *total* of the unity of the masculine and the feminine name of *Hashem* is what?"

"Ninety-one."

"Exactly! And what did we say is the total of the word *sukkah*? Also ninety-one! So the word *sukkah* represents the union of the male and female aspects of *Hashem*!"

"Cute! Real cute."

"*Cute*?! That's all you have to say? Look, the *sukkah* represents the union, or *yihud*, of the masculine and the feminine aspects of *Hashem*. In fact, the first and last two letters of the word *sukkah* – the *samech* and the *heh* – equal sixty-five, which is the value of the feminine name. But the middle two letters, *kaf* and *vav*, equal twenty-six, the value of the masculine name. So perhaps we could say that the *sukkah* stands for the enveloping of the masculine within the feminine . . ."

"Chaim, you're not making all this up, are you?"

"Of course not, Dovid!"

"Sorry. Just kidding."

"Well, to be honest, the idea about the outside letters 'enveloping' inner letters is something I just thought of. I don't remember seeing it in any *sefer* – in any book. But the idea that the *gematria* of the word *sukkah* adds up to the *gematria* of the two names of God – that's ancient."

"Interesting. So, anyway, you said there was something ironic about all this. What's the irony?"

"Isn't it obvious? The gematria of *sukkah* – ninety one – represents the union of the masculine with the feminine aspects of *Hashem*. Yet, like I said before, the customary practice is *not* to have marital relations in the *sukkah*. Don't you see the paradox?"

"Well, yes. That does seem ironic, I guess. So is that what Kabbalah is all about? Numbers? *Gematria*?"

"Dovid! First of all, numbers are important. The world is based on numbers. Don't you agree? The Torah says that God created the world in six days and rested on the seventh. Is that just an accident? Of course not! But Kabbalah is not just about numbers either. That's just the tip of the iceberg. The numbers and *gematrios* are hints at deeper *yesodos*, or fundamentals. Take, for example, the very idea that *Hashem* has a masculine and a feminine aspect, and the idea that there can be a *yihud*, a union of these two aspects. A lot of Kabbalah deals with a proper understanding of this union of the masculine and feminine aspects of *Hashem*. This is much deeper than just numbers!"

"Yes. That part does sound pretty interesting."

"And when you study Kabbalah, you can really see how many of the *mitzvos* tie into this concept of this union. Like for example, all the prohibitions regarding sexual behavior really only make sense when understood from this angle. In fact, when understood from Kabbalistic perspective, the sexual act itself between man and wife of course, takes on profound meaning."

"I'd like to learn more about that."

"There's more."

"Like what?"

"Like learning how to apply the Kabbalah to your life, to the worship of *Hashem*, to the observance of *mitzvos*."

"Really? How do you do that?"

"Dovid, I can't explain it all on one foot! But that's what I was talking about earlier when I said, the whole focus of Torah is really, *ivdu es hashem be-simha*, serve *Hashem* with joy. True joy consists in unifying the different aspects of *Hashem*, the Divine Name, which stands for the manifestation of the infinite God. You see, there is a kabbalistic explanation for everything in Torah, whether it's keeping Shabbos or keeping kosher or whatever. And just a moment ago we were talking about *mussar*, right? So, there's a kabbalistic approach to developing yourself, working on your character traits, relating to others. When you study Kabbalah you see how everything falls into place, and that's why they say that if you really want to have true emunah, true faith without any doubt, you have to study Kabbalah. There's even a kabbalistic approach to prayer. Until you learn about the kabbalistic approach to how to understand the levels of prayer, I'd say you can't really appreciate what prayer is all about."

"This is really beginning to sound very interesting. And it also makes me wonder: if the Kabbalists are mystics, that would mean they'd probably be into some kind of meditation. Is that true?"

"Of course! There's an elaborate system of Jewish meditation."

"Wow! I never knew that!"

"We call it *hisbonnenus*. A lot of it has to do with meditating on the divine name. And – *oy, vey!* Sorry, Dovid! I just realized I have to cut this short! I'm late for *minha*!"

"Sorry? Late for what?

"*Minha*, the afternoon prayer!"

"Oh, sorry, Chaim. It's my fault. I got you all distracted."

"No, of course it's not your fault! We'll just have to continue this discussion another time. I think I can still make it to the yeshiva in time if we take the car. Sorry to rush off. But hey, Dovid, why don't you come with me?"

"I really need to get back to the subway and head back to campus."

"C'mon. Come with me to *minha* and I'll give you a lift to the subway right after. I just need to say a quick blessing on the tea and honey cake, and then we can go."

13

"Hey, David. What's going on?"

"Simon! How are you?"

"Where've you been hanging out?"

"With my second cousin, Chaim. I've told you about him, haven't I?"

"You mean the black-hat guy who came to your mom's funeral?"

"Yes. He's really a nice guy. He said he would come up and visit me on campus one day. And he knows all about Kabbalah – you know, the Jewish mystical tradition."

"No, actually I *don't* know, but that's OK. Anyway, I hope he doesn't brainwash you too much."

"Don't worry, Simon. Don't you remember our agreement? We said that we won't let my interest in Jewish things get in the way of our friendship. Right?"

"Sooner or later, if you keep heading in that direction, it's going to get tough!"

"Why do you say that? I accept you just the way you are."

"David, let me ask you this: Are you still smoking the good essence?"

"Of course! You should know that smoking is an important part of my . . . uh . . . spiritual path. It expands my . . . uh . . . consciousness. I smoke a little, then meditate on the divine name. It's pretty powerful stuff."

"David, come on. Nobody mixes drugs and religion any more. That's out of fashion. How many religious Jews do you know who get high? Of course I knew guys in high school who smoked, but they weren't the real religious ones. And I don't think you'll find too many rabbis approving this practice. Hey, why don't you ask your cousin what he thinks of it?"

"Maybe I will sometime. But look – just to prove to you that I haven't really changed, how about we try some right now? Do you remember what stands behind the City of God?"

"Yes, of course."

"Well, here's the pipe. And here's the lighter. You do the honors, Simon."

"Great! Thanks. This makes me feel a little better! But still – I've got to say, you really seem to be getting more and more into it."

"The truth is, I go through stages with it. Up and down. Like right now I'm very interested in learning more Kabbalah. But I'm still struggling with keeping Shabbos. Especially when it comes to smoking!"

"Sure you go through stages, but overall, you're getting more and more into it as time goes by. You're up a lot, down a little, up a lot, and eventually you'll be walking around with a beard and *payes*!"

"No way, Simon! *Nu*? Are you lighting the pipe?"

"Yes, I am. And don't 'nu' me! But seriously, even the fact that you say you're struggling with keeping Shabbos shows how much it all means to you. I'm telling you, you're changing."

"Does that mean we can't be friends? I'm still friends with Ravi and George."

"They're different. First of all, they're religious. And they're not even Jewish, so you don't expect the same things from them. Sooner or later, there's going to be tension between us."

"Why should there be? I'm not trying to change you. This is just about me, trying to find my own way."

"But if you really believe in it, isn't it your obligation to spread the word, at least among other Jews? Wouldn't it be your duty to try to change me?"

"Maybe, but you've got to want to change. Otherwise it's just going to backfire. I know you've got problems with Judaism, and I don't blame you for that."

"I don't see how you could be an Orthodox Jew and not disapprove of my lifestyle. Here's the pipe."

"Thanks. Ah, that's some good essence! Well, in the sense that you're an avowed hedonist and atheist – yes, I suppose that's true, in some sense, I disagree with you. But I don't judge you."

"How can that be? And actually there's something else about me that you should know."

"Simon, I'm not blind or deaf. I already know. How can I not know?"

"Fine. So you do know. Well? Can an Orthodox Jew accept that?"

"Who said I'm Orthodox anyway? I'm not Orthodox!"

"That's what you keep saying. And that's why I said that if you keep heading in that direction, there could be a problem."

"Simon, trust me. I will always be your friend, no matter what."

14

Chaim met David in the afternoon and they headed to the park. It was a crisp, cool day in late autumn. The trees stood out sharply against the clear, blue sky. They found a secluded path and walked in silence for some time. Soon they were enveloped in a canopy of brown, yellow and red leaves. They found a huge rock and sat down. Chaim and David could barely see the sky above.

"Chaim, this reminds me of being in your *sukkah*."

"Yes, it's kind of like that. And it's secluded. An ideal place for sharing secrets."

"So can we talk a little more about Kabbalah? I wanted to ask you about something you said last time in the *sukkah*."

"Sure. What is it?"

"You said that the whole Kabbalah can be understood as a commentary on the divine name."

"Yes. I did say that."

"Well? What does that mean? It sounds like it can't really be taken literally. How could the whole Kabbalah be a commentary on one word?"

"Dovid, it's not just any old word! It's *Hashem*, the name of God! Look, let me try to explain. But first, can I give you a little introduction?"

"Go ahead. Do you mind if I smoke? A cigarette, that is?"

"Well, it's not healthy, you know that. So I'd be lying if I said I didn't mind. Do you know the verse *u-shmartem es nafshoseichem*? There's a *mitzvah* to take care of yourself. Of course, one cigarette's not going to kill you, but I thought you said you were a runner. Do you smoke a lot?"

"No, not really."

"Well, the smoke itself won't really bother me as long as you sit downwind."

"OK. I'll just have one cigarette, then."

"Fine. Now, let's talk about the divine name. First I want to show you that this idea of focusing on God's name is not some strange or crazy idea. It's what the Torah is all about. David, do you know the *bracha* on the Torah that we say every morning?

"Yes, sort of."

"We ask *Hashem* to make the words of his Torah 'pleasant in our mouths' . . . and that we should all become *yodei shmecha* – 'knowers of your name' and *lomdei torasecha* – 'students of your Torah,' *lishmah*."

"Right. I remember that prayer."

"So, this is obviously a really important *bracha*, right? And what do you suppose we're asking for when we ask that God help us become *yodei shemecha*, knowers of his name? What does it mean to be someone who knows *Hashem*'s name?"

"I'm not sure. It can't just mean to know what the name is. That wouldn't require too much help on God's part unless we're talking about some secret pronunciation that's very difficult to grasp without God's help."

"But you don't think that's what we're asking for, do you?"

"No, I doubt it."

"And what could it mean to study the Torah *lishmah*?"

"To study Torah *lishmah* is to study it for its own sake."

"And what does that mean?

"Ah, that I know. It means to study it just because it's intrinsically the right thing to do, and not for any other ulterior reason."

"Very good. But did you know that the word *lishmah* can mean something else? A more literal translation is 'for the sake of the Name' – that is, for the sake of *Hashem*'s name itself."

"Sorry, I don't get that. What can it possibly mean to study Torah for the sake of Hashem's name?"

"I'll try to explain. First of all, to 'know' God's name is not just to be acquainted with God's name. It's to understand the true significance of the name. Now, what do you think it means to understand the significance of the Name?"

"I'm not sure, but I know that the Tetragrammaton is etymologically related to the root of the Hebrew word for being. Dr. Maimon taught me that."

"Very nice! But does that explain what's going on in this blessing? Are we asking God to help us understand that his name is connected with being?"

"I'm not sure. I don't know."

"Dovid, let me tell you that you can't really grasp the true meaning of this *bracha* until you understand what the Kabbalah says about *Hashem*'s name. So listen carefully to what I am about to tell you. This is the *yesod*, the basis of everything in Kabbalah and actually, the basis of everything in the world."

"OK. I'm listening. But first can I ask another question? You keep saying that the Kabbalah says this and the Kabbalah says that. I hope you don't mind if I ask, but how do we know that what the Kabbalah says is true?"

"Dovid! Kabbalah is part of Torah. So you might as well ask how we know that anything in the Torah is true."

"OK. How do we know that?"

"First of all we know the Torah is true because of tradition, which in Hebrew is *mesorah*. The word *mesorah* comes from *massar*, which means to transmit or hand over to someone. By the way, that's also where we get the word *mussar*, which, as you know, means 'teaching' or 'discipline.' Now, the word *kabbalah* comes from the word *kabbel*, which means 'receive.' So, when a person learns Kabbalah properly, that means he receives or accepts the tradition. It is no longer just something transmitted, but something that is received. And when a Jewish person accepts or receives the *mesorah* properly, he knows inside that it's all true because something clicks inside his soul. To understand this, you really need to know more about the Jewish soul, and I can't explain that right now. But the more a person learns, and the more he delves into Kabbalah, the more he knows inside that the Torah is *emes* – that is, true."

"OK, I've heard something like this before, but you're giving it a new twist. You can tell me more about the Jewish soul some other time. Anyway, you were about to explain something about the divine name. What was it?"

"Right. Listen up. The Divine Name itself refers to certain aspects of God. Each of the four letters hints at a different aspect. And the unity or oneness of the name hints that despite the fact that *Hashem* has these different aspects, nevertheless they are all unified. In fact, the Kabbalah teaches that our task as Jews is to bring about the *yihud*, or unification, of the divine name – that is, a unification of the various aspects of God. That's really what it means to do something *lishmah*, for the sake of *Hashem*, the Name. And the path toward fulfilling that unification or *yihud* is by learning and fulfilling the Torah, God's teaching. And that's also why before we do a *mitzvah*, we're supposed to have in mind that we are helping to unite the different aspects of God, to bring about the unification of the name. That's why before doing many *mitzvos* we recite the kabbalistic formula, '*Le-shem yihud kudsha brich hu u-shchinteh*,' which means, 'For the sake of the unification of the Holy One, Blessed be He' – that's the male aspect – 'and his Shechinah' – that's the female aspect. This statement is a declaration of intent to do the *mitzvah* in order to unify the male and female aspects of God."

"Chaim, this all sounds very interesting, but it's also puzzling. I'm wondering – how can God be one and yet have different divine aspects, as you put it? And if he does have different aspects, how can they be more unified at some times and less unified at other times? And how can anything we humans do unite these supposedly different aspects of God?"

"Good questions, Dovid! It's such a joy to talk to you about this because I can tell that you're really trying to think it through. But I'll explain. Basically you have to distinguish between God's *atsmus*, or essence, and God as he manifests himself in the world. God's *atsmus* is *ein sof* – that is, *infinite*, which means, unlimited and indescribable. In his essence, all of the divine aspects are perfectly one. And the essence itself never changes. But insofar as God is manifest in the world, that's a different story. God is manifest in a fragmented and incomplete way, especially at the beginning of creation. And at various times, God is more or less manifest in the world. The purpose of keeping the Torah is precisely this – to bring about the most complete and perfect manifestation of God's essence in the world."

"OK. I think that makes sense. Continue, then."

"Like I said, God's essence is *ein sof* – that means 'without end' or 'infinite.' But God is manifest in the world through what are called the ten vessels or *kelim*, which are also known as the ten *sefiros*. The *sefiros* are like spiritual energies through which the *ein sof* manifests itself. We interact with the essence of God only indirectly, through the *sefiros*. The ten *sefiros* also fall into four basic groups or categories, each of which is hinted at by one letter in the divine name, the *shem ha-meforash*."

"Wow. This is getting complicated. But before you go on, can I ask you a question? You spoke about the infinite essence of God. Do you think of that essence as *a* being? And these *sefiros* that you mentioned – are they also entities or beings as well?"

"Of course. The infinite essence is a being – that is, an infinite being. And the *sefiros* are spiritual entities or beings too. Why do ask? What else would they be?"

"Never mind. Let's not get sidetracked. Go on."

"OK. But let me say that you're right – Kabbalah is complicated. Why shouldn't it be? The world is complicated. Even the structure of an ant or a crab is complicated. All the more so, we should expect the spiritual realm to be complicated!"

"I guess you're right. So tell me – what are the ten *sefiros*, and how do they correspond to the four letters of the name of *Hashem*?"

"Well, I don't think we can finish in one day, but we can certainly get started. As you know, the name has four letters, *yod*, then *heh*, then *vav*, then *heh*. Let's start with the last letter of the Name, which is the *heh*. Here, let me draw the letter *heh* in the ground with a twig."

ה

"This is a *heh*. It's the last letter of the divine Name, but it's also the second letter of the Name. The last *heh* of the Name is often called the 'lower *heh*' to distinguish it from the 'upper *heh*' – that's the second letter of the Name. The lower *heh* stands for the *sefirah*, or divine energy, called *Shechinah* – that's the divine presence, the aspect of God that is most accessible to us. This is also the feminine aspect of God. Are you familiar with the *midrash* that says that when the people of Israel go into *galus* – exile – the *Shechinah* goes into exile with them?"

"Yes, I've heard that one."

"What do you think it really means?"

"It means that they always have some special connection with God, even in exile."

"Right. But it's more than that. There is an aspect of God that is transcendent, beyond time and space. And there are aspects or levels of God that are not readily accessible except to the *tzaddik* or the true *hacham* – the very pious or the very wise. Yet there is a certain aspect of God that is always available to us, to every Jew, even in the depths of our physicality, even in the depths of sin or *galus*. That's what the lower *heh* stands for. That's the *Shechinah*. This aspect of God is also the *sefirah* or divine energy of *malchus*, which means kingdom or kingship. It is through the *sefirah* of *malchus* that the *ein sof*, the infinite God, manages the affairs of the world, like a queen who manages the affairs of state. There are other, more transcendent aspects of God, just like there are other, more remote aspects of a king's personality which he keeps hidden from the people."

"OK. I think I get it so far."

"Good. Here's another way to think about the *Shechinah*. Let's suppose you're involved in something, and you haven't been thinking about God or Torah for some time. You're running on the track or writing a paper or something like that. Then, suppose you start thinking about God. Whenever you begin to think about God, whenever you begin to approach God spiritually, your first step is the level symbolized by the lower *heh* – that's the *Shechinah*, the outward manifestation of God. Again it's also God's feminine aspect. Incidentally, that's why if you look at the letter *heh*, you'll see that it is an "open" letter. Unlike most other Hebrew letters, it's completely open on the bottom. That symbolizes our access, our approach to *Hashem*. Actually, the *heh* is open in two ways – at the bottom and at the top as well. This corresponds to the fact that there are two ways in which a woman is 'open': physically and intellectually. The physical is obvious. The intellectual way in which women are open is that they are in general more receptive to new ideas. They're less stubborn, in general."

"Hmmm. This is all very interesting. Excuse me for a second, I'm just going to light another cigarette. Now let me ask you this. Didn't you say last time that the feminine aspect is symbolized by the name *Adonai*? Yet now you're saying it's symbolized by the lower *heh* of the Tetragrammaton."

"Good question. Both are true. In Kabbalah, the central name is the *Shem ha-meforash*, the Tetra – whatever you call it. That's the name that holds all the other aspects in unity. The *yod keh vav keh* is the only proper name, and that's why it's the holiest name as well. But all the other aspects of God have a name of God associated with them as well. The *Shem ha-meforash* never has a non-holy use, but all the other names do. For example, the name *Adonai* can also mean *master*, and it can sometimes be used to refer to a human. And by the way, you said you were only going to have *one* cigarette."

"Yes . . . well, just one more. OK?"

"I'm just reminding you of what you said."

"Thanks. But look, I have another question. Does it really make sense to say that the feminine aspect of God is called *malchus* or kingship? That sounds like a pretty masculine notion to me."

"Good question! But actually, *malchus* does have a feminine aspect. The *Shechinah* is referred to as a queen, or *malkah*. Feminine does not necessarily mean *passive*. It means *receptive*. There's a difference. A good queen – or king, for that matter – has to be receptive to what his people need or want. Even in a man, the capacity for receptivity may be viewed as a feminine quality."

"OK. I suppose that's true."

"Look, I could say a lot more about the *heh*, but let's move up to the next letter of the Name. Like I said, God manifests himself through the lower *heh*. But what does he manifest? The most obvious thing he manifests is His character. The character or personality of Hashem is represented by the *vav*, the next letter in *Hashem*'s name. So let me draw a picture of the *vav*."

|

"The *vav* represents *Hashem*'s character traits or *middos*, His ways of acting. The *vav* also stands for God's masculine aspect – that is, God as *mashpia*, one who generates activity. As I said before, in this respect, *Hashem* is referred to as *Ha-kadosh baruch hu*, or in Aramaic, *Kudsha brich hu*, which means 'the Holy One, Blessed be He.' One significance of the *vav* is that aside from the *sefirah* of *malchus*, there are six *middos* or character traits. As you know, the *vav* is the sixth letter of the *aleph-beis* and has the *gematria* of six. These are sometimes called the *shesh ketzavos*, or 'poles,' because some of these character traits or *middos* are, in a sense, opposites of other ones. It's kind of like branches on a tree that grow in different directions but that are held together by the center, the trunk."

"You're saying that God has specifically *six* character traits? No more and no less?"

"Yes, exactly. These six are the roots, or *ikkarim*, of all the ways in which God manifests his character. Let me describe what they are and then you can tell me whether you still think this is an odd idea."

"OK. But before you get to that, I've got another question. This is kind of like my earlier question about the *Shechinah*. You're saying the *vav* represents the masculine side of God. But last time, you said the masculine aspect is represented by the *shem ha-meforash* itself."

"Again, good question! The simplest way to answer is that basically, the *yod keh vav keh* has two senses. In one sense, the divine name hints at *all* of God's aspects, including both masculine and feminine. But in another sense, it is the name associated specifically with the *vav*, the masculine aspect. The reason the *vav* has this special role is because the *vav* is the central branch that holds the whole name together."

"I'm not sure I get it. How can one name have two senses?"

"It's just like the name Yisrael, or Israel. Sometimes, this name refers just to Yisrael, our patriarch. But sometimes, it's used as the name of the entire people. Though Yaakov – that is, Yisrael – wasn't the first of the patriarchs, he was the central branch of our people. This is related to the point I made earlier about the six *middos* being like branches on a tree. It's also like the word 'Torah,' which sometimes refers to the entire *Tanakh*, and sometimes only refers to the first five books."

"OK, I think I'm with you now."

"Good. So, I need to tell you about the six *middos* or character traits. The six are divided into two groups of three. These are sometimes called the *upper three* and the *lower three*. There are many different names for the *sefiros*, but for now we'll just say that the three upper ones are *hesed*, *din* and *rahamim*. Have you heard these terms before?"

"I've heard of *hesed* and *din*. My professor explained those to me. They're benevolence and justice. But what was the third one?"

"*Rahamim*, which is compassion. It's a middle point between the other two."

"How so?"

"I'll explain. *Hesed* means an outpouring or overflowing of generosity and giving. It is through *hesed* that *Hashem* created the world. When you give someone a gift that is totally undeserved, and for which you expect nothing at all in return, that's an act of *hesed*. On a human level, a classic example of *hesed* would be inviting a stranger over for lunch. You don't owe this person anything, and you don't expect anything in return. That's *hesed*."

"OK."

"On the other hand, *din* is different. In a sense, it's the opposite of *hesed*. *Din* has to do with giving people exactly what they deserve. When *Hashem* punishes the wicked, that's an act of *din*. When *Hashem* rewards the *tzaddikim*, the righteous, that is also considered an act of *din*. Another example would be paying back a loan or paying someone for a job they've done for you. Any case of giving someone what they deserve is *din*."

"OK. That makes sense."

"Finally, *rahamim* is usually translated as mercy or compassion. That would be doing an act that is in some sense deserved, but in some sense not deserved. In Kabbalah, *rahamim* is considered a *mizug* – that is, a blend of *hesed* and *din*. That's why *rahamim* is also called *tiferes*, which means beauty or harmony."

"Hold on a second. Can you explain that? Either something is deserved, or it isn't. How can you have a balance of *hesed* and *din*?"

"I'll give you an example. Take the idea of giving someone who deserves punishment a second chance. What a criminal deserves by the strict letter of the law is punishment. That would be strict *din*. But if he truly regrets his offense and resolves never to do it again, he doesn't 'deserve' mercy, but in some sense it is the right thing to have mercy on him."

"Ah, I see. That's a case of deserving it in some sense, but not in another."

"Exactly. And that's why, by the way, when we pray for forgiveness, we often appeal to God's *rahamim*. We ask God to forgive us because we have done *teshuvah* – that's repentance. If we've done *teshuvah*, in some sense we deserve to be forgiven, but in some sense we don't. So you'll find that throughout the davening, whenever we ask God to forgive us for our sins, the term *rahamim* keeps popping up over and over."

"But wait. Doesn't the word *hesed* come up too?"

"Sure it does. We have to appeal to God's pure *hesed* too, because maybe our repentance is flawed. But even the fact that we're appealing to God is something in itself. So the main thing we appeal to when we try to do *tshuvah* is really God's *rahamim*."

"OK. That seems right."

"And another classic example of *rahamim* is that of helping the poor. That's also a mixture or a *mizug* of *hesed* and *din*. By strict *din*, the poor don't deserve our help because they haven't earned it in the way that someone who works for you would be entitled to a wage. Like I said, paying a worker is a matter of *din* or justice. If you don't pay him, you're doing something wrong. But if someone knocks on your door, asking for charity, you don't really owe him anything. If you send him away empty-handed, you haven't done anything unjust. On the other hand, in general you should help the poor. They do have some kind of claim on us, even if they haven't worked for us. That's because nothing we own is really ours, and if things were different we could just as easily be as poor as they are, and we would want them to help us. So even though they don't deserve our help, it is proper that we help them. And that's why helping the poor counts as *rahamim*."

"OK, I think I get it."

"Good. So, in summary, the three major character traits of *Hashem* are *hesed*, *din*, and *rahamim*. These are the energies, or *sefiros*, through which God runs the world. Everything that God does in this world can be viewed as an act of *hesed*, *din* or *rahamim*. That is, either the act is totally undeserved, totally deserved, or it's a mixture, somewhere in between. These are the upper three of the six *sefiros* symbolized by the *vav*. Of course, I still need to explain the lower three *sefiros*. But it's starting to get dark, and maybe we'd better head back."

"Chaim, this Kabbalah stuff is really interesting. I'm anxious to hear more about how this all relates to prayer, and about Jewish meditation."

"Sure, we can talk about that, too. Actually, I can recommend some good books on that. But you should also know that we've barely scratched the surface.

Maybe you can come over for a Shabbos some time? Then we could spend a lot more time talking together."

15

"David, how are you?"

"Pretty good, Esther. Really, I'm doing much better."

"That's nice to hear. I hope you're not too upset with me."

"No. I'm not upset with you. But I did really want to see you that night."

"David, I'm sorry, but you sounded a little desperate on the phone."

"Maybe I was. Still, I think you could've been a little more receptive. But I'm not mad at you. Let's forget it."

"OK, thanks, David. So what have you been up to lately?"

"Actually, I've been learning Kabbalah with my cousin, Chaim."

"*Kabbalah*? With your *cousin*?"

"Yes. I think you'd approve. He's very Orthodox, married with three kids, going on four. He's totally *frum*, black hat and all that. He's studying to be a rabbi, and he's been teaching me some really interesting things about Kabbalah. Actually, I'm supposed to go over there for Shabbat."

"Wow! I'm glad to hear that. I didn't know you had relatives like that."

"Neither did I until he showed up at my mother's funeral."

"I see. What yeshiva does he go to?"

"Sorry, I don't remember the name. But I can find out. Esther, do you know much about Kabbalah?"

"No, not at all."

"It's really interesting stuff. I don't know if I believe in all of it, but still, it's really interesting. What's even more surprising to me is that there's a whole system of Jewish meditation that I never knew about. Do you know anything about that?"

"No, sorry. Never studied that at all."

"Maybe you should study Kabbalah sometime."

"No way! That stuff's too deep for me. Really, David, I'm glad to hear you're learning more. But still, it's a little strange that your cousin is teaching you Kabbalah."

"Why? Is it supposed to be a big secret?"

"Maybe your cousin knows what he's doing, but as far as I know, you're not supposed to learn Kabbalah till you're really advanced. In fact, I've heard some people say that if you study it before you're ready, Kabbalah could be dangerous."

"Really? Maybe I'll ask Rabbi Low what he thinks about that."

"Good idea, David."

16
—

From: dgoldstein@cuniv.edu   Sent: 11/ 1/ 01 7:22 AM
To: rlow@ahavattorah.org.il
Subject: Kabbalah

Dear Rabbi Low,

How are you? I'm doing much better. I wanted to thank you for all your kind words in the past few months. I really appreciate it. I haven't thanked you enough for all your help. I also wanted to let you know that I've met a new friend, who's actually a relative of mine. His name is Chaim. He's Orthodox, studying to be a Rabbi. He's very into Kabbalah, and he's been teaching me some really fascinating things. I'm also starting to get into Jewish meditation. But I don't remember your referring to any Kabbalistic ideas at all in any of our previous emails. So I wonder: what is your view on Kabbalah? Is it true that a person should study it only if he's really advanced? Do you think there is something dangerous about studying it?

David

From: rlow@ahavattorah.org.il   Sent: 11/ 1 / 01 8:39 PM
To: dgoldstein@cuniv.edu
Subject: RE: Kabbalah

Dear David,

It's wonderful to hear from you. It sounds like your interest in Judaism has been reinvigorated through your meeting with your cousin. Great!

The word Kabbalah in the sense which you are using refers to the "*sod*" or "*nistar*," or secret tradition of Judaism. I think it's important for every Jew to be familiar with the basic concepts of Kabbalah at some point. However, you've got to be careful about in-depth study of Kabbalah with the right person, and even then only after mastering the basics of Torah. Without trying to dampen your enthusiasm, I feel obligated to give you a word of caution.

One reason why Kabbalah is secret is because it is dangerous in the sense that it's both difficult and deals with the essentials of Judaism. Since it is difficult, it's easy to make a mistake, and since it deals with essentials, any mistake becomes a serious mistake. Getting into meditation, for example, sounds like an exciting thing, but there are some dangers. Many people who have studied Kabbalah improperly end up straying from traditional Judaism, including the false messianic movements of Shabbetai Zvi and Jacob Frank. (Have you heard of these people? Easy to check out in the *Encyclopaedia Judaica*.) To some degree, the controversy

over the Chassidic movement (do you know much about that?) had to with
the question of to what degree Kabbalah should be studied without intensive
preparation. Obviously, Chassidism is less of a divergence from traditional Judaism
than these false messianic movements. But even today, there is the phenomenon
of Lubavitch Chassidism. Many adherents believe that the late Lubavitcher Rebbe
is Mashiach (some believe he really never died but many of them believe he will
come back from the dead to be Mashiach.) To the rest of Orthodox Jewry, this is
all very strange and in fact smacks of Christian notions. It could be argued that
the roots of this divergent (some say heretical) view can be traced to improper
dabbling in Kabbalistic/mystical teachings.

Don't get me wrong. There is great value in much Chassidic and specifically in
Lubavitch teachings. In the yeshiva that I run, one of the teachers, a Chassidic
rabbi, teaches a course in Chassidic concepts (but this is not directly Kabbalistic). I
have deep respect for the Chassidim in general, but there were and still are some
strange excesses found in some Chassidic groups. I wonder, is your friend/relative
a Chassid? Do you know for sure that he is a legitimate teacher of the topic? Is
it possible that he is throwing in his own ideas and passing them on to you as
Kabbalah?

Final word. The Torah says *bi-krovai ekadesh*, which means that those who wish
to be especially close to G-d are in some respect in "danger" because they are
held to a higher standard. The Talmud says that G-d judges the righteous with
more exactitude than he does others. People who seek to be close to G-d through
Kabbalah are seeking an extraordinary closeness to G-d. This is great, but it
needs to be approached with the proper reverence. Again, far be it from me to
discourage you from studying Kabbalah altogether. I'm just trying to give you a
word of caution.

Rabbi Low

17

David arranged to stay with Chaim and his family for Shabbos. After the long
subway ride, he arrived just barely before sunset on Friday night. When he met
Rochel, David was surprised to see how pretty and young she looked. She could
have passed for a college freshman. *She looks like a slightly older version of Esther,* he
thought to himself. Yet she had already three children and was expecting a fourth.
And she also had a career.

David was about to change into his dress clothes, when Chaim knocked on his
door and handed him a towel. He insisted that David quickly take a hot shower
in preparation for Shabbos. Finally, Chaim, David, and Moishe set out for *shul*.
Chaim's wife Rochel stayed home with Rivky and Yankel. When they returned,

Chaim made *Kiddush* and they washed for bread and had *challah*. It seemed to David that Rochel had prepared a special feast, but Chaim insisted this was quite usual.

The entire dinner, from start to finish, seemed to be focused on the children. What was Moishe learning in school about the weekly Torah portion? What beautiful artwork did Rivky produce in kindergarten? Yankel also got a lot of attention. Chaim held him on his lap during most of dinner, during the course of which Yankel knocked a cup of wine over and some of it spilled on Chaim's clothes. Unfazed, Chaim calmly asked Rochel to remind him not to wear the same pants the next day. They ate, they sang Shabbos songs or *zemiros*. Finally, they said the blessing after the meal.

After the kids went to bed, Rochel excused herself, claiming she was exhausted. David thanked her for the dinner, but she waved her hand as if to say it was nothing.

"I'm glad you enjoyed it," she said, and disappeared up the stairs.

Chaim and David still sat at the Shabbos table. Suddenly, the house was quiet. The candles were beginning to flicker. Chaim brought out a bottle of Vodka.

"Are you allowed to have a small drink? You're not driving anywhere, right?" Chaim laughed and poured out two shots.

"I tell you," said Chaim with a sigh. "It's impossible to have an adult conversation with the kids around."

"Yeah, but the kids are wonderful. And your wife, she is really . . . a good cook!"

"Thanks. Well, anyway . . . *l'chaim*!"

"*L'chaim*!"

"You know, you're lucky to have a name like Chaim. Every time a Jew takes a drink, he's drinking to you!"

"Very funny! Sorry, but you're not the first to crack that joke."

They sat in silence for a moment. David watched and listened as Chaim closed his eyes and started humming a melody, very softly. Gradually, the melody rose and fell, rose and fell. Eventually, Chaim's voice trailed off.

"Chaim, that's a very beautiful tune. What is it?"

"That's a *niggun* from Rabbi Nachman of Breslov. You know what a *niggun* is?"

"A tune?"

"Yes, but not just any tune. It's a special tune, a spiritual tune. In fact, there are different *niggunim* for different occasions, different *niggunim* for different moods. Rav Nachman of Breslov was one of the most famous Chassidic Rebbes. The *niggun* I just sang is a *niggun* for a special purpose. But before I explain let's have another shot of Vodka. Here you go . . . *L'chaim*!"

"*L'chaim*! Thanks! Chaim . . . you really seem to enjoy your intoxicants!"

"Why not? Intoxicants have their place. Don't you agree?"

"I sure do, Chaim. I sure do. Actually, I myself . . . uh . . .".

"What?"

"Oh, never mind."

"What? What is it?"

"It's nothing, never mind."

"Come on, out with it!"

"Actually, I just wanted to ask . . . Chaim, are you a *chassid*?"

"*What*? No, of course not. Our family is not *chassidish*."

"So what? Why should that stop you?"

"You don't understand. It's important to keep the customs of your parents, unless you have some serious reason to change. Actually, I think the Chassidim were really onto something, with their emphasis on joy, and also their more vigorous and open study of Kabbalah. The *Ba'al Shem Tov* – the founder of *Chassidus* – taught that in our day and age, most of the reasons for keeping Kabbalah hidden no longer really apply. I've even studied with some Chassidim here and there. To be honest, my father and my brothers – I have four – they think I'm a little strange, with my interest in Chassidus and Kabbalah. When I was a teenager they were really worried, but now they realize I'm normal enough! But, no, I'm not a *chassid* and I don't see the need to become a follower of any particular Chassidic Rabbi – and that's really what defines a person as a *chassid*."

"OK, I think I get it. So . . . anyway, what were you going to say about the *niggun*?"

"Ah! I was going to say that the *niggun* I sang is supposed to be sung before learning Torah. It's supposed to arouse the soul with the love for Torah."

"I see. So, is that what we're about to do – learn Torah?"

"You didn't come just for the food and drink, did you? Seriously, we need to continue our conversation about the four letters of the divine name. Are you up to it now?"

"Yes, of course. I love that stuff."

"So, *nu*, remind me, where were we up to in our discussion of the holy name, that is, the *Shem*? Can you summarize what we did so far?"

"I'll try. You said that each of the letters of the name stands for some aspect of God, and that the last letter or what you called the lower *heh* stands for the *Shechinah*, the most revealed aspect of God. And you also said that the *vav* stands for God's masculine aspect, which is, the six character traits. But you only got through telling me about three of those traits – *chessed*, *din*, and *rachamim*. You had said there were three 'lower' traits as well, but we didn't get to those."

"Ah, right. Now, the other three *sefiros* are *netzach*, *hod*, and *yesod*. But wait . . . let me get something which might be helpful."

Chaim stood up, walked over to a bookshelf and pulled out a prayer book or *Siddur*. He came back to the table and sat down. When he opened the *Siddur*, he carefully removed a single, laminated page that had been stuck inside the book. Chaim gazed at it for a moment.

"What's that?" David looked at the page curiously.

"This is a chart which shows how the Kabbalah interprets the *Shem*. It's an oversimplification of course, but it's useful."

	Left	Central	Right
י *yod*		KESSER (crown or will)	
			CHOCHMAH [father] (wisdom)
ה *heh*	BINAH [mother] intelligence		
	DIN (judgment)		CHESED (benevolence)
ו *vav*		RACHAMIM [son] (compassion)	
	HOD (majesty)		NETZACH (victory)
		YESOD (foundation)	
ה *heh*		MALCHUS or SHECHINA [daughter] (kingship) (presence)	

"Very interesting. It looks like a mandala. What's it doing inside your *Siddur?*"

"The whole order of *Shacharis* – that's the morning prayer – is based on a certain understanding of the *Shem*. The morning prayer has four different parts or stages, corresponding to the four letters of the *Shem*."

"I didn't know that. I mean, I knew there were parts, but not that they were connected with the four letters of the Name."

"Well, don't feel bad, because most Orthodox Jews who've been praying for years still don't know this either. Especially if they're *Ashkenazim*. But it's not an accident that the prayer book is called the *Siddur*, which comes from the word *seder* or order. And it's not just *any* order, it's the order of the *Shem*. When I daven, I use something like this page to focus on the various stages of prayer and how they correspond with the Name. The one I use now is all in Hebrew and more complicated. In fact, you can keep this. But I'll have to explain the connection between the *Shem* and the morning prayer some other time. Meanwhile, just take a look at the chart."

"The chart shows the four letters of the divine name, the ten *sefiros*, and how the *sefiros* are connected with each letter. On the bottom, you can see the lower *heh*, the *Shechinah*. Above it, you see the *vav* with six *sefiros*. Still above that, you see the upper *heh* and then the *yod*. You can also see that the ten *sefiros* are divided into right, left, and central groups. I'll get to that later. But right now we need to talk about the *sefiros* of *netzah*, *hod*, and *yesod*. Basically, *netzah* derives from *hesed* and *hod* derives from *din*. To say that one *sefirah* or attribute 'derives' from another means that one *sefirah* or divine energy depends on or is caused by another. Ultimately, all the *sefiros* derive from the *sefirah* associated with the first letter at the top, the *yod*, which itself derives from the *ein sof*, the infinite essence of God. But, within the six *sefiros* of the *vav*, some *sefiros* are derived more closely from others. So, *netzah* is especially derived from *hesed*, and *hod* is especially derived from *din*. *Yesod* is the *sefirah* that draws its energy from all of the other five *sefiros*. Also, *yesod* is the *sefirah* that links the *vav* and the *heh*. That's why the *mekubbalim* sometimes say that *yesod* is like the 'lower tip' of the *vav*. Do you follow so far?"

"I think so."

"Good. Now, in order to explain *netzah* and *hod*, I need to backtrack for a second. The three *sefiros* we've already talked about – *hesed*, *din* and *rahamim* – have to do with *tov* and *ra,* that is, good and evil. *Hesed* refers to the capacity for doing totally undeserved things that are good. *Din* refers to the capacity for doing things that people deserve, whether good or bad. Finally, *rahamim* is a combination or harmonizing of the other two attributes. Right?"

"In other words, these three *sefiros* represent God's *moral* qualities."

"Ah! That's a nice way to put it. But you know, God has other qualities or character traits as well that are not obviously moral. For example, take God's capacity for power or sheer force. This aspect of God is displayed, for example, in the creation of the universe. It's mind-boggling to think of the infinite power that is exhibited in the natural world. But would you call that power or sheer force a moral quality? Isn't it theoretically possible that a being could be powerful – indeed, very powerful – without being benevolent – that is, without having *hesed*?"

"Sure, that's true. Some people have a lot of power but no *hesed* at all."

"Exactly. So the notion of power is not the same as the notion of *hesed*. That's why Kabbalah designates God's capacity for sheer force as the *sefirah* of *netzah*. The word *netzah* itself means eternality, victory, dominion. This is not obviously a moral quality at all, so it is distinguished from *hesed*."

"OK, that makes sense."

"However, Kabbalah also teaches that in the end, *netzah* is derived from *hesed*. Any time God uses sheer force or power, though it may appear not to have a moral quality, it actually does in the end."

"I see."

"Now, just as *netzah* is derived from *hesed*, *hod* is derived from *din*. *Din*, you will recall, means judgment. We are fearful of God because of his *din*. Yet there is another aspect of God that also inspires fear and trembling, yet it is not obviously a moral quality. That's what *hod* is all about. *Hod* means majesty or awesomeness, for lack of a better term. There is something about God that is frightening or awe-inspiring, aside from God's capacity for *din*. Again, this is displayed in many ways in creation. Think of the awesome nature of the sea, or the mountains. Think of the awesome, majestic nature of the heavens, the stars. Think of the awesome, frightening nature of an earthquake or a volcano. This awesome aspect of God is not obviously a moral quality. Is it?"

"No, it's not. One could imagine a very awesome creature without any moral qualities at all."

"Exactly. The Kabbalah designates this awesome quality of God as *hod*. Yet Kabbalah also teaches that this quality of *hod* is really derived from *din*. God's awesomeness is not 'free-floating' awesomeness, so to speak. It may look that way at times, but in the end, God's awesomeness, or *hod*, is really just an offshoot of his attribute of judgment, or *din*."

"Hmm. This is very interesting."

"Glad you find it so. Now I need to explain *yesod*. But first, perhaps we should moisten the palate. Ready for another drink?"

"Sure."

"Here you go, then. *Le-chaim tovim u-le-shalom!*"

"Ah, thanks! But what was that, Chaim? I heard '*le-chaim*' but you added something else there at the end."

"Yes. *Le-chaim tovim* means 'to a good life,' and *le-shalom* means 'to peace, wholeness, completion.'"

"Is there a special time when that's said?"

"Not really. I was just feeling inspired for a little extra blessing, a little extra *brachah*. As you'll learn, there is a connection between the *sefirah* of *yesod* and *shalom*.

You see, *yesod* is a really critical *sefirah*. That's because *yesod* is the culminating *sefirah* that takes all the energies from the other five *sefiros* associated with the *vav* and harmonizes them before they are transmitted to the lower *heh*, the *Shechinah*. It connects the six *sefiros* of the *vav* with the lower *heh*. *Yesod* is the name for the attribute by which God brings all of the other previous *sefiros* into harmonic balance. And that's why it is associated with *shalom* – peace. It is only through the *sefirah* of *yesod* that God finalizes what energy the *Shechinah* will receive."

"Very interesting."

"But there's another function of *yesod*, one that I haven't directly mentioned yet."

"What's that?"

"*Yesod* is the *sefirah* that is associated with reproduction. Let me explain. I've already said that the *ein sof* acts in the world in certain ways, through the *sefiros*. But the *ein sof* also seeks, in some sense, to reproduce itself within the world. I don't mean that literally, of course. God doesn't seek to replicate himself – that's impossible. But God does seek to reproduce himself, or perhaps I should just say – place his stamp, or what's called His *hasimah*, within creation. One of the ways God does this is by creating the human being. Dovid, how do you interpret the meaning of the *pasuk* – the verse – that says, 'God created the human being in His own image?'"

"I think it means that the human being is rational, just like God is rational. That's what Maimonides says in the *Guide to the Perplexed*. Of course, our rationality is very different from God's. Still, there is a similarity."

"That's very nice, but the Kabbalah interprets the *pasuk* differently. The Kabbalah says that the human being, both man and woman together, represent God's qualities or *sefiros*. This includes rationality, but it includes all the other *sefiros* as well. As you remember, the lower *heh* is God's feminine aspect, and the *vav* is His masculine aspect. That's why here the *Shechinah* is sometimes referred to as the daughter, while the six *middos*, particularly *tiferes*, are referred to as the son. As you'll see later, the upper *heh* also has a feminine aspect, and the *yod* has a masculine aspect. That's why the upper *heh* is called Mother, and the *yod* is called Father. But the point right now is that the human being, both male and female together, represent *Hashem*'s attributes."

"I see."

"But there's more. Look at the diagram again. The Kabbalah teaches that all of the ten *sefiros*, taken together, are represented within the human form, both male and female. This is one of the major teachings of Kabbalah. The lower *heh*, or *Shechinah*, corresponds to the legs or the feet. *Hesed* corresponds to the right arm, and *din* corresponds to the left arm. And that's not coincidental. There's a reason why *hesed* is on the right and *din* is on the left. The right side is always the predominant side, and the left side is always the secondary side. God's *hesed* predominates over his *din*. By the way, that's why most people are right-handed and that's why it's a Jewish custom that whenever you have a chance, you're always supposed to start from the right side rather than the left. It's not some silly superstition. It expresses a profound teaching. Anyway, since *hesed* is right and *din* is left, the center represents the harmony or balance of the other two extremes. Like I explained once before, *rahamim* is a balance of *hesed* and *din*. So *rahamim* is represented by the chest or heart, which is at the center of the body, between the right and left arms. *Netzah* and *hod* are represented by the right and left thighs, because each one stems from *hesed* and *din* respectively. *Yesod* corresponds to the sexual organ. And, as I'll explain probably some other time, the upper *heh* and the *yod* stand for God's intelligence, wisdom, and will, and these three correspond to parts of the head. So, the entire structure of the *shem ha-meforash* — God's proper name — is represented or reproduced within the human being."

"In other words, you're saying that there's an isomorphism between the structure of the human being and the structure of God's *sefiros* or qualities."

"Iso . . . what'd you call it?"

"Isomorphism. It means a similarity in form or structure."

"Very nice! I like that word. Yes, that's exactly what I'm trying to say. But there's still another way in which God places his stamp within creation."

"What's that?"

"Are you familiar with the midrash that says that the human being is an *olam katan*? It means that man is a 'small world' or microcosm. In some sense, the human contains within himself the entire universe. Not only is God represented or reproduced specifically within the human being. Rather, the entire cosmos is an expression or representation of God's *sefiros*. For example, the heavens correspond to the *vav*, or masculine *middos*, and the earth corresponds to the *heh*, or the feminine aspect of God."

"Chaim, that's an idea found in many traditions."

"Is that so?"

"Sure. Haven't you heard the idea of 'Mother Earth'? This was very popular with the American Indians, for example. The earth is often viewed as feminine, and the rain coming from the heavens is like the seed that comes from the male and impregnates the female."

"Well . . . that's interesting. I didn't know that. Anyway, the basic idea is that God is represented not only within the human being but within the entire universe as well."

"OK, I think I follow you. Anyway, where were we? What does all this have to do with *yesod*?"

"If all God wanted to do was to act in the world — to be benevolent, just, merciful, and so on — then there would be no need for the *middah* of *yesod*. But God also seeks to reproduce himself within the world, that is, to place His own stamp on the entire creation. So *yesod* is that energy through which God acts in order to reproduce himself within the world."

"I think I get what you're saying. But what does that have to do with what we said before about the need for balance and harmony? Earlier, you said that *yesod* is the harmonizing principle of all the other *middos*. How is that connected with the idea that *yesod* is the reproductive principle?"

"But that's exactly the way a human reproduces. In order to reproduce, you need to bring together all of the various aspects of yourself into one single, unitary whole. Physically, that would correspond to the production of seed. That's why there's a correlation here between *yesod* and the male reproductive organ. The *sefirah* of *malchus* is also sometimes correlated not only with feet, as I said before, but also with the female sexual organ."

"Wow. This is really very interesting, Chaim."

"I'm glad you think so. And you know what? This is a good place to stop. It's late – time to go to bed. Tomorrow we'll continue. You want some tea or something? Help yourself if you do."

"Thanks a lot for having me over, Chaim. I'm learning so much!"

"It's a pleasure to have you. It's nice to have someone I can share these ideas with. The truth is – I don't find too many willing listeners. So let's continue tomorrow."

"Yes, let's do that."

"Good night, Dovid. *Gut Shabbos!*"

"*Good Shabbos,* Chaim!"

18

In the morning, David, Chaim and the children went to shul. After the service, everyone went into a large auditorium for *Kiddush*.

"Come with me," said Chaim. "We'll find something to drink and make a nice *le-chaim*."

Chaim led David through the crowd to a table in the corner.

"Ah, here's something nice. A single-malt scotch! Just what we need."

"Excellent," David said.

Chaim poured a shot of whiskey into a plastic cup. He then rattled off the *Kiddush*, said a blessing over the whiskey, and drank half the cup.

"Here," said Chaim. "You have the rest. And have some crackers. You need to eat something. Otherwise, it doesn't count as *Kiddush*. Have some fish, too."

"Thanks." David took a cracker and a tiny ball of gefilte fish. Chaim started to speak, but the noise in the room was deafening.

"Chaim, it's pretty noisy in here. I can barely hear myself think."

"Let's go outside. I know the perfect place where we can talk. The kids always want to play with their friends for a little while after shul, before we go home. Take your drink and follow me."

They went down a narrow hall, out a door into a courtyard. Suddenly it was pleasant and quiet. They sat down on some wooden benches.

"So? Are you enjoying Shabbos?" said Chaim.

"Yes, I am. But what I really enjoy most is learning from you," said David.

"You've been keeping Shabbos pretty regularly?"

"On and off. I was keeping it for a while. Then I kind of slipped."

"Why? What's the problem? Do you find it hard because of school or something?"

"Actually, I was keeping it more or less for a while, and it just got difficult. Then, after nine-eleven . . . I don't know. It just got even harder."

"Oy! What does that have to do with anything? I thought we went through that already."

"Yeah, we did. Intellectually, I agree a lot with what you said. Still, I find it difficult. When I first started keeping Shabbos, it was new and fresh. Then it sort of lost its glow."

"Dovid, I think that if you truly understand the meaning of Shabbos, you'd never hesitate to keep it!"

"Oh? I think I understand its meaning."

"You think so? OK, tell me. What is the meaning of Shabbos?"

"Well, like you just said in the *Kiddush*, it's a remembrance of God's creation, a remembrance that God rested on the seventh day. It's also a remembrance that we were slaves in Egypt and God took us out so that we would rest and even give our slaves and cattle a rest. And it's a sanctification of time. It creates a space for meditation. Let's see . . . what else am I missing?"

"Actually, Dovid, as far as meditation goes, I personally meditate more on the weekdays than I do on Shabbos."

"Really? That's surprising."

"We must be thinking of meditation differently. It's like this. On Shabbos I feel that I don't need to meditate as much to have a deep connection with *Hashem*. This is related to the fact that the main prayer, the *Amidah*, is so much shorter on Shabbos than it is during the week. During the week, you need to work harder to achieve a level of closeness with *Ha-kadosh baruch hu*. But on Shabbos, it's just all there, naturally."

"That's an interesting idea."

"Also, there's something else about Shabbos that I think you're missing."

"What's that?"

"During the prayers of Shabbos, we ask *Hashem*, "*Ve-taher libenu le-ovdecha be-emes*" – that He should purify our hearts to serve him in truth. This is a tremendous prayer. We never recite it during the week. Why? Because, first of all, on Shabbos you have a *neshama yeserah*, an extra soul. You enter a higher level of spirituality. During the week, when you engage in work, you are also working on yourself, improving your soul. But when you get to Shabbos, you're able to rest and then enjoy the spiritual benefit of what you've accomplished. The Talmud says that Shabbos is "*me-ein olam ha-ba*" – like the World to Come. In the World to Come, you will experience the reward for all the good deeds you did while you were alive.

Similarly, even here in this world, on Shabbos you get a taste of the true spiritual reward for all the good things you did the previous week. And that includes even all the good deeds that you did which required *melachah* or work, which on the Shabbos itself is forbidden. But the catch is that you only get that taste if you keep Shabbos!"

"Interesting."

"Interesting? It's *gevaldik*! I mean, amazing. And there's something else. Shabbos is not just the culmination of the past week. It's also the head, the start of the next week. So on Shabbos, if you pay real close attention, you're able not just to grasp what you accomplished spiritually in the last week, but also to see what you really need to do spiritually in the coming week. Speaking for myself, that's why it's usually on Shabbos that I make decisions about what I'm going to do the coming week. Not just in spiritual things, but also in family things and other stuff. It's not that I dwell on issues that have to do with the work week. It's just that the right decisions sort of come to me. Do you get what I'm saying? If you keep Shabbos, it's such a tremendous opportunity! And by the way, that's why there's a custom for men to go to the *mikveh* on Friday – to prepare ourselves to reach that higher level of *taharah*, of purity, that is found on Shabbos."

"I've heard of men going to the *mikveh* but I've never met anyone who does it. Do you go to the *mikveh* on Fridays, then?"

"Of course. It's more commonly done before the holidays. But some do it before every Shabbos. You should try it some time. Going to the *mikveh* is really important. When you submerge yourself in the water – it's hard to explain, but it's an amazing thing. I can't tell you how many insights and ideas I've had after going into the *mikveh*."

"Well, then, maybe I'll try it some time."

"Really, you should. And I just thought of something else, while we're on the topic. Maybe I could just quickly tell you one more idea before the kids come looking for me. You said before that when you first started keeping Shabbos, it was something new for you, and you were really into it. Yet lately it seems to have lost its glow. It's kind of like a dry spell."

"Yes, that's exactly what it feels like."

"So, let me explain some thing really important. Kabbalah talks about the process of going from *katnus* to *gadlus*. That means growing from spiritual childhood to spiritual adulthood. When that first happens, it's a tremendous thing, and a person feels great. But after a while it sometimes feels old and stale. In Kabbalah, this is called reaching the level of *katnus sheni*, or second childhood. At this point, a new level of growth is required. A person needs to take on a new appreciation or new understanding of what they're doing. They need to take it to a higher level. In other words, from this second childhood a person needs to grow once again into *gadlus sheni*, or second adulthood."

"Interesting. But what's your point with all this?"

"My point is that you have to understand that the dry spell you're experiencing is normal. You shouldn't be frustrated that it's happening. The same thing happens with learning Torah. What I mean is: when you learn, you sometimes reach a point where you think you really know the whole structure, and the rest is just filling in the details. And then, you may get a little bored. But then, if you stick with it, soon you realize there's an entirely new plane that you haven't seen before. That's when you reach *gadlus sheni* in Torah learning. And of course, the cycle repeats itself again and again. You're on that new plane for a while until it's time to grow once again. And actually this whole thing is hinted at in the name of *Hashem*."

"Really? How's that?"

"The lower *heh* and the *vav* represent the transition from *katnus rishon* to *gadlus rishon*. When you meditate, or when you advance spiritually in any way, you start off at the lower *heh* and then you advance up to the *vav*. But soon you reach the point where you realize you need another level of growth. When you have this realization you're now at the upper *heh* – that's *katnus sheni* or second childhood. Although it may seem to you like you've fallen backwards, the truth is that second childhood is really higher than first adulthood. That is, you're at a *heh* again, but you're at a higher *heh*. Then, when you advance to *gadlus sheni* or second adulthood, that's like moving from the upper *heh* to the final *yod*."

"Interesting. Actually, that reminds me of something in Plato's *Republic*. Are you familiar with the famous allegory of the cave?"

"I've heard of Plato. But what's the allegory of the cave?"

"It's Plato's way of describing intellectual growth from knowing the particulars of the physical word to knowing the eternal essences of things. Imagine a man in a cave who is chained facing a wall, seeing shadows of puppets. At some point he realizes that the shadows are only copies of the puppets. At that point he thinks the puppets are real. Later, he gets out of the cave and sees real things. Then he realizes that these are the real things and the puppets were images of real things. So, there's something going on here that's exactly like what you're saying about the two stages of growth. The first maturity is from the shadows to the puppets. And the second maturity is from the puppets to the objects outside the cave."

"Wow. It's pretty interesting that Plato –"

Suddenly the children came running into the courtyard, laughing and screaming gaily at the top of their lungs.

"*Abba*! *Abba*! Pick me up!"

"Sorry, Dovid. I guess we'll have to finish this later."

"No problem, Chaim. No problem at all!"

19

After lunch on Shabbos, Rochel walked the children to her sister's house to play with their cousins. David lay down on his bed in the guest room to read Chaim

Grade's story, *My Quarrel with Hersh Razeyner*. But soon he dozed off and fell asleep. He dreamt he was turning pages in a book, trying to find some obscure passage, but without success. He stirred an hour and a half later, when Chaim knocked on his door. It was time for the traditional third meal or *shalosh seudos*.

Chaim and David helped Rochel set the table. They washed for bread and sat down to a meal of gefilte fish, half-sour pickles, and left over potato kugel. Since the children were out, the house was quiet.

"An opportunity for conversation. Great!" said Chaim.

"Aren't we lucky?" Rochel quipped.

"Very lucky," answered Chaim. "But first, let's sing *Yedid Nefesh*." From the bookcase nearby, he took two booklets with songs and prayers, and passed them to David and Rochel. "You know this one? It's on page fifty four."

Without waiting for an answer, Chaim closed his eyes and started singing. The tune was slow and pensive, almost melancholy. Rochel didn't sing aloud, but David noticed her humming softly. David tried to hum along, but his mind became engaged in puzzling through the translation of the Hebrew words.

Soul's beloved, merciful father	ידיד נפש אב הרחמן
draw your servant toward your will	משוך עבדך אל רצונך
may your servant run like a deer	ירוץ עבדך כמו איל
let him bow toward your majesty	ישתחוה אל מול הדרך
may your caresses be more pleasant to him	יערב לו ידידותיך
than flowing honey or any other taste	מנפת צוף וכל טעם
Beautiful, majestic shining light of the world	הדור נאה זיו העולם
my soul is love-sick for you	נפשי חולת אהבתך
please, O God, please heal her	אנא קל נא רפא נא לה
show her the charm of your shining light	בהראות לה נעם זיוך
then she shall be strengthened and healed	אז תתחזק ותתרפא
and have eternal joy	והיתה לה שמחת עולם
Eminent one, please feel compassion	ותיק יהמו נא רחמיך
have mercy upon your beloved son	וחוסה נא על בן אהובך
how long I have yearned	כי זה כמה נכסף נכספתי
to see your harmony, your strength	לראות מהרה בתפארת עזך
that is my heart's desire	אלה חמדה לבי
so have mercy, do not hide	וחוסה נא ואל תתעלם
Reveal yourself, my beloved, and spread over me	הגלה נא ופרש חביבי עלי
your canopy of peace	את סכת שלומך
let the earth shine with your glory	תאיר ארץ מכבודך
let us celebrate and rejoice in you	נגילה ונשמחה בך
hurry, make love, for the time has come	מהר אהוב כי בא מועד
show me favor as in days of yore	וחננו כימי עולם

When the song was over, Chaim spoke. "You know what that *zemer* is really all about?"

David looked at Rochel, hoping she might answer. But she just smiled and said, "Go ahead. I think he's asking you."

"Well, it's obvious that each stanza starts with one of the letters of the *shem ha-meforash*."

"Excellent," said Chaim. "And what else do you notice?"

"It seems the poem is all about the desire of the *nefesh*, the soul, to love God. And it sounds like the soul is asking God for help in bringing about the fulfillment of this love."

"Yes, it's about that, of course," Chaim answered. "But it's not an accident that each stanza starts with a letter from the *shem*. If you examine the poem closely, you'll find that each stanza contains many allusions to the *sefiros* associated with each letter. For example, look at the last stanza, which corresponds to the lower *heh* or *Shechinah*. Here the soul asks *Hashem* to spread over her the *sukkah* of *shalom*, or 'canopy of peace.' The soul also asks that the *eretz* – the earth – shine with *Hashem's* glory. Don't you remember? We said last night that the *sefirah* of *yesod* is *shalom* – peace, completion, fulfillment – and that *yesod* collects all the divine energies of the higher *sefiros* before transmitting them to the 'earth' – that is, the *Shechinah*."

"I see." David examined the poem again. "It also hints at the idea that the *Shechinah* is the most revealed aspect of God. It's only in this last stanza that the soul finally asks God to *reveal* himself."

"Very good, Dovid! You're starting to think like a *mekubbal*! In fact, you could look at the whole *zemer* as a way of asking *Hashem* to let all the divine energy flow through the *sefiros*, from the highest and most sublime – the *yod* at the top – to the lowest of them all – the *heh*, or the 'earth' that is mentioned in the last stanza."

"Interesting. Now that I look at it, I see that some of the six *sefiros* of the *vav* are hinted at in the third stanza."

"You're absolutely right. There are several hints of that. The third stanza is the only one which mentions compassion or mercy. That's an obvious reference to the *middah* of *rahamim*, which is the central *middah* of the *vav*. And I'm sure you remember that the *vav* symbolizes God's masculine aspect. That's why we mention the 'beloved son' in this stanza. Also, here we mention *tiferes* – beauty or harmony. Like I said once before, *tiferes* is another name for *rahamim* – the balance between *din* and *hesed*. And, finally, in this stanza, the *lev* – the heart – is mentioned. That's because the bodily part associated with *rahamim* is the chest or heart, which is the central branch that holds all the six *sefiros* together."

"OK. But what about the first two stanzas? You haven't taught me much yet about the upper *heh* and the *yod*."

"Right. So let's get into it right now."

"Not too much time, if you want to finish before *minha*!" Rochel interjected with a smile. "Can you really do justice to the *yod* and the *heh* in forty-five minutes?"

"We'll do what we can. Basically, the upper *heh* signifies intelligence or the *sefirah* of *binah*, and the *yod* signifies two *sefiros*: *hochmah*, or wisdom, and *kesser*, which literally means 'crown' but also is known as *ratzon*, or will. Kabbalah teaches that the *yod* itself signifies *hochmah*, but the very tip – that's called the *kotz* of the *yod* – signifies *ratzon* or will."

"Wait a second," David said. "What's the difference between intelligence and wisdom?"

"Let me explain. Obviously, both are powers of *comprehension*. But *hochmah* is higher than *binah*. Basically, *hochmah*, or wisdom, is the actual grasping or knowledge of truth. On the other hand, *binah*, or intelligence, is the ability to analyze or explain the knowledge that one already has, as well as to deduce or derive information from that knowledge. When you learn some totally new truth from someone else or discover some new knowledge on your own, that's called *hochmah*. But when you explain what you know, or when you work out the implications of a given thought – that's *binah*. Have you ever had the experience of gaining some insight that you knew deep down had some truth and validity, but you couldn't quite explain or articulate that insight?"

"Yes, I have."

"Well, that's the difference between *hochmah* and *binah*. When you have a flash of insight, that's *hochmah*. Sometimes it happens that you may not be able to explain the insight or put it into words, or to understand its implications. But when you take that insight and develop it and work out its implications, that's *binah*."

"I get it. Very interesting."

"Now, like I said, wisdom is higher than intelligence. That's why wisdom is represented by the *yod* and intelligence by the *heh*. And, if you remember my chart from last night, that's why *hochmah* is on the right side and *binah* on the left. But let's not underestimate *binah*, which also includes the capacity for analysis or making distinctions. That's why in Hebrew the word *'bein'* is used to mean a difference between two things. It is through *binah* that we distinguish, for example, *bein kodesh le-hol* – that is, between sacred and profane. And *binah* has a wider meaning as well. For example, when you construct a system with parts that are logically related, that's also a use of *binah*. That's why the word *binyan* in Hebrew means building or construction, something made out of parts into one. It is through *binah* that one makes a *binyan*."

"Very nice! I didn't realize the Hebrew language was so rich."

"Of course it is. That's why it's called *lashon ha-kodesh* – the holy tongue. Anyway, getting back to the song *Yedid Nefesh,* here's another point. In Kabbalah, a symbol of *binah* is light, or *ziv*. This is why the term 'shining light,' or *ziv*, is mentioned in the second stanza. That's because the stanza that corresponds to the upper *heh*, or *binah*, is intelligence, which includes logical comprehension. Notice that the word for light is mentioned twice in this stanza, precisely to emphasize this point. And –"

"Wait," said Rochel. "The word 'light' is also used in the last stanza, where it says, "*Tair eretz mi-kevodecha*" – Let the earth shine with your glory. If light is associated with *binah* and belongs in the second stanza, why does it appear in the last stanza?"

"Good question, Rochel," Chaim said. "In the last stanza, the soul asks that the 'light' which stems from a higher source – that is, *binah* – shine upon the *earth* – that is, upon or through the *Shechinah*. The difference is a little clearer in the Hebrew. In the second stanza, the word *ziv* is used, translated here as 'shining light.' But in the last stanza, a different word – *ta'ir* – is used, which is here translated, 'let it shine.' In other words, there are really two forms of light."

"OK," she said. "I guess that's a good answer. Go on."

"Now, let's get back to *hochmah* and *binah*. I've been talking about how these concepts apply to human beings, but now let me explain how they apply to *Hashem*. *Hochmah* is *Hashem*'s power to grasp the truth. Now, regarding *Hashem*, we can't say that *hochmah* is the power to learn new things that he does not already know, since his knowledge is infinite and eternal. Of course, *Hashem* has the ability to grasp or comprehend truth. That's *Hashem*'s *hochmah*. On the other hand, *binah* is God's comprehension of the distinctions between things, and also the relations between things. It is also *Hashem*'s understanding of the implications and consequences of what He knows. For *Hashem*, the two stages always go together. He doesn't grasp a truth and understand its implications or figure out its consequences only later. For *Hashem*, it's all one! *Hashem* never has that experience of having an insight and yet not being able to explain it. When *Hashem* grasps the truth, he fully understands it at exactly the same time. And that's the reason why the Kabbalah teaches that *hochmah* and *binah* are like 'two friends that never separate.'"

"That's an interesting metaphor," David mused.

"Now, finally, we need to talk about *kesser*, or *ratzon*. That's the highest *sefirah* which is signified by the very tip, the *kotz*, of the *yod*. Kabbalah teaches that the *ratzon* or will of God is something that goes beyond *binah* and *hochmah*. Precisely because of that, it's hard even to talk about *ratzon*. But another name for the *sefirah* of *ratzon* is *kesser*, or crown. This hints at God's will or power, just as a crown symbolizes the sovereignty of a king. Since a crown also goes on top of the head, it stands for something that goes beyond the intellect or even wisdom. All these things are hinted at in the first stanza of the song we just sang."

"How's that?" asked David.

"Look at the text again. The *nefesh* asks *Hashem* to draw it toward His *ratzon* or will. It also uses the term *avdecha* – your servant – not once but twice. A genuine servant is obedient to the will of his master whether or not he understands his master's commands. The *nefesh* also asks that it should enjoy the caresses of *Hashem* 'above any *ta'am*.' In our translation, the word *ta'am* means 'taste.' But the word *ta'am* can also mean a reason for something. In effect, the *nefesh* seeks to enjoy the master's 'caresses' in a way that goes above and beyond reason. This is clearly a reference to the *sefirah* of *ratzon* or *kesser*, the divine will that goes beyond *hochmah* and *binah* – that is, beyond all forms of comprehension."

"This is all very interesting." said David. "But do you really think the person who wrote this song had these things in mind?"

"Of course. No question about it."

"Hold on a second, Chaim," Rochel said with a frown. "You said the first stanza in the poem stands for *hochmah* and *kesser*. And you explained the hints to *kesser* in that stanza. But where do you find an allusion in the first stanza to *hochmah*?"

"That's easy, Rochel! It's right in the opening words, '*Av ha-rahaman*,' which means 'merciful father.' In Kabbalah, 'father' is a code word for *hochmah*."

"Ah, right," she conceded. "I should have remembered that."

"Let me just explain this point better for David. Remember, we said a while ago that the lower *heh* has a feminine aspect while the *vav* is masculine. In the same way, the *mekubbalim* say that the upper *heh*, or *binah*, is considered the 'mother,' and the *yod* – that is, *hochmah* – is considered the 'father.' They are called 'mother' and 'father' because the seven lower *middos* are derived from them. Like a father, *hochmah* provides the germ or seed of insight. Like a mother, *binah* takes that seed and constructs or bears the 'children' – the son and the daughter, which are the *vav* and lower *heh*."

"OK, I think I get it. To put it all together, you're saying that the *sefirah* of *Shechinah*, which is symbolized by the lower *heh*, and the character traits or six *sefiros* which are symbolized by the *vav*, are all governed or directed by the rational part of God – his intelligence and wisdom, which are themselves symbolized by the upper *heh* and the *yod*."

"Well said, David! You just have to add that, ultimately, *kesser*, or will, is the highest *sefirah*. It is the source of wisdom and intelligence. That final *sefirah* is symbolized by the *kotz* or tip of the *yod*."

"Whew! This is a lot to take in, but I'm following, I think!"

"Great. Now, going back to the first stanza of *Yedid Nefesh*, we see mention of the term *av*, or 'father,' in the very first stanza. Actually, it is possible to read the phrase '*av ha-rahaman*' not as 'merciful father' but rather as 'father of the merciful.' This alludes to the fact that the *middah* of *hochmah* is the 'father' or source of the *middah* of *rahamim*. The feminine aspect of *binah* is clearly hinted at in the second stanza as well, by the repeated use of the feminine term '*lah*,' which means 'for her.' This contrasts with the term '*lo*,' which means 'for him,' used in the first stanza. Unless you interpret these allusions by way of Kabbalah, it is very difficult to explain why the author of this song would switch suddenly from the masculine to feminine."

"Possibly," Rochel said. "I'm still not sure there's such a convenient match between Kabbalah and this poem. Here's another question I have. If what you're saying is correct, why is the reference to *sukkas shalom* – that's the canopy of peace – made in the very last stanza, which corresponds to the *heh*? Isn't the *sukkas shalom* an allusion to *yesod*, which is one of the six *sefiros* of the *vav*? If that's the case, then shouldn't the reference to the *sukkas shalom* be in the third stanza rather than the last one?"

"Rochel, good question! I have an answer. The *sefirah* of *yesod* is the very last of the six *middos*, the one that is supposed to unify or bond with the *heh*. Now, the point of the whole song is to unite the *middos*, to bring them together. That's the idea of *'yihud shem'* – the unification of the divine name. Therefore, the *mekubbal* who wrote this *zemer* placed the allusion to *yesod* in the last stanza in order to unify the Name."

"I don't know, Chaim. That seems like a stretch to me."

"Do you see that, Dovid? Unbelievable! She's still skeptical after all these years!"

"And now it really is getting late," said Rochel, rising from her seat. "You'd better *bentsch* and go to *shul* if you want to be on time for *minha*!"

"You're right," said Chaim.

"Finally, you admit I'm right about something!"

Quickly, they recited *birkat ha-mazon*. Chaim and David got up to leave.

"Thanks for the meal, once again. Can I help clear up?" David asked.

"No, thanks, guys. Go ahead. You'll be late. Just go! *Gut Shabbos!*"

20

"Well, David? Do you like this place more than the last one?"

"To be honest, Ravi, I really liked the food at the other place better! But this is better for me since it's vegetarian."

"I see. So explain this thing again to me one more time. You said you're *not* becoming a vegetarian, right?"

"No, I'm just trying to keep kosher. Basically, anything vegetarian has got to be kosher, so I'm OK eating here."

"Well, I'm a vegetarian too. But I don't mind eating at the other place where we used to eat all the time. They have a lot of meat, but they also have vegetarian dishes, you know."

"Yes, but since they also have meat there, it's hard to know that those vegetarian dishes are really vegetarian!"

"I guess I'm not as meticulous about it as you. But couldn't you say the same about this place? I mean, how do you know it's purely vegetarian unless you check all the ingredients?"

"Ravi, I've got to draw the line somewhere. Many Jews who keep kosher eat only in certified kosher restaurants. But this is going far enough for me."

"OK, that makes sense, I guess. Well, anyway, what about meditation? Are you still doing that?"

"Yes, actually, I'm starting to get into Jewish meditation."

"That's great. I don't know anything about Jewish meditation. What do you do when you meditate? Are there breathing exercises? Do you use mandalas of any sort?"

"Most of it involves focusing on God's attributes, which correspond to certain human attributes, and also to certain letters, words, and divine names. So I guess you could say there are mandalas."

"Sounds interesting. Are you doing this meditation regularly?"

"I do it once or twice a day, or sometimes once a week. It depends how I feel."

"Ah, I see. Well, any serious meditative form of life involves discipline. Actually, that reminds me – there was something else I was curious about. I heard you were selling marijuana in the dorm. Is that true?"

"No, not really. It's just that I have a little extra to get rid of."

"I see. Well, you should be careful about that."

"It's not a big deal, really."

"Anyhow, you're still smoking the stuff."

"Of course. I really think it enhances and advances my spiritual life. I mean, when I use it, everything's intensified, and it's just so much more obvious how everything is all interconnected. I see things so much more deeply than I would otherwise."

"Don't you think it's odd that you need some kind of drug to – as you know, I hate using this phrase – 'advance' spiritually, as you put it?"

"Ravi! I'm sure you know that intoxicants are used in many religious rituals. And in some cases, some spiritual people use mind-altering substances like marijuana or peyote. That's precisely because it has an effect on the consciousness."

"Well, it's not found in all religions. Look, I really think those things – drugs, alcohol, and, for that matter, cigarettes and caffeine – are crutches. No yogi would touch any of them."

"I'm not a yogi. I'm a Jew."

"Good point. But I suspect you'd be better off without them. If you're really serious about the spiritual quest, at some point you've got to give up these artificial aids."

"Hmm. Maybe you're right. But right now, I guess I like the extra kick it gives my spiritual life . . . ."

21

"Hey, Esther! How about we go out to a movie for a change?"

"Sorry, I can't go to the movies just now."

"Why not?"

"It's *sefirah*. Do you know about that?"

"*Sefirah*? Isn't that the Kabbalistic concept of divine energy? I learned about all that from –"

"No, that's not what I mean. Maybe there's some connection, but that's not what I'm talking about."

"What *are* you talking about, then?"

"I'm talking about the time period we're in now – the period between the holidays of *Pesach* and *Shavuot*. The word *sefirah* means 'numbering' or 'counting.' Actually, it's called *sefirat ha-omer*, the counting of the *omer*. It's in the *Siddur*, the prayer book, at the end of the evening service."

"Oh, right. Now that you mention it, I remember seeing it in the *Siddur*. It started on the second night of Passover."

"Right. We're supposed to count the days and the weeks from the second day of *Pesach* until the forty-ninth day. Seven times seven, that is. The fiftieth day is the festival of *Shavuot*, which means 'weeks.' That's why it's called the Festival of Weeks. Actually, that reminds me – your birthday's coming up on *Shavuot*. School will be over by then, and I'm going to be in Israel. So unfortunately, I won't be able to be with you!"

"Israel? Wow. How long are you going for?"

"Just a few weeks. I'm going for a wedding."

"Wow. Have a great time. And take care of yourself."

"Thanks. Don't worry about it. And that also reminds me – you know . . . last year, I never got you the present . . . ."

"That's OK. Don't worry about it. But we're getting off track. Tell me, what does *sefirah* have to do with not going to the movies?"

"OK. It so happens that this is kind of a sad time because many Jews were killed during this time of year. Did you ever hear of Rabbi Akiva, one of the great sages of the Mishnah? Twenty-four thousand of his students died in a plague at this time of year."

"That's a lot of students!"

"There were other massacres of Jews committed this time of year in later eras. So there's a custom of not having weddings, not listening to music, and not gathering for parties or doing fun things together, like going to movies during *sefirat ha-omer*."

"OK. Sorry, but what's the *omer*?"

"It all comes straight out of *Vayikra*. On the second day of *Pesach*, there was a special offering brought in the *Beit ha-Mikdash* – that's the Temple – from the new crop of barley. This offering is sometimes called the *omer*, which is the name of a certain dry-measure that was used for raw produce like barley. In the land of Israel, the first grain crop is barley, and it comes in the early spring, around the time of *Pesach*. The Torah commands us to count forty-nine days after the *omer* is brought, until we reach the fiftieth day when we celebrate *Shavuot,* which involves another offering – this time for the new crop of wheat. Only, instead of bringing raw grain, this time the offering involved the *shtei ha-lechem* – two loaves of bread, made from the new wheat crop."

"I see. So *Shavuot* is basically a harvest festival. Yes – now I remember that

Dr. Maimon talked about this a little bit in my class last year. Maimonides has a discussion of the harvest festivals in the *Guide of the Perplexed*."

"Hang on. I'm not quite finished yet. It's not just a harvest festival. The Talmud teaches that *Shavuot* is also the time we celebrate *matan Torah*, the giving of the Torah. The Jews came out of Egypt on the first day of *Pesach* and received the Torah at Sinai seven weeks later. In fact, there's a *minhag* – a custom – to stay up all night to learn on *Shavuot*."

"Really? Do you do that?"

"No. It's mostly men who do this."

"Oh. Well, do you know anybody who does this?"

"Lots of guys do it. I'm sure your cousin Chaim does."

"I guess it's the original all-nighter!"

"Actually, I think there's a *midrash* which says the idea of staying up all night is to make up for lack of interest the people of Israel expressed the first time around. The story is that the Jews woke up late on the day of *matan Torah*. God was not impressed."

"I can only imagine!"

"Seriously, the point is that by staying up all night to learn, we show our eagerness to receive the Torah. It's written somewhere that a person who stays up to learn on *Shavuot* night has the chance to see the divine presence."

"Wow. Maybe I should consider doing it, then."

"Absolutely!"

"Well, look. There's still something I don't understand. What's the point of counting the days between *Pesach* and *Shavuot*? I mean, do you literally count the days?"

"Yes, of course. Every night during the *sefirah* we make a blessing to thank *Hashem* for giving us this *mitzvah*, and then we count the day as well as keep track of the weeks. Even I do that."

"Why do we need to do all that?"

"The Torah doesn't say why. It just says that's what we should do. But I can tell you something I remember learning about this."

"Yes, please do."

"On *Pesach* we were released from physical bondage, but we were still subject to spiritual bondage. On *Shavuot* we received the Torah, which allows us to achieve spiritual freedom. The Maharal – that's Rabbi Judah Lowe of Prague – adds something else. He points out that the barley offering comes during *Pesach*, while on *Shavuot* we bring the offering of loaves of wheat bread. The Maharal says that barley is typically an animal food. But bread, especially when made from wheat, is considered the essential human food. In fact, bread is a sign of human civilization. Now, animals can be physically enslaved, and they can also have physical freedom. That's why the barley offering is connected with *Pesach*. But only humans can be spiritually enslaved, and only humans can have spiritual freedom, which is achieved through Torah. So, that's why the bread offering from the new wheat is brought on *Shavuot*. So the effect of counting day by day is to link *Pesach* and *Shavuot* together. It reminds us that the whole purpose of *yetziat mitzrayim* – the exodus from Egypt – was ultimately to give us the Torah."

"Very interesting! But does Torah make you free? It seems like Torah is a system of rules and regulations. How can all that obedience make you free?"

"Sure, there are lots of obligations and rules, but by studying and keeping the Torah, we free ourselves from the physical world and live a spiritual life."

"OK. Can I go back to something you said before?"

"What is it?"

"Didn't you say at first that there is some connection between the counting of the *omer* and the Kabbalistic idea of the *sefiros*?"

"Yes, I did say that. I don't know too much about it, but I can tell you the little that I know. When the Jews were slaves in Egypt, they were deep in idol worship and in *tumah,* or impurity. There are forty nine 'gates' of *tumah* that the Jews had to pass through before they could receive the Torah. So from the second day of *Pesach* till the day they received the Torah – each day they went up one level of *taharah*, or purity. We repeat this cycle every year by counting the *sefirah*."

"I see. So there's a spiritual progression or growth that goes through stages. That makes sense. But why specifically forty-nine?"

"That's where Kabbalah comes in with an explanation. I know this only because this is reprinted in the *Siddur*. Like I said, it's at the end of *ma'ariv*, the evening prayer. There are seven *sefiros* that correspond to the seven weeks. I can't remember all of them, but –"

"I know them: *hesed, gevurah, tiferes, netzah, hod, yesod* and *malchus*."

"Very good, David! Your cousin's doing a good job. So, he must have also told you that each of these seven *sefiros* has seven *sefiros* within itself. For example, within *hesed*, there are the seven *sefiros*; within *gevurah*, there are seven *sefiros*, and so on."

"No, he never told me that. That sounds very strange. Are you sure?"

"Of course I'm sure. Just don't ask me to explain it. I'm just telling you what I know. Each of the seven weeks between the first day of *Pesach* and *Shavuot* represents one of the seven *sefiros*, and, each day of each week represents one of the seven *sefiros* within each *sefirah*. That's how we get seven times seven, or forty-nine stages of impurity."

"I haven't heard this twist before. I wonder what it means to say that each *sefirah* contains the other *sefiros*. But just a second. Do you know there are actually ten *sefiros*, not seven?"

"Yes."

"So shouldn't there really be ten weeks for ten *sefiros*?"

"David, I told you – I really don't know anything about Kabbalah."

"But didn't you say all this stuff is in the prayer book? Don't most religious Jews have to know what all this means?"

"No, of course not. Very few people really understand all this stuff. They know about the seven *sefiros*, and about the *sefiros* within *sefiros*, but they don't really know what it all means."

"I find that so bizarre. It's got to be important if it's in the prayer book."

"What can I tell you? I really don't know much about it. If you want to find out more about it, you'll just have to ask your cousin."

"Yes, I guess I will."

"Meanwhile, even though we're not going out to the movies, you can still take me out for dinner!"

22

May 12, 2002 BS"D

Dear David,

Hi! I'm here in Israel and already I miss you. You probably thought I forgot about your birthday, but I didn't! You told me you were staying with Simon for a few weeks after school before you go over to Chaim's house for Shavuot. So I sent this package to Simon's house (I called him and he was kind enough to give me the address). I have to confess I actually didn't buy you new ones because I couldn't afford that. But I managed to get them second-hand from my cousin who's a sofer – which, as you probably know, means a scribe. I told him about you and he gave me a great deal. They are gently used, but they are in very good condition. By now, you can guess what they are! I hope you like them!

Have a great birthday and a great Shavuot!

Yours truly,

Esther

23

In the late afternoon on the eve of *Shavuos*, David reached Chaim's house. Chaim took David to the *mikveh*. It was David's first time. The water was very warm, almost hot. When he submerged himself under the surface, he felt like a fetus inside his mother's womb. When he shared this with Chaim, the latter smiled and said, "Very interesting. You should keep track of these things. Next time you go in the *mikveh*, who knows what'll occur to you?"

In the evening, they went to *shul* and then came back home for a light dinner.

Afterwards, Chaim and David went to the yeshiva together with Chaim's eldest son, Moishe. Chaim had assured David there would be many different classes on various topics all night long at the yeshiva. While Chaim went off to the study hall to learn with his son, David went to a class entitled "The Meaning of the Three Festivals." When the class was over, it was already eleven o'clock. David came out to the lobby of the yeshiva, where coffee, cheesecake, and soda were set out on long tables. Men and boys of all ages were lounging about, chatting, drinking, and eating, doing almost anything but learning.

Moments later, Chaim came out of the study hall with Moishe, who insisted that he wasn't tired at all. But Chaim told David he was going to take Moishe home to bed, and then come back himself and study more. While Chaim was gone, David went to another class entitled "What Makes a Marriage Jewish?" When the class was over, David came out to the lobby. It was already one-thirty in the morning. The class wasn't bad, but David felt himself beginning to fade. He poured himself some soda. Just then, Chaim reappeared, seeming as energetic as ever.

"Dovid! *Gut yom tov*! *Nu*, how's it going?"

"Not bad. I'm a little tired, though."

"Already? The night's just getting started. Let's look at the program. Ah, here's something you might be interested in. There's a class coming up at two o'clock called 'The Jewish Concept of Moshiach' – that's the Messiah."

"Yes, I know. I'd like to learn more about that. I'll go to the class. But what should we do for the next twenty minutes?"

"How about we learn something together till the next class? Come, follow me."

"Sounds good. Can I take my soda?"

"Yeah, sure. Take your soda, and take the bottle with you."

Chaim led David out of the lobby, down a hallway, through a door, down another hallway and down three flights of steps."

"Chaim, where are we going?"

"You'll see. I call it my *mikdash me'at*, my private sanctuary. It's a little room with a nice little library that's really quiet. Just come with me."

Chaim led David to a door and unlocked it. Inside was a small room with a table and two chairs, and two bookshelves lined to bursting with books. A bright fluorescent light illuminated the room. Not a sound could be heard from the lobby or study hall above.

"So this is your private sanctuary? Nice, very nice."

"Thanks. I finagled it from one of the Roshei Yeshiva. I come here when I need to get away. Please, have a seat."

David sat down while Chaim scanned the bookshelves, evidently looking for something specific.

"Let's see. How about learning a piece from *Mesillas Yesharim*? I think there are two copies here. Ah, here we are! In English, it's called *Path of the Just*. It's by the great *Mekubbal*, Rabbi Moshe Chaim Luzatto, known also as the Ramchal. Do you know this *sefer*?"

"Sorry, Chaim. I'm not familiar with it."

"That's OK, I excuse you! Seriously, you should study it. By the way, a lot of people don't know this, but originally, this *sefer* was written in the form of a dialogue."

"Interesting! That's like Plato's works. Actually, a lot of stuff in philosophy of religion was written in dialogue form."

"Plato wrote in dialogue form, too? I didn't know that."

"You mean you haven't read Plato?"

"No, sorry."

"That's OK, Chaim. I excuse you!"

"Touché!"

"Anyway, Chaim, tell me more about the book – the *sefer*."

"*Mesillas Yesharim* is real strong stuff. It was, and still is, a real important book for me."

"What do you mean by that?"

"This book is really a classic – in fact, *the* classic work – in *mussar*. You know the word *mussar* means 'teaching' or 'discipline,' but it's also related to the word *yissurim*, which means 'pains' or 'afflictions.' The book is organized into a series of nine stages, or levels, in which a person goes higher and higher in his service to *Hashem*."

"It sounds like you're talking about stages of spiritual growth."

"Yes, that's correct."

"Why is it such an important book for you?"

"We'll talk about that some other time. How about we study the *hakdamah*, the introduction to the book itself?"

"First I'd like to hear an answer to my question."

"I can't go into that now. It would take too long. Your class is going to start in fifteen minutes."

"Chaim, how about if I skip the class and instead we stay here for a while and you give me the answer? Tell me, why is the book so important for you?"

"OK, OK! Dovid, you win! I'll try to explain. You didn't know me when I was younger. I wasn't always as into being Jewish as I am now. I mean, I was always religious, Orthodox, of course. I suppose that, as a little kid I was very devout, you know, in the way that only little kids can really have that pure belief in *Hashem* and be afraid of Him. But by the time I became a teenager, for the most part I did it all by rote. I didn't do it because I really wanted to do it. I just did it because it was the thing to do. It was what my family did. It's not that I disliked it or anything like that. I was happy the way I was, at least as far as I could tell. I didn't have doubts, *has ve-shalom,* or anything like that."

"Heaven forbid that you should have doubts!"

"What can I say? I just didn't have doubts. Do you find that so shocking?"

"No, not really. I've met a few other people like that. Sorry to interrupt. Go on."

"Then, one day in high school, one of my *rebbeim* – my rabbis – told us that we were going to spend a half an hour each day studying *Mesillas Yesharim*. That was the first time I was exposed to the book. Right off the bat, I felt a closeness with the author. After all, his middle name was Chaim. And once I started reading, I started to realize what being a religious, pious Jew really meant. I'd always thought I was *frum*. I thought my family was *frum*. I thought we were all *frum* Jews. But when I started to read *Mesillas Yesharim*, that's when I started to realize what it means to be really *frum*. The Ramchal really lays it all out for you, all the stages you need to go through, all the character traits you need to develop, how you need to work on yourself, not just your actions, but also your words, your thoughts. This opened up a whole new world for me – the world of *mussar* – and, through that, ultimately, the world of *Hassidus* and Kabbalah. Dovid, to really serve *Hashem* with *ahavah* and *yirah* – with love and awe – and to come close to *Hashem* – *oy!* – it's an amazing, awesome thing! And Ramchal had such an amazing mind, such an ability to conceptualize and systematize. He put everything into perspective, into a structure so you could see the whole plan from beginning to end. Dovid, to really understand what I'm saying you have to study the book – and even then, not just to study it, but to live it. So, from the time I started studying *Mesillas Yesharim*, I decided that I would take Torah seriously. Since then, I've never been the same."

David and Chaim sat in silence for a while. Finally, David spoke.

"Chaim, that's really amazing. It's interesting how one book can make such an impact. And it certainly makes me interested in reading the book. But, I wonder – you said he discusses nine stages in the book, right? I'm just curious: where do you place yourself now? I mean, at what stage are you right now?"

"Well, I'd have to say that in certain ways, I'm still at the first two stages."

"What? I don't see how that could be. You're so devout. What faults could you possibly have?"

"Well, I do have my faults, you know! I'm working on them. I've tried to come up with ways of dealing with them. But of course I have faults."

"As an Orthodox Jew?"

"Of course. You know, I think I'll have a little of that soda."

"Sure, have some. But I wonder – what faults those might be?"

After a few sips, Chaim looked David right in the eyes and spoke.

"Look, Dovid, I'll make you a deal. The truth is that ever since we've met, you really haven't told me much about yourself. You're a great listener to everything I have to say about Kabbalah, and you ask good questions too. But I really don't know what's going on with you inside. So I'll make you a deal. I'll open up to you if you open up to me. And I'll tell you what I think my faults are, if you'll tell me what you think your faults are. What do you say, Dovid? Is that fair?"

"Yes. That's fair."

"And I'll also tell you how I'm trying to deal with my faults. And let's also promise that we'll keep it all in confidence, and that we'll make a pact to help each other try to overcome our faults. Actually, they say that the Ramchal used to do that with his companions. He and some of his fellows would agree to be like spiritual partners, so to speak. They would admonish each other and give each other advice. *Nu*, what do you say?"

"That's quite a proposition. But I'm not sure I *have* any faults to speak of!"

"Very funny, Dovid!"

"Seriously, Chaim. I'm sure I'll think of something!"

"So you agree! Very good. OK. Why don't you go first?"

"What? Why should I go first, Chaim? This was your idea, wasn't it?"

"OK, Dovid, here's a compromise. Why don't you tell me three things about yourself that you haven't already told me? They don't have to be faults, just three important things about yourself that I don't already know. Then I'll tell you about myself. I mean, I'll tell you about my faults. After that, it will be your turn to tell me your faults."

"OK. That sounds fair."

"Great. So, tell me three things about yourself that I don't already know."

"All right. First of all, I don't think you know that *Shavuos* is my Jewish birthday."

"Really? Fantastic! Mazal Tov, Dovid! That's such a *zechus* – a merit – to be born on *Shavuos!*

"Thanks."

"You know that reminds me of something I've been meaning to tell you. The original Reb Dovid that you're named after – in other words, your great-grandfather . . . ."

"Yes? What about him?"

"He was *niftar* – he passed away – around the time of *Shavuos*. Actually, we don't know exactly when he died. But we know that the Nazis deported the whole family to the death camps in the spring of 1944. So we consider his *yahrzeit* – that's the anniversary of a death – to be on *Shavuos*."

"I didn't know that. So I guess it's kind of a coincidence that I'm named David, isn't it?"

"I don't think so. In fact, that might be why they named you Dovid, since you were born on the anniversary of his death."

"I see. I guess that's possible."

"OK, so you've told me one thing about yourself. So, *nu*, what's the second thing?"

"I don't think I've told you that I happen to have a Jewish girlfriend."

"Oh, that's nice. I'm glad to hear that. Is she religious?"

"Very. FFB. I think you'd approve."

"Dovid, I hope you're not doing anything inappropriate."

"*Has ve-shalom!*"

"Ah! Well said! I'm glad to hear that. But really, the whole idea of girlfriends is foreign to me. In my circles, when you're ready to get married, you go out on pre-arranged dates to find the right one. But at least she's Jewish. So, OK . . . what's the third thing?"

"I'll tell you what she got me for my birthday, which came to me in the mail earlier today."

"What's that?"

"Tefillin."

"*What*?"

"You heard me. She got me a pair from her cousin and sent them to me."

"Wow! That's amazing . . . . I've never heard of such a thing. She sounds like she's a really special person, and she must really like you a lot!"

"Yes. I think so."

"So are you going to start wearing the tefillin?"

"I'm going to give it a try."

"Great! That's fantastic!"

"OK, Chaim. I did my three things. Now it's your turn."

"Well, all right. This isn't easy to do. The problem is that there's a paradox here, because it's hard to do this without sounding a bit vain. I guess I can't talk about my faults without actually committing one of them."

"Ah! So I deduce that vanity is one of your problems."

"Exactly. Actually, I see myself as having two major flaws. The first is *ga'avah*, and the second is *anochius*."

"Translation, please?"

"*Ga'avah* is vanity, arrogance or haughtiness. I have to confess that I consider myself special, unique."

"Well, you *are* special. So what?"

"Yeah, but I consider myself *really* special. I mean, for one thing, I consider myself to be a really good keyboard player."

"Well, so you *are* a really good keyboard player. What can you do about that? Start playing poorly?"

"No, but what I mean is, I let it go to my head."

"What's that supposed to mean?"

"Well, sometimes I play just to play music, to bring *simcha* – you know, joy – to people. Oh by the way, this reminds me, I have a wedding to play at in a few weeks. Your year of mourning is over, and now that *sefirah* is over, there are a lot of weddings. I'd really like you to come so that you can see a real Jewish wedding with Jewish dancing. Do you remember our conversation about dancing?"

"Yes, I do."

"Good. I hope you'll be able to come."

"I'll plan on it."

"Anyway, what was I saying? Sorry I got sidetracked. Oh, yes – the problem is that sometimes I find myself playing to impress people. I'm playing so that people will say, 'Wow, what a great keyboard player that guy is.' That's *ga'avah*, vanity or pride. And there's something else."

"Yeah? What is it?"

"Well, I haven't told anybody this – not even Rochel, my wife."

"Uh oh. What is it? You're having an affair?"

"Dovid, please! This is serious!"

"Well, what is it?"

"Will you promise not to tell a soul?"

"Yes."

"OK. Actually, I'm writing a *sefer*, a book. That's really why I have this secret room. I do my writing here."

"Chaim, that's great! What's the book about? And, what's so terrible about writing a book? I don't get it!"

"Well, the book is kind of like a guide toward spiritual growth. Actually, this is one thing I had in mind earlier when I said that *Mesillas Yesharim* had such an influence on me. I didn't really want to get into it, but . . . somehow it came out. *Mesillas Yesharim* is one of the models for my book. And my book is also written in the form of a dialogue between the *sechel* – that's the intellect, and the *nefesh* – that's the soul – or, to be more precise, the lower part of the soul, the part that deals with actions and emotions. That's a technique Ramchal uses in several of his works, aside from the original format of *Mesillas Yesharim*. I think he got it from Bachya, who used the dialogue form in his much earlier classic work, *Hovos ha-levavos*."

"Very nice. I like the idea of a work in the form of a dialogue. But wait a second – are you referring to *Duties of the Heart*?"

"Yes, exactly."

"But that's not in dialogue form. I've looked at that book myself."

"You didn't look closely enough, I guess. True, most of the book is not a dialogue. But look at *Sha'ar ha-avodah*. Chapter 5 shifts into dialogue form with a conversation between the *sechel* and the *nefesh*."

"Ah, that's interesting! I didn't get that far into it. You know, I used to think that it was better to write discourses or tracts, just stating directly what you believe – like Maimonides's *Guide of the Perplexed*, which is definitely not a dialogue. But over time, I've come to think that dialogues are better. There's much more room for various levels of meaning."

"Actually, what you just said about the Rambam's *Guide* is not entirely true, either."

"What do you mean?"

"Don't you remember the preface to the *Guide*? The Rambam dedicates his book to his student, Joseph, with whom he had many conversations before he wrote the book. In fact, the Rambam sent him some of the chapters while he was in the middle of writing it, and I wouldn't be surprised if Joseph wrote back while the Rambam was still sending him more chapters. So actually, there was something of a dialogue there."

"Hmm. That's very interesting. I'd never thought of that. Still, the *Guide* itself is not written in dialogue form."

"True."

"Anyhow, getting back to your own book – it's on spiritual growth? I can't say I'm surprised. I'd love to hear more about the book. But I still don't get why you're not telling anyone you're writing this book. What's the big secret? What does this have to do with vanity?"

"Oy! You really don't understand, Dovid. Look – I'm kind of young to be writing a book like this. I mean, spiritual growth – that's a deep, serious topic, the kind of thing only a great *talmid hacham* should write about."

"Wait a second – how old was Ramchal when he wrote his book?"

"Very young. He died in his thirties. But you obviously don't understand! The Ramchal was a *tzaddik*, a *gaon*, a *mekubbal*. He had visions and visitations from angels!"

"Is that so?"

"Yes, it is. So I can't even begin to compare myself to him."

"So, are you saying that you shouldn't be writing the book after all?"

"Well, no, because I think I have something to say. And I'm convinced that if a person thinks he has a *hiddush* to make, then he has a *mitzvah*, an obligation, to write it down."

"A *hiddush*? What's *that*?"

"A new idea, something novel in the world of Torah. You know, something no one has ever thought of before."

"I see. So, you feel you have something to say. What's the problem then?"

"The *ga'avah* problem is that I feel special because I'm writing this book. The feeling is not there all the time, of course. Sometimes I'm just working on the book, without thinking about the fact that I'm writing it, if you know what I mean. But sooner or later, that feeling creeps in. And the paradox is that here I am, writing a book on spiritual growth, when the very writing of the book itself has me tied up in a character flaw!"

"I see the irony there. But Chaim, I think you're being a little hard on yourself."

"No, I don't think so."

"Well, anyway, what's the other flaw? What'd you call it?"

"*Anochius*. That means being egoistic, self-centered."

"OK. How is that different from vanity?"

"*Ga'avah*, or vanity, is thinking you're really special or great when you aren't. *Anochius* is putting yourself before others. Theoretically, you could have someone who isn't vain at all but who thinks only about himself. I mean, such a person would know that he's really nothing special, but still, he acts only for his own sake. On the other hand, you could also have someone who thinks a lot about others and even makes sacrifices for others, but nevertheless thinks very highly of himself. Do you see?"

"I think I do. So what makes you think you're self-centered?"

"I'm so concerned about my own *neshamah*, my own soul, my own spiritual growth, that sometimes I tend to neglect others around me. Again, it's not like I'm totally selfish. I care about my wife, my family, my friends. I'm not obnoxious or anything like that, *has ve-shalom*. I take care of my kids when I have to. But half the time I do those things as a chore when I should really be doing them with *simha*, with joy – with *hislahavus* or excitement. You'd think that someone who grows spiritually would be less and less selfish and more and more selfless as he advances. We're supposed to have in mind the welfare of *klal Yisrael* at all times, you know, not only our own welfare but the welfare of all Israel. But sometimes I wonder about myself. It seems like the more I grow spiritually, the more sensitive I become to other people's flaws and failings! And take this room for example. As I told you, I call it my *mikdash me'at*, my private sanctuary. Here, I'll tell you something I haven't spoken to anyone about in years."

"What's that?"

"When I was a little kid, like four years old, I made a small model of the *mishkan* – that's the tabernacle that the Jews had in the desert – complete with a *mizbeah* – that's an altar. I kept the *mishkan* in my closet. No one else knew about it, except one of my older sisters. Sometimes I would cut little pieces of paper shaped like animals. Then I'd go into the closet and offer them as sacrifices on the *mizbeah*. Once I even took some *besamim* – that's aromatic spices – from the *havdalah* set – you know what *havdalah* is, right? Anyway, I took the *besamim*, went into the closet, and made believe I was offering incense in the *kodesh kodashim*, the Holy of Holies . . . ."

"Well, that's very interesting. But seriously, Chaim, what's so terrible about all that? It only shows how devout you were, even as a child."

"Maybe so, but my point is that in a way, I haven't changed. I still think mostly about myself. I still come to my private sanctuary in order to get away, in order to meditate and work on my soul. I have to confess – you know what one of my favorite sayings in the Talmud is? It says that if anyone murders a human being, it's as if he killed the entire world. Why? Because the whole world is worth having been created just for one person."

"Wow. That is an amazing statement."

"And it means that *my own individual life* is incredibly worthwhile! Of course, the same statement also means that *your* life is incredibly worthwhile too . . . but somehow I can't quite internalize it in the same way that I can for myself."

"Chaim, really, you're being too hard on yourself. Actually, you know, that's one thing I like about you."

"Oh? What's that?"

"You're really serious about working on yourself, and that's maybe why events that happen around you or outside of you don't seem to shake you. Like nine-eleven, for example. You know, I gotta say – the first time I met you and we had that conversation about nine-eleven, it was actually a little scary for me to see how unfazed you were by the whole thing. But after I thought about it, I began to see your point of view. Well, anyway, you said you were – how'd you put it? – working on yourself, trying to improve. So what exactly are you doing to improve?"

"Well, about the *ga'avah* thing regarding my playing the keyboard, I think I found a *tahbulah* – that's a trick, a technique – to deal with the problem."

"Really? What is it?"

"You're going to think I'm a little crazy. But my trick is actually based on a story I once read. Can I tell you the story?"

"Of course."

"One day some years ago, I was browsing through some of the tales about the Hassidic masters in Europe. I came across a story about a certain Reb Yehoshua, who lived in the town of Shtok. He happened to be a great *ba'al koreh* – a Torah reader. Well, Reb Yehoshua read the Torah beautifully every Shabbos, without any mistakes at all. His tune was perfect, and he never missed the slightest vocalization or punctuation. He had a remarkable memory and a great voice.

"But one Friday afternoon in the weeks leading up to Rosh ha-Shannah, he went to the *mikveh* as usual, and the minute he submerged in the water, the thought flashed through his mind that he had become a *ba'al ga'avah* – that he had become prideful because of his reputation. Of course, he was very disturbed. Friday night, as he went to bed, he contemplated the fact that the next morning he would again be chanting the Torah in shul, and again he would be taking pride in himself. He lay awake in bed, unable to fall asleep. Then, suddenly, he came up with a solution. He decided that at some point during the reading, he would make a mistake on purpose! What a stroke of genius, he thought. That way, people would think he had made a mistake by accident, and they would no longer think so highly of him, and then he would no longer have any reason to be arrogant. He went to sleep happy with himself for finding a solution.

"But later that night, he woke up in a cold sweat, thinking to himself, 'Wait a minute! Am I allowed to make a mistake in the Torah reading on purpose, just for this reason? After all, that would be selfish, too!' He wrestled with this dilemma for some time, and he couldn't sleep. Finally, he decided to go to the rebbe of the town to discuss the matter with him. The rebbe had a reputation of staying up to learn every Friday night. Surely, he thought, the rebbe would give him a *heter* – that's rabbinic permission – to make just one small mistake on purpose in order to eliminate his arrogance problem. So Reb Yehoshua got out of bed, got dressed and went to the house of the Rebbe of Shtok to ask for a *heter*."

"What happened?"

"The rebbe heard the knock on the door and invited Reb Yehoshua into his private study. He listened carefully as Reb Yehoshua told him everything that happened. Then he asked, 'When did you first realize this was a problem?'

"'When I went into the *mikveh* on Friday afternoon,' Reb Yehoshua answered.

"The rebbe thought for a moment and said, 'Reb Yehoshua, I'm afraid I must tell you that it's forbidden to make mistakes in the Torah reading on purpose. I cannot give you a *heter* to do such a thing.'

"Dejected, Reb Yehoshua got up to leave. But the rebbe told him to sit down and listen to an *etzah* – that's a piece of advice.

"'Reb Yehoshua, did you know according to the *midrash*, when *Hashem* gave Moshe the Torah, it was written with black fire on white fire?'

"'Of course,' Reb Yehoshua said. 'Everybody knows that *midrash*. What about it?'

"'Listen, then, to the proper interpretation of this *midrash*. The Torah is *Hashem*'s light in this world. But there are two types of light. There's infinite light and there's finite light. This means that there are two ways in which *Hashem* reveals himself. He reveals himself in a finite way, but He also reveals himself in an infinite way. The infinite light is the *or mekif*, the light that surrounds us, like a *tallis* that we go under when we pray, like the water of the *mikveh* that we enter. The finite, tangible light is the *or penimi*, the inner light – that's like the human being who is created in the image of God, and who is inside the *tallis*, or submerged in the *mikveh*.

"'Now, which light is more spiritual, more divine? Obviously, the infinite light is more spiritual. Yet it's also less tangible, less accessible to us. As finite creatures, we are more easily able to grasp the finite than the infinite. If *Hashem* were to reveal Himself only in an infinite way, we wouldn't understand Him at all. It's only because He reveals himself in a finite way that we have some idea of his infinity.

"'The letters of the Torah represent *Hashem*'s finite light or 'black fire.' It's called 'black' to contrast with the 'white' fire that represents the infinite light. Because the black letters are expressions of the finite light, they have particular shapes and sounds, and they form particular words that have concrete meanings. These are the words that we can read and understand. These are the words that we can pronounce and chant with a tune. But the infinite light of *Hashem* is the 'white fire,' the background against which the black letters appear. Unlike the many different black letters, the white background is the same everywhere. Without the background, the black letters could not exist. Obviously, you can't have a letter with a specific shape unless you have a contrasting background against which it is written. So the finite expression of *Hashem* is possible only because of the infinite background against which it occurs. Reb Yehoshua, are you following?"

"'Yes, Rebbe,' he said. "But what does all this have to do with my problem?'

"'My dear Yehoshua,' continued the Rebbe, 'Your problem is that when you read from the Torah, you concentrate solely on the black light of the Torah, the finite words that can be read, the audible tune that can be chanted. You pride yourself on being able to read this black light. So here is my advice: when you read the Torah, focus on the infinite white light, too – the light that goes beyond all expression. I guarantee that if you do this, you will find that your *ga'avah* will dissolve by itself. Now, go home and go to sleep so you will be well rested for tomorrow's Torah reading.'

"Somewhat puzzled and disheartened, Reb Yehoshua thanked the rebbe and went home. The next morning he went to *shul*, resolved to not make a mistake on purpose as the rebbe had told him. And as he started to read the Torah, in the back of his mind he started to think about what the rebbe had said about the black fire on the white fire. Then, for one split second, he took his mind off the letters and looked at the white of the *klaf*, the page. And suddenly, for the first time in his life, he made a mistake!"

David burst out laughing.

"From that point on," Chaim continued, "everyone knew he was fallible. And even though he never made a mistake again, that one mistake was enough to bring back his humility!"

"Good story, Chaim! Good story! But what was the point?"

"Don't you remember? We were talking about my *ga'avah* problem when it comes to playing the keyboard."

"Ah, right. What's the connection?"

"Well, as soon as I read this story, it hit me right away that the same principle applies to my situation."

"What do you mean?"

"The notes or sounds played on the keyboard are like the letters in the Torah or the black fire. The silence or empty space in between the sounds is like the white fire. I was focusing too much on the sounds and not enough on the empty space – the silence in between the notes that allows the music to exist. So what I decided to do is to keep in mind that even while I play the notes, I can only play them against the infinite, empty background – the background of silence. And that reminds me to be humble, because to be truly humble is to recognize that we are nothing in the face of the infinite."

"Wow. That's got to be somewhat difficult to do while you're playing. Has it helped?"

"Yes, I believe it has helped, *baruch Hashem*. Actually, I think I'm even a better player now than I was before. Isn't that strange? I'm actually a better player, but less vain!"

"That's pretty ironic. So that helps you in the case of keyboard playing. What about in the case of writing the book?

"That's harder to do, of course, but the same principle still applies. I remind myself every day that whatever work I do, whatever I accomplish in writing this book, it's all done against the background of this infinite, white light. I really believe that, with *Hashem*'s help, the book will be better because of this, and that the *ga'avah*, the vanity problem, will gradually dissolve. In fact, do you know what? Right now my plan is just to work on the book and not even think about publishing it at all, ever. In fact, I don't even know if I will succeed in finishing it.

But that's not the point. Right now, I'm writing the book just to write the book! Even if it never gets published or even finished, it will have been done *lishmah*, for the sake of Heaven. This way of looking at things has really helped me in my battle with *ga'avah*."

"Well, I'm glad it's working for you. As far as I'm concerned, I hope you do publish it!"

"Now, regarding the *anochius* issue – I mean, the issue of egoism – well, that's another story. I'm still working on it. I think that the main thing is to force myself to do things for other people even when I'm not in the mood. For example, I make a point of taking the kids out after school once a week, or something like that. I'll tell you one thing: you've been a big help in all this."

"Me? How so?"

"Isn't it obvious? Look, here you are – in my own private sanctuary! You've given me the chance to work on helping someone else and not just myself."

"I see. Well, I've certainly learned a lot from you."

"Thanks."

"So, Chaim, how about telling me more about your book? What's it called? Does it have a title?"

"You really want to hear about the book?"

"Of course. Is it something I could actually read?"

"I hope that some day, you could, but not right away. For one thing, it's written in Hebrew."

"Can you just tell me about it a little more?"

"Look, I warn you, once I get started talking about this, I could go on and on non-stop. Let's not forget that you're supposed to tell me your faults too."

"There's plenty of time for that. We've got all night. Remember, you said you wouldn't push off my questions. So, *nu*, tell me about the book!"

"Well said! All right, you win. You asked about the title. The title is very important. It's called *Sefer ha-Chaim*, which means 'The Book of Life,' but it also could mean 'The Book of Chaim.'"

"Really? Well, well! Talk about humility now!"

"Do you find it strange for an author to name a book after himself? Look, when you write a paper for college, don't you put your name at the top? When someone writes a book, doesn't his name appear on the cover?"

"But that's different from putting your own name in the title!"

"I guess so, but there is a long tradition of doing this, especially when the title is based on a phrase that comes from the Tanakh. For example, the great Rav Chaim of Volozhin, a student of the great Vilna Gaon, called one his books *Nefesh ha-Chaim*, which means 'the soul of Chaim.' The same thing is true in Jewish poetry. Often a famous poem will contain an acrostic of the poet's name. For example, the famous *Lecha Dodi* that we sing as part of *Kabbalas Shabbos* contains the name of the author –"

"Wait, I know it. It's Shlomo ha-Levi."

"Right! But there's a reason for all this. Remember how we talked about *gematria*?"

"Yes. That's the numerical value of words."

"The gematria of the word *sefer* which means book is *samech, peh, resh* – that's 340. Do you remember how to say 'name' in Hebrew?"

"Yes. It's *shem*."

"Right. That's *shin* and *mem*, which also add up to 340! So you see that there's a connection. A *sefer*, or book, is an expression of one's *shem*, or name!"

"Cute. Very cute."

"Oy, Dovid. I hate when you say that! This isn't just a cute idea. This is an important *yesod* – a fundamental principle! Our sages say that when a person writes a book, especially a work of Torah, he leaves an imprint of himself in the world. In fact, this is like the idea that *Hashem*'s name is itself a reflection of his own nature. This is also like what the *midrash* says about the Torah in relation to *Hashem*."

"What's that?"

"The idea is that *Hashem* writes the Torah, and leaves an imprint of himself within the Torah. In fact, the *Zohar* says that the Torah can be read as one long divine name."

"Wow. That's quite a long name!"

"And there's another custom that's been around for a long while concerning the Torah scroll that is relevant to this. I'm sure you know that the Torah is written in the form of columns. Now, in almost any Torah scroll, you'll find that the first letter of every column always begins with the letter *vav*. That's a hint to the *vav* in *Hashem*'s name, of course, which signifies the *sefirah* of *rahamim*, which is also connected to the *Torah she-bichtav*, the written Torah. But there are six specific columns that must begin with the letters *beis, yod, heh, shin, mem*, and once again, *vav*. This series of letters spells out the phrase 'be-yah shmo,' which means, 'His name is expressed in the *yod* and the *heh*.' The *yod* and the *heh* together are shortened version of the *Shem ha-meforash*. So here again we find the idea that *Hashem*'s name is hinted at in the text itself. In fact, the famous Reb Tsadok of Lublin said something that goes even further. He said that the mark of a *sefer kadosh* – that's a holy book – is one where the author and his content are *one and the same*."

"OK. Now I see what you're getting at. A book or creative work is an expression of the author himself. That's an idea I've heard before, actually. And as far as putting a signature inside the work itself – that idea is found outside of Judaism too."

"Really? Where?"

"For example, some of the great composers would occasionally imprint or encode their name within their compositions. I learned this in my music class not long ago. Bach's *Art of the Fugue* is a good example. Are you familiar with that?"

"I've heard of Bach. But that's about it."

"The Art of the Fugue is one of his greatest works, which he wrote toward the end of his life. At the very end of this work, he invented a fugue based on the notes B, A, C and H – that was the German symbol for what we call B flat. It's kind of like a signature at the end of a book. Actually, in his case, it was a signature at the end of his life."

"Very interesting! But that reminds me of something else – not about Bach or music, but about the Torah. The last verse of each of the five books of the Torah contains a name. In the last verse in *Bereshis*, the name *Yosef* is mentioned. In the last verse of the other four books, the name Yisrael occurs in each of those verses. And the very last word of the Torah is the name Yisrael."

"I suppose you're going to say that's not an accident."

"Of course it's not an accident. Dovid, you should know that in *Yiddishkeit*, names are very important. I'll never forget what my father said in his *derash*, his speech at my bar mitzvah. 'Chaim,' he said, "it's your task and your destiny to help bring *chaim* – that is, *life* – to this world." For some reason, those words always stuck with me. I haven't talked about this with my father since then, but maybe I'm trying to fulfill my father's wishes for me by writing this book."

"That reminds me of something the rabbi said at *my* bar mitzvah."

"Really? What was that?"

"It's got nothing to do with my name. It was just the phrase, 'Never let not trying stop you.' In fact, that's about one of the few things I remember about my bar mitzvah at all. It was a quotation from the great basketball star, Heyward Dotson. The saying always stuck with me, and it's been very helpful to me sometimes."

"That's actually not such a bad saying. But maybe your rabbi could have tied it in with your name somehow. You know, Dovid ha-Melech – King David – was a special person. He also had a lot of hard times, but he was tenacious and never gave up. By the way, he also wrote a book."

"Did he?"

"Of course! The book of *Tehillim*, or Psalms. Didn't you know?"

"Oh, right. I guess so. Did he imprint his name in his book too?"

"Sure. Many of the psalms begin with 'A Psalm of David' or 'A Song of David.' He wasn't bashful at all about putting his name right at the beginning of many psalms."

"I see. Anyway . . . can we get back to *your* book?"

"Well, aside from the association with my name, there's another reason why I chose this title. I'm sure you're familiar with the concept of the Book of Life?"

"That's the idea that God writes some people in the Book of Life on Rosh ha-Shannah. Other people don't make it into the Book of Life, and, supposedly, they die. In a deeper sense, the Book of Life is the 'book' we're all trying to get into. I mean, it's life in the full sense. It's life as it's supposed to be lived. That's where we all want to be."

"Very good, Dovid. So, the reason my book is called the Book of Life is because the book is meant to be sort of like a guide, a road map for life, in the full sense. Of course, the real road map is the Torah itself. In fact, Torah is sometimes called the 'way of life,' or *derech chaim*. My book is meant to be an aid toward putting Torah into practice. But really, the single most important thing about the book – even more important than the dialogue form – is its structure. The book has four parts, following the pattern of the name of *Hashem* and the corresponding structure of the human being. As I said, the whole book deals with spiritual growth. But the First Part deals with things that pertain to the lower *heh* or the *sefirah* of *malchus*. Part Two deals with the *vav*, or the next six *sefiros*. Part Three corresponds to the upper *heh* or *Binah*, and Part Four corresponds to the *yod*, which stands for *hochmah* and *kesser*."

"So the book has a very definite structure. That's real good. I learned this while writing papers for school. It's always important to have a good outline or structure."

"Exactly. In fact, I was hesitating to write the book for a long time until I came up with the idea for the structure. A good book is like a tree with branches growing from a central trunk. And in Kabbalah, the *shem Hashem* is sometimes called the *etz chaim*, the tree of life, because the *shem Hashem* holds together the ten *sefiros* like the trunk of a tree that holds all of its branches. So, what could be a better outline for a book than the holy *Shem* itself? And even the length of each of the four parts is important. The first and third parts are very similar in length, since they correspond to the lower *heh* and upper *heh*. The longest part of the book is the second part, since that corresponds to the *vav*, which symbolizes six out of the ten *sefiros*. The shortest part of the book is the last part, since that corresponds to the *yod*, the smallest letter."

"I get it. Brilliant! But now, tell me more about the content of the book."

"Yes, I'm coming to that. Each part discusses spiritual growth, moving from lower levels to higher levels. Like I said, the first part corresponds to the *Shechinah* aspect of *Hashem* and the lower part of the human soul. So, in the first part, the *sechel* discusses mainly the ideas of *shiflus* and *anavah* – that's humility – and *heshbon ha-nefesh* – that's self-examination, taking stock of yourself. Just like the *Shechinah* is the lowest aspect of *Hashem*, so too, these are the very first steps in spiritual growth. Only a person who is humble is willing to undertake a true self-examination to see what his life amounts to. As the *sechel* explains, humility is the kind of thing that doesn't necessarily require a great deal of detailed knowledge. Some of the most humble people actually know very little. But that's just a start. Because if you don't actively take interest in self-examination, you'll never begin to grow spiritually. At this first stage, a person has to pray in his own words to *Hashem* to guide him along the spiritual path and to help him succeed in this self-examination. Also, a person needs a mechanism to examine and keep track of himself. So, the *sechel* recommends to the *nefesh* the idea of keeping a *pinkas* – that's a notebook in which a person writes down his major faults and limitations. A person can also begin to describe his innermost thoughts, even dreams and such, so he can get to know himself better and figure out where he needs to go."

"Chaim, you're talking about a kind of spiritual journal. That's common to many traditions. But I didn't know the idea of writing down your dreams was a Jewish idea."

"Sure it is. First of all, it's in *Sefer Daniel*. Daniel had a dream, and then he wrote down the main points. Later on, it became incorporated into the Book of Daniel. Lots of *mekubbalim* wrote down their dreams, and later incorporated them into their *seforim*."

"Very interesting. Please go on."

"OK. Still in the first part, the *sechel* also discusses physical or bodily *mitzvos*, because these are the easiest and most basic ways in which a person can begin to grow spiritually. Actually, they're easy in one way and hard in another way. It's hard to break certain physical habits. But it doesn't take a lot of brain work. It just takes action. Now, humility and self-examination are also the gateways to the other good character attributes. So this leads naturally to the second part, which corresponds to the *vav* and the next six *sefiros*. This part discusses the six major character traits of *Hashem*, and deals with what a person has to do to develop into the kind of person that *Hashem* wants us to be. Here, we're talking not so much about physical or bodily mitzvos, but more about emotional or character traits. The *sechel* talks about how a person has to take stock of himself and reflect not only upon his bodily actions, but also on what his motives for acting are. A key idea here is that you can't become a *tzaddik* – that's a righteous person – all at once. If a person truly wishes to advance, he has to identify the one or two most important faults or failures that he has and the specific things he can do to improve them. Or it could be that a person has to identify the single most important thing that he could be doing better. Or perhaps it could be a character trait that needs improvement. Also, a person must also make specific resolutions that involve thought, speech, and action. This is a key to battling against one's *yetzer* – one's inclination. Again, a person has to write down in his *pinkas* what his flaws are and what steps he's taking to improve his actions. Again, he must pray for help from *Hashem*, but this time at a more sophisticated level and in more detail regarding his character faults. Do you follow?"

"Yes, I do."

"Good. Now, toward the end of the second part, I talk about *ahavah* and *yirah* – that's love and fear of *Hashem* – as well as how it's necessary to combine the two. That's a whole topic in itself that I can't go into now. Anyway, at the end of Part Two the *sechel* emphasizes that the *nefesh* has got to do her job, no one else can do it for her. In other words, the key to advancing in the first two stages is to realize that despite everything the *sechel* has taught the *nefesh*, at these lower stages, it's not really about the *sechel*, it's about the *nefesh* just doing what it's supposed to do. On the first and second levels, the key is action, not thought."

"I get it. It sounds very interesting, Chaim. So, what's in Part Three?"

"Part Three deals with *Binah* – understanding. This part gets more theoretical. This part is all about trying to understand *Hashem* and His Torah. This includes trying to understand the cosmic plan, and the role of the Jew within that plan. The *sechel* lays out for the *nefesh*, in relatively simple terms, an overview of the Kabbalistic system, starting from the basic concepts of *ein sof, tzimtzum, briah, behirah, Adam, sefiros*, working down through *am Yisrael, Torah, mitzvos, gilgul neshamos, moshiach, geulah, olam ha-ba*, and so on. At this point, the *nefesh* turns —"

"Hang on, Chaim. I don't know some of the terms you just mentioned. Can you explain them briefly?"

"Yes, but first let me finish what I was going to say. Just as the *sechel* is beginning to explain these concepts, the *nefesh* turns to the *sechel* and asks, 'Why are you explaining these concepts to me? Isn't it *your* job to understand these things?' To which the *sechel* responds, "Certainly it's the job of the *sechel* to understand these things in depth, but even the *nefesh* needs to have some basic understanding in order to do its task better. In any case, the *sechel* needs the encouragement and the participation of the *nefesh* in order for it — the *sechel* — to understand these things properly. And here, too, it's important for the person to pray to *Hashem* that he should help the person understand these deep concepts as best as possible."

"Interesting. But can you go back to that list of basic concepts which you mentioned earlier?"

"Yes. *Ein sof* is the infinite, indescribable essence of *Hashem*. We've already talked about that once before. *Tzimtzum* is the idea that in order to create something other than himself, there must be a kind of 'contraction' or 'self-limitation' that the infinite places on itself in order to make room for creation. In order to create something that is other than Himself, *Hashem* has to limit the way He expresses His infinite essence. If He did not do this, His being would overwhelm anything and everything else, and nothing could possibly be other than *Hashem* Himself."

"I'm not sure I get how that's possible. How can that which is infinite limit itself? Isn't that a contradiction?"

"I thought we went through this once before. Insofar as the essence of *Hashem* is in itself, it is infinite, and cannot be otherwise. The essence of *Hashem* remains infinite and unchanging. But insofar as the infinite creates or reveals itself to others, it can certainly choose not to create or reveal itself in the fullest way possible. I'll put it another way. In creating something other than itself, the infinite essence cannot express itself fully, for then, that which was created would be identical to the creator, and it wouldn't be a creation after all. So that requires that there be a *tzimtzum*, or contraction, at the moment of creation. Do you follow?"

"I'll have to think about that. Please go on. What were some of the other terms?"

"Let's see. *Beriah* is creation, and *bechirah* is free choice . . . ."

"OK, I'm familiar with those terms."

"And *geulah* means redemption. Are you familiar with that?"

"Yes. That's the idea of the ingathering of the exiles to Israel and the reinstatement of the worship in the Temple."

"Right, but I mean it in the cosmic sense, which includes not just that, but also the unification of all the divine aspects into one, so that the infinite essence can be fully manifest as one."

"OK. I sort of get that."

"And what about the idea of *gilgul neshamos*? Are you familiar with that?"

"No. What is it?"

"That's the idea that the same soul can go through a cycle of different bodies before fulfilling its proper state of *tikkun* or 'rectification.'"

"You mean reincarnation? That's not a Jewish idea, is it?"

"Sure it is! It's taught in the Zohar and other writings of Kabbalah as well."

"Really? I was told that reincarnation was a non-Jewish idea."

"What can I say? You've been misinformed!"

"Well, I'd certainly like to hear more about it. But we're getting off track from the structure of your book. The explanation of all these concepts is in Part Three. Is there anything else in that part?"

"Yes. I also discuss the importance of learning Torah for its own sake, which relates to the idea of *herus,* or freedom. The concept of *herus* is tied into another concept that is crucial in the third part – *simha,* or joy. It is only through understanding that true joy is possible. When you understand the depths of things, you really appreciate what's going on, and then you experience true joy in worshipping *Hashem.* You're able to accept things as they are with *hishtavevus* – I'm not sure how to translate that word. A person who has *hishtavevus* is a person who never loses his temper and is always cheerful, or at least in a good mood, no matter what. *Hishtavevus* comes from the word *shaveh,* which means equal. But there must be a better translation."

"Equanimity?"

"Yeah, that's it! Thanks, Dovid. And the last thing I talk about in Part Three is how, once a person gains a theoretical understanding of the system, he now has to go back and improve or elevate his behavior. He has to bring his physical actions to a newer, more sophisticated level. In other words, once you get through stage three, you've got to redo the first and second stages – but this time in a higher way. This relates to the idea of *katnus sheni* and *gadlus sheni* – second childhood and second adulthood, which we talked about once before. Really, the truth is that a person has to keep going through the same four stages over and over in different ways, but at a higher level each time."

"Actually, I have a question about that. I understand the idea of a *gadlus rishon* and *gadlus sheni,* a first adulthood and then a second adulthood. But if what you just said is true, that you keep growing and growing, then there should be a third childhood and a third adulthood, and after that a fourth childhood and a fourth adulthood, and so on. So why does the Kabbalah speak only of a first and a second adulthood?"

"That's a good question. I don't know what to say. I'll have to think about it."

"OK. Well, let's not get sidetracked. You still need to tell me about Part Four of your book."

"Ah, yes. Part Four is really my favorite part. It's also the trickiest and most difficult part because here, even the *sechel* realizes that it's approaching its own limits. The *sechel* confesses to the *nefesh* that from this point on, it can't quite explain everything as well as it's been doing till now."

"Why's that?"

"Don't you see? Part Four corresponds to the *yod* of the *Shem* – that is, to *hochmah* and *kesser* – wisdom and will. Among other things, this part deals with *hisbonenus*, or what you would call meditation. Actually, there are many different kinds of meditation that one can engage in. But an important thing is that *hisbonenus* is different from *binah* or understanding, which is back in Part Three. At the third level, you're trying to understand things logically and conceptually, in such a way that you can analyze and break down what you're understanding. But here, at the fourth level, you're not trying to do that any more. Instead you're trying to achieve a connection or bond between your *sechel* – that's your own *hochmah* – and *Hashem* himself."

"I see. You know, the mystics have a term for that. It's called non-discursive contemplation."

"Sounds nice, but I'll stick with *hisbonenus*. Now, in order to do this properly, a person needs to accept that there are limits to how far he can understand *Hashem*. So in the fourth part, the *sechel* confesses to the *nefesh* that it can't understand everything, and it starts discussing *emunah*, or faith in *Hashem*. It also discusses the concept of *bittul* or self-nullification. At this point, the *nefesh* consoles the *sechel* by saying that it, the *nefesh*, is used to being in a subservient position all the time, and that it's really not so bad after all. Finally, toward the end, the *sechel* discusses the effort to achieve *devekus* – a bond between one's own *ratzon* – one's will – and *Hashem*. That's beyond *hochmah* and *binah* altogether. *Devekus* goes completely beyond reason, and it's the pinnacle, the climax of the whole process. Of course –"

"What'd you call it?"

"*Devekus*. It means bonding or connecting. It's the highest of the high."

"But Chaim, I don't get that. Why do you say that *devekus* comes at the end of the process? It sounds to me like the whole process, from the very beginning, is all about trying to achieve a bond with God."

"In a sense, you're right. From the very beginning of stage one, you're keeping the *pinkas*, working on yourself, getting closer to *Hashem*. So everything is about *devekus*. But in the first three stages, the connection or bond is indirect. It's a connection that one attempts to achieve through physical actions, through keeping the *pinkas*, through working on one's character traits, and through one's intellectual ability to understand things. But in the fourth and highest part, the goal is to achieve a direct bond between one's will and *Hashem*. So *devekus* itself becomes the goal. Of course, if one can really do this, it has an effect on the other, lower aspects of the self as well. Again, a person who goes through stage four will have to redo the earlier stages as well. For one thing, a person who goes through stage four will see new ways in which his character needs improvement. Those new insights will have to be investigated and refined by the power of *Binah*, or intelligence, and then put into practice both in one's character and physical behavior. I'll give you my own example. Do you think I noticed my own *ga'avah* so easily? Not at all! It was only after working through the four stages that I finally realized that about myself."

"Yes, well . . . it's not so easy to see your own flaws, even ones that have been there for some time."

"True. Now, in the fourth stage, a higher level of *mesirus nefesh* – that means devotion, or giving over one's soul to *Hashem* – becomes crucial. Another thing happens as a result of stage four, something really amazing."

"What's that?"

"After working for some time on stage four, a person's mind will expand. In Kabbalah it's called *mohin de-gadlus*, as opposed to *mohin de-katnus*. The word *mohin* basically means consciousness. The words *gadlus* and *katnus* are, again, maturity and childhood, like we said before. I guess you'd say that in *mohin de-gadlus*, a person reaches a higher state of consciousness. He will truly think and experience like an adult and not like a child. This will affect his actions and emotions, of course. But another great thing that happens at this level is that here, a person uncovers new insights in Torah that neither he nor anyone else has ever noticed before. This relates to something we talked about earlier – the idea of coming up with *hiddushei Torah* – that is, original insights of Torah interpretation."

"Wait a second. I thought stage three was the learning or understanding stage."

"Yes, but there's a difference between learning, or even deriving things from what you learned already, and seeing totally new insights."

"Ah, that's true."

"So, I'm saying that after engaging in *hisbonnenus*, – or what'd you call it? – non-discursive contemplation? – one of the results is that you begin to uncover new insights of Torah. And the next task is to write down those Torah thoughts. When you write these things down on paper in a concrete way, what's happening here is that you're going back down the chain again, from the highest to lowest."

"What do you mean?"

"Like I said, level four is the stage of wisdom or *hochmah*, but now that you've got new Torah insights, you need to formulate those thoughts in speech and ultimately in writing, which is of course a physical manifestation of thought. There's also a process of *berur* when you write things down. Do you know what that means?"

"No. What's *berur*? I never heard of that."

"This is an important concept in Kabbalah. *Berur* means clarification, purification or refinement. In the very act of writing ideas down concretely, there is a purification, a refinement of the very ideas themselves, and also a refinement or purification of the one who is writing them down."

"Yes, I know what you mean! When you write things down, it helps you realize better what those ideas are in the first place. I've definitely had that experience."

"Ultimately, these writings can be shaped and edited into the form of a *sefer*, a book, which can be shared with others. In this way, what once was started as a personal or private *pinkas* is now transformed into a *sefer*, a book that can be made public. This also represents the transition from *katnus* to *gadlus*."

"Very interesting, Chaim. This is really amazing stuff!"

"Actually, there's a verse in *Tehillim* that supports the idea of using a book as a mechanism to purify oneself and come close to *Hashem*. I think it's in Chapter 40 where Dovid says, 'Then I said, Behold, I have come with a scroll of a book – *megillas sefer* – written upon me.' This is a very difficult verse. What does it mean to 'come, with a scroll of a book written upon me'? Why does he use the phrase 'scroll of a book' rather than just 'a book'? My interpretation is that Dovid is saying that he has 'come' – that is, he has approached *Hashem*– with a 'scroll of a book' written 'upon me' – that is, 'about me.' In Hebrew the word 'upon' can sometimes mean 'about.' That would appear to be the scroll or draft of the book of *Tehillim* itself. As we know, *Tehillim* is filled with Dovid's personal reflections, prayers, and so on. So *Tehillim* – or, rather, Dovid's version of it before it was published, was his own personal journal, which served as a *berur* for him in order to approach *Hashem*. Of course, since Dovid represents the soul of the people of Israel that means this book has a very special status as a *berur* for all of *klal Yisrael* – the whole Jewish people."

"Wait a second. Are you saying that what started as a sort of personal journal for David later became public?"

"That's exactly what I think. He must have been composing prayers and formulating praises for many years, keeping a record of some sort, until finally at some point he collected and maybe even edited them into a form he could share with others."

"I wonder what the uncut version looked like."

"It certainly could be that he edited out certain things that he felt were too private. But anyway, I think it's important to take a lesson from David. It's a great *zechus* not only to write a *sefer*, but also to publish or at least disseminate the book so that others can read it, as long as it doesn't contain anything inappropriate that shouldn't be shared. Of course, what should be kept private can always be edited out or perhaps just hinted at so that only the wise will understand. One interesting thing is that for the person who writes the book, it can obviously take a long time – maybe even a lifetime to write, and also it's sometimes very difficult or painful to make that *berur*, or purification. But once the book is written, many other people can read it in a relatively short time and also achieve a certain *berur*, or purification, just by reading it. It won't be the same *berur* for the reader as it is for the writer. But the process of *berur* is really a collective process, a process for all Jews. And that's why it's important to not only write but also share one's writing as well."

"Chaim, I wonder: could a work of fiction also involve this kind of *berur?*"

"Fiction? I doubt it. But I really don't know anything about that kind of writing at all. Why do you ask?"

"Never mind. Well, anyway, when you were talking about gaining new insights, expanding the mind, reaching a higher state of consciousness, it reminded me of a question I've been meaning to ask."

"Sure, go ahead."

"I'm not sure you're going to like it."

"*Nu?* What is it? Come on, come on! I promise I won't be upset. What is it?

"It's about marijuana."

"Sorry, I don't have any."

"*What?*"

"Gotcha there, didn't I?"

"Chaim, you really had me there for a moment!"

"I couldn't resist. *Nu*, go ahead. What's your question?"

"Well, you were talking about the spiritual quest. Now, some intoxicants seem to enhance a person's consciousness. In my opinion, marijuana is one of those intoxicants."

"OK. So, what's the question?"

"Well, I just wondered, what you thought about using something like marijuana to enhance one's spiritual consciousness."

"Ah, I see. Well, as far as I know, the Torah doesn't speak directly about psychedelic or mind-altering drugs. There's no record of the prophets, the rabbis, or any of the *mekubbalim* using them. And even though they of course used wine and occasionally drank other intoxicating beverages, as far as I know, there is no connection between drinking wine and going into meditative states. I know the incense that was burned in the Temple must have had quite a scent. Maybe it could affect one's mind as well. I don't know. As far as the *avodah* or service in the Temple goes, it is forbidden for a *kohen* to serve *Hashem* while intoxicated. That's also why it's forbidden to pray while under the influence. But maybe there's a difference between prayer and prophecy or *ruah ha-kodesh*. Now that I think of it, there's a statement in the Gemara. I think it's in *Yoma* somewhere: "*Yayin ve-reah tov marhivin es daato shel adam*," which I guess you could translate as "Wine and pleasant fragrances expand human consciousness.""

"Yes, that's sounds exactly like what I have in mind. It seems that the Talmud does support what I'm saying. I'm beginning to like the Talmud quite a lot!"

"Hang on. I'm not finished. Ha-Rav Moshe Feinstein wrote a *teshuvah* on marijuana."

"He wrote a what? Doesn't *teshuvah* mean repentance? And who's Rav Moshe Feinstein?"

"A *teshuvah* is also a response to a halachic question, written by a rav, or rabbi. Rav Moshe Feinstein was one of the greatest *poskim* – halachic authorities – of recent times."

"Oh. So what did he say?"

"Well, someone once asked him what is the Torah opinion on marijuana. He wrote that it's *assur* – forbidden."

"Why's that?

"I can't remember all of his reasons, but basically, he wrote that it's unhealthy for the body and messes up your mind. It makes you incapable of learning and davening properly, and it increases your desire for food and drink, which is improper. There may have been some other reasons too. Obviously, if it's unhealthy, you shouldn't do it, just for the same reason you really shouldn't smoke cigarettes, like I once told you. And there's another thing Rav Moshe didn't mention which he might have, and that's the concept of *dina de-malchusa dina*. That means: *the law of the land is binding law*. If it's illegal in the country of your residence, then that law is binding upon you. But there's some question about whether that principle applies to all non-Jewish laws, or whether that principle applies only to certain aspects of monetary or business law. Maybe that's why he didn't bring it up. I'm really not sure about that point. He also says that smoking marijuana can lead to other greater *averos*, or transgressions, but I'm not sure what he has in mind. There's also an issue of *hillul Hashem* – that's profanation of *Hashem*'s name if you get caught. I mean, if you're Jewish and you get caught, people might say, 'See what this Jew did?' That brings shame upon the Jewish people. So, for all these reasons, Rabbi Feinstein said that it is forbidden."

"Chaim, first of all, I can tell you that the chances of getting caught are pretty low. And I don't really accept the idea that it's unhealthy or that it makes you incapable of learning Torah or davening any more than drinking wine or whiskey does – unless, of course, you overdo it, which could happen in the case of wine or whiskey too. And what 'greater transgressions' might it lead to? Adultery? Murder? Idol worship?"

"I don't really know. I'm just telling you what the Rav said. But Dovid, may I ask, why are you asking about marijuana?"

"Well, I confess . . . I occasionally smoke it."

"Really? I'm shocked!"

"Seriously, I find that it enhances my perception of reality. I see connections between things that I don't usually see. Everything is more intense."

"But it's a mind-altering drug. Maybe it doesn't enhance your perception of reality. Maybe it only distorts it."

"Well, it's a little hard to explain, but some of my best insights have come when I was under the influence."

"Dovid, let me tell you this. Do you know about the Gra, otherwise known the Vilna Gaon? He was a great sage who lived several hundred years ago. He used to have visitations from *malachim* – angels – who wanted to give him insights of Torah."

"That sounds like the man you mentioned earlier."

"Yes, like the Ramchal. Actually, the Gra admired Ramchal very much. But listen to this: the Gra prayed that *Hashem* not give him any insights into Torah through *malachim*. He wanted to come up with the insights on his own, not through a power outside himself. So, *le-havdil elef alfei havdalos* – that means there are thousands of degrees of separation between his case and yours – what I'm saying is that in the long run, maybe you'd get even better ideas if you just kept Torah and *mitzvos* more carefully and didn't use any mind-altering substances."

"You don't understand, Chaim! Have you ever tried it?"

"No, never. But you know, it does remind me of something amusing."

"What's that?"

"In high school, I knew a guy who made up an imaginary page of the Talmud – it was all a joke – which discussed whether you should say a *bracha* – that's a blessing – before smoking marijuana. It sounded and looked like an authentic page of Talmud. He even printed up copies and distributed it throughout the Yeshiva on Purim. It really caused quite an uproar."

"You've got to be joking! Did he get in trouble?"

"No, not at all. It was Purim Torah."

"Purim Torah? What's that?"

"You know what Purim is, don't you?"

"Of course. That's one of the days you're supposed to get intoxicated."

"Exactly. But also, Purim is kind of like 'Topsy-Turvy Day,' if you know what I mean. Everything is upside-down. So, Purim Torah is satirical Torah. It's Torah for fun. It's customary to make up Purim Torah and share it on Purim. The guy got away with writing the satire only because he did it on Purim. I think I have it somewhere. I'll show it to you some time."

"Yes, I'd like to see it. You know, it makes me wonder. Are there are any other religions that are able to poke fun at themselves like that? I can't imagine Purim fatwas, for example . . . ."

"Fatwas? What's a fatwa?"

"I guess you haven't been following the news. That's the Islamic version of a religious opinion, an Islamic *teshuvah*, you might call it. I'm just saying that I can't imagine Muslims doing anything like that."

"Sorry, I really wouldn't know!"

"Anyway, let's put marijuana on the back burner. You were telling me about the last stage of the book, where a person reaches a level of expanded consciousness and starts seeing new insights. Is that where the book ends?"

"No. Even then, there's still more work for the *nefesh* and the *sechel* to do."

"And what's that?"

"I confess I'm still working on this part. It's kind of hard to explain, but I'll try.

At this very advanced stage, one begins to delve into the attempt to understand the *shoresh* of one's soul, one's 'soul root.' Are you familiar with this idea?"

"Not at all. What's a soul root?"

"Actually, it relates to the idea of *gilgul neshamos*, or reincarnation."

"Oh. Well then, I'm a little skeptical. But I'd love to hear about it."

"Good. Because it also relates to something I wanted to say about the *kaddish yasom*, the mourner's *Kaddish*. Now, first let's go back to the basic idea that the human was created *be-tzelem Elokim* – in the image of God. Just as *Hashem* has ten *sefiros*, the human being also has ten aspects that correspond to them. To explain the concept of soul root, I need to add something new. There's the human being in general, and there's each and every individual human being. The human being in general is represented by Adam, the first man. So, obviously, Adam had ten aspects corresponding to the ten *sefiros*. But each individual human being also has ten aspects corresponding to the ten *sefiros*. So the question arises: are there any differences in the way those ten *sefiros* are represented within each and every human being?"

"Good question."

"What would you think the answer would be? Reason it through and tell me what you think."

"Well, it seems that if we're all human, then we should all have basically the same nature. But you could also argue that human beings are very different from one another. We all have different personalities. Of course, a lot of that has to do with the fact that we are placed in different environments and we have different experiences as humans. But still, from the very beginning, it seems that some aspects of our personality are just inborn. So if our personality comes from the fact that we represent the divine nature, then, each of us must represent that divine nature in a different way."

"Excellent, Dovid! Good thinking. But just a moment. You say that our personalities are very different from one another. Isn't it also the case that in addition to the fact that we're all human, some people are very similar to others? For example, there's the intellectual type of person, the emotional person, the bold type, the meek type, the gregarious type, the loner, and so on."

"Yes, that's true."

"So, perhaps the divine nature is represented differently, not within each individual person, but rather within each personality type."

"Sorry – I'm not sure what you mean."

"Let's assume that there's a certain personality type which we'll call the intellectual type. So we could say that all people who fit into this intellectual type represent the ten *sefiros* in just such a way that the intellectual aspect – say the *sefirah* of *binah* – is more dominant in these people than in people who do not fall in to this type. And let's assume that there's a certain type which we'd call the aggressive type. So in all persons of that type, perhaps the *sefirah* of *gevurah* is somehow more dominant. And something similar would be true for all personality types."

"OK, now I get what you're saying. But there's an obvious problem with that. Even among people who fit into any particular type, there are still differences in personality. What would account for that? And besides, there are only ten *sefiros*. Obviously, there are more than ten basic types of personality. So you couldn't say that all differences in personality are accounted for by the fact that in some people, one *sefirah* is more emphasized than others."

"Exactly right. Obviously, something more complex must be going on. Let me try to explain what I think it is, according to Kabbalah. You may be familiar with the idea that each of the lower seven *sefiros* has within itself the seven other *sefiros*."

"Yes. I once discussed this with my girlfriend. That concept comes up in the case of counting the *omer*. But I really have no idea what that means."

"Then I'll try to explain. First of all, the truth is that all ten *sefiros* contain within themselves aspects of *all* the other ten. For example, we can speak of the *sefirah* of *hochmah*, but we can also speak of the ten *sefiros* within *hochmah*."

"So, each *sefirah* has ten sub-*sefiros*, you could say."

"Very nice. I like that!"

"I still don't get it, though. What does it really mean?"

"The basic teaching of Kabbalah is that the ten *sefiros* are the ten major divine attributes, or ten basic ways in which *Hashem* manifests Himself in the world. But the *sefiros* aren't ten isolated attributes. All ten *sefiros* are interrelated."

"OK. So?"

"So for each *sefirah*, there must be within it some aspect that allows it to relate or interact with each of the other nine. So, for example, there's an aspect within *hesed* that allows it to relate to *gevurah*, and there's another aspect that allows it to relate to *tiferes*, and so on. That's why we can speak of the *gevurah* within *hesed*, the *tiferes* within *hesed*, and so on."

"I guess that makes some kind of sense. But still, why speak as if one *sefirah* is 'within' another? For example, there's an aspect of this chair that allows it to relate to the table, and another aspect that allows it to relate to the floor, and so on. But we wouldn't speak of those aspects as the 'table within the chair' or the 'floor within the chair.' Besides, I've got another problem. Suppose you do need to postulate a *hesed* that's within *gevurah* in order to allow for the relation between *hesed* and *gevurah*. But once you've done that, what would be the need to postulate *gevurah* within *hesed*? Both would boil down to the same thing – namely, something that allows *hesed* to relate to *gevurah*!"

"Great questions, Dovid! Let me give you an analogy that I think will answer both of them at once. Consider a family. You've got a father, a mother, a teenage son and a baby girl. Now, the father relates to the son in a certain way. To do that he's got to sympathize or feel in some way like the son does. He can't feel exactly the way the son does, of course. But, there's some aspect within the father that allows him to do this. That's the son within the father, so to speak. The same thing goes for his relationship with his wife and his daughter. The father has an aspect which allows him to relate to his daughter. That's called the daughter within the father. But now, in addition, the daughter relates to the father. When she does that, she's got to in some way sympathize or feel the way the father feels. And that's the father within the daughter. So, the father within the daughter is not the same thing as the daughter within the father. Do you follow?"

"Yes, I think so. Very nice explanation."

"And something similar is true for all the other relationships in the family."

"OK. But wait – given what you just said, what would the father within the father be?"

"Ah, very simple. Once you distinguish aspects in which the father relates to the others, it also makes sense to say that there's a certain aspect of the father which is just what the father is, and not insofar as he relates to others. That aspect is the father within the father."

"Ah, I see."

"Good. Now, let's go back to the *sefiros*. Each *sefirah* has an aspect that allows it to relate to each of the other *sefiros*, and an aspect that is just what it is. Since there are ten primary *sefiros*, that means there would be one hundred sub-*sefiros*, as you called them. But now, consider just one of those sub-*sefiros*. For the same reason we said that there are sub-*sefiros*, we'd also have to say that there are ten further *sefiros* within each sub-*sefirah* as well!"

"Why's that?"

"The reasoning is the same. After all, each sub-*sefirah* is related to all the other sub-*sefiros*. So, that means there has to be some aspect within each one that allows them to relate to others too. Hence each sub-*sefirah* itself must have ten sefiros within itself!"

"I guess we would call those sub-sub-*sefiros*."

"Very good! I like that. Like *Adam ha-Rishon*, you philosophers are very good at coming up with names! Now, if there are a hundred sub-*sefiros*, and each one of those has ten sub-sub-*sefiros*, that means you'd have a thousand sub-sub-*sefiros*."

"Chaim, isn't this getting out of hand? Does it really make sense to talk about the *gevurah* of the *binah* of *hesed*, or the *tiferes* of the *yesod* of *hochmah*, and so on? And once you go down that road, you'll have to say there's ten *sefiros* within each sub-sub-*sefirah*, and so on, and then eventually you'll have an infinite number of *sefiros* within *sefiros* within *sefiros*! This is beginning to sound pretty weird to me."

"It sounds weird, but don't you see how, by using this idea of *sefiros* within *sefiros* within *sefiros*, we can now answer the question we had earlier?"

"Sorry, I lost track. Which question?"

"The question was: what is the Kabbalistic explanation for the fact that although we are all humans and are made in the image of Hashem, we are also all individuals?"

"Oh, right. No, I don't see how that answers the question."

"Then I'll explain. Remember, we said that human nature parallels the nature of *Hashem*. So just as *Hashem* has ten primary *sefiros*, human beings have ten major aspects. We had also said that the differences in human personality types could be partially explained by the fact that in certain people, certain *sefiros* dominate more than others. But our problem was that since there are only ten *sefiros*, how would this account for the variety of human personality types? But now we've seen that while it's true that *Hashem* has only ten primary *sefiros*, it turns out that there is an infinite number of *sefiros* within *sefiros*! So we can say something like this: each and every human being has ten major aspects. All humans have that in common, and in that respect, we're all alike. But then, once we take into account the *sefiros* within *sefiros*, we realize there's an infinite number of different possibilities of how the ten primary *sefiros* might be represented, depending upon which particular unique combination of *sefiros* within *sefiros* are dominant. Get it?"

"I think so. But it still sounds kind of bizarre."

"Let me give you an example. Take two imaginary people – let's call them Reuven and Shimon. They're both human, so they're both created in the image of *Hashem*. Both have the same ten basic aspects that correspond to the ten *sefiros*. So in that respect, they're exactly alike. And let's say they are both pretty intellectual people. So in both of them, the *sefirah* of *binah* dominates. But it still could be that Reuven and Shimon have very different personalities, depending on what combination of *sefiros* within *sefiros* dominates in the *binah* of their souls. For example, it could be that in Reuven's soul, the *hesed* of *gevurah* of *binah* dominates. That would be, so to speak, the blueprint of Reuven's *neshamah*. And that's what we could call his soul root. Whereas, in Shimon's soul, it could be that the *hod* of *yesod* of *binah* dominates. Therefore, the soul roots of Shimon and Reuven would be similar but still different. Do you follow?"

"Yeah, sort of. But wait a second. There's still going to be an infinite number of different possible combinations of *sefiros* within *sefiros* . . . ."

"Why is that a problem?"

"Because there aren't an infinite number of actual human beings in existence, nor has there ever been."

"So what? All that shows is that no matter how many different souls *Hashem* creates, there would never be a complete and total representation of the divine nature within the species of human beings. Still, each actual human being represents a slightly different version of the divine image. In fact, the Talmud says that someone who willfully does not engage in procreation is *memaet ha-demus* – that is, he diminishes the divine image. That's because each and every human being represents the divine image in a certain unique way. By the way, that's related to another amazing teaching in the Talmud . . . ."

"What's that?"

"I'm not sure you're ready for it. You might make fun of it."

"I promise I won't. Come on. What is it?"

"It's about spilling seed in vain. Do you know what the Talmud says about that?"

"Do you mean to tell me the Talmud talks about that, too?"

"No topic, great or small, is foreign to the Talmud. It's all there, from the highest to the lowest."

"Amazing. Well, what does the Talmud say about it?"

"Spilling seed in vain is like committing murder, improper sexual relations, and idol worship combined."

"*What?* That's absolutely the most ridiculous thing I've ever heard!"

"See, I told you. And you just promised that you wouldn't make fun of it!"

"Seriously, Chaim, how could that possibly be true?"

"Look, I don't want to get off track. It's really a whole discussion in itself. But if you really understand on the basis of Kabbalah what it means to be a human being, and what it really means to be with a woman – especially your wife, who is married to you – then you'd see the wisdom of this teaching. But I don't want to get off track."

"Well, this seems like one digression worth taking."

"OK, I'll try to explain it briefly. The true purpose of having relations is to further the process of *yihud shem*, the unification of the divine name. The act of having relations is holy or at least can be holy, whether it produces children or not. That's because the unification of the male and female in the physical realm parallels the process of the unification of the divine energy that flows through the *sefiros*, which, as we've talked about before, have a male and female aspect. The *zivug*, or coupling, in this world parallels the *zivug* of the male and female *sefiros* on high. Do you follow so far?"

"Yes, I think we've talked about this before."

"Now, when a man has relations with a woman who's not his wife – well, at least he's got going for him the fact that she's a woman! So his physical act still in some way parallels the unification of the *sefiros*. But when a man spills seed without completing the act with a woman, then, in some sense, that's much worse! The unification parallel is missing, and that's why it's like idol worship and in some sense like improper sexual relations, because the energy is flowing but without the proper vessel in place. If such a thing were to happen in the realm of the *sefiros*, imagine how horrific it would be! It would be like divine energy running rampant, without a proper vessel to receive it. And it's obviously like murder because the seed that's wasted has missed its chance to unify with the feminine source. That's true regardless of whether or not a pregnancy results from the act. Do you follow?"

"Hmm. Well, I sort of understand."

"Good. Now, where were we before we got on to that? Oh, I remember. We were saying that it's no surprise that theoretically, even an endless number of human souls would not completely represent all the possible ways in which the divine image could be expressed in the human being. So what we do have to say is that it's up to *Hashem* to decide how many different personality types he wants in His world before He brings about the final cosmic redemption. It's hard, if not impossible, to know exactly what that number is. Some would say it's a *sod*, a secret that is connected with the coming of *moshiach*."

"What do you mean?"

"The Talmud teaches that when the desired number of souls is reached, the *moshiach* will come. Nobody really knows what that number is. But I'm getting ahead of myself. There's something else I wanted to bring up. This is where the idea of *gilgul neshamos* or reincarnation comes in. Earlier I gave you an example where two people, Reuven and Shimon, have soul roots which are similar yet slightly different. Do you remember?"

"Yes, of course."

"But if He so desires, Hashem could arrange things so that the exact same personality type could be expressed in two or more different individual human beings. Do you get what I'm saying? This is really an amazing thought."

"I'm not sure how that could be."

"Simple. Theoretically, it's quite possible that two or more different human beings could have the exact same soul root, that is, the exact same combination of sub-*sefiros* and sub-sub-*sefiros* that are emphasized or dominant within their soul."

"Wait! Isn't that like saying that two different people could have the exact same personality? That's impossible."

"No, no. You're forgetting what you said earlier. First of all, any two different people would have different bodies. In fact, they could be born at different times and different places. They could have different experiences, different teachers, different environments, and so on. And to top it off, they would still both have free will to choose how to act. Remember, the Torah teaches that we all have *behirah hofshis*. The fact that you have a certain personality type does not dictate how you act. So two people who have exactly the same soul root could still act very differently."

"Chaim, I don't know if this all makes sense. I have to think about this a little more."

"Fine. But still, now you understand the basic idea of the soul root, at least as far as I've explained it. So now you can begin to understand what *gilgul neshamos* means."

"How's that?"

"Based on what we've just said, the next step is really quite simple. Two different people, living at different times, could have the exact same soul root. In fact, many different people, living at many different times, could have the exact same soul root. In other words, the same soul root can be 'recycled' in different bodies, in a manner of speaking."

"Well, I guess that makes sense given what we've already said."

"The Kabbalah teaches further that each person in this world has a certain job to do, a certain *tikkun* or 'fixing' in order to help bring about the unification of *Hashem*'s name. So based on what your soul root is, your job may be very different from mine. But for two people who have the same soul root – their job would probably be similar. Again, let's not forget free will. In one bodily existence, a given soul may fail, and in a later life, that soul may succeed. Kabbalah teaches that in one life, a soul might be a *rasha*, or wicked person, and then in another life the same soul might be a *tzaddik*. For example, do you remember the story of Pinhas in the Torah?"

"I think so. Wasn't he the one who took a spear and killed a man and woman right in the middle of the sexual act?"

"It wasn't just a sexual act. It was an act of sexual immorality. There was a plague raging at the time that killed twenty-four thousand people. When Pinhas killed the couple, the plague stopped."

"Yes, I remember that story."

"Good. Well, the man's name was Zimri ben Salu, and the woman was Kazbi bas Tzur, a Midianite princess. So listen to this. It's written in the *sifrei kabbalah* that Zimri ben Salu came back as Rabbi Akiva!"

"Wow, that's interesting. But I can't imagine how anyone would be able to *know* that, even if it were true."

"And those twenty-four thousand people who died in the plague? According to Kabbalah, they came back as the twenty-four thousand students of Rabbi Akiva. Kazbi bas Tzur came back as a wife of a Roman governor. She tried to seduce Rabbi Akiva, just like Kazbi seduced Zimri, who gave in to her. But this time, Rabbi Akiva resisted. Later, after the governor died, she ended up converting to Judaism – and marrying Rabbi Akiva!"

"That sounds . . . well, beyond belief."

"Dovid, I'm not making it up. I'm just telling you some of the secrets of Kabbalah. Maybe I shouldn't be doing this. You'll probably make fun of the whole thing."

"I'm not making fun. But just a second. Those twenty-four thousand people who came back as students of Rabbi Akiva . . . didn't they die in a plague during his lifetime as well?"

"Yes, that's right. They still didn't get it right, even the second time around!"

"I still don't see how anyone can possibly know all this, even if it were true. How can you really know whose soul is whose?"

"Well, it takes a very high level of spiritual attainment, of course. Only very few people, the prophets and the great *mekubbalim*, could reach such levels. The Ari ha-Kadosh was on that level. He was one of the greatest *mekubbalim* of all time. Based on his teachings, there is an entire book that discusses whose soul was whose in a previous life."

"Right. Well, while we're on the topic of Rabbi Akiva and the plague, that reminds me of something else I wanted to ask you. The period between *Pesach* and *Shavuos* is supposed to be a period of spiritual growth. Right?"

"Yes, that's correct."

"And the seven weeks between *Pesach* and *Shavuos* correspond to the seven lower *sefiros*, right? And during each week we're supposed to purify the aspect of our personality that corresponds to that particular *sefirah*."

"Yes."

"But in fact there are ten *sefiros*, not seven. So why are there only seven weeks between *Pesach* and *Shavuos* rather than ten?"

"Ah! Good question, Dovid. Of course, you might as well ask why there aren't ten days in the week as opposed to seven, or why there aren't ten years in the sabbatical cycle instead of seven."

"Yes. I was thinking of asking you that, too."

"Then let me explain. The *sefiros* of *kesser*, *hochmah* and *binah* are called the *gimel rishonos*, or three first sefiros, precisely because they are always more hidden than revealed. They are distinguished from the *zayin tachtonos* – or seven lower *sefiros* – that have to do with God's character traits – I mean, his actions – and his presence in this world. Now, the upper three *sefiros* represent aspects of *Hashem* which He has, even before He creates the world. Before *Hashem* creates the world, he is powerful, wise, and intelligent. But you can't really talk about a benevolent or just God until the world is created. Of course, God has the potential to be benevolent before the world is created, but he has actual benevolence only after it already exists. And you certainly can't talk about God's presence in the world until there is a world where he can be present. So the seven lower *sefiros* are a more outward manifestation of the *ein sof*, the infinite divine essence. That's why there are seven days of the week and seven years in the sabbatical cycle. The days of the week and the years of the sabbatical cycle correspond to the seven lower *sefiros* even though the seven lower *sefiros* are rooted in the three upper *sefiros*. Do you follow?"

"I think so. Still, how does that explain why we only have seven weeks of the *omer*?"

"I'm getting to that. As I was saying before, the *sefiros* are represented within the human being. Just as God has will, wisdom, and intelligence, so does the human being. And just as *Hashem* has seven character traits or *middos*, so do humans. Now, the first three *sefiros* are not subject to corruption or *tumah* in the same way that the lower *sefiros* are. Actions can be good or bad. Character traits can be good or bad. The same is not quite true of the mind, nor of the will, for that matter. A person may have bad thoughts, but in general, that's not so terrible unless he acts on those thoughts and does something wrong. Similarly, the *ratzon*, or will, is always pure. That's why the Kabbalah teaches that *teshuvah* – repentance – is rooted in *binah*, the lowest of the three upper *sefiros*. The mind and the will always remain pure. A person who has done bad things has corrupted himself and needs to become pure. He needs to change his actions, his character traits. But Kabbalah teaches that no matter how low a person has sunk in terms of his actions, he still knows, deep down, that what he's doing is wrong, and he has the power or will to change his ways, to do *teshuvah*. So, the mind and the will are not subject to corruption in the same way that one's character traits are. That's why the period of *taharah* or purification takes seven weeks, not ten. And since there are seven lower aspects within each of the seven, that's why there are forty-nine levels of impurity that we need to pass through before we can receive the Torah on *Shavuos*."

"OK. I think I follow."

"By the way, this is related to the fact that we verbally count only forty-nine days and not the fiftieth day itself, when the festival of *Shavuos* is celebrated. It's the same principle at work. The fiftieth day corresponds to a level that transcends the lower seven *sefiros*, and we're only counting as a means of purification anyway. So, once we've reached the fiftieth level, there's no need to count any longer."

"I see. That makes sense."

"Good. Well, now that you understand the basic idea of soul roots, I can finish up the summary of my *sefer*."

"Yes, please do that. But you were going to say something about the mourner's *Kaddish*. I'd like to hear that."

"Right. Toward the end of the book, the intellect describes to the soul a process that goes on at the highest level of spiritual development – the process of delving into one's soul root. This is something a person can engage in only after going through the first four stages over and over again, each time at a higher level. Remember, the book starts out with the ideas of *anavah* – that's humility, and *heshbon hanefesh* – that's self-examination. At the final stage, there's also self-examination, but at a higher level. The self-examination in the first stage was rough and uneducated. No knowledge of the *sefiros* or anything else in Kabbalah was assumed. But by the end of stage three, a person has gained an understanding of the whole kabbalistic system, so the potential for self-understanding is now much deeper. By that point, a person has worked on his character and refined it. Also, in stage four, a person has practiced *hisbonenus*, or meditation, and attained some more direct level of *devekus* with *Hashem*. Now, I'm not saying that one can figure out precisely what one's soul root is in detail. Like I said, that's something only the great *mekubbalim* can do. They also know certain meditative techniques that allow them to enter the inner chambers, if you know what I mean. That's why only they can identify which *neshamos* are *gilgulim* of which, including their own. But anyone who really puts himself into it and works at it really hard can discover his soul root. It means getting in tune with who one is, one's role in the scheme of things, one's true destiny. At this point, a person realizes what kind of a person he is because he's already filtered out all the garbage, so to speak. He's worked on himself and refined his character to the point where he knows what his soul is all about. He knows where his true weaknesses and strengths lie. He's aware of what kind of challenges and temptations will be difficult for him to face, and what kind of contribution he can make toward fulfilling the purpose of *Hashem*'s creation. That doesn't mean he knows the future or anything like that. It certainly does not mean he can identify his own prior or future *gilgulim*. But it does mean that he has a good idea of what kind of *tikkun* he is supposed to do. By the way, that's why the great rebbes were so good at giving personal advice. Remember the story I told you earlier about Reb Yehoshua and the Rebbe of Shtok? A spiritual master could penetrate a person's soul, see who that person really was, and determine what he needed to do in order to accomplish his *tikkun*."

"OK, I think I get the picture. Now, wasn't there something you wanted to say about the mourner's *Kaddish*?"

"Yes. Thanks for reminding me. Basically the *Kaddish* is the sanctification and glorification of *Hashem*'s name. The obvious question about the *Kaddish* is: what does this sanctification of *Hashem*'s name have to do with the soul of the dead person?"

"Yes. I've wondered about that myself."

"Once more, let's go back to the basic idea that the human being is created in the *tzelem*, or image, of *Hashem*. Again, the ten *sefiros* are represented or paralleled in the human being. Remember that the ten *sefiros* are hinted at by the divine name. Now we've added that there's a specific way in which different *neshamos*, or types of *neshamos*, represent the divine name. Consider your mother, for example. I know that you just finished saying *Kaddish* for the year, but still you're going to continue saying *Kaddish* on her *yahrzeit*, the anniversary of her passing. Now, there's a specific, particular way in which the *neshamah* of your mother represents the divine nature, depending on which particular *sefiros* within *sefiros* are emphasized within her soul. Of course, that soul root is not completely unique to her because others before her have had the same soul root and so will others after her. But still, there is some particular combination or emphasis of *sefiros* within *sefiros* that make up the blueprint of her personality. And, like we said earlier, each individual person has a job to do, a *tikkun* to perform, by bringing about a certain particular *yihud shem*, or unification of the divine *sefiros*. Of course, different people accomplish this task at different levels and in different ways. Some don't accomplish it at all, and almost nobody does it perfectly. I'm sure your mother fulfilled her *tikkun* to some degree, given her circumstances, her background, and so on – although, like I said, nobody's perfect. Anyway, when you say *Kaddish* for her soul, what you're doing is helping to further the process of the *tikkun* for her *neshamah*, which helps to complete the process of unification for the Name of *Hashem* himself. That's why the *Kaddish* is completely focused on the sanctification and glorification of the name of *Hashem*. Since you're her son, it's primarily your responsibility to do that. No one else can do it in quite the same way. And that's what it means to advance the soul's place in heaven."

"Wow. That really is very interesting. Is that how the book ends?"

"Almost. The book ends with a discussion of *ruah ha-kodesh* or what you might call divine inspiration, the holy spirit. A person who works through the four stages over and over again has prepared himself to receive *ruah ha-kodesh*. But here I use an idea of Ramchal, which is also found in Rambam. And that is that even though a person may be well prepared to receive *ruah ha-kodesh*, that doesn't mean *Hashem* will grant it. You can't force *Hashem*'s hand. It must be part of His plan that a particular person receives *ruah hakodesh*. And like I said before, it is part of *Hashem*'s plan that a certain number of souls be created in order to bring about the final *tikkun* that's necessary for completing the purpose of this world. Still, there are certain specific prayers and meditative techniques that can be used when a person reaches this stage, which involves preparing for *ruah ha-kodesh*. Truth is, I'm still working on developing this part of the book. But eventually, if we – I mean the people of Israel – keep at it, *Hashem* will grant us *ruah ha-kodesh*. In its highest form, *ruah ha-kodesh* is *nevuah*, or prophecy. When the Jewish people bring themselves to the point where they are just about ready to perform their proper *tikkun* – in unison – that's precisely what must happen in order for *moshiach* to come and bring the final redemption or *geulah shlemah*, may it come speedily in our days!"

"So, Chaim, we've gotten around to talking about *moshiach* after all."

"Yes . . . and I'm beginning to wonder: what time is it?"

"I don't know, but it's probably close to morning by now."

"Really? *Oy vey!* I'm supposed to be reading the Torah at *shaharis*! We'd better go upstairs!"

"Then let's go, Chaim."

"I guess we'll have to discuss your faults another time."

"That's OK. I already told you: I really don't have any!"

24

May 20, 2002

What a conversation we had on Shavuot night! Tired at the beginning, but once I got my second wind, barely noticed the time fly by. Chaim really opened up. I wonder if he would be surprised to know I've got my own "pinkas" after all. I'm sure he has one. That's probably how he started writing his book. I wonder if he's got any other flaws he didn't share with me. Nobody's completely honest when it comes to their own flaws. That night, I never got around to confessing my flaws. Kept joking I didn't have any. But what would I have said, if he'd gotten around to asking?

One problem I used to have was depression. It sure got pretty bad sometimes. Lying in bed for hours, staring at the wall, smoking cigarettes, wasting myself away. The "nothing matters" or "what's the point?" syndrome. I think I inherited it from Mom. But is that fair? Depression itself is not a flaw. But succumbing to depression – that's a real flaw. It's not always your fault if you're depressed. The real issue is, what do you do about it? ~~Everything~~ Most of what you get in life is not your own doing. I could've been born defective, or in a concentration camp. Or I could've been in some terrible accident. You can't blame someone for being depressed in that situation. But some people in those situations don't give up, and instead do incredible things. So the real question is: how do you deal with what you have?

I'm sure many people would say that the most constructive thing to do for depression is to go see a shrink. But I think I've figured out how to get out of the kind of depression that I get. I sit down and I write, and I go back to my basics, my rock-bottom beliefs, and work from there. Lately it seems I've been doing pretty well. I really haven't been depressed in a while.

So, back to the question: what flaws do I have? Smoking, drinking, wasting myself away. These are things I still do on occasion. Could all that stuff be a fault or a flaw? As for cigarettes, that's surely wrong if a) life is good, and b) cigarettes damage your health or shorten your life. Since I believe that b) is true, it all depends on whether a) is true. Of course, when you're depressed, you <u>don't</u> think life is good, or at least, you think its goodness is questionable. But right now this is one of my rock-bottom beliefs:

LIFE IS GOOD. (Basically, that is.)

So I really shouldn't smoke cigarettes. At least not as much as I do. Why do I smoke so much? I guess it does give me a little buzz. But I also like the feeling of having something in my hand, something to do with my mouth. If you have nothing to do, you can always do this: have a smoke! So basically, it's a crutch. Why do I need a crutch? I'm not really sure. I guess I have to admit: there's a weakness here. All right, here goes. Time for a resolution:

I HEREBY RESOLVE TO ~~QUIT~~ CUT DOWN ON SMOKING CIGARETTES.

Mom would be proud. I admit now that I do feel guilty a little bit about lying to her about whether I was smoking, drinking, etc. But I only did it so as not to make her worry. In general, I am very honest.

Then there's the drinking. I admit that I go overboard sometimes with that. Not that I'm an alcoholic or anything like that. But why do I do it then? Just because it's <u>fun</u>? Do I enjoy being intoxicated? Is intoxication an end in itself? Is it a kind of <u>escapism</u>? Maybe so. As for smoking the good essence, it's definitely not <u>wrong</u>. The rabbi that Chaim mentioned the other night had no idea what he was talking about. It's not really unhealthy. And besides, what great transgressions has it led me to commit? That's absurd.

But I guess it is a kind of intoxication or escapism. Escapism. Need to ponder that. Escaping <u>what</u>? Escaping reality, I guess. Living a fantasy life, avoiding the truth. But so what? Is it wrong? I guess it all depends. If reality is nothing special, or if nothing is really or truly good, then what's wrong with escaping reality? Nothing! But, if by escaping reality you're avoiding what's truly or really <u>good</u>, then, escapism is not only bad, it's <u>really</u> bad. So, if there is such a thing as what's <u>truly</u> or <u>really</u> good (as opposed to what's only apparently good or not really good) then escaping reality — or at least, escaping that <u>part</u> of reality which is good — is bad! (I'm beginning to sound like Plato.) Now, do I believe there is something that's <u>really good</u>, as opposed to something that's <u>really bad</u>? Yes, I do. So it follows that I <u>do</u> think escapism is bad. But even so, this only shows that avoiding the <u>really good</u> is bad. It doesn't show that avoiding <u>all</u> <u>reality</u> is bad! So it doesn't show that fantasy or escapism is <u>always</u> bad!

But here's another argument against escapism: what if reality or truth is <u>inherently good</u>? That's what Dr. M thinks: <u>being</u> or <u>reality</u> is intrinsically good. (That's <u>why</u> life is good, as I wrote above. Because it is a kind of being.) As far as Dr. M is concerned, that's basically what it <u>means</u> to believe in God. (If it's true, it sure would be nice. What could be better than living in a world where being, or reality itself, is inherently good? But now I'm beginning to sound like Rabbi L.) Anyway, if Dr. M is right that being or reality is inherently good, then escapism (=avoiding reality) is inherently bad! Q.E.D.

But wait. Is smoking really escapist? Is that assumption valid in the first place? I know myself at least this well: I'm <u>not</u> interested in avoiding truth. I <u>want</u> truth, I <u>want</u> reality. So escapism is <u>not</u> something I want. The blessed essence takes me to a higher level of reality, a closer look at truth. I perceive things that I would never perceive otherwise. I come up with thoughts that I would never come up with while straight. I get more creative. It opens up channels that are not getting opened otherwise. It makes my sensations more intense. So it's not an escape! It's getting me to another, higher level of reality. Therefore, it's OK. In fact, it's good!

Then again, I can just hear what Ravi would say, "David, can't you get to that higher level without the 'artificial means' of a mind-altering substance? If you practice meditation, you will develop the ability to open up those channels of perception with your own natural powers." Now, if Ravi is right, then the blessed essence is a kind of shortcut or crutch after all. And Chaim said pretty much the same thing. And maybe it's a bad crutch, because once you become dependent on the stuff for your insights, it corrupts your ability to open those doors with your own natural powers. It's kind of like taking a pill to be happy when you're not naturally happy. It might corrupt your ability to be happy naturally. The same thing might be true of wasting yourself away. Maybe it corrupts your ability to have a true or real experience later on.

So it boils down to this: does the good essence take me to a place that I could never get to naturally — that is, without using it? If it does, then it's _not_ a crutch or shortcut. It's rather a ticket to another place. But if it can't take me to a place I couldn't get to naturally, then it _is_ a crutch, and probably a bad one. (Consider the story Chaim told me about the Gra.)

So the basic question is: does the essence give me a shortcut to truth even as it corrupts my ability to get there on my own? I guess it's possible that it _could_ get me to some place in reality that I'd never get to on my own, and _still_ corrupt my ability to get to some _other_ part of reality, that I could've gotten to if I didn't use the good essence.

I must confess — I don't like the conclusion to which this argument is leading!

Anyway, what other flaws do I have? I really, seriously can't think of any.

25

"Nu, Dovid, are you enjoying the wedding?"

"WHAT DID YOU SAY? CHAIM, IT'S TOO NOISY. YOU'LL HAVE TO SHOUT!"

"I SAID: ARE YOU ENJOYING THE WEDDING?"

"OH! YES, I AM. THE MUSIC IS GREAT AND THE DANCING IS AMAZING! I THINK I MAY HAVE DRUNK ONE TOO MANY. THE SEPARATION OF MEN AND WOMEN ISN'T SOMETHING I'M USED TO. STILL, IT'S ONE OF THE BEST WEDDINGS I'VE EVER BEEN TO!"

"GREAT! I ALSO DRANK A BIT, SO I'M TAKING A BREAK. DO YOU WANT TO GO SOMEWHERE QUIET FOR A FEW MINUTES AND TALK?"

"GOOD IDEA, CHAIM!"

"THEN, FOLLOW ME. THERE'S A QUIET ROOM WE CAN GO TO."

"Ah, that's better. Hey, Chaim, sorry to boost your ego, but you really do play piano very well!"

"Thanks. So now that you've seen it in action, do you think Jewish dancing counts as exercise?"

"Definitely. Some of those guys are really incredible."

"But I haven't seen you out on the dance floor. Are you going to try it? You'll see, Jewish dancing has an effect on your whole *neshamah*, not just your *nefesh*, but also your *sechel*, your intellect. You've got to try it!"

"Yes. Maybe later."

"Don't you remember what I told you that first day you came and visited me in the *sukkah*? *Ivdu es Hashem be-simha*. Serve *Hashem* with joy. Dancing is the ultimate expression of joy, and Jewish dancing is the ultimate expression of joy in *Hashem*."

"I remember your saying that. You know, Chaim, I really have to thank you. I've learned so much from you."

"And there's so much more to learn. Dovid, my *haver*, my friend! I've been meaning to ask you this for a while – did you ever think about going to yeshiva?"

"No, I never did. Why?"

"Why not? You should really think about learning in yeshiva sometime, probably right after college."

"Nah, I don't think so."

"Look, I'm not talking about becoming a rabbi or anything like that. Most people who learn in yeshiva don't become rabbis. They learn for a few months or maybe even a year, and then they go on to whatever profession they want. Really, a year in yeshiva could change your life."

"I don't know if I'm cut out for yeshiva. Well . . . I'll think about it. But that reminds me – I was going to ask *you* something."

"What?"

"Chaim, you're obviously a bright guy . . . ."

"Yeah, so?"

"And you've also got a talent in music . . . ."

"Yeah, so? *Nu*, what is it?"

"Did you ever think about going to college?"

"College? Nah, I don't think so. Why should I go to college?"

"You would learn so much about the world, about science, about literature, history, philosophy, music, the arts, everything."

"Dovid, look, all I really need and want to learn is Torah. All that other stuff – it's essentially for the *goyim*."

"Really? Is that what you believe?"

"I could sugarcoat it if you wanted me to. But I'm a little drunk right now, so I'm telling you up front what I think. Look, *Hashem* gave the Jewish people the

Torah, and that's God's wisdom. We're commanded to study and teach the Torah, it's the highest commandment. That's what feeds our *neshamah*, the Jewish soul. Every minute that's free should be taken up with studying Torah if possible. Of course, we have to learn about the world for practical purposes. And if I were going to be a doctor or a lawyer or something like that, of course I'd need to go to school in order to learn what I'd need to know. But especially when it comes to things like literature and philosophy – why should I study that? I'm probably going to end up as a rabbi teaching somewhere in a yeshiva or a school. So why should I go to college?"

"Chaim, don't you think it's important to be a well-rounded person?"

"Are we talking about a well-rounded human or a well-rounded Jew?"

"Isn't a Jew a human?"

"Yeah, but the soul of a Jew is different from the soul of a non-Jew."

"I don't know if I accept that. But even if it's true, a Jew is still also a human being. So, shouldn't a Jew be well rounded as a human?"

"What does 'well-rounded' mean? Does it mean learning things that are irrelevant to the service of *Hashem*? If that's what it means, I'm not interested. The Jew was created to serve *Hashem* and unite His name, to study and keep the Torah."

"Wait a second, Chaim! Are Jews supposed to keep to themselves and have nothing to do with the rest of the world? Don't Jews have a mission to carry the teaching of monotheism to the rest of the world? How can they do that if all they do is stick to themselves?"

"Jews have a 'mission'? Ha! What you're saying reminds me of a joke. When the Reform movement took hold in Europe, a lot of Jews were leaving the traditional ways. In one of the Reform seminaries, a student went to his rabbi and asked, 'Rabbi, if we don't believe the Torah is from heaven, how can we still believe the Jews have a mission?' In full seriousness, the Rabbi responded, 'Of course, we have a mission! The mission of the Jewish people is to be "*mishin*" – that means mixing – with the *goyim*!'"

"Very funny, Chaim, but what's your point? Seriously, don't Jews really have a mission to the rest of the world?"

"Dovid, the whole idea that Jews have a 'mission' to teach the rest of the world monotheism was invented by people who really don't believe in *Torah min ha-shamayim*. If they did believe that the Torah was from heaven, they would know that the true purpose of the Jew is to remain separate from the non-Jews, to keep the Torah, and not to worry about what the *goyim* think!"

"I don't know. Even if you're right, I still think a Jew should be well-rounded."

"Dovid! I'll tell you what 'well-rounded' means for a Jew. It means that you have a family, you have a job or some form of *parnassa* or support, you're a *ba'al hesed* or generous person, you *daven* with a *minyan* every day, and you're knowledgeable in all areas of Torah, including Gemara, Kabbalah, and all areas of *halacha*. That's what 'well-rounded' means!"

"Really, Chaim, I find that very difficult to accept."

"That's because maybe you don't really believe in *Torah min ha-shamayim*. No, wait. I take that back. Sorry – I'm still a little drunk. You *do* really believe it. Deep down, you really do believe it. But you still haven't got used to accepting what it means. Part of you still believes that all knowledge is just as important as any other knowledge, that the Torah is only one way of life among many possibilities, that all religions are equally valid. This is what you were brought up to believe, and it's hard to change overnight. But you should also know there are some serious halachic problems with studying some of the things that you mentioned."

"Like what?"

"Some of the things you're talking about are not just a waste of time. I know, I know, you don't even agree with that – but aside from that, studying some of those things could lead a person to *kefirah* – heresy. For you, coming from a background of heresy anyway – no offense, of course – it's maybe not such a big issue. But for me, coming from a position of truth – there are serious problems studying things that can lead one astray. Can you deny that a person who is born Orthodox or *frum*, and who studies philosophy or . . . what do you call it, things like Biblical Criticism, might be lead to reject the divine basis of the Torah?"

"Sure, that can happen. But don't you believe in a sincere and honest quest for the truth?"

"*Vey iz mir!* You really don't get it. Dovid! We've been *given* the truth! We *know* what it is. *Hashem* gave us the Torah, and that includes the *Torah she-be'al peh* – the oral tradition – and the Kabbalah as well. You have doubts about that, and I'm sorry that you do. I don't hold it against you, of course. It's not your fault. But I'm telling you now that it follows from what we've been given that we should be studying Torah full-time!"

"And how do you know those 'givens' are true?"

"Didn't we discuss this once before? Deep down, a Jew knows that Torah is true. And when you accept it and live it, then you feel and you know that it's true. Of course, there's always a level of *emunah* that goes beyond reason. Dovid, what's wrong with faith?"

"Look, a Christian or Muslim or even an atheist might say just the exact same thing. They have faith that they're right, and you have faith that you're right. Who's to say who's right, unless we try to use reason to figure out who's right? Besides which, if you base everything on faith, you might end up with some crazy views – even as a Jew. Like for example, the people who believe the deceased Lubavitcher Rebbe is *moshiach*."

"I don't know about that. Is that really so crazy?"

"What? You mean you don't think it's crazy?"

"Not necessarily."

"Chaim, I can't believe my ears! Do you really think the Rebbe – who is not even alive anymore – might be *moshiach*?"

"Maybe. I don't know. I'm not saying yes and I'm not saying no. But that's not the point. And of course, you can and should use *sechel*, or reason, but within the limits of the Torah. The Torah gives the parameters, the limits of what a person should believe. You can't just believe anything you want and call it Torah! The question about who is *moshiach* boils down to a *halachic* question – does the Torah allow the possibility that *moshiach* might be someone who comes back from the dead? Are you so sure the Torah rules that out? Have you studied this question?"

"I know enough to know that *moshiach* is supposed to be a *living* leader – a person who unites the people of Israel under the worship of God and observance of the Torah . . . someone who is essentially a great political leader and also has . . . what's that called again . . . *ruah ha-kodesh*, divine spirit."

"Fine! So, maybe a person could die, and come back from the dead, and then be recognized by the *hachamim* – the sages of the generation – as *moshiach*. What's so crazy about that?"

"Chaim, your whole approach is too irrational for me!"

"Dovid, you just don't like what I'm saying, so you're calling it irrational!"

"Well, either way, irrational or not, there's a whole wide world out there that God created. I can't believe that God left it only up to the non-Jews to study the world!"

"Sorry . . . I guess we'll have to agree to disagree on this one."

"Chaim, I'll make a deal with you. If you go to college, I'll go to yeshiva!"

"Very funny, Dovid, very funny! And anyway, I think it's high time for me to get back to the keyboard!"

26

June 5, 2002

Today, difficulty davening. I put on tefillin and I wanted to say the words, but I just couldn't. Part of me wants to believe it's all true, but I just can't honestly say I believe it. If I think of God as Dr. M does, then at least I can say I believe in Being, without a question. And I believe that Being is essentially good. But can I say I believe the Torah is genuinely divinely revealed? Or do I believe rather that Torah is ultimately a human creation that is an attempt (sometimes valiant, sometimes feeble) to obtain a special relationship with Being? And, maybe, sadly, that relationship just can't be had? Or maybe it can be had, but in some other way than thru Torah? If I go pragmatic, as Rabbi Low suggests, I should choose to follow at least <u>some</u> system which says it's possible to have the best relationship with Being. But I keep struggling with the fact that I can't just create an <u>authentic</u> belief by means of a pragmatic argument. So instead of saying the words of the davening, I tried to meditate on Being. I felt a little better afterward. But not much.

The Kabbalah is a fascinating system and there's definitely something to it. I'm not sure I can buy all that stuff about sefiros and soul roots and reincarnation, but it's still pretty amazing. And I was pleasantly surprised to find how much attention Kabbalah pays to sexuality. That's only one facet of it, of course, but it's still important and I'm sure there's even more to it than I've heard so far. I definitely want to learn more Kabbalah. But that conversation I had with Chaim at the wedding really was bizarre and frustrating. It made me realize how different we really are. At times he seems so thoughtful and rational when it comes to explaining Kabbalah. How can such an intelligent person not see value in ~~going to college~~ studying the world around them?

It's still puzzling to me how most Orthodox Jews seem to know so little about Kabbalah. Like E for example. I already know more about Kabbalah after studying with Ch for a few months than she does even though she's been Orthodox all her life. Speaking of E, I think she must be in love with me. The tefillin were an incredible gift. I wrote her a letter thanking her. The more I learn, the more she seems to fall in love with me. She's really getting serious about me. It's almost a little scary sometimes.

Getting back to Kabbalah, I wonder what Dr. M thinks of it. I've got to get up the courage to ask her. I'm a little afraid to ask. Why? I think it's this: I'm afraid to ask because I'm afraid she'll tear it apart. And right now it seems Kabbalah is my lifeline to Judaism.

Last night, the dream came back, this time a little different. It started as usual in the museum. Once again I'm in the room with the shoes. But this time, Chaim is there, and he's holding a shoe. He looks at me, without saying a word. And then, I'm moving off the ground, going up on levels, toward the top of the room. This time, the smoke is heavy. Sweet smell again. Is it incense? My eyes are teary, I can hardly see anything, till I'm out of the room, floating in the sky. Then, the rushing wind and the high-pitched sound starts. I keep going upward, the smoke is dissipating, the sound is getting louder and now I can see the museum below me. But the building seems to have changed, maybe it's no longer the museum. Lots of people seem to be milling around. They didn't seem to be looking at exhibitions. They are doing things, going places, from room to room. I can't see the building too well through the smoke but somehow I can tell that it's an impressive building, medieval-looking, like a castle. Then I wake up.

What does it all mean? Where am I going with all this? Of course, there are still details that I have questions and problems with. For example, I still wish I had some better understanding of kashrut. Reminds me: ask Chaim what Kabbalah says about it. But even about the bigger questions, I'm still confused. When I broke up with Helen, I thought this process would take a few weeks. Then I realized it's more complicated than that. But now I've thought and analyzed the issues through and through, and still can't come to a clear decision about whether ~~or not to believe~~ I am a believer. I can't keep going on like this. What's next?

,

SENIOR YEAR

From: rchgoldstein@rchgoldattorney.com   Sent: 9/2/02 9:32 PM
To: dgoldstein@cuniv.edu
Subject: law school

Dear David,

How's it going? Did you start classes yet? What courses are you taking? What else is going on?

I know things were difficult for you last year, but I really hope you'll be able to get back into the swing of things.

Is there any help you need from me in your applications for law school? By the way, I still know some people at Harbridge.

Dad

From: dgoldstein@cuniv.edu   Sent: 9/3/02 10:15 PM
To: rchgoldstein@rchgoldattorney.com
Subject: Re: law school

Dad,

I'm doing fine. Classes start tomorrow. I'm taking music, existentialist philosophy, medieval history, and Jewish philosophy. I was hoping to take a course in Jewish mysticism but none is being offered this year. Instead, I'm taking a course in modern Jewish literature.

Yes, I will apply for law school. No, thanks – I don't need help.

David

September 11, 2002

One year after 9/11. I can't believe it's my senior year of college. I've got to make the most of this year. Of course my favorite so far is the Jewish Philosophy class with Dr. M. But the other classes are also interesting. In the Jewish Lit class we're reading some authors who wrote in Hebrew, some in English, and some in Yiddish (in translation, of course). I didn't realize how much literature there is, by both secular and religious Jews, from the medieval period all the way up to modern times. There is also a lot of literature from the Holocaust and we'll read some of that, too. We started off with some religious poetry from the Middle Ages. I didn't know that Yehudah Halevi (author of the Kuzari, which is the first thing we're doing in Dr. M.'s class) was a famous poet as well as a philosopher. I like the poetry but I'm still fascinated by the (philosophical) question — which is higher (deeper? more important? more true?) — poetry or philosophy? I still think philosophy is higher. But maybe by the end of the year I'll change my mind!

My other favorite class so far is existentialism. Lots of non-philosophy majors in the class, a lot of them literature majors. It is interesting that many existentialist writers wrote poetry and fiction as well as philosophy. The prof's name is Dr. Breslow. He seems like a really peculiar guy, but a great teacher. On the first day, he gave an overview of existentialism, using Sartre and Kierkegaard as his main examples. It's very different from anything I've had before. There are religious existentialists (like Kierkegaard) as well as atheist existentialists (like Sartre). But all existentialists agree that the most important fact about the human being is not <u>what</u> he is, but <u>that</u> he is. Their slogan is "Existence comes before essence." The fact that a person exists is more important than the kind of thing a person is. According to Sartre, human beings don't even have an essence or pre-ordained set of defining qualities. He uses this to criticize all traditional philosophers. According to Sartre, Plato was wrong when he said that the essence of the human is the intellect; Aristotle was wrong when he defined the human as a rational animal, and Descartes was wrong when he said that the essence of the human is consciousness. Also, the materialists were wrong when they said that man is essentially a bodily thing; the empiricists were wrong when they claimed that man is essentially a sensory being, and the romantics were wrong when the said that man is basically an emotional creature. Of course it's true that humans <u>have</u> intellect, rationality, consciousness, sensation, emotion, body. But none of these things <u>define</u> the human. The existentialist says that the human has to define himself by <u>what he chooses to be</u>. What an amazing idea. By acting, by committing oneself to a certain way of life, a person "defines" himself!

According to Sartre, there is no God, so there's no "objectively" right or wrong way of defining oneself. The responsibility is on you alone to decide what kind of person you're going to be. According to Kierkegaard, faith is the act of commitment to God. It is by choosing to have faith that a person defines himself as religious. Genuine faith cannot come from reason. It is just a pure commitment. And that never changes throughout one's life. It never becomes rational to have faith. It is always an "existential commitment."

Kierkegaard was a Christian, but could this idea work for Judaism? Can a person just choose to be a religious Jew as an existential commitment, without reason? Maybe you can't prove the Torah is divinely given or that there really is hashgacha pratis. But you can still just choose to believe in spite of that. Is this what Rabbi A was saying all along, that it's all about emunah or faith? Maybe Rabbi A is a Jewish existentialist! Maybe he's more sophisticated than I thought.

I'm definitely excited about my courses this year but I also hope I have time to delve more into Kabbalah. I need to call Chaim. (Don't forget to ask him whether there's a kabbalistic explanation for kashrus.) Despite our differences, I want to continue learning with him. But it's a trek to get over to his house. I wish there was someone I could study with on campus. Maybe I should go visit R. Abraham again. Maybe he'd be willing to study Zohar with me or find someone else who will.

I should call E also. I missed her call the other day and she's going to be upset that I haven't called her already. Call her soon!

<u>3</u>

"Hey, Chaim! How are you?"
"Dovid! How are you? How nice of you to call! What's going on?"
"I'm back in school. This is my last year. What's new with you?"
"Well . . . actually . . . over the summer I got smicha."
"Wow! So now you're officially a rabbi. Congratulations! Or should I say: mazal tov!"
"Thanks. And what's new with you? How's your Jewish flame?"
"You mean my soul?"
"No, tzaddik! I mean your girlfriend!"
"Oh! Sorry!"
"So? Are you engaged yet?"

"Very funny. No, we're not engaged. But I'm still seeing her."

"Good. All in good time. So when are you coming over to visit?"

"I'd love to come over. I'm just real busy and it's hard to get over there."

"Yeah, I understand. Actually, I've started doing some teaching, so I'm pretty booked up. But maybe we can do some learning over the phone."

"Are you serious?"

"Why not? Lots of people do it. What would you like to learn?"

"More Kabbalah, of course! By the way, there is something I wanted to ask you."

"Go right ahead."

"You've said many times that Kabbalah gives the real explanation for the mitzvos."

"Yes, definitely."

"But how many Jews — I mean, even Orthodox Jews — really understand the proper kabbalistic intention of the mitzvos?"

"Very few, I'm sorry to say. That's why we're still in galus, *in exile. The Zohar speaks very harshly of those who fulfill the mitzvos without the proper intent. Still it's better to do a mitzvah without intent than not to do it at all. Are you familiar with this saying?* Mi-toch she-lo lishmah, ba lishmah. *It means —"*

"Yes, I've heard that before. If you start out doing mitzvos without the right intention, eventually you'll end up doing them with the right intention."

"Very good! But look, Dovid . . . you shouldn't get the idea that I'm saying that the reasons for all the mitzvos are completely understood. There are still secrets, even within the Kabbalah. A person could be a great mekubbal, *a great sage or even a prophet. Yet there might still be aspects of certain mitzvos that he doesn't understand."*

"Can you give me an example?"

"The classic example is the parah adumah *or red heifer. Very few people — maybe no one — understands the reason for it."*

"Ah, yes. Now that you mention it, I think I've heard of that before. But why would that be? Why would God keep things secret from the great mystics?"

"Well, first of all, God's wisdom is infinite, and human wisdom is finite. So there's a limit to what we can understand, and that includes the wisest among us. But it's more than that. Do you remember the order of the sefiros? Kesser, *which represents God's* ratzon, *or will, is higher than* hochmah, *which is wisdom. Since* kesser *is higher than* hochmah, *it's got to be the case that certain things flow directly from God's will without reason or explanation."*

"Interesting idea."

"And even for those things which could be understood with great effort, there might be some great potential for misunderstanding, which could be very dangerous. And besides, not all knowledge is a good thing. For example, take the knowledge of how to split an atom. We wouldn't want this kind of knowledge to be too widespread, would we?"

"Well, I can see how the knowledge of splitting an atom could be abused. But I don't understand how the knowledge of kabbalistic secrets could be abused. Anyway, speaking of explanations for mitzvos, I've been meaning to ask you about the mitzvah of keeping kosher."

"Yes? What about it?"

"*Is that also something that we don't understand? I mean, why are we allowed to eat certain animals and not others? I've heard some interesting theories about this, but I was wondering whether there is a kabbalistic explanation.*"

"*As far as I know, there is an explanation, but only up to a point.*"

"*What's the explanation? Can you tell me?*"

"*It's a very deep topic, and it involves an area of Kabbalah I haven't managed to explain to you so far. I can't give you all the details, but maybe I can give you the basic idea.*"

"*I'll take whatever I can get.*"

"*OK, I'll try. As I explained some time ago, all of the mitzvos have to do with advancing the process of the* yihud, *the unification of the sefiros. For example, the mitzvah of taking the* arba minim – *the four kinds of species on Sukkos – has to do with the unification of the sefiros, since each kind represents a different sefirah or set of sefiros.*"

"*Yes, I'm familiar with that idea from the* Siddur."

"*Great. Well, eating is a holy act, or at least it can be and should be. Food contains energy, and when you eat, you are elevating the food into energy that you are then going to use for a holy purpose – that is, to serve God, which means unifying Hashem's name. So eating should be done* lishmah, *too. Do you follow?*"

"*Yes, I think so.*"

"*Now, I've already explained to you that the ten sefiros are the basis for everything that exists in this world. This means that everything that exists in the physical realm has a spiritual root, or source, in the sefiros. For example, as I've said many times, the human being parallels the entire set of ten sefiros. That's what the Torah means when it says that Adam was created* be-tzelem Elokim. *Furthermore, the male represents* tiferes *while the female represents* malchus. *And the union that takes place between husband and wife parallels the unification of the sefiros of* tiferes *and* malchus. Right?"

"*Yes, I remember all that.*"

"*There are many other examples. The Kabbalah teaches that heaven, or* shamayim, *represents* tiferes, *and* aretz, *or earth, represents* malchus. *Also, they say that the sun represents* tiferes *and the moon represents* malchus. *The same applies to many other things in the world. In fact, the four* yesodos – *the four basic building blocks of nature – air, fire, earth and water – they all have their spiritual root in different sefiros.*"

"*Hang on, Chaim. Did you know that those four building blocks you just mentioned are the four elements of matter in Aristotle's physics?*"

"*Sorry, no. I don't know anything about Aristotle. All I know is that in Kabbalah, air represents* tiferes, *fire represents* din, *water represents* hesed, *and earth represents* malchus. *And that's not arbitrary. There are reasons for why each of these things corresponds to a specific sefirah.*"

"*I'd like to hear more about that, but let's not get sidetracked. What does this all have to do with explaining the kosher animals?*"

"*Hang on, I'm getting there. First, there's another* yesod – *a fundamental teaching – that I have to explain. You see, just as there are positive divine forces in the world, there are negative forces in the world, too. One kabbalistic name for the whole system of negative forces in the world is the* sitra ahara, *which means, literally, the 'other side.'"*

"Hmm. Do you really believe in that? It sounds like something out of Star Wars."

"Where do you think they got the idea from? But seriously, Dovid, haven't you ever heard of the yetzer ha-tov *and the* yetzer ha-ra*?"*

"Yes. The good inclination and the evil inclination."

"OK. So – do you believe in that?"

"I guess so."

"There are also good angels and bad angels. For example, there's the angel, or malach, *Rafael, who is the angel of healing. There's an angel called Michoel, who tries to encourage the Jewish people and help them to keep mitzvos. But there's also the angel of death, the* malach ha-maves, *who is sometimes equated with the Satan, or the angel that brings people to sin. There are other angels that correspond to the seventy nations of the world."*

"Chaim, do you really believe in angels?"

"Of course. What's the big deal? I believe in Hashem, so why shouldn't I believe in angels? Angels are forces created by Hashem to do His will. Look, let's talk more about angels some other time. My point is that just as there are positive spiritual forces in the world, there are negative forces as well. Both the positive and the negative forces are created by Hashem, ultimately for the greater good. Now, it's obvious why there are positive forces. God is good, and He wants to make the world a better place. The negative forces are there to challenge us, to give us a role in bringing about the yihud *of the divine name. Without the negative forces in the world, there would be no* behirah, *no free choice. Without death and injury and sickness, there would be no challenge in life for us to save people or help people. Don't you agree?"*

"I can agree with that, but I'm not sure we need to postulate negative and positive forces in order to explain free will. But never mind. Please go on."

"All right. Now, in Kabbalah, the positive spiritual forces are referred to as kochos ha-taharah, *that is, the forces or powers of purity. And the negative forces – the forces of the* sitra ahara – *these are referred to as* kochos ha-tumah, *or the forces of impurity. Got that?"*

"Yes."

"And remember, I said earlier that all things in the natural world have their root in the spiritual realm."

"Yes."

"Well, that's what explains the whole realm of tumah *and* taharah – *purity and impurity. Some things have their root in the* kochos ha-tumah, *while other things have their root in the* kochos ha-taharah. *For example, death and certain kinds of diseases have their root in the* kochos ha-tumah. *That's why contact with death and certain diseases make you* tameh. *This is also related to the* tumah *of the* niddah – *that's a woman who menstruates. Water, on the other hand, which stems from* hesed *and is closely associated with life, comes from the* kochos ha-taharah. *That's why in many circumstances, immersion in water – that is, in a* mikveh, *can make a person become* tahor, *or pure."*

"OK. Very interesting."

"The same thing is true of living creatures, whether bird or beast. All animals represent and in some way embody the spiritual forces. Now, different animals have different kinds of

qualities and powers. For example, there are animals that climb, walk, or run. There are animals that bite and tear. There are animals that crawl, scurry, and slither. Each of the different species does these things in different ways. Furthermore, since Hashem has an infinite number of powers, there's an infinite number of possible species."

"OK. I'm still with you so far."

"Now here's the main point: the animals that are tahor *have their source or root in the positive forces, the* kochos ha-taharah. *The animals that are* tameh *come from the negative spiritual forces, the* kochos ha-tumah.*"*

"I see."

"And though I cannot give you a reayah *— that's a proof — of what I'm saying, nevertheless there is a* siman, *a sign, that what I'm saying is true."*

"What's that?"

"You'll notice that many of the animals which the Torah says are tameh *are repulsive in some way. This is certainly true of the creepy-crawly things, or things that slither and slink on the ground. Almost all of those things are not kosher. Also, you won't find a single kosher animal that is poisonous. In fact, most of the animals which are* tahor *are either docile or easily domesticated. Almost all the kosher animals are herbivores rather than carnivores. Regarding the birds, almost all the non-kosher birds are birds of prey that attack and tear other animals apart. Now I'm not saying that the reason why some are prohibited while others are permitted has to do with their behavior. What I'm saying is that the way these animals and birds behave is an expression of their spiritual source or root, either in the* kochos ha-tumah *or the* kochos ha-taharah. *Do you follow?"*

"Yes."

"Still, there is a lot we — or at least I — really don't know or understand about tumah *and* taharah. *Like, for example, why is it that having split hooves and chewing one's cud makes an animal kosher? Or why is it that having fins and scales makes a fish kosher? I really don't know why that is, and I've never seen a Kabbalistic explanation for what's behind that. But what I do know is that the kosher animals come from the* kochos ha-taharah, *and the non-kosher animals come from the* kochos ha-tumah.*"*

"Chaim, I think I get the basic idea, and it's really interesting. But I've got one question. Let's suppose that some animal does come from a negative spiritual force. Still, what's wrong with eating that animal, especially once it's dead?"

"Ah, well, that goes back to what I said earlier — namely, that food has a certain energy that is released into the body. But the energy stored in the body of a non-kosher animal is energy that comes from a negative spiritual root. When you eat the meat of a non-kosher animal, you release the negative energy that was in that animal into your body. Of course, that's very bad, especially if you're trying to live a holy life like a Jew is supposed to do. By the way, do you know who the Ramban was?"

"I think so. Didn't he write a commentary on the Torah?"

"Yes, and he was one of the greatest mekubbalim *as well, though he only hints at kabbalistic ideas in his commentary."*

"I see. Well, what about him?"

"The Ramban wrote in his commentary on the Torah that if you eat certain non-kosher animals, you might take on their characteristics. Now, many people mistakenly think that what he's saying there is that if you eat the meat of a fierce and vicious bird of prey, you'll become fierce and vicious, too. That's not really what he meant. He was hinting at this kabbalistic idea. What he meant was that if you eat the meat of a non-kosher animal, the negative source or root from which it stems might affect your mind or soul. But when you eat the meat of a kosher animal, you release the energy from a positive source, and you can now use that positive energy to serve Hashem and do mitzvos. Do you follow?"

"Yes, I follow. I don't know if I believe it all, but you've certainly given me a lot of food for thought!"

"Ah! I knew you'd be skeptical. That's why I hesitated to get into it."

"No, Chaim. Seriously, I'm glad you've told me about it. It's fascinating. Well, I guess we did some learning over the phone after all!"

"Hey, Dovid, it was nice talking to you, but I've really got to go. Call again some time and we'll learn some more."

"Yes, I'll do that. Thanks so much!"

4

"Hello? Rabbi Abraham?"

"Yes? Who is it? Come in."

"It's me, David Goldstein. How are you, Rabbi?"

"Well, well! How nice to see you! I haven't seen you in ages. Please, please come in. Have a seat!"

"Thanks, Rabbi."

"What's new? How are you getting along?"

"I'm good. Real good."

"*Baruch Hashem.* Please, sit down."

"Thanks."

"Well, what can I do for you?"

"Actually, there are two things I wanted to ask you about. First, have you ever heard of existentialism?

"I've heard the term, but I really don't know what it means. Why?"

"I'm taking a course in existentialism, and it turns out there are religious existentialists who think of faith as a commitment that is not rational. Based on some of our conversations we had back when I was a freshman, I was wondering whether you'd consider yourself an existentialist."

"What a question! I'm impressed that you remember our conversations so well. And I'd be honored to think of myself in such fancy philosophical terms! But really I don't know enough about existentialism to answer your question. I would recommend that you look at an article called *The Lonely Man of Faith* by Rabbi

Joseph Soloveitchik. Have you heard the name? He was one of the greatest modern Jewish thinkers of our century. From what I gather, Rav Soloveitchik is considered something of an existentialist thinker, but I'm not even sure that's correct."

"OK, maybe you can give me that reference later. Still, Rabbi, isn't it your view that basically the human is not a rational creature and that faith is a completely non-rational commitment, totally going beyond reason?"

"Well, yes and no. I don't think I'd want to say that the human is essentially not a rational being. If I remember correctly, all I said is that a person has to take the first step, the leap of *emunah*, faith, in order to reach knowledge of Hashem in his heart by learning Torah and doing the *mitzvos*. But later, once you get to that knowledge of Hashem, then you come to know in your heart that Hashem is real. So, at that point, your faith is very rational."

"Hmm. So once you attain that knowledge, you don't need *emunah* any more?"

"No, that can't be right. You always need *emunah*. Any knowledge of Hashem that a person has is always limited and can grow further. You still need *emunah* because your knowledge of *Hashem* will collapse, and certainly not grow, without it."

"Interesting. I'll have to think about it. I'm not sure whether your view counts as existentialist. But it doesn't really matter what you call it. Anyway, let me get to my second question."

"Sure. I hope it's an easier one!"

"I think it is. Do you remember you once said that you could find someone who might be able to learn with me on a weekly basis?"

"Ah! You're interested in learning? Great — no problem! That *was* an easy question! What would you like to learn?"

"I want to study the Zohar."

"Ah, well, that's a different story! How did you latch on to that?"

"A friend of mine told me about it. Actually, he's my cousin. He's very Orthodox. Why? What's the problem? Is there something wrong with the Zohar?"

"*Has ve-shalom!* There's nothing wrong with the Zohar! It was written by Rabbi Shimon bar Yohai, one of the greatest of the tannaim. Look, I'm glad you want to study Torah. But you know, Kabbalah is very advanced. So David, I appreciate the fact that you want to learn, but I really can't help you with the Zohar. You know, there are four levels of Torah: *peshat, derash, remez* and *sod.* Have you heard these terms?"

"No, I don't think so."

"David, you don't even know this basic terminology and yet you want to study the esoteric meaning of the Torah?"

"I don't know those terms, but maybe I do know what they mean. Can you explain them?"

"Yes. *Peshat* is the plain meaning of the Torah. *Derash* is the rabbinic interpretation of the plain meanings, drawing connections, making analogies, going beyond the plain meaning. This is what you find in the Talmud. *Remez* is what the Torah hints at through *gematrios* and allusions that you couldn't get at through strict interpretation. You will find some of this in the Talmud as well. But *sod* – that's the inner meaning, the secret meaning of the Torah. That's what the Kabbalah is really about. There are only slight hints of this in the Talmud."

"OK, so actually, I knew those concepts. I just didn't know them by those names. It's interesting that you say there are four levels. That sounds kind of like the four levels of the name of Hashem."

"I wouldn't know about that. What I do know is that *sod* is the deepest level of the Torah, the secret meaning that's taught by the Kabbalah and the Zohar. And it's secret because it's not known to the average person – I mean, even the average religious Jew, who keeps Torah. And before you can learn the *sod* level, you must master all other levels first. That's just the way it is."

"But Rabbi, is it important to study Kabbalah at all?"

"Yes, but only if you're prepared for it. David, have you been learning *Tanakh* like I told you?"

"Uh, off and on."

"Have you *mastered* the *Tanakh*?"

"No, of course not."

"What about the Talmud? Have you studied it?"

"I've studied *Pirkei Avot*, like you suggested."

"Great. But is that it? Have you studied anything else in the Talmud?"

"No, not really."

"Do you have any idea how vast the Talmud is?"

"Sort of. Not really."

"Well, *that* I'd be happy to help you with! Look, in order to study Kabbalah, a person should really master the first three levels – *peshat*, *derash*, and *remez*. That means *Tanakh*, Talmud, *halacha* – all the aspects of Jewish law."

"And how many people ever get to that stage?"

"Very few indeed."

"How about yourself, Rabbi?"

"*Me*? Well, I can't say I have mastered the Talmud. I've been through the entire Talmud once, and several parts of it many times. But that's not mastery."

"So you've never studied the Zohar or Kabbalah?"

"No, not really. I know a few things about it. Some things everyone knows – I mean everyone who is Orthodox."

"Like what? Like the idea of the seven *sefiros* which are associated with the seven weeks of the *omer*?

"Right, exactly."

"And like the '*le-shem yihud*,' the kabbalistic prayer of intent which is said before davening and before doing certain *mitzvos*, such as shaking the lulav?"

"Yes, that too. I see you've been reading the Siddur. Very good! Sure, I'm familiar with things like that. But frankly, I have no clue what it all means. Anyway, David, let's talk about you, not me. Did you know that there's a customary minimum age rule for studying Zohar? You're supposed to be forty before you study Kabbalah."

"No, I didn't know that."

"Yes, and even though – thank God! – I'm over forty, well, I just don't think I'm there yet! And another thing is all the terrible popularization of the Kabbalah that's come about in recent years. It's become a fad, with all sorts of people setting themselves up as authorities on Kabbalah when they don't even keep *mitzvos* or know the basics. You know what the Talmud says about studying the secrets of the Torah? You should only study the secrets if – I'm paraphrasing a little bit – if you've 'filled your belly with the meat and potatoes' of the Torah laws governing everyday life. In fact there are dangers involved in studying Kabbalah before the proper time. What need do most of us have for the mysteries and secrets of the Torah when just learning and doing the basics is challenging enough?"

"I thought the Kabbalah is supposed to be what gives meaning to learning and doing all the basics. That's why I want to study it. I figure if I understand the inner meanings of things, then maybe I'll want to keep the *mitzvos*."

"Well, I certainly admire that thought. But really, you're supposed to keep the Torah regardless of whether you understand the deeper meanings. David, have you been keeping Shabbos?"

"Yes, pretty much."

"How about kashrus?"

"Lately, I've been pretty good about that too. I even have *tefillin* now, which I put on at least once a week."

"Excellent! I'm really glad to hear that!"

"So? What's your final decision? Will you help me study Zohar?"

"Sorry, no. I personally couldn't help you study the Zohar. But like I said, I can help you if you want to study Talmud. I'm going to be teaching a beginner's class in Talmud, starting up next week. Why don't you join? Look, if you're really serious about Kabbalah, you've got to study Talmud anyway. That's the plain and simple truth."

<u>5</u>

"Dr. Maimon?"

"Yes, David. Please, come in. How are you? Have a seat."

"Thanks."

"What's on your mind? Are you enjoying the class?"

"Yes, I am. But actually, there's something else I wanted to ask you about."

"What's that?"

"I wanted to get your opinion about Kabbalah, and, in particular, the Zohar."

"Kabbalah? The Zohar? David, how did you get interested in that?"

"Well, I have a friend — actually, he's a relative of mine, who is really into Kabbalah. He's been teaching me a few things about it and I'm really interested in learning more. But I noticed you haven't made any reference to it at all in our conversations. So I just wondered: what do you think of Kabbalah?"

"Well, it's all very fascinating from a literary and historical and psychological point of view, but I must tell you that if you're looking for truth, I wouldn't go there."

"Why not?"

"Hmm. Where to begin? Let's talk about the text of the Zohar first. Some scholars claim that the authorship of the Zohar is a complex issue. But to me it's pretty clear that it was largely a hoax. It was probably written in the thirteenth century by Moses de Leon himself. Yet it purports to be a record of much earlier writings dating back to Shimon Bar Yohai, who lived during the first century. That's historically a preposterous claim. The Zohar clearly contains material that stems from other, later schools of thought such as Neo-Platonism and theosophy, with some elements of medieval philosophy thrown in. The style and language of the Zohar is clearly post-rabbinic. In fact, some of the literary quality of the Zohar is rather poor. The Zohar purports to be a *midrash* on the level of other *midrashim* such as those collected in Midrash Rabbah and other similar collections, but there is no comparison between them. Even the legends and tales told in the Zohar are second-grade level compared with the stories in Midrash Rabbah. The actions and speeches attributed to Shimon bar Yohai and his circle just could not have happened the way they are described in the Zohar. Honestly, it's been a while since I looked at the Zohar, but it's always the same story told over and over again. It's always something like this: 'So-and-so was traveling on the road, and he was studying a certain text. Then he met a stranger who didn't appear to be Jewish, but the stranger said such-and-such' — at this point, some passage is interpreted in terms of the Kabbalistic doctrine of the *sefirot*. Then the text continues — 'And the traveler responded, "What a profound teaching!" Then he asked the stranger who he was, and he turned out to be Jewish. He kissed him on the head and said, "Thank God there are still people like us who teach the secrets of the Torah!"' Again and again, the same story. These are clearly fabrications."

"Wow. I didn't know all that."

"Well, you should. Given these facts, don't you think we should be suspicious of the doctrines in the Zohar as well? And since the Zohar is the central work in the history of Kabbalah, it throws the entire Kabbalah into serious question. Besides, the doctrines and teachings of the Kabbalah are very problematic. The doctrine of the *sefirot* smacks of paganism and polytheism. The idea that God has elements and parts, and that through our actions we are able to assist in the unification of these parts, sounds very pagan to me. That's what the standard kabbalistic prayer, the *le-shem yihud*, is all about. It seems to me that the kabbalists were very much influenced by pagan ideas. Also, the sexual imagery so central to the Zohar is rather peculiar, to say the least."

"Well, sexual imagery's not exactly second-grade level stuff!"

"David, when I made that comment, I meant that the stories or tales in the Zohar are not very imaginative. But the use of sexual imagery is a separate issue."

"Oh, I see."

"Furthermore, there's the Kabbalistic idea that the Jewish soul is *helek eloka mi-maal* – a part of the divine. That sounds very heretical indeed! There's also the doctrine of reincarnation –that's completely unheard of in any of the Talmudic literature. This demonstrates two things: the Zohar contains non-Jewish doctrines, and, the Zohar couldn't have been written during the time of the Talmud. This is not normative Judaism! Moreover, the Kabbalah has encouraged superstitious and magical practices."

"Oh? Like what?"

"Palm-reading, face-reading, fortune-telling, automatic writing – you name it!"

"Automatic writing? What's that?"

"It means writing under a trance. For example, it is known that Yosef Karo wrote a work called the *Maggid Mesharim*, which was supposedly the record of communications of an angel to him."

"Sounds bizarre. Hey, wait – isn't Yosef Karo the author of the *Shulhan Aruch*, the code of law?"

"Yes. That's a very different kind of work. That's a halachic code, and it is written with a great deal of logical and analytical rigor. Anyway, getting back to Kabbalah, another problem with Kabbalah is the false messiahs it has spawned. I'm thinking of Shabbetai Tzvi, Jacob Frank, Breslov messianism, and the latest incarnation – pardon the expression – of this problem, the Lubavitch heresy. The whole Hasidic movement is founded on the work of the Baal Shem Tov, who claimed that Kabbalah should be taught to the masses because we are supposedly nearing the coming of the Messiah. The followers of the Baal Shem Tov practically deified him, and it's not surprising that they have practically deified their leaders. It's all a result of the unbridled charismatic approach fostered by Hasidism, driven by the Kabbalah. And to top it off, the Kabbalah, as far as I can see, is inherently anti-rational and anti-philosophical."

"For you, that must be the worst thing of all."

"What can I say? Kabbalah tends to minimize the ability of the human mind to understand God rationally and without special divine help. In fact, that has a lot to do with its superficial popularity today. Everything the Kabbalah teaches is through divine inspiration, not rational inquiry and analysis. The next major figure after the Zohar was the Ari, who claims to have his information directly from Elijah the prophet himself. In his system – which, I must say, I could never make head or tail of – things get even more absurd, and more explicitly sexual, too, I might add."

"Well, Dr. Maimon, it sounds like you really want to discourage me from studying it."

"You're a big boy, and you'll do whatever you want to do. Like I said, Kabbalah is a fascinating development from the point of view of the history of religion, and it's had a powerful effect on the development of Judaism – a negative effect, if you ask me. Certainly, it's worth studying as a phenomenon. But if you're looking for Truth with a capital T, I wouldn't recommend it. Do you want to study *Tanakh*? That's wonderful. Talmud? That's fine, too. Halacha? That's OK. But if you really want the truth, my advice is: stick with Jewish philosophy. If you ask me, that's the most intellectually mature version of Judaism. That's really what you're looking for, I think."

6
—

From: dgoldstein@cuniv.edu   Sent: 11/5/2002 3:35 PM
To: rlow@ahavattorah.org.il
Subject: Zohar

Dear Rabbi Low,

Not long ago I had a discussion with Rabbi Abraham about the Zohar. He thinks the Zohar is authentic, and that it was written by R. Shimon Bar Yohai. I reread your email from last year and it seems you agree a lot with him. But then I discussed the Zohar with Dr. Maimon, and she thinks the whole thing is pretty much a hoax and that many of the doctrines taught by Kabbalah are actually heretical.

I was curious – what is your view about the Zohar? And is it really true that people should study Kabbalah only if they are over forty?

David

From: rlow@ahavattorah.org.il   Sent: 11/7/02 6:18 PM
To: dgoldstein@cuniv.edu
Subject: Zohar and Kabbalah

Dear David,

Good to hear from you. I know you too well to think you're just asking a theoretical question about the Zohar. I see that you are persistent in your desire to study Kabbalah. Good for you! But like I said in my email last year, there are some issues to be careful about.

Although I'm not an expert on Kabbalah, I'll try to answer some of your questions. First of all, despite the fact that the Zohar is widely regarded as the central text in kabbalah literature, it is certainly not the first or the only text. There are earlier texts such as Sefer Habahir and Sefer Yetzirah. There is also a sefer called Shaarei

Orah which was written by Rabbi Yosef Gikatillia before the Zohar became known. It contains many doctrines that are similar to the Zohar. (Even the name Shaarei Orah – Gates of Light – seems deliberately chosen to parallel the name of the Zohar, which means "Shining.") Shaarei Orah, which was written in Hebrew, actually has been translated into English and I would say it is very accessible. If I were you I would start with the Shaarei Orah rather than with the Zohar. By the way, the Shaarei Orah was written in response to an inquiry from a student! I would also recommend R. Moshe Chaim Luzatto's *Derech Hashem* as a starting place, and also his *Daas Tevunos*, both of which are available in English.

Regarding the authorship of the Zohar, this is a fascinating and complex question that has not yet been resolved. Personally, I think that even from a strictly "academic" point of view, it's quite mistaken to say that the Zohar is a hoax. There is evidence that at least some of the teachings of the Zohar and the Kabbalah go back to Talmudic times. There is evidence of esoteric schools that thrived throughout Jewish history long before the Zohar was published. The Talmud itself mentions the concept of "megilas sesarim" – that is, hidden texts, or texts studied only within certain circles. So it is known that there were groups or circles of scholars who had secret traditions, and who wrote down some of these traditions. It stands to reason that these circles included some of the great tannaim of the Mishnah period. Hence it is plausible that secret traditions were passed down from generation to generation, from ancient times until the time came when some Kabbalists in the late thirteenth century saw fit to publicize them. Some of the tannaim, such as R. Shimon Bar Yohai and his group, were known to be more adept at these mysteries. So it is not surprising that he is the central figure quoted in the Zohar. Now, in my view, it is quite possible and even likely that over the centuries, these doctrines might have evolved or been reinterpreted anew in each generation. If it is stated in the Zohar that Rabbi Shimon said "such and such," it does not necessarily mean that the historical Shimon actually made that statement verbatim. Rather, the content of what he said has been retained even if the form of its expression has been altered. One might go so far as to view Kabbalah as one legitimate interpretation or theoretical framework in which to place Judaism, recognizing that other theories such as, for example, Maimonides' more rationalistic framework, are also legitimate.

I'm sure Rabbi Abraham would disagree, but I tend toward the hypothesis that Moses de Leon or someone living roughly around that time wrote a good portion of what we know as the Zohar today. Whether or not this is true, I still believe that the bulk of the Zohar is based on esoteric traditions, some oral, some written, that go back to the Talmud, and even farther back to more ancient times. To me, it seems preposterous to say the entire Zohar as we know it was written by a single person. The Zohar is like the Hebrew Scriptures or the Talmud in this way. It contains too many different strands, too many different voices, too many different kinds of texts and views to say that it was all written by one person. (However, it is possible that one person or two people could collate and organize different texts into one final whole, as did Rav Ashi with the Talmud.)

Today, it's impossible to separate the strands of the Zohar into ancient, authentic, invented, interpolated, etc. In fact, great Orthodox scholars such as Rav Yaakov Emden claimed that much of what we know as the Zohar is not of ancient origin. But other authorities regard it as a holy book, and over time the Zohar has been universally embraced by the Orthodox. Indeed, the fact that the Zohar has received general acceptance among the mekubbalim and among the people of Israel generally gives it a certain sacred status, as is the case, say, with other works such as Rambam's Mishneh Torah and Rav Yosef Karo's code of law, the Shulhan Aruch. So even if some things have crept into the Zohar and Kabbalah that do not originate with rabbinic teachings, it is still a *sefer kadosh*, a holy book.

Dr. Maimon claims the Zohar contains heretical doctrines. This is a charge often made by those who prefer a more rationalistic and more mythologically sanitized approach to Judaism. Many of the great mekubbalim were knowledgeable and pious sages, and they were sensitive to the fact that some of the Kabbalistic doctrines seemed heretical (e.g., attributing parts to G-d, or attributing change within G-d). Many mekubbalim responded in great detail to such charges and though I have not made a study of this literature I am confident that they knew what they were up to. It is somewhat arrogant to accuse these great sages of heresy.

An entirely different question is whether and how *you* should study Kabbalah. As I said in my last email to you on this topic, there really are some dangers here. The rule about being over forty is not universally agreed upon, so that's not such an issue. Still, there is no question that in an ideal situation, you would first master at least the basics of Tanakh, Talmud, Halacha, etc., before delving into Kabbalah. The Talmud says one should "enter the *Pardes*" only if one has "filled one's belly" with the study of practical law." It is not entirely clear that here the term "enter the *Pardes*" refers to the study of what is today commonly called "Kabbalah" (such as the doctrine of the sefiros, the notion that G-d has male and female aspects that need to be united, etc.). Perhaps here the Talmud is referring to something else. (Maimonides thought it referred to the study of physics and metaphysics.) But let's assume that "entering the *Pardes*" does mean something like delving into Kabbalah. It seems to me that the phrase "filling one's belly" connotes a subjective criterion – that is, for certain people, more study of practical law may be necessary than for others before they go on to study Kabbalah. David, have you "filled your belly" with the study of practical law? I would certainly agree with R. Abraham that you should at least get more solid grounding in Talmud – if not before studying Kabbalah, then at least in the process of doing so.

Above all, you need to be careful to study with the right people and the right frame of mind. And you must be careful not to lose your grounding in the basics of Torah practice . . . which leads me to my next set of (now predictable!) questions. Are you back into davening again? What about keeping Shabbat? How about tefillin? Are you being truthful and honest in your relationships with others and with yourself? I believe that without practice of the basics, study of the kabbalah is at best an academic exercise, and at worst, a form of spiritual experimentation that can lead one astray from the Truth.

Sincerely,

Rabbi Low

From: dgoldstein@cuniv.edu   Sent: 11/ 7/ 2002 10:02 AM
To: rlow@ahavattorah.org.il
Subject: Re: Zohar and Kabbalah

Dear Rabbi Low,

Thanks for your response. To answer your questions. I'm getting back into davening lately, though still struggling with the issue of repetition. I've got a pair of tefillin which I use regularly and I've been keeping Shabbat, though not 100 percent. I'm still interested in exploring Kabbalah and Jewish meditation some more. But I'm realizing more and more that Judaism is a package deal, and if you try to keep parts of it without others it doesn't work so well. You've convinced me that at least I should also study Talmud. Even though I don't see eye to eye with him on so many other things, I'm going to take a class with Rabbi Abraham.

Thanks again for your help!

David

7

"Good evening! I'm Rabbi Abraham, and today we are starting our first Talmud class. Will everyone please open up to the first page? This is meant to be an interactive class, so you're supposed to interact both with me and with the text! You're looking at the first page of the *Talmud Bavli*, also known as the Babylonian Talmud. Notice that the Talmud Bavli starts on page *beis*, which means page two. You see the *beis* in the left top corner? Circle it with your pencil! Remember, always bring a pencil. You're going to want to mark up your text! Now, why does it start with page *beis*, or two? Shouldn't it start on page *aleph*? *Nu*? Any ideas? I'll tell you why! It's a reminder that this is an oral tradition! If we started on page *aleph*, you might get the wrong impression that the whole thing can be written down,

עין משפט
נר מצוה

מסורת הש״ס

פרק ראשון ברכות מאימתי

RASHI

מאימתי

Tosfos

מאימתי
"FROM WHEN"

MISHNA

GEMARA

רב נסים גאון

and that's false! Now, the Talmud is made up of two layers of text, the *Mishnah* and the *Gemara*. The Mishnah was composed and compiled from earlier sources by Rabbi Yehudah ha-Nasi about a hundred years after the time of the Second Temple. Rabbi Yehudah was the head of the Jewish community at the time, and he was also a descendant of King David. The *hachamim*, or sages, quoted in the Mishnah are known as *tannaim*, which means 'teachers.' Generally speaking, the Mishnah is very concise, and it states mostly practical laws. Sometimes it mentions disagreements among the *tannaim* over matters of practical law. Rarely does the Mishnah explain how the laws have been derived from the written Torah, or why the *hachamim* disagree on a particular point.

"On the other hand, the Gemara was compiled later than the Mishnah. It was composed over several centuries and was put into its final form by Ravina and Rav Ashi, who lived in Bavel in the fifth century of the Common Era. That's why it's called the Talmud Bavli. The *hachamim* who lived at this later time are known as *amoraim*, which means 'masters.' Another version of the Gemara was composed in Israel, and that's known as the Jerusalem Talmud, or Talmud Yerushalmi.

"The Gemara is written mostly in Aramaic because that was the spoken language at the time. Unlike the Mishnah, the Gemara is not concise at all! The Gemara goes into lengthy, detailed conversations and explanations of the Mishnah, including things like how the *tannaim* derived practical laws from the Torah, the rules for interpreting scripture, the basis for their arguments, under what circumstances those laws apply, and the final ruling of law in cases of dispute. The Gemara includes other things as well, such as *midrash* and *aggadah* – these are commentaries on the stories in the Torah, homiletical interpretations, stories about the sages themselves, sometimes even things like medical remedies, matters of health, potions, you name it! The Gemara very often goes off on tangents. It doesn't always stick to the topics covered in the Mishnah.

"Now, on the inside of your page, you'll find Rashi's commentary on the Talmud. It's really impossible to learn Gemara without Rashi! Rashi lived in France in the eleventh century. On the outside of your page you'll find Tosafos, which means additional commentaries. They were written by later scholars, some of whom were Rashi's students and descendants who lived in France and Germany. Generally, the Tosafos goes into greater depth and analysis of the Talmud, sometimes disagreeing with Rashi's commentary. Every page of the Talmud follows this pattern: the inside is Rashi, and the outside is Tosafos. Now, do you see the largest word on the page? What does it say? "*Me-emasai.*" That's the first word of the first *mishnah*. So let's jump into the first *mishnah*. "*Me-emasai korin es shema be-arvis?*"– which means: from what time do we read *shema* at night? And the Gemara answers . . . ."

8

"Esther! How are you?"

"I'm OK. But how are *you*? You've been pretty busy lately. What have you been up to?"

"Oh, different things. Applying for law school, learning . . . ."

"And what've you been learning lately?"

"Actually, I've been taking a Talmud class with R. Abraham."

"Oh? That's great!"

"And I'm really busy with my Jewish Philosophy course with Dr. Maimon."

"Of course. That goes without saying."

"But Esther, what I've been meaning to tell you is that I've been making good use of the *tefillin*."

"I'm glad to hear that! David, to be honest, I was beginning to wonder."

"About what?"

"You know, you haven't even called me in *two weeks*!"

"Really? Has it been that long? I'm sorry, Esther. I've just been so distracted."

"David, can I ask you a question?"

"Uh-oh. This sounds serious. What is it?"

"I just want to make sure – is everything still OK between us?"

"Why? Don't you think so?"

"David, I guess it's partly my fault because we never really talk about how we feel about each other."

"Esther, don't I tell you all the time how attractive you are?"

"I'm not talking about that. David. I'm sorry to bring this up, but do you remember when we had dinner together about a year and a half ago – the night you told me that your mother was planning to visit?"

"Yes, I remember."

"I don't know about you, but I felt something that night – something special. Did you?"

"I think so. But look, I'm sorry – everything that happened afterward put a big cloud over everything that happened before."

"David, this is a little hard to say – but ever since your mother passed away, I really feel that something changed. Not in me, but in you. Of course, it's natural. You needed some time to deal with your mom's passing. But still, I feel something changed. You just don't look at me the same way you used to."

"Really, Esther, you're one of the most important people in my life. I mean it."

"OK, that makes me feel better. But I'm sure lots of people are important in your life."

"So what are you asking, then? Are you asking whether I love you?"

"I don't know. I guess maybe I am asking that."

"Well, I wish I knew what love was. Then I could tell you."

"David, stop being such a philosopher! Anyway, it's impossible to define love. You just know it when you feel it. Look, I admit I wasn't expecting things to work out this way. I just feel really strongly about you. But I'm beginning to wonder whether the feeling is still mutual."

"Esther, I feel strongly about you too. Really, I do . . . ."

9

November 17, 2002

I need to work on those law school applications. But first, three things to write about today: running, Talmud, and existentialism.

About running. Just couldn't get into it today. Odd, because I've cut down on smoking quite a lot. So that's not it. Don't know what it is. This is not good. If this keeps up I know I'll go into a tailspin. But right now I'm not in a bad mood at all. In fact, I'm feeling pretty good. But I know that if I don't exercise, eventually I get depressed. Make sure to go running tomorrow.

Next, Talmud. An entirely new world. The class is going well, even though we're still only on the fourth page after a month and a half. Rabbi A. is a good teacher after all. I got the Artscroll edition for Tractate Berachos. I've been browsing through it. On the tenth page there's a passage that compares the relationship between the soul and the body to the relationship between God and the world. For the five ways in which the soul relates to the body, there are five corresponding ways in which God relates to the world. It made me think of Aquinas's five ways, which we studied back in sophomore year. I also see in the Artscroll a commentary that links this discussion to the Kabbalistic teaching about the five parts of the soul. This made me think of the five halleluyahs, which I've been thinking about ever since I started davening. Maybe there's some connection between the five halleluyahs and the five parts of the soul? Need to work on that.

Chapter 9 of Berachos is fascinating (about dreams). I've been trying to go through the English myself. It's amazing how much commentary it can take to explain even just a few lines. The classic edition of the Talmud is even more unbelievable. I looked in the back, and of course I can't read it. But all that tiny, tiny print! There seems to be no end to the detailed complexity of it all.

Commentaries on commentaries on commentaries. Rabbi A. said in
one of our classes that the Talmud is an "unparalleled intellectual
edifice." I wonder if Phil has any idea of what the Talmud is like.
Would that change his view about Judaism? Of course not. Still, he
would have to be impressed by the "intellectual edifice." I should talk
to him about it.

And yet so much of the Talmud is puzzling to me. Like the "thirteen
middos" of Rabbi Yishmael, the exegetical rules by which the Torah
is interpreted. That's not in the Talmud, but I found it in the daily
prayer book. It's in a collection called the Sifra, which is part of the
midrash, that dates back to the time of the Talmud. I'm still trying
to understand how these rules work. Like the "gezerah shavah,"
which says you can derive a law from the fact that the same word
occurs in two places, so that what's true in one case must be true
in the other. For example, in talking about marriage the Torah says
"when a man <u>takes</u> a wife," but it doesn't describe exactly how
a marriage is accomplished. But it says elsewhere that Abraham
"<u>took</u>" a field from Efron and gave him money for it. (Interesting
that there's an analogy between a wife and a field.) So the Talmud
says since both cases use a form of the word "take," we can derive
from the case of Abraham that one way of "taking" a wife is by
giving her money. This concept I sort of understand. But doesn't the
word <u>take</u> occur many other places as well? So how do you know
which one to use for your gezerah shavah?

There are other rules, too. Sometimes the sages are able to derive
laws from an extra word or even from an extra letter in the Torah.
That seems really bizarre. How do they know exactly what to derive?
Or sometimes they derive something from the fact that there are
dots over a word in the Torah, which is kind of like telling you that
the word has been crossed out. For example, in Bereshis where it
says that Esav kissed Jacob, the word "and he kissed" is written
with dots over it, which some say it means to imply that he really
didn't kiss him wholeheartedly. This idea actually makes some sense
to me, because if you were reading someone's journal and found that
they had crossed something out, you could probably learn quite a
lot if you could see what they had crossed out. But others say that
the dots on top of the word are to emphasize that in this particular
case, Esav acted out of character and did kiss Jacob wholeheartedly!
So the first guy interprets the dots on top of the word to be a cross
out while the other interprets it to be an underscore! How do you
know who's right?

I got a hold of a book that has selections from the Talmud in English. One thing that's striking is all the rabbinical decrees that keep coming and coming. Some of them make sense. Like, you need to say Shema before midnight even though you can really say it all night long, lest you fall asleep and don't say it all. But others seem so strange or unusually demanding. Like how you can't blow the shofar if Rosh ha-Shannah falls on Shabbat because someone might carry it more than four cubits in a public domain in order to show it to an expert to see if it's a kosher shofar. Or how you can't eat chicken with milk because people might get confused and think it's ok to eat beef with milk, which is a divine prohibition. I guess negiah is like this too. You can't even touch a woman other than your lawfully wedded wife lest you end up sleeping with her. One thing might lead to another!

On second thought, maybe that one does make sense after all. For example, if I had touched E, it would have been hard to stop there. Not having touched E all along, it really had an effect on our relationship. I have to admit that lately I don't really think about her that much. Sometimes I have to force myself to call her. It's weird, because she's attractive, but I don't think about her that way any more. Maybe I don't really love her. But what is love? That's a question that's bothered me for some time. Is E right that no one can define love? In class, Dr. M has been talking about love of God in medieval philosophy. But what does she know about love itself? She seems like such a cold person sometimes. No, that's not fair. She's reserved, unemotional. But she must have asked herself once or twice what love is. I wonder, does she have her own theory on love? Got to find some way to ask. But ~~she~~ this is a tangent.

Getting back to the Talmud, what's really strange are some of the stories, the aggadah. Like the one about Moses being over six cubits tall. Or the story about how King Og survived the flood by hanging on to Noah's ark. I can't imagine anyone taking these stories literally! And some of the stories about the sages of the Talmud are also pretty strange. Like the one about the debate between Rabbi Elazar and the sages. He calls upon the natural forces to prove that he's right, and streams start flowing backward, a tree falls, and all sorts of weird things happen. A fascinating story, but can you really believe that things happened quite this way? And then there are the really weird things like demons, charms, medicines. Then there's a fascinating section toward the end of Berachos on dreams, and some of the interpretations of dreams are really incredible. I think the most amazing one is that if I dream I'm having sexual relations with my mother, it's a sign that I will gain understanding. Even more bizarre: if I dream I'm having relations with a goose, that's a sign I should expect to become the head of an academy or rosh yeshiva! I could never imagine a Catholic theologian or a Muslim imam saying such a thing. (Maybe a Zen monk, though!)

Idea: Keep a notebook with weird things from the Talmud.

I've started going through Pirkei Avot again, this time with commentary. I'm in the last chapter now, which deals with Torah study. Some things in there are pretty straightforward. Others are a little more perplexing. Like the one about how Torah study makes a person "free," based on a play on words. (Ask Rabbi Low about that one.) Those guys sure thought highly of Torah study! Of course, if you believe it's the best and holiest way of life and that it's divinely ordained, of course it's important to study it! But is it higher or better than prayer or meditation? Why should that be? Why doesn't that make you free just as well? And what does "freedom" mean here anyway? (The importance of freedom. Reminds me of existentialism! Get back to that later.)

It seems there's a kind of tension between learning and davening/meditation. The first is an intellectual process, the other is a non-rational, or "transrational" process. Of course, prayer has a rational structure, but you climb the structure and then transcend it. When you meditate, it's almost as if you're trying to lose the critical thinking mind altogether (sink into the pool and become one with it). On the other hand, learning is always an intellectual process. No matter how deep you go, you still maintain your ability to be critical and skeptical. Which one is better? I guess it depends on whether the relationship with God is more intellectual or more ~~emotional~~ spiritual. (Emotional and spiritual are not the same thing.) If the relationship is more intellectual, then learning should be higher. If it's more of a spiritual thing, then prayer should be higher. Still, this doesn't resolve the question as to which is higher. (Could this be related to the question of which is higher, poetry or philosophy?)

On to Existentialism. Now that we've read "Existentialism is a Humanism" and discussed it in class, I think I understand Sartre a little better, and I also think I see some of its problems. I am still interested in the question of whether Existentialism can somehow fit together with Judaism. Dr. Breslow gave us an assignment to write a paper on Sartre, so I thought I would work out some ideas for a rough draft right here in my journal.

Tentative title for the paper: "Is Existentialism a Humanism?"

Sartre claims that the human does not have an essence or a fixed nature. He chooses what kind of being he will be. Man is "radically free." At first, this seems like an incredibly liberating and exhilarating view. There is no human "telos," no goal or purpose that comes from outside of man himself, whether it's God or nature. Man has to choose his purpose or way of life, without reason and without looking to some outside source to dictate what is the "right" choice. Even the choice to live a hedonistic life is itself a choice, and it is not the only option. (I couldn't stop thinking of Simon when I was reading Sartre. Simon considers himself a hedonist. But maybe he misunderstands himself. He's not a hedonist. He's an existentialist.) One might possibly choose an altruistic life, or a life of achievement, or a philosophical life. But none of these choices are objectively right or wrong. According to Sartre, all attempts to prove God's existence or to prove that there is some objective Good are flawed. (He doesn't bother to show this. He just assumes that it has already been shown. That's a flaw, but let's put that aside.) Sartre admits that the idea that there is no objectively provable right or wrong way of choosing how to live is a scary one. When a person faces up to this, he experiences "anxiety" and "dread." The existentialist has no illusions: there is no objectively right way of deciding what makes life meaningful or good.

Yet Sartre claims that he is not a pessimist, but rather a humanist, which basically means that he believes all people should be treated with equality and respect. Right away, Sartre raises an objection against himself as follows. If there is no rational way of making the choice about how to live, then there is no rational way of evaluating any commitment that a person makes. So, for example, there is no rational way of saying that the choice to be a humanist is any better than the choice to be a Nazi! This is especially a problem for Sartre because he claims not only that he is a humanist, but that existentialism is a form of humanism. (This is exactly the same problem which Hersh raised against Chaim in The Quarrel. Chaim claimed to be a humanist. Hersh criticized this by claiming that if there is no God or objective standard of goodness, there is no way of saying that what the Nazis did was really "bad.") Sartre responds to this by saying that when a person chooses a way of life, he

<u>implicitly chooses that way for all humankind</u>. This is a bit difficult to understand, but it seems to mean that when you choose a way of life, you must ask yourself whether all humans would choose that way of life. So for example, would you really commit yourself to a way of life in which other humans were treated as subhuman and were tortured? Would the Nazi be willing to make the choice to be a Nazi even if he put himself in the shoes of the Jew? Sartre says, of course, the answer is no! Or at least, that's what he expects most people will say.

But there's a serious problem with Sartre's answer. First of all, if Sartre's premises about human nature are correct, then, when a person chooses his way of life, why does he need to implicitly choose that way "for all humankind"? On the contrary, it seems to follow from Sartre's existentialist premises that when an individual chooses his way, he is choosing just for himself! Why should he care one way or the other about whether his way of life is a possibility for "all mankind"? I don't think Sartre has a good answer to this.

So this takes us back to the problem of how the existentialist philosopher can evaluate certain choices as "good" or "bad." We discussed in class that sometimes Sartre seems to be saying that from the existentialist's point of view, the only way to distinguish between "good" or "bad" choices is to ask whether a given choice was "authentic." In other words, did the person himself really choose his way, or rather did he let someone else choose for him? Did the choice really stem from the person himself, or did it stem from some source outside the self? In a way, the existentialist is saying, "Be true to yourself."

A problem with this is that it seems possible for someone to choose to be a Nazi "authentically." As long as a person does so, there is no way that the existentialist can claim that this choice is objectively bad or wrong. But Sartre could argue that almost no one would choose to be a Nazi authentically. For example, if a person chooses to be a Nazi because of peer pressure, or because it's the popular thing to do, or even because of some false belief about oneself (such as the supposed superiority of one's race), then the choice is inauthentic and therefore "existentially flawed." (Self deception is a big existentialist no-no. That's one of the things I really like about existentialism: it demands self-honesty.) An existentially authentic choice has to flow from something within the person, and not from something that is phony or external.

But there are two problems with this. One is that someone could just say something like this: "I don't care about whether my choice is inauthentic. Sartre's claim that my choice is flawed because it is 'inauthentic' is unjustified." Now, I'm not sure that this is such a good objection to Sartre since, in practice, very few people would admit that their commitments are inauthentic. For example, a Nazi would not want to admit that his choice to be a Nazi is inauthentic. Second, a more serious problem is that if we're saying that a person's choice should "flow from the person" — what does that really mean if — as Sartre himself believes — the person has no essence or fixed nature? The only way Sartre can define an authentic choice is "negatively" — that is, by saying what it is <u>not</u>. As long as my choice is not based on some source outside myself, it is authentic. But still, that seems pretty weak as a criterion for evaluating choices. Imagine a case where a person is faced with a choice between two very different ways of life — for example, the choice between being a Humanist or a Nazi, and without any pressure or false beliefs or self-delusions, the person just happens to pick one way over the other. It would follow that no matter which one I picked, the choice was equally authentic, and therefore equally "good" from an existentialist perspective!

One way out of this jam is for Sartre to say that although the human does not have an essence or a fixed nature, he still has what is called a "history." (Footnote: Dr. Breslow mentioned this was an important idea for another existentialist thinker, Ortega y Gasset. Find reference.) Sartre talks about the idea of a "history" at the end of the article. The idea is that, over time, a person builds up a set of character traits, or a <u>personality</u>. A given personality is not essential to man, since it is changeable, but it is still there in the person. So Sartre might say that a person's choice is authentic only if his choice stemmed from his personality. The choice must flow from the person's past or history or character. You can't simply pick one choice at random and call it an "authentic" choice.

But now, the problem remains that the existentialist has no way of criticizing any choices that flow from a person's personality, no matter how rotten or cruel that personality is. For example, once a person has made certain choices that build up the personality of a Nazi, it now turns out that the existentialist should encourage the Nazi to act as a Nazi, for otherwise he would be acting inauthentically!

My conclusion is that Sartre has no way of defending "humanism," and no way of distinguishing "good" or "bad" choices, without falling back on the idea that the human does have some nature or essence. Perhaps Sartre should have said that he is an existentialist, and that he <u>chooses</u> to be a humanist, but he should have admitted that that's just his choice. He could have claimed that it follows from existentialism that humanism is no more and no less rational than any other life choice. But he should not have asserted that existentialism <u>is</u> a humanism. He should have asserted that he is an existentialist who chooses also to be a humanist. That would have been more honest!

The thing I'm still left wondering about is whether existentialism can fit together with Judaism. (Probably won't include this stuff in the paper. Maybe I can do my term paper on this? Ask Breslow.) If it's possible to be an existentialist humanist, maybe it's also possible to be an existentialist religious Jew? Of course, Judaism is not atheistic, and in that sense it strongly disagrees with Sartre. Also, the human being has a soul, which is given or created by God, so it is not correct to say that man has no essence. There is a purpose and a goal for the sake of which man was created by God. Still, maybe you could look at the commitment to be a religious Jew as an existentialist choice. The idea would be that a person does not choose to be religious because it is rational. Rather, a person chooses to be religious as an existential commitment. In a way, this is a convenient view for a religious Jew to have, since all the arguments for and against God's existence, all the doubts and questions about the truth of the Torah or the truth of hashgacha pratis, become irrelevant to the question of whether or not a person should make the commitment. The commitment would be "authentic" if the choice were not coerced and if it stemmed from the person's essence or soul. So if the person were actually Jewish and had a Jewish soul, then it would be authentic. But, according to the existentialist, there would be no way of proving that there is a God, that one has a soul, etc. A Jewish existentialist would be in the awkward position of never being able to know through reason whether his religious commitment is authentic. (Does this make any sense at all?)

This journal entry has gone on and on. I just leafed through my journal and this is definitely the longest entry in it. I practically wrote an entire paper here. I better stop this and get to work on those law school applications. Ugh!

IO

From: dgoldstein@cuniv.edu   Sent: 1/10/03 12:38 AM
To: rlow@ahavattorah.org.il
Subject: Question about passage in Pirkei Avos

Dear Rabbi Low,

How are you? I wanted to ask you about a passage in Pirkei Avos. This is an example of one of those many passages that I find both frustrating and intriguing at the same time. I'm sure you know it, but the passage goes as follows:

Rabbi Joshua the son of Levi said – quoting the Torah . . . *"The tablets were the work of God. The writing was the writing of God, engraved – harus – on the tablets." Don't read it as "harus,"* which means "engraved," *but rather as "herus,"* which means "free," *for no person is free except for one who involves himself with study of Torah.*

The obvious problem is that a person who involves himself with the study of Torah is not free at all. Quite the opposite, he is bound to a way of life with lots of rules and regulations. How can it be that only a person who involves himself with Torah is free?

Second, what about the play on words with the term *harus* and *herus*? Is this just a kind of game, that the word *harus* can be read differently to read *herus*? Can the rabbis just do this arbitrarily?

David

From: rlow@ahavattorah.org.il   Sent: 1/12/03 2:00 PM
To: dgoldstein@cuniv.edu
Subject: Freedom

Dear David,

You raise some excellent questions about what I think is a very deep passage. I once gave a talk on this mishnah and I am happy to share some thoughts on it with you. I don't think the play on words is arbitrary. I believe that whenever the rabbis engage in this kind of word play, there's a real conceptual link between the two concepts, in this case the concept of engraving (*harus*) and the concept of freedom (*herus*). In fact, I think the notion of word play is itself a crucial part of the drasha, as I shall explain below.

The mishnah may be understood in light of the doctrine that the Torah is the purest expression of G-d's supreme free will. Indeed, the Torah is the truest expression of G-d Himself. The midrash says that the Torah was created "before the world." I don't take this literally, but rather what it means is that the Torah is the blueprint for creation. Another midrash says that G-d looked into the Torah and created the world. Surely, if G-d had the Torah before the world was created, that must mean that in some sense, the Torah was within G-d himself.

On the other hand, the human being is also an expression of G-d. The human is created *be-tzelem Elokim*, in the image of G-d – that is, with intelligence and will, with the capacity for choice and responsibility. But precisely because he has free will, man can do good or evil. So man is not complete or perfect. Rather, it is the Torah that expresses G-d's will, and that teaches how the human being should behave in order to express G-d's will fully.

We find a connection between the *luchos* (= the tablets) and the human being. Just as the human is created *be-tzelem Elokim*, the tablets are called *ma'aseh Elokim*, the work of G-d, and even the writing is called *michtav Elokim*, the writing of G-d. (The phrase *ma'aseh Elokim* occurs nowhere else in Tanakh.) Just as the human being is an expression of G-d, the *luchos* are, in some way, also an expression of G-d. The *luchos* are that portion of the written Torah which were, at least in the first instance, written by G-d Himself. It is interesting that there were two versions of the *luchos* – a first one that had to be destroyed because the Jews sinned and a second version that came after the Jews repented. Moshe himself engraved the second one. This is kind of like the idea of a "second draft." Sometimes, when you write something, it doesn't work out and you need to fix it. The phrase "set in stone" is actually a misnomer. Even things that are set in stone can be redone! The same thing is true in the case of human beings. This is related to the concept of teshuvah. If you don't like what you are, you can fix it. This ties back to the concept of free will. Our free will is so powerful that even if we've chosen a certain way of life, we still have the power to change ourselves.

Now, here's the next crucial point: The fact that the *luchos* were written or engraved is integrally related to the concept of free will. There is a special connection between writing, or the ability to communicate in a written language, and free will. A being that cannot engage in a written language is a being that is not free. Humans are the only known animals that use written language. Similarly, humans are the only known animals that are responsible agents. (Some animals communicate verbally and with other signs, but none use written symbols.) This is also related to the uniqueness of handwriting. Everyone has a slightly different handwriting, because even though we are all human beings, we are all different due to our own free choice.

And that's why writing is so important. I mean real writing, the kind that expresses your self. G-d Himself expresses Himself in the *luchos* and in the Torah, which are written texts. We emulate this when we write a *sefer Torah*, which must be handwritten and not produced by a printing press. Thus every *sefer Torah* that is written is unique. But we also emulate this process when we write our own *divrei torah*. When we write *divrei torah*, we emulate, or perhaps even partake in G-d's expression of Himself in Torah. What an amazing thing it is that we humans have the ability to do this!

It is not accidental that this lesson (that true freedom comes through concern with Torah) is taught through a play on words. Word play is a form of wit or humor, which is also a crucial sign of our humanity. (If I can indulge in some word play myself, notice the similarity between *humor* and *humanity* – though there is actually no etymological connection between the two!) A life without humor would be inhuman. And as far as I know, while some non-human animals engage in *play*, and some engage in *communication*, no animals other than humans tell jokes or engage in word play. Our capacity for humor is a crucial sign of our humanity – that is, our freedom. But that's only a starting point. G-d is the Supreme Person, and so He is supremely free. And G-d expresses Himself in the Torah. Of course, humans have freedom, but our freedom is limited and dependent on G-d. When we involve ourselves in Torah, we involve ourselves with the truest and purest expression of G-d's supreme freedom. That is why only the person who involves himself with Torah study is truly free. The highest, most refined involvement in Torah is when we ourselves reach new insights of Torah or *hiddushim* – when we ourselves create new Torah, so to speak.

Speaking of learning Torah, I realize this must be your senior year. I was wondering if you had plans for the summer. We have a great summer program here at the yeshiva that might interest you. I'm sure you would really get a lot out of a session of intensive Jewish study. Besides, have you ever been to Israel? It's definitely worth a visit!

Rabbi Low

II

"Hello, Phil. How are you?"

"Not bad, David. How've you been?"

"Great, really great."

"What a response! I can't remember hearing anyone say that recently, much less you. I see you've got some books. What's that big tome you're toting?"

"It's a volume from the Talmud. Actually, it's something I wanted to ask you about. Have you ever studied the Talmud?"

"No, I haven't. Why do you ask?"

"I just wondered if you were familiar with it. I've just been starting to study it lately and it's really quite amazing."

"Is that so? Well, why don't you show it to me?"

"Here, take a look."

"Wow, this does look quite dense. And it's all in Hebrew."

"And in Aramaic."

"There's a lot here. Is all this material from the Second Temple period?"

"Some of it is. But most of this volume is commentary from the early medieval period on down through the centuries. Some of the stuff in the back of the book is very recent."

"Well, if this is the Talmud, obviously it would take a long time to get through it even once, let alone to master it."

"Phil, this is just one volume."

"Oh? How many more volumes are there?"

"Around twenty or so."

"*Twenty* volumes? Just like this one?"

"Yes. And that's only the Babylonian Talmud. There's also the Jerusalem Talmud."

"Goodness gracious! What's in there?"

"A lot of it is Jewish law. Since Jewish law covers all areas of life, the Talmud gets into all sorts of things – agriculture, business, ritual law, marriage, sex, divorce, even medical stuff. But it's not written like a code, it's mostly in the form of records of conversations."

"Now *that's* interesting."

"There are also other things, like interpretations of the stories in Scripture. There's homiletical stuff too. Some really thought-provoking things . . . ."

"Like what? Can you give me an example?"

"Sure. Do you know what tefillin are?"

"Yes. The little black boxes – phylacteries, they're called."

"Right. Well, the Talmud says that God wears tefillin."

"Hmmm! I wonder what Maimonides would say about that!"

"But it's not just the content of the Talmud that's so impressive. The other thing I wanted to say is that some of the logical structures of some of the arguments in the Talmud are really complex."

"Is that so?"

"The exegetical strategies of the Talmud are very interesting and unique. I bet there's nothing else like it in the world."

"Exegetical strategies? What do you mean?"

"I'm talking about how the Talmud interprets and derives things from the scriptures. Actually, I brought something else for you to look at. Here – this is a *Siddur* or prayer book. As part of the morning prayer, we read something called the thirteen exegetical rules. It's part of the Sifra, which is actually another rabbinic work, similar to the Mishnah, the earliest layer of the Talmud. Here, take a look at these thirteen exegetical rules. You can just look at the English, on this page."

"Whew, this *is* complex! It reminds me of medieval logic! What's this doing in the prayer book, I wonder? It's not a prayer at all!"

"True. It's not a prayer at all. But as part of the daily ritual we're supposed to do some learning, so it was included in the *Siddur*, the daily prayer book."

"Well, as far as religions go, I admit, Judaism is a rather intellectual religion."

"That's what I'm coming to realize more and more. And you know, the Talmud kicks off a whole body of literature that extends from the time of the Second Temple through the Middle Ages and right up to this day. Of course, it really all started with the Hebrew Scriptures, going back much earlier. The Torah is the single longest-standing continuous legal tradition in the world."

"I guess that's true. There were other ancient systems of law that were also quite detailed and complicated. But I guess they're not around in any living form today."

"Exactly."

"So do you now plan to become a Talmud scholar, David? You're obviously pretty taken with it."

"I guess I am. There's a statement in the Talmud that says, 'Turn it over and turn it over, for everything is in it.'"

"Everything? David, let me ask you this. Is there anything like *philosophy* in the Talmud?"

"That's a good question. I hadn't thought of that."

"David, I bet the Talmud doesn't come close to criticizing its own fundamental assumptions. And so, despite its complexities and intellectual subtlety, there's really nothing in the Talmud that is philosophical. It reminds me of the great scholastic systems of the Middle Ages, which took both Aristotelian science and Scripture for granted. So despite the logical sophistication and complexity of some of these systems, they were, so to speak, castles in the air. At least those systems were *somewhat* philosophical. But the Talmud isn't philosophical at all. Isn't that so?"

"I guess that's true. But the Talmud doesn't *exclude* the possibility of philosophy. Maybe the assumptions underlying the Talmud can be defended philosophically."

"Maybe, maybe not. My point is that philosophy is the free, rational inquiry into fundamental questions, and the attempt to give answers with rational support. Does the Talmud even encourage such a thing?"

"What about the great Jewish philosophers of the Middle Ages – people like Saadia Gaon and Maimonides? How do you explain them?"

"Your examples only prove my point. The names you just mentioned are not in the Talmud. It's only through the influence of the Greeks that these people did what they did. And they were, in some sense, great thinkers, but ultimately, in my opinion they were not true philosophers since, like the scholastics, they accepted certain things on faith and revelation and were unwilling to criticize certain assumptions. And if you tell me that in fact Maimonides himself was willing to entertain such a critique, I still bet that you won't find any such willingness in the Talmud itself."

"Probably true . . . but still . . . people like Maimonides managed to do both.

Maimonides was not only a philosopher, but one of the greatest masters of the Talmud."

"I know that. But wasn't Maimonides controversial within the Jewish community precisely because of his all-too-healthy interest in philosophy?"

"Yes, but ultimately he and his works were accepted in the Jewish community."

"I'm not so sure everyone in the Jewish community accepts Maimonides wholeheartedly. David, let's face it! Obviously there's a conflict there, or at least a tension. Look, the issue really is not about the Talmud *per se*. It's about the Scripture just as much. We're back to the same old argument we've been having ever since we met. It's Athens versus Jerusalem all over again! You could have come in here with a copy of the Hebrew Scriptures and you could have claimed that the Scripture is an impressive work, and I'd have to admit it that in some sense, of course it's impressive. The time frame described by the Hebrew Scriptures spans several centuries. It's a vast work composed by many people over many years. It's much more impressive than the New Testament or the Koran, each of which covers a much smaller period of time, and each of which is really much thinner in substance. The Hebrew Bible is a very rich work from a literary and historical point of view. Maybe it's the greatest literary work of all time. But again, it's not philosophy in the slightest sense!"

"What about the Book of Job? That's philosophical, isn't it?"

"Not really. It deals with the problem of evil and suffering, but in a very different way from how a philosopher might deal with it. As I recall, it ends with a revelation, not a philosophical explanation. Right?"

"Yeah, you're right. So if it involves revelation it can't be philosophical?"

"Of course not. The two are antithetical."

"I'm not sure I agree with that. But look – maybe not everything important can be known through reason. Maybe some things can only be learned through revelation or religious experience."

"Here we go again. Haven't we discussed this once before? Both of us agree that there is such a thing as ultimate truth and that the pursuit of truth is a worthy endeavor. But this is the difference between us: I hold that anything important about ultimate truth can be learned – if at all – through reason, which is universally available to all people. But you hold that God can reveal certain things, including directives or 'commandments' about what we should or should not do, which we would never know using reason alone."

"Yes. That certainly seems possible to me."

"And as far as I'm concerned, the problem you need to address is why would we even think that ultimate truth is accessible in any way other than through reason."

"Wait a second – don't we learn about the world through experience?"

"Of course."

"Well, revelation is a certain kind of experience."

"It's not ordinary experience, is it?"

"No, it isn't."

"So let me restate my claim. Anything that I could know through ordinary experience, or through reason, I don't need God to 'reveal' to me, and therefore, I don't need to accept 'on faith.' On the other hand, if I am given something that's purported to be revelation, but which I could not have known through ordinary experience or through reason, I should come to the conclusion that God's revelations are nonsensical and that his directives are irrational or arbitrary."

"Well, wait a second. I think I have an answer for that. You see, Phil, there's an even deeper crucial difference between us."

"What's that?"

"You think of ultimate truth as impersonal. But I think of ultimate truth – that is, God – as personal. In other words, ultimate truth has a personality, a character."

"OK – so what's your point?"

"Well, if ultimate truth is a person, then, it stands to reason that ultimate truth would manifest or reveal itself as a person would. A person manifests himself in different ways than a non-person would. Don't you agree?"

"I suppose that's true. So?"

"Well, isn't it the case that people surprise us all the time by doing and saying things we would have never thought they would do? But once they do them, we can sort of understand why they did them. We can make sense out of them. For example, take a great artist who produces a work of art. A great work of art is not predictable ahead of time, but once it's done, it can be recognized as great. And that means it is not considered arbitrary or capricious."

"OK. That's an interesting point. Where are you getting this from? Did you think of it yourself?"

"Not really. I'm kind of putting together some things I heard from Dr. Maimon with things I've learned from others."

"Great. Anyway, go on."

"So, if God is personal, then it is bound to be the case that God may reveal certain things that are not predictable or knowable to us if we just rely on reason or ordinary experience. Yet once they are given, they might make sense, given God's personality."

"Hmm. David, I must admit – I'll have to think about what you're saying. You're right that I don't believe that ultimate truth is personal. But if it were personal, then I suppose what you're saying would make sense. In the meantime, I give you my blessing to study not only Scripture, but Talmud as well!"

"Thanks, Phil!"

12

"So, Dovid, you want me to help you do some Jewish meditation. I don't usually do this sort of thing, but let's give it a try. Like I said once before, there are different kinds of Jewish meditation. Today we'll do a very basic one that's focused on the letters of the name of *Hashem*. Once I teach you this meditation, there's no reason why you can't do it on your own. You could also use it as an introduction to the davening in the morning. As I once mentioned, the four letters of the name correspond to the four stages of the morning prayer. Dovid, are you ready?"

"Yes, Chaim."

"Sit up a little straighter in your chair."

"OK. You don't want me to lie down?"

"No, you're not going to sleep! You're not even going to relax. You're going to focus very intently on the name of *Hashem* and what it really means. But first, I want you to read this short prayer of intent. I think you're familiar with it, but I adapted it for this purpose. The idea is to state your intention to meditate on *Hashem*'s name, for the purpose of bringing about a unification of the name, which means, the unification of the different aspects or *sefiros* of God. So, please say after me:

לשם יחוד קודשא בריך הוא ושכינתיה. בדחילו ורחימו ורחימו ודחילו. ליחדא שם י"ה בו"ה ביחודא
שלים בשם כל ישראל הנני מוכן ומזומן להתבונן בשם.

*For the sake of unifying the Holy One blessed be He with His Divine Presence, in fear and love, in love and fear, to unify the name **yod heh** with the **vav heh** in complete union, in the name of all Israel, I am now ready and prepared to meditate on the name of Hashem.*

"Good. From this point on, speak only if and when I ask you to. Now, close your eyes. I am going to ask you to recite a certain *pasuk* – that's part of a verse – from *Tehillim*. Say this *pasuk* slowly. I'll say it in English too: *Shivisi Hashem le-negdi tamid*. Now, in English: *I have set Hashem before me always*. Excellent. Now say it three times, very slowly, with *kavvanah*, with intent. Visualize the Name of *Hashem* in your mind's eye. As the *pasuk* says, set the name before you. Now, recite the *pasuk* slowly three times.

"Good. Now, you're going to focus closely on each of the four letters of *Hashem*'s name, starting with the last letter or the lower *heh* and moving gradually to the first letter, the *yod*. At each level, you will focus not only on the letter itself, but the *sefirah* or *sefiros* with which it is connected, as well as the divine name associated with that *sefirah*, and the *middos* or qualities associated with that *sefirah*. For each letter, you will also focus on a certain aspect of the soul, and also on one stage or part of the morning prayer. First, imagine a white canvas, a blank *klaf* or white parchment. As I ask you to imagine or picture each letter in your mind, you will start on the left side of the *klaf* and work your way to the right side. Now, focus on the letter *heh*.

הֵ

"This is the last letter of the name of Hashem, the lowest aspect of Hashem, the level in which God's presence, the *shechinah*, is always here in the world, even in the lowest of the low places, even in exile, even when we sin. This is the *sefirah* of *malchus*. The divine name associated with the *Shechinah* is *Adonai*, which, like the word *aden*, means a socket or receptacle. The *heh* corresponds to the first stage of the morning prayer – that is, the morning blessings, which focus mainly on thanking God for the bodily functions. This stage also includes the recitation of the morning sacrifices, which involves the body of an animal, and other physical *mitzvos* such as burning incense and lighting the Menorah. As you focus on the letter *heh*, focus on your body, particularly your legs, the lowest part of the body. Notice that the *heh* is open at the bottom. The *heh* accepts and receives. Focus on your ability to accept and receive. The *heh* is a feminine aspect of *Hashem*: a woman, a bride, a wife. Focus on the *middah* of *anavah* or humility, and on the mitzvah of helping others in need, especially those less fortunate than you.

"Now I will be quiet for several minutes as you connect your mind, heart, and soul with the lower *heh* and all that it represents.

"Now . . . let's move up to focus on the *vav* of *Hashem*'s name. Picture the *vav* in your mind . . .

ו

"The *vav* is long and narrow. This is the aspect of *Hashem* that is called *Ha-kadosh Baruch Hu*, the Holy One, Blessed Be He. This is the masculine, active aspect of *Hashem*. The *vav* represents the six character traits or *middos* of *Hashem*. These are *hod, netzah, yesod, rahamim, din, and hesed* – self-restraint, perseverance, peace, compassion, justice, and benevolence. The *vav* is the central letter in *Hashem*'s name, like the trunk of a tree that holds the tree together, and so, the name associated with the *vav* is itself the *shem Hashem*, the *yod keh vav keh*. Now, think of your chest and your heart as the central part of the human body and as the locus of your emotions and your spirit, or *ruah*. Think of your right arm and hand as the vessel by which you do acts of kindness and benevolence. Think of your left arm as the vessel by which you do acts of righteousness and justice. The *vav* corresponds to the second stage of the morning prayer, which are the *pesukei de-zimra*, or verses of praise. The main purpose of this stage is to sing the praises of God with your *ruah*, your spirit.

"Now I will be quiet for some time as you focus and connect your mind with the letter *vav*, and all that it signifies . . .

"Good. Now it is time to focus on the upper *heh*.

הֵ

"This *heh* also represents a feminine aspect of the divine, but think of this *heh* not as a bride or wife, but rather as a mother. This *heh* is associated with the *sefirah* of *binah*, or understanding. Again, this letter has an opening. But here, focus not on the *lower* opening of the *heh*, but rather on the *upper* opening, which represents the opening we have for comprehension and understanding. The divine name associated with this *heh* is the name *Elokim*. Focus on your head, especially on your eyes and your ears. Focus on your ability of intellectual comprehension and understanding. The upper *heh* corresponds to the third section of the morning prayer, which includes the reading of the *Shema*. In this section, we focus on acknowledging and understanding God as the Creator and as One. Focus on your ability to intellectually study and comprehend the Torah. Focus on the mitzvah of Torah study.

"Now I will be quiet for a time as you connect with the upper *heh* and all that it represents . . .

"Very good. Now it is time to move up to the last and highest letter, the *yod*.

י

"The *yod*, the smallest letter, stands for the most hidden aspects of the divine name. The *yod* is associated first with the *sefirah* of *hochmah*, or wisdom. The divine name here is the name *yod keh*, or *Kah*. This represents the wisdom through which God created the world, and through which God wrote the Torah that is in heaven. Focus here on your ability to attain new thoughts. Focus here on the mitzvah to be *mehadesh divrei torah* – that is, the commandment to arrive at new insights in Torah. The letter *yod* corresponds to the fourth part of the morning prayer, which is the silent *Amidah*. Here we have the ability to speak to God as we wish. We do not merely praise God or acknowledge God. We actually pray to God to bring about new things, to change the world, to change ourselves. But now you are about to go one step higher. Focus specifically on the *kotz* or the lower tail of the *yod*, which signifies the *sefirah* of *kesser* or crown, the highest aspect of God – that is, *ratzon* or will. This is associated with the name *Ehyeh*, which means "I shall be." Focus here not on your power to do something or think something or know something, but on your will itself, your power or capacity. Focus on the mitzvah of *devekus*, the mitzvah of cleaving to *Hashem*, the mitzvah of bonding your will with *Hashem*'s will. This corresponds to the final stage of the prayer at the end of the *Amidah*. Here we seek to connect to God with our will. In your mind, mentally say this *pasuk*: *Yehyu le-ratzon imrei fi ve-hegyon libi*, which means: 'May the words of my mouth and the inner, silent thoughts of my heart be in accord with the *ratzon* or will of Hashem.' Now, I will give you a final *pasuk* to meditate on – a *pasuk* which contains your own name. Meditate on the verse, '*Kalu tefillos Dovid ben Yishai*," which means: "The prayers of David, son of Yishai, are now complete."

"I will be silent for some time as you focus on connecting your will with the will of *Hashem* . . .

"Dovid, you have reached the pinnacle of the *Yod Keh Vav Keh*, but of course even this holy name, and all it represents, is only a manifestation of the *ein sof*, the infinite, indescribable essence of *Hashem*. You are at the precipice of the infinite.

Like a flame, your will and your soul and your mind and even your body want to go higher. But now is not the time to go higher. Dovid, you have visited with *Hashem*. You have been strengthened and energized. Now it is time to bring that new energy back with you into this mundane world. So turn back and come down the ladder now. Direct your focus away from the *kotz* or tip of the *yod*. Come back now to the whole *yod*, back to the *sefirah* of *hochmah*. Then come back down to the upper *heh*, the *sefirah* of *binah*. Next, come back down to the *vav* . . . the *shesh ketzavos*, or six lower *sefiros*. Finally, come back to the lower *heh*, the *Shechinah*. Come back to this physical world, ready to bring down and apply in practice all the holiness and insights that you gained from this *hisbonnenus*, from this meditation on the name of *Hashem*.

"Now, Dovid, open your eyes."

13
―

"Ah, there you are, David. Come in. You made an appointment to see me?"

"Yes, Dr. Maimon. I did."

"So, have a seat. What's up?"

" Dr. Maimon, we've been talking a lot about the idea of love of God in the medieval Jewish philosophers."

"Yes."

"But I was wondering – instead of talking more about the medievals, can you tell me about your own idea of love of God?"

"*My* idea? Here we go again! Sure, we can talk about that if you wish. But that requires a theory of love, in general."

"So . . . do you have your own theory of love?"

"Yes, I do."

"Great. Can you tell me about it?"

"Yes, if you insist. First, let's go back to the theory of objectivism we once talked about some time ago. You remember that conversation, don't you?"

"You mean the conversation we had a couple of years ago, when I asked you to explain what it means to do what's right or good for its own sake?"

"Exactly. Do you remember my claim that it is a rational judgment to say that certain beings are intrinsically better than others, insofar as they are beings?"

"Yes."

"And I claimed that respect for a being has to do with recognizing the intrinsic worth of that being, insofar as it is the being that it is?"

"Yes, I remember."

"Very good. Well, my theory of love is just an expansion of that theory. Any particular being has two aspects. It's a being of a certain *kind*, and yet it's also a *particular* being. Take you, for example. David Goldstein is a being of a certain kind – namely, a human being. In this respect, he is similar to countless other human beings. But David Goldstein is also the particular individual that he is. And in this respect he is rather unique. Isn't that right?"

"Yes. I hope so."

"Now, to respect a being is to recognize and appreciate its intrinsic worth insofar as it is a being of a certain kind. For example, when you respect a human, you do so because you recognize his worth or dignity insofar as he falls into the class of human beings."

"OK. I get that."

"So respect is basically impersonal. By that I mean that respect has nothing to do with the particular human being in question. It has to do with the fact that he or she falls into a certain category – the class of human beings. Do you follow?"

"Yes, I think so."

"Good. Now, before I get to love, let me say just a little more about respect. Respect has mainly to do with *not* doing certain things. First, let's talk about respect for non-persons – that is, creatures who do not have intelligence or the capacity for choice. The way you respect non-persons is by not treating them wantonly, which means destroying or trashing them for no constructive reason. So, for example, causing an animal unnecessary or excessive pain is disrespect. I also think that trashing the environment unnecessarily is disrespect for nature. But if you slaughter animals for consumption and use natural resources responsibly that's not disrespect."

"OK. That makes sense, I think."

"Now let's talk about respect for persons. Basically, if you respect someone as a person, you don't violate or frustrate their personhood – that is, their intelligence and free choice. Of course there are exceptions to this, such as, for example, when it is necessary to frustrate or foil someone's free choice in order to prevent him from frustrating or degrading someone else's free choice. Still, in general, respect takes the form of not doing certain things that would violate or degrade the intrinsic worth of other things or beings."

"I follow."

"Good. So much for respect. Love, on the other hand, has to do with the recognition of worth of a particular being, not merely insofar as it falls into a certain class, but also insofar as it is the particular being that it is. Thus, for example, I can respect many people, even people whom I barely know. But I can only love someone whom I know as an individual. Thus Maimonides says that love is always in proportion to knowledge. The more you know an individual, the more you can love that individual. And so, if you know someone superficially, your love for that person must be superficial indeed."

"Right. That makes sense."

"So, in fact, one has a great potential to love oneself."

"Really?"

"Yes, because one is most intimately familiar with oneself. Of course, self-deception is always a possibility. But barring that, one has a great opportunity to know oneself very well."

"So it's OK to love yourself?"

"Certainly. Don't you remember the verse 'Love your neighbor as yourself'? It's implied right there that one should love oneself!"

"Ah, I see. Of course you're right. But Dr. Maimon, can I ask you a question?"

"I'm still in the middle of my exposition, but go ahead."

"Do you think love is rational?"

"Absolutely, yes. I think genuine love is very rational indeed. While an 'irrational love' is perhaps possible, it is not a genuine form of love at all. I'll explain why. Remember, I have already argued that it's rational to think that certain beings have intrinsic worth insofar as they are the kind of being that they are. In fact, it is rational to think that certain beings are intrinsically superior to other beings. It follows that it is rational to respect certain beings more than others. Thus for example, human beings are due a greater respect than dogs. But I also think that certain particular beings are more intrinsically worthy than others, insofar as they are the particular beings that they are. For example, the individual human, David Goldstein, is more intrinsically worthy as a particular being than the individual dog, Lassie. That's because David Goldstein is a higher being than Lassie. It follows that it's more rational to love David Goldstein rather than to love the particular dog, Lassie. Sorry, I keep using you as an example!"

"No problem. OK, I think I get it so far."

"Back to my exposition, then. Whereas respect for a being is expressed mostly by our *not* doing certain things, love is expressed mostly by *doing* certain things. If you love someone, you want to see them flourish and you want to help them flourish. Every being has a certain potential to be greater and greater as a being. And so, if you truly recognize and appreciate the being of that individual, then you want that being to flourish. A person who loves you wants to nurture you and help you grow. Of course, different particular beings need different kinds of nurturing. Children need a special kind of intensive nurturing. They won't flourish without a lot of help and attention. Adults need a different kind of nurturing. Sometimes they don't flourish unless they are left alone, at least some of the time! In any case, the more intimately you get to know a person, the more you can love them and the better you are able to help them flourish as individuals. Last but not least, if you love a person, you always want to get to know them at deeper and deeper levels, to the greatest extent possible. Don't you agree?"

"Yes, that sounds right."

"Another thing I would add is that you can't really love someone without respecting them too. But the reverse is quite possible. You can respect someone without loving them at all. That's because respect requires merely the recognition of the worth of a being insofar as she is a being of a certain kind. But love requires the recognition of the worth of the being or individual insofar as she is the particular individual which she is. And you can't know a given particular being without knowing what kind of being it is. Are you following?"

"Sorry, I'm not sure I got that last point."

"It's really pretty simple. Look, if all I know about you is that you are a person, I can respect you insofar as you are a person and still not know anything about you as an individual. I might not even know your name or anything particular about you. Thus, I can have respect for a stranger whom I meet on the street even though I do not love that stranger at all. But if I love you, then I must know at least some particular facts about you, and certainly I must know that you are a human being! So, if I genuinely love you as a particular being, certainly I must respect you insofar as you are a human being. Do you follow?"

"Yes, I think so."

"Good. So much for my theory of love in general. But what you really wanted to know about is my theory of love of God. So, we have to ask, how does all this apply to God? In other words, what does love of God amount to? Of course, in my theory, God is not *a* being. Rather, God is Being itself. But that only makes God even more special and more unique. God is, so to speak, off the charts when it comes to being. Necessarily, there is only one of a kind when it comes to God."

"Right, I get that."

"Well, since God is not just the best being but rather Being itself, it follows rationally that God is intrinsically worthy not only of the greatest respect, but also of the greatest love. One might go so far as to say that one's love for God should be of a radically higher order than one's love for particular beings, no matter how great those particular beings might be."

"OK. I think I'm with you there too."

"In my opinion, that's why it says in the Torah, that you should love God 'with all your heart and all your soul and all your might.' It's very interesting that this phrase occurs nowhere in the entire *Tanakh* but here, in the context of the commandment to love God. The lesson is that the love one should have for God is all-engrossing and all-consuming. If your love for God is partial or halfway, then, in some sense, it's not the real thing. That's because God is objectively worthy of the highest kind of love. If you have anything less than the highest love for God, something's amiss."

"And it also seems to follow from what you're saying that our love for any human should not be total or all-consuming."

"Yes, that's absolutely right. People make a very big mistake when they try to find a human being to love with an all-consuming or total love. That's irrational and, I might add, immature. An all-consuming love should only be reserved for God. Also, people make a mistake if they think they need to find that one particular Mr. Right – or Ms. Right, as the case may be. Of course, all human beings are unique, but none of them is radically unique in the way that God is unique. Only

God is the true unique One, and that is why God is supremely worthy of total love. It's no accident that the commandment to love God follows right after the verse in which we declare the Oneness – that is, the uniqueness – of God. First, we say, 'Hear, O Israel: the Lord our God is One' – or, as I would prefer to translate, 'Hear, O Israel: the Lord our God is radically unique.' Only then do we say, 'And you should love God with all your heart, with all your soul and with all your might.' That's because, as I just explained, true love is driven by the recognition of the particularity or uniqueness of the beloved. By the way, my theory also solves another question which people sometimes ask – namely, how can love be commanded? The answer is that indeed, love can be commanded because God is eminently worthy of love. And as I just indicated, the Torah gives the reason for why God is worthy of love just before it states the commandment to love God. Again, God is eminently worthy of total love precisely because God is radically unique."

"Wow. This is really interesting, Dr. Maimon."

"Thanks, but I'm not quite done. If we put this all together with what we said earlier, we can make good sense of the Torah's teaching that all humans have an obligation to respect all other humans, as well as to respect God. Respect for God manifests itself primarily in not doing certain things, such as blasphemy and idol worship. But when it comes to love, things are different. As I said before, you can't love someone that you don't know. So only those who have experienced the revelation of God have an obligation to love God. And that, of course, means the Jewish people, who experienced the revelation of Torah."

"I see."

"Furthermore, my theory makes sense of the fact that the Torah does not say that we have an obligation to love our fellow human being."

"It doesn't? Didn't you yourself just quote the verse, 'Love your neighbor as yourself'?"

"David! To use a Talmudic phrase, let your ears hear what your mouth just uttered! The verse does not say, 'Love all humankind.' It says, 'Love your neighbor' – that is, those with whom you are familiar. Again, you can only love someone with whom you are familiar. In my view, all the talk one hears about 'mutual love for all humanity' is misguided. We should rather talk about respect for all of our fellow humans and reserve the term 'love' for more intimate relationships."

"Yes, that makes sense."

"Anyway, I was saying that if you love someone, you want to help them flourish. Now, you might ask, how do you help God flourish? The answer is that God has projects, so to speak. Remember that we once spoke about the idea of divine self-expression?"

"Yes, of course."

"So if you love God, you want to fulfill God's will, keep God's commandments, and contribute to the divine self-expression. But most importantly, if you love God, you want to know God, in the most intimate way possible."

"And that's an intellectual thing, according to you."

"Yes, of course."

"Dr. Maimon, this is all very interesting. But I just thought of another question. You said you were expounding a theory of love. But do you believe there is such a thing as romantic love – between humans, at least?"

"Yes, I suppose so. Sure, there is such a thing."

"So, how does romantic love fit into your theory?"

"Well, frankly, I haven't worked out a theory of romantic love. But if you're interested in that, let's think it through together. Is it fair of me to assume that when you say 'romantic love,' you have something in mind that involves sexual attraction?"

"Yes."

"OK. Well, of course there's a broader thing which we might call physical attraction – like the maternal attraction that a mother has for her child. But since you asked about romantic love, let's focus on the kind of physical attraction that is sexually charged. If it is a passing attraction, we can call it infatuation. If it is more lasting, we could call it passionate sexual attachment. If it is excessive, we could call it sexual obsession. Obviously, one could be in any of these states without loving the person in question. For example, you could be sexually obsessed with someone you barely know. But a passionate sexual attraction to someone could conceivably exist in conjunction with genuine love – that is, the kind of love we were just talking about a few moments ago. Perhaps that's romantic love."

"Sorry I'm a little confused. Can you explain that again?"

"I'll try. My suggestion is that if you have a mere sexual attraction to a particular person, that would be lust. But, if in addition to that, you also had true love for the person – that is, a recognition and appreciation of her intrinsic worth insofar as she is the individual that she is, then the combination of those two would constitute romantic love."

"Ah, very interesting. I wonder, though – aren't you saying, in effect, that romantic love is socially sanctioned lust? The lust is OK as long as it's combined with the other, higher kind of love."

"No, not at all. The lust should be transformed and elevated by the love for the person. The lust is then no longer lust. Instead of mere sexual attraction, it becomes sexual affection. Do you see?"

"I guess so. Well, I had a different question. I was wondering – in your theory, could there be such a thing as a romantic love for God? I mean, obviously you can't have a sexual attraction to God, but still – could there be something like romantic love for God?"

"Ah, that's a good question. Let me think. I suppose . . . well, yes. There might be an analog. You know, the Jewish philosophers draw the following analogy: the soul is to the body as God is to the world. And –"

"Yes. I've heard that idea before. It's in the Talmud."

"It is? Where's that?"

"It's in *Berachos*. It says there are five ways in which the soul relates to the body, just as there are five ways God relates to the world."

"David, I'm impressed. You've been studying Talmud?"

"Yes, I have."

"Good for you. Well, you're right. It is in the Talmud, now that you mention it. I'd quite forgotten about that passage. But I think it's in Philo first. I'll have to check. Anyhow, it's an ancient idea. And I was just thinking that, using that idea, there might be an analog to romantic love with God."

"What do you mean?"

"I'll explain. Suppose you're sexually infatuated with a certain person. We could say then that you're not really relating to that person's soul. You're relating to that person's body. That's not romantic love – that's just lust. Now, let's allow ourselves to speak very loosely – and I mean, *very loosely* – of the physical world as God's body. So, a person who focuses solely on the material world – a materialist or a crass hedonist, for example – is like someone who's passionately attracted to God's 'body' while ignoring God's 'soul.' That's parallel to the case of lust. But, if in addition to finding the material world attractive, one also had a genuine love – that is, a recognition and appreciation of God insofar as He is Being Itself – then we could legitimately say that the combination of those two amounted to a romantic love for God. What do you think of that?"

"It sounds interesting. Still, it seems difficult to carry out. How do you combine the two in practice?"

"Ah, that's not easy. The challenge is to keep both going at the same time. It's all too tempting to become absorbed in the physical world of pleasure and to ignore Being itself altogether. On the other hand, for some people it's easy to live an ascetic life and seek to have a direct relationship with Being itself while forgoing all pleasures in this world. I don't think that's the Jewish way, though. What's hard is to do both at the same time. That is, it's hard to live in the material, physical world, and also recognize and appreciate God insofar as God is Being itself. And as I said before about lust, the higher kind of love for God should transform and elevate the desire for pleasure. But you're right – it's not easy!"

"Well, Dr. Maimon, thanks a lot. You've certainly given me a lot to think about."

"Not at all. David, I should be the one to thank you for helping me to refine and develop my theory . . . in rather unexpected ways."

14

March 20, 2003

I missed the minyan this morning so I davened in my room. I just finished davening and I still have my tefillin on as I sit down to write. My mind is popping with ideas and new connections and I don't want to lose them so I'm going to write them down. Maybe this is the 'mochin de-gadlus' that Chaim mentioned once? So many things are beginning to click. Like Rabbi L said, blaze your own intellectual trail when it comes to Torah. That's when all the depth really comes. It's also related to what Chaim said about the level of the yod, where you come up with new, original ideas.

I did Chaim's meditation this morning before starting to daven. It felt really good. It hit me how similar yet different Chaim's meditation is when compared with the meditation I did with Ravi in freshman year. (The ladder, the progression from bottom to top, etc., but very different at the end. Write that up some time.)

I felt more comfortable saying the Shema today, though sometimes it seems easier to do this when praying with the minyan. Need to try to wake up for that, maybe at least once a week beside Shabbos. But then, at the minyan they go so impossibly fast. Are they really saying all the words? I don't see how. Some of the Orthodox guys seem real nice and it's great to be part of this group, but sometimes I really just want to be myself, on my own. I guess I'm struggling with the tension between being part of the group and yet not wanting to lose my individuality in the process. Honestly I don't see how that tension is ever going to be resolved. Maybe I just have to accept it?

Meditation also made me think more about the relation between body and soul and about the five ways in which the soul/body relationship is like the God/world relationship. I was thinking: maybe there's a connection between these five ways and the five halleluyahs? And this also makes me think again of the five parts of the soul in Kabbalah which I read about somewhere. There's got to be a connection there.

I just pulled out my Gemara Berachos to look at the original source. It's on page 10a, where the five ways are linked to the five times that the phrase "let my soul bless Hashem" occurs. So obviously there's a connection with the five *Halleluyah*s, since that also talks about praise for God. Also, at the very end of Tehillim is the verse, "Let the entire soul praise Hashem." (Actually that verse is repeated during the morning prayer, but not repeated in the original chapter in Tehillim. Why?) Obviously, the five *Halleluyah*s reach their climax in the fifth one, which is the last chapter in Psalms where it says, praise Hashem with music, cymbals, tambourine, and dance.

Dance. Dance vs. running. As Ch once said, the ideal Jewish exercise is religious dance. Integration of body and soul. So maybe that's what I should be doing? Dancing instead of running?

God, this is amazing. I'm not having a mystical experience or anything like that, but so many things are beginning to click. (Mochin de-gadlus.) And this also relates to the idea of intellectual maturity. Dr M. mentioned it when I spoke to her about Kabbalah. I didn't think of it till now, but it's basically the same thing: intellectual "gadlus" as opposed to intellectual "katnus." It's strange. Sometimes Dr. M and Chaim's views seem so different, yet sometimes their views seem so close. I guess that's not too surprising, since they come out of the same tradition. They agree on some kind of commitment to Torah and mitzvos. Sure there are differences in the way they practice, but there's a lot they have in common. The big difference is in their interpretation of what it really all means. Dr. M thinks God is not an entity, and she thinks of God's attributes as the basic principles or metaphysical laws of the universe. Chaim believes in God as an entity, a being. He also believes in the sefirot as well. The sefirot are entities or spiritual beings. I agree more with Dr. M that God is not an entity. To believe in God is really to believe that the universe has a certain structure, that it manifests Being, and so on. But the doctrine of the sefiros seems so rich, so "powerful," as Dr. M would say. Yet maybe there's some way of combining the two views? Can't a person believe in ein sof and still <u>not</u> think of ein sof as an entity? Need to think about that.

And maybe some compromise between Dr. M and Chaim can be made on the idea of reincarnation. Dr. M says she rejects the whole idea. But why? She claims we should understand the soul as a principle or structure that underlies a given human body. So why couldn't she also agree that theoretically, the very same principle that underlies one body at a certain time could underlie another body at a different time? And if different bodies that have the same underlying principle can come to be, that would make "reincarnation" possible! And maybe olam ha-ba is a case where the soul, as a principle, is the underlying structure of something which is different from the human body as we know it, but is in some sense similar. Just like the same way in which a principle can be the structure of a person, as well as of a book or a text which the person writes. (Reminds me of the idea of being "written in the book of life" on Rosh ha-Shannah. Maybe that's the whole point of the book metaphor. Like what Rabbi A said in his RH speech last year. "Book" is to "meaning" as "body" is to "soul.")

Idea: Look for compromise or unification of Dr. M with Chaim, Dr. M with Rabbi L. And so on.

Another thing is that Dr. M thinks it's very rational to be a religious committed Jew, and she tends to denigrate pure faith. Chaim thinks that the system of the sefiros makes rational sense, but in the end you have to just have emunah. Is there some way of unifying the two views, so that it's both rational and a matter of emunah as well? Maybe it is rational up to a point, and then emunah kicks in. This makes me think of the existentialist approach. Will that work?

Maybe the real dispute between Dr. M (the philosopher) and Chaim (the Kabbalist) is really about this: Is it reason or free will that is really the highest thing in the end? The Kabbalists say that in the end, reason takes you pretty far, but ultimately God transcends reason and if you want to connect with God in the highest way, you've got to take a leap beyond reason. That doesn't mean you give up reason. You just transcend it. You do the same thing in the case of relationships. Like love. A relationship can be rational. It can make sense that I loved my mom. But there is always an element that goes beyond reason, too. I can't agree with Dr. M that love is completely rational.

This makes me think of a new idea on the question of whether Judaism could fit together with existentialism, based on something in Kabbalah. When I wrote my paper on Sartre I was thinking that Judaism is completely different from Sartre, since according to Judaism man has an essence and a telos, since he is created by God. But what about <u>God himself</u>? Does God have an essence? Could it be true to say that according to Kabbalah, for God, "existence precedes essence"? That seems true, since, according to the Kabbalah, God's essence is ein sof. Then there are the sefiros of kesser (will), hochmah and binah (rationality) and hesed, gevurah, tiferes (moral qualities). But still, these traits or qualities do not <u>define</u> God. Of course, God has a will, and God is rational and moral, but his essence doesn't consist in will, rationality or moral behavior. So God doesn't have a defined essence, which is exactly what existentialism says (about man, though).

And if man is created in the image of God, even though we have a "given" essence of some sort, that essence must in some sense be like God's essence. So, even though man has a soul, and even though man has a telos, his essence is indefinable, just like Sartre said. Man's essence is <u>expressed</u> in will, reason, and emotion, but it is not reducible to any of those things, either. So maybe, in the end, a Jewish existentialist could say that the commitment to God is an irrational choice that a person decides to make when he acts in accord with that indefinable essence within himself (and within God).

An amazing idea, but is it right? Even if man's essence is indefinable and even if man's will is more basic than his rationality, does it follow that the choice to be committed to God is ultimately <u>irrational</u> or <u>non-rational</u>? Maybe all that follows is that the choice to be committed to God always contains a non-rational component, but not that it will be completely irrational. That definitely makes more sense to me. This seems like a compromise between existentialism and rationalism. Beautiful!

I'm now going to pause and meditate and see what comes to mind. Looking for more unifications.

OK, I'm back. I had two thoughts. One about kashrus and one on the Zohar.

On kashrus: Chaim's Kabbalistic theory of kosher animals (the idea that some animals have a pure spiritual root and some have an impure root) could be combined with Low's theory that the kosher animals are perfect specimens of their type whereas the non-kosher animals are "in-betweeners." Come back to this one later.

The Zohar: As far as Dr. M's criticism of the Zohar goes, the thing I really don't understand about her view is why can't she say the same thing about the Zohar as she does about the Torah. Suppose Moses De Leon wrote a lot of it, or even most of it. Even if, historically, the Zohar does not contain actual conversations of people who lived during the time of the Second Temple, and even if many of the conversations are fictional, it could still be the case that the teachings of the Zohar are divinely inspired in the same way, more or less, as she herself believes the Torah is divinely inspired. Dr.

M herself thinks that the historical veracity of the Pentateuch is irrelevant to whether the teachings are regarded as divinely inspired. So if that's the case, why can't she say the same thing or something similar about the Zohar?

On the other hand, I don't agree with Low's point that the Zohar couldn't have been written by one person because of all the varieties of texts and styles in the Zohar. I can easily imagine one very clever author imitating a lot of different texts and styles and even many different types of conversations. Of course, it's still most likely that there were different authors. It seems to me like a lot of the Zohar could have been written by someone who was undergoing visions or trances, or sort of like a dreamlike state in which the author "met" a soul of some person who may have actually lived a long time ago. In Dr. M's theory of the soul, that could mean that for a certain period of time, the soul of the author takes on the structure, or even just part of the structure that is the soul of the deceased person. In this way, maybe the Ari could have experienced a visit with the soul of Elijah the prophet, who lived ages before he did. This sounds far out, but really isn't all that different from what Dr. M herself said regarding her interpretation of the idea that souls live on after the body dies — which is that the thoughts, words, and deeds of dead people have major effects on the world even after those bodies die. Perhaps De Leon's soul really did periodically adopt a structure similar to the souls of his characters, such as Shimon Bar Yohai. And of course all of this could be happening in virtue of the underlying structure of the world, which is to say, because of God.

Wow. I'm sure if I were stoned, I'd be saying that this is absolutely the most profound thing ever written. I'm not stoned, so I'm not saying that. But still, this stuff is amazing.

So many things to read/learn/think about. Need to make a list:

a) Brachos (with class), continue chapter nine on my own

b) Finish Avos (Ethics of Fathers) with commentary by Maimonides

c) Moshe Chaim Luzzatto's "Derech Hashem"

d) Aryeh Kaplan's book on Meditation and the Bible (I finished the one on Jewish Meditation).

e) Maimonides's Guide to the Perplexed for Dr. M's class

So much stuff to study and read, I barely have time for school. ~~What will Dad think~~

Oh, God. I can't believe after all that's happened, I'm still worrying about what Dad will think! Why can't I admit that ~~what I really want is for Dad to go to hell. No. I don't mean that. I can't say that. But~~ I've got to face up to the question. Do I really know what happened that night? Did Mom do it on purpose? Did she OD by accident? Did she find out he was having an affair? Can I say that I know? Am I going to ask him? Will I ever know the truth? I've got to admit these questions have been bothering me ever since the day she passed away. And I haven't till now faced up to these questions.

When I think about all this, part of me feels like just putting the pencil down and going back to bed and moping. But I won't allow myself to. I've got too much I'm interested in, thinking about, working on. Like all the stuff I just wrote about above. I've got to accept that I don't know what happened that night and I probably never will. But can I blame him for drifting away from Mom? For not being there when she needed him? Yes, I can. Actually, I pity him. What an empty relationship he had with her in the first place. The rest was just a consequence of that. What a fool he's been. She was a beautiful woman. So whether he had an affair or not, whether she knew or not, <u>I don't want to end up like him</u>. And maybe all of this bad history is messing up my mind when it comes to E. Maybe that's it. Is this why I'm avoiding her? She's really getting serious and I'm getting cold feet. Maybe I need to put the past behind me and move on?

God, I'm growing up. And this journal, thanks to Ravi, has so much to do with it. Looking over my journal I see that mostly the content has become less and less about me and my personal life (self-analysis) and more and more a journal of the ideas that I've been thinking about. It reminds me of what Ravi said. After a while, he stopped keeping a journal. I don't want to stop keeping a journal, but maybe it's becoming a different kind of journal.

Katnus to gadlus again. Yet this time, on that second level which Chaim spoke about, gadlus sheni. Looking back, I changed so much from freshman to sophomore, but now I changed again from junior to senior. In freshman year I had H, in sophomore year I tried to seduce E. Then in junior year I still chased after E. And now, I've moved beyond that. To what, I'm not entirely sure. That conversation with Dr M about love was one of the best. But I'm still processing it and I still can't figure out where I am with E.

Another thing just clicked. The transition from katnus rishon to gadlus rishon and then katnus sheni to gadlus sheni is like the four years of college. A freshman is a katan. Even the word "freshman" hints at the idea of childhood. Now, when you go from freshman to sophomore, that's a big transition. Sophomore is first maturity. The problem is you think you know it all, but you really don't, and that's why it's called the "sophomore" year, because in some sense you're wise, but you're also a moron! Then, when you get to your junior year, you kind of fall back, because now you begin to realize once again that you're actually still a katan, a minor in certain ways with so much room for growth. That's why it's called junior year. But since you now <u>realize</u> you're a katan, you're actually on a much higher level than before! Then, when you get to senior year, you've grown again. Now you're at gadlus sheni and that's why it's called "senior." And you're more mature now because you realize that you don't know it all and there's always so much more to know.

And now I realize the answer to the question I once asked Chaim. Why does the Kabbalah speak of only two cycles if there's always going to be more growth? Why isn't there a third katnus/gadlus, a fourth katnus/gadlus, etc.? The answer is that of course you grow again, after senior year. But once you go through the process of going from second childhood to second adulthood, you know that there is always more room for growth. Maybe that is the essence of the second growth, knowing that the first growth was only one stage in a long process yet to take place. When you grow the first time, you think: that's it, I'm now mature. But when you grow the second time, you implicitly know that the process of learning and growth will go on and on.

This turned out to be more phenomenal than I thought. But I'd better take off the tefillin and get to class. I'm late already!

15

Hey, David! It's been a while since we got together. How's it going?"

"Good, Simon. How are you?"

"Well? What've you been up to lately?"

"I finished my applications to law school."

"Good boy! Dad will be proud, I'm sure."

"Thanks. What are you going to do next year? Do you know yet?"

"I signed a contract with the Village Circle Theater. I'll be doing stage setting and some dramaturgy for them. I think it's a good start."

"That's great, Simon!"

"So, what else is going on? How's your love life?"

"Oh, pretty uneventful at the moment."

"What's up with What's-her-name?"

"You mean Esther? Not much. Actually, lately I've barely seen her. I've just gotten so distracted with other things."

"Like what?"

"You know . . . tests, papers, law school applications . . . ."

"But you just told me that's all over now."

"Well, I've just been busy."

"It sounds like it's gone cold between you two."

"No, I've just been busy with other things."

"Right. Well, anyway – do you have anything good to smoke?"

"Yes, I do. Take a look behind the *City of God*. I got a new supply a few weeks ago, but I've barely had any of it lately."

"Man, you've got a lot here! This must be at least a pound! Why do you have so much?"

"Remember that time I got some stuff for your friends? I went to the same place. I really didn't want to get so much, but that was the deal. All or nothing."

"You'd better be careful. Don't leave it around here too long. Well, shall we have some?"

"Sure. Why not?"

"You don't seem too enthused."

"I'm just trying to cut back on smoking."

"It's really hurting your running?"

"That's part of it."

"I thought you said you like smoking because it stimulates your mind to get deep ideas. And here I was, hoping to have a deep conversation! What's going on?"

"I'm just trying to cut back a little. And we can still have a deep conversation."

"Ah, I knew it! Let me guess – this has something to do with being a religious Jew."

"Not necessarily."

"Come on, David. Be honest! Your not wanting to smoke has something to do with your getting more religious. I knew this would happen sooner or later."

"I just said I want to cut back, that's all. I said I'd have some, didn't I?"

"Good. So here goes. Here, take some."

"Thanks."

"And while you're smoking, tell me about why you're cutting back."

"All right. Look, here's what I think. When you smoke, it opens up channels and pathways in the mind that aren't open. It loosens some inhibitions, it makes some of your sensations more intense."

"I agree. So?"

"So some of the ideas that you get while under the influence are going to be ones you would not have had at that time, unless you used the stuff. But that doesn't mean that all those ideas are valid ones that will last. First of all, some of the ideas actually seem deeper at the time than they really are because you're intoxicated at the time. But that's not the whole story. Some of those ideas really *are* deep. The thing is that the inhibitions and blocks in the channels may also be reality checks in some way. They're like filters for those ideas. Maybe the ideas are deep, maybe there's a lot of truth to them. But maybe if you were to avoid the drugs and work naturally to get at the truth, you'd get those same ideas later on, and once you did, they'd be more properly filtered. Do you get what I'm saying?"

"I'm not sure. Maybe if I take another hit, I'll think more deeply, and then I'll get what you're saying! Seriously, either the ideas are deep or they're not. If they're deep, you should be glad you smoked. If they're not deep, you'd know that once you weren't high anymore. But you just agreed that some of the ideas are deep, even after you're stoned!"

"Simon, what I'm trying to say is that using the stuff is like a shortcut to the truth. In a sense, it's a good thing. But maybe because you used the shortcut, the idea is not properly channeled when it comes out. It's kind of like using drugs to stimulate a woman to give birth prematurely. Had you waited longer and taken the natural course, the baby would have come later, but it would have been more mature. In the long run, if you're really interested in deep, valid ideas, maybe you're better off without the stuff."

"I guess that's all possible. But the bottom line is that it stimulates the mind to get deep ideas. You can always worry later on about whether they are valid or true. And besides, like you said, it makes your sensations more intense. I don't know about you, but I find that certain things are much more intensely pleasurable when you're high. Don't you agree?"

"Yes, I definitely agree."

"So, that alone would be a reason to smoke – in order to experience pleasure more intensely. Like, for example, I don't know about you, but I find the pleasure of sex far much more intense if I'm under the influence than if I'm not."

"Well, I have to agree with that. And there's nothing wrong with pleasure *per se*. The thing is, though, that if you're overly focused on the pleasure, you might neglect something else about the experience."

"Ah! This goes back to an old argument between us. We disagree on whether pleasure is the highest good. Meanwhile, here – take another hit."

"Thanks. Wow. I admit, this *is* good stuff. Look, Simon, I don't think we're going to change each other's minds about that. But don't you agree that there's a difference between having sex and making love?"

"No, I'm not so sure there's really a difference."

"Don't you agree that you can sleep with someone you barely know at all, and it can be quite physically pleasurable?"

"That's certainly true."

"And you might sleep with someone you love, and – well, it may or may not be so intensely physically pleasurable. I mean, you'd hope that it is . . . but that's still making love, isn't it? The point is that making love includes the physical dimension, but it goes beyond it."

"Yes, I guess I'd have to agree with that."

"So here's what I'm trying to say. If you sleep with someone while under the influence, then the physical sensations of pleasure could be very intense. But sometimes the physical pleasure might be so overwhelming that you barely pay any attention to the one you're with."

"Yeah, that can happen."

"At that point, you're so into the physical aspects that you might as well be having sex with someone else, or even with a prostitute."

"Maybe so, David. But I don't think there's anything wrong with that, either!"

"Look, do you agree that making love is better than having sex?"

"Well, that depends on the person. It depends on what the person wants."

"Then I will put my claim hypothetically. If making love is better than having sex, and if you agree that smoking marijuana intensifies the physical pleasure of the experience to the degree that you even forget about the person you're with, then you should agree that smoking interferes with the love aspect of the relationship."

"I don't know. I'm not convinced. Meanwhile, since we're neither making love nor having sex, would you pass me the joint, please?"

16

From: dgoldstein@cuniv.edu
To: richgoldstein@rchgoldattorney.com
Subject: Law School

Sent: 4/21/ 03 2:22 PM

Dear Dad,

How are you? Things are going well. I'm really enjoying my Jewish Philosophy independent study. I've also been studying Talmud a couple of times a week. I've continued to get more and more into Jewish things.

By the way, I got some good news yesterday. I got into Harbridge Law School.

David

From: dgoldstein@cuniv.edu   Sent: 4/21/ 03 2:30 PM
To: richgoldstein@rchgldattorney.com
Subject: Re: Law School

Hey David,

CONGRATULATIONS!!!! Great news! I guess that settles what you'll be doing next year.

Dad

17

"Dovid! It's nice to finally see you in person instead of talking on the phone."

"Thanks, Chaim. Same here."

"So, *nu* – how's the Gemara class going?"

"Good. I enjoy it. It's perplexing, puzzling, intriguing, and sometimes bewildering – all at the same time!"

"Great! That's exactly the experience you're supposed to have."

"Right. Anyhow, I wanted to ask you about that parody you once mentioned. I think it was on last Shavuos. Do you remember?"

"Ah! You mean the parody of a Talmudic discussion about smoking marijuana?"

"Yes, that's it."

"I think I have it somewhere in this desk. Just a second. You probably want to see the English version. Ah! Here it is. Have a look."

"Chaim, this is really clever! It sounds exactly like real Gemara!"

"Glad you like it. Like I said, one of my friends did it."

"He must have worked pretty hard on it."

"What are you talking about? It probably took twenty minutes for him to do it!"

"Does he do more serious stuff too?"

"Sure. He's got some really good *divrei Torah*, some interesting *hiddushim*."

"*Hiddushim?*"

"New ideas, new Torah thoughts."

"Oh, right. That reminds me – I had a new thought myself. At least I think it's new."

"So, *nu*, let's hear it!"

"It has to do with the five *halleluyahs* that we say in the morning. You know, that's the last five chapters of Psalms, each of which starts and ends with the word *halleluyah*."

"Yes, of course. But unless we're davening, we usually use the word *hallelukah* in order to avoid saying God's name. Anyhow, what about them?"

"Well, for a long time I had this question, whether it's just an accident that there are five *hallelukahs*, or whether there's some significance to the number five.

hemp. this is a certain plant from which leaves are dried and made into a substance that is smoked through a pipe. It affects the soul and intensifes certain pleasures. **Sharp one.** That is to say, smarty pants. **Ointments and hemp.** Ointments affect only the skin, but hemp enters the body and affects the soul. **To which is smoking more similar, etc.** Food, drink, and scents enter the body and affect the soul, as does smoking hemp. **We make a blessing over all things.** The tanna should have said: We make a blessing over *these* things: food, drink, and scents. Why did the tanna say, on *all* things? Surely it is to indicate that this list is merely a set of examples and not an exhaustive list. **Rabbi Tanaka came from the east.** In the east smoking hemp was more prevalent. **Was he smoking hemp at the time?** Smoking hemp can make a person prone to forget things. **tabbak.** This substance does not affect the soul in the way that hemp does. **Don't give me your lungs and don't give me your soul.** A nice way of saying: the distinction you suggested is absurd. **When is the blessing made?** In general, a blessing over enjoyment should be made *before* the enjoyment takes place.

Rabbi Gidi asked: "Should a person recite a blessing before smoking hemp?" Rabbi Bimi responded: "Isn't this obvious from a mishnah?! For it was taught, 'Rabbi Yehudah said: He who takes enjoyment from this world without reciting a blessing is considered as if he has stolen from the Holy One, Blessed Be He!' Rabbi Gidi retorted, "But we learned [in a *baraisa*]: 'We make a blessing over all things — these are drinks, foods, scents. We do not make a blessing over ointments.' Now, if we do not make a blessing over ointments, obviously we do not make a blessing over *all* enjoyments!" Rabbi Bimi retorted, "Sharp one! Is this a proper comparison? Here we are talking about ointments, and here we are talking about smoking hemp! To which is smoking more similar? To drink, food, and scents? Or to ointments? Moreover, what does the phrase 'We make a blessing over all things' come to include? It comes to include smoking hemp!" When Rabbi Tanaka came from the East, Rabbi Gidi informed him [of the entire exchange]. Said Rabbi Tanaka, "Mother of Abraham! Was R. Bimi smoking hemp at the time? Surely even a child knows the following ruling: 'No blessing is made on smoking!'" Rabbi Gidi responded, "Perhaps 'smoking' here refers only to smoking tabbak? And if it refers to smoking tabbak, how can you compare smoking tabbak with smoking hemp? One affects the lungs, the other affects the lungs and the soul as well!" Answered Rabbi Tanaka, "Don't give me your lungs and don't give me your soul! Smoking is smoking, and no blessing is made on smoking." Rabbi Garbonus asked, "According to Rabbi Bimi's opinion that a blessing is made, when is the blessing made? Before lighting a match? Or after? And if after, is it before taking a smoke? Or after? And if after, is it before the hemp affects the mind, or after?" Perhaps the act of smoking begins with the lighting. Therefore, one should make the blessing before lighting. Alternatively, if one makes the blessing before lighting and the light goes out, one will have made the blessing in vain! Furthermore, is the smoking itself an enjoyment, or is it the effect on the soul that is the enjoyment? If the former, one should make the blessing before taking the first smoke, and if the latter, one should make the blessing after the first smoke, but before it affects the mind! Let the matter stand [unresolved until Elijah comes].

We do not make a blessing over all enjoyments. This is obviously true, since there are many enjoyments over which we do not make a blessing, such as massaging, tickling, and the like. Why do we make a blessing over some enjoyments and not over others? Rabbi Nosi of Narbonne answered that we bless only on those things that supply enjoyment or pleasure to all, and not merely to some. Not everyone finds ointments enjoyable, and the same is true of massaging and tickling. However, this is difficult for if so, why does Rabbi Bimi hold that we make a blessing on smoking hemp, since not everyone enjoys this? Thus instead Rabbi Tosi of Toledo answered that we make a blessing only on those enjoyments that involve ingesting a substance. Eating, drinking, and smelling involve ingesting, whereas ointments, massaging, and tickling do not. Smoking is surely ingesting a substance, and the dispute concerns whether smoking hemp counts as an enjoyment, or rather as merely a frivolous activity. **Before the hemp affects the mind, or after.** This is difficult, for if one waits until the hemp affects the mind, one will have taken pleasure in the hemp before reciting the blessing, which violates the stated dictum that one must not take pleasure from this world without a blessing! Rabbi Tosi answered, perhaps the hemp is bad and will not affect the mind, and then one will have recited the blessing in vain. Hence it seems the right thing to do is to wait until it affects the mind a little bit, and only then recite the blessing!

It didn't really bother me that much. But once you told me that numbers are really important in Judaism, I started wondering about it some more."

"Dovid, that's an excellent question! Why are there exactly five? Do you have an answer?"

"I think so. In our Gemara class we came across the teaching that the phrase 'Let my soul bless' occurs five times in Psalms, and that corresponds to five ways in which the soul relates to the body, and in which God relates to the world."

"That's in Berachos, *daf yod. Nu*, go on."

"I was thinking that maybe the five *hallelukahs* also correspond to those same five ways."

"Very interesting, Dovid!"

"And maybe this also has something to do with the fact that, as you once pointed out to me, *Tehillim* is made up of five separate books. And by the way, the Gemara's discussion reminded me of the famous 'Five Ways' in which Thomas Aquinas tried to prove God's existence."

"Thomas who?"

"Thomas Aquinas, the great Christian philosopher. I guess you haven't heard of him. He lived after Maimonides. In fact, Aquinas quotes Maimonides every so often. He refers to him as Rabbi Moses."

"Sorry, I haven't heard of him. But what you're saying is interesting because – do you remember I once told you about the book, *Shomer Emunim*? In it, the author Rav Irgis explicitly uses the five ways in which the soul is similar to *Hashem* as a basis for five arguments for God's existence."

"Are you serious? I wonder if he was copying Thomas Aquinas's famous five ways!"

"I doubt it. But really, you should look at that *sefer* some time."

"Yes, I'd like to. Is it in English?"

"No, I don't think so. Anyway, getting back to your *dvar Torah* . . . you want to say that the five *hallelukahs* correspond to the five ways in which the soul is like God?"

"Yes. But there's something else. Somewhere I came across the idea that Kabbalah teaches that there are five levels or aspects of the soul."

"Right."

"So, maybe the five *hallelukahs* correspond to the five levels of the soul."

"Dovid, excellent! You're *mamash* bringing tears of joy to my eyes. What a *geshmak* idea!

"Sorry? What does that mean?"

"That means – what a delicious, tasty idea."

"What a compliment! Thanks. The next thing I need to do is study the content of each of the five *hallelukahs* and see if somehow they match up with the five aspects of the soul."

"Good idea. By the way, you may be interested to know that the five parts of the soul also correspond to the five fingers on the hand. Maybe you could work that in somehow as well."

"I'll have to think about that. Another thing I was thinking about has to do with the author of the five *hallelukahs*."

"That would be Dovid ha-Melech, or King David."

"Exactly. Didn't you once say that Dovid is considered something like the collective soul of all Israel?"

"Yes, that's a big idea in Kabbalah. All souls are in some way interrelated and interconnected. And there is an idea that the soul of Dovid, which is also the soul of *moshiach*, is somehow the essence of the soul of the people of Israel. That's why he's the king, that's why he's the *moshiach*. That's also why when we *daven*, we generally say *Tehillim* – that's Psalms – as part of davening. And so much of *Tehillim* is in first person, as if Dovid were praying just for himself. But that's also a hint that when Dovid spoke about himself, he spoke for all Israel as well – past, present and future generations."

"Right. Now, do you remember what you said about how in the Jewish tradition, it's customary to sign one's name inside a book that you're writing?"

"Yes."

"And sometimes it's at the beginning, but sometimes it's at the end, as when a person signs a letter."

"Of course."

"Well, it would make sense that if David wrote the book of *Tehillim*, he might have put his own imprint at the end of the book somehow."

"Indeed so. You know the verse at the end of the second book, which says, 'This completes the prayers of Dovid, son of Yishai'? If you recall, that's the verse I gave you to use at the end of your meditation. But I don't know of anything like that at the end of book five."

"So that's exactly what I wanted to explain! I was thinking that if David is the collective soul of all Israel, it would make sense that at the end of *Tehillim* there might be some kind of signature – that is, an imprint of the soul. And that would be the case if the five last psalms correspond to the five parts of the soul."

"Ah, very good! Again, excellent idea! Dovid, you're definitely on to something! You should work on it and write it up when you're done."

"You think it's that good?"

"You should definitely write it up. Why don't you email it to me when you've got it done? I'd love to read it, and I'm sure others would, too!"

18

From: dgoldstein@cuniv.edu Sent: 5/2/03 11:44 PM
To: rlow@ahavattorah.org.il
Subject: Dvar Torah
Attached: The Five Hallelukahs.doc

Dear Rabbi Low:

I've written up an essay – or I guess you could call it a dvar torah – on the five Hallelukahs. I thought you might like to read it. I also want to say, I'm planning to have a graduation party to which I will invite my close friends and teachers, and I was hoping that if you were in the States by any chance, maybe you'd come. It will be the night after the graduation.

David

The Five Hallelukahs by David Goldstein

The last five chapters of *Tehillim* (Psalms 146–150) are recited as part of the daily morning prayer. Each of these chapters begins and ends with the word *hallelukah* (praise *Hashem*). For this reason they are often referred to as "the five hallelukahs." Is it just an accident that there are exactly five *hallelukahs*? Or is there some significance to the number five?

The Talmud does not explicitly address this question. But it does give an explanation for why the phrase "*Borchi nafshi et Hashem*" (let my soul bless *Hashem*) occurs five times throughout *Tehillim*. In *Berachos* 10a, R. Shimon ben Pazzai says that there are five ways in which the soul relates to the body that correspond to five ways in which G-d relates to the world. He then continues, "Let the soul, which has these five aspects, come and praise Him who has these five aspects." The five aspects of the soul are as follows:

1. Just as the soul fills the entire body, *Hashem* fills the entire world.
2. Just as the soul sustains the body, *Hashem* sustains the world.
3. Just as the soul sees and is not seen, *Hashem* sees but is not seen.
4. Just as the soul is pure, *Hashem* is pure.
5. Just as the soul sits in inner chambers, *Hashem* sits in inner chambers.

The Zohar (*Terumah* 158b) also discusses the idea that there are five aspects of the human soul which correspond to five aspects of G-d. The five aspects are (from lower to higher):

1. *Nefesh*: the power that governs the body (the "animal soul")
2. *Ruah*: the power to have emotions or character traits (the "heart" or "spirit")

3.   *Neshamah*: intelligence (*binah*)

4.   *Hayah*: wisdom (*hochmah*)

5.   *Yehida*: free will (*ratzon*)

The main theme of the five *hallelukahs* is the soul's praise of *Hashem*. This leads naturally to the idea that the five *hallelukahs* correspond to the five aspects of the soul. This would explain why there are exactly five *hallelukahs*. I will support this idea by showing how each chapter speaks of the praise that is fitting for each aspect of the soul (from higher to lower). The result is that at the end, all parts of the soul praise Hashem, and together, the entire soul praises Hashem.

1.   The first *hallelukah* begins with the phrase "let my *nefesh* praise *Hashem*." The main theme of the first *hallelukah* is the mortality of man, which is contrasted with the fact that *Hashem* is "maker of heaven and earth." In reciting the first *hallelukah*, a person praises *Hashem* insofar as he is a creature made of flesh and blood. This psalm clearly corresponds to the lowest level of the soul, the *nefesh*.

2.   The second *hallelukah* is much more upbeat. This psalm corresponds to the second level of the soul, the *ruah*. We begin by saying that it is good, pleasant, and fitting to praise *Hashem*. At one point we say, "Sing to our G-d with the harp." The theme of this psalm is *Hashem*'s special providence and grace over the world, over Jerusalem, and over the people of Israel. In this psalm, *Hashem* is praised not only as the maker of heaven and earth, but as the one who sustains the flourishing of the earth and all that it contains, including plant life, animals, birds, as well as humans. It is interesting that this is the only one of the five *hallelukahs* which contains any form of the word *lev* or heart. In reciting the second *hallelukah*, we praise *Hashem* insofar as we have a *ruach* or spirit.

3.   As we have seen, the first two *hallelukahs* focus on what *Hashem* does for the inhabitants of the world, for humans, and for the people of Israel. The third psalm is a song of praise for *Hashem* as creator of all. Here we call upon even the angels and the heavenly hosts to praise *Hashem*. We call upon the sun and the moon, the stars, the heavens and even the "heavens of the heavens" to praise *Hashem*. We call upon all earthly creatures (animals, birds, humankind) to praise *Hashem* – not out of thanks for what *Hashem* gives us, but out of recognition of His glory. This third psalm is less joyous, but also more reverential than the second. We do not say anything here about joy or song, nor do we mention any musical instrument. In reciting the third psalm, we praise *Hashem* as intelligent beings who are capable of grasping the awesome universe that *Hashem* created. Therefore, the third psalm corresponds to the third aspect of the human soul, *binah* or intelligence.

4.   The fourth *hallelukah* starts off in a unique way: "*Shiru la-Hashem shir*

hadash" – "Sing to *Hashem* a new song." This is associated with the fourth part of the soul, or *hochmah* (wisdom), which is the power to come up with new insights or innovations. But what exactly is new or different about this psalm? The focus of the fourth *hallelukah* is not on *Hashem* as creator of the human body, of the earth, or even of the cosmos and all that it contains. Instead, the focus is on the fact that *Hashem* has a special relationship with those who are devoted to him. The new song is the one that is sung by those who are righteous or devout (*hasidim*). This ties in to the fourth aspect of the soul and Hashem as taught by the Talmud. Just as Hashem is pure, and therefore capable of good actions, the soul, too, is pure and capable of good actions.

5. The last *hallelukah* is the shortest of all five. After describing the various reasons for why Hashem should be praised in the previous four psalms, the only thing left is simply to praise *Hashem*. The fifth psalm is the only one of the five *hallelukahs* that mentions any form of the term "*kadosh*" (=holy or transcendent). The highest level of praise is not praise of *Hashem* insofar as He has created the world, but rather insofar as He is the Almighty, pure and simple. Of all the five psalms, only the fifth mentions a whole bunch of musical instruments. Music is a form of *non-verbal* expression. And that is precisely the point of this fifth psalm, which goes beyond the verbal realm and into the non-verbal realm. Hence this psalm corresponds with the fifth level of the soul namely, *ratzon* or free will. In reciting the fifth psalm, we praise *Hashem* with that aspect of our soul which goes beyond words, the will itself.

In conclusion, each of the five psalms corresponds to one of the five parts of the soul. The five *hallelukahs* go in a progression from the lowest part to the highest part. The fifth and final psalm concludes with the phrase *Kol ha-neshamah tehallel kah, hallelukah*. During the morning prayer this verse is repeated. Why? Perhaps it is repeated because the word *kol* can have two meanings. The phrase *kol ha-neshamah* can mean every soul, or it can mean the entire soul. Perhaps we mean it in one way when we say it the first time, and we mean it the other way when we say it the second time. The first time we say it, we mean, "Let every soul praise *Hashem*!" The second time we say it, we mean, "Let the entire soul – that is, all five parts of the soul together, praise *Hashem*!"

19

From: dgoldstein@cuniv.edu   Sent: 5/20/03 10:15 AM
To: eapplefeld@cuniv.edu
Subject: Graduation Party

I tried your number in the dorm, you must be studying or something like that. I wrote an essay on the five hallelukahs. Would you like to read it? I'll email it to you if you like. By the way, I'm planning a graduation party the night after graduation on the night of May 28. That's my birthday! Please, would you come?

From: eapplefeld@cuniv.edu   Sent: 5/20/03 11:29 AM
To: dgoldstein@cuniv.edu
Subject: Re: Graduation Party

David, I'm in the library working on my last paper due tomorrow. I'd love to see your dvar Torah on the five hallelukahs, so just print it out and give it to me next time I see you, which I hope will be soon.

As for the party, I'd love to come but I can't. It would be nice finally to meet all the people you keep telling me about. But my cousin's wedding is that night! I have to go out there earlier in the day and I'm not even sure I'll be able to make it to the graduation at all. I was also going to ask you if you might be interested in going to the wedding with me. Can you change your party to another night?

Esther

From: dgoldstein@cuniv.edu   Sent: 5/20/03 11:35 AM
To: eapplefeld@cuniv.edu
Subject: Re: Graduation Party

Congratulations on the wedding – or should I say, mazal tov! I wish I could go with you. I really love Jewish weddings. But I'm sorry – that won't work. It's already set that the party has to be that night. Maybe you can come to the party after the wedding? I'm sure the party will go late.

From: eapplefeld@cuniv.edu   Sent: 5/20/03 11:37 AM
To: dgoldstein@cuniv.edu
Subject: tomorrow?

The wedding will go late too, believe me. Oh, well. Meanwhile, what are you doing tomorrow?

From: dgoldstein@cuniv.edu   Sent: 5/20/03 11:39 AM
To: eapplefeld@cuniv.edu
Subject: Re: tomorrow?

I have my Gemara class tomorrow late afternoon. But I should be back in the evening. I'll call when I'm done.

From: eapplefeld@cuniv.edu   Sent: 5/20/03 11:40 AM
To: dgoldstein@cuniv.edu
Subject: Re: tomorrow?

Great. Maybe we can go somewhere nice for dinner? See you!

20

"Dovid?"

"Yes?"

"Hi! It's Chaim! Are you busy?"

"I just finished my Gemara class. I need to call Esther soon but I can talk for a bit. What's going on?

"I just had to call you, Dovid! I just read your dvar Torah on the five hallelukahs. It's great! Yasher koach!"

"Thanks, Chaim. That's so nice of you to say."

"Seriously, it's really gevaldik! One day, maybe you'll study what the Ari had to say about the five hallelukahs, but never mind that for now. You know, when you work out an idea like that, you really take on Tehillim as your own. If you've thought about the five hallelukas on such a deep level and you've brought out a hiddush or novel point about them, then, every time you read the five hallelukahs, it's almost as if you wrote them yourself!"

"I think I know what you mean. Every time I say the morning prayer and go through the five hallelukahs, I think of this dvar Torah. It makes the whole thing so much more meaningful."

"Exactly. So you must be really getting into davening, then."

"Yeah, mostly I am."

"You don't sound too sure."

"There's still something that bothers me about the prayers."

"What's that?"

"As I learn more, I get more and more interested in the daily prayers. But still sometimes it gets a little rote. I feel like adding something new. It doesn't seem like there's really any place to do this."

"Dovid! Sure, you can add your own prayers! Didn't we talk about this once? I think it's really an important thing. As Dovid ha-Melech says, 'I pour out my soul in prayer.' The idea of pouring out one's soul before Hashem — it's something people used to do much more often. Nowadays, a lot of Jews think you have to be a tzaddik in or-

der to do this. I think everybody should do it as long as they follow some simple rules."

"Oh? Like what?"

"Well, there's a time and place for personal prayers. You can't just insert a personal prayer at any random point in the davening. But you can always insert a personal prayer in the bracha of shema kolenu, even in English. And you can also do so in the section of the shemoneh esreh that starts 'Elokai, netzor leshoni me-ra.' Or you can add something after davening as part of Tahanun, though that is usually reserved for prayers for forgiveness. But, aside from the regular prayers, you could just decide you want to pour out your soul and pray. The thing is, you should always start off by acknowledging Hashem's goodness, maybe by saying some of the Tehillim that talk about God's greatness. That's one reason why we say Ashrei before davening minha. As to the prayer itself, you should only ask for things that you know are good to ask for. It's always safer to be more general than specific. Like, if you want to get married, you shouldn't pray that you get married to a specific person. You should pray that you get happily married. You shouldn't pray that a specific business deal go through. You should rather pray for wealth and material success. But sometimes it's OK to be specific, as long as you pay attention to what you're doing. Like if you're praying for someone who's sick, you definitely should mention their name. Actually, what I think a person should do, if he really wants to make a personal prayer, is to write it up first before they actually pray it. Just like what I once said about writing up hiddushei torah. When you write something down, you naturally spend more time figuring out exactly what it is you want to say. Remember what I taught you about berur and writing? Just in the act of writing it down, you clarify or refine yourself, as well as your prayer. And you know what's the most important thing?"

"What's that?"

"The bottom line is to realize that the main reason we pray is actually not so much to get the thing we want."

"No? Why else would we be praying, then?"

"We pray in order to become closer to Hashem. That's why we say that, no matter what, even if Hashem chooses not to answer our prayer, he always hears our prayer. In other words, prayer always brings us closer to Hashem, even if the prayer is not answered."

"Hey Chaim, hang on a second. I'm getting another call. Maybe it's Esther. No, it looks like it must be my friend, Ravi. Can you hold on a second?"

"Yeah, sure. I'll hold."

"Hello? Ravi?"

"Hey, David. This isn't Ravi. It's Simon. Can you talk?"

"Simon! Why are you calling on Ravi's phone? Look, I'm on the other line with Chaim. Can I call you back later?"

"Sorry, David, but this is real important. We have a problem. Did you hear what happened up here in the dorm?"

"No. Hang on, Simon. Let me just say bye to Chaim and I'll be right back."

"You do that."

"Hey, Chaim! I've got to take this other call. I'll call you back later. OK?"

"Sure thing. But Yasher koach again on the dvar Torah! And remember what I said about *your own davening. All the best. Bye!"*

"OK, Simon, I'm back. So? What's up? What's going on in the dorm?"

"David, I was doing some work in your room when the guys from campus security knocked on the door . . . ."

"Really? What did they want?"

"Well, they were looking for illegal substances."

"You're joking."

"No joke, David. The security guards came. They asked a few questions. Then they checked the room – and, believe it or not, they found what stands behind The City of God. David? Are you still there?"

"Yeah, I'm here – just barely. Oh, man, I'm in trouble now. How could I have been so stupid? I shouldn't have kept that whole stash in my room!"

"Don't dwell on that now. Just be calm and think practically."

"Right, right . . . what should I do? What do you think is going to happen?"

"I'm not sure. I guess it depends. If they go to the police, they could charge you with dealing."

"No way! I'm not a dealer. You know that!"

"David, I hate to say this, but that's what it looks like. I was thinking . . . if they want to, they can probably trace everything, including things from last year, like some of our emails and cell phone calls. By the way, that's why I'm calling you from Ravi's phone. He was kind enough to let me use it. Look, David – you have to think about what you're going to say when you talk to security."

"All I can think of is that I'm in trouble. This is really going to mess me up."

"Look, don't panic. You're a philosopher, aren't you? Be calm, and just think logically about what you're going to say. They're going to question you when you get back. So will the police, if they get involved. The thing is – if you lie, you have to do it right. That's why I'm calling."

"My father's going to kill me."

"David, calm down. Listen to me. They asked me some questions, too."

"What did you tell them?"

"I said I didn't know anything about how the stuff got into your room."

"Great. So what am I going to say? I can't say the same thing!"

"Sure you can."

"If they can recover some of our cell phone calls, they'll find out that we talked about buying some stuff."

"Yeah, but they can't prove that you actually bought this stuff. You can say that all the phone talk was just bull, and you never actually bought anything, and that someone else put this in your room. Things like that can happen in a dorm."

"What? Simon, they'll never believe that!"

"I think that's your best shot if you want to get off the hook. I don't know what else to tell you. Look, they said they'd come back later to talk to you. Anyway, David, I've got to go. I suggest you make a point of being here. Otherwise, they might call your dad."

"All right. I'll be right over."

21
—

"David, have another cup of coffee. Come on, you've got to think positive."

"Simon, I don't know where to turn. I can't even talk to anyone about this, except you of course, and you're already involved. I can't believe I screwed up like this. All that time I smoked the stuff, I thought about all sorts of problems – my running, my health, my lungs, how I lied to my Mom about smoking. I even thought about whether it was ruining my brain, and about whether it goes against Judaism. But I never thought about getting in trouble with the cops!"

"That's life, man. It's what you least expect that sneaks up and hits you in the rear. Anyway, you'll get out of it somehow. By the way, have you considered praying?"

"Very funny, Simon!"

"Just kidding, David. But seriously, is it really all that bad?"

"Of course it is. I'm in deep trouble. I mean, aside from the trouble with the police itself, which is bad enough – this is going to wreck my life."

"David, get real! You're obviously exaggerating."

"Do you think they'll let me register in law school this fall? Man, I could be charged as a felon!"

"They could charge you, but that doesn't mean they'll convict you. You have a good chance of arguing that they had no right to search the room."

"Yeah, right. Even so, if there's a trial, it could drag on for months. Besides, my dad is definitely not going to like this. I emailed him and told him I need to come home and talk to him about something. I'm really afraid about how he's going to react. He'll probably disinherit me. Or at least stop supporting me. In which case, how will I be able to afford law school anyway?"

"Oh, come on. He won't do that. He's your dad. He might be angry, but he wouldn't do anything permanent."

"You don't know my dad."

"David, people make mistakes. I'm sure he knows that. Don't you think your dad knows what goes on in college dorms?"

"I'm sure he does."

"So? You made a mistake. He knows you're not a bad son."

"I didn't just make a mistake, I got caught. From Dad's point of view, that's what's bad! And – oh, my God – what about Esther?"

"What about her?"

"She won't have anything to do with me once she finds out about this. I don't even know what to tell her. In fact, I've been avoiding her altogether."

"Just tell her the truth."

"No way. She won't be able to handle it. She'll never want to see me again."

"If that's so, she doesn't love you."

"But she does."

"Did she say so?"

"Not in so many words. But I know it. She wants me . . . to make a commitment."

"Really? You didn't tell me about that! So then, she loves you. If so, she'll stick by you through thick and thin. Isn't that what love is about?"

"Yeah, but look – this would just be too much, I think. It's not only the stuff itself . . . it's the embarrassment of getting in trouble with the cops. I'm sure her parents will forbid any contact between us. You know, her background . . . ."

"Yeah, I know the background! Remember, that's where I came from!"

"So you know what I mean."

"Look, if she can't get over this because of her background, she's not for you whether you're guilty of a felony or not. If she really loves you, she'll overcome it. She'll forgive you. It's not like you murdered your mother or something . . . . Oh, no, that was really stupid of me. David, I'm sorry. Really, that was just a total slip. I didn't mean that the way it sounded at all –"

"It's OK, Simon. It's OK. Forget it. I know what you're trying to say."

"Thanks, David. Well, anyway, getting back to Esther. Do you think they're all so kosher over there? They have people getting in trouble with the cops all the time: drugs, spousal abuse, tax evasion, securities fraud, you name it!"

"I don't know. I don't think she'll accept it. Anyway, there's another thing."

"What's that?"

"Did I tell you I was thinking about possibly studying in yeshiva in Israel over the summer?"

"Surprise, surprise! Are you sure it'll be just for a summer? Many times, people who go for a summer end up staying for a year."

"I can't go for a year. I've got law school to go to. But what's the difference? Look, do you think a yeshiva will admit a student who's been charged as a felon?"

"Why not? Those yeshivas are filled with crooks! Well, I'm exaggerating a little bit. But believe me, the yeshiva world is no stranger to drug users and crooks. You'll fit right in!"

"Very funny. Seriously, the place I want to go is very small, very elite."

"I see. In that case, you may have to go to a different yeshiva. What's the big deal?"

"No, it has to be this one – the one where Rabbi Low teaches. Anyway, there's another practical problem."

"What's that?"

"It's not going to be easy to leave the country."

"Ah, I didn't think of that. You've got a point there. At least, you might be stuck here for a while. I guess you are in a bind after all. Of course, to me, all of these problems are manufactured."

"What do you mean?"

"Well, if you didn't have this need to go to yeshiva, and if you didn't have this relationship with your dad, and if you didn't have a relationship with this Orthodox girl, and if you didn't have this relationship with Judaism, then this wouldn't be such a big problem after all! In other words, if you were just like me, you'd confess, muddle through, and eventually you'd put it all behind you."

"Maybe so. But I'm not you, and you're not me."

"Small problem there."

"God, I don't know. Maybe it is time to start praying after all."

"Well, David, at least you haven't completely lost your sense of humor!"

22

May 25, 2003

I'm really not sure what to do next. I really don't know what to do. It's going to be really tough facing Dad. And I really am in trouble. Am I being punished for something? Is this my punishment for delving into the secrets of Torah? I can't believe that. Is it punishment for something else I did? For dishonesty? No, I can't believe that. But who knows?

Maybe I should pray after all. What do I have to lose?

I guess I could say some Tehillim. OK. Here goes.

I just said Psalm 23. Somehow that didn't quite do it. I need to just say what's on my mind in my own words. It's not so easy. Chaim said: If you're going to pray to God, think about what you're going to say before you say it. Why should this be any easier than writing a letter to Mom or a friend about what's really going on in your life? That's not so easy. If you were going to speak with the President of the U.S. or the king of another country, surely you would take some time to figure out exactly what you want to say before you got there. You wouldn't just ad lib. So maybe I should write it up before I say it. And like Chaim said, don't be too specific unless you really mean it. And be honest. As it says, "Pour out your soul." And always start out with a preface of thanks. OK. Here goes.

BS"D

God, thanks for all the ~~stuff~~ things you've given me. Thanks for my body, my brain, my mind, my will, my emotions. Thanks for giving me life, thanks for sustaining me, thanks for all the knowledge you've given me. Thanks for this great, beautiful world. Thanks for all the people you've led me to meet, especially over these past few years. I've learned so much.

Now, as it says in Tehillim, I shall pour out my soul in prayer. O God, please help me out of the ~~mess~~ trouble I've gotten myself into. I'm really sorry for my silly, foolish actions. I'm sorry I ~~smoked~~ broke the law. I'm sorry I've done things that are unhealthy for my mind and body. I'm sorry I lied to Mom about not smoking. I just didn't want her to get worried. But it was still dishonest. Obviously, ~~(if you exist)~~ you know my thoughts and you know that I feel that things like that shouldn't be illegal. ~~And I still don't understand why it should be forbidden by the Torah, except maybe for health reasons. But~~ The fact is that it is criminalized in this country so ~~I guess~~ I shouldn't be doing it. You know my innermost thoughts. So you know I have trouble regretting smoking. But it's criminalized. Maybe I bought that stuff from a true criminal, and who knows where my money went? And anyway, I'm definitely sorry for being irresponsible. I feel ~~a little~~ ashamed asking you for help in this. I admit that so much of this is about my own personal desires getting frustrated if this whole thing comes out in the open. But God, some of those desires are for good things. God, you know that despite all that's happened I'm ~~assuming~~ hoping my father is innocent and I'm trying to have some kind of positive relationship with him. Please, God, help me to attain this goal. And another thing is that I don't want to ruin what I have with Esther. I don't want her to get scared away. You know I've been thinking more and more about what to do after college. Maybe I should really go and study with Rabbi Low in Israel. Of all the people I've talked to and learned from about Judaism, he's the one who's the most on my wavelength. But actually, I really don't know what to do about that, either. Maybe I should find some place local to study. Or maybe I should study more with Chaim. Anyway all that is down the drain right now unless I can get out of the trouble I'm in. The bottom line is — please, God, help me to get out of this trouble. God, you know that I doubt your very existence. I'm sorry about that, ~~I feel like Augustine writing his confessions~~ but I don't exactly think that's my fault. Anyway, I'm ready to seek you out if you're there, and I'm asking you to meet me halfway. I wish I could have true, genuine knowledge of you, O God.

(Conclude with my own adaptation of Chaim's prayer:) Hashem, please guide my thoughts, my speech and my actions so that I may do and be that which is right and proper in your eyes, so that I achieve the best relationship with you. ~~And please help get me out of this trouble I'm in!~~ Kalu tefillos David ben Yishai. So may it be your Will. Amen.

———

Well, I said it, and then I said it again, and then a third time.
Chaim was right. When you write down a prayer, one thing leads
to another, in ways you didn't expect. I sure hope He's up there
listening.

23

"David, I got it all worked out. Your problems are solved."

"What?! Simon, what do you mean?"

"You're off the hook. I spoke with the cops this morning. They still might want to ask you some questions. But I'm pretty confident. You're good to go."

"Wait! What's going on? What did you tell the cops?"

"Simple: I confessed."

"Simon! That's ridiculous!"

"Calm down. I told them it was all my stuff, not yours . . . which is kind of true, because we shared it all the time."

"Simon, you can't do this. I'm going straight to the cops."

"Don't bother. They won't believe you anyway. They'll think you're trying to protect me. And you'll only get me in more trouble if you do that, because they'll start thinking that I've lied to them."

"What are you talking about? I can prove that it was mine."

"Really? How? Do you have a receipt from the store where you bought it? A credit card slip, maybe?"

"Stop joking!"

"Look, seriously, I've already proved it was mine. I hung out in your room all the time. Everyone knows that. My fingerprints were all over the stuff, all over *The City of God*. I'm telling you, they bought the whole thing. You're in the clear."

"Simon, no. This is crazy. It doesn't make any sense. What about the phone calls, the emails?"

"Don't worry, I thought about that, too. I went through all that with the cops. Guess what? Those calls and emails don't show anything at all. All they show is that you went looking for stuff to buy. But, in fact, they seem to show you were rather unsuccessful! So I told them that in the end, I went downtown and bought it all myself."

"This is crazy, Simon. Why are you doing this? You're going to get in trouble."

"Trouble? Not really. I already worked out a plea bargain. I thought I could do that better myself rather than if you tried to do it. Of course, I could have coached you through it. Or maybe a good lawyer could have done it. Speaking of which, maybe you're really not cut out to be a lawyer after all, given your inability to handle matters of the law!"

"Wait a second — you worked out a plea bargain? What do you mean?"

"Well, it's not over yet, but they really seemed eager just to close the books on this. But they still have to decide whether they're going to accept my offer."

"Offer? What offer?"

"Look, they really had no right to search the room. I told them I would plead guilty, but only if they reduce the charge from sale to possession. For a first offense, that'll carry a fine and some community service. How nice! On the other hand, if they charge me with selling, I'll get a lawyer and argue that the search was improper — which it was, by the way. At least, it was questionable. So I think they'll take me up on the offer!"

"Simon, I don't know what to say. Are you sure this is going to work?"

"Absolutely. Why wouldn't it?"

"Simon . . . why are you doing this for me?"

"What's the big deal? That's what friends are for, isn't it?"

24

From: dgoldstein@cuniv.edu   Sent: 5/26/ 03 5:11 PM
To: richgoldstein@rchgoldattorney.com
Subject: Israel

Dad,

Maybe I don't need to come home and talk to you about the situation. Really, what I wanted to ask you about is, I'd like to go study in a yeshiva in Israel. Is that OK with you?

David

From: richgoldstein@rchgoldattorney.com   Sent: 5/26/03 5:40 PM
To: dgoldstein@cuniv.edu
Subject: Israel

David,

So that was the big secret? What a relief. You really had me worried.

I guess so, if that's what you really want to do. I hope it's safe. Where exactly would you go? I'd like some more details. Financially, how much can that be just for the summer? Not too much. I guess we could work something out.

Dad

25

The evening after graduation, Simon and David threw a party at Simon's apartment. Simon insisted that David invite any guests he wished. David told Simon that he would agree, but only if he could be in charge of the food and drink. Of course, everything had to be strictly kosher. Simon also had to promise to keep the music down and allow smoking – of tobacco, nothing else – only on the outdoor balcony. David invited several guests, including some of his teachers and friends. He didn't think they'd all show up, but in the end, they did. Phil, George, Ravi, and even Chaim were there. Dr. Maimon and Rabbi Abraham also came, but they insisted they couldn't stay too long.

The party got into full swing at around 9:30 p.m. Simon's friends congregated on the balcony near the den. David's guests gathered in the living room, where it was much quieter. They found themselves sitting in a circle, sipping wine and eating cheese and crackers.

"There's still a lot of wine left. Please have another glass!" David walked around the room, filling each glass with wine.

"Wait a moment," said Phil. "If you're going to pour us a glass of wine, why don't you propose a toast?"

"OK, let me think," said David.

"In fact, instead of a toast, how about a speech?" said Phil.

"Great idea!" said Rabbi Abraham.

"Yes, make a speech." said Dr. Maimon.

"A speech? About what?" said David.

"Let's see," said Phil. "What about the nature of ultimate reality? No – that's too complex, and might take too long! How about your college experience? No, that's too personal. How about what you plan to do after college? Could that be more interesting? Maybe, maybe not. Ah, I've got it! Now that you've reached your senior year, presumably you've grown wiser over the last four years. How about this as a topic: what is wisdom, and why is it worth pursuing?"

"Excellent idea! Let's have a speech in praise of wisdom!" said Dr. Maimon.

"No way! I can't give a speech on wisdom!" exclaimed David. "The only thing I know about wisdom is that I don't have any!"

"How Socratic," Phil retorted. "But actually, you must know something about wisdom after all if you can say you don't have it!"

"Very clever, Phil!"

"Come on, Dovid," said Chaim. "I think you can do it. Now that you're a senior, a real grownup, you must know something about wisdom."

"Look," said George. "It doesn't have to be a long speech. Why don't you just tell us in plain words what wisdom is and why it's worth having? It can't be that hard to do."

"Really? How can I dare speak about wisdom in the presence of such honored sages? George, if you think it's so easy, why don't you give a speech on wisdom yourself?"

"Well, maybe I could, if I were allowed to use Christianity as my source. But I don't want to be the only one to give a speech. You guys will tear me apart!"

"No, we won't," said Rabbi Abraham.

"Wait! I've got it," said Phil. "Why don't we have a little symposium on wisdom? We can all take turns giving a short speech on what we think wisdom is, how you go about getting it, and why it's worth having. And we can all feel free to draw on whatever sources we wish."

"That's a splendid idea!" said Dr. Maimon.

"I'm game," said Ravi.

Everyone else nodded.

"But who will go first?" said George. "It seems like that would be unfair. People who go later can just build their ideas based on what the first person says."

"Actually," said Dr. Maimon, "it will be easiest to go first, since it will be easy to say something original. It will get harder and harder to say something fresh each time. Besides, I'm sure we'll all have very different things to say about what wisdom is."

"You're right, Professor. I stand corrected," said George.

"In fact," Dr. Maimon continued, "I think we all have to be prepared to accept that some of us are going to disagree with one another, maybe very sharply. It will be impossible to state our views clearly without some critical discussion of the others. But we could all agree not to be too harsh, of course."

"Fine," said David. "Hey, I just thought of something else. After each speech, we could all take another drink of wine. That would give each person a chance to collect their thoughts before they speak. And it will also be kind of like what they did in Plato's *Symposium*."

"Or like what we do at the Pesach *seder*," said Rabbi Abraham. "Four cups of wine, one during each segment of the *seder*. Except here, it looks like we'll have more than four cups!"

"How interesting," said Phil. "I never knew that about the *seder*."

"Why, of course!" said Dr. Maimon. "The rabbis purposely modeled the structure of the Pesah seder along the lines of a Roman feast. You know, the whole bit about reclining while eating, being served by waiters, and so on. All with a Jewish twist, of course. No dancing girls, for example!"

"Indeed!" said Phil, "But Plato's *Symposium* is about love, not wisdom. So maybe the wine and women made more sense there! Anyway, I say we let George go first, since he seems the most willing. Then we can continue around in a circle to his left."

"No," said Rabbi Abraham. "Always go to the right. That's what the Talmud says, anyway."

"OK, then. To the right it shall be! If we start with George, next is Rabbi

Abraham, then Phil, Ravi, Dr. Maimon, Chaim, and last but not least, David. Are we all agreed? Great! Well, George, are you willing to start?"

"I don't mind going first. Only please give me a few minutes to collect my thoughts."

Everyone sat quietly, sipping their wine, waiting for George to start. After a few moments, he began.

"OK, I think I know what I want to say. We tend to think wisdom involves knowing a lot of important facts. We think that someone who's wise is really special and unique – someone who's super-intelligent and smart. But actually that's a mistake. That's not real wisdom. That's fake, worldly wisdom. Real wisdom is – like the Bible says, foolishness compared to worldly wisdom. As it says in the New Testament, *"the foolishness of God is wiser than men."* The Bible teaches that the simple, plain person, who may seem like a fool is, in the end the truly wise person. And the complicated, highly intelligent person is really the fool when it comes to eternal matters. That's because in the end everything that's important is really simple. Remember that famous book title? *All I Really Needed to Know, I Learned in Kindergarten.* Of course, you do learn things after kindergarten that you need to know – in order to make money and to get along in the world. Otherwise, I wouldn't have gone to college! But the values, the fundamental beliefs, right and wrong, how to act and behave, how to share and to love, how to have faith in God and what's eternally important – all *that* you can learn in kindergarten because it's all so incredibly simple! The wise person lives life simply, without trying hard to figure it out and without trying to get something out of it through craftiness. The crafty person is always trying to find an 'angle' – trying to get something out of life – something for *himself*, that is. No craftiness or super-intelligence is necessary to live a moral, religious life. In fact, a really simple-minded person tends to be more righteous, more generous, and more kind than most super-smart people you meet – present company excluded, of course! Have you ever noticed that the nicest people around are often the so-called 'dumbest'? That's because they're only 'dumb' in the worldly sense. They're actually wise in the true sense of wisdom. They may get shafted in this world. But in the next world, their reward is the greatest. And even in this world, they live the best, the happiest, and the most meaningful lives. Perhaps that's why, for many people, childhood is the happiest time of life. That's because children are simple and uncorrupted. Later in life, when we think we know what the world is really all about, and when we get worldly wisdom – that's when we lose our innocence and become unhappy. Yet, sometimes it takes just one quick moment to realize that life's true values are all so simple! If we allow that moment to happen, then we become like children again, for the rest of our lives. If we can do that, that's the greatest wisdom of all. And that's all I have to say about wisdom."

For a moment the room was silent. Then everybody clapped.

"Bravo!" Ravi said.

"Well done!" said Rabbi Abraham.

"Nice going, George!" said David.

"Quite profound, yet simple too," said Phil.

"And just off the cuff – really a good statement of Christian wisdom!" said Dr. Maimon.

David went around the room and filled up each person's glass with wine.

"Here's a toast to George!" he said.

"To George!" everyone said.

"Hey, what's going on here?" Simon appeared at the doorway. "I was just going to the kitchen to refresh my vodka tonic and I heard clapping. What am I missing?"

"We're having a symposium," David explained.

"How very intellectual. On what topic?"

"We're each giving a little speech in praise of wisdom. George just finished his, so we gave him a round of applause."

"How nice! I'm sure it was well deserved."

"Would you like to join us?" said George.

"Thanks, but I don't think so."

"You mean you don't have any view on wisdom?" George asked.

"Not really. And I better get back to my guests on the balcony. I don't want to be rude, you know! That wouldn't be very wise, would it?"

"Ah," said Phil. "So you do have some idea of what wisdom is after all!"

"Well, I suppose I do." said Simon.

"Come on, then. Step into the ring," said Phil.

"Look," said Simon. "If you want to hear it, it won't take very long. It's a thirty-second speech. But like I said, I've got to get back to my guests. I can't stick around for the refutation."

"Wow," said Phil. "Wisdom in thirty seconds. We really do want to hear that!"

"Cool it, Phil," said Ravi. "Look, no one's refuting anybody here. It's just an open mike."

"Come on, Simon," urged Rabbi Abraham. "Why don't you sit down and tell us what you think?"

"That's OK. I'll just stand here in the doorway and give my speech. Ready? It's very simple. Wisdom is knowing what you want, and how to get it. And that's why it's good to be wise. The problem is that lots of people around don't realize what they want. Look, I don't want to offend anyone. Let's just say . . . basically people don't admit that they want what makes them feel good – in other words, pleasure. Of course, different people find different things pleasant. And there's no telling what that might be. Money, sex, power, religion, sports, art, philosophy, even God – whatever! And, unfortunately, some people think they know not only what they want, but also what everybody else wants, or should want. Anyway, if you know what you want, the next step is knowing how to get it. Sometimes you have to be ruthless, you have to be tough. And sometimes you have to be soft and gentle. Sometimes, you have to learn a lot of information, sometimes you don't. It all depends on what you want. Either way, like I said, wisdom is knowing what you want, and knowing how to get it. And now, I better get back to the balcony. Cheers!"

Simon tossed back his drink, turned sharply and left the room.

"Well," said Dr. Maimon. "That's a perspective I think we've heard before. Shades of the hedonistic sophists and the Dale Carnegie school of thought. In his view, wisdom amounts to knowing how to win friends and influence people!"

David got up from his seat. "Actually, I'm not so sure that's what he's all about. Anyway, it's time for another round of wine. And it looks like it's Rabbi Abraham's turn next."

"Yes. I'm thinking." He stroked his beard for a minute or two.

"All right," he said. "I think I'm ready. I really don't have much to say about Simon's speech, except to say that I disagree with almost every word he said. I don't think people do only what makes them feel good because otherwise, I wouldn't be here. I'd be . . . I don't know, maybe out on the balcony! On the other hand, George made some good points. But pardon me if, in my speech, I make some critical remarks as well. First of all, what George said about dumb people being nice and gentle is not entirely correct. There are many dumb people who are cruel and abusive. Also, while a dumb person may be very nice and gentle, they will never accomplish great things. As it says in *Pirkei Avos* – that's *Ethics of the Fathers* – an ignoramus cannot be a *hasid* – that is, someone who does extraordinarily good things. If you'll notice, the really great people who do things on a great scale for humanity are usually pretty thoughtful. Of course, there are also some really nasty people who are 'smart' in a technical sense. So I agree with George that wisdom is not the same thing as just being smart. Hitler and Stalin were 'smart' in some sense. Still, I do not think that wisdom is simple. It's a matter of knowing very profound and important things.

"George quoted the New Testament to support his view. But if you look in the *Tanakh* – the Hebrew Scripture – you will find that wisdom is something that needs to be sought out, investigated, and delved into with great effort. I'll get to what wisdom is in a moment. But first, regarding what George said about that clever book title – all you need to know you learn in kindergarten – that holds true only if you had good teachers. There are actually a lot of kindergartners who can be quite naughty and really almost cruel. It's the same with dumb people. Some are very nice, and some are cruel. Have you ever seen the way a child can torture a small animal or be cruel to his fellow classmate? So it all depends on their teachers and their parents. If they have good teachers and good parents, then they are set with a solid foundation for life. But that doesn't mean they don't have room for improvement. And, more importantly, you've got to ask: where did the parents and the teachers get their information from? From their teachers and parents? If so, where did they get their information from? Well, ultimately, in my opinion, it all goes back to God and the revelation of His will. And that's where wisdom comes in, at least from a Jewish perspective. Wisdom is the acceptance of God and God's revelation – in particular, God's revelation about what is good or bad, and about how to live. And don't ask me for a proof of God's existence and divine revelation, because I think it's impossible to prove. It's a matter of faith – or, in Hebrew, *emunah*. And it's something you'll accept only if you have true humility and fear. The Torah says that Moses spoke to God face to face and received the divine revelation. It also says that Moses was *anav mi-kol adam,* the humblest of all people. It also says in *Mishlei*, or the Book of Proverbs: "The fear of the Lord is the beginning of wisdom." Now, wisdom isn't the same thing as fear of the Lord. Rather, fear is necessary for wisdom. After all, God is the source of all truth, all knowledge and understanding. So we only get wisdom if we have fear of the Lord. As it says in *Pirkei Avos*, where there is no fear, there is no wisdom.

"Now, getting back to children – they may have a little bit of this fear naturally, and so they can have a little bit of wisdom too – if they accept the teachings that are communicated to them by their parents. But as a person grows and becomes more intellectually mature, he has the capacity to understand more and more of God's revelation, and therefore to become more and more wise. Yet at the same time, he must also increase his fear of God step by step. Otherwise, he will not grasp God's revelation. He must also follow God's words and instructions. Otherwise, he will not understand God's revelation adequately.

"It follows that a truly wise person is someone who has a deep understanding of God's revelation. He is also someone who follows God's will very closely. Although he may not have a technical knowledge of how to succeed in this world, he will learn whatever technical skills he needs to in order to fulfill God's will properly. But, surely, he won't be a simple person. Again, Moses is the role model of a wise person in Judaism. Moses was surely not a simple person. He must have been quite intellectually capable. And even Moses needed forty days and nights to grasp the Torah. That's because grasping God's revelation is not something that one can do overnight or suddenly. It takes a lifetime of work and continuous study. The Torah teaches that God's revelation is not a simple matter. It's extremely detailed and complex. So I disagree with George's definition of wisdom as something simple. But I agree with George that a truly wise person will be blessed and happy in this world, and even more blessed and happy in the next. Thank you!"

Again, everyone clapped.

"*Yasher koach,*" said Chaim.

"Sorry? What does that mean?" said Phil.

"It means, 'May your strength be renewed.' It's a customary way of saying 'Well done!'"

"Oh, I see. Well in that case, *Yasha koa*, Rabbi!" said Phil.

"Thank you. And sorry, George – I hope I didn't offend you in any way," said Rabbi Abraham.

"Not at all," George answered. "Thanks for taking my speech seriously enough to criticize it. I'll have to think about what you said."

"You're very gracious," said Rabbi Abraham.

David got up to refill everyone's glass.

"Well," he said, "I guess it's your turn next, Phil. Do you also need a few minutes to collect your thoughts?"

"No, I don't think so. I've thought about this question once or twice before, so I have something ready to say. And I'm sure that if I disagree with Rabbi Abraham, he will be just as generous with me as George has been with him. Actually, I think the rabbi and George are really not as far apart as it may seem. As far as I'm concerned, wisdom is knowledge of the ultimate truth – that is, knowledge of the most fundamental reality or realities. If you have a lot of knowledge of trivial things, like baseball statistics, or like how many threads are in every carpet in this building, that doesn't count as wisdom. But if you have knowledge of the most basic, important truths or realities, then you have wisdom. Of course, it is a matter of dispute as to what those basic truths are – and I'll get back to that point in a minute.

"First, I need to make it clear that when I say 'knowledge' I mean understanding or comprehension, which is a rational process. It isn't an emotional matter, but a cognitive one. So, in my opinion, no fear or any other emotion is necessary in order to pursue wisdom. In fact, fear would just be a distraction. It's more likely to be more of a hindrance than a help in the pursuit of truth! Even if I thought the ultimate reality was a single, personal God, I still don't think I'd change my mind about that. And I'm quite confused as to how fear of God can precede knowledge of God, which is what Rabbi Abraham said. You shouldn't – or, rather, you can't fear something you don't even know! As the rabbi himself says, you can't prove there's a God, and so, you can't know him! It follows that even if God exists, God cannot be the proper object of wisdom. And so, this is where I disagree with both Rabbi Abraham and George. If you believe in God, that must be a matter of faith, which is very different from reason. Belief in God, or faith, is not a matter of genuine wisdom, since, like I said, wisdom is a rational matter. Anyway, I don't believe that ultimate truth is a personal God. That's precisely because I've yet to see any convincing argument for it. In fact, Rabbi Abraham himself admitted that there isn't any such proof.

"You may ask: what do I think ultimate truth is? Well, if I knew that, I'd be wise! But I'm not wise. I'm not even sure there is only one ultimate truth . . . maybe there are multiple ultimate realities. That, too, is a possibility that I have not ruled out. However, I can say a few things about what ultimate truth is not. Some of these things are obvious, and some are not. First, as I already said, ultimate truth is not something that one can comprehend completely. I don't believe that this is a temporary situation that will be overcome some day in the future. In principle, it is impossible ever to know ultimate truth completely.

"Many philosophers over the centuries have shown this to be true in various ways. I can't rehearse them all here. For one thing, our knowledge of the world is always relative to our sensory apparatus. Creatures with different sensory apparatus would have a completely different view of the world. Second, our rational capacity is finite and fallible. The best available scientific theory changes from time to time. There is no definitive statement of ultimate truth, and there never will be one. But the thing that many people don't realize is that it follows that it is impossible to have any definitive knowledge of ultimate truth at all. This, I admit, is a somewhat pessimistic conclusion to reach, and it is very difficult for people to accept. Many religious people try to say that although we can't know God completely, we can still have at least some partial knowledge of God, such as his attributes, his ways of acting, his purported teachings and revelations. But the hard truth is, if you don't know something completely, you really don't know it at all. For example, if you have partial knowledge of some organism, but not complete knowledge, then you really don't know definitively even the parts you think you know. Suppose you knew that some organism had what appeared to be a finger, but you didn't have any knowledge of the rest of that organism. Could you really say that you definitively knew the 'finger' of that organism? In the scheme of the whole organism, that finger-like appendage might play some role that is utterly unlike a finger altogether. Similarly, since we don't know ultimate truth completely, we really have no definitive knowledge of it at all.

"Now, although I said I am not wise, I am committed to philosophy – that is, the love of wisdom, the pursuit of understanding or comprehension of ultimate truth. The true philosopher is the one who accepts the fact that we have no definitive knowledge of ultimate truth whatsoever. It is the philosopher who criticizes and debunks all purported claims to definitive knowledge, whether proposed by religion, or science, or even by other so called 'philosophers,' who claim to have definitive knowledge – usually either by falling back on faith or on dogmatic assumption, or by making an error in their reasoning.

"You may ask: why be committed to this quest if indeed it is impossible to succeed? David and I had this discussion a couple of years ago. My answer at the time was that the quest for truth – that is, ultimate truth – is the noblest task to which we can aspire. I believe that the mind is the noblest aspect of the human being, and its noblest use is in the pursuit of ultimate truth, even if it cannot succeed. For the philosopher, all other passions and pursuits are secondary to the love of wisdom. And while we cannot know ultimate truth, we can often demonstrate or show what ultimate truth is *not*. The job of the philosopher is a negative one, you might say. And whereas Rabbi Abraham just claimed that humility is a prerequisite for wisdom, my view is quite the opposite – that is, humility is a consequence of philosophy. Once you truly realize that we have no definitive knowledge of ultimate reality, you are humbled. Many religious people, who believe they possess definitive knowledge of ultimate truth, tend to be the most arrogant – present company excluded, of course. In any event, to sum it all up: wisdom is knowledge of ultimate truth – but we, unfortunately, can't get it. The best we can do is engage in philosophy, which at least gives a clear understanding of the limits of our capacity to grasp ultimate truth. I thank you for your patience in listening to me."

When Phil stopped talking, the room remained silent for a time. Everyone seemed to be deep in thought. Phil cleared his throat and spoke.

"What? No applause?" he said with a smile.

Ravi spoke first. "On the contrary, it was so profound, yet so pessimistic, that we don't even know how to react. Perhaps we're not sure whether to clap or cry!"

"Aw, shucks," Phil said. "It's not that bad, really. Despite the fact that it is doomed to failure, the pursuit of wisdom can be quite entertaining."

David stood up. "Quite thought-provoking, Phil. Meanwhile, as we're busy trying to comprehend all that, let's all have another round of drinks."

"I think I've had quite enough to drink," said Rabbi Abraham.

"And since it looks like my turn is next," said Ravi. "I think I'll also forgo this round. Unlike Phil, I will need several minutes to formulate my thoughts. Much as I am not used to public speaking, I hope you won't mind if I speak in my customary way, which is more dialogic. Actually, I agree with a lot of what has been said so far. Yet there is much that I disagree with as well."

"Take your time," said David, as he poured drinks for the remaining guests and sat down. Ravi closed his eyes for several minutes. Finally, still with his eyes closed, he began to speak.

"In one respect, Phil is right. Ultimate truth is beyond intellectual understanding. We cannot reason our way to an understanding of ultimate truth. Yet, at the same time, Phil is mistaken. Ultimate truth is accessible in another way, in a manner and mode that goes *beyond* intellect. The critical question is: what is ultimate truth? I believe that ultimate truth is not a personal God, but rather an ineffable Oneness that transcends all distinctions and polarities, even the distinction of person versus non-person, even the distinction between good and evil. Now, if we have no intellectual understanding of ultimate truth, and if ultimate truth is not a personal God who might simply reveal his will to us, how can we have access to ultimate truth? The answer is: through mystical absorption in the One. Another word for this is enlightenment, or wisdom.

"The process of attaining wisdom is not primarily philosophical or intellectual. It is a process that involves meditation, discipline, living a certain way of life. All over the world, many meditative traditions recognize that ultimate reality is one, and that the diversity and change that we see in ordinary experience is an illusion to be overcome. To recognize the ultimate Oneness, a person must give up his own ego, his own self. And this is where discipline comes in, both in meditation and in one's way of life, which must be utterly selfless. Of course, this is very difficult for most people. And that is why so many religions have proliferated, with detailed mythologies about God or gods, and about how one might get into God's good graces so as to attain bliss in this world or the next. Some of these mythologies are very simple, and some are more complex. Most of them involve interpreting ultimate truth as a person or set of persons, which is a way of initiating the masses into some kind of relation with the One. In any case, only a small number of people are able to reach true enlightenment or wisdom. But the difficulty is not an intellectual one. To gain wisdom, one need not know a lot of complicated facts or data. Rather the difficulty is a cognitive one, that is, a matter of effort and will. And here I agree with Rabbi Abraham: the pursuit of wisdom certainly does require a great deal of humility – in fact, an extraordinary kind of humility – that is, self-denial.

"This is not to be confused with low self-esteem or asceticism or nihilism or anything suicidal. As the term is commonly used, a person has low self-esteem if he judges himself to be worthless by some false standard of worth such as how smart, good-looking, wealthy or popular he is. The person who has low self-esteem mistakenly finds value in these false standards, and when he sees that he falls below them, he feels pain. Of course the pain is a pseudo-pain because it is based on a false belief. Such a person may reach such a low level of self-esteem that he commits suicide. But low self-esteem is not to be confused with genuine humility. Genuine humility, the kind that leads to wisdom, is a recognition that there is no self apart from the One – or, as the Hindus say, *Tat tvam asi,* which translates as *Thou art that,* meaning: you are the same as the One, the Absolute. This realization may make a person less fearful of death, but it is not grounds for suicide. In fact, it is tantamount to attaining genuine happiness or bliss.

"Thinking here of what Simon said, one might be tempted to say that this is what everyone really wants deep down – that is, everyone wants or desires ultimate happiness. But that is also a profound mistake. Enlightenment is not a matter of wanting at all. It's a matter of ceasing to want, ceasing to strive. It is this cessation of desire that unites the soul with the One. Now, in my opinion – here I agree with Phil – we cannot know whether there is a next world or some kind of other realm in which the soul goes on to live after its existence here. But it really doesn't matter. Whether or not there is a next world, it is possible for us to reach enlightenment. And nothing can surpass the bliss that comes in realizing the union with the One . . ."

Ravi's voice trailed off. No one was sure he had finished, until he opened his eyes. For a moment, no one stirred.

Finally, Phil spoke. "Very soothing. Very profound. After that speech, the only appropriate response is one hand clapping – which is why you can't hear anything, I guess!"

"Whoa, Phil! That's hitting below the belt," said George.

"Not at all," Ravi said. "I take Phil's response as a compliment."

"Of course. It was meant as one." said Phil.

David rose once again to pour wine for his guests. "Thank you, Ravi, for that most enlightening discourse. Well, Dr. Maimon, it looks like you're next. Are you ready?"

"Yes. I'm ready."

"Uh-oh," said Phil. "This spells trouble for all of us, I think. Prepare to be torn to shreds."

"Oh, don't worry," Dr. Maimon began. "There are elements of truth, bits and pieces of things that I agree with, in everything that's been said so far. Even Simon is right that wisdom has something to do with getting what you really want. What he doesn't realize or accept is that deep down, although everyone wants the same thing, it isn't pleasure. It's knowledge! Also, George is right that there is something we can call worldly wisdom, which is quite different from genuine wisdom. But he is mistaken about what genuine wisdom is. Rabbi Abraham, you're also right in saying that wisdom is not simple, it is quite complex. But I disagree with your claim that our belief in God is a matter of faith, or something that is opposed to reason. I think there are good reasons for belief in God, but let's not get into that debate here. Instead, I would point out that right after saying there's no proof for God's existence, in the very next breath you spoke about how Moses saw God face to face and received the revelation. Surely, Rabbi Abraham, you would agree that Moses knew that God existed! He had reason to believe in God, just as much if not more reason than he did to believe in, say for example, the existence of his brother or sister! Of course, he had faith too, and that consists in trusting God, which is what the word *emunah* means in the Hebrew Scriptures. But trust in God is not the same thing as belief in God's existence.

"Now, Phil is right in claiming that wisdom is the noblest goal we can aspire to, because the intellect is our noblest quality. Phil and Ravi are both right in claiming that wisdom is a kind of knowledge of the ultimate truth, and that reason cannot completely know ultimate truth. But they both make a mistake in claiming that, because we cannot know ultimate truth completely, therefore we have no definitive intellectual knowledge of it at all. This pessimistic conclusion is false! We *can* have partial knowledge – and not just negative knowledge – of ultimate truth. And Ravi, you make the mistake of substituting some kind of pseudo-knowledge or bogus mystical knowledge in place of intellectual understanding. I agree with Phil on this point, and that's why Phil and I are both philosophers rather than mystics. As far as I'm concerned, there is no form of knowledge or understanding – no form of "enlightenment" or wisdom – other than intellectual or rational comprehension.

"Having made these critical observations, let me state my own position more directly. The question on the table is: what is wisdom? Quite simply, wisdom is the intellectual comprehension of ultimate reality, to the best of our ability. Using reason, we can know quite a lot about ultimate truth. For example, we know that ultimate truth is one, that it is self-identical, that it is eternal and necessary, and, that it manifests itself in an infinite number of ways. All the things we experience in ordinary life – the earth, the sky, the sun, the trees, the tables and chairs, human beings, and so forth – everything is in some way an expression of ultimate reality or being. Now, a big question is whether ultimate reality is best understood as a personal God. In my opinion, strictly speaking, ultimate reality itself is not a person. Rather, ultimate reality is being itself. But I also think it is rational to believe that there are certain metaphysical principles which describe how Being itself is manifested in our world, and that, due to these principles, the universe operates as if it were under the direction of a Supreme person. I won't try to support these claims here because it would take too long. David's been through my arguments on these matters. But it's very plausible to believe that history is heading in a certain direction, one that is ultimately beneficial for all humankind. Speaking in the language of the common human being, we can describe Being itself using terminology which is usually applied to persons, such as, when we say that "God thinks" or "God acts" or "God has providence" or "God directs history." Scripture speaks in this mythical way as well. As the Talmud says, and as Maimonides reiterates, 'The Torah speaks in the language of human beings.' Human beings believe that the ultimate reality is a personal God, while the wise know that this is only a metaphorical or mythic way of speaking.

"Now, let's see, what else did I want to say? Ah, yes. Let me explain what I think is the true relationship between wisdom and humility. Obviously, the pursuit of wisdom requires some humility, because if you don't set your ego aside and put your biases behind you, you won't be able to see your way clearly to truth. But listen! Pursuit of the truth also requires a kind of brazenness, or *hutzpah*. Rabbi Abraham, what you said about Moses was interesting, but you know that Moses was a *navi* – that means a prophet – which is different from a *hacham*, or wise person. Sure, the Torah says Moses was the most humble of all people. But think about what Scripture says about Solomon. He was the wisest of all, and he is nowhere depicted as humble! Or think about what Maimonides says about Abraham – namely, that he came to discover the existence of God after realizing through an intellectual process that polytheism must be mistaken. Abraham was an iconoclast – literally, a smasher of idols! The Talmud also talks about the *hutzpah* required to be a *talmid hacham*, a wise student. The Talmud also says, "*Hacham adif mi-navi*" – that is, a wise person is better than a prophet! So just as humility may have been important for Moses, a certain kind of arrogance has its place in the pursuit of wisdom. Perhaps it's no surprise that many intellectuals and philosophers are not the most humble people around . . . present company excluded, of course!

"Having said all that, I think there is another type of humility that is a result of wisdom. It is a result of the intellectual realization of God, or Being Itself. Once we recognize God as ultimate reality, we are humbled. Now, I disagree with Ravi in that I think we do not and cannot be mystically 'absorbed' into the One. However, I do agree that upon reaching an intellectual realization of God, we are deeply humbled and awed in two ways. First, we are awed by the majesty and power of God. Second, we are humbled by our realization that despite our intellectual comprehension of ultimate reality, there are limits to our understanding of God. This is the kind of humility that Phil was talking about – a humility derived from recognizing our own limits. In sum, genuine wisdom requires a certain type of humility, yet also a certain type of arrogance, as prerequisites. It also leads to a different kind of humility as a consequence. And that's all I have to say about wisdom . . . unless you have any questions, of course."

"*Yasher kochech*," said Rabbi Abraham. "That was really very interesting. Actually, I think I'd have to hear it again in order to understand it fully. I certainly do have some questions, but I think I'll wait till another occasion."

"Me too," said Phil. "*Yasher* . . . sorry – how's that go?"

"*Kochech* – that means 'your strength' in the feminine," said Rabbi Abraham.

"Ah, very good. I second the motion!" said Phil.

"I do too." said Ravi. "Really, that was very intellectually stimulating."

"I must say," Chaim said, "I also found that very interesting. Thank you, Dr. Maimon."

"No problem," said Dr. Maimon. "But I'm a little parched. Perhaps now I'll also take that glass of wine!"

"Great," said David. "Who else is having more wine?"

"I will," said Chaim. "And I'll need some, because it's my turn to give my speech!"

David poured more wine. Chaim took a large drink, put down his cup on the table, and began to speak.

"A lot of things people have said tonight remind me of a fundamental *yesod* – a basic idea – in Kabbalah. There's a distinction between *hochmah*, or wisdom, and *binah*, intelligence. David and I talked about this once before, so I hope he doesn't mind the repetition. Clearly, Dr. Maimon and Phil are talking about rational comprehension, or intellectual understanding. That's *binah*. *Binah* is the power to understand things logically and to analyze them. It's the power to derive new things from things that you already know. *Hochmah*, or wisdom, is something else. It's more like what Ravi was talking about. It's a certain kind of intuition. It's the ability to grasp something that goes beyond what is rationally comprehensible. Without *hochmah* we could never grasp the *ein sof*, the infinite essence of God. Of course, even through *hochmah*, we can't completely grasp it. We grasp it only partially. It's like a flash of insight when it happens. The Rambam – that's Maimonides – talks about this flash. It's something unpredictable and you can't sustain it for too long. What you learn in this flash is not derived from something you already knew. Rather, it's a divine gift. Like a seed, that new insight is something from which you can derive new things using the power of *binah*. *Binah* takes the insights from *hochmah* and converts them into something that is applicable to action. But, using *binah*, you can never completely break down the insights from *hochmah*. There will always be some aspect in that insight that escapes complete understanding. Anyway, both *hochmah* and *binah* are important, and you can't really have one without the other. If you didn't have *hochmah*, you wouldn't have insight into *ein sof*. If you didn't have *binah*, those insights would be worthless, because you wouldn't be able to apply them, interpret them, or put them into practice.

"Now, the way it works is that first you get insights through *hochmah*. Then, if you analyze and apply those insights – and I mean if you live in accord with those insights, if you live a certain way of life – then you end up getting newer and deeper insights through *hochmah*. Again, those new insights become seeds that can be analyzed and applied by *binah*, and so the cycle continues endlessly. So, basically, wisdom or *hochmah* is intuitive grasping of the *ein sof*. *Binah* is the rational comprehension and explanation of the insights that are attained through *hochmah*.

"There was some discussion about whether ultimate reality – that's *ein sof*, the infinite essence – is a personal God. I find myself agreeing and yet disagreeing with Dr. Maimon on this issue. This is a little complicated, so please *halt kop* – I mean, keep your heads, or bear with me – as I try to explain. The *ein sof*, the infinite essence of God is an entity that is beyond description. It is not a person, not an intellect, not a will – there's no way to describe it except negatively. However, Kabbalah teaches that *ein sof* manifests itself through the ten *sefiros* – that is, ten entities that are the intermediaries between *ein sof* and the rest of creation. The ten *sefiros* include aspects that correspond to the structure of the human being. I can't go into the whole theory now. But it's because of the *sefiros* that we are able to think and speak of God as a person. The Kabbalah says that even God's holy name – the tetragrammaton— refers not to the infinite essence of God, but only to that essence insofar as it manifests itself through the *sefiros*. So, when we say that God is a person, we're not talking directly about *ein sof*. Rather, we're talking about a mask that *ein sof* has adopted in order to reveal himself. But here's where I disagree with Dr. Maimon. She thinks that really, God is not a person, and only the common people or ignorant people think of God that way. But I'm saying that while *ein sof* adopts a mask, the mask is real. To say that God is a person is not just a metaphorical way of speaking. That's a big mistake. Even though the *sefiros* do not fully encompass or express the *ein sof*, the *sefiros* are real entities.

"Now, another question is whether *hochmah* is the greatest thing a person can aspire to, and how it relates to other qualities, such as humility. In Kabbalah, the *sefirah* of *kesser* is higher than *hochmah* or *binah*. This is true both for God and for human beings. *Kesser* corresponds to *ratzon*, or will – that's the ability to choose. So God's will is ultimately higher than God's *hochmah* or *binah*. Now, to connect with God through *hochmah* and *binah* is very great and very high. But it is even higher to connect to God through one's *ratzon* or will. Of course, when you connect with God through *hochmah* and *binah*, that in itself is one way of connecting with God through your will! The will is manifested in many ways, one of which is through the mental capacities of *hochmah* and *binah*. But the will is also manifested in acts of benevolence, justice, and compassion. So when you do those actions, you also connect to God with your will. And that explains why, sometimes, connecting with God through such actions is just as high, and sometimes even higher, than through the mental capacities of *hochmah* and *binah*.

"Now, a question arises as to whether you can connect with God purely through your will, without any other *sefirah* being involved. In a way, the answer is no, because any connection to God with the will involves the whole person, so all aspects of the person will be affected – mental as well as emotional capacities. But in a way, the answer is also yes. I don't think you can ever reach the state of absorption or union with the *ein sof* that Ravi seemed to have in mind. That's impossible because you can never completely break down the divide between the infinite and the finite. That's also why I think that total denial of the ego is going too far. I don't think Judaism expects that of a person. You always have to maintain a distinction between yourself and God, no matter how close you get. So, if you can't become one with God, what's the next best thing? You can achieve *devekus* – that is, a bond with God – just with your will, by bonding your will to God's will. Like I said before, this is the highest connection with God that is possible. How do you do this? Simply by choosing to do so! And I didn't expect to say this, but here's where I actually agree with George. In the end, despite all the complexities of the *ein sof* and the *sefiros*, there is something remarkably simple about what is really the most important thing a person can do. Of course you have to have some knowledge of God, some understanding of what God is and what He wants, in order to be able to do this. Still, it's not the knowledge, it's the commitment itself, or the making of this commitment – accepting God upon oneself – that is the highest bond a person can establish between himself and God. And that commitment is a very simple, easy step. But still – and here's where I agree with Rabbi Abraham – the more you know about God and what He wants from us, the greater and deeper this commitment becomes. The more wisdom, the deeper the commitment, and the more impact it has on one's mind, emotions, and actions.

"Well, in order to make this commitment, guess what you need, aside from a little knowledge about who God is and what He wants from us. Obviously, as Rabbi Abraham said, you need humility, because that's the basis of any true commitment to another person, but especially a commitment to God. And getting back to wisdom, you obviously need humility in order to get wisdom too. God doesn't grant insights to those who are arrogant. In fact, you need more than humility – you need what's called *hisbatlus* in the face of the *ein sof*. I wouldn't call this self-denial like Ravi did, but rather self-nullification. In Jewish law there is a principle that if a tiny drop of milk falls into a pot of meat, the milk is *batel* or nullified if the proportion of milk to meat is one-sixtieth or less. This doesn't mean the milk has become meat, or that the milk has magically disappeared. It means the tiny drop of milk has no separate significant status relative to the meat. Similarly, this is what *hisbatlus* means before God. It does not mean merging with God, or denying one's self before God. Rather it means accepting that one has no significance – or even reality – apart from a proper connection with *ein sof*. This is what Moshe was able to do at the highest level, and that's why he was the greatest prophet. And, Dr. Maimon, although he is not called a *hacham* in the *Tanakh*, he clearly was a *hacham*, a wise person. When the Gemara says that a wise person is better than a prophet – it's only talking about a certain type of prophet – namely, one who isn't a *hacham* also! In fact, the Gemara says that Moshe understood certain things in the Torah that Shlomo – I mean King Solomon – did not understand, such as the reason for the commandment of the *parah adumah* – that's the red heifer. So Moshe was wiser than Solomon after all."

"Excuse me," said Dr. Maimon. "I'm sorry to interrupt you there. I don't want to get into a dispute about how to interpret that text, but may I ask a simple question?"

"I'm finished, so you're not interrupting. Sure, ask a question."

"Haven't you contradicted yourself? Earlier you said that wisdom is a matter of gaining insight, and that it's not a matter of rational comprehension. But now you're saying that the evidence that Moses was wiser than Solomon is precisely because he understood the rational meaning of a certain commandment. This seems to support my view rather than yours. Moses was wiser than Solomon because he had more rational comprehension!"

"Ah, but wait a second. Like I said before, any time you have an insight through *hochmah*, it's like a seed that will yield information through *binah* or intelligence. So the fact that Moshe knew the reason for the red heifer means that he had higher insight through *hochmah*, and then, using the power of *binah*, he worked out the reason for the red heifer!"

"Hmm. I wonder," said Dr. Maimon. "Maybe he was just better at *binah* than Solomon. And besides, this still leaves me wondering: what is the non-explicable content of that insight – aside from that content which is intelligible through *binah*?"

"Sorry, Dr. Maimon. I don't get the question."

"Please, call me Sofi. But look. You said that *hochmah* is some kind of intuitive grasping that goes beyond intellect. In other words, it has some non-explicable content. And you just said that Moses had an insight about the red heifer through *hochmah*. Then, using *binah*, he worked out a rational explanation. So I'm asking: what is that non-explicable content of *hochmah* that is left over after *binah* has done its job?"

"Ah, I think I get the question now. But I can't answer it! If I could, it wouldn't be . . . how did you say it? Non-explicable."

"So the non-explicable element in *hochmah* is like a ghost with no palpable substance. Hmm! Well, can I ask you one more question? You said that God's wisdom is the *sefirah* of *hochmah*, and God's will is the *sefirah* of *kesser*. Right?

"That's correct."

"And these two *sefiros* are two entities?"

"Yes."

"So God's wisdom is a separate entity from his will? I fail to see how this is consistent with traditional Judaism. If God is one, then he can't be composed of entities. I just don't under —"

Ravi cleared his throat and spoke up. "Excuse me. Your discussion is very interesting, but haven't we violated the rules of the game? It seems we're getting into a testy conversation. And anyway, it's now David's turn to give his own discourse on wisdom."

"Ravi! What a spoiler!" said Phil. "I was just beginning to find the conversation interesting."

"No, no," said Dr. Maimon. "Ravi's right. And I'm sorry. I did get a little carried away."

"It's OK by me, Dr. Maimon," said Chaim. "But actually I'm curious to hear what David has to say. So maybe we should let him speak."

"Absolutely," said Dr. Maimon.

David poured out the remaining wine for his guests and then returned to his seat. He was still holding a full glass in his hand when he started to talk.

"To be honest, at first I wasn't sure I had anything interesting to say. But actually, listening to all of you speak and argue, I think I now know what I want to say. Chaim made a distinction between *binah* as intelligence and *hochmah* as intuition. According to Chaim, wisdom is mysterious or goes beyond reason. But if you say that, you get into some of the objections made by Dr. Maimon. Not that these are necessarily devastating objections, but they are at least problems to think about. So, while I agree with Chaim that rational comprehension or *binah* is not the same thing as wisdom, still I have a different take on what wisdom is. I think that *hochmah* or wisdom is not a mysterious intuition, but rather the ability to think creatively, or the ability to think of new ideas or concepts. I guess another way to say it is that wisdom, or *hochmah*, is creative insight.

"I can support this idea in a couple of ways. Most of you quoted some text, so I'll quote a text too. There's a verse in *Tehillim* that says, "How great are your works, you made them all through wisdom." I know this verse because it's in the daily morning service. This verse indicates that God's wisdom has to do with his creative ability. And it's obviously a power that we humans have, too. I don't think there are many places in the first five books of the Torah where the term *hochmah* is mentioned. But one place it's mentioned is where the Torah says that the artisans who constructed the *mishkan* had *hochmah*. Here we see that *hochmah*, or wisdom, has to do with creative ability.

"Now, there is definitely something mysterious about how our creative power works. But everyone knows we have it. And it's different from intelligence or reason. For example, through reason I can demonstrate a geometric proof of the Pythagorean Theorem. But how did Pythagoras come up with the theorem in the first place? *That's* wisdom! Or take the story of how Solomon solved the dilemma he was facing about which woman was the true mother of the baby. You all know that story, I'm sure. That was a brilliant stroke of genius, a creative idea. We follow Solomon's logic after the fact, but it took some special ability to come up with the idea in the first place. Dr. Maimon, you've got to admit there's something mysterious about this process. There is no program or recipe for getting creative insights. Yet everybody knows that we definitely have this ability.

"Here's another reason I think wisdom has to do with creative insight. A person with a good sense of humor is called a wit, which is obviously related to the word 'wisdom.' Why's that? Well, if we think of wisdom as creative insight, we can see that there's a strong connection between wisdom and having a sense of humor. A person is considered witty only if they can think of things or perceive things in ways that are new or unexpected. That's always the secret to a good joke, by the way. A logical argument is not a failure if the conclusion is predictable based on the premises. But a joke sure fails if its punchline is predictable! Wit, or wisdom, is also the secret to irony. Something is ironic if its plain meaning is one thing and its real meaning is the opposite. That's also a form of unexpectedness. In fact, God's free creation of the world could be considered the greatest example of a radically unexpected event. Just imagine: there was God, in His eternal solitude – and suddenly, there's creation, something other than God! At the same time, once He's created it, it makes sense that He's done it. I guess it follows from what I'm saying that if God is wise, He must also have a sense of humor!

"Now, obviously, wisdom occurs in many fields. There's creative thought in science, math, politics, the arts, technology, even sports. When a coach comes up with a creative idea about how to get his players to play better, that's wisdom. When someone comes up with a new idea for a scientific hypothesis, or produces a new invention, that's also wisdom. When someone writes a work of fiction or a poem or a play, or comes up with any great work of art, that's also a sign of wisdom. And the more creative a work is, the more wisdom it must have required to create it! But I think we can all agree that some forms of wisdom are deeper or more profound than others. We could call the deepest form metaphysical wisdom, which is the ability to come up with new insights into the ultimate nature of reality, or being, or truth. Now, if we believe that ultimate reality is God, then what we might call religious wisdom would be the ability to come up with new insights regarding God. Of course, if God is ultimate reality, then metaphysical wisdom overlaps or coincides with religious wisdom. But whether we believe in God or not, the deepest form of wisdom is having new and creative insights into the nature of ultimate reality.

"Now, if I may poke my head in between great mountains, I have something to say about the dispute between Chaim and Dr. Maimon about whether God is an entity or not. On the one hand, I agree with Dr. Maimon that God is not an entity. I like to think of God's essence as being itself, and that's not an entity. On the other hand, I don't see why we can't think of being itself as *ein sof*. We could use the name *Havayah* to refer to *ein sof* or being itself, or we could use it to refer to that set of ways in which the *ein sof* manifests itself. And also, we can say something similar about the *sefiros* as well. We don't need to think of the *sefiros* as entities. We can think of the *sefiros* as the ways in which the *ein sof* — that is, being itself — manifests itself. After all, Dr. Maimon agrees that there are certain metaphysical principles in accord with which reality operates. So, perhaps the Kabbalistic theory of the *sefiros* is just another way of talking about these metaphysical principles. In other words, *hesed* and *gevurah* and the other *sefiros* may be understood not as entities that exist apart from one another, but rather as ways in which *ein sof* manifests itself. And once we say the *sefiros* are not entities, we realize that the doctrine of the *sefiros* is not saying that God has parts, but rather that God manifests Himself in different ways. I'm not sure, but I think Dr. Maimon could accept this position.

"Getting back to the topic of wisdom, I have one idea about the relationship between wisdom and humility. On the one hand, I agree with Sofi — sorry, I mean Dr. Maimon. To be creative sometimes takes a little arrogance because it involves thinking independently. But it also takes humility. An arrogant person thinks he knows everything there is to know. A humble person realizes how little he knows. And that's the first step to creativity. A truly creative person has to be open to new thoughts, new ideas, and maybe even new feelings. An arrogant person is usually closed-minded and rigid, not open to new ideas at all. Of course, you might be arrogant in one area and creative in another. For example, you could have an arrogant but creative sports coach. But if you're arrogant even in one area, you're not going to be creative about deep things or about life in general.

"Now, if I was right earlier in saying that there's a connection between wisdom and having a sense of humor, it should follow that there's a connection between humor and humility. A very special teacher and mentor of mine, Rabbi Dr. Low, once suggested to me that there might be a connection between humor and humanity. But couldn't we also say that there's a connection between humor and humility? The best comedians are the ones who can poke just as much fun at themselves as they do at others. On the other extreme, an arrogant person is often someone who lacks a good sense of humor. I'd bet that Hitler and Stalin didn't have a good sense of humor at all. So maybe there is a deep connection between humor and humility.

"Finally, about the question of what's so important about wisdom, or why should one have wisdom. As I see it, this question boils down to: what's so important about developing creative insight? To be creative is to be your own person, to be unique. I think everyone has the potential for creativity at least in some way. When we're creative, we're kind of like God, who created the world. Just as life is boring without a sense of humor, life is also boring without creativity. Where would we be if people were not wise? We wouldn't have inventions. We wouldn't have science, literature, philosophy, art, comedy, music, you name it. So, wisdom is a great thing that we should all aspire to in whatever way we can. And that's my speech on wisdom. Cheers, everyone, or perhaps I should say . . . *le-chaim!*"

"*Le-chaim!*" everyone responded, drinking their cups of wine.

"*Yasher koach!*" added Chaim and Rabbi Abraham, speaking almost as one.

"Excellent!" said Ravi. "Really, quite creative."

"My sentiments, exactly," said Phil. "I withdraw my earlier theory and I now concur entirely with you!"

"See?" said George. "It wasn't so hard after all!"

"Honestly," said Dr. Maimon, "that was very well done. I'll have to think more about your suggestion about how to reconcile my view of God as Being itself with the Kabbalistic view regarding *ein sof* and the *sefirot*. But my goodness – what time is it?"

Rabbi Abraham looked at his watch. "*Oy vey!* It's almost two o'clock!"

"Oh, well. I *really* have to go. My babysitter's going to kill me," said Dr. Maimon.

"I trust you don't mean that literally! " said Chaim.

"Yes, me too," said Rabbi Abraham. "I mean, I've got to get going also."

"And I'd better get going also," said Chaim. "I have a long drive back home."

"Are you sure you don't want to sleep over here?" said David. "I'm sure Simon wouldn't mind if you slept here overnight."

"No, thanks! I'll be fine."

The guests stood up and stretched.

"I've got to tell you all," said David, "that this has been a special night for me. I mean, after four years, to get all of you in the same room and have this discussion . . . it's been really interesting."

"I think it's been quite interesting for all of us," said Dr. Maimon.

"Yes, me, too," said Chaim. "I must confess that I learned quite a lot!"

"We all did," said Ravi.

"Especially me," said Phil.

"And me," said George. "And I really have to turn in. I'm exhausted!"

Rabbi Abraham and Dr. Maimon left first. Shortly afterward, Chaim and George left. Phil, Ravi, and David sat around talking until dawn. Finally, Ravi and Phil left to go out for breakfast. They invited David to go out with them, but he said he was too exhausted. After they left, he said a few *berachos* and *shema*. Then he collapsed on the sofa.

26

From: dgoldstein@cuniv.edu   Sent: 5/29/03 11:27 AM
To: rlow@ahavattorah.org.il
Subject: graduation party

Dear Rabbi Low:

Last night was the graduation party I told you about. I really wished you could have been here. I invited some friends and some of my teachers and we really had a great time. Toward the end, we had a discussion about wisdom. Everyone gave a speech on wisdom from their own point of view. I wonder what you would have said had you been here!

I've been thinking more and more about your idea to come learn this summer. I'm getting closer to a decision.

Incidentally, did you ever get a chance to read the dvar torah on the five hallelukahs?

David

From: rlow@ahavattorah.org.il   Sent: 6/2/03 8:15 PM
To: dgoldstein@cuniv.edu
Subject: your dvar torah

Dear David,

I just got back to my office after a trip and checked through some of the backlog in my inbox. I read your dvar Torah on the five hallelukahs and I couldn't believe it! I read it several times over. It's fantastic! You make excellent use of kabbalistic ideas to explain what's going on in the peshat of the Tehillim. I had a little difficulty with your analysis of the fourth hallelukah and how that fit into the scheme, but never mind that for now. Thank you very much for sharing it with me. Anyone who reads your dvar Torah will never be able to say the five hallelukahs again without thinking of some aspect of your dvar torah! And since I daven every day, that means I will think of you every day as well.

Sorry I missed your graduation party! It sounds like you've got some really interesting friends. With regard to the topic of what is wisdom, I'm not sure what I would have said. I wish we could discuss it in person . . . which brings me to my next topic.

Over the last three years I've come to know you pretty well. I want to invite you formally to come and spend not just the summer, but an academic year at our yeshiva, Ahavat Torah, in Jerusalem. I know this is very short notice, but there is a discount ticket available for one seat on a plane that leaves next week that will be carrying a group of students. I think the time is right for you to study seriously all aspects of Judaism, which you will be able to do here. We have classes in Tanakh, Gemara, Mahshavah (Jewish thought and philosophy) and Halacha. I think you'll enjoy the group of guys here. Almost all are college graduates, quite a number of whom are *baalei teshuvah*, or people coming back to their Jewish roots. Study takes place mostly in English but there are some classes in Hebrew. If you think you've had some great conversations in America, wait till you come here and spend time in yeshiva!

Now is the time for you to really delve into Judaism. Now is the time not just to visit but to live in Israel for an extended time. Being in Israel will also be a tremendous experience for you. You'll visit the sights and get to know the people. There's an incredible diversity here of all sorts of Jews from all over the world. You'll learn and grow so much just by being here. I strongly urge you to come. The new session starts next week with a new group of students, so the best time to come would be as soon as you could.

I know this is a little sudden, but I hope you'll consider this very seriously.

Sincerely,

Rabbi Yehudah Low

27

"Esther? Hi! It's me, David."

"Yes?"

"Esther, you don't sound right. What's wrong?"

"Nothing, nothing at all. Just . . . where've you been? Don't you remember that day two weeks ago when you said you'd call, and you didn't? I thought we talked about this once before."

"Oh, yes. Sorry about that. Something came up and I've been busy . . . really busy."

"I see. So now you're not busy, so you thought finally you'd call?"

"Look, Esther, I'm sorry. But believe me, I really have been busy."

"With what?"

"Well . . . things going on with my dad . . . and some new plans."

"Plans? Plans for what?"

"Well, actually, I . . . I'm going to Israel next week."

"What? What did you say?"

"Yes. I'm going to Israel. To learn at Rabbi Low's yeshiva. Esther? Are you still there?"

"Yes, barely. Did I just hear you say that you're going to Israel next week?"

"Yes. And I think I'm going for the whole year, if it works out."

"What? I . . . I really can't believe this."

"Esther, I honestly thought you'd be happy to hear this."

"David, that's great for you, but I . . . . Look, I really have to say I'm a little confused too. About us, that is."

"Uh-oh. What did I do now? What's the problem?"

"David, don't you think you could have at least told me about this before? Don't you think we could have discussed this at least a little? Is this what you've been busy doing the last few weeks? You've been so busy that you couldn't even call the person who connected you with Rabbi Low in the first place? And now, dropping this on me out of the blue, a week before you're going away, probably for a year? I can't believe this. You know what? I just can't talk any more."

"I'm really sorry, Esther. But really I wasn't thinking seriously about it till just this past

week, when Rabbi Low emailed me and invited me to come —"

"David, you could have at least told me you were thinking about this! Look, I don't even want to have this conversation. I don't think I can talk with you any longer. I'm hanging up."

"Wait a second. Don't hang up! You sound like you're beginning to cry. Esther, I'm really sorry. Can we meet and talk about this in person? I really want to see you once more before I go."

"What for? We can say goodbye on the phone. Nesiah tovah, David. You know what that means? Have a good trip. Goodbye. I'm hanging up now."

"Esther —"

[Click.]

28

June 9, 2003

Dear Esther,

I'm writing this letter to you to try to explain what happened. When we spoke last on the phone, obviously I didn't get a chance to do that. One thing for sure is that you've been so important in everything that's happened to me over the last few years, and I certainly don't want to hurt you. But obviously I already have and I'm really sorry. There were a few things I kept secret from you, and I see that caused us trouble. So I thought I'd write you this letter. Some things are more easy to say in writing than in person. Some of what I'm going to tell you might be a little hard to take, but anyway, here goes.

The truth is, you know that when I first met you, I wanted to be physically intimate with you, but that wasn't what you wanted, and I tried to understand that. It wasn't easy — and, to be honest, I thought for a long time that I would eventually succeed in winning you over. But as time went on, I gave up on that, and eventually I stopped even wanting to seduce you. I related to you more and more as a person. When I lost some of that raw lust for you, I thought that meant I didn't love you. Now I realize that's not correct. I do truly love you, and I love you deeply. You are a wonderful, precious individual. I just got so immersed in other things I was doing that I stopped paying enough attention to you. That was no excuse and I'm really sorry.

You're probably still upset with me, so maybe it's all over, but maybe it's not. But I'll continue in the optimistic hope that you will forgive me. Sometimes when we spoke, it seemed you were looking for me to make a commitment to you. Obviously, one of the things that complicates our relationship is the fact that I'm not ~~yet~~ as committed to Orthodox Judaism as you are. I think I have difficulty sorting out or distinguishing how I feel about you from how I feel about Orthodox Judaism. But that's why I need the time now to learn, so I can sort out the commitment. I'm pretty sure I'm committed to Judaism in some form. But I've still got to work out exactly what that form of Judaism is.

I'm still trying to find my way, and I don't know where all of this will end up, at least for me. But over the last couple of months one thing has become clear. There isn't a lot I know for sure. But I do know this: I <u>must</u> learn more about Judaism, from the original sources of Judaism, and in the original language, as much as I can. You know the passage in the prophets that says something like, "All those who are thirsty, come and drink"? Honestly, that's how I feel – thirsty. And what are the sources? Obviously, the Torah, the Tanakh, the Talmud, the Midrash, but also the commentaries, the Jewish philosophers, the Kabbalah, the whole history, how Jews in later centuries responded to it all. It's such a rich, vast tradition, and it never ceases to amaze me how the more you learn, the deeper and richer it all becomes. One thing I can say is that some of the problems I had in the past with Judaism got ironed out as I learned more, so I am pretty confident that whatever problems I still have with Judaism will probably be ironed out as I learn even more. So I've got to immerse myself in it for some time, not just intellectually, but also practically and spiritually. But to "immerse" myself doesn't mean to fool myself into believing things I don't really believe or even understand. That's one thing I still worry about – brainwashing myself, becoming a fundamentalist. But the <u>learning</u>, that's the main thing. I realized that whatever decision I make will be a better decision if I learn, than if I don't learn. And I realized that now's obviously the time, before grad school, before I get involved in pursuing a career, or anything more serious. I've got to figure out where I stand on Judaism, and that's going to take some time.

And so the next question was: where should I learn? Of all the people I've talked to and learned from over the last couple of years, Rabbi Low is the one who speaks to me most on my wavelength. Not that I agree with him on everything, of course. And for your helping me make a personal connection with Rabbi Low, I am truly thankful. If not for you, I would have never developed a relationship with him. But of course, he's in Israel, so I had to think about that. Honestly,

I am a little nervous about going to Israel, what with all the terrorism, etc. But looking at it purely from the question of where would be the ideal place to learn Torah, it seemed obvious that Israel would be the best place. I'm sure there will be so many dimensions of learning there, not just book learning, but the whole atmosphere, the place, the history and so on. Besides, Israel is the Jewish state. So where else better than to learn Judaism than in the Jewish state? So I thought about going to Israel for the summer. And then something else happened.

Here's the thing that was keeping me preoccupied in the days before, during, and shortly after graduation. I hope this doesn't come as a shock, but I had one habit in college that happens to be illegal. I smoked marijuana. This may be difficult for you to understand, but for me it wasn't just about getting high and goofing around. It was about getting into a higher state of consciousness. Anyway, a few weeks before graduation, the campus police came in and found a large amount of ~~the good essence~~ stuff in my room. I hope you don't find that too upsetting. If you do and you never want to speak to me again, well, that's too bad for me. But I hope you'll read the rest of this letter first. The police were going to charge me with drug dealing, which really was false. I was worried that this would make it impossible to leave the country for Israel even just for the summer. I couldn't bear to tell you all this because I thought it would destroy our relationship. Maybe I was wrong. I won't know about this until I hear back from you, if I ever do. But I couldn't even call you because I knew you'd be able to tell something was going on, and I felt I would have to lie. If there's one thing I'm tired of, it's all the lies people tell all the time, including myself. I realize now how dishonest I've been in so many ways over the past four years. And if there's one thing I admire about Judaism, it's its emphasis on emes, on truth. So I didn't want to call and then lie. But I didn't have the strength to tell you the truth either. So I just avoided calling altogether. It wasn't right, but that's what I did. I'm sorry.

Anyway, I was so desperate that I actually prayed to G-d to get me out of trouble. The next day, my friend Simon told me he had told the police that all the stuff was his. He claimed that he had bought it and stashed it in my room without my knowledge. I couldn't believe he had done this. He did it just for my sake. What a true friend. Anyway, at first I didn't want to go along with this but he convinced me that it would only make things worse if I tried to undo what he'd done. The truth is that we used to take turns buying the stuff, so it could have just as easily been his. He insisted it really wasn't a big deal for him and that the police record would have no impact on his future. I still feel bad about all this, but Simon insisted. So, as far as the police were concerned I got off the hook completely. When things calmed down I finally called you, but by then it was too late. You were already upset for my not calling you before and I couldn't explain things over the phone. That's why I'm writing this letter and laying it all out, so that you'll at least know what happened.

If you want to stop reading this letter right here I would totally understand. But if you can forgive me, I hope you'll continue.

I know this may be a little weird, but I wanted to tell you about a dream I had that very night after I prayed, which was also the day before the police decided to drop the case against me. This is definitely something I would find very hard to tell you in person. It's much easier to do it in writing. The reason I'm telling you about this dream is because it has a lot to do with my decision to go to Israel for a year. I'm never sure how much to make of dreams, but at least it says something about what's going on in my head. Actually, the dream is a recurring dream that I've had before. Only each time I have it, it's somewhat different. And it usually happens that I get this dream sometime in the springtime around Shavuot, and I think I figured that out too (I'll get to that later). What I'm writing here is the latest version of the dream which I had just a few weeks ago.

The dream starts off in the Holocaust museum in Washington. I'm in a room where the main exhibit is a huge picture of a pile of shoes that were taken from the victims of a certain city before they were killed. And then, someone appears in the dream, an old Jew. He's wearing tefillin, and he's holding a shoe, looking at me intently. He says to me, "Here, take, take." I can't tell who he is, but he seems familiar. Then, slowly, I begin to realize I'm not in the museum after all, rather I'm actually in a concentration camp, and the old Jew is about to be murdered. For some reason, I'm not about to be killed. I'm an observer, an outsider. I'm there and not there at the same time. The old Jew doesn't seem anxious at all. He's quite calm. And then, the place starts filling with smoke, and my eyes get teary and I can't see anything. I'm groping around trying to find the old Jew, but I can't. I want to scream or cry out, but I can't. I smell a burnt odor, which I now realize must be the smell of the burnt flesh from the crematoria. I'm beginning to black out. But then, there's a rushing sound, like a wind, and, then, suddenly,

I'm being lifted, slowly, off the ground. I'm rising into the air, going higher and higher, until I'm at the top of the room. As I go up, the wind gets louder and louder, and I keep going up, until finally, I'm beyond the room, in the sky, looking down. The smoke has begun to dissipate, and I can see the outlines of a structure below me. All I can see now is a thin stream of smoke, rising straight in the air. It's not the museum or even the concentration camp any more. Slowly the vision becomes clearer. At first I'm looking down on a grand medieval castle of some sort. There are beautiful, majestic buildings of golden bricks, and trees, flowers, ponds, gardens, everywhere. Instead of the burnt flesh, I smell a wonderful, intoxicating scent, the odor of incense. There are people walking about, going places, doing important things, but I can't tell exactly what they're doing. Suddenly, in a flash I realize, this is the city of G-d, the city of Jerusalem. And then I wake up.

You may think this is crazy, but it's pretty clear to me what this dream is saying to me, at least about what's in my head. I don't think I ever told you that my mother's grandfather, whose name was also David, was murdered in the Holocaust in June 1944, around the time of Shavuot. He's the David I was named after. And as you yourself first taught me, my Hebrew birthday is on Shavuot. To me, the interpretation of the dream is pretty clear. In 1944, during the Holocaust, a man named David was murdered for being a Jew. Today, sixty years later, another David is about to set out for Jerusalem in order to carry on where the first David left off.

So here I am, writing to you as I sit on the plane to Israel, to go study in Jerusalem at Rabbi Low's yeshiva, not just for a summer but for a whole year. To my surprise, my father agreed to support the idea. That could also be interpreted as a miracle!

Esther, I know I've hurt you. Again, I'm sorry and I really hope you will forgive me. You're a special person, a unique individual, and I really respect and love you. I'll be mailing this letter to you as soon as I get off the plane in Israel. I'll be sure to include the address – I'll be at the Ahavat Torah Yeshiva. I hope we stay in touch. Of course, I can't know where you'll be a year from now, but I hope we can pick up where we left off.

Will you write back? I sure hope so.

Love,

David

Acknowledgments

The author would like to acknowledge the following individuals for their material support to make possible the publication of this book: Max and Harriet Behr, Alison and Bret Caller, Cathy and Moises Dreszer, Nicole and David Goldstein, Roy and Janie Hyman, Phyllis and David Leibson, Jerry Leibson, Lester Levin, Rae and Benny Lewis, Raquel and Daniel Rosenberg, Belinda and Victor Schwartz, Jonathan and Stephi Wolff, Carolyn and Simon Wolf, Bill and Judy Yesowitch. Aside from the very capable editors at Urim, many individuals commented on earlier drafts of the book. The following deserve special thanks: Ayala Golding, Olga-Maria Cruz, Daniel Rosenberg, Brandon Kenney, David Shatz, Joseph Castriota, Michoel Stern, Arie Michelsohn, Paul Herrington, Joshua Khavis and Penny Miller Harris.

About the Author

JOSHUA GOLDING is a professor of philosophy at Bellarmine University in Louisville, Kentucky. He has held research positions at the University of Haifa and at the University of Notre Dame. He is the author of *Rationality and Religious Theism* (Ashgate, 2003). He has published articles in *Religious Studies, Faith and Philosophy, Modern Schoolman, Tradition*, and *Torah U-Madda Journal*. He also has rabbinical ordination (Hilchot Shabbat) from Yeshivat Sulam Yaakov in Jerusalem.